Mermaid in a
Bowl of Tears

Go n-éirí an bóthar leat.

Andy Brandner

Also by Cindy Brandner

Exit Unicorns (Book 1 - Exit Unicorns Series)

Mermaid in a Bowl of Tears (Book 2 - Exit Unicorns Series)

Flights of Angels (Book 3 - Exit Unicorns Series)

Mermaid in a
Bowl of Tears

by

Cindy Brandner

Starry Night Press

For my own Patrick,

without whom there would be no words.

Acknowledgements

A book this size requires the efforts and expertise of far more than one person and I am deeply indebted to the following.

My patient and supportive family- my daughters who never complain about takeout because mom forgot to cook yet again! My wonderful husband who puts up with all sorts of artistic moaning and whinging and supports me one hundred and fifty percent.

The ladies and gent of Shamrocks and Stones, my online social club- you all are the best and I thank you for all the laughter, tears, encouragement and fun that we have together on a daily basis. Peggy Busby who runs the place with a firm hand and a kind heart- thanks for the world's only bottling of 'Connemara Mist' – I'm saving it for a truly special occasion.

Michelle Moore for giving me what is surely one of the most beautiful websites on the internet- you are an amazingly talented lady Michelle. Do go check out her work- www.exitunicorns.com. Thank you also for all the lovely designs for the mugs, mousepads, t-shirts etc for all the 'Exit Unicorns' paraphenalia that is out there.

Shannon Curtis- aka 'Jamie's girl'- my gratitude for your beautiful Chapter Charms that honour the spirit of both 'Exit Unicorns' and 'Mermaid in a Bowl of Tears'.

Lee Ramsey for her endless well of patience with the job of editing such a large manuscript, Carla Murphy for her clear eye for what works and what does not- you bring the spirit of Newfoundland to all you do and it's a lovely thing woman. Jane Hill for double checking all those Boston scenes and for making certain that my hooker sounded suitably low class. Tim Crowley for his expertise in all things Boston.

My circle of 'first readers'- Fran Bach for reading the whole thing in a few days and for loving every page of it. Dorine 'Dreen' Lamarche- honey you are the world's worst critic and for that I just loves ya. Elaine Pontious- you are my Anam Cara woman and I thank you for all the hyacinth. Mahri Newton for all the inspirational pics of our Col- keep 'em comin'. Noelle Delieto- part of my Irish posse, with you at my back I cannot go wrong in this world. Sallie Blumenauer for reminding me every now again that the words alone are, indeed, worth it. Tracy Goode- you have the world's best heart girl.

Mick O'Neill for showing me a side of Republican Belfast that few outsiders are ever allowed to see. It was an amazing day and I will be forever grateful.

Bobbie Thornton and Rhonda Rawling for being my friends for oh so long now and always encouraging me on this journey of mine.

My parents Marvin and Wanda Brandner for teaching me to follow my dreams no matter how long and bumpy the road.

My grandmother Violet Brandner who loved words as much as I do. I miss you Grandma, and I thank you for always being so proud of me.

Last but never least- I thank the readers for all your letters, gifts, cards and mostly for loving these characters of mine and taking them into your lives and hearts as friends. I know the wait was long for many of you and I thank you for your patience. I hope when you turn the last page you will feel it was well worth the wait.

Until next time,

Rath Dé ort

Cindy

www.exitunicorns.com
cindy@exitunicorns.com

Table of Contents

Part Three - Nothing Sacred

Part Four - When the Dark Night Seems Endless...

Part Five - An Aran Idyll

Part One

If This is Love...

Chapter One

Conversations With a Gull

"WHAT'LL YE HAVE?" The bartender, clothed like an impeccably starched penguin, looked as though he'd rather be anywhere than stuck behind the bar at a three hundred dollar a plate political fundraiser. Casey Riordan, bowtie and top stud of his crisp white shirt undone, knew the feeling all too well.

"Have ye got any Connemara Mist?" Casey asked, as he sat on one of the highly cushioned brass stools next to the bar.

"Aye, ten year malt, sixteen year reserve, an' the special blend."

"Give me a double of the single malt," Casey said, rummaging in his tuxedo jacket for a cigarette before remembering his wife had rather pointedly removed them, saying they ruined the line of his suit. He sighed audibly, and the bartender set a pack of cigarettes in front of him.

"Thanks," Casey said gratefully, tapping one out and sliding the pack back.

"Take a couple," the bartender said, "ye'll need the fortification."

"Look that thrilled to be here, do I?" Casey asked.

"About as thrilled as I feel, an' I'm gettin' paid," the man replied, setting a generous tumbler of whiskey on the polished wood of the bar.

Casey picked the glass up, sniffed appreciatively, and took a sip. It slid gold and warm down his throat, leaving tendrils of fire in its wake.

"What bit of Belfast are ye from?" the bartender asked, opening a split of champagne and setting it in a silver bucket of dry ice.

"The Ardoyne," Casey said, and swallowed the remainder of his drink, closing his eyes around the taste, feeling the welcome heat in his belly. "An' yerself?"

"Donegal, little village up near Malinhead, population of about eighty an' that includes the sheep," the bartender replied with a wistful smile. "How long have ye been over?"

"A few months," Casey said. "How about yerself?"

"Three years."

"Do ye get homesick?"

"Sometimes," the man shrugged, "though when I was home I couldn't wait to get over here an' now that I'm here I wonder what was the rush. How 'bout yerself, longin' for the old sod?"

"Aye," Casey looked down into his empty glass, "at times."

"The land of milk an' honey not all ye expected?"

"Not entirely, but then I suppose home would not seem the same to me now either."

The bartender set the bottle of malt whiskey in front of him. "Have another. It's on the house, least I can do for a fellow countryman."

"Thanks, man."

The bartender whisked a rag over the spotless gleam of the bar. "I went back home the once, an' it was as if I belonged neither here nor there. I've a foot in both worlds but I'm not standin' firm in either, if ye'll know what I'm sayin'."

"Aye, I'll know," Casey agreed, "ye're a man without a country."

Just then, a voice at his left elbow said, "Cognac. Hennessey if you've got it."

"Boring crowd," drawled the voice, and Casey knew without turning his head what he would find—floppy blonde hair, long thin-bladed nose, ice-blue eyes and a jaded, world-weary expression. He poured himself another two fingers of whiskey and stared straight ahead at the vast array of bottles lining the mirrored wall of the bar.

"Say, can I just have the bottle as well? Good man," the voice said, as the bartender, now expressionless and silent, placed the cognac at the man's elbow. "Good turnout, though, and plenty of old money; Eliot should do well for himself tonight." A long, slender hand—pale and refined—stuck itself in front of him and Casey sighed.

"Charles Reese-David, though everyone calls me Chip."

"Of course they do," Casey muttered, giving the hand the briefest of shakes and then, taking another swig of his drink, turned most reluctantly towards the voice that had already saturated the floor with its dropped *r*'s.

The man looked exactly as he'd predicted to himself—hopelessly overbred English, though his ancestors had likely come over with the Mayflower. Casey wondered if everyone on that particular boat had looked this way, bloodless and effete, yet somehow still managing to convey an innate superiority.

"You look familiar," the man continued as Casey turned back to his drink. "Were you at Harvard? I was in Law there. Went to Choate as a boy, is that where I know you from?"

"Don't think so," Casey said with as much politeness as he could muster, hunting in his inside pocket for his wallet. The bartender shook his head at the bills and Casey returned the money to his pocket with a nod of thanks. He was just sliding off the stool when the man next to him let out a long, low whistle.

"Get an eyeful of that will you?"

Casey turned and saw the object of the man's interest making her way across the floor of the ballroom. In a roomful of heirloom jewelry she wore only a pair of tiny ruby earrings and a plain silver band on her left hand. She stopped to have a word here, two there, smiling and charming the people who'd paid and paid well to get on the political express train of Eliot Reese-David.

"She's my brother's PR person if you can believe it. Bastard's always been terrifically lucky with women. Even he couldn't believe his luck, though, when Love Hagerty gave her to him for the campaign."

"Gave her?" Casey said raising his eyebrows, his tone making the bartender look up warily from the case of Cristal he was unloading. Charles Reese-David, however, had no such instinct, and continued heedlessly on.

"Yes. She's Love Hagerty's piece on the side, apparently. She's married to one of his thugs. Eliot's had no luck with her at all. He's hoping to change all that when he goes to Washington, though. Thinks maybe she's afraid of Love Hagerty; in Washington she'll be at a safe remove; even that backroom-dealing Irish crook's tentacles can't stretch all the way there."

"Mr. Hagerty's a born an' bred Bostonian, I believe," Casey said lightly.

Chip snorted derisively. "There's an old Beacon Hill saying about that— 'you can take the mick out of the bog, but you can't take the—'"

"Bog out of the mick," Casey finished coldly.

"Heavens, is she coming this way?" Chip straightened up, shooting his cuffs and casting a surreptitious glance in the mirror over his shoulder. "Met her at Eliot's office a few weeks ago. Apparently," he smiled creamily, "I left an impression."

"I don't doubt that," Casey said, his voice coming as close to friendliness as it had all night.

The object of Chip's interest reached them a moment later, gave him a polite 'hello', and sliding her arms around Casey's neck, tucked her face into the curve of his shoulder and said, "Casey, take me home will you?"

"Aye I'll take ye home. Are ye all finished with yer business for the evenin', then?" he asked, sparing a sideways glance for Chip, who was looking even more bloodless than he had a moment before.

"Mmhm," she said sleepily, "Eliot can manage on his own, it'll only be the stragglers left soon anyhow and I'm exhausted by this crowd." She slid one hand inside his loosened collar and whispered silkily, "Take me home to bed."

"Ye're goin' to cause a scandal woman, can I not take ye anywhere?" He said with mock sternness.

She whispered something else in his ear and he found to his consternation that he was blushing.

"Is that even legal in Massachusetts?" he asked. "Ye have to remember this place was settled by Puritans."

"I think," she said, tongue touching the rim of his ear in a highly distracting manner, "that several of them are here tonight."

"Well I'd best get yer wrap before I'm forced to carry ye out of here over my shoulder," Casey said, with a grin, noting that Chip was still staring in stunned disbelief at the two of them.

When he returned with the coats he found his wife in conversation with Eliot Reese-David the Fourth, and took a deep breath before approaching. He'd loathed the man on sight, something in his Hibernian soul recoiling from the very first meeting. Eliot was old Yankee, Boston Brahmin all the way. Like his brother, he was Choate and Harvard educated, housed on Beacon Hill, heir to a fortune that exceeded the fiscal resources of many small nations, and far, far too fond, Casey thought—watching with fury as the man laid a hand on Pamela's shoulder—of his wife.

"Ready then?" he asked, settling Pamela's plush black velveteen jacket around her shoulders.

"Pity you have to leave so soon, we didn't even have a chance to chat." Eliot said to Casey, his eyes like two ice chips.

"A great pity," Casey returned, the heavy sarcasm in his voice lost on none of them.

"Well Pamela," Eliot turned a much warmer aspect on his public relations assistant of the last two months, "we pulled off a very good evening here, I'd say." The man managed to make the *we* sound distinctly cozy and Casey had to bite his tongue sharply.

"*You*, Eliot," Pamela said, "it's your baby now, there's only a week left until the election and then you're off to Washington and I'll go back to working for Mr. Hagerty."

"We'll see," Eliot said, and Casey thought of how he'd dearly love to throw the man the length of the bar.

"Good night, Eliot," she said and there was just the slightest edge of dismissal in her voice, as though she had laid a hand on his arm and pushed him gently, but firmly, away.

The man blinked, a slight flush staining his face. "Good night."

Pamela tucked her arm through Casey's and leaned into his side in a gesture of casual and sure intimacy that was not lost on their two-man audience. Casey smiled and nodded goodbye in a way that managed to be dismissive, and then at the last moment leaned back towards Chip and said, "'Twasn't at Harvard we met, for I wasn't schooled there, as ye may have guessed."

"Indeed," Chip said frostily, "where were you schooled?"

"Streets of Belfast, an' then I matriculated up to a little institution called Parkhurst, on the Isle of Wight. Was there at the invitation an' leisure of her Majesty the Queen. Class of '68, got my degree in the finer points of how to take a man's life, or how to make him wish I had." He paused for a moment, his dark eyes making certain contact with Chip's pale blue ones. "If ye feel a certain fraternal fondness for yer brother, I'd advise ye to tell him that my wife is well taken care of an' in no need of his attentions. D'ye understand my meanin'?"

Chip nodded, Adams apple bobbing up and down nervously.

"I see ye're a fast learner. Good fer you, it's a valuable survival skill," Casey said in a deceptively amiable tone before turning to escort his wife out of the ballroom.

"You really think the man will win?" Casey asked, after they'd hailed a cab and begun the long ride from Beacon Hill to South Boston.

"I certainly hope so," Pamela said, wrapping her arms around his waist and laying her head on his shoulder. "I only wish Congress sat in Zimbabwe or some equally remote place."

"Ye know he's goin' to ask ye to come to Washington with him, don't ye?"

"I've already turned him down twice."

"The sleeven bastard!" Casey said, vehemently. "Ye know why he wants to take ye there?"

"Of course," she said lightly, "for my diverse talents. Now let's not talk about him anymore, it'll ruin the rest of the night. And I have some very specific plans for tonight."

"Do ye then?" Casey said as a hand found its way underneath his onyx-studded shirt.

"Oh yes, Mr. Riordan," she said and removed the loosened bowtie with one tug of her fingers, "I do."

"Well then, Mrs. Riordan," he stifled a gasp as a hand slid down the front of his impeccably creased trousers, "we'd best get ye home quick like."

HOME WAS AN OLD walk-up triple-decker in Southie. Pamela and Casey occupied the top floor of the shabby red-brick Victorian, and so, as Pamela had optimistically said, had a view to the stars. Casey was less romantic in his view and saw a rundown hovel with slanted floors, where the windows were so thick with ice that, even now in November, a man couldn't see out of them. The pipes groaned like an old man on his last legs, and the stairwell stank of beer and piss. Pamela belonged here about as much as a priceless diamond belonged in a cesspit, Casey thought, sitting on the bed and taking off his cufflinks, studs, and shirt, before lighting a desperately needed cigarette. He hated the damn place, but it was what they could afford on their wages and still have enough left over to put in the bank for the house they hoped to buy sometime in the near future. Still, it pained him to keep her here.

He sighed and leaned against the wall at the head of the bed. The room was bathed in blue light from the neon sign across the street and he watched Pamela in the dim as she took off her pumps and pulled the pins out of her hair. She headed for the bathroom to take off her makeup and begin all the mysterious rituals that she couldn't seem to go to bed without.

"Don't," he said huskily, "undress out here. Undress for me."

She looked over her shoulder at him, giving him a glance that made his breath stop in his throat. Then she reached for the zip on her dress.

Her back was blue-brushed ivory in the night, the dress a delicate, slithering web that dropped slowly to her hips and then, aided by her hands, fell to the floor.

He took a deep breath as he saw the stockings and the garters, all frothy lace, that held them up. She was slender and supple, but she had a woman's body, the stuff of which a healthy male's fantasies were made.

She unclipped the garters, one snap at a time, her hair falling over one shoulder, black ribbon against the white lace of her brassiere. She rolled the stockings down with slow deliberation, making an art of it. He stubbed his cigarette out, stood, and walked across the room. He stopped only inches away, drinking in her scent, feeling her heat, not yet touching.

She shivered.

"Cold?" he asked softly.

"No, I can feel your eyes on me." She drew a shaky breath. "Touch me, Casey."

He rested his hands on her shoulders, hooked his thumbs under the straps of her bra and slid them slowly down her arms.

"All those men lookin' at ye tonight," he said and ran his lips feather-light down the side of her neck, "an' I know what they're thinkin', that they're imaginin' ye like this, an' still they don't know the half of it. I sit there," he ran his hands down over her collarbone, across the pale skin of her chest, "an' I think 'if ye knew the truth of her, boy, ye'd go mad. Ye wouldn't be able to breathe or sleep proper again, if ye knew what it was to touch her so," his hands came around and under, spreading across her belly, his voice like rough silk in her ear as she leaned back into his chest, "ye'd be addicted for life, ye'd be like a man drugged, never able to get enough." She moaned softly as his hands, rough with calluses, slid up to cup her breasts.

"And what about the women looking at you?" she asked, reaching behind her to unfasten the button on his trousers.

"What women?" His tongue flicked the edge of her ear. "I didn't see any other women there tonight."

"Well they saw you. Women always look at you."

"Do they?" he asked, hands slipping inside the rim of her little white panties and pushing them down until they fell to the floor and she stepped daintily out of them.

"Oh, do they? They look at you like alcoholics look at whiskey."

"An' what do ye think when they look at me?" He put an arm under her knees and swung her up, depositing her on the bed.

"I think..." she undid the zip on his pants, watched them fall to the floor and then pulled him over onto the bed. "I think—don't even imagine it, sister, 'cause he's mine, every inch mine and you couldn't handle him anyhow."

"Do ye, then?" Casey murmured, tongue making butterfly kisses on her navel and then proceeding down until she gave a sharp cry, crumpling the sheets in her fists and arching up to meet his questing mouth. She tangled her fingers in his hair, gave it a gentle tug, pulling him up, guiding him urgently between her legs.

"Patience, Jewel," he said, easing in slowly, gasping at the tight, fevered fit, raising her hips for deeper penetration, their bodies already moving in an undulating rhythm that threatened to push them both over the edge in short order.

"Mmmnn," Casey said in not-convincing protest, ceasing his movement altogether, "I plan to take it slow. It's just you an' I, darlin', an' the night is long." He thrust with slow deliberation and she cried out, arching off the sheets, head turned to the side, hair drifting across her face. He loved this moment best of all, when she was all soft and hot beneath him, crying his name like she was in pain and only he could bring her release. He thrust again deep into her and she arched tightly to him, giving a soft, shattered sob, arms flung out to the sides. He collapsed against her, face buried in her neck as she wrapped her arms around him, all sweet, living, burning cells.

The night was never quite long enough however, Casey thought some time later. The hands on the clock at their bedside read four a.m. He swung his legs over the side of the bed, bowing his head and rubbing his face with his hands.

"Do you have to go?" Pamela's arm wrapped around him from behind, hand stroking the soft skin of his belly.

He picked her hand up, kissed the back of it firmly and laid it down on the sheet. He glanced back at her. "Ye know I do."

"It's barbaric the hours he makes you keep," she said grumpily, sitting up and pushing her hair away from her face.

"He keeps them himself an' longer many nights."

"What sort of business is done at four in the morning?"

"Ye know I don't question Love about his business."

She sighed, twisting her wedding ring about her finger. "Maybe we ought to question it, Casey."

"An' both be out of work?" he asked lightly, pulling his shirt on and buttoning it up by feel.

"I left a letter on the table for you yesterday," she said, changing tack. He could hear the sheets rustle softly as she laid back.

"I saw it," he said shortly.

"Damn it, Casey, how can you be so stubborn? He's your brother."

"I know who he is," Casey said, rolling up his cuffs, "an' the last time I saw him he told me to stay the hell out of his life. I've done my best to honor his request."

"And now he wants to patch things up. Why won't you at least read his letters?"

"Because they're addressed to you, not me. I take that as a fairly broad hint."

"It's only because he knows you'd throw his letters away unread."

Casey sighed. This topic was not new to the two of them and it was an issue they could never see eye to eye upon.

"How is he, then?" he asked, tucking his shirt into his pants and reaching for his cigarettes.

"Good, though he'd be better if you'd at least give some signal that you know he's alive." She paused, and he sensed there was something she wanted to say to him but hesitated to do so.

"Ye'd best out with it or it'll go straight to yer spleen—at least that's what my daddy used to tell us."

"It's just that...well what with Siobhan and Desmond coming for Christmas I thought it would be nice if Pat and Sylvie could come as well."

He was silent for a long moment, digesting this shocking suggestion.

"I suppose ye can ask," he said gruffly, "but I doubt the boy will accept yer invite."

"He already has," she said quietly.

Casey sighed and turned around to look at his wife. Her eyes slid swiftly away from his gaze.

"An' may I enquire what bold little tale ye told him to get him to agree to come?"

"It wasn't," she said with slow reluctance, "entirely a tale."

"Oh." He quirked his eyebrows questioningly, "half fable an' half truth, was it then?"

"I only told him what I know to be true," she said defensively, drawing the sheet up over her breasts. Casey tugged it back down firmly.

"Ye once told me it was harder to lie when ye're naked, darlin', so now that ye're naked," he cast an appreciative eye along her length, "tell me what it is exactly that ye've told my brother?"

She tugged vainly at the sheet, which he held tight in his fist.

"Only that you were sorry and that you missed him."

"Forgive me if I can't see where the nugget of truth is buried in yer little story," he said, voice rich with sarcasm.

"You do miss him," she said softly, "I know you do. I've lived with you every day for over a year now, Casey, I know what the silences say as well as the words."

"All right," he admitted, "I do miss the little bugger but I'll not say as I'm sorry. What I said to him still holds true, he's stirrin' up a cauldron of snakes with that organization of his, an' what I said was said out of concern for his safety—for his damned life, truth be told. But he's too stubborn to see truth even when it comes armed with a bullet."

She reached up and stroked his face softly, her eyes searching his own. "He's like his brother that way, aye?"

He caught her hand in his own, pressing the knuckles hard against his lips. "Can ye not allow a man his illusions every now an' again, darlin'?"

"Not when it's this important. He's your family, Casey, and I want family around this Christmas," she said firmly, eyes suddenly dark and opaque, like heavy green glass.

"Is this about the babe, then?" he asked, voice subdued, hand stilled against hers.

"No," she said too quickly and then, with her free hand, dashed away a quicksilver glitter of tears, "maybe, I don't know. We'd have our baby soon, you know, if I hadn't lost her."

"Aye," he lowered himself onto the bed beside her, stroking her hair back from her forehead in a soothing motion, "I know. She'd be a bitty wee thing, but she'd come in a rush like most Riordans. But darlin', it wasn't yer fault. Ye know what the doctor said."

"Oh yes," she replied in a gritty voice, "I know what the doctor said. I also know they say the same damn words to every woman who loses a baby, it's just nature taking care of things, there'll be more babies—but it doesn't matter, it's all just words and I wanted that baby. It was just a bit of blood and bone to him, but Casey, it was our *child*, someone we created out of love, and I wanted *that* particular person."

He put his lips against her forehead, felt the pulse of her blood in the veins under the fine skin, and closed his eyes against the sting of tears. It still took him unawares, this flood of sudden emotion for someone he'd never known, never would know. Someone who'd had a steady, thrumming heartbeat, rapid like the whir of a hummingbird's wings. Someone who, though unseen, had been felt by his hands, turning and fluttering under the small mound of his wife's belly. Son or daughter, it hadn't mattered to him, only that it was their child.

The thought of that night was like a knife cutting a valley through his heart. He'd been away, working late as usual, when Love himself had come out to the warehouse where Casey was supervising the unloading of a shipment from the Caribbean.

He'd known something was wrong at once, Love would never have shown his face at the warehouse otherwise. He liked to keep a safe distance from the grittier aspects of his business. The gritty aspects were Casey's job.

The baby had already been removed to the morgue by the time he'd arrived at the hospital, Pamela sedated, drifting in and out of drug-induced sleep. But she'd felt his presence, half-opened her eyes and whispered, "Sorry, so sorry, Casey." And then as he'd leaned down to comfort her, she'd said, "Make them give me my baby; they won't let me see our baby."

And so he'd gone to the nurses and asked to see the baby, and been told politely that it wasn't policy to allow the mothers to see the baby when the child was dead. It was better for the mother, they'd continued, if the child remained a stranger.

In a voice that seemed to emerge from someone else's throat, he'd told them in no uncertain terms that he would see his child, and see it now. And the nurse, quite obviously frightened by something in the dark, grief-stricken face in front of her, had acquiesced, calling a doctor up to speak with him. When it became clear that the doctor would be unable to dissuade him from his purpose, the baby was brought to Casey on a cold steel cart, covered by a sheet reeking of disinfectant.

He'd held the tiny, otherworldly, pearl-pale body that would have been his daughter and thought he'd die from the pain of it. Then he'd wrapped her carefully in the coarse cloth, placing the translucent, frond-like fingers against the impossibly fragile chest. She was covered in a soft golden down, her tiny ears no bigger than the pad of his thumb—delicate, wee pointed ears like an elf. Her eyelids were milky blue and sealed perfectly against a world she would never see. He'd taken her then to her mother, saying in a rough voice, when the nurses protested, that a mother had a right more than any did to say goodbye to a child she'd carried in her own body.

He'd gone in the hospital room, closed the door behind him and locked it. And due to the interference, in low and charming tones outside the door, of Love Hagerty, it had stayed locked all night. He later learned that Love had made a substantial donation to the hospital in order to buy them a little privacy.

Eight hours they'd had, the three of them. Eight hours with the baby tucked carefully between the two of them on the narrow hospital bed.

Somewhere in the wee hours Pamela had said, "I'd like to name her Deirdre."

"It's my mother's name," he'd responded in surprise.

"I know," she'd answered quietly and bent to kiss the terribly still form between them. "Do you object?"

"No," he said, and so the tiny, translucent girl, with the ears of an elf, had become Deirdre. Deirdre of the Sorrows, how tragically fitting, he'd thought.

Eight hours, the minutes unfolding like the petals of a flower which has only a night to bloom. Eight hours to say hello and goodbye and all the things in between which need a lifetime to be said.

With dawn's light, he'd unlocked the door and watched as people in stiff, starched uniforms took his child from her mother's arms. Watched with a clarity that was painful, edged in a sharp, hard light that seared his eyes, and yet still could not comprehend that he was not to be anyone's father, and yet would be a father for all the rest of his days.

Beside him the clock's hands pointed halfway between the four and the five. Beneath his lips Pamela's forehead had cooled, her breathing even and deep. She was asleep, tear trails soft silver lines radiating out into her hairline, where small puffs of blue-black curls had absorbed and hidden her grief. He gave a small prayer of thanksgiving that she was well again, that she had begun, as impossible as it had once seemed, to laugh again, to respond to outside influences. Then he got to his feet, exhaustion deep in every cell and trod, barefoot, toward the kitchen.

The kitchen faced east towards the water and beaches that seemed unimaginable from this vantage point. The room was filled with a soft, ashy light, the silver coffee pot glowing hazily on the counter by the sink. Casey lifted his hands to rub them over his face and was caught short by the scent of Pamela's skin on his palms. He closed his eyes to breathe more deeply and wasn't surprised by the thickening of his throat this time. He'd gone soft of late he supposed, when something as small as the smell of a woman's heat on his hand could cause such a rush of gratitude and wonderment. But then, this was not just any woman, this was his wife, and he loved her with a primal ferocity that shocked him at times.

Faith found him in such small moments. He had wondered at first why it came at all to someone who had never found it in easy supply, and then had thought that perhaps it was the convenience of it, for he'd more to lose now than ever before.

He drank his coffee standing, feet cold on the patched linoleum, and contemplated the meeting that was before him. He wasn't, it could be fairly said, looking forward to it in the least.

He took his rapidly cooling cup of coffee over to the window, scraped away the frost that had gathered in the night and looked down at what lay below him. Running off to the south into the housing projects of Old Colony, Old Harbor and D Point was Dorchester Street. To his left, and slightly out of view, was Broadway, a street lined with grocery and liquor stores, coffee shops, and barrooms that were filled to overflowing most nights. Directly facing him was a neon shamrock, gaudy green and buzzing in the dim light. Graffiti lined the dingy brick walls of most businesses, and decorated the labyrinth of triple-deckers down turgid alleyways and on street fronts, where afternoons found tired mothers half-heartedly supervising the play of their offspring from the vantage point of crumbling stoops.

Against the dark blue morning sky, a gull rose and fell on the air currents, a greater black-back who'd wandered inland, seeking more exotic fare than the incoming ships could provide.

Casey took a slice of bread from the paper wrapped package on the counter and unhasped the kitchen window. The sash gave with a shriek of protest as he levered it up with his shoulder. He winced, hoping the noise wouldn't wake Pamela. He waved the bread out in the morning air, sucking in his breath as the chill of it flowed past him through the window.

Attracted by the noise and movement the gull swooped in closer for a fly-by inspection, gave him a cursory once-over, and returned in a graceful arc to take the chunk of bread. It settled on the fire escape railing and set to gulping this unexpected morning treat.

"Up with yer thoughts, were ye?" Casey asked softly, watching as the bird tucked its sooty feathers in with a quick ruffle.

The gull eyed him beadily, a torn strip of bread hanging from its ocher beak.

"Not to worry, *beag cara*, I'll not hurt ye."

The gull tilted its head to the side, the red dot on its beak no more than a darker blot in the faint light.

"Ah, ye'll not have the Gaelic, then?" Casey asked conversationally. "I've only called ye 'wee friend', so there's no need to be lookin' at me as if I've insulted ye."

If the gull had a discernible eyebrow, Casey felt certain it would have raised it at this point.

"It'll be a rare hour to be up an' about for either gull or man, ye'll admit, though?"

The gull bobbed its head from side to side and uttered a soft *coo-uh, coo-uh*, its pinkish legs doing a funny little side step in time with the bobbing head. It looked hopefully at his coffee cup. Casey smiled.

"My daddy always said ye should offer food to yer company, said 'twas the least ye could do for them, considerin' they were trapped in yer home for politeness sake an' would have to listen to ye whether they liked it or no'." He tore off another strip of the mealy bread.

"Now ye understand, ye'll owe me the kindness of a listenin' ear," he told the gull, holding out the bread. The bird hesitated only momentarily, keeping a wary eye on the broad calloused palm from which it received its meal.

"In Boston for the winter, are ye? It's not so bad as cities go, though ye might want to look for a better neighborhood than this one."

He took another slug of coffee, which was distinctly bitter now, handed the gull another piece of the bread and turned his gaze toward the outlines of the neighborhood. A light was on here and there, wakeful babies with exhausted parents, drunks stumbling home believing the last of the dark would hide their sins, and people that simply could not sleep. There were streets here, particularly in Southie, where he could almost believe he was back in Belfast.

But it wasn't Belfast, and the streets here were not controlled by political mobs, instead they were controlled by the *actual* mob. Everything that stretched below him—the buildings, the streets, and the people inside the graffitti-littered brick homes—was owned lock, stock and smoking barrel by his boss, Lovett Hagerty. Including the building in which he and his wife were housed.

The two of them had arrived in Boston on a beautiful September day, exhausted, uncertain, and in Pamela's case, four months pregnant. Love Hagerty had sent a car to meet them at Logan airport, had arranged their housing, and had found Pamela a doctor and Casey a job within his own organization.

The pregnancy had surprised the both of them. Pamela had only missed her monthlies the one time and so when the doctor told her she was four months gone, with a child due to arrive early in the new year, she had been, to say the least, surprised. As had he. After surprise had come a sneaking happiness which had made both of them discuss the future with anticipation and a fragile hope.

Pamela had gone to work for Love Hagerty soon after their arrival. Casey viewed the job offer with some cynicism. He was used to men staring at his wife, used to the desire that rose unbidden in their eyes even as she passed them in the streets. Generally speaking, though, a sharp look or an arm about her shoulders made them turn away, faces flushing with shame. Not so with Love Hagerty. Pamela had assured Casey, however, that she could handle Mr. Hagerty, and so had gone to work on a campaign that was faltering in its final furlong toward Election Day. Pamela had replaced an assistant who had suddenly, and rather conveniently, Casey thought, found herself quite ill.

The work itself had put Casey's antennae up. Pamela's own father had been involved in Irish American politics and she had been, in part, groomed for the rough and tumble etiquette of that world. Casey knew this only after long, late night conversations about his wife's childhood. How Love Hagerty had been so certain that she would fit this world like an ivory hand within a velvet glove was something that worried him a great deal. There was, however, little use gainsaying the woman when she made her mind up to a task. And he trusted her implicitly, even if he trusted Love Hagerty less and less with each week that passed.

Shamed as he was to admit it, he had been surprised to find Pamela within her element in the world of Boston politics. She knew how to smooth ruffled feathers, cajole money and time from the wealthy, and make every constituent feel as though their vote was the only one that mattered. She was a priceless asset, he only wondered how Love Hagerty had so swiftly and clearly seen that which had astonished him.

The baby they had begun to build an entire world around was lost a mere month later. Through it all Love had expressed concern, sent flowers and small treats, and finally one afternoon arrived on their doorstep to lure Pamela back into the world of politics he had instinctively known would be her saving grace. While grateful for the return of his wife to the world, Casey had been less pleased about the method employed. For Love Hagerty, smooth and polished as sapphire on the outside, was, behind the sparkling façade, a much darker stone altogether.

Love, who had dreams of one day dwelling in the governor's mansion, had a crooked finger in every pie South Boston had to offer. Though his own fingers—should they be inspected—were squeaky clean. Love controlled the neighborhood, but he did it intravenously, through the corrupt line of Blackie Brindle.

Blackie, who ran his office out of the back of a pub called *The Shamrock and Shillelagh*, was feared and respected throughout the whole of South Boston. Born to first generation Irish immigrants Blackie was raised on the streets of South Boston, where the code held that a man took care of his own and kept his mouth shut about all he knew and saw. As Love Hagerty's right-hand man, he oversaw the vast majority of sports betting, numbers running, loan-sharking, and drug dealing that occurred south of the Fort Point Channel. And that was not to mention the prostitution rings, paid protection, and deals that were cooking between Southie and Boston's North End, where Giulio Bassarelli and his family held court—and the reins of power—for New England's mafia.

"Do ye know what it is to have knowledge of things that ye've no wish to know, to have things that ye've seen an' heard be a burden?" Casey said softly, the last piece of the bread lying on his palm.

The gull took the bread, less cautious now. Ruffling its feathers, it sank down onto webbed feet to enjoy this final bit of breakfast.

Born to a Republican family in a hard neighborhood, incarcerated in a British prison for five years, Casey was no stranger to trouble. But he'd never really felt as frightened as he did this moment. Belfast was a tough city, but he understood its rules, knew which streets were safe and which were not. Even prison, though terrifying, had operated within a set of parameters that he learned to adjust to. South Boston, and the two men who had a stranglehold on its streets and rundown tenements, was a different kettle of fish altogether. Just when he thought he had a grip on things, they shifted, presenting him with a whole new face, unfamiliar and unwanted. On his own he could manage, but now he had a wife to take care of, and it was this fact that made fear a constant presence in his life.

The gull stood and stretched, giving its wings a couple of flaps, while stretching its neck out towards Casey with a questioning look.

"I've no more, wee fella," Casey said, showing his hands to the bird, palms up.

The sun was no more than a watery hint against the mirror of sky as the gull took its leave, the underside of its wings catching a fleeting green glow off the neon shamrock.

Casey watched until the bird became a mere speck caught between the rising sun and the sea, and wished fervently that he could leave his own troubles behind with such ease.

He stood, shut the window and glanced wearily at the clock above the stove. Blackie was waiting. It was time to go to work.

Chapter Two

True Love

IF THE SMALL TRIBAL enclaves of South Boston could be called a kingdom, then Lovett Hagerty was undoubtedly its king. To outward appearances he was a benevolent ruler, a true son of South Boston, with a curious mix of Brahmin and Southie genes.

Most residents of South Boston's neighborhoods had known Love since he was wearing booties and a bonnet. They had watched him grow from an angelic faced altar boy to a twelve year old entrepreneur who'd invested in his own string of newspaper kiosks. To a man who everyone feared, who ruled his empire with a dark velvet smile and an iron fist. Rumor had it that he'd made his first million before his twentieth birthday.

His childhood was the stuff of legend on the streets of South Boston. How at thirteen he'd stood his ground against a notorious Italian gang, armed only with a baseball bat and sheer bravado, when they tried to sell drugs on his block. How at fifteen he'd convinced a group of old Boston Brahmins to fund the building of a Boys' Club in the City Point district. And Love always gave back, the old timers said, more than he took.

Each Thanksgiving and Christmas without fail, five hundred turkeys would find their way onto the doorsteps in Southie that needed them most. Public works jobs could almost always be found for new immigrants over from the 'auld sod', in exchange for votes, favors and blind eyes. Love had the neighborhood tied up so tight that most of its occupants didn't dare breathe without asking his approval first. Women with problem sons and husbands with problem wives sought his counsel, and woe betide any man caught committing a crime on his turf.

Love didn't keep the normal gangster hours of mid-afternoon to the wee sma's, he kept a politician's hours—available twenty-four hours a day, seven days a week, even during mass should someone need a willing ear, a lending hand, or a shoulder to cry upon.

But there were also the whispers, like a transparent black ribbon, furtive and sinuous, that unfurled behind closed doors and under the influence of too much drink. Of how Love only cared if drugs were being sold on his streets if the profits weren't making their way to his pocket. That he'd killed George Kellen, the man who'd helped him get his start on the streets, to ingratiate himself with the Somers gang, who, if the rumors were to be believed, had all found themselves behind prison bars, courtesy of Love's involvement with an FBI agent who'd grown up in Southie and was still bedazzled by Love's legend and charisma. But the whispers stayed just that—from fear, from need, from a neighborhood code that meant outsiders, especially those in the law enforcement industry, were not welcome, nor expected to understand the rules by which this most Irish of neighborhoods conducted its business.

For the one truth everyone understood was that the police usually didn't get there fast enough to save you if you crossed Love Hagerty. Certainly it was Blackie who did the dirty work, or contracted it out, but everyone knew it was Love you didn't cross. Because the Irish charm and good looks were only a surface veneer, something far colder and uglier lay just beneath the skin.

SOUTH BOSTON WAS TRIBAL by nature. Some streets in Southie were microcosms of Irish counties, blocks where only emigrants from Galway lived, or Cork, or Kerry.

Love Hagerty knew this, and used it to his own advantage. South Boston, called Southie with pride and affection by its inhabitants, was a geography he understood intimately.

He often walked in his old neighborhood in the small hours, when the streets were mostly empty and he could keep his silence and not have to glad-hand a hundred strangers. He liked to picture it as it had once been—pastures and orchards filled with peach, apple and plum trees, the magnificent stands of elm that had once surrounded the houses of the original land barons who had been part of the English invasion of these shores. Those English had quickly become Americans, though, and were the beginning of the brash young colony that would eventually banish the British army back to their homeland, and write a constitution for the nation that was based on liberty, equality and justice. Though that justice would not initially extend to the immigrant tide that would flood Boston in the seventeen and eighteen hundreds.

For though the English had established the first foothold, there was no doubt that this was an Irish city. The Irish were the backbone of this country, and this was never truer than in the great cities of the East Coast. The railroads, canals and mines were built upon the back of Irish labor. A journalist of the times once said,

"There are several kinds of power working at the fabric of the republic—water-power, steam-power and Irish-power. The last works hardest of all."

Love was the product of a Boston Brahmin mother who'd been disowned by her family when she'd married his first generation Irish American father. He had been born to a family that, while not poverty stricken, certainly understood what it was to worry where the next meal might come from.

Tonight he stood upon his favorite bit of the old neighborhood, the eastern portion of the peninsula, called City Point because it looked out over the vast expanse of the Atlantic Ocean. Love liked a horizon that was without limits. It was how he viewed his own life.

The Point had become an area for many institutions over the years, its fresh salt air and broad green pastures seen as the ideal spot for hospitals, poorhouses, mental asylums, and a house of corrections for adults guilty of misdemeanors, as well as a separate institution for juvenile offenders. The maze of all these brick buildings slowly ate away the green pastures, fruitful orchards and lovely homes that had once graced this neck of land on the edge of the Atlantic. The resentment shaped by the city construction of these places was the seed of discontent that would make South Boston turn in upon itself, become self-sufficient, and forge the 'us against them' mentality that would become a theme in Southie.

The refrain of an old song flitted through his head and he smiled,

> *It will make you or break you,*
> *But never forsake you,*
> *Southie is my home town.*

It was an attitude that had seen Southie through many crises: the influenza epidemic of 1918, the Great Depression that swept through factory-laden Southie with a particular vengeance, labor disputes, and gang turf wars. Southie survived it all, due in large part to the interconnected family network that was the hallmark of the community. Those who had little gave to those who had less. Doors were open, beds available and an extra place at the table could always be managed. In many ways, the culture was a continuation of the old Irish village way of life.

It was a way of life Love understood, and subverted to his needs. It was easier to keep things quiet when outsiders weren't spoken with, when police weren't trusted, when people were afraid and grateful all in the same breath.

Every once in awhile, however, a person came along who didn't understand the status quo in this neighborhood. Or they understood and thought they were an exception to the rules. Casey Riordan was such a person. He was becoming a problem that Love didn't want to deal with anymore. He'd liked him at first, had thought he'd work well within the tight knit organization Love ran. It hadn't been long before he realized he'd sorely miscalculated the man's character.

He had to admit he didn't think a man who'd come looking for IRA funding would also be in possession of a conscience, or of a wife who literally took the breath from Love's body.

Love Hagerty was used to getting what he wanted and he had never wanted anything more than he did Pamela Riordan. He had known it from the first time he set eyes upon her.

It had been a Sunday dinner at his house, and he'd invited the two of them to join his family. She had come in behind Casey, laughingly picking leaves from her hair, where they'd fallen in autumnal splendor amongst the blue-black curls, and he had been stopped cold there in the marble entryway of his Beacon Hill home.

Had she been merely beautiful, and God knew she was certainly that, he was sure the obsession would have run its course. However, as he'd drawn her into conversation during dinner, she had revealed herself to be witty and intelligent, with a sense of humor and an ability to read situations very clearly.

It had taken only days to get the rest of the information on her. How she'd grown up. He'd whistled when he realized just who her father had been, it explained a whole hell of a lot about her level of sophistication, her knowledge of Irish American politics and business, and her polish in dealing with social situations.

Her history with the Clann na Gael he'd found very interesting. Details were scant, but through his contacts, he had been able to determine that she'd done some work for the Clann, which was ostensibly the American wing of the Irish Republican Army.

And then she had fled to Ireland and to the house of James Kirkpatrick. That tidbit of information had given him pause. He didn't know the man, but had been able to glean enough from the reports he'd received to know he wasn't someone to be trifled with. His fiscal resources exceeded that of many small nations, he was also an MP for West Belfast and a man that stirred up talk and speculation everywhere he went. He was particularly popular with the ladies, and Love wondered exactly what Pamela's relationship to him had been. It couldn't have been more than dalliance, he surmised, for she had married Casey less than a year later.

It was as though she'd been born and bred to sit at his side. The queen he'd been waiting for, even though he had not known it. His marriage of twenty-four years suddenly seemed not the comfort it had previously been, but an impediment. He'd never been faithful, and his wife was resigned to it, as long as he exercised discretion. He'd had a series of affairs over the years, but they had been merely a satisfying of physical lusts. This was different. This was the woman destiny had foreordained for him.

There was a glitch, however, for she loved her husband. It was apparent in the way she looked at him, in the way their eyes would meet in an intimate look that excluded everyone else in the room, even though it was not consciously done. The heat in the air around them near to scorched those within their aura. It was a powerful bond, and he knew better than to underestimate the depth of such a thing. Love, however, not one to admit impediments, saw this as merely a temporary setback.

He took one last look out over the water. The fog was heavy, shrouding the rest of Boston from view. From this vantage, Southie was the whole world. His father used to bring him to the Point when he was young and tell him that all of America lay before his feet.

"It's yours for the taking, boy," he'd say.

Love nodded to himself, as though he could hear his father's voice in the here and now.

Something would have to be done soon about the Irishman. He didn't like all these sleepless nights. They made a man sentimental.

Chapter Three

Agent Gus

THE WIND COMING in off the Atlantic scoured the streets of Boston with an icy breath that left a sparkling frost in its wake. While pretty, it was also fiercely cold to be walking in. Particularly for an Irishman used to the milder winter exhalations of Belfast.

Weather notwithstanding, Casey liked these walks to work. Today he was driving one of Love's 'associates' down to Hartford. It made for a long, boring day and he would have preferred to unload the shipment of furniture that was docked at a warehouse in Southie. The driving paid better, though, and with his godfather Desmond's visit looming imminently in his near future, Casey wanted to be sure that he was on as secure a financial footing as possible. He knew Desmond had his doubts about the wisdom of what he saw as a precipitate move across the Atlantic. In spite of, or perhaps because of, his own doubts as to how wise they had been in this venture, Casey wanted to put as good a face on their situation as possible. Desmond would see that he was a man well able to look after his own family, no matter how small said family might be.

Though he had experienced a few bouts of homesickness, altogether he liked Boston. It was a brash city with enough Irish running in its arteries that he didn't feel entirely adrift.

During Colonial times, Boston had been a tiny pear-shaped peninsula connected to the mainland by a narrow strip of land. Each day when the tide came in Boston became an island. Due to its size, Boston's residents had little need for horses and carts, and walked wherever they needed to go. Thus it became a city of winding footpaths—between home and church, church and business, business and tavern. Over streams, around rocks and trees and other natural obstacles.

The ghosts of these obstacles remained in the meandering way of the paths, which became cobbled streets and then eventually paved roads. It left Boston with the unplanned charm of the old cities its inhabitants had left behind in Europe.

Casey enjoyed the history of these streets, the narrow wee laneways with oaks and elms overhanging the pavement.

He was just two blocks shy of his destination when he spotted the man. He cursed softly under his breath and put his head down into the wind, hoping the man wouldn't see him. He turned left instead of the right he had intended to take and picked up his pace considerably, breaking into a half run. He'd just have to approach take the Chatham approach rather than his usual route up Congress.

He glanced over his shoulder. The man had disappeared. He heaved a breath of relief and turned the corner. The man stood directly in front of him, a deceptively amiable smile on his face.

"Christ on a piece of toast!" Casey exclaimed. "Ye're lucky I didn't smack ye, poppin' up like a friggin' jack-in-the-box."

"Sorry about that, but you've given me the slip ten times in the last two weeks, so I had to get tricky."

"Has it occurred to ye," Casey said dryly, "that I've given ye the slip because I've no desire to talk to ye? I've already given ye an answer to the question ye keep askin'. My mind isn't goin' to change."

The short, slightly pudgy agent with the disarming smile and crew cut hair had become, for Casey, the stuff of nightmares. The sort you desperately wished to wake from, but couldn't quite seem to.

He'd first seen him two weeks before when it became evident to him that the short man in the bad suit was following him and not merely taking the same route to work. This was exactly what Agent Gus had claimed to be doing, when Casey had waited around a corner and confronted him. Casey had responded with threats that were not veiled in the slightest, assuring the man that he knew a federal agent when he saw one.

"Thought it was the best time of day to talk with you, before everyone is out and about."

Casey cast a quick glance around and blew air onto his hands in a futile effort to warm them. "Listen, I told ye I'd nothin' to say to ye the four days past. Not a thing has happened to change my opinion in that time."

Agent Gus smiled like a friendly dog that doesn't understand when it's being told to get lost. It was a trait that was beginning to grate sorely on Casey's nerves.

"I think you might change your mind one of these days," the agent replied cheerfully, sticking his own hands in the brown polyester armpits of his suit to warm them.

"Aye, if I want a hole or two in my skull, or to be found floatin' facedown in the Charles. Until then I'll thank ye to keep yer distance." He nodded curtly and made to move around the man.

Agent Gus, however, was nothing if not persistent. "That girl you drove home the other night—the pretty one with the blonde hair?"

Casey froze in place, wondering what angle the agent was playing now. "What about her?"

"Do you know what she does for a living?"

"I've not time to play twenty questions here man, if ye've something ye wish to say, say it an' let me get on my way."

"She's a hooker—didn't used to be though. She used to be Hagerty's girlfriend. That's what he does with people, uses them up and then throws them away. That's the sort of man you're protecting."

Casey had an uncomfortable memory of the woman, crying in the back seat of his car, makeup smeared and face anguished. She had been inadequately clad for the bitter chill of the day and pathetically grateful to him for driving her home to an area of Jamica Plain that had seen far better days. He shook his head to rid himself of the vision.

"Maybe it's not him I'm protectin', maybe it's merely self-preservation."

"We could protect you."

Casey shook his head and snorted. "Ye must think I'm terrible naïve. Ye've no doubt had a good look at my own past. That alone ought to tell ye how likely I am to rat a man out."

Agent Gus shrugged. "Doesn't make it any easier to sleep at night, though, does it? You think about it, Mr. Riordan and when you decide you'd like a conscience you can live with again, give us a call. We'll be waiting."

Casey took a deep breath and walked away from the man. He got half a block before turning back to look. Agent Gus was still standing there waving cheerfully.

Casey cursed under his breath and continued down the block. Agent Gus was even more annoying when he was right.

Chapter Four

Have Yourself a Merry Little Christmas

"CASEY RIORDAN," PAMELA said with a smile, "I do believe you're nervous."

Casey twitched uncomfortably at his starched collar. "Damned right I am," he said, "this is no friendly visit, ye know."

He stood in the middle of their bedroom, clad in gray dress pants and a stiff white shirt that had him looking as miserable as a scalded cat. Desmond, Siobhan and Patrick were due in at Logan in slightly less than three hours. Sylvie had decided against the trip to Boston, taking the opportunity of Pat's absence to visit her family in Derry for the holidays. It couldn't be Pat making him nervous, for the two had settled their estrangment once Casey knew Pat had accepted the invitation to come to Boston for Christmas.

Pamela undid the top button of his shirt, smoothing the white cloth along his shoulders, more in an effort to calm him than rid him of imaginary wrinkles. "What on earth are you talking about?"

"Just what I said, this is no friendly visit on Dez's part, he'll be coming to see how we're set up over here, if I'm providin' well for ye, an' how I'm farin' on the wrong side of the pond. His words," he added apologetically, "not mine."

"It will all be fine," she said, brushing an errant lock of hair behind his ear and kissing the tip of his nose. From either side of it he glared down at her.

"I don't know how ye can be so certain of that."

"Because," she replied softly, "they love you, so whatever they think of our home, or this city, it will all be well so long as they see that you're happy. That's why they're really coming, you know—to see if you're happy."

"Well, that I am," he replied, voice still a tad gruff with nerves. He narrowed his eyes at her. "Though it'd be better had ye put a bit of weight on, leastways then Dez would know I'm feedin' ye."

She arched a sooty brow at him. "I'm starting to feel like the autumn sow here."

He looked her over with a critical eye and sighed, as if he would be much happier if she were in as full flesh as an autumn sow.

"Ye just look a wee bit thin in yer clothes, Jewel. Now out of them," he waggled an eyebrow at her, "it's another matter altogether."

She put her hands on her hips. "Are you saying I'm fat out of my clothes?"

"No, never," he assured her, pulling her into his embrace, "only that ye've lines to ye that can only be fully appreciated when viewed in the altogether."

"Mmnn," she murmured, not fully convinced.

Casey grasped her hips and rather firmly made it clear that he was currently appreciating her lines, despite the fact that they were hidden from view beneath a sweater and jeans.

She undid another of his buttons, feeling that a return appreciation of his own lines was only polite under the circumstances.

"Lord, woman," he gasped a moment later, "I've not the time for this. I'll be late for the plane."

"Oh well, in that case," she removed her tongue from the hollow at the base of his throat, only to have him pull her directly back.

"Not so hasty, I've a minute or two, besides it'll help relieve my tension."

She looked up, catching the glint in his dark eyes and knew that whatever he now had in mind, odds were it was going to take a lot longer than a minute or two.

"I might wrinkle you," she said, taking a last stab at preserving the virtue of his unmolested clothes.

"D'ye know," he grinned, and pulled his shirt off over his head, "I think I'll risk it."

IT HAD LONG BEEN A RIORDAN family tradition that the host toasted all those who sat at his Christmas table. Casey, standing at the head of his own table, a glass of red wine in hand, remembered the eloquence of his own father, and felt justifiably nervous.

But then he looked at the people gathered round him, and a warm glow set up within him that had little to do with the whiskey he'd shared with Desmond and Pat before dinner. These were people he loved, who knew him, who would forgive him a tongue less than silver, should his nerves get the better of him.

The table, scarlet-clothed, was near to groaning under the weight of turkey and potatoes, candied yams, those nasty wee cabbage thingies that Pamela called Brussels Sprouts (as if that would fool him into putting one in his mouth) stuffing, cranberry sauce, carrots and the omnipresent coarse Irish soda bread. At least, he thought with some satisfaction, Desmond would see that he was capable of feeding his wife, and occasionally a few others as well. He turned his attention to the man in question, who sat to his left hand, and cleared his throat to begin his small Christmas speech.

Desmond and Siobhan, childless themselves, had long considered Casey and Patrick their surrogate sons. During his years in prison, Siobhan had written weekly, though Casey had rarely had the heart to respond. Truth was he'd been too ashamed, because they, more than anyone, knew how he had been raised, and how disappointed his own daddy would have been in him.

It was with a pang that he noted the gray in Siobhan's hair, and wondered how her heart was doing. When he asked, she was wont to say 'fine' and leave it at that. But he saw the vague worry that hovered in the back of Desmond's eyes every time he looked at her, and wondered what the doctor down in Dublin had to say at her last check-up.

Then there was Desmond himself, still with the look of a slightly tipsy owl about him, but formidable nonetheless, a man whose judgement and advice Casey had always respected and sought.

"To Desmond and Siobhan, thank ye for makin' the trip over an' for takin' over the parentin' of Patrick an' myself when our daddy no longer could."

Desmond nodded, as if to say no less could have been expected of them, but Siobhan surreptitiously wiped tears with a linen napkin.

His eye moved further along the table, alighting on Pat, his brother, a man now, long of line and pleasing to the eye. As dark in color as he himself was, though leaner and with a more sensitive look to him. A strong man, driven by the things he knew to be right. Casey felt a stir of pride, and wished his father could be here to see how fine a human being this younger son of his had become.

"To my brother who has been my best friend and who has become someone I am proud to know. *Tá grá agam duit*, Patrick."

Pat nodded. "Likewise, brother, always."

Casey took a deep breath, wondering if it was the wine that had made him so sentimental. Whiskey didn't bother him, but he'd never developed a head for wine.

At the foot of the table, emerald eyes smoky in the candlelight, sat his wife. Smiling at him as he stood, carving tools laid out near his right hand, the warm aromas of turkey and thyme, sage and brown sugar rising up in a comforting vapor around him.

Her hair was pulled up and away, exposing the long length of her neck. His rubies glowed like living things at her throat and in bright drops at her ears. He winked and blew her a kiss, and she flushed, a trait he found incredibly endearing considering the sorts of things that they got up to in bed, yet a simple kiss in front of others could make her color up like a schoolgirl.

This morning he'd given her his gift by the tree, while it was still dark and everyone else slept, the apartment quiet around them. She had opened the box with eager anticipation, and when she saw what lay within had clasped her hands together like a small child before drawing the gift forth from its careful wrapping. She had held it in her hands, wordless, eyeing it as though it were some sort of sacred artifact.

He had found it in the bowels of a dusty, dark hovel of a secondhand store two months before, and had then set about the painstaking job of finding someone to bring it back to its original state. It was a 35mm Leica, a camera around which myths had been built for the quality of its photos. It was a photographer's camera, to be used with the passion and intensity of the artist, and Casey had known it belonged in his wife's hands from the moment he'd seen it.

"D'ye like it, then?"

"It's amazing," she had breathed out, eyes bright with tears. "You're amazing," she whispered later, pulling him down for a kiss that left him in no doubt as to the depth of her gratitude. He'd been bemused at her emotion, thinking as he often did that women were a mystery, but this one was a puzzle he never tired of trying to solve. To him it was a wee box, but to her it was that intangible link between the vision in her head and the story—in a thousand shades of gray—that her pictures would tell.

Finally there was the one empty chair near his own, which he'd been puzzled by, for it was set complete with china and cutlery, and even a wine glass that Pamela had filled along with all the others.

"It's for our fathers," she'd said simply, and it had been his turn to feel that rush of gratitude for her understanding of the things within his heart.

He turned his head toward the empty chair, seeing in mind the two men who had had the shaping and forming of their lives. And the two women as well, who were still in the world and yet more absent somehow than the fathers who had died.

"For those who are no longer with us in body, but remain in spirit," he said toasting the chair, where the candlelight glowed, lambent as gemstones, within the belly of the wine poured for those missing, but always remembered. Everyone raised their glass in silent homage.

Casey turned again to his wife. "Pamela, *mo mhúirnín bán*," he said with great tenderness, "the jewel at the center of my heart, who is the gift God saw fit, for no reason I can fathom, to give me and for whom I am truly grateful. Without you, I would be lost."

She raised her own wine in salute, the delicate glass casting trembling gold prisms over the fine skin of her face and neck. Tears pooled on the thick edge of her lashes.

"And I without you, you bloody Irishman."

He grinned and put his wine glass down, picked up the carving knife and put it to the turkey.

"Let's eat then, for my stomach, despite all evidence to the contrary, thinks me throat's been cut."

LATER, WHEN EVERYONE else had gone to bed, Casey made his way up to the roof, where he now sat watching as snowflakes, like delicate, miniature stars, fell upon the heavy swirls of tar, lending a transient beauty to that which was not beautiful. Funny how at a distance all things seemed lovely, even the light-ridden city laid out below him.

Somewhere in the distance he could hear, faintly, the sound of *Silent Night* being played on an organ. Father Kevin, perhaps, playing his arias to a distant God in the hollow heart of the Church of the Assumption.

"'Tis a pretty night," Pat said.

"Aye, 'tis," Casey replied, having sensed his brother's presence as soon as he'd lit upon the roof. "Thought ye were sleepin', man."

Pat shook his head, coming to sit down beside Casey in the chill, wet air, huddled against the cold in a lumpy old coat that had been left behind by the previous tenant. It smelled mildly of stale beer and smoke, but it was warm.

"What are ye thinkin' about?" Pat asked, attempting to burrow his hands deeper into the misshapen pockets of the ugly coat.

Casey shook his head, looking out through the separate veils of snow, seeing the dull pink glow of Dorchester on the horizon. Then decided to tell the truth.

"Mam. I was thinkin' about mam."

"Because it's Christmas?"

Casey shrugged, flicking the remnants of his cigarette off the edge of the roof, watching its faint red light turn over twice and then disappear into the snow and the street below. "I suppose. I can put her out of my mind most other days, but Christmas tends to bring her back."

"I don't remember any Christmas with her," Pat said quietly.

"Aye," Casey looked down at his hands, clearing his throat, "I suppose ye were too young. She was good at Christmas, though, seemed like she came out of the darkness an' all the space about her would be lit up for those few days. It was enough," he paused, throat unaccountably thick, "to keep ye lovin' her for the rest of the year."

"She left on Christmas Eve, didn't she?" Pat asked.

"She did."

"Do ye remember it?"

Casey shook his head. "Only in bits an' pieces, not the whole of it. I think daddy tried to shield me from the knowledge until Christmas was over."

Pat cleared his throat. "I got a letter from her 'bout eight months back."

"Did ye, then?" Casey asked, voice stiff.

"Aye, I did," Pat replied, "she said she'd written ye years back, but ye'd not responded. She asked after ye."

"Kind of her." He wanted to ask where she was now, and what she'd had to say for herself, but couldn't bring himself to do it around the pain that had formed in his chest. Pat however, being like to their daddy, didn't need him to ask.

"She's still in England, little village in Sussex. She's married to a nice man, she says. They own a wee shop that sells the papers an' candy."

"What happened to the Indian man?"

Pat shrugged. "She never said."

"Did ye write back?" Casey asked, digging in his pocket for another cigarette.

"I did."

"Mmphmm," was Casey's only reply to this.

"We've written back an' forth a few times since." When this statement was met with stony silence, Pat sighed heavily.

"Would ye rather I'd ignored her, as ye've chosen to do?"

"No, ye're grown, 'tis yer business whether ye've to do with her or not."

"An' what about you?" Pat asked.

Casey shook his head, sending a cold spray of snow down the back of his collar. "She doesn't exist for me anymore."

Wisely, Pat changed the subject. "Do ye remember that Christmas Eve ye got legless on rum an' eggnog, an' passed out under the tree?"

Casey smiled ruefully. "Aye, I remember, 'twas the night Mrs. McLeod found us out pissin' our names in the snow."

Pat winced slightly at the memory. "Never could see her after that without thinkin' that she knew exactly what my backside looked like."

"Was that same Christmas Daddy gave ye yer telescope."

Pat nodded, a white halo of fluffy snow sitting on his short-cropped curls. "I never did understand how he managed to afford it. I'd expected a secondhand book, maybe a sweater or somethin' but when I opened it, 'twas magic."

"He sold his books," Casey said.

"He what?" Pat asked sharply.

"He sold all the books granda had left him, some of them had a bit of value to them. He said that ye might have to have yer feet on the ground, but he'd do what he could to keep yer soul out there amongst the stars where it belonged."

Pat shook his head. "I never knew," he said. "Times I wonder if I ever knew daddy at all."

Casey shrugged. "He was a good man, an' the best father anyone could ask for. Beyond that he kept himself to himself."

"He was terrible private about himself, but mighty free with his opinions when it came to us."

"I think," Casey said slowly, "that he sensed at times that he'd not be with us for very long, an' so he tried to cram all the things he wanted to teach us in the time he did have."

"I used to think his tongue lashins' were the worst thing about livin' with him, but once he was gone, I realized the silence was much harder to bear. There's still days I'd give anything to have him take a strip off me, or tell me he'd never known a more stubborn fool. Though I think he bestowed that title on you more often than me."

"Aye, well, that particular shoe fit me rather well. Still does, I suppose."

"Ye won't find me disagreein' with that statement," Pat said, then shivered, "I'm for bed, man, are ye comin' in?"

"No, I'll bide for a few minutes more. Sleep well, brother."

He heard the door creak as Pat slipped through it, and then the deep silence descended once again. Even the occasional car that went past seemed muffled and far away.

Casey hadn't been entirely truthful with Pat, he did remember that Christmas Eve. He'd only wanted to forget, but had never managed to erase it from his memory.

They'd come from Midnight Mass, Pat asleep on Brian's shoulder, a stick of candy someone had given him, still clutched tight in his toddler's fist—red and white stripes with a fine ribbon of green running between them. Casey eagerly anticipating opening the one gift he was allowed before bed.

The table was set with holly and red candles. There were candles in the window as well, gleaming against the faultlessly polished glass. The smell of Christmas food provided a warm welcome. But there was no feeling of content, only a strange flickering emptiness, a silence that was not peaceful.

Many years later, he would look back and see it as one of those strange pivotal moments where the world you know slips away to be replaced by a completely new one, and as much as things look the same—the walls, the table, the streets, the sky, your father—they aren't even similar to the way they were before. At the time, though, he only felt a strange hunger in his belly that had nothing to do with food. Even at six, he understood that much.

Somehow, the still had told him without words what his father tried carefully to explain to him the next day. But for those first moments of realization they had remained silent, both father and son, as if the web of quiet would somehow buy them a few more moments of ignorance.

"Blow the candles out, will ye, son?" Brian had said from over top of Pat's head, the wee lad boneless and heavy against their father's chest. Casey had gone, window by window, seeing in each of them his own pale face, reflected starkly against the night that huddled tight to the glass. And had blown the candles out, watching his face disappear in tendrils of smoke, and seeing in the face of that boy the knowledge that Christmas, however many might come, would never again be the same.

He stood up, body damp and chilled from sitting so long in the snow. He was tired, and wanted the comfort of his wife and his bed. He glanced upward before turning towards the roof door. The snow still fell thickly, melting as it touched his skin.

"*Nollaig Shona Duit, Mathair*," he said softly, not to the mother that sold papers and sweets in England, but to the one who'd cleaned the windows and lit the candles before she'd left his life forever.

Chapter Five

Judas Kiss

THERE WAS BLOOD. A great deal of it. Casey couldn't see it, but he could smell it. That earthy fecund scent carried on the wind. No one could lose that much blood and live. He tried not to breathe too deeply. Was it possible that only two hours before he'd dropped off Love Hagerty at his Boylston Street office, and had been about to take the car to the garage where it stayed overnight, and then catch the train home?

Just as he'd been turning the car around, Emma had dashed out from the shadows of the office wall and knocked on the driver's window. He had rolled the window down, thinking that maybe she needed a ride; he'd driven her home a few times. As usual, she was dressed too skimpily for the weather, and her hands were red and chapped with the cold.

There was a low-pressure system sitting off the coast, brewing up a brutal nor-easter that was expected to dump huge amounts of snow on the city overnight. He wanted to be home before it hit, but he knew he'd not rest easy with himself if he didn't make sure she was safe home first.

"I...I need a ride, but not home," she'd said and he saw that her shaking wasn't just from the cold, she was afraid of something.

"Get in the car, it's perishin' out there."

She scuttled around the car and got in, her cheeks bright red and her nose tipped in cherry. He handed her his fur-lined driving gloves.

"Thanks," she said pulling the gloves on. Then she had turned to him, and he saw beneath the winter-chilled flush, she was white with fear. Pale gold hair framed a face with high Slavic cheekbones and amber eyes. Emma was the prostitute Agent Gus had spoken of. Emma was also a friend of sorts. The first time Casey had met her had been when he found her crying on the front steps of the office building, seemingly oblivious to the people staring at her as they walked by. He had given her a tissue, put her in the car and driven her home. Since then he checked in with her occasionally, let her warm herself in the car when he saw her walking. Fed her hot tea from a thermos and gave her the extras from his lunch.

When he had explained this odd relationship to his wife she had sighed and said all things considered, it didn't surprise her. Whether this was compliment or insult, or merely a commentary on his general nature, he did not know, though he noticed that his lunch increased markedly in quantity right after.

"How can I help?" he asked.

That misguided question was what had landed him here, in the snowy pine woods in the foothills of the White Mountains. Boston was now three hours behind them. The last town he'd seen was a good eight miles back. The foothills were the beginning of a stretch of fir and granite that ran up to the border of Canada. The place he found himself now was as remote as the backend of hell, and twice as inhospitable. They had turned off the I-93 and taken four different secondary roads, to finally wind their way down a narrow twisting road that was rutted with autumn's hard frosts, and swiftly being obliterated by the driving snow.

"Are ye certain this is the place?" Casey asked dubiously. The property sat in the notch between two mountain slopes. It was a curved hollow with a lake cradled at its lowest point. Tall white pine coated the steep slopes that rose darkly from the shores. A small cabin and a weathered boathouse faced each other across a space of blowing snow. Both were dark and empty.

"Y...yes," Emma said through chattering teeth. "I'm sure. She gave me directions in case she needed me to come up here. I thought she meant in case her car broke down or something."

Casey blew on his hands. They'd had to leave the car back a ways, as the snow had simply gotten too deep as the road narrowed. Whatever reason Rosemary had for giving Emma directions to this isolated area, he didn't think it was to provide transportation. The reasons that occurred to him weren't designed to comfort either of them.

"Did she say why or who she was meetin'?"

"No, she said it was wicked dangerous for me to know. I don't know why. Rosemary and I always tell each other where we'll be, and with who. We watch each other's backs. That alone worried me. It had to be bad if she couldn't tell me." She shrugged, "You were the only person I could think of that might help me."

He checked the cabin first, a measure that was more avoidance than actual belief that it held Emma's friend. The cabin was cold and damp, but it smelled of earth and dried wood, not blood. A lone set of tracks led up to its door, but they turned on the porch and ran in a wavering line down to the boathouse.

The back end of the boathouse stood upon pilings that were rooted deep in the frozen innards of the lake. He walked beside the tracks, careful not to step in them himself. The odd one was still clear where the woman had passed under overhanging tree boughs and the snow was light on the ground. And it had been a woman; the toe was narrow and the heel pointy. Fashionable boots that were as useless as bare feet in terrain and cold such as this. Emma followed behind him, her own suede boots completely inadequate to the weather.

He hesitated outside the boathouse door, Emma clutching tight to his coat. The wind was moaning eerily through the tops of the tall pines, and neither of them was eager to see what lay behind this door. There were no tracks leading away, so unless Rosemary had somehow crawled out the back onto the icy surface of the lake, Casey knew she had not left this building.

He pushed the door open and walked in, Emma so close behind that she trod on his heels. He flicked on the torch in his hand. The shadows danced ghoulishly up the two-by-six planking and rough plywood walls. Nothing there. He moved the torchlight down to the floor.

The cold had congealed the blood so that she lay in a blue-black pool of it. Tiny wisps of steam rose from the pool, but even as he touched his fingers to her wrist, Casey knew the woman was dead. Not long dead, though, there was still a residual warmth to her skin. He cursed under his breath, though it wouldn't have made a difference had they gotten here earlier, she would have bled out anyway. Without a doctor and an emergency room, there was no way to stop a hemorrhage like this one.

O MOST MERCIFUL JESUS, lover of souls,
I beseech Thee, by the agony of Thy most Sacred Heart...

He muttered the prayer; in the face of death, his Catholic upbringing always asserted itself.

"Her throat's been slit." His voice was matter-of-fact. He knew there was no good way to relay such information. He slid the torch away from the gaping wound, the yellow-white of the large vessels of the neck were clearly visible and he did not want Emma to see them.

Emma nodded, still standing at a distance. Obviously, she too was familiar with the look of death, and had held no hope that the woman was still alive. He looked back at the dead woman. Dark red curls spiralled out from a narrow skull, the ends of her hair glistening black with blood. She was fair-skinned, with a handful of freckles splashed across the bridge of a sharpish nose. The eyes that stared unseeing into the beam of the torch were a pale green. An Irish girl, he thought. At least her ancestors were. It struck him hard, all the tragedies that had played out for the people who had come here with the very last of their hope. Hope so small that it could fit in a thimble, and yet had been enough to cross an ocean and begin life in a new and strange land.

"Why here d'ye think?"

"Far away enough from anything that no one would hear her scream."

Casey nodded, the same thought had occurred to him. Whoever had drawn the woman here must have known the place was deserted all winter, and must have planned to kill her once she arrived.

"I'm goin' back to the car to get a blanket," he said as he stood up. His knees were damp with blood and the clammy touch made his stomach clench.

Emma nodded, still standing stiff and dazed, staring down at the corpse that had been her friend. A woman for whom she had cared enough to run to her in the teeth of a terrible gale, in the hopes that she would arrive in time enough to save her.

By the time he reached the car Casey knew they would not be going anywhere this night. Already the car was up to its axles and the snow was falling both thicker and heavier than it had been when they'd arrived. The wind was lashing the myriad flakes into small tornadoes that stung his face and eyes. He looked up the small knoll, where the cabin sat like a dour old man with an eye patch, the one good eye looking out over the silver frosted lake. Then his gaze, narrowed against the stinging ice, swept back towards the lake.

Other than their own and Rosemary's, there were no tracks in the snow between the cabin and the boathouse, and had not been for some time. There had to be another set coming in from a different direction—maybe the man had come across the lake itself. The wind was roaring down the mountain slopes and blowing snow in great gusts over the ice. Any visible prints might already be obscured. He would have to check now.

Twilight was fast falling toward night as he walked out onto the ice, testing each step gingerly before applying his weight. The winter had been cold, though, and the ice was thick. He was right; the tracks were there, leading right from the window at the back of the boathouse. A man's boots, well treaded enough that the ridges in the sole were still visible when he blew the snow away. Given a few more hours, they would have been completely obliterated.

In his mind he could see the man coming across the ice in the twilight, early on enough in the storm that he'd be obscured from the sight of the other cabins that dotted the shoreline, but he could still make his way fairly easily. And he could see him waiting with the cunning patience of a natural hunter. The face on this hunter was one only too familiar to him. The cold Arctic gaze of Blackie Brindle, pale as the snow itself and twice as frozen. There was no direct proof and yet he sensed the man's presence, no longer here, just the dark energy he left in his wake.

Emma was waiting, huddled by the half-open boathouse door. Her lips were blue with cold, the shadow of storm and night scooping hollows out beneath her eyes and cheekbones. She looked like a corpse herself, the bones too close to the surface of her fragile skin. He needed to get her out of the cold.

"We'll have to hole up in the cabin for the night," he shouted over the whistle of the wind, his cheeks numb from the walk to the car and back. It was fiercely cold, but the towering white pines that grew down to the eastern shore of the lake would protect them from the worst of the wind.

Emma nodded, her own words lost on the wind and turned back one last time to look at her dead friend. He wanted to warn her not to do that, that to look back at a corpse was ill luck—that you risked taking the discontent of their spirit into your own by the act of seeing.

They followed their own footsteps back, the hollows already filling up over their ankles. They stamped their feet when they reached the tumbledown porch and went in the cabin.

Inside they found an old rusted bed frame with a lumpy and damp mattress on it. A little potbellied tin stove with a box of dry pine behind it, two half-burned candles thick with dust and another box filled with musty old newspapers. There were also two rickety chairs and a table with three legs. He had a book of matches in his pocket; for once he was grateful for his cigarette habit. He wasted no time in getting the stove lit, and they huddled near it, both chilled to the bone.

The full fury of the storm was over top them now, the wind shaking the frost-laden window panes. Drafts of cold air and small puffs of snow blew in through the logs. Casey stuffed the cracks with the old newspapers, his hands numb and clumsy.

By the time he was satisfied that he'd blocked out the worst of the wind, the fire had built up to a good blaze and it was warm in the old cabin. It was well built, and would serve to wait out the storm and the night. He thought of Pamela waiting for him to come home, torn between fury and fear, wondering why he didn't call. There wasn't much he could do, though, it would be near suicidal to attempt the long, treacherous drive back to Boston in the teeth of a fullblown snowstorm. It could not be helped. Though he doubted that the idea of him spending the night holed up in a cabin with one bed and a prostitute for company was going to be a point in his favor.

"We'll have to dig out an' then call the local police in the mornin'." It was not a prospect that cheered Casey. When you had grown up Catholic in Belfast you developed a healthy aversion to law enforcement of any kind. He'd brought a measure of this skepticism across the sea with him, and so wasn't thrilled about the questions that would have to be answered, and the detailed reports that would need to be filed.

Emma looked at him with a rather large dose of her own skepticism. "The cops ain't gonna care. She was a hooker, dead whores don't rank all that high on the police priority list. Getting killed is like an occupational hazard kinda thing—at least that's what the cops seem to think."

"But someone purposefully drew her here to an abandoned cabin in the woods. It was premeditated, that ought to..." he trailed off at the look of world-weary defeat that filled Emma's eyes.

"I think you come from a hard neighborhood," she said softly, "but you still don't understand what you're dealing with here. She wasn't a person; she was property—a whore like me. As a human she has no value, but as a commodity she had plenty. Now that she's dead," she shrugged eloquently, "she's worthless."

Casey looked over at her. In the glow from the candles her silhouette was softened, and she appeared very young. As she must have once been, before Love Hagerty got his clutches into her.

He took a deep breath and the smell of blood flooded his senses. He had washed his hands in the snow, but knew his nails were still rimmed in red.

"I had an abortion; it was Rosemary who held my hand through that."

"Aye," Casey said quietly, his tone giving her the space to either tell him her story or not, as she chose. The recounting of life experience was often the only exorcism one could perform in the face of a violent death. Because no matter the reason, there was no making sense of such a death.

"I was nineteen—went to a back alley clinic, was this lady who did abortions in the evenings. Like after it was dark. I couldn't have had a baby, I was doing heroin then and my whole life revolved around getting that Judas kiss everyday."

"Judas kiss?"

She nodded, the fire sparking off the copper in her hair. "You think it's your friend, it makes you feel good when nothing else can, it gets you through the day, makes life bearable. Until one day you realize you're living for it, that it's got claws so deep in you that you ain't never really gonna get them out. And you will do anything for it. I thought it was the only thing that had ever loved me unconditionally; it made me feel safe. Your view of the world and everything in it gets twisted, you see it all through the eye of the needle. I knew that was no life for a baby, and I wasn't ready to give up the drug. But the drug always betrays you in the end, makes you do things you never thought you would, double-cross and hurt people you love. Steal, cheat and lie all to make certain you get your hit that day. So I had the abortion and I figured it was the right thing to do. But smack lies to you and justifies all your actions."

"So what made ye quit?"

"How do you know I have?"

"Because ye don't tend to wear overmuch in the clothing department, an' I'd have noticed fresh tracks did ye have them."

She smiled, but it wasn't a humorous expression. "You'd be surprised the places on your body a junkie can find to shoot up. But you're right, I'm clean, have been for five years now. Cause I got knocked up again. And this time I did love something more than the smack. Rosemary was there for me the whole time. Cleaning up puke, sponging me down when I was hot, bundling me up when I was cold. Forcing broth down my throat when I was being the biggest pain in the ass you can imagine. God, I don't think I slept for a year after I came off and then Jakey was born and *he* kept me up at night. When he got croup and I thought I was gonna' totally lose my mind, Rosemary walked the hall with him nights. Walked a path right into the carpet." She wiped at the tears that had spilled down her face, as though their presence angered her. "Did you ever have a friend like that? One who had your back no matter what?"

"Aye," Casey smiled, "I did—once."

"I thought you might have, you seem like a man who people can trust. I think it's why Love Hagerty is afraid of you."

Casey snorted. "Afraid of me? I don't see why. The man's got Southie zipped up so tight no one can breathe without his permission, an' what he doesn't hold the strings on his pals in the Bassarelli clan do. Besides how could ye know such a thing?"

"Well whores don't inspire a lot of loyalty," she said, with a bitterness that Casey knew was hard earned. "But people often use them as a shoulder, I hear things and I've got a long memory." She sniffed, her nose running now that she was warm. He leaned forward and handed her a tissue from the stash Pamela had neatly placed in his inside coat pocket.

"I do wish ye'd quit callin' yerself a whore."

She narrowed her eyes at him. "It's what I am. It's honest, is all. I have no illusions about what I do. I don't expect to wind up in some street version of Cinderella or anything."

"It's what ye do, it's not necessarily what ye are," Casey said. "I drive car an' offload questionable cargo, does that mean the sum of me is drivin' and haulin' boxes?" He shrugged with a nonchalance he didn't necessarily feel. "I am more than that, an' so are you. No human bein' is that simple, or can be summed up that tidily."

"Are you for real?" She cocked her head, eyes bright with doubt. But the tough stance was gone and suddenly she seemed horribly fragile, a lost soul in a world that surely seemed like one of the interior circles of hell. "Because if you say that you don't think of me that way, that you don't just see a whore when you look at me, I'll believe it, I'll believe you."

He lifted her hand to his mouth and kissed it gently, and his dark eyes met her own with a clear honesty. "Not for a minute have I thought of you that way. I see a woman, no more, no less."

She laid a hand on his wool-clad leg, the fingers trailing northward in unmistakable invitation.

"I could use some warmth," she said, "couldn't you?"

He clasped her hands between his own, stilling her. He realized suddenly that the kiss on her hand might have been grossly misinterpreted. He also understood that this was a natural coin for her to deal in.

"Ye know I'm married, I don't take that lightly."

"Your wife doesn't need to know," she said, and he could feel her trembling beneath his hands.

"But *I* would know," Casey said.

"We could just kiss, for you it'd be free," she trailed off as he gave her a very stern look. Tears suddenly flooded into the topaz eyes, making them glitter like cat's-eye in the firelight.

"Yer an attractive woman, an' I'm flattered, but what ye don't understand is that it wouldn't matter who I was kissin' or makin' love to, I would still be kissin' my wife, makin' love to my wife. D'ye see what I'm sayin'?" he asked gently.

She nodded, the smoke-gold eyes filling with tears. "I hope she knows how lucky she is."

"Aye," he grimaced, thinking of how upset his wife likely was at this point. "I hope she knows it tomorrow, leastwise. Now ye'd best get some sleep, we've the devil of a day facin' us tomorrow."

He dragged the bed over near the stove, and then halved the blanket so she could wrap herself in it. He'd meant to lay the blanket over the dead woman, but when he'd realized they were stuck here for the night, he knew they needed it much worse than she did.

Emma huddled to one side. "There's room for you. I promise to behave."

"I'll bide for a bit," Casey said, "I'm not tired just now." Which wasn't strictly true, but he knew he could not sleep just yet. He sat in one of the chairs, alert in every cell and fibre of his being, the hairs on his arms still standing up, despite the glow of the potbellied stove.

Emma apparently was feeling some of this same current in the air, for she tossed and turned a bit before sighing and saying, "I don't think I'll be able to sleep."

"Why not? Yer safe enough. I'll keep watch for the night. It'd have to be somethin' supernatural to get through a storm such as this one."

Emma looked toward the door as though she half expected some terrible spectre to come out of the blinding snow and howling winds. He shivered. He half expected it himself, truth be told.

"I...I'm used to the noise from the streets. It's too quiet here. You have a good voice; I've heard you sing down at the Rose—sing something."

"Have ye a favorite?" Casey asked, thinking a song might soothe his own mind.

"My mom used to sing this lovely one about living in marble halls and longing for a lost love—do you know the one I'm talking about?"

"Aye I know it. It's a sad one, are ye certain yer in the mood for it?"

"Yes," she said, the domed lids half-closed over her eyes, making her look absurdly young and fragile in the sift of candle flame.

He started in low and soft on the gentle sway of notes. It was one his own mother had once sung to him. How he remembered this he did not know, most memories of his mother he had blocked out or lost in the wash of time. But the music remained.

I dreamt I dwelt in marble halls
With vassals and serfs at my side...

The notes themselves were arranged like a slow waltz, danced alone after the lights had dimmed and the other revelers had gone home, and you were alone in the ballroom with the scent of dying flowers and regret for chances lost. His mother had sung it so, and he wondered what in her heart had infused the music with such pain that he could feel, even now so many years later, the lingerings left behind.

But I also dreamt (which pleased me most)
That you loved me still the same,
That you loved me,
You loved me, still the same...

Emma slept now, her breathing deep and relaxed. He was tired himself, could feel the fatigue of the day pulling on him, though he knew were he to close his eyes he would only see the image of the dead girl, cold and blue with ice crystals forming in her red curls. Nor did he want to face thoughts of the morning—of police and questions and the great dark danger he felt as heavy as the scent of blood in the air. And so he sang. For Emma, whose sleep was so often troubled, for himself, and the pain he felt for the Irish girl outside, whose American dreams had come to ashes. He sang to drown the sound of wolves howling in the distance, and the hissing of ice against the windows. And last, just before his eyes closed, he sang for the mother who had once sung for him.

That you loved me
You loved me, still the same...

CASEY WAS ON HIS BREAK, having a smoke outside the warehouse, where a shipment of televisions from Japan was being offloaded. It had been two weeks since he and Emma had sat in a squalid little police station in a New Hampshire village, and explained *ad nauseum* their story regarding the murdered prostitute in the boathouse by the lake.

The sheriff had been mildly skeptical, but had let them go after taking their addresses in Boston. Thus far, Casey had heard nothing; there hadn't even been a whisper of the murder in the newspapers. The cold chill of that night persisted though, the feeling of darkness hovering just out beyond his line of vision. As though something was coming, and he would not be able to stop it.

"Casey."

The voice startled him and he dropped his cigarette on the ground, where the dirty snow extinguished it immediately.

It was Emma. He had not seen her since dropping her off at her apartment late in the afternoon the day after Rosemary's murder. She did not look as though she came bearing glad tidings.

"Can we talk?" she asked, looking about her in a furtive manner.

"Aye. I'm the only one mad enough to come out in this weather for a smoke. No one else is about." He rubbed his hands together and blew on them, noting that she was still wearing the driving gloves he'd loaned her.

"The state police in New Hampshire called me, and then they sent an investigator down to talk with me. They were asking some questions that really scared me."

The chill in his hands and feet seemed to have spread into his bloodstream. "Such as?"

She swallowed hard and he knew he wasn't going to like what he was about to hear.

"Mostly about you. Were you sleeping with Rosemary, and stuff like that. Did I know your past? Some of it seemed routine, like they were trying to clear you away before getting focussed on hunting for the real killer. But then the detective came back again. He...he," she sniffed, "was angry and said I was covering for you, that someone had told them you knew Rosemary real well. And that you'd had the motive to kill her, 'cause she was pregnant and they figured it was your baby."

"WHAT?!" The snake that had ridden in his belly since that cold night by the lake, uncoiled and slithered in an oily ribbon through his intestines.

She shrugged, eyes bright with tears. "What are we gonna' do?"

"We—what d'ye mean *we*—they're not tryin' to pin it on you too, are they?"

She shook her head miserably, "No, but I feel responsible for asking you to take me up there."

"It's not yer fault...I...this makes no sense." His chest was suddenly tight, and he had to fight for his next breath. How the hell could this be happening?

"You should go, get out of Boston."

He narrowed his eyes at her. Something was strange here, she sounded far more desperate than she ought, considering it wasn't her neck they were neatly tying a noose around. And for that matter, why the hell hadn't the detective come to see him, if they were so certain he'd murdered the girl?

"I didn't do it, so I've nothin' to fear," he said with a bravado he simply did not feel, despite his innocence.

"It's not just the cops, though," she said, looking around again as if she suspected a thousand ears were trying to listen in on their conversation.

"No," he said quietly, "who is it, then?"

"Blackie. I think he's setting you up for a fall."

"Why would he do that?" His tone was still quiet, but Emma stepped back a bit, eyeing him warily from under mascara-clotted lashes.

"I don't know. Maybe because it's convenient, maybe because he did know Rosemary real well." She glanced back over her shoulder again, and Casey wondered just who it was she was so terrified of seeing in the blue shadows that hung about the warehouse.

When she turned back he sensed that she was trying to tell him something without actually using the words. "Look, this isn't a Hollywood movie, the lone hero doesn't get to walk off into the sunset at the end. These are very bad people, Casey and even if you managed to get rid of several of them, there would always be more waiting."

"I take it we aren't talkin' about the police anymore?"

"I'm talking about all of them," she whispered, tears glittering in the corners of her reddened eyes.

"Then what the hell d'ye suggest I do?"

"Get out of town for a bit, until the heat dies down. They can't order you to stay put until they actually lay charges."

"I can't just leave," he said, "I've a life here."

"If you want to keep that life, you'd be better off elsewhere. It might be convenient," again the fearful look over her shoulder, "if they don't know where you are. You'd have a better chance of moving around undetected."

Casey rubbed his temples in frustration, "I feel as if you're giving me only half the picture here, Emma."

"I can't afford to give you any more. I'm sorry—I really am." she said, and now the tears were slipping freely down her face, soot black lines of mascara like dirty rivers destroying her makeup.

"Don't be sorry," he said wearily, fishing in his pocket for a tissue and handing it to her. This gesture only served to make her cry harder.

Suddenly she clutched his hand, the supple leather of his gloves far too big for her tiny hands. "I need you to know that I am sorry though—for all of this."

And then she was gone, the wind catching the cheap material of her short skirt and flaring it around her cold-stippled skin.

Casey stood frozen to the spot, his most prescient thought being what the hell he was going to tell his wife.

THE INTERIOR OF THE BIG CAR was wonderfully warm after the bitter chill of the warehouse yard. Still, Emma thought she would rather walk a hundred miles in the teeth of a blizzard than ride next to the man in the seat beside her.

Right now he was looking at her, a question in his face.

"It's done," she said in a small voice.

Love nodded to the driver in the mirror and the big Lincoln slid out into traffic.

Emma huddled in the corner of the luxurious leather seat, as far from Love as she could manage. She watched him from the corner of her eye. He wore a triumphant look on his face, not a hair out of place, clothing impeccable, hands smooth, cologne discreet. Objectively viewed, an attractive man, made all the more so by the power he wielded and the money he had. Subjectively speaking, though, she thought she'd never seen an uglier human being.

Once she had loved the smell of him, the discreetly expensive cologne, the scent of French milled soap and cigars. These days, though, all she could smell around him was the corruption that rose from his white skin like wisps of brimstone. It smelled a lot like blood.

Chapter Six

Priest and Friend

THERE WAS A SOFT WHICKER as the ball curved around the hoop, then tilted in Casey's favor and swished through the net.

"Luck of the Irish," Father Kevin said, between wheezing breaths.

"Believe what ye need to if it helps ye sleep at night," Casey grinned, feeling jubilant despite his scraped and stinging palms.

"Come on, let's go sit down for a minute," Father Kevin suggested, hands on knees, blood trickling from raw knuckles.

Casey nodded, flapping his sweaty t-shirt away from his body. The gym had been used only an hour before by two teams of overheated, hormonally charged teenage boys, and a thick fug of perspiration still clung to the air.

"Jaysus," Casey hit the outside door, welcoming the rush of freezing cold into his lungs even as his skin protested the assault. "Did they not teach ye that mercy was a virtue in the seminary?"

"Mercy," Father Kevin said emerging onto the steps, his red hair sticking up in sweaty spikes and giving him the general appearance of a pissed off leprechaun, "has no place on the basketball court. You weren't holding back yourself out there."

"I was fightin' for my life," Casey protested, wiping sweat out of his eyes with a broad forearm, while digging in a crumpled pack for a cigarette.

"If you'd stop puffing on those coffin nails you'd be able to keep up," Father Kevin said sweetly.

"Ye know, for a priest ye've the devil's own guile," Casey responded, lighting the cigarette with two bruised and swollen fingers. "But it'd take a saint's patience to wean me off these things—ahh—there's somethin' more like it," he breathed out a long stream of blue smoke, eyes closing in pleasure.

"I'm surprised Pamela lets you."

"Ah, ye've noticed the woman's a fearsome will on her, have ye?"

"It's a little hard to miss," Father Kevin said with a smile, "she has a quiet way about her that kind of sneaks up on a man before he realizes he's outmaneuvered."

"I take it she got her playground equipment for the wee ones in the Flats?"

"Oh, she got it all right," Father Kevin said, "appropriated the funds from no less than the Cardinal if you can believe it."

Casey laughed, "Oh I can believe it, she'd flirt with the twelve disciples did she think it'd improve things for that lot of ankle-biters down there."

"She's a good woman," Father Kevin said, voice suddenly and unaccountably sober.

Casey narrowed a dark eye at him, "I know it man, an' if I forget for a minute or two, sure the woman sees fit to remind me of it. So tell me why ye're givin' me the confessional tone?"

"It's just that you seem like a man with something on his mind, something that's bothering the hell out of you."

Casey sighed. Father Kevin was nothing if not direct. It was, for the most part, one of the things he liked best about him.

"Do I strike ye as completely mad?" he asked, tapping his ashes carefully onto a broad leaf that lay on the top stair.

"Near to it, but no, not completely. Why do you ask?"

"Because the woman'd have my ballocks neatly stuffed an' roasted did I so much as cast an eye on another female. Besides, I meant it when I married her," he added gruffly.

"I think most couples do when they are standing before the parish priest, but life can get complicated, as we both know."

"Well, Pamela an' I are not most couples," Casey said firmly, "an' I've a notion yer talkin' around the edges of the apple when ye really want to discuss the core."

"The spirit may be strong but the flesh can still be tempted," Father Kevin said, face turning red and muting the white spaces between freckles.

"It's not like ye to speak in priestly platitudes. It doesn't sit well on yer tongue, so whatever it is ye feel ye have to say, say it plain."

"A man in your position has a lot of temptation thrown his way, and not to belabor the fruit metaphor, but you've been walking around with a face on you like an apple with a worm for a conscience. So I'm thinking," Father Kevin ran a stubby-fingered hand through his bright hair, making it stand on end, "maybe you've done something you shouldn't have and it's eating you up."

"Are ye speakin' as a priest or a friend?" Casey asked sharply.

"I'd like to think I can manage both for you," Father Kevin said, expression unruffled by the hostile tone.

"Aye, well," Casey said warily, "'tis nothin' to do with my wife."

"Your employer?" Father Kevin asked, tone carefully neutral.

"Maybe," Casey gave him a slant-wise look, taking a long draw on his cigarette. "How much are ye willin' to hear, man?"

"Am I friend or priest now?" Father Kevin asked quietly, eyes fixed firmly on the pebbled surface of the ball he held.

"Both, I hope," Casey rejoined softly, trying to still the shaking in his hands, feeling a mix of fear and relief that unsettled his body. "What will ye know of the man?"

Father Kevin suddenly threw the ball away with a quick, violent thrust. "Enough to have to ask God several times a month for forgiveness for the hatred in my heart toward him."

Casey let out a breath that was mostly made of relief. "Then ye know."

Father Kevin nodded and turned a hard eye on Casey, "How much did you know before you went to work for him?"

Casey returned the hard eye in full measure. "Not enough, obviously." He shook his head, stamping his feet to keep them warm. "Hindsight is twenty-twenty though, aye? I can look back now and think maybe I knew somethin' was off, didn't smell right, that I always scented the reek under all that cigar smoke and expensive aftershave. But I don't think I did. At least that's what I tell myself at three a.m. when I can't sleep."

"Lord preserve us, the boy's got a Catholic conscience after all," Father Kevin said lightly, though the brevity didn't come off as he'd intended. Then he took a deep breath and asked the question that might well end the friendship he was coming to value dearly.

"How much do you know now?"

"Too much," Casey said bluntly. "Do ye know what it is when ye've seen too much an' ye know yer not innocent anymore, that the blood is on yer hands as much as the man who committed the crime?"

"I'm a priest, man. I know it everyday."

Casey nodded, as if digesting Father Kevin's words, but Kevin knew him well enough to see that he was weighing how much he could now safely say.

"When ye were anglin' about before, were ye askin' because of Emma?"

"Yes. She comes to confession occasionally. She has feelings for you. And there's gossip as well."

"Is there?" Casey took a fierce drag on his cigarette, the ash lit up like a hot coal, and two red spots were reflected in the man's dark eyes. "Did she tell ye about Rosemary, then?"

"No," Kevin said, sorting through his recollections of Emma's various friends. Then he had it, a pretty girl with red curls who came for both the Thanksgiving and Christmas dinner the parish held every year. "What about her?"

"We found her murdered up at a place in New Hampshire. She'd called Emma and Emma got scared an' asked me to come up there with her. I did, but the girl was dead by the time we got there. An' now it seems the New Hampshire state police are lookin' at yours truly for the crime."

"What?" Kevin could feel the blood rush down toward his knees.

"Aye, ye look about as well as I did when Emma told me they were questionin' her."

"Have they questioned you?"

Casey shook his head. "No, that's the odd bit—I've not heard a word from the police."

"Something isn't right here," Kevin frowned.

"She did mention as Blackie was close with Rosemary."

"That I don't know," Kevin said, "Blackie hasn't darkened the door of a church in a lot of years. But it's possible, though generally he likes them blonde and—*ahem*—rather well built."

Casey narrowed his eyes thoughtfully. "There's a deal here not addin' up. I did a wee bit of pokin' around up in New Hampshire. Got a look at the property title on the wee cabin an' the land it sits upon."

"How'd you manage that?"

"A wee bit of Irish charm an' a strip of blarney will get a man a ways in this world."

"I see," Kevin said dryly, "the title clerk was female. So what did you find out?"

"The property belongs to a man named John Mullins—which is about as common as carrots in a stew, so that didn't give me a great deal to go upon."

Kevin shook his head. "Sorry it doesn't mean anything to me."

"Aye, well, it didn't mean a great deal to me either, until I found out Emma's father used to have an old partner by that name. Did ye know that Emma's father was a policeman?" Casey blew out a stream of smoke and stubbed out his cigarette, wrapping it up neatly in the brown leaf. It was one of things that Kevin had noticed about him from the start. That he never left a trace of himself behind, other than the strong impression he made on people.

"No, I didn't." Kevin felt suddenly weary of all the corruption. How did a policeman, of all people, end up with a daughter turning tricks in the streets? He knew there was an answer, though, and it was obvious enough. Love Hagerty.

"There's connections here an' I feel as if I can almost see them an' then they run underground an' don't poke back up again for several feet, so to speak." One fist hit the iron stair rails. "It's just damn frustratin' trying to figure this out while the noose is bein' fashioned to fit my neck." He looked at Kevin squarely. "Ye've not asked me if I'm guilty."

"Give me some credit. I do have a bit of judgement; priests tend to cultivate it after awhile you know."

"Aye, well, ye were fishin' about to see if I was commitin' adultery a moment ago."

Kevin waved a hand in dismissal. "I didn't really think you were indulging in that either. I've seen you with your wife. I would have been terribly disappointed if you really were having an affair. I knew something was bothering you, though, and couldn't think of a more tactful way to approach it."

"Thanks for that—for not thinkin' the worst of me." Casey sighed, "I don't come from a place where things were prettied up. But there's a certain value in that and an honesty that lets a man know where he stands. Belfast is hard city, aye, but I knew how to deal with that. A wolf seems a wolf there, an' isn't likely to be dressed as a sheep." Father Kevin suppressed an unseemly smile at the thought of Love Hagerty in the guise of a sheep. "This," he put his hands up in a hopeless gesture, "this mystifies me. Can ye tell me why evil seems worse when it smells good an' looks like ice cream?"

"Because it ought to stink and look bad, just to make things simple, if for no other reason."

Casey laughed, a humorless sound. "Could ye put in a request with the man upstairs then, Father, ask him to simplify it a bit for us fools?"

"You could ask him yourself," Father Kevin replied, not quite managing to keep the bite from his tone.

"Are ye angry at me, then?" Casey asked, "Do ye wish I'd kept it to myself?"

Kevin sighed, "No of course not. I'm just a little surprised at your naïveté."

"Aye, looks stupid in retrospect, but I ask ye how many people know what he is? Outside of these streets, I mean?"

"No one," Kevin admitted reluctantly. "Blackie is the front man for all the business they conduct. I just thought, considering the capacity you met him in, it might have occurred to you that he wasn't a shining example of civic duty."

Casey laughed. "Now who's bein' naïve, Kevin? Have ye any notion of the places ye might find people who support such causes? Particularly that of a United Ireland."

"Don't tell me you've been soliciting the Cardinal as well?"

Casey laughed, and the tension between them broke.

"No, I've left my arms-dealin' days behind me. It'd take a better man than I to beard the Cardinal on such a subject."

"I don't know, you weren't afraid to approach Hagerty, there's not many would do that in such a bold manner."

"Aye, well, I didn't know who I was dealin' with at the time."

"And now that you do?"

Casey gave the priest a hard look. "Were ye trained by the Jesuits, Father? What would ye have me say? I'm only one man, I can't take him on alone."

"You wouldn't have to. I saw a man talking to you back of the Old City Hall, not too long back. He had the look of a member of a certain Federal organization."

Casey sighed and shook his head. "D'ye think they could save me, should it all go to shite? They've their own interests. An' there's more than one agent at the local field office that comes from the man's own neighborhood. For all my address is on those streets, *I* am the outsider—not him."

Father Kevin wanted to deny the truth of the statement, but could not. Corruption was not limited to the streets, nor to the flaking gold leaf of the halls of politics. Love was a man of powerful charisma, and he had held much of Southie in a thrall for three decades now. Even those that had good reason to hate him feared him enough to crumple under his rule. But this man standing beside him, though young, seemed made of something strong enough to stage an uprising and maybe, just maybe, get away with it.

Yet, he was right, he was an outsider and there was nothing worse a man could be in Southie—even Christ would be suspect in that neighborhood. Old loyalties lay deep, sanctified in the blood of the past, and pacts made between small boys who were too small to understand what the future could hold, still held firm as a warrior's oath. Ironically enough the roots of such fierce loyalty lay in the small Irish villages most of these people's ancestors had originated in. Small huddles of cottages that contained a wealth of tangled relations, loves, hates— in short, all the salt and blood of life.

Though Belfast was ostensibly a city, Kevin knew it too retained the fierce tribal loyalism of a much smaller center. The Scots had brought their clannishness with them, and made the Irish outsiders in their own land. Yes, Casey understood how deep such loyalties lay, and how history could affect the future for hundreds of years. Casey was right, Southie was not safe and he could not take down an empire single-handed. Should he attempt it, all doors would be closed to him, and he would be in the merciless streets alone. With a stocky, red-headed priest at his back mind you, but that wasn't likely to be of much comfort to the man.

"If something should happen to me," Casey said, voice flat, "will ye see to it that my wife gets out of this city? I don't trust what might happen if I'm not here."

"With Hagerty?"

"Aye," he nodded, eyes a savage gray, "I've seen how the man looks at her, like he'd have her whole for breakfast if he might. He's no respect for what is another man's, nor does he understand that a woman might not choose to have him in her life or her bed. It's as if no one ever has told him no in his life."

"Some have," Father Kevin said, "but they've generally lived to regret it."

"Or not lived," Casey added tersely.

Father Kevin nodded his agreement.

"Listen I've got a cousin who runs a fishing boat out of St. John's up in Newfoundland. You'd be out a month at a time, but it would keep you off of Hagerty's radar for a bit."

"Quit an' go to sea?" Casey said, the joking tone of his voice not quite coming off.

Kevin turned to him questioningly. The man had gone the color of a fish belly.

"I've no great love for the water."

"Are you serious? You come from an island, for heaven's sake."

Casey snorted derisively, "An' what the hell has that got to do with anything? For all it's an island, the Irish are hardly a seafaring race, man."

"No," Kevin conceded, "they are not. Strange that—surrounded by water on all sides and yet not a great many sailors. Yet they had the courage to cross the Atlantic in search of a better life here. I wonder how many felt they'd found it once they arrived."

"Do ye think of them, Kevin? What it was to be torn from all ye'd ever known or understood an' come to this wild an' fierce place dirt-poor, with barely a shirt to call yer own, knowin' ye were not welcome in the least?"

Kevin nodded, "How could I not, with half the city originating in Ireland?"

"An' yer own people?"

"Cork," Kevin said, rolling a small bit of ice under one flattened palm.

"Ah," Casey laughed knowingly, "the chosen people."

"Should I call my cousin with the fishing boat?" Kevin asked, not looking at the man beside him, but at the bleak yard in front of the two of them, the deserted swings swaying lightly in the cold breeze.

There was a long silence and then the answer came, soft and defeated.

"Aye, call him."

Chapter Seven

Devil's Deal

BOSTON GREETED SPRING with an explosion of green. Everywhere one looked there was green-flagrant, riotous and trembling with life. Between the cracks of sidewalks, sprouting out from crumbling walls, round the graves of long dead patriots and tumbling up from the esplanade in a rolling crescendo. Spring in Boston did all the things it did to the human psyche in other cities—couples kissed on street corners, skin was exposed to the returning sun in all its shades of glowing winter white, children played kickball in the street and mothers in sundresses pushed baby carriages while chatting with other mothers. The Redsox returned to Fenway, and a certain ebullience filled the air and infected all from eight to eighty. For all its Brahmin heritage, Boston was a brash city, full of working class values and middle man morals. This was never more apparent than in the spring, when the city assumed the character of a freckle-faced tomboy up to bat and ready to show her stripes.

With the arrival of spring, Pamela had taken to having her lunch in the park. The Back Bay Fens were part of the long, linked choker of parks that encircled Boston's throat with its fabled Emerald Necklace. It was a peaceful respite from the business lunches Love often required her presence for, pleading that he needed her intuitive reading on possible business ventures. More often than not, she felt she was merely there to distract the latest sucker Love was looking to swindle.

The week before, she'd come across a bench, tucked in the lee of a horse chestnut, delicately braced by a ribbon of ferns. It was an ideal spot to sit and let thoughts meander along with the spring breeze that smelled enticingly of slow-moving sap and just blossomed flowers.

When Agent Gus showed up amongst the fern fronds, looking unmistakably agent-like in his navy suit, he stuck out like a monk at a bacchanal. She sighed in resignation and indicated the empty stretch of bench beside her with a tilt of her head. The agent had become a familiar sight over the last few weeks.

He took the invitation with alacrity, placing himself on the weathered gray wood under the deep canopy of the chestnut, with a breath of relief.

"Don't be nervous, you're not in any trouble," he said, though the 'all work and no play' expression he wore said otherwise.

"Forgive me," she replied acidly, "but I'm not used to having my lunch interrupted by a federal agent."

"I'm supposed to look like a businessman on his lunch hour," he said, tucking his sunglasses in his jacket pocket and squinting under the onslaught of unfiltered sunlight.

"Lose the jacket, loosen the tie, roll up the cuffs and you might pass, though I doubt it." She angled her head, "If you were younger you could be mistaken for a Mormon missionary, but a businessman—no way."

Though Agent Gus was hardly a pillar of granite, she noticed that today he seemed particularly fidgety. He was swallowing compulsively, avoiding her eyes and plucking at the buttons on his suit jacket.

"There's something I need to discuss with you." He swallowed again, sticking a finger inside his collar, under which the flesh was growing increasingly red. "I don't know exactly how to say this."

"I'm guessing you're not here because you had a desire to share my tuna fish with me, so you'd best out with it before it chokes you."

"That obvious?" he asked, chagrin written clear across his features.

"Like you've a dozen fish bones lodged in your craw."

"So much for subtlety."

"Not," Pamela said, though not unkindly, "one of your virtues."

"Right then," he took a breath and loosed the rest of his words on a rush of air, "we need someone close to Hagerty to help us out. Someone that he trusts." There could be little doubt exactly whom he meant by *someone*.

"I thought you had informants or agents on the inside to handle these things," she said, feeling a bubble of panic lodge behind her windpipe.

"We did," Agent Gus said grimly, "we found him with his throat slit from ear to ear, facedown in the Charles River last month."

"Oh," she said faintly, unable to block the image of Casey in the same condition from her mind.

"I don't know, Mrs. Riordan, how much you know about your boss," Agent Gus continued uncomfortably, "but we're not talking about an amateur here, the man has got people in his pocket from thugs on the street to detectives on the force. Had a judge from the housing court stand up to him four years back. The man refused to put the person Hagerty wanted into an open clerkship, Hagerty leaned a bit then backed off. Six months later legislature passes through the State House that has the judge's pay cut back, staff reduced, and then his court is folded into another judiciary branch effectively ending any power the judge had. Hagerty's willing to wait for his revenge and he's got a long memory. And now," the agent chanced a quick look at her, "he's in bed with the Bassarelli family, and that's a poker game with the highest stakes you can imagine. Want a hot dog?" he asked, nodding toward a vendor at one of the cross paths of the pretty little park.

"Don't tell me, he's one of yours?"

"He is, as a matter of fact, but he has real hot dogs just to make him look legitimate."

"You're kidding," she said incredulously.

"Of course I am," he said without cracking the slightest smile. Just her luck to get a G-man who thought he was a comedian.

Agent Gus held up two fingers to the man who nodded and dug in the cart with his tongs.

"Listen," the agent continued, "I know all this seems a little cloak and dagger, but the truth is Love Hagerty is one of the most dangerous men in Boston. He's got such a chokehold on Southie that we can't get a whisper out of anyone close to him."

"And that, I suppose, is where you think I come in." Pamela said, feeling the figurative noose tightening rather quickly about her own neck.

"Sorry," he said, face flushing beetroot red. "It's just that things are getting a little desperate. If Love merges his set of criminals with the Bassarelli clan, we're talking about complete control of all the organized crime on the Eastern Seaboard from Maine down to New York, and that's a big stretch of real estate. We have to nail this bastard now or never. Excuse me for a second," he said. He walked over to the hot dog vendor with the odd bouncy step that was his trademark.

He came back with two napkin-wrapped hot dogs and two bottles of Coca-Cola tucked under his elbow. She waved off the hot dog but accepted the Coke, grimacing as the agent loosened the cap with his teeth before handing it to her.

"Sorry, that always bothers people, makes my wife crazy when I do it."

Agent Gus had a wife? She had a sudden vision of him in boxer shorts brushing his teeth and took a quick swallow of her drink to cover the laugh that accompanied the image.

"Thought they just hung us up on a hook, suit and all, at the end of the day?"

She flushed, realizing he'd read her thoughts as easily as she could see the rush of trapped carbon in her soda.

"Something like that," she smiled ruefully, wondering if she was ever going to develop the ability to hide her thoughts. She took another swallow of soda, feeling the tiny sting of bubbles as they rushed over her teeth and tongue. "So, Agent Spencer, why me?"

"Because you're the only one in Hagerty's inner circle that's got something we can barter for."

She raised her eyebrows at him. "Care to define that?"

"Your husband," he said bluntly, and then bit into his hot dog, bright yellow mustard leeching through the white napkin. She waited patiently for him to chew and swallow.

Then she repeated the agent's words back to him, "My husband?"

"Mrs. Riordan," he said tone apologetic, "I don't need to tell you that there's bad blood between your husband and Hagerty. I think you also realize your husband is in a rather tenuous position legally, he's seen things it would be better if he hadn't and that makes him guilty by association. He won't talk to us; he's made that clear, even though he's got to know he's in a bad situation with Hagerty."

"By bad situation you mean he wants my husband dead?" she said, voicing the words that had been gnawing a hole in her mind for weeks now.

"Yes," Agent Gus said, and she saw clearly the core of steel in the man that made him equal to his job.

"Wouldn't you be better off approaching the mistress? I'd think she'd know a thing or two."

Agent Gus shook his head. "The pretty little apartment in Brookline is empty, though he's still paying the rent on it. He cleared her off his calendar about a month ago. Had the place cleaned, repainted and swept for bugs. He knows we know, he's just arrogant enough to think we can't catch him. The mistress left no forwarding address, but we traced her to Las Vegas, where she's working in a casino and has little memory of anyone named Love Hagerty. I don't think she knows anything anyway, he's pretty damn careful."

"Why'd he get rid of her if she doesn't know anything?"

"I think, Mrs. Riordan, it's a case of out with the old and in with the new. Perhaps he thinks you'd prefer Brookline to Southie."

"Me?" she squeaked, horrified at the implications. "But I..." she shook her head, speechless, understanding suddenly why the man had wanted to speak with her.

"I don't think," the agent said quietly, "it matters a lot to him whether you're willing or not, he's so corrupt he thinks everyone is seducible given the proper inducement. He just thinks he hasn't found your upper limit yet."

Above her head, in the spreading branches of the horse chestnut, a scarlet tanager emitted its optimistic *burry-shureer-shureet-shuroo* and a flutter of filmy pink-white petals dropped upon Agent Gus's impeccable navy blue suit. One petal clung to the fine dew of condensation on her soda bottle, tearing when she tried to set it free.

"I love my husband," she said, not knowing why she felt the necessity of stating it to this man.

"Enough to help save his life?" Agent Gus asked, taking another bite of his hot dog. The smell of mustard mingled with the scents of new mown grass and the bitter undernote of the chestnut. She watched, mesmerized, as a petal drifted from the agent's sandy crew cut to land precariously on the knife pleat of his trousers. She knew the next question was hers.

"What exactly are you suggesting, Mr. Spencer?" she asked, hands cold and lips numb.

"I think you know, Mrs. Riordan, what I'm suggesting. It would kill two very nasty birds with one stone. If Love Hagerty doesn't take a fall, and soon, you are going to have the rather unpleasant task of burying your husband. If not," he shrugged, "well, knowing about a crime makes him an accessory, and that'll buy him some unpleasant time in a federal prison at the least. At worst Hagerty finds him in there and you're a widow anyway. It's up to you."

"Anything I could get from Mr. Hagerty would be hearsay," she said, desperately looking for a way out of this tangle of thorns she'd suddenly found herself in.

"We'd tape it. We've been waiting for this bastard to screw up for about twenty years now. You're the first real shot we've had."

"You're going to tape it? Where exactly," her voice was thick with sarcasm, " would you suggest I hide the wire?"

The agent shook his head. "No wire, there are any number of places to hide a bug in a bedroom."

She flinched at his use of the word 'bedroom' but somehow was glad of the bluntness and that the man wasn't trying to couch this in nicer terms. They wanted her to screw Love Hagerty for information, not make him fall in love with her. She clasped her hands hard around the Coke bottle to stop them shaking. "It's not illegal or inadmissible to record his private life?"

"We can't place bugs with impunity but if we have reason to think that we'll get something solid that will lead to conviction, we'll get the go ahead. I've got reason to think he'll open up to you, he'll be vulnerable in a way he just isn't with anyone else."

"Forgive me if I'm not flattered," she said dryly. "I want to know what we're talking about here, how long do you actually think you can put this man away for?"

"RICO's given us some leverage. If we can establish a pattern of organized crime we're talking hard time here; twenty years or more in prison is something even the mob takes seriously."

She knew a bit about RICO. It had been in the news, touted as the most potent weapon the government had ever held against organized crime. The Racketeering Influenced and Corrupt Organizations Act had been passed by congress only that year. For the first time operating a criminal racket became a federal offence, carrying huge prison terms. The FBI finally had the power to crack the back of the Mafia and those who gained from their affiliations with it. Affiliates like Lovett Hagerty.

"What's the protocol in these situations?" she asked, tone remarkably calm, almost as if she'd sensed the inevitability of this from her first meeting with Love.

"Generally speaking you'd have to have a face-to-face with my supervisor, but I told them all bets would be off if they insisted on it. I thought maybe," he gave a half-hearted smile, "it'd be easier if they couldn't put a face to the voice they'd be hearing."

She swallowed, feeling slightly dizzy, "That was decent of you, Agent Spencer."

"Call me Gus," he said.

"I'd rather not," she replied.

"Fine," he shrugged again and then his face softened, looking once again like the bumbling young man she was used to. "As soon as he starts talking we'll call the whole damn thing off."

She shook her head. "Don't lie to me Agent Spencer. You haven't yet, I'd rather you didn't start now."

"Okay, I apologize. You're a tough one, Mrs. Riordan."

"Agent Spencer, if you keep calling me Mrs. Riordan I'm not going to be able to go through with this."

"Point taken," he said. "Now is there anything you need, anything we can do for you?"

She raised her eyebrows, feeling a hot core of anger opening inside her. "Like what? Lingerie? Champagne? I already feel like a whore, I don't want a wallet left on the dresser to confirm it."

His face remained implacable, "I thought you might want your husband removed to somewhere safe."

"Safe for whom? Him or me?" she asked, feeling a scalding rush of tears damming up at the back of her eyes.

"For the both of you, I imagine. You may want to give some consideration to where you want to be when all this is over."

"I suppose Boston is out of the question," she said sarcastically.

"I'd avoid the entire Eastern seaboard," he said, with a slight twitch of his lips that might have been a smile. "Your husband's an Irish citizen."

"Are you suggesting we go back to Ireland?" she said incredulously.

"Do you want my honest opinion?"

"Yes."

"Put an ocean between yourself and what's happened here. When Love Hagerty goes down there's going to be an awful lot of unhappy boys in the neighborhood looking for a scapegoat. You don't want to be in that line of fire. I used to work homicide in the North End. Twenty-four corpses in a six month period, burned, strangled, cut from ear to ear, and all of it the Bassarelli family's handiwork. Hagerty's going to want to cut a deal, and that means ratting out his contacts in the North End."

"And they'll want their vengeance?"

"They're Italian, aren't they?" he said and this time there was no sign of humor in his face. "When they're done in Southie there won't be a man left standing. We're expecting a bloodbath and we're rarely wrong about these situations. This is your chance to get out before we put the fire to the mob's feet, probably the only chance you're going to get."

She nodded, slightly dazed by the revelations of the last hour. "How much time do I have?"

"It's got to be in the next month, sooner if possible, we've got agents out there undercover that need to be pulled back in before someone sniffs them out. You pick a target date, tell me and I'll get it set up."

"That simple, hey?" she said, wanting nothing more than to go home and shower. She knew the filth of the day was going to take more than hot water and soap to clean off though.

"For us," he said, "yes. For you, no."

"All right," she took a deep breath, "give me a week to figure this out. Mr. Hagerty's going to be suspicious if I spring this on him. I've been resisting his advances for months. Give me a week and then get my husband the hell away from here, somewhere they can't find him and he," she pressed the dewy bottle to the burning skin of her cheek, "can't find me."

"Done," Agent Gus Spencer said, thinking he'd never put in a harder hour for the Bureau than the one he'd just gone through.

He swallowed the last of the liquid in his bottle and then held it away from him, the vagrant sunshine curving thickly through waves of pale green glass.

"Coca Cola designed this bottle to feel like a woman's body—see how it's nipped in at the waist—so that subconsciously a man would connect it with the female form in his mind and like the snug of it in his palm."

"Seems to have worked," she said, wondering if he had a point or was just making conversation.

"I've always thought females were the ones with the real power," he said quietly, turning the bottle around in his hand, "it just comes with a price. Is the price going to be too high for you?"

"Considering what's at stake, no," she said, "it's just a body after all, right? Mine to give if I so decide."

"It's a lot more than that and we both know it."

"Try not to remind me of that too often," she said bleakly.

He looked at his watch, uncomfortable now that she'd agreed to consider his deal. She wondered if he'd ever be able to look her in the eyes again.

"I've got to get back to the field office," he said awkwardly, and she felt a certain detached sympathy for him, knowing he was an honest man simply trying to catch a dishonest one, and that he didn't like the methods he'd had to resort to.

She sat for a long while after the agent's dark-suited form had disappeared from view. Sat while couples strolled past arm in arm and mothers headed home with sleepy babies. In the distance, she heard the distinct crack of tight leather against a bat. She knew she had to get back to work before Love wondered what had happened to her. She couldn't afford to raise his suspicions now.

She gathered her uneaten lunch, her unread book and the bottle of soda that was still three-quarters full, then set them back down and closed her eyes for a moment against the brightness of the sun. She took a breath, the smell of crushed ferns so pungent that she could taste it on her tongue.

Once she'd asked Jamie how he'd borne the pain of his marriage, the loss of three children and the sanity of a woman he'd loved most of his life. How he'd managed not to question the existence of a God who would allow such pain. He'd replied quietly that love didn't ask a lot of questions, it just provided the answer that made life bearable. She could see him suddenly in her mind's eye, with a sharp clarity that she had not allowed herself in a long time.

"Oh Jamie," she whispered forlornly, "what do I do now?"

Against her hand, she felt a sudden tickle of movement and opened her eyes to find that a ladybug had landed on the upturned palm of her left hand.

She watched as the bug spread its bright lacquered wings and a stray breeze set loose a waxen rain of chestnut bloom, tipping the glossy bug forward into the crease where the lines of heart and life merged.

"Don't bother flying home, lady," she said cupping her hand to shelter it from the wind, "the house is already in ashes."

Chapter Eight

The Whale Road

THE SNOTGREEN SEA. *The scrotumtightening sea.*

Casey Riordan, standing on the deck of *Jeannie's Star*, recalled the words of his famous countryman, and thought Joyce had definitely been onto something in his description.

The contents of his own scrotum, had they the choice, would have gladly climbed up into his body and stayed there until he was back on land. Oddly enough, he had found his sea legs quickly, and after the first day hadn't experienced any nausea. But a natural born sailor he would never be.

Jeannie's Star was an old tug, once used to haul warships and barges across the North Atlantic. She'd been found, bleeding rust and lying low and dull-eyed in the Scottish harbor of Perth. The inexperienced eye would have passed her over for junk, destined to go to a watery grave in a North Sea port. But Jack Blythe, a seaman from Petty Harbor, Newfoundland, saw the spirit in the abused tugboat and bought her for a song, had her refitted in Perth, and then took her home across the icy road of the North Atlantic. Once tucked in the rocky inlet of Petty Harbor, she was converted to a fishing boat.

At one hundred and fifty-six feet, and 650 gross tonnes, *Jeannie* was oversized for a stern trawler, but that was what she was fitted out as. Her below deck spaces were generous, with the living quarters aft and the freezers to the stern. She had a big open deck space on which to land and begin the processing of the fish. Her hold would take 400 tons of cod. In Newfoundland, and on any boat that ported out of her, fishing meant cod fishing. The word fish itself was synonymous with cod, other fish would be called by their individual names, but a Newfoundlander who said fish meant one thing and one thing only—cod.

Jeannie's crew consisted of fifteen men, an oddly assortment of men from the brutal northern shores of Newfoundland, Nova Scotia and Labrador. There was also an Icelander named Hallbjörn, which roughly translated—Casey was given to understand—meant rock-bear. The name was apt, as Hallbjörn was an enormous man with a well-furred face and hands the size of dinner plates.

He was as silent and taciturn as the rock he was named for, but when it came to sussing out the weather, he was akin to an Old Testament Prophet. As far as Casey could tell, the man didn't speak to anyone other than Captain Jack, and even that was only when strictly necessary.

Olie had assured Casey, though, that the big Icelander liked him well, for he would occasionally clap Casey on the shoulder, fix him with a hard gaze and nod. This, Olie told Casey, was a sign that Hallbjörn considered him one of the crew.

Olie himself was of Norwegian descent, though his family had been in Petty Harbor for three generations.

"We were the only Norwegians in a miniature Ireland. Accents on the people there—three, four generations away from the old country an' ye'd think they'd just come from Ireland the day afore."

Casey wisely forebore to mention that Olie's own accent sounded as though its roots were square and deep in the soil of County Kerry.

Olie had the ruddy skin of a seaman, and the intense blue eyes of his Nordic forebears. And like so many of those Norse ancestors, the sea flowed hard through his veins. He had fished all his life and the taste of saltcod was mother's milk to him.

"I fished with my father everyday afore school. Was good times, those. Afternoons, if the clouds come scuddin' in, we'd have to leave school, run down to the harbor to the fish flakes an' turn the salt cod skin side up to save it from ruinin' in the rain."

Unlike Olie, Casey did not have seawater in his veins. The work of fishing was hard and often brutal, particularly when the weather took an unkind turn. Being no stranger to physical labor, however, Casey had picked it up quickly enough. Though a man, or woman as the case might be, could be forgiven, he supposed, for thinking he was completely out of his element in the undertaking of such a job.

In fact, Pamela's response when broached with the notion had been distinctly unflattering. "*FISHING?! Fishing?! Have you completely lost your fucking mind?*" The conversation had gone progressively downhill after that.

The answer to his wife's question might well be a resounding and heartfelt yes, Casey thought, standing upon *Jeannie's* slimy deck, the reek of fish enveloping him. Hallbjörn had been on deck minutes before, had stared long at the sea, sniffed the wind, and shook his head at the horizon. As far as Casey could see, this was tantamount to a normal man breaking down and having full-blown hysterics.

The sea was relatively calm that morning, though there was a long low swell like the ripple of birthing pains that lofted the boat and then dropped it in a deceptively gentle manner. Something about the weather made Casey uneasy, and it wasn't just Hallbjörn's actions, but rather an electricity that jumped along the surface of his skin. When he related these fears to Olie, the reply was succinct and not made to ease his nerves.

"Aye, weather breeder, that's what a day like this is, me son, damned weather breeder. Means something ugly is brewin' herself up below the surface for tomorrow."

Casey gazed up at the clouds, lit like pale gray pearls on their undersides. The sea was exactly the same color. He shivered beneath his layers of fog-dewed wool, the small hairs on his neck rising. Olie was right; he could feel something brewing dark and furious beneath the surface of the water.

"No worries boy—we'll get ye drunk enough, ye'll pay no mind to the weather."

This didn't do a great deal to comfort Casey either. He'd already had one hangover out on the water, and didn't relish the thought of another.

The rum Olie had shared with him, two nights out from St. John's, was the blackest, foulest concoction that Casey had ever drank. And considering that he was no stranger to *poitín*—that lethal Irish brew that many said was the cause for such an abundance of leprechaun sightings in the Emerald Isle—that was really saying something.

When he had, in what was his last intelligent act of that night, attempted to re-cork the rum, Olie had shaken his head vehemently. Casey was quite certain he could hear the contents sloshing about in the man's skull as he did so, though perhaps it was only his own wits trying to surface before being drowned completely.

"Ack," Olie croaked around a mouthful of the fiendish brew, "don't be after doin' that, son."

"Doin' what?" Casey asked, numb brow furrowed.

"Puttin' the cork back in the rum, 'tis ill luck to do so. Ye uncork it an' ye drink it to the dregs, no mistake, or the evil spirits will be loosed."

"I think," Casey said, forehead still wrinkled in an effort to marshal his thoughts. "Th' evil spirits are loosed already."

"Nay," Olie shook his head with the vehement seriousness of someone in the clutches of a royal piss-up, "ye have to drink it all down so's the bastards are trapped in yer belly. 'Tis the only way to be certain yer safe."

To Casey's reeling mind, this had the form and substance of fuzzy genius. And so they drank the bottle to the dregs. In the morning, Casey had wished with every fibre of his being, that God would take him, quickly and without hesitation. For the demons, no doubt unaware of the rules governing these things, were trapped (and seemed very unhappy about their incarcerated state) firmly inside his skull. Where they stayed for three full days.

A great hissing exhalation in the mist pulled him back to the present. The sound was followed shortly by the musky scent of the deeps. There—only thirty feet out from the starboard rail—was the great misty balloon of a humpback whale surfacing. He wondered if it was the one he'd taken to calling Soot, for the deep gray, speckled with paler ash, color of it. He was an old male, to judge by the numerous scars that carved a long and elaborate story on his back and tail flukes.

He wondered if the humpbacks were the sirens of the old Greek myths. The ones whose haunting song drew sailors to their death on the rocks. He shivered. Two nights before, the whales had been floating around the boat, their long misty exhalations drifting out over the strangely calm water. Overhead had been a sky drenched with stars, and all the men had stood on the open deck, silent, small and fragile. And he'd had a sense then of the planet, moving, drifting, unanchored in space, itself a lost seafarer borne along on the currents of a universe so merciless that it took the breath from a man's body in pure terror and wonder.

Near the boat, small slick patches had formed on the water. They were the strange footprint-like shapes that humpbacks left in the wake of their dives, glassy patches on the surface of the water, as though a ghost walked upon the cold, gray waves.

The Anglo-Saxons had called the ocean the Whale Road, and Casey could certainly see why. This realm belonged to the Leviathan, those big, half-dreamed creatures that swam among mountains higher than anything ever seen by man, through great rift valleys and salty abyssal plains, over steaming jets and through wonders both beautiful and terrible.

Aye, it was a water world indeed, with the continents only minor intrusions in the vast seas. So why then, out here on the limitless deeps, did he have the sense that someone was watching him?

He turned from the railing. It would be time to haul in the nets soon, and then he would be too busy to feel the hairs rising on the back of his neck.

The scrotumtightening sea indeed.

Chapter Nine

The Nature of Love

THE ITALIANS WERE THE KINGS of the Boston underworld. The Irish, princes in their own small principalities. The Italians ran their criminal vassals on the hard and fast rules of an army. Capos, soldiers, consiglieres. The Irish still ran on tribal rules, with the attendant internecine warfare, and thus had become subcontractors to the more powerful *La Cosa Nostra*. It was a reverse of natural order, for the roots of American organized crime were not in the rich soil of Italy, but rather in famine-stricken Ireland.

The Irish countryside, long the victim of failed rebellion and squashed political uprisings, spawned many resistance societies: the Molly Malones, the Peep o'Day Boys, the Whiteboys and the Ribbonmen—underground movements in which membership was a fiercely guarded secret. They professed to be the guardians of their own communities, but were as likely to prey upon their own people as they were to rebel against the Crown. This was the mentality that survived the brutal Atlantic crossing and found succor in the tarnished coin of American politics.

By the time the Italians began to emigrate in search of the elusive American Dream, the Irish mob was already established along the eastern shore of the United States. They were the gangs that strong-armed for Tammany Hall, that provided the struts for the infrastructure of a corrupt political machine. Tammany was the machine, and the Machine was the only way to achieve the dream. The Irish found their way through the cogs and wheels, becoming ward bosses, aldermen and precinct captains. Extending favors, exerting control, building a cultural dynasty that had begun in small turf-roofed cabins, muddy laneways and pestilential fields.

Despite the initial dominance of the Irish, though, it was the Italians who seized the ascendancy in Boston during the Prohibition. When the Irish tried to take over bootlegging operations in Boston Harbor, the Italians sent them a very clear message by murdering two of their gang leaders. The Irish mob retreated to South Boston, making it their private fiefdom, and hiring out as enforcers and hit men for the Italians.

In the early seventies, the Italians still ruled out of a small office in Boston's cobble-streeted North End. Their undisputed head a tiny, aged man with glasses so thick they gave him the appearance of a myopic gnome. He looked entirely harmless, but anyone who had ever crossed him knew the lie of appearances. He behaved like an old world gentleman, but he had the soul of a Sicilian butcher. Lovett Hagerty might control South Boston, but it was only a small corner of the empire that Guilio Bassarelli ruled over, and it was he to whom Love Hagerty owed his allegiance.

Pamela knew this acknowledgement of the godfather chafed at Love's very soul. And that his ambition, as such fires will, was rapidly outpacing his common sense. That, as far as Pamela could see, was the biggest chink in his armor. It was here that his pride and ego might well get him into trouble from which his charm and connections could not extract him.

She was beginning to feel a little like a bird attempting to build a solid nest out of invisible thread and faint whispers. Every time she managed to grasp hold of one, it led nowhere, or petered out in denials and shrugged shoulders. She knew that with every question she asked she was putting herself in greater and greater danger. For whatever else he might be, Lovett Hagerty was not a stupid man.

It was a delicate dance, played out upon the edge of a razor so fine it could not be seen. But she did not have a waking moment anymore when she was not completely aware of the swift and absolute laceration that awaited her smallest misstep.

There were two other fissures that could be exploited—one was fraught with danger, the other was the one she had hoped to avoid, though it seemed less likely that she would be able to do so as the days passed.

Two days previously he had given her a gift, producing a box from his dinner jacket with the flourish of a magician. A choker of emeralds that glowed with a deep, green fire there in the dim of his office. In allowing him to place them around her neck, she knew she was taking an irrevocable step forward that could destroy the foundation of her life. While fully aware that if she did not, she might well lose her husband altogether.

The emeralds felt like a vise around her neck, '*half a million dollars,*' Love whispered in her ear as he placed them about her throat, '*half a million, and next to that skin and those eyes they're nothing but dime store baubles.*'

Half a million in stones cut from the hide of people like Emma, carved from the conscience of Father Kevin, who'd been forced to look the other way in order to keep his flock safe. Half a million dollars for a chunk of rock with which to keep her tightly leashed.

For a man did not choke a woman with five hundred thousand in jewels unless he expected something in return. And she knew what he wanted, it flamed hot as the arc of a welding torch in his eyes, it was there in the random touches that caused a surge of sickness in the pit of her stomach.

It was not, however, his desire that worried her the most. It was that the man seemed to be falling in love with her. That it was not just her body he desired, but rather all that she was. She didn't fool herself into thinking that even this was any more than another acquisition for him. His innate ruthlessness had given him everything he'd wanted in the past; she was merely another challenge. Yet, the fact he had not yet tried to take her to bed told her much. He wasn't going to rush, for he had bigger things in mind. He was paying her court, wooing her as best might a man who was still married to another woman, and always mindful of his political future. The man wanted her for a wife.

She was well aware of the irony of her position. For he was exactly, mob connections aside, the sort of man she had been groomed for all her growing years. A wily Irish politician with boundless ambition and an eye constantly to the future. And the truth was she did love the legitimate side of his world— the shenanigans, the backroom dealing, the assiduous charm and outright chicanery that were the hallmarks of Irish politics and that was somehow, at the same time, so quintessentially American. Like every glittering coin, though, the underbelly was equally dark.

Through all of this, she kept thoughts of Casey at bay. Worry for him, out on the ocean (a more unnatural set of events she never could have imagined) was a constant, like a nagging pain under her ribs that could not be ignored, but must be lived with.

Just the thought of another man touching her seemed a gross betrayal of what she shared with Casey. The trust between them was a thing of quiet strength. It lay at the core of their marriage. For Casey, after the years in prison, trust had not been a thing easily given. And yet he had given it and she, for so long rootless and lonely, had found in him a home in which she placed complete faith. Which only made the game she was now engaged in that much more difficult. It would be a betrayal of so much more than the flesh.

And so that brought her down to the last option. Blackie. Blackie and Love together comprised a closed universe that even the oldest of Southie insiders could not hope to be allowed entrance to. Blackie was Love's right hand, the hand that got dirty and bloody, the hand that held the gun, even if the order came from Love.

If it were at all possible, Blackie frightened her more than Love. He did not make a secret of what he was and what he had done. Even his physical appearance put the hair up on the back of her neck. He was so pale as to be nearly albino, his eyes an icy blue without a spark of human warmth, his hair so blond it was almost white. His mouth, subversively, was a full and bloody red, and was twisted up on one side by an old scar he'd gotten in a knife fight, giving him a perpetual sneer. He looked like a cold-blooded reptile that wouldn't think twice about tormenting its prey before eating it leisurely.

Where Love could not afford to be seen, so went Blackie. It was exactly this state of affairs which had provided her with what she thought might be her ticket to divide and at least have a shot at conquering. For she had seen Blackie talking to a man that she knew Love would find most interesting.

She waited for an opportune moment to mention it. They were drinking red wine in a tiny North End restaurant where the cooks and wait staff were paid extra for averted eyes and sealed lips. It was one of the few places Love could safely take her. It was a small, dark restaurant with a very select clientele. Which meant the Bassarellis ate here, and anyone else the old man gave the nod to.

But Love had other things on his mind this night. He had finished his steak, always rare to the point of oozing blood, and was now eyeing her as though she were merely another cut of meat. Something to be devoured.

"I like to see you in the clothes I've bought."

Outwardly, she had smiled. Inwardly she had thought that his street manners were never too far from the carefully cultivated surface. It was a sore point, for she had refused the first delivery of clothes that had landed on her doorstep, a stunning array all in the discreet packaging of half a dozen different couture boutiques. She had not even looked in the expensive boxes, but had sent them directly back to Love with a polite note attached.

Agent Gus had gently rebuked her, saying that in order to cultivate trust Hagerty needed to believe she was falling in love with him as well. Which meant accepting his gifts and appearing to cater to his tastes and whims.

She had acquiesced with an ill grace. And now had a closet filled with the fabrics that whispered voluptuously in threads of silk and taffeta, chiffon and organza, linen and lace. The names all French—Chanel, St. Laurent, Dior and Balenciaga. For the French did certain things better than the rest of the world—food, wine, perfume and clothes. Because they understood one thing, it was all about sex, every last detail of it.

The little apartment in Brookline was filled with such things. Every room speaking its own dialect in the language of seduction. Tumbling, slipping sweet-smelling piles of lingerie in rich jewelled shades, with the tiny hand-sewn labels of the small Parisian boutiques from which they'd been ordered. In the bath oils and liquids infused with dark flowers and spices—cinnamon, cloves, jasmine and roses. Perfumes in Baccarat bottles murmuring of the east, of souks in Morocco and Tunisia, perfumes named for moonlit Indian gardens and English schoolgirls who'd once broken a French boy's heart.

In the kitchen—wine. The pale gold of the semillons and sauvignon blancs, the richer autumnal tints of the chardonnays on through the blooded hues of the reds—merlots and burgundies, bordeauxs and sangioveses and the smokey oak-casked cabernets.

And all of these things speaking in scent, taste and touch of one thing desire and the satiation of it. He would wait, but not much longer. Nor, did it seem, would the FBI, for Agent Gus had informed her that the bugs were now in place and ready to operate. So she put from her thoughts of her husband, and did what she must to keep him.

The dress she wore tonight was black, a filmy thing of silk with chiffon overlay. Black was not a color Casey liked, so for him she did not wear it.

"I knew black would suit you," Love said smugly, "it's that hothouse skin of yours." There was a faint sheen on his forehead and upper lip, and he flicked his tongue across his bottom lip in a manner she could not mistake. It was an opportune moment to change the subject, so she had clutched her napkin in a clammy palm and made the opening move in this dreadful chess game, where there were no pawns to sacrifice.

She was as vague as could be managed, saying only that she had seen Blackie chatting with a redheaded man, who looked like a businessman from the cut of his suit.

Love lowered his wine glass from his lips, a dark mask coming down over his face that chilled her to the core.

In the cold face, his eyes simmered.

"Was he? If he thinks he can end run me, he'd better think again."

Pamela stiffened her backbone, though her natural instinct was to flee from the anger that pulsed from his skin like an electric current.

"The neighborhood is mine, the people are mine. I look after them and they look after me. Blackie is nothing but a punk that I hauled out of the goddamn gutter like some crossbred mutt. He may need reminding of that."

As much as she loathed Blackie, Pamela's spine gave a sympathetic shudder for the man. In Love's world, being reminded of your place was likely to result in permanent injury if not permanent sleep.

The man she had seen Blackie talking with was a man she had also seen leaving Love Hagerty's office a number of times. Though always at night, when the streets were dark enough for a man to move about in anonymity.

His name was Mark Ryan, and he had grown up in Southie. He was a man who had never quite outgrown his boyhood worship of the neighborhood king, whose eyes were still dusted in the glamor of Love Hagerty, the man to whom everyone pretended a connection even if they didn't have one.

Which begged the question of why he was having cozy chats with Blackie away from Love? For the most interesting thing about Mark Ryan was his job. He was a federal agent.

Chapter Ten

Mermaid in a Bowl of Tears

C ASEY AWOKE TO ELECTRIFIED DARKNESS, the world no more than an upside down bowl filled to the brim with stark blue light. He awoke to fear, disoriented, thinking he was back on the damn boat, the smell of fish and blood heavy in his nostrils. The sound of thunder, crashing like a steel-plated drum through his consciousness brought him back to himself, calming the fear. He took a deep breath, filling his lungs to their limit and releasing it just as harshly. Near the ocean, yes, but thank God and His little green men, not on it.

He was between fishing trips, with an entire week behind him and a week still to come. He'd met Pamela here on the Cape, where she had rented a cottage for the two of them near the town of Yarmouth.

He reached for his wife, wanting the luxury of her skin beneath his hands. Wanting to wake her gently, with lips and fingertips, until she cried for him in need and sweetly stirred desire.

But her side of the bed was empty, and judging from the temperature of the sheets, she'd been gone awhile. Surely, the woman wasn't mad enough to go out in a storm, though. He sat up in the bed, knowing the answer to the question. When she was troubled she always wandered the shore, as if the roar of the surf and the icy salt spray of the sea could tell her what she needed to hear.

He stood, grabbing his pants in one hand and a sweater in the other, going to the window that overlooked the bluff. Beyond the glass, the night seemed a great devouring beast, illuminated by neither star nor man. He waited for the next flash of lightning, and when it came in a pouring blue sheet, he scanned the shore below him quickly.

He thought he caught movement in his peripheral vision, there and gone as quickly as the stark light. He dressed swiftly, not bothering with socks and shoes. The sand would only fill them anyway, bare feet were easier.

Outside the air was cold, the wind so strong it whined against his ears, blowing the rain at a forty-five degree angle. He hunched against it, tasting salt and sand on his lips. The waves must be high for the spray to blow up this far.

The sand, where the sea had slowly eroded the bank away over time, crumbled under his feet, causing him to slide precipitously down the bank several yards at a time. Dune grass, slick and icy with spray, left a chill dew on his skin where the two touched in passing.

He half slid, half tumbled to the bottom, barely managing to keep to his feet. The rain drummed harder, relentless in its sheer power. The core of the storm must be close to hand. He stopped, feet sunk in sand up to the ankles and waited for the next flash. It came quickly, seeming to expand from its center like a living thing drawing breath, showing him all the world around him down to its finest grain.

She was down the shore from him, where the sand arced out into a rounded point and the waves gathered and submerged the narrow spit, again and again. He turned in her direction, feeling the cut and crunch of abandoned shells beneath his soles. His shirt was soaked through to the skin and he could feel sandy grit where the waves had thrown it up beneath the worn denim of his pants. The woman *was* mad to be out in this godforsaken night. And himself as lunatic to come after her.

The next flash of light showed her on her back, perhaps forty yards distant, entirely naked and, despite the distance, a world away. He halted as though a hand had come up hard against his chest.

He knew the moods the sea provoked in her, how vital it was to her, as necessary as breath. It was what was foreign to him about her, a thing that, at times, he felt the separation of—that she needed the ocean, felt its every thrust and slide in the running of her blood.

Lightning split the world again and fired a path along the sea, a light-shattered vee that opened its arms wide as it neared the shore. To embrace or to seize? He never knew which himself, but he knew what his wife felt.

The eldritch light in that split second had carved all her lines onto his retina like cored ivory—line, curve, dip, hollow. She appeared oddly weightless, as if she had become an empty vessel ready to receive the sea. Even her breasts, which his hands well knew the weight of, seemed like cups awaiting the bounty and benevolence of the ocean gods.

And what if, one day, the water claimed her, if the terrible sea kings took what was theirs? For she was foolhardy in her love, courted it, danced on its edges, allowed the current to first caress, then grasp. It was a mating as sure as any other and one that made him jealous.

There were other things separating them, he knew, the words they were not saying being foremost at present. Secrets that pilfered from the all too brief hours they had together. It made him restless and it was obviously doing the same to her.

She lay in the sand, the waves first rushing over her naked form and then pulling back with cold frothy fingers, leaving her skin only to rush back again, swimming over length of leg, reaching with splayed white fingers around her thighs, surging into the heated core of her. Foam skimmed like lace across her belly to encircle her breasts and curled with a sigh through the heavy lines of her hair, which glistened in the odd light like gelid streams of kelp.

Another flash and he saw that her eyes were closed and knew she was fathoms deep, gone into that far kingdom where valleys ran a hundred miles wide and mountains would seemingly reach the moon if they were not rooted to the ocean floor. Born to the sea, she was, a mermaid in a bowl of tears. And he with his feet planted firmly in the earth.

The Atlantic that his wife loved so well had been called *'the bowl of tears'* by the Irish poet John Boyle O'Reilly, and for good reason. Two million Irish, in a desperate bid to outrace death, had taken to the sea upon vessels so decrepit and unseaworthy that they were known as 'coffin ships'. Ships with rotten rigging, uncaulked timbers and leaking hulls. Ships without provision, nor berths, nor adequate water. Ships that would become fetid prisons of starvation, thirst and black fever. Still, the Irish, often unaware of the perils of ocean travel, preferred to take their chances upon the cold, unforgiving waters of the North Atlantic rather than face certain death in the land they'd been born to.

Casey saw them clear in his mind at times—the poor, the destitute, those abandoned by God and man, forced to flee the only security they'd known in a life that had been desperate at best. And he saw those too weak in spirit or flesh, too poor or enfeebled by their labors to take flight from a doomed land.

The scent of them lay thick along the shore. So many had come and so many had not survived, but they'd left their legacy in strong backs and stubborn minds. He could smell them everywhere, the smell of dispossession and displacement, of longing and fear. He knew the smell well for it was on his own skin—the fragrance of a man without a country. His own ancestors had come here once, and then returned to Ireland. The father-in-law he'd never known had come and stayed.

He wondered what Pamela's father had thought of this, this raw country that could break a man if he wasn't born knowing how to bend. She'd told him the basics—how her father had landed at Ellis Island, a thirteen year old orphan from the rough end of Limerick, without a dime to his name and only the clothes he carried on his back. Forty years later he'd been one of the wealthiest Irish Americans in the United States. She might have been telling the story about anyone, though, and that told him far more than her words ever could. He'd never pushed her about her past, had always backed off when she shied away from his questions, knowing too well there were some things that could not be said, things for which there weren't words in any language. But it bothered him to realize that somewhere inside her was a core of loneliness that he could not penetrate, a loss that was shrouded but not healed. Bothered him that the sea somehow gave her a relief that he could not. His wife, and yet there was always some element of her that eluded him.

It wasn't that he didn't understand what it was to have such a core. He'd his own, after all, like a lead-lined box harnessing the pain of his years in prison, a wee box to be certain but locked tight against the interference of outside eyes.

Another flash of light and movement caught his eye, snapping him abruptly from his reverie. Beyond Pamela, something had moved in the dark. Casey blinked, moving forward instinctively, panic lighting his nerve endings and burning quickly in toward his core. Who the hell would be out on a night such as this one? He cursed the sand as it slogged his steps, seeming to enlarge the distance between him and Pamela. The rain was coming harder now, blurring his vision, making him doubt the amorphous shape that he could have sworn had emerged from the dark only seconds before.

He began to run, feet sinking into the loose icy sand. He shifted his path down closer to the tidemark where the drenched sand provided firmer purchase. Pamela had once told him that the shore was an edge place, where two separate and spinning planes met, providing some sort of crack in the fabric of reality. It was why seabirds always uttered such desolate cries as they neared shore, she said, they saw the rip in the fabric of time and space, sensed it as humans could not, creatures of air that they were. He remembered the goose bumps rising on his skin as she'd told him this, green eyes as uncanny as a witch's, as though she too had seen into this abyss and was lured by its siren call.

'Perhaps,' she'd said dreamily, 'perhaps it's where monsters hide. The ones you're so certain of as a child, the ones you know are just waiting in the shadows with jaws held wide to snap you up. The ones your subconscious remembers as an adult. The ones that snatch away the innocent and the afraid, whose very innocence or fear was the thing that allowed them to stray too close to the edge of that spinning plane in the first place.'

He ran faster, insides icy with fear, seized by the certainty that his wife was about to fall into one of those nightmare rifts if he didn't reach her in time. But the sand kept giving beneath his feet, the lightning distorting the atmosphere into an alien sphere, as though he were trying to scale an arc that remained resolutely flat beneath his feet.

He yelled her name, feeling the wind and rain spit the frail syllables back into his face. There was no way she could have heard him within the howling wind, and yet her head turned toward him and he saw her hand come up in invitation and demand.

"Come back to the house!" he yelled, close enough now to see something wild in her face, something reckless. He shouted at her once more even as he dropped to his knees beside her, pulled by a need that emanated like fire through the air and water.

She shook her head; his words were lost in the wind in the bare foot between them. Her own intent was clear, though, as she grasped him behind the neck, pulling him over on top of her, arching against him in a passion that was nine parts desperation, matched only by his own to have and possess—to leave this shore with the scent of her heavy on his body, the touch of her molded to his skin, the heat of her lingering upon him.

She looked like a sea creature in the strange storm light, eyes as enigmatic as the ocean itself. He had a sudden fear that he would drown in them and never belong to himself again. Would wake to find himself imprisoned in a soul cage at the bottom of the sea.

Even through the rain, he could smell the tang of seaweed in her hair, and taste the salt in her mouth. He was dizzy with her, as though the world moved with them, rushed over them, took away and gave back. She was as fully open to him as the gates between worlds this night and thus he could see her dark side and know it the twin of his own.

"Harder," she whispered, urging him against her with body and words, "I want to be able to feel you after you're gone."

He groaned, lost already in the heat that only needed a look, a bare touch, to spring into a blaze that threatened to consume them both. How many times had he made love to this woman? And yet he never tired of it, never slaked the thirst for her that gripped his very innards. He'd been afraid those first few times they made love that such a fire would have to peak quickly, leaving only ashes in its wake. But it hadn't happened. He still came hungry and needing to her every time and occasionally left her in the same condition. It frightened him, the force of such a passion. It was as elemental as breathing, and as necessary to life for him now.

After she held him tightly through the aftershocks of the flesh, the world lit an eerie blue all about them.

They half walked, half ran back in silence, only partly clothed, the world wild about them and the rain falling hard against their skins.

Casey looked back only once, but behind him, the shore was empty. Still, he shivered, primal brain alerting the spine of some danger that couldn't be seen, but was no less real for its invisibility.

Nor could he rid of himself of the idea that his wife had been trying, between himself and the sea, to exorcise something—some intangible demon—from her very soul.

Chapter Eleven

Tales From the Fourth Dimension

OUTSIDE THE WIND HOWLED, shrieking round the boughs of stunted trees and the salt-licked corners of the cottage. Inside all was snug, the chimney drawing well despite the clamor, firelight reflecting warmly off the polished pine boards. Regardless of the cozy surroundings, Casey shivered, unable to rid himself of the feeling that he *had* seen something on the beach—the form and shape of a man—and yet when he'd reached out—nothing. He eyed the tightly shut curtains, knowing there were no cracks through which they could be seen, and yet he couldn't shake the feeling that someone—*something*, was watching them still.

Pamela had made a fire in the grate, boiled the kettle, ordered him under the blankets and brought him a cup of hot chocolate to ward off his chills.

"Christ, are ye not human, woman?" he asked, as another shiver struck out from his spine, shaking him to the ends of his fingertips. "Ye've not so much as a goose bump on ye, an' here I am blue to the gills."

"Landlubber," she said unsympathetically, adding another two logs to the fire now that it was well caught and poking it up into a blaze that scorched the fine hair on his arms.

"If not bein' a landlubber means splashin' about naked in the ocean on such a night, I'll take the title an' wear it proudly." He shivered again, teeth chattering against each other. "Woman, come warm me. That'll wait 'til mornin', will it not?" He nodded his head toward the pile of wet clothes from which she was shaking sand.

She nodded. "I suppose they will, though they'll smell awful."

"I've reeked of fish guts for weeks now, a pile of wet clothes isn't likely to offend my senses. Please come to bed." There was something odd in his tone—a note of fear that made her turn sharply, wet clothes forgotten.

"What's wrong?" she asked, brows drawn down in fine inked lines.

"Pamela, please," he said, a hand emerging from the blankets to pull her down into the makeshift pile of quilts and pillows.

She took the hand, allowing herself to be drawn into his embrace. He held her tightly and she could feel the tremors that shook him from head to toe, though his skin emitted a healthy warmth. He smelled of wood chips and brine and the co-mingled scents of their recent lovemaking. She breathed deeply, wishing she could stay here with him, by the fire, indefinitely.

"Talk, man, you're warm as toast and shaking like a leaf," she said as the worst of his tremors seemed to have passed.

"Well..." he drew the word out uneasily, "it's only that I could have sworn I saw someone out there with ye."

"What?" she said, hoping he didn't notice the sudden tension in her body.

"Wasn't so much someone as some*thing*," he said, tone heavy.

"Some *thing*?" She glanced up to see him looking positively sheepish. "Casey, what on earth do you think you saw?"

"Don't look at me that way, woman, I've not taken drink," he said, a tint of indignation coloring his tone.

"I haven't accused you of drunkenness," she said, arching an eyebrow at him, "now just tell me."

"A ghost," he said.

Both of her eyebrows shot up as she leaned up on one elbow, to better see the expression on his face. She put a hand to his forehead, which he swatted away irritably.

"'Tis no joke, I'm serious," he said, meeting her incredulous look with a black glare.

"*You* believe in ghosts?" she said in disbelief.

"Mmphmm, well," he began, uncomfortably, making one of those indecipherable Celtic noises that said he wasn't thrilled with the direction the conversation was taking.

"Do you?" she insisted, noting that he was now studying the edging on the worn quilt with great interest.

"Well," he frowned visibly in the firelight, "I'll not say as I do, but I'll not say as I don't."

She eyed him narrowly and he capitulated with the deep sigh of an Irishman who knows himself backed into a corner. "It's only that a man will have experiences that can't be explained in the normal run of things, aye? An' mayhap it's only somethin' that cannot be understood as yet, an' mayhap it's beyond explanation altogether."

She raised her eyebrows at him and he sighed again. "Alright then, I'll try to explain what I mean, but I'll need a cigarette to get my thoughts together."

She watched him as he reached for the crumpled pack, pulled a cigarette out, and lit it with an unusually elaborate set of motions. For some reason the mention of ghosts had made him uneasy in the extreme.

"Well, as I see it, it all comes down to subatomic particles," Casey said, after taking a long drag off his cigarette.

"What?" she asked, momentarily confused by the jump from ghouls to the netherworld of quantum physics.

"Bear with me, darlin'. I've given this matter some real thought."

He shifted in the blankets, propping a pillow up against the armchair behind him, then leaned back against it and tucked her in the curve of his free arm.

"Now there is an actual ghost behind this, or at least I think there is, but I'll get to that later. See, I'd an experience in prison that I could never find a reason for, an' I'd pretty much given up on explainin' it to myself. Until one day when I was browsin' through one of them scientific journals Pat is so fond of readin', an' I stumbled across somethin' that seemed like a possible explanation."

"An explanation of what?" she asked.

"Patience, woman," he said, "I promised ye a ghostie, an' I'll deliver. I bet ye couldn't wait for dessert when ye were a wee one either, could ye?"

It was her turn to make an indecipherable Celtic noise.

"This article was about subatomic particles, see? An' they were explainin' how these particles didn't occupy space or move through it in any way that was familiar or quantifiable. An' the really odd thing—an' this was the thing that struck me—was that these particles came in pairs that even when separated were affected by interactions happenin' to the one. The scientists couldn't figure out how. It made no sense, as information travellin' from one half of the pair to the other would have to exceed the speed of light. Which we know is impossible. That left them with no answers, so they called it a phenomenon. Which I think is the name assigned to anything scientists don't have the answer for. The conclusion bein' that it wasn't explicable in human terms, as it didn't behave in a rational or orderly manner that could be classified. But it seemed to me that such a thing was very human, as so much of our behavior is inexplicable. Ye cannot slice a cell an' divine by it why one man is a coward an' another a hero. Some say it's environment an' experience, but I always thought it went deeper than that somehow." He shook his head, as if absorbed momentarily by some inward melody, something only he could hear.

"Anyhow it brought back to me some of my schoolin', both the formal an' the informal," he smiled ruefully, "there was, as ye may well imagine, a great deal of time for readin' in prison. Well, I remembered a passage of some book that said matter could neither be created nor destroyed, an' it went on some further way down the page to say that matter was really just another form of energy, an' that energy was really tricky, as it could exist—even just the potential of it—in absolute nothingness. So I pictured it as this void, where something could be, an' then just as swiftly, not be. An' if that were so—an' these men seemed to think it was—then it made definin' where the borders of reality were a little difficult. Do ye follow me so far, Jewel?"

"I think so," she said slowly, the hairs on her arms rising in the night air.

"Well if ye take it as a given of our story here, that the borders of reality are merely a matter of the creature perceivin' them, then ye can follow the next bit of what I'm goin' to say. We're three dimensional creatures an' so it follows that we live in a three dimensional world, right?"

She nodded and he paused to take another drag on his cigarette, the glowing red tip of it punctuating the dark that was gathering around the edges of the dying firelight.

"But suppose, darlin', that a two dimensional creature existed in our sphere, an' to be honest we've no way of perceivin' that they don't, what do ye suppose this cigarette end would seem to it?"

"Well I suppose that would depend on the angle of the ember, wouldn't it, and whether or not this two dimensional creature was circumnavigating the cigarette?"

Casey snorted. "We're not talkin' about the Magellan of two dimensional creatures, just an ordinary run-of-the-mill entity, sittin' firmly in place with no desire to move. Ye understand?"

"Ah," she slapped a hand to her forehead, "I think I do, this is an Irish, male, two dimensional creature, nursing a pint of ale."

"Woman," Casey eyed her sternly, "do ye wish to hear the rest of this tale or not?"

"Pray, go on," she said with mock seriousness.

Casey shot her a purely Irish look, cleared his throat and continued. "Alright then, suppose ye're seein' the burnin' end as a two dimensional creature. Imagine there's a knife slicin' the cigarette an' ye can only see where the knife cuts, not above it, nor below it and only on a flat plane out to the sides. But at the same time this figurative knife is cuttin' at an angle, so what do ye see?"

"A red line for a split second and then nothing."

"Aye, like a flash in the corner of yer eye, but when ye turn yer head, it's gone an' so ye presume there was naught there. Now, Jewel," the red ember in question danced in graceful curlicues in the air with the movement of his hands, "supposin' that we three dimensional creatures are that knife, we see neither above nor below and only on a flat plane out to the sides."

"A fourth dimension."

"If ye must stop there, then aye, let's presume a fourth dimension. So three dimensional creatures drifting through four-dimensional space will see only shadows of things, an' not the reality, because it's outside the sphere of their dimension."

"Are you saying ghosts exist in this hypothetical fourth dimension?"

"Well," he drew the word out reluctantly, "I don't know exactly *what* I'm tryin' to say. Only that there are things, as yer Englishman said, between heaven an' earth, that have no explanation, but it doesn't make them less real."

"Ghosts?"

"Aye, ghosts," he leaned over to the side and stubbed out his cigarette, face drawn into the dark-inked lines it always assumed when a topic bothered him. He leaned back into the pillows and took a deep breath.

"Now, Jewel, I've never told a soul this story, 'cause I thought I was mad at the time an' that I'd only imagined it all in retrospect. An' ye know, I'm not so overfond of talkin' about my days in prison at any rate. Well prison, as ye can well imagine, is not a pleasant place for any man to be, but it's altogether less so for an Irish Republican militant who's incarcerated in a British facility. An' truth be told, though I'd acted like a pig-headed fool an' deserved the punishment I got, I was still a boy. An' I was scared out of my wits an' still grievin' my da an' missin' Patrick somethin' fierce. An' maybe these elements combined provided a rip in the fabric of reality—who's to say?

"I think, too, that whatever thin thing it is that separates us from the animals, that civilizes us, it's not so much in existence in prison. Humanity on the outside is a fragile thing. It doesn't take a great deal to reduce us to violence an' murder, but in prison even the pretence of that is gone, an' it's every man for himself."

She shuddered. She could well imagine, a little too clearly perhaps, what life had been like for him. Nineteen and defiant on the outside, but still a boy needing his father's love and assurance on the inside. His innocence and inexperience would have stuck out like a sore thumb as well. Tall, dark and by no means ill-favored in the looks department, which would have attracted all sorts of unwelcome trouble for him. The sum of this equation meant he would have been a magnet for the uglier side of what prison life had to offer.

"Things didn't go easy on me right from the start, but I'd expected some of it," his tone shifted, his look faraway, "but there are things a man cannot imagine unless he experiences them. I'd no real notion of how brutal one human bein' could be to another. I thought I'd seen all there was to see of hatred an' anger an' violence in my own streets. But in prison, my education was, shall we say, to be broadened extensively."

He gazed down, stroking absently at the quilt that covered the two of them, and she knew he'd gone back in his memory and did not register the squares of velvet and flannel, worked in shades of deep purple and lavender, but instead saw the high, dark walls of Parkhurst, as clear in his memory as if they'd been outlined with charcoal and then burned into his synapses by tempered steel.

"It was October an' near to the end of it. A time, my daddy used to say, when the gates between one world an' the next briefly stand open. About a week before Hallowe'en..."

It was autumn, and though he could not define it by the usual set of signs, he could smell it in the air—the smell of smoke and mellow sunshine with a whiff of decaying earth accompanying them. If he closed his eyes and breathed in deeply he could almost feel the crunch of leaves—amber, copper, brown, bronze and gold, under his feet, releasing the silk-fine dust of death as they fractured under thick-soled shoes. At night, if he scrunched his large frame tight against the damp, mildewed concrete of his cell he could just see, through the barred window, a wedge of the moon and a scraping of stars. Autumn was the least spectacular of the seasons in the sky, the first magnitude stars all but invisible in the great galactic haze of the Milky Way, with only summer's lingerings left.

His father had begun to teach him the names of the stars when he was four. Gave the words to his soft child's tongue, where they rounded into natural forms and he could, even then, taste the sand and honey of their root language. Stars named fell from his tongue in streams, in buckets and cascades to form bright burning bridges in his subconscious for all time. Sometimes he thought the repetition of these things, the focus on something so far from earthly care and woe, was the only thing that kept his sanity intact.

He was on kitchen duty that morning, stirring the dirty gray industrial slop that passed for breakfast, reciting grimly to himself from the table of chief spectral classes. He'd just worked his way through examples of orange stars, 'Arcturus, Pollux, Alpha Ursa Majoris' and was beginning on the characteristics of red stars, 'rich spectra showing many strong metallic lines with wide bands produced by titanium oxide,' when he was hit sharply between the shoulders by something narrow and hard. He barely missed overbalancing into the porridge pot, cursing out loud as he swung around to face his attackers.

They stood in a loose semicircle, five of them, all gripping paddles identical to the one he held in his own hands.

Fear, his constant companion of late, hit hard, grabbing him in the knees and stomach. Just as quickly he put it to the side, his brain sizing up the opposition. Five men, none as large as him, granted, but, as he'd long ago learned, sheer number made up for a lack of size every time. They were familiar to him, prison being the small world that it was. Henchmen of the Baron of 'D' wing, where all illicit items could be bought and sold, if you had the coinage, be it in prison currency or blood.

"Well lads, who do we have here then?" asked the one in the middle—the corporal to the Baron's general, and likely the man who would decide his fate in the next few minutes. Any talk would have to be directed at him.

"I'm mindin' my own business, doin' my job here, an' not lookin' for any trouble," Casey said, keeping his voice polite but not allowing for the weakness of actual civility.

"Did I say ya could speak, ya Paddy bastard?" said the corporal, smiling nastily and revealing a row of rotting, broken-off teeth. He looked, Casey thought, like a weasel in need of dental work.

"I wasn't aware I needed yer permission," Casey replied as coolly as he could manage, though his intestines felt as though they'd turned to icewater.

"Ya need my permission to take a piss round here, boy, it's only a right div as would forget that."

"Aye well," Casey said, half-turning back towards his cauldron of bubbling oats,

"I'll bear that in mind next time nature calls."

"'E's a smart mouth on 'im lads, an' we know as what happens to smart mouths in here, don't we."

From the corner of his eye Casey could see the four henchmen nod as one—well-trained and likely bluntly stupid. Unfortunately, that made them all the more dangerous. They'd do as they were told and wouldn't give a thought to consequences. He angled his back carefully, casting a quick look about him. Not an ally in the place, the other men in the kitchen had their eyes carefully averted, hands on their assigned tasks. He was alone, utterly and completely. The brain, wondrous weapon that it was in many situations, was of limited use when the physical odds were squarely against one. He'd have to do the best he could with size, agility and his paddle and hope to God they didn't kill him.

Not only did they nod as one, they moved as one and he could feel the force of their coming in the air as it began to push against his skin. He tensed himself for it—muscles contracting, skin pulling back toward the sanctuary of bone, body trying desperately to find a fixed anchor in the sea of adrenaline that poured unrestrained through him.

They were almost to him now, he could smell their body odor—onions, piss and, oddly enough, rosewater. Then, again as one, they stopped dead, only a foot and a half away, close enough to grab, close enough to hit. He slid his hands lower down the haft of the paddle, cursing the sweat that slicked their path and wondered, rather wildly, if he would live to see the next hour.

He could feel the tremor of their muscles through the air, the violence that heated their blood as one, making of man an animal. He braced himself, knowing the first blow was always the worst. Then suddenly their eyes flicked to the left, and they backed away an inch or two, the expressions on their faces changing almost comically. He didn't relax, but dared a slight intake of air. He knew something had put up their guard but couldn't afford to turn and look.

"Somethin' goin' on here, lads?" Casey judged the gruff voice to be a few yards behind and to his right. It was one of the screws, a Welshman by the name of Manfred. He was known to be fair-minded and honest. He'd never treated Casey any worse or better because of his nationality. It was a gesture that was appreciated; most of the screws weren't so unbiased. Casey dared a larger breath, the flood of adrenaline tapering down to a stream. He'd been given a reprieve, though he knew it wasn't likely to last long.

"I asked a question, lads, if you've not an answer I suggest the bunch of you clear off and let this boy finish his work."

Casey could feel the guard standing close behind him, his stick tapping rhythmically against a calloused palm.

Wisely the four men backed off, though the postponed threat still there in their silence. Casey let the haft of the paddle slide down, his arms suddenly the consistency of the sticky porridge that bubbled beside him.

"Thank ye," he said quietly.

"Be careful, laddie, those ones are not done with ye yet," Manfred said, before casually strolling the length of the kitchen, as if he were out for a Sunday meander.

Casey returned to stirring the porridge, though every hair on his body remained alert and prickling. He remained wary throughout his shift of kitchen duty, through the cleanup, the scrubbing of the large pots, the mop up of the floor. He didn't relax until he sat to eat his own breakfast. He was aware of other men milling about, but the hunger in his belly overrode all other sensations, even that of caution. He was, after all, only a boy, one still growing, and seemed to be hungry all the time. The food prison provided barely took the edge off the gnawing in his belly. He was just finishing up the last of a glass of milk when someone called his name. It was the surprise—the sound of his Christian name after months of not hearing it—that made him turn without thought.

The scalding oatmeal took him full in the face, blistering his skin on contact. The pain was enough to make a man scream, but he bit down hard on the inside of his lower lip, willing the sound to stay inside his body.

"Whaddya have to say now, ye paddy bastard?" Weasel Tooth asked, his flinty little eyes glittering maniacally, dripping paddle still held in his hands.

"Well," Casey said, wiping the sticking mess from his face with a dismissive gesture designed to cover his badly shaking hands, "I've heard as oatmeal is beneficial to the complexion, though I imagine they meant it to be taken cold."

"Have a nice day Paddyboy." The man gave him a nasty wink. "We'll catch up with ya later."

The threat was implicit, but Casey couldn't think far enough past the pain in his face to give it the importance he needed to.

He hadn't bothered going to the infirmary, determined not to give the bastards the satisfaction of his hurt. So he gritted his teeth through the pain and waited until he got back to his own cell before giving in to the raw searing agony. But he didn't cry, for he no longer knew how.

In the night, they came for him.

HE'D NEVER DREAMED *they'd come back for him so soon. Later, he would damn himself for a fool. He'd been dreaming when they came, one of those odd half-waking dreams where the border between reality and the night of the mind is blurred. Dreaming of home, the narrow streets, the curling wallpaper in his bedroom, and the sound of his brother murmuring in his sleep beside him. And so when the first man touched him, he'd thought it was Pat, grabbing him in the grip of one of the night terrors he'd been afflicted with since childhood. Then knew just as certainly that it was not Pat.*

His recollection of the night would never be entirely clear, though even years later it would seem as if it had lasted many nights, not just the hours it had been in reality. Though one thought would remain clear many years later—he was going to die and was going to wish death would take him quickly many times before it did.

They blindfolded him with a sack over his head. Small bits of dirt and fiber found their way into his nose, eyes and mouth as they dragged him down the corridors of the prison. He recognized, with a bitter chill, the smell of potatoes on the inside of the bag.

He fought to gain his feet, but was kicked solidly behind the knees, buckling his legs and causing them to scrape the uneven stone. Blind and in pain, he quickly lost track of the twists and turns they took. The entire world was reduced down to the sound of harsh voices, brutal hands and the scent of blood that raced in panic too near the surface of tender skin.

A minute, or a lifetime later, they stopped, throwing him face-first onto the floor. Then they pulled the sack off his head. He wished they'd left it on. He wasn't thrilled about witnessing his own murder.

It was not an area of the prison with which he was familiar. Granted it was damp and freezing like the rest of the place but it was also pitch black. With only the rough grate of stone under his face and the taste of moss in his mouth to go on, he'd no idea what wing they'd taken him into. There were empty areas of the prison, rooms that hadn't been used in years for one reason or another. He suspected this was one of them, which meant it would take a while for them to find his body. Though there'd be a full-scale alert once they found he was missing from his bed. Unless of course the screws were in on it, which was entirely possible.

They removed the gag, wanting the sound of his torment, as well as the physical struggle, though he only screamed once and then the pain was beyond the relief of sound. He was frozen by it, suspended by raw terror and an agony beyond his comprehension in some odd fugue state where ordinary time had no meaning.

The first cut of the knife felt like a shard of fiery cold in his back. He didn't realize what it was at first, rational thought was not possible, only the deafening clamor of instinct screaming inside his skull.

Their voices reached him as though from a great distance, as if he were hovering up near the ceiling of the tomb they'd dragged him to. Some words reached far enough to impress themselves upon his ears, others did not.

"Kill the bastard! Feel that, paddy? Not so cocky now, are ya? Fuckin' little terrorist, we'll teach ya real terror, won't we lads?"

He felt as though his soul pulled itself away from the shell of bones and flesh and shrank down until it was only a small thing, hiding in a corner, hoping only to remain unnoticed, knowing that was the only chance. It was this small part of himself, disconnected from the conscious mind, that ensured his survival. By not asking, not begging for release or mercy, by maintaining a silence that was beginning to frighten his captors, it saved his life. It would be a long time before he could find a shred of gratitude for this foreign part of him, though he knew it would always reside in that dark corner of him, waiting, should he ever need its assistance again. He hoped to God he never did.

Odd things registered—the smell of the sacking still thick about his face, a loose bit of stone digging into his stomach, the sucking hiss of a cork being withdrawn from a bottle, the sound of liquid pouring, and the realization of what that liquid was.

Acid like razors with horrible small teeth, bent on gnawing its way through to his core. When he felt the first smoking rush of it in the open channels of his back, he thought it was water, that they were trying to keep him conscious. What was left of his mind at that point quickly corrected that first impression and mercifully he finally lost consciousness, profoundly grateful that death had seen fit to come take him at last.

CASEY COULD HEAR *what sounded like the pages of an old and well-thumbed book being turned in haste, and amongst those rustlings a vaguely cross murmur.*

"...-now where is that damned recipe, can never remember from one day to the next...is it the Velvet Flowers for the bloody flux...hmm, Moonwort—to open locks an' unshoe horses, no doubt handy in some situations but hardly applicable to us here. Ah there—bleeding, vomiting, blows an' bruises, an' to consolidate fractures an' dislocations, bit of a miracle plant that one, but we'd best be after coverin' all the bases as we can."

He heard a heavy tread then, and the movement of displaced air where he lay.

"Open yer eyes then, laddie. Come now, ye can do it. Ye must wake up now, if only for a bit."

Though his eyelids felt as if they'd been forged shut with molten lead, Casey made a great and terrible effort to open them, and promptly wished he had not done so. For above him stood a fearsome giant of a man, with a great bushy black beard and eyes so blue they cut like an unsheathed knife.

"I'm yer nurse," the man said with a smile.

"Kill me now," Casey muttered, wanting merely to sink back into oblivion, dark and painless.

"Don't go to sleep on me boy, ye canna just yet."

"Let...me...be," Casey said, realizing in some dim way that his words seemed to come with long lapses of time between them.

"Nay, 'tis not my job to let ye be. Come lad, sick as the thought makes ye, I'll need to look at yer back."

Even the slight breeze that came from the crack in the window felt like harsh fingers flicking across his raw nerves. The man busied himself, his touch surprisingly light, the running commentary punctuating his touches.

"Hmm, it's none so bad as I thought, though it'll never look the same. An' I'll say the one thing for the wee doctor, for all he's the face of a puckerin' lemon on 'im, he's a dab hand with the needle. 'Twill take all my skills though, hm—is there any of the Adder's Tongue left? An' we'll need a pinch of the Graveyard Dust for sleep, an' some burned nettle round about the room..." he mumbled on but Casey was drifting towards unconsciousness again and so was only vaguely aware of the things that took place over the next few days.

Poultices that smelled of bitter rooted things were applied to his back. Their scent was brimstone, but their touch was cool and soothing. He was given what he could only think of later as potions, to drink. Things that left the taste of earth and tart green-ness upon his tongue and lodged firmly at the back of his throat. The drinks made him sleep, made him dream—of ships, of the sea, of terrible black things that slunk beyond the edge of his nocturnal horizon.

Sometimes the drinks tasted of flowers, and when they did, his dreams were considerably kinder and were often of women. Or rather one woman, whose touch healed and burned him all at the same time, though he never could see her face.

Time became a vortex, into which he sank dizzily, unaware of hour or day or month. It was some time before he realized that Angus and the doctor, who checked in on him twice a day, were never present at the same time. This puzzled Casey, but his fevered brain would turn fretfully away to its kaleidoscope of unconnected dreams and dread-filled nightmares, and he would wonder no more about the oddity of this arrangement.

During the day, the doctor would feel his forehead, change his dressings, force more antibiotics down his throat and then shake his head. Casey, even in his dire straits, understood what that shaking head meant. The doctor wasn't putting odds on his survival.

At night, Angus would rumble his disapproval over the doctor's methods of treatment, "Christ the man couldna' cure a flea of the dogs." And then he would remove the dressings, saying that the wounds needed air, and apply his own poultices.

The room seemed different at night, as if the sterile furniture and implements transformed themselves into something more organic and soothing in the darkness. For instance, Angus had a big old battered sea chest, replete with salt-rusted hinges, that Casey had never noticed during the day.

The sea chest sat in a corner and had strange symbols burned into its body. From his bed, he could make out a few of the figures. There was a three-headed beast with the body of a lion, a mermaid with talons and snakes in her hair, and a very large five-pointed star, with what looked like Hebrew lettering inside of its angles. One night while Angus was rootling through it muttering about gathering some sort of fungus now that the moon was full, Casey asked him about the chest.

"An' what do ye call that thing?" Casey asked.

"It's my wizard's chest," Angus replied simply, as if the title explained it all.

"An' all the wee symbols on the outside?"

"'Tis so nosy buggers like yerself won't open it. Scares people, aye, if they don't understand. They think there's like to a hex on the box."

Casey had glimpsed what lay inside the chest—old books, instruments of brass, weights and stones, small packets of herbs, glass vials and velvet wrapped tools, as well as other oddments of the healer's trade.

His interest was short lived. Even sustaining any kind of coherent thought exhausted him. Sleep called him constantly, became his lover, and he was grateful to sink into the dark arms and stay there for longer and longer periods of time.

He knew he wasn't getting better and in fact was getting worse. Infection had invaded his body and his soul. Dark thoughts clustered near at all hours, his dreams all of darkness and fire, his defences dissipating like smoke before wind. He was, he realized, in the process of dying. He could feel the veil between one world and the next getting thinner and thinner. Sometimes he even thought he could glimpse shadowy figures that existed in that other realm. They did not frighten him, but merely seemed to offer a vague sort of peace.

One night he came around sufficiently to find the room in darkness, stifling with heat, the only light that of four white candles that burned steadily without a trace of breeze to dance upon. Angus was poised over a basin of water, a low guttural crooning coming through closed lips and a vial of dark fluid that looked like ink held in his hand.

"Awake are ye, boy?" Angus had said gruffly. "Here, drink this."

A drink was put to his lips and he gulped thirstily, it tasted of honeyed flowers, though, and did little to calm the raging thirst that plagued his very dreams.

Angus sat upon the floor, and through bleary, fever-impaired vision, Casey noted that he was wearing an odd sort of garment. It was white and loose, and seemed to ripple, though the air was tremendously still.

"What are ye doin'?" Casey had asked, barely able still to rise, the weakness invading every cell of his body.

"Conjuring angels," Angus said, and continued to sway gently, with that terrible crooning over the water. Within the water, the inky fluid snaked out, in long slinking vapor trails, taking on strange shapes, forming under the man's dreadful chant.

Words singled themselves out in the multitude, and Casey could hear amongst them fragments of Latin and something far older and guttural, the very sound of it alone sending the hairs up on the back of his neck. There were names, ancient ones, that seemed as though they must predate man, must have been born in the depths of the ocean, and that the uttering of them would bring about terrible beings.

Casey's skin crawled upon his frame, but he'd not the strength left to move. He was drifting in and out of consciousness as it was, when a sharp smell jerked him back fully.

Angus stood above him, the taper of a burning stick in his hands. The smoke stung Casey's eyes and clogged his throat, the scent bitter and ammoniac.

The man seized his face hard between his huge hands, his eyes occluded still by the drugs or the trance he had put himself in. But the look speared Casey, fastened his soul to a point from which it could not escape, and then Angus spoke in a voice which wasn't recognizable.

"At the darkest time of night there is a turning point. From darkness to light, from death to life, a journey completed, a new journey begun. You must make the choice—light or dark, death or life? CHOOSE, BOY!"

Casey's body had spasmed, and he felt as though the man had seared his soul with that one look and seen inside him the terrified child who could not fathom all that had happened to the young man's shell. It broke something in him, tore down walls with its bare hands, that look.

Then Angus said in a voice so soft, it was like a mother's caress, "Look up, boy."

Casey thought the man must be mad, trying to make him move now when even the slightest sussurration of air on his bare skin made his stomach heave with nausea. But in the end he managed it, and only threw up once from the effort.

"For Christ Jesus' sake, don't lean against the bed," the burly man said as Casey, reeling with dizziness, began to sag back towards the support of the blood-streaked sheets. "Lean into my arm, I'll not let ye go."

Casey did as bid, feeling as weak as a newborn baby and disoriented by the dark, smoky surroundings.

"There now, I've put the bed next to the window. Look up, do ye see?"

Casey obligingly looked up, his head swaying drunkenly on his neck, muscles still weak with shock from the abuse they'd endured. At first his eyes refused to focus, eyelids thick and heavy from the drugs, but then he did see. A faint line in the north-eastern sky, and then another and another, until it seemed as if a fine spray shot of silver dusted the horizon. The name came from somewhere in the recesses of his subconscious, a place too deep to be damaged by the week's terrors.

"The Orionids," he said blearily, tongue sticky with disuse.

"Aye, the Orionids," his erstwhile nurse replied, "reminds one that pain comes an' goes, an' so does the tiny scrap of time we call life, but the stars, they endure. It's all a river, ye see, the sky above an' the earth below, an' our time in it no more than the barest ripple from a summer breeze. An' yet for us, the ripple, momentary as it is, matters greatly. Do ye see what I'm tellin' ye, laddie?"

The tears, when they came, were painful. He'd not cried since he was a child, eight years old, to be precise. He'd seen tears as weakness, though his father, wisely, had tried to teach him otherwise.

'The Good Lord, in his wisdom, wouldn't have made us with tears if we weren't intended to be weepin' creatures.'

But he'd never given in to tears. It had just been another test of willpower, another brick in the arsenal. And then it had become habit. His life had demanded toughness, and tears had become the hard thing. An ability he no longer possessed.

That they came now shocked him, even though in his pain and weakness he couldn't have stopped them had he wished to. For somehow the great arched backbone of night, with its arteries and veins of stars, the limitless horizon its ribs and its pour of blood the Milky Way, reduced him to tears as the knives had not been able to. It was undeniable and inescapable, a great meandering river of light, spilling over its banks in immense billowing clouds of celestial gas and dust.

"Ye see just a particle," Angus said, and his voice sounded familiar once again. "One of the whole. That is what we are, one step into the infinite. But a vital step, laddie, a vital step."

The night after he cried, Angus was gone, never to be seen by Casey again.

In his wake he had left Casey with the will to survive, and he healed quickly after that. Indeed, it was only a short time later that the pucker-faced doctor discharged him from the infirmary and he took his place once again amongst the prison's general population.

Something had changed, he knew, something in his very cells that showed in his every movement and expression. He saw the reflection of it in the faces of the other prisoners as he was walked back to his cell, heard it in their very silence. He'd gone to a place they all had nightmares about and he'd come back from the fire made of a substance that was more refined and much harder to the touch than he'd been before his baptism.

He was two days free of the infirmary when he came face-to-face with one of his captors. He said nothing, merely smiled at the man, not blinking, nor moving, so still he seemed as a statue made of stone. The man blinked several times, gave him a wide berth, and continued on his way muttering. Casey took a breath and continued on his own way. Behind him, he could hear the murmuring arise, and knew that to them, he was now a creature apart.

No one ever touched him again.

"WHAT DO YOU THINK he gave you in that drink?"

"Opium of some form, mayhap."

"You never saw him again?" Pamela asked, her low tone like a shockwave to the web Casey's story had wrapped them in.

"No, an' for good reason."

"Why?"

"Because there was no Angus," Casey said, face turned away from her as he stubbed out his cigarette. A small wraith of smoke shivered in the air from the eclipsed coal and then disappeared.

"What do you mean there was no Angus? He healed you, he protected you."

"Aye," Casey answered wryly, "I was there. Still the fact remains, Jewel, that I never did see the man durin' the day, nor outside of the infirmary."

"That doesn't mean he didn't exist, for heaven's sake."

"Perhaps not, but when I tried to find him afterwards there was no record of him in the rolls. I'd a friend in the library, wee quiet man named Milton, who'd no love on this earth save books. If Angus had been in that prison, Milton would've found him. Though in a sense he did find him, just not in the way I'd expected."

"What do you mean?"

Casey shifted forward, clasping his arms around his knees so that only his back was visible in the dying firelight. "What I mean, Jewel, is that the man did exist, just not in my own time."

"When?" she asked through lips that felt tingly with pent-up oxygen.

"About a hundred an' fifty years before either you or I took our first breath on this planet. Milton had compiled all the prison records, ye see, goin' back to ledgers from the original prison that was situated under the foundation of Parkhurst itself. He came to my cell one night, about a week after I'd made my initial request of him to look through the current records. He was shakin' like a leaf, half-excited, half-terrified, I think. Said he'd somethin' to show me.

"I followed him back to the library an' the man never said a word all the way there, just kept tuggin' on his ear the way he did when he was particularly agitated. When we get there, he tells me to sit. At this point I'm feelin' a wee bit anxious myself, bein' that we're not supposed to be in the library in the middle of the night. On the table there's this big book, an ancient thing with its pages all grimy an' burnt lookin' about the edges. Well he opens it up an' steps back a bit an' says 'there he is, there's yer man.' I looked where he was pointin', an' certain enough there was Angus' name, with the same stiff letters as I'd seen in his wee herbal. I felt a bit relieved, truth be told, for at least I knew I'd not hallucinated the whole thing, or so I thought for that one second. Then Milton says, 'look ye, look to the head of the page."

'I looked an' saw all the column headings an' how the ink was faded clear away in some places. 'Aye I'm lookin',' I said. Well Milton tugs real hard on his ear then an' says 'Look at the date, ye daftie!' Despite the insult to my intelligence, I did as I was told. I saw the date an' then I just slid down straight onto the floor, half-fainted I think."

"Had he been a prisoner?"

"Aye, but as I said the date was a hundred years an' more before my own time."

"Do you know what he was imprisoned for?"

"Aye, he'd murdered his wife an' her lover when he'd caught them in his own bed."

Pamela felt as though all the blood had left her extremities and sought shelter at her very core.

"I'm surprised they didn't hang him."

"I was as well. But he'd medical training. He was a bit in the way of a wise man it would seem, so perhaps his skill saved his life. He became the resident doctor at the time, from what little Milton could scrounge up on him. He died of consumption after thirty years in prison, seems though he'd cared for many men, there was none to care for him in the end."

She shivered involuntarily.

"Still an' all, I'd have maybe thought I'd somehow seen the information, an' my fever addled brain had twisted bits an' pieces together an' given me a fine set of dreams, but for that he'd given me a wee amulet. 'Twas chased silver, with a leather thong to hang it about my neck, an' he'd filled it with ground bits of wood betony an' a wee cross of rowan tied about with red string. He said 'twas for protection from evil, both high an' low, by which he meant spiritual an' physical. Aye, dinna' wrinkle yer forehead at me; Jewel, I read up a bit on such things after. I wore that amulet between my shirt an' chest everyday until I got out of that damned prison."

"Do you have it still?"

"Aye. Ye'd best believe it goes to sea with me now."

"I've never seen it."

Casey looked down at the quilt. "I didn't want ye to think me a superstitious fool. Ye'll maybe not have as many of the old beliefs, not growin' up in Ireland, but such things are powerful an' sometimes a man needs all the comfort he can find."

"You forget I had an Irish nanny," Pamela said, "I was chockful of superstition and morbid stories from the time I was wee."

"Perhaps I was attributin' my own shortcomin's to ye, Jewel, for I'd a tendency to look down my nose at such things when I was young. Thought I was too much of a rational man for such tomfoolery, but my da said 'twas arrogant to think that the people of old hadn't had their fair share of the world's wisdom too, an' that a man should never mock what he couldn't fully understand.

"There was a lady lived a street over when I was growin' up, had her dead sister round for supper every Tuesday evenin'. We thought the woman was a few pegs shy of a full washline, if ye take my meanin', but," he shrugged expressively, "who's to say what others see an' feel in this world. I never looked at her the same after my time away."

"I wish I'd been there to protect you," she said fiercely, heart aching for the boy he'd been, furious with those that had taken advantage of his youth, who had made him achieve manhood through an ordeal of fire. And grateful to the ghost who had nursed him back to health.

"Ye're here now, Jewel," he said, stroking her hair back from her face, "an' that takes a great deal of hurt out of the past."

Her hand stilled on the grooves of old scars, feeling the odd quiet of twisted, wounded flesh next to the pulse and quiver of whole, fresh skin.

"My old nanny Rose," she said, "believed in spirits. You could only countenance half of what she said. But she once told me that we were all surrounded by ghosts—some personal, some not, and that some we could sense, while others we couldn't. But that they were always there, nevertheless."

"I think perhaps ghosts come to us in any manner of ways," Casey said, long moments later when the fire had died to a vague glimmer, his voice soft as ether in the dark, "like the spirits of forgotten ancestors."

"Do you feel your daddy around you?" she asked quietly.

"Aye, I do at times. Though it's rare an' it's one of those things that ye talk yerself out of believin' five minutes after it happens. But when they touch ye, it lingers, aye?" He looked slantwise down at her, the dawn light quenching the colors that defined his face, painting him in shades of ash and coal. "I sensed him on our weddin' day. Thought I felt his hand on my shoulder, just large an' warm, the way it was when I was a child. An' I knew I had his blessin', that he must have approved of my choice if he'd decided to make his presence known."

"I feel that way sometimes when I'm looking in the mirror," she said, "that if I were to touch the surface it would melt, and I'd touch fingertips with that mirror self, and maybe she'd be younger or older. Myself in another time."

"Aye, mirrors are sometimes eerie that way. Pat used to swear he could see our grandda in one."

"Brendan?" she asked, mesmerized by the way the soft, growing light lent more and more detail to Casey, and yet shrouded the rest of the room with a ghostly hand.

"Aye, Brendan. Pat scared Da an' I with his imaginins' at times. He'd fix his eyes just beyond ye, as though he could see through ye to someone that wasn't there an' yet more there, if ye'll take my meanin', than yer own self was. An' when we'd ask him what he was lookin' at, he'd just say 'tis only grandda, don't get yer ballocks in a twist.' Well, that right unnerved daddy 'cause it's what his own da used to say to him when he'd get upset over small things, an' Pat had no real way of knowin' that."

There are more things in heaven and earth, Horatio,
Than are dreamt of in your philosophy.' She quoted softly.

"Sometimes, Jewel, I think that's too true for comfort's sake." He looked off out the window towards dawn, seeming suddenly weary.

"You need to sleep," she said.

"Aye," he said on the rise of a yawn, "I suppose I do at that."

Moments later he was asleep, and she moved quietly about the room, tidying up, banking the fire against the chill of the night. Casey snored lightly, ghosts forgotten, the bones of his memories once again buried deep. His face was relaxed, one arm thrown above his head, the other stretched out on her side of the blankets. She hoped he was having pleasant dreams, enough for the both of them.

She knew finding her in the water had disturbed him. Always she had loved the ocean, which for a man who viewed the sea as one of the lesser circles of hell, was admittedly a little hard to understand. For her it was both baptism and redemption, a cleansing of spirit that nothing else could give her.

Once, when she was very young, her father had taken her to Nantucket for a holiday and they'd watched the sunset hissing into the ocean and he'd told her that they stood on the very edge of the new world. She had been frightened, believing she was going to fall off that edge, knowing in a visceral way that if she began the fall it would never end. So he'd tipped her head back so she could right herself and find her balance in the night sky.

Through a million years of dust that turned the sky bloody, one star had glimmered, a faint beacon from another time, reassuring in its very distance. She'd watched it, a quiet messenger of the infinite, steadying her breath with its brightening aura against the paling backwash of night. Then realized that it was getting larger, leaving a fire mist trail in its wake.

"Daddy it's falling," she'd said, remembering the horrible panic which had seized her entire body at the realization, the weakness in the knees, the tightness in the chest, the blood falling away from the brain.

"Make a wish," he'd said, face rapt, not noticing her terror.

She'd wished, with teeth clenched and heart pounding, that the damn star would quit falling, but of course it hadn't. It had plunged into the sea, its fiery trail no more than a vague, fuzzy outline on her cornea. And she had known then that the world was not a safe place, that wishes did not always come true, that nothing lasted forever.

"Just think," her father had said, eyes still on the heavens, "of all the stars that have fallen, the sea is full of them. Such a fall from grace, from the heavens to the deeps in seconds."

The idea had taken hold in her young mind, the romance of it not lost on her youth. She never entered the sea without remembering that around her flowed the remnants of stars that had fallen from favor of the Divine.

It comforted her somehow to know that as she lay there the sediment of dead stars washed over her, that in her they again knew a form of life, of flaming through the cosmos, never knowing where the trajectory would land one. And that through those same dead stars, long quenched, she would again know life long after her own death. There was continuity in such knowledge. Sometimes it was enough to know these things and breathe, to merely exist. It could take away the stain of yesterday, the grime of everyday life, the pain of a week ago Tuesday. At least long enough to allow her to catch her breath and meet her husband's eyes without shame.

The bedroom in the Brookline apartment had been lit with candles, and every luxury had been attended to. Of course, one would never expect less of Lovett Hagerty. The bed, a cloud adrift in a blue carpet sky without stars. He'd plied her with champagne, which she'd drunk, desperately wishing it were whiskey, something that would shear the edge off her nerves and blot out the smell of his cologne and the smoothness of his skin against her own.

She'd hoped, foolishly, she supposed, that he'd talk before the inducement of the pillows, but he'd been intent on one thing and one thing only.

And she, smiling, had put her soul in a corner, and given it to him.

The betrayal had not gone deep enough for him though, he had wanted more, he'd wanted emotion to go along with the body. Then she had understood, Love had wanted what she gave to her husband, he had wanted the emotion of response. She only hoped her imitation of it had fooled him.

She shivered. Rose had been right. There were, indeed, ghosts all around, and not all were dead.

She turned from the window and saw pale fingers of light stealing through beneath the curtains, outlining Casey in rosy-gold corona. He'd turned over onto his stomach and the scars on his back were faintly luminescent, borrowing light from both morning and the fire. The just curling ends of his hair, stiff with salt, rose in clockwise whorls away from his scalp. Sleep's restorative hand had smoothed the lines of worry from his face. He looked terribly vulnerable and she felt a fierce surge of protectiveness come over her at the sight of him. Whatever she'd done to keep him safe had been worth it and she would not regret it, she would do whatever was necessary to keep him alive and whole. He stirred beneath her gaze, half-rising on an elbow, looking up at her, voice rough and tender with sleep.

"Come back to bed, Jewel, ye look as though ye could use the warmin'."

"In a minute," she said quietly, knowing he'd drop back to sleep instantly. She glanced out the window one last time, where the sea surged against the shore, giving and taking in one swift movement. Continuity, here long before she had drawn her first breath, here long after she had drawn her last. But for now she would take the allotment of time given to her and love the man in the bed behind her without impediments or guilt, knowing that without her sin he would not be here to love.

She could feel the heat of his body the minute she slid under the blankets. He rolled over, arm tucking her to him instinctively, hand curving across her belly.

"Ye alright, darlin'?" he asked sleepily, bestowing a kiss on the back of her neck.

She stroked the forearm that lay protectively about her.

"I'm just cold," she said.

Chapter Twelve

Emma

THE BUILDING WASN'T SO DIFFERENT from her own. A little more rundown and desperately in need of paint, but the same basic layout. A three-decker with sagging windowsills and cracked sidewalks, where weeds grew through the seams. Dandelion fluff floated in the humid air and there was the slightest hint of salt wind off the Point.

A shattered nameplate stated that E. Malone lived on the second floor. Pamela tried the buzzer, found it was broken and so tried the door. It too was broken and swung open the minute she put her hand to the knob. Security was obviously not a priority.

The building stunk inside of stale, greasy cooking, and cat urine. The stairs leading up to the top two floors were canted to the left and covered with filthy green indoor-outdoor carpeting.

E. Malone, the nameplate had stated, was in unit number 4. It was on the right-hand side, a lime green door whose battered surface testified to the fact that it had once been red. Pamela took a deep breath and knocked, waiting for what seemed a small eternity before hearing a slow shuffle on the other side of the door.

The woman who answered the door could have been thirteen or thirty; she had the small-breasted, slim-hipped androgyny that was so loved by the fashion industry. A slimness accentuated by the boy's tank shirt she wore. Once you got a glimpse of her face, though, you saw your mistake clearly. Over thirty with the eyes of eighty. A photojournalist she knew called that look 'the thousand yard stare'. He had seen it plenty in Vietnam. People who'd simply seen and done too much.

A mop of badly cut pale gold hair framed a face with cut-glass cheekbones and hostile amber eyes. You want somethin', lady?" The voice was hard, dragging the last word out into an insult.

"I'm looking for Emma Malone," Pamela replied, hoping she wasn't making the biggest mistake of her life.

"You're lookin' at her. Hey," the door opening narrowed a little, "you that bitch from DYS keeps callin' here?"

"No," Pamela answered hastily, "I'm here about Love Hagerty."

The door stayed where it was.

"How do you know Love?" Emma's face was hard and the tone of voice no less so.

"I work for him," Pamela answered, her own tone even but not friendly.

Emma gave a bitter little grin. "You must be the one I been hearin' rumors about. Heard the bastard was smitten with someone else's wife, heard she had a face on her like an angel. Can't be two of you wanderin' around lookin' like that so I figure it must be you." The door opened, "You wanna' come in, or you gonna stand out there all day?" She turned and wandered back into the dishevelled apartment, as though it made very little difference to her what Pamela did.

"So what's Love want? Gotta say his messenger service has gone uptown in a big way," Emma flicked a jaded glance over Pamela's pale linen outfit.

"I didn't come on behalf of Love. He's got no idea I'm here, actually." She took a deep breath, "He thinks I'm home sick with 'women troubles'."

Emma snorted. "Yeah that'd keep the squeamish bastard from getting too curious. So what d'you do for him?"

"Public relations."

"Yeah, I could see where he'd need some help there." The woman went to the fridge, opening it and glancing idly inside it. "You like workin' for him?"

"He's not so bad, though he's under the impression he's next to Jesus in this neighborhood," Pamela said mildly. Emma gave a short bark of laughter, face an unhealthy gray in the light issuing out of the refrigerator. She was terribly thin.

"Well he ain't no savior, but I guess you could say he looks after people," she said, taking two icy beers from the fridge and popping the caps off on the bottle opener attached to the edge of the counter. "Like a pimp looks after his hookers." She shrugged, handing one of the stubby bottles to Pamela. "He's a way of life here, people don't know any different from Love. Not so many nice, white urbans looking to get in this neighborhood, and most of us," she sat, hooking her legs over a stool, "forgot long time ago that we ever wanted out. So what exactly do you want with me?"

"I came to talk to you about my husband."

Emma's eyebrows shot up. "Really? Can't say I know him. Pretty sure I didn't bang him—so what's the problem?"

"Casey Riordan is my husband."

Emma tilted her head, a thick lock of golden hair sliding over her eyes. "That the big one, real tall, dark—looks like he'd be hell between the sheets, but the kind of hell a woman'd gladly burn in 'bout ten times a week?"

"Yes," Pamela replied dryly, "that would be my husband. And I know you were friends with him Emma. He told me everything."

"Yeah, that so? Wouldn't be so sure about that, lady."

"He told me about the murder of your friend up in New Hampshire," she said softly, but there was no warmth in her tone.

"What's your point?" Emma was feigning nonchalance, but a small vein beat rapidly in the thin skin of her throat.

"You must have thought he was a real chump. The situation looked a little too pat to him though. He checked into just who owned the property where Rosemary died. Turned out the man who owned it was your father's former partner, John Mullins. And then I got thinking about how a girl with a cop for a father and teacher for a mother ends up on the streets. So I went to see Mr. Mullins. Turns out he remembers you really well Emma, and *very* fondly I might add."

"You got a real nerve coming in here and—"

Pamela cut her off, "No I think you're the one with the real nerve here, Emma. I've done a little homework, studied your past, and suddenly it's looking to me like you're not so much a victim as a manipulator. John Mullins was your father's partner and best friend. Best man at your parent's wedding; you even called him Uncle John. You set out to seduce him. He left his wife and three kids for you. You wrecked his life and then dropped him like a hot potato. So then I ask myself why you'd do such a thing?"

"Yeah, so what? I was only eighteen, he shoulda known better. Besides that's all ancient history."

Pamela shook her head slowly and then took the picture from her pocket that John Mullins had given her, in an attempt to exorcise himself of the ghosts he'd been haunted by these many years. She put it on the table and slid it over where Emma could clearly see it. This time she knew she didn't imagine the flinch.

"History has a funny way of catching up with a person, Emma. Particularly when a crime is involved. You see, when a cop gets murdered that really never becomes history for his colleagues. They take it fairly personally, and they have long memories."

"I don't know what you're talking about," Emma said, but her hand kept compulsively smoothing the hair around her ear.

"Don't you? Look at the picture Emma. Lieutenant Robert O'Donnell. A good honest cop. And maybe one of the only ones with enough courage to attempt to break the stranglehold Love Hagerty has over Southie. Disappeared one autumn on a hunting trip up in New Hampshire. In the White Mountains somewhere. They never did find his remains, but I've got to wonder if they might show up if the police were to excavate John Mullins' property. What do you think Emma?"

"I think you need to go, lady, that's what I think." She made to stand up, but Pamela caught her wrist in her fingers and squeezed until she could feel the frail bone bend. The woman hissed at her, but she hung on.

"You see," she pulled Emma down by her wrist, halfway across the table, making sure the woman could not mistake her intentions. "This is what I think. I don't think a man called Rosemary at all. I asked around a bit, and Rosemary sounds like she was a pretty smart girl. What I think is that you called her. You told her you had to meet someone up there and that you were scared and she ran to your rescue just like she always did. Only it wasn't you waiting when she got there, was it? It was Blackie. You set her up to be slaughtered and then tried to get it pinned on my husband. Just like you set John Mullins up years ago to take Robert O'Donnell out on a hunting trip. And then blackmailed him with pictures of the two of you in bed afterwards to make sure he kept his mouth shut, knowing it would destroy his career, which was all he had left when you were through with him."

"You can't prove it," the woman said sullenly.

"I don't need to, all I have to do is call the police and drop a few hints and suspicions and they'll prove it.

"What do you want then?"

"Love Hagerty."

"Why?"

"Because he's going to kill my husband if I don't find a way to get him locked up for a really long time."

"What makes you think I got anything on Love?"

"Because it was him that you seduced John Mullins for, him that wanted Robert O'Donnell dead. Him that you were setting my husband up on murder charges for. Am I right? It's just that Blackie did the dirty work of killing that poor girl."

Emma's lip twisted up in an unattractive sneer. "You think you're Trixie Belden or something? Pretty little detective in her expensive clothes. But those clothes were paid for with dirty money."

"You jealous?" Pamela asked, trying to disguise how badly the remark had unsettled her. Emma might be fishing, but she didn't look as though she was making lucky guesses.

"Jealous?" She shook her head. "I hate him. I hate him like I ain't never hated anybody in my life. And not for the reasons you're thinking, either. Yeah, I whore for him, I have for a long time. I done a lot of things for him that I ain't proud of. But I hate him because he killed my brothers."

"What?"

"You let my wrist go so I can have a cigarette and I'll tell you what you want to hear."

Pamela let go, keeping a wary eye on the woman.

Emma tapped a cigarette out of a nearly empty package, the shaking of her hands making the task take a minute. "You want one?"

Pamela shook her head, feeling a sudden terrible pang for Casey. Ridiculous as it seemed, she even missed the smell of his smoking.

Emma took a long drag, sighing as the nicotine hit her blood stream. "My daddy, as you know, was a cop. Big, freckle-faced Irish bastard, and my mom came from Polish immigrant parents. That's where I get the blonde hair. Joe and Anna Malone, sort of the walking, talking version of the American dream. Couple of working class kids with immigrant parents making their way in the promised land. I was the oldest, and then there was my twin brothers, Stephan and Donal. Two blonde angels when they was little," she said, "couple of hellraisers when they wasn't so little."

Emma looked down, skin tightening over the Slavic cheekbones. "I miss them. People always thought my baby brothers were nothin' but trouble, but I still remember when everything about them was pure, y'know? I'd help momma bathe them, and after they'd smell so sweet, all those gold ringlets damp on their necks. That's how I remember them."

"What happened?"

"Drugs," she shrugged eloquently, "what the hell else ever happens in this neighborhood? Stephan overdosed on heroin on his twenty-first birthday; he'd started using when he was fifteen. But he'd been clean for six months by then, no one believed that later, but I knew. I'd held his hand through the shakes and helped him to the toilet when he had to throw up. He went cold turkey, thought it'd kill us both before he was through. But he made it, thought he owed it to Donal." She paused to take another long drag, yellow eyes heavy with memory. "Donal got shot 'cause someone mistook him for Stephan. Stephan was into his dealer for a big wad of cash, somebody was putting pressure on the dealer and I guess the dealer thought he'd warned Stephan enough. Big old Eldorado drives past him on Broadway one night and *bang* he's dead. Only it ain't Stephan, it's Donal."

She tapped the ashes off her cigarette into a tin can on the table. The short-bitten nail of one thumb dug into the scarred melamine surface of the table.

"A week later Stephan decides he's gonna' go join Donal an' ODs. Didn't take, though his heart stopped a coupla' times before the doctors were sure he'd survive. It changed things for him though, an' he went straight after that. Six months clean, had a job at a garage down on Lancaster, wasn't much but he was there every day on time, had regular pay. Then he goes missin'. Didn't think much of it at first, I knew he was havin' a hard time without Donal. Two days later he's still gone, though, an' hasn't shown up for work. I knew he was dead then. Cops call my mom 'bout a week later an' tell her they need her to come an' identify a body some jogger saw stuck in the shallows in the Neponset. It was Stephan alright, still had the black rubber tubing round his arm. Cops figured he stumbled into the river when he was high an' that was that. Case closed."

"But you knew better?"

"Yeah I knew better, but what did that prove? Cops knew Stephan, knew he'd been a junkie for years, he sure as hell wouldn't have been the first to fall off the wagon an' go back on the shit."

"Why would anyone want him dead then, surely he wasn't a threat?"

Emma shook her head. "It don't need to make any kind of sense in this neighborhood. There's people here, you piss 'em off once an' that's enough. They'll bide their time."

"People like Blackie?"

The thumb had moved from digging at the table to scratching at the scars on Emma's inner elbow, "Maybe, maybe not. You wouldn't be the first to suspect it lady, but provin' it, that's somethin' else. Besides, Blackie's not the one givin' orders, he's just following 'em."

"I don't understand," Pamela said, thinking aloud, "Love's been rich now for years. He doesn't need the money anymore. What's in it for him?"

"It's not the money," Emma shook her head resolutely, "he likes to own people, he likes to have their soul right there in the palm of his slick little hand. He's like the devil that way—wants your soul and then when he's got it he moves on to the next victim. You think you know, lady, but you don't, 'cause you ain't made him mad yet."

"How do you know that?"

"You're sittin' here with me ain't you? Mmn-mn, you don't know."

"Then tell me, Emma, tell me who this man really is."

Emma gave her a hard look, eyes like dull metal. She hugged her arms across her thin chest, shivering though it was abysmally hot in the small apartment. Pamela could see ancient track marks crisscrossing the delicate underside of the woman's arms. She'd been an addict, but had been clean for a while to judge by the scars.

"Maybe you can't tell so much anymore, but I was real pretty at one time. Half the boys in Southie had the hots for me. Never looked like you, mind, but I was pretty enough to turn heads in the street. I knew it too, wore tight little dresses and high heels, painted my toes and fingers bright red all the time, did my hair up in one of those slick little French twists. I thought I was something else, was gonna blow this neighborhood and never look back," she smiled wistfully, "never made it farther than Haverhill on a Sunday afternoon." She sighed. "This neighborhood does something to you, takes something out of you that makes you feel scared everywhere else. Like bein' from Southie is all you got, y'know? You can be somebody here but when you take the train up north of the river you're just another face in knock-off designers and cheap shoes. An' you realize the only place you're ever really gonna' be somebody is in Southie."

"Why didn't you leave, Emma?"

Emma gave her a weary look, "You can't guess?"

"Love."

"Got it in one, lady. But don't get me wrong, I was in trouble before he came along but maybe there was a minute or two I'da had a chance to get clear of this fucking neighborhood if he'd never looked my way."

"Five years ago," Emma squinted as though trying to peer backward into her mind, "a boy got pushed off the top of an apartment building down in Old Colony. People said it was an accident, but everyone knew he didn't just fall. Story was he got in an argument over drug money with this black kid from Jamaica Plains, but nobody could ever put the finger on who this mysterious black kid was. Truth was he didn't exist; whisper got round that Blackie had pushed the boy off, 'cause the kid was mouthin' around town that Love Hagerty was his daddy."

"Was he?"

Emma gave another expressive shrug, "Don't know for sure, bastard's actually pretty discreet with the ladies, generally. Only God an' the FBI know who he's banging." Pamela just barely missed spitting her beer out at that statement. Fortunately, Emma was too deep in her story to notice. "Anyway the kid looked like him, sure enough, but then black hair an' blue eyes ain't exactly rare in this neighborhood."

"What do you think? Was the boy his?"

Emma looked down, thumb still digging at the table surface. "What I think, lady, is that if a man is willing to kill a boy that might be his own kid, then that's a man you better be real careful around."

Pamela nodded and took a deep breath, knowing the sort of chance she was taking asking this woman for help. "What I need, Emma, is help taking him down. I need something big, something that will assure he doesn't see the outside world for a very long time."

Emma's mouth hardened into a tight line and Pamela's heart began to thud as she wondered if she'd made a fatal mistake in coming to this woman. Then Emma seemed to find what she was looking for in the face before her, and nodded.

"There's a pipeline of heroin that runs the East Coast up from Florida. Everybody knows the Bassarelli family's got the market tied tight from Albany on up to the Canadian border. But even they need a little help keeping their turf protected. Huey Somers and his boys used to provide the muscle, but Love provides it now. Through Blackie, of course, but everybody knows who really sent the Somers gang up the river. There's been a flood of the stuff on the streets in the last few years, lotta' dealers between here and Roxbury, Jamaica Plains, City Point and the Flats, but there's only one supplier. But *that*, lady," Emma's hand picked at the hair around her ear again, "ain't something that just anyone knows. That's the sort of information that can get you killed."

"So what do I do, Emma?" Pamela asked, voice quiet but with a core of steel at its center.

"You watch Blackie, he maybe ain't so careful as he once was, somewhere there's a trail leading back to Love."

"Just how far back do those two go?"

"About a thousand miles on a piece of real bad road," Emma said. "They met as altarboys at St. Thomas' when they were about twelve. People said Love looked like an angel in his robes, but that Blackie just looked like the little crook he was, even then. Blackie's bad, but he don't ever pretend to be anything else. You need to be careful, even if you got Love fooled now."

"What makes you think I've got him fooled?"

"Hear people tell it, he'd hang the moon an' stars off your ears if he could."

"What people?" Pamela asked sharply, panic cutting a cold slice through her middle.

Emma gave her a speculative glance. "You're scared of him, ain't you, lady? Smart to be scared of Love." There was a challenge of sorts in the woman's eyes. "Maybe not just God an' the FBI huh?" Emma said softly, "Why you doin' it, lady, if you hate him so much you wanna' destroy him?"

"I'd like to keep my husband alive. I don't much care what it takes to do that."

"Oh Jesus, the feds got you on a string don't they?" Emma's face had gone from gray to ash, "You be careful, lady, you are in the middle of one big shitstorm you don't know the first thing about. They'll promise you anything to get what they want. You wired up now?" There was real fear in the woman's face for the first time.

"No, they don't know I'm here either. I've got the day off, so to speak."

Emma laughed, but there was nothing humorous about it. "Well they don't look like your average pimp but I guess they got some real motivatin' forces on their side. They tell you they can keep your man safe?"

Pamela nodded.

"You must love him an awful lot, takin' a chance like this?" Emma said, voice slightly wistful.

"More than anything," Pamela replied honestly.

"I think that's where Love underestimated the both of you. That you got something real. He don't know what that looks like."

"Did you ever love him?"

The thin fingers were flicking at the hair around her ear again. "I was only eighteen the first time he took me to bed, he was thirty-three, he had this kind of glamor—like a movie star or somethin', y'know? I never had a prayer."

"I'm hardly in a position to find fault," Pamela said quietly.

Emma nodded, lashes flicking down to the tabletop. "He's in love with you."

"I know," she replied, "but I never wanted him to be."

"Gives you a lotta' power, lady, I don't think he ever even loved his wife. Gives you somethin' on him ain't nobody else ever had."

"Never, Emma? Didn't he love you?"

The amber eyes met her own once more. "No, I loved him, but he didn't never love me. I know that now."

"How?" Pamela asked, an icy shiver travelling along her spine.

Emma ran a hand under her nose, eyes suddenly bright with tears. "'Cause I seen his face when he talks about you."

"Does he still come here, Emma?"

Emma blinked, tears replaced with wariness. "No, not much these days. It's how I knew, see, that he had someone else, 'cause before he'd talk about you but I knew he couldn't have you, 'cause he kept comin' here to get laid. Round three months ago he stops comin' here at night, an' I knew he'd got what he wanted. Three months sound about right?"

Pamela nodded her head, aware that she was flushed with humiliation.

"You an' me, lady, we're just two sides of the same coin, got the same name though. Now I think if you heard what you need to, it's time for you to go."

Pamela nodded, then stood. A movement near the bedroom door caught her eye.

She stopped breathing, fear making her entire body tingle. Was Love here? Could he have driven here and beat her to her destination? Then her heart resumed its job. The movement was that of a little boy, trailing a worn blanket, thumb stuck solidly in his mouth.

"Jakey," Emma stood abruptly, voice sharp with panic, "you come here to mama."

The child obeyed, still half asleep, coming to lean into his mother's thin comfort.

He peeked shyly out from beneath Emma's bruised elbow, sleepy cobalt eyes still dreaming, jet hair ruffled, a mangy teddy bear with round bandages for eyes clutched tightly to his chest. Pamela smiled at him but knew the gesture didn't reach her eyes.

Emma caught the look and pulled the boy closer to her side.

Pamela met her eyes, managing to keep her smile in place, despite the cold ball of fear that had settled in her stomach, "You said it yourself, Emma, blue eyes and black hair aren't so uncommon in this neighborhood."

Emma nodded, bones sharp against her pale skin, "Maybe they ain't so common, either. I think you better get going now, lady." The woman's eyes had gone opaque, as still as amber in an ancient forest.

Pamela opened the door, the reek of the hallway hitting her in the face instantly. Emma's voice, soft and flat, halted her momentarily.

"I'll pray for you, lady," Emma said, a sobriety in her tone that made the hairs go up on the back of Pamela's neck. "Pray that the bastard doesn't make a fist before you manage to get out of his palm."

Chapter Thirteen

After Camelot

NORTH PHOTOGRAPHY WAS A HOLE in the wall establishment that sat above an old-world cobbler's shop in Boston's North End. The proprietor was a man by the name of Lucas North, who just happened to be an old friend of Jamie Kirkpatrick's.

Pamela had met him when she lived in Jamie's home and Lucas had been passing through on his way back from France where he'd been photographing the student riots in Paris. The majority of his time was spent now in Vietnam where he was often months in country, following the baby-faced soldiers as they fought to survive a jungle and a culture that was completely foreign to their innocent American psyches. He strung for the big dailies: *The New York Times, the Boston Globe, the San Francisco Chronicle* as well as occasionally having his work featured in *Time* and *Life*.

When his last assistant had left for New York, Lucas contacted Pamela, stating that Jamie thought she might be interested in helping him out, at least short term. He was on one of his brief furloughs and it was either close up shop or find someone to replace the lost assistant immediately.

Lucas North wasn't long on charm. He was terse, didn't tolerate fools gladly, and was the best damn photographer that Pamela had ever seen. She learned more in the rare hour he could spare for her when in Boston than she ever would have in school. She had spent three days with him the first time and done two weddings and a bar mitzvah under his supervision. She had also attended two crime scenes, as Lucas had connections within the force and had done a lot of homicide scene photos during the early sixties. Back then, he told her, it had been mostly mob hits. There had been twenty-four factions of the mob in Boston and they had kept both the police and Lucas fairly busy. He had also attended a few of the Strangler scenes.

"It was unbearable in the city when the Strangler was on the loose. Women were afraid of their own shadows, and rightly so, for months. It's frightening how one man can hold so many people hostage for such a long period of time."

Lucas and she had developed the photos from each event together, and he'd looked them over with a critical eye afterwards. Then he had merely said, "You have the eye."

She had floated on air for a week after. Those few words were as good as a shower of praise from another person.

Despite his words, she didn't fool herself, knowing that it was geographical proximity more than any God given talent that had landed her the job. But she was willing to work hard, and the focus that photography required allowed her to immerse herself within its colors and nuances, its elusive and frustrating compositions, its art and workmanship. And then she could forget about the other parts of her life, even if the relief was only temporary.

On weekends she hovered and arranged and smiled, and shuffled youthful wedding parties. Searching for that grace note in the faces of red-nosed uncles who'd had too much to drink, harassed fathers who wondered how much her services were costing them, and the slightly disillusioned faces of married women who were taking bets in the kitchen on how long the union would last. She loved the weddings herself, though she knew many photographers considered them one of the lesser circles of hell.

She loved the gauzy-netted butterfly bridesmaids and the queen bee bride decked out in tulle and taffeta. She loved the uncertain grooms and beer-drinking ushers. Her favorite pictures were the ones she took in the evening, as the reception wound down and the cake had been cut and crumbled, when the bride was swoony in her new husband's arms and he wore a look of protective possession that was aeons old. She loved the old grandmas in their net stockings and flowered dresses. The rough talk of the men out back of the hall in the harsh sodium lights, shirt cuffs rolled up and ties abandoned. The sleepy children collapsed on relative laps, faces sticky with sugar and heat. In all these faces, she saw the promise America had always held for the Irish. In the broad faces and curly hair, the quick wit and rough camaraderie. Not the streets of milk and honey some had believed they would find, but the America they had hewn out with their own hands and spirits. An America that was now post-Camelot, without the gilded prince at its head. In these moments, it was tempting to wander the forbidden territory of what might have been. What if Kennedy hadn't been killed at the peak of his powers? What if America's Camelot had not been sacked in the hour when her flags were about to fly golden and glorious above the world, a beacon of idealized pragmatism led by a man whose grandfather had sold dried goods in the streets of Boston?

John Kennedy's death represented the end of an age and a chance to the Irish in America. As if there had been a moment when they might all, the entire country, have grasped that golden ring and held it for eternity. But it seemed as if the dream had slipped past, eluded all their hands by the merest slice of time, and now that dream was behind and they were pressing forward into unknown territory, with only some realization that Camelot lay back there on the dark continent, and was now irretrievable. It was both the sorrow of lost promise and the stubborn survival of a people who had known little peace that she saw in their faces.

It was after a wedding at St. Catherine's one Saturday afternoon in late October that she spotted a man in the crowd of guests that was all too familiar. He was slim, red-haired and clad in a very expensive pale gray suit. She frowned, keeping him in her peripheral vision as she changed the film in the camera and pulled black netting over the lens, fastening it in place with a rubber band. It was a trick she used when photographing the older ladies in attendance, it softened all the lines and wrinkles and gave a soft glow to the picture that they always appreciated.

Inevitably at these events, she always attracted the attention of some young Turk that would follow her around for the afternoon and evening, packing her equipment, assessing whether she was a likely prospect. Some cleared off once she made it clear that she wasn't available, but others would still hang about, chatting. These she put to work, which they always did with a good natured air, most of them slightly drunk by early evening, but perfectly amiable and still fit enough to pose in front of her camera as she adjusted the frame and focus on their black coats and then measured the light against their white shirts.

At this particular wedding, it was a young man named Charlie. He was twenty-eight and had done three tours of Vietnam, the most recent of which had left him with a leg full of shrapnel and hands that shook constantly. She had first met him at the O'Connell 25th wedding anniversary five weeks previous. At first he had made her slightly nervous as he had stared at her throughout the festivities. Finally, though, he had approached her and apologized.

"Sorry, I know I've been staring all night. It's just that I've seen a lot of ugliness these last few years and looking at you kind of makes me feel like I'm erasing some of that." After that, his stare hadn't bothered her. His presence also had the added bonus of keeping the 'Hopefuls' as Charlie had taken to calling the men, young and old, that inevitably clustered around her at these functions, at bay.

Southie's social structure being what it was, she tended to see many of the same faces at the various social functions. Charlie seemed to be on everyone's list, as this was the fourth wedding at which they'd found themselves together.

"What do you know about him?" she asked Charlie, nodding toward the agent. He was chatting with a group of men in the gathering dusk near the parked limousine that the bride and groom had arrived at the hall in. He stood with them, yet the men all held themselves warily; none were truly relaxed, which told her volumes about how well Mark Ryan was trusted within his old neighborhood.

Charlie looked over from his perch in front of a mostly naked cherub. "Mark Ryan. He's from the neighborhood, moved back not too long ago. He's a feeb."

"Do he and Love Hagerty know one another?" she asked, striving for a casual tone.

He raised a thick, sandy brow. "Sure they do. Anyone who grew up in Southie knows that. Mark used to follow Love around like a pup on a leash for years. There's ten years between them. Love tolerated him, gave him money for ice cream, things like that. He likes to have someone looking up to him; Mark fit the bill, so Love always treated him well. Twisted a few arms is what I heard to get Mark into the field office in Boston. Otherwise someone his age would be working out of Podunk, Idaho."

She merely nodded and smiled, though a sick feeling rooted in her stomach. Charlie was absolutely right. If Mark Ryan knew Love Hagerty that well and if he still retained the old neighborhood ties—and it seemed he did as he'd moved back into his family home in the Old Colony projects—then it wasn't likely he was protecting anyone other than Love Hagerty himself.

It was true that Love seemed all too charmed. Even armed with what Emma had told her there still didn't seem to be a crack anywhere in the man's life either professional or—unless she counted herself—personal. That neither he nor Blackie had ever been charged with any sort of crime, had never done time in prison, and in Love's case had even managed to keep the whispers to a low enough level to not harm his political career, had the waft of a week old can of tuna. Unfortunately, these musings led to one conclusion—that Love had several well-placed contacts in all levels of law enforcement watching his back. This was something she had understood before, but now realized it reached into the echelons of the FBI. Which made her own current position even more of a tightrope act than it had previously been.

When she came up with the extra lens she'd been rooting for in her camera bag, Mark Ryan was standing right next to her, so close she could smell the harsh reek of his scotch and the starch in his shirt. Charlie had wandered off to find a drink and so she found herself alone with the agent.

"Pamela Riordan, I believe," he said, though she knew he was fully aware of just who she was.

"Yes." She adjusted the aperture on the lens, affecting a nonchalance she did not feel. This man put the fine hairs up on the back of her neck and she was quite certain he knew it.

"How's that husband of yours?" he asked, leaning casually against a low stone wall that skirted the grassy area.

"He's fine," she said stiffly, "though I wasn't aware you were acquainted with him."

"I heard he'd gone out on a cod boat," he said, eyes narrowed, assessing her reaction to his words.

"Yes, he did," she said, as calmly as if they were engaged in an ordinary conversation.

"Dangerous occupation," he said, swirling the ice cubes in his glass before taking a long swallow of the whisky. "Uncle of mine got gaffed on a boat, tore his arm right through. Died from the infection few weeks later. There are an awful lot of memorials up and down this coast to dead fishermen."

She didn't dare blink right now, nor swallow, nor show any weakness to this man. Even if he'd just voiced her very worst nightmare about what might happen to her husband out on the sea. Still she realized his words were meant more in the line of a threat. That anything could happen to Casey and she would be powerless to stop it. Only perhaps not as powerless as he believed.

The smell of crushed grass rose in her nose. Mark Ryan's eyes flickered the slightest bit, and she knew Charlie had moved into place behind her.

"I think you better move along, Agent Ryan," Charlie said, and though his voice was low, it carried a heavy threat that was unmistakable. Mark Ryan merely raised a red brow and then poured the rest of his whisky into the ferns behind him, straightened his tie and nodded at Pamela.

"Until later then, Mrs. Riordan."

She was silent, the lack of words as effective an insult as any. Her senses remained on full alert as he moved off into the dusky shadows that were lengthening across velvety lawns, reaching out darkly from crooked oak boughs.

"What the hell was that about?" Charlie asked.

She took a breath, realizing she'd been holding it the entire time Mark Ryan had stood near her. A cold trickle of sweat was running down her spine, causing her to shiver involuntarily.

She summoned up a weak smile for Charlie. "Nothing, he was just asking after Casey."

"Your husband?"

She nodded.

"Mark Ryan doesn't ever just 'ask after' anyone."

Pamela shrugged, knowing her show of casual indifference wasn't well feigned.

Charlie gave her a sharp look. "Just stay away from him. He's bad news and if he ain't tied tighter round Love Hagerty's finger than a wedding ring then I miss my guess. Most will tell you the connection between them is just rumor, but me, I think where there's smoke there's a mighty big fire."

She could have told Charlie that it was more than rumor; three nights before she had been out walking on Carson Beach in the wee hours, an occupation which would have made Casey furious with her. Admittedly, it wasn't the safest thing to do, but she had trouble sleeping these nights and could not bear the empty bed nor apartment in those hours.

There had been a big gray Plymouth sitting in the parking lot, the only car there. She had hesitated, leery of walking past it alone. Suddenly all the warnings her husband had peppered her with came back to her. Somehow she knew, though, that the men in the car hadn't seen her, nor sensed her presence nearby. Still she stood frozen, instinct laying its warning down the length of her spine.

Then a hand had held out a lighter and flicked it on. The tiny flame illuminated a small circle within the car. But it had been enough to recognize the occupants. Love Hagerty's profile was unmistakable. It wasn't Love's presence that she found so worrisome, though, it was the other man. For the fire had lit upon the unmistakable flame of red hair.

It was one thing to know that Love's back was covered by the law, but to know that he was holding secret meetings with a federal agent meant something else altogether. It meant there was something other than old neighborhood ghosts and ties at work here. And that made her own dance upon the razor's edge that much more lethal.

Love's surprise, however, when she had mentioned seeing Blackie in the company of Agent Mark Ryan had seemed genuine. His anger even more so. The only question that seemed to remain was whether it was Love double-crossing Blackie or Blackie double-crossing Love.

She was going to have to arrange a meeting with Agent Gus to discuss this latest turn of events.

Chapter Fourteen

In the Blink of an Eye

HE WAS DREAMING OF WEE DEIRDRE. *In the dream, she had grown from the tiny babe he'd held so briefly to a tot with a mop of dark chestnut curls and eyes the color of spring oceans—pure unending green. He picked her up, savoring the warm heft of her in his arms. He held her close, feeling the desperation of one who knows time is a finite thing, even in dreams. He tucked his face in the crook of her neck, and breathed in. The scents of new mown grass and strawberries crushed under bare, tender feet satiated his senses and brought a prickle of tears to his eyes. Her arms about his neck were fine-boned and unbearably soft.*

Daddy's girl.—the words were silent and yet he knew both he and she heard them in the reverse laws of nature that existed in dreams. She drew back, and put chubby hands to his face and looked him directly in the eyes.

"Daddy," she said in a voice like silver fairy bells.

And then he woke.

Olie was standing above him. "Wake up, lad!"

"What's goin' on?" Casey asked, sitting up on one elbow, right hand going to his face in an effort to clear his bleary vision. He could still smell strawberries and his throat was tight with the dream's lingering.

Olie was hastily grabbing supplies and stuffing them into a canvas sack. "There's been a bad accident north of here, sealin' boat got stuck in the pack ice off Horse Island an' the damn fools thought they'd blow the ice away with explosives, set the goddamn boat afire instead. Don't know the details, but it sounds right bad."

"Sounds terrible," Casey agreed, trying to remember where he'd left his cigarettes last night. An awful thought seized him suddenly and he forgot his cigarettes entirely.

"What," he asked, dreading the answer, "does the accident have to do with us?"

Olie rammed his filthy toque down to his grizzled eyebrows before answering. "We're closest to the boat so we go an' see what can be done."

"But *Jeannie's* a fishin' boat," Casey protested, "what can we do?"

"We're takin' a load of nurses an' doctors up, medical supplies an' some food an' water. Besides, *Jeannie* was a salvage vessel once, afore Captain Jack turned her into a fishin' boat. She's the soul of a hero in her, twelve hundred horsepower in her belly, go nose first into a trough an' come up 'thout a sputter. She knows how to get the job done, this girl, an' does it without the dancin' an' fancywork of a rich man's boat." Olie rubbed his hand across a brass fitting, long gone green with verdigris. "If any boat can get those men out safe, 'tis *Jeannie*. I don't know how far into the pack we can get, so pray God you wee Catholic fiend, for the souls of those poor bastards out on the ice." He spat into a tin cup for emphasis. "An' maybe add a word or two on our behalf while you're at it. Dress warm, eh?" Olie said before ducking under the doorframe of their quarters.

Wee Catholic fiend that he was, Casey muttered his way grimly through the first quarter of the rosary while putting his clothes on. Two sets of the wool socks Pamela had put in his bag last time he'd been home, long johns, undershirt, heavy wool sweater and an oilskin coat over top of it all. On his head he put the scarlet toque Olie's girlfriend had knit for him. It was a fine balance in cold like this. Dress too warm and your range of motion was limited and you'd sweat and find yourself miserably cold despite your layers. Dress too lightly and you'd be dead within the hour.

The air on deck was breathtaking—literally. Casey could feel his lungs protest the vicious cold, trying to seal off the opening to his throat. He gulped three times and felt the icy shear of Arctic outflow along all the tender membranes that made up his respiratory system.

The doctors and nurses had already been loaded on with as many medical supplies as could be gathered in such a short space of time. The distress call had only come in an hour before. It was just luck that *Jeannie* was in port that night.

The trip to Horse Island took an hour and a half. During which time they all strained at the railing, looking out into the dark night, as though they could project themselves forward to the tragedy. This was the country of icebergs, and so the boat had to take its time amongst the great floating beasts which had calved from the mating of tides and glaciers. Ancient blue-white ice, spawned in medieval storms, compacted over centuries into frozen diamonds that floated free through cold seas to string themselves in a dazzling chain, here near the top of the earth. Ice that could crush the iron hull of the boat, as though it were no more than foil.

Jeannie's Star slowed to a crawl three miles out from the Island. The ice pack had been driven together by strong gales over the last two months, and was as impenetrable as concrete.

"What now?" Casey asked, squinting out over the stretch of frozen water. Low cloud on the horizon had formed an ice-blink and it illuminated the burning skeleton of the sealer and smaller humps on the ice that were debris and men.

"Walk, crawl, run, whatever it takes, but *Jeannie* sure as hell is goin' no furder," Olie said, hands already around a dory rope. The plan, hastily sketched in by Captain Jack, was to pull the dories *Jeannie* was in possession of out onto the ice and pull them back filled with the wounded. The boat herself would be set up as a triage center, with half the doctors and nurses staying behind to prepare for the incoming wounded, and the other half coming with *Jeannie's* crew out onto the deadly ice.

Within minutes the crew was spread out in a thin and fragile ribbon, each man hoping to God he'd make it back to the boat alive and with all his fingers and toes intact. They all knew the risk they took in this sort of climate.

Casey crawled belly down across the ice, feeling the slush in the cracks where the day's sun had tried to melt the floes without success. There was a fine blue thread that separated the edge of the world from the sky. In between himself and that shifting line, the fire still roared without mercy.

Jesus, he didn't see how anyone could have survived such an explosion. His mind couldn't help but see the irony of burning to death in a frozen hell. He stopped for a second, flexing his fingers to keep the blood flowing, noting how much they'd stiffened since his last such stop. The dory rope was stiff as steel pipe and frozen to his gloved palm. He put his mouth and nose to his forearm and took a deep breath, trying to protect his lungs from the worst of the freezing air. Then he continued the relentless half-walk, half-crawl forward again, every inch of his skin fine-tuned to the shifting of the ice.

It was an agony to move so slowly, but the cracks between chunks of ice became broader, small patches of water opening up underfoot without warning. Some of them requiring him to walk around, every step a breathless prayer that he wouldn't plunge into the killing water. The average mean temperature of the water this time of year was a heart stopping zero degrees. Even with protection the survival time was under fifteen minutes. The bits of clothing which had come into contact with the water were already frozen solid, bumping like thin planks of wood against his body.

Suddenly the ice rocked under him and the bottom dropped out of his stomach. Christ, he could feel the breath of the water beneath him, waiting to pull him in and swallow him in one steel-jawed bite. He scrambled forward and the ice went down in the other direction, the horizon tilting up sharply in opposition. He went to his stomach, not daring to breathe until the rocking subsided beneath him. He closed his eyes and swallowed hard—that had been too damn close. The water had slopped up to his knees in the mad scramble and he could feel the ice moving along his skin already.

Ignoring the discomfort, Casey leaned on his elbows and pulled himself towards the edge of the patch of ice, hoping to God that it would bear his weight just a little longer. It held and he managed to bridge the gap to the next piece of ice, which was much firmer and larger than the last.

A few feet more and the smell hit him, strong enough to halt him. Though he'd never smelled burned human flesh before he knew the reek for what it was. The cold seemed to sharpen the smell to a point, so it drove directly into his senses. He gagged slightly, then clenched his teeth and continued his slow crawl toward the one thing he could see moving in the charred pile. Somebody was still alive.

As he crawled closer, he began to make out details. Limbs became distinct from torsos, blackened clothing still letting off wisps of smoke. The sound of the other men shouting back and forth was disembodied and shifting, likely a result of the brutal wind that sheared along the surface of the ice.

He almost crawled over the man, and it was only the feel of something warm and soft beneath his hand that made Casey pause. The man was face-up, as though he'd simply lain down in the hollow where Casey found him. Laid down, and given in to the creeping numbness, given way to the delicately forming arches, the needling lances and the pricking crystal spars that were death by ice.

A fine frost had formed in the man's hair and lashes already, and was spreading out across his face. He was dead, of that there was no doubt. Beyond the stillness, he'd the look of it in his face. The spark gone, the pain over, and the curious peace that followed already at rest upon his features. Casey passed a hand over the man's eyes, closing them against the fiery night. He braced himself on one knee, and then froze in place, the small fine hairs on his neck rising like separate entities, and he knew that whoever had been watching him on the boat, stood behind him now, and that he did not wish Casey well.

He turned carefully, so as not to startle the man.

It was Olie. He stood no more than six feet away, and in his hand was a gun, glittering with reflected flame.

"Why?" Casey managed to croak out.

"Money o' course. Money, hard-earned, mind—ye're a bloody hard bastard to kill. Tried on the boat twice, but ye're a bit like the cat that just kept comin' back. Was startin' to think ye were indestructible."

"Paid by whom?" Casey asked, though he knew the answer only too well.

"Love Hagerty. I owed him money indirectly for a drug run gone bad off the coast of Maine. He said if'n I were to kill ye, he'd call his goons off an' throw in some money to make certain I kept my nerve. I don't know what ye did but the man seems to want ye dead like a drunk wants whiskey."

"An' now?" Casey asked, trying to gauge the odds of making the jump across the dark water to the floe behind him, and then trying to outrun the man. He was bigger, stronger and, he'd no doubt, faster, but not as strong, nor big, nor as fast as the water would be should he misstep, and the odds of falling in were astronomically high.

"And now, I just want it done, so's I can stop havin' nightmares about it."

"Aye well, I'll apologize for any disruption plannin' my murder may have caused to yer sleep," Casey said dryly.

"Still maintainin' yer humor I see. I can admire that, it's almost a pity to kill ye."

It wasn't movement that attracted his eye, and later Casey could not say what had drawn him to look over Olie's shoulder, other than maybe a sense that it simply was not his time to die, and therefore something or someone was going to have to intervene.

Beyond Olie, Hallbjörn stood, braced on a floe of ice which had broken free of the main pack and floated in a deadly open space of black water. The ice was no more than a shoulder span but the big man stood with the confidence of a natural hunter, the only movement that of the long fur of his coat waving in the breeze. In his hand he held the small harpoon sometimes used on sword fishing boats. A small and deadly length of steel, tipped to razor sharpness.

Something in his own face must have told Olie that the two of them were no longer alone, for he looked about wildly, the wind catching his sandy curls and haloing them out about his head. He'd lost his cap somewhere along the line.

"*Hey Mömmuriðill*," Hallbjörn called out softly. Casey had no idea what the word meant but he guessed it wasn't a compliment. Olie swung about, the ice he'd chosen to stand upon secured by a thin thread to the main pack.

Hallbjörn threw, the ice floe beneath him rocking, though he kept his feet, as only a man born to the impermanent shifting of ice could.

The deadly iron hissed, parting the curtain of frigid air, and Olie rocked back on his heels with the impact, then dropped slowly to his knees. It was a true hit, slightly to the left of the sternum, and lodged firmly in the heart.

Casey didn't think, but got to his feet and jumped across the expanse of water toward Olie. He knelt by the injured man's side. The harpoon was lodged deep and fast within the chest. To move it, to pull it out, would mean certain death even under ideal circumstances—in a hospital for instance. Out here on the ice, he would bleed out quickly, despite the bitter cold.

"Dinna' bother," Olie said, his breath a rasp in his throat, lungs laboring for oxygen, as the heart began to fail.

The gun had fallen away and lay now, a cruel length of steel upon the ice, well out of Olie's reach. Though just to be certain Casey picked it up and tucked it inside his coat.

Olie was laying awkwardly, legs bent under him at an uncomfortable angle. Casey straightened them out and put his own cap under the man's head.

"Look up," Olie said, and it was then Casey noticed the odd shifting colors crossing through the man's eyes. He looked up. The sky was moving in a vast curtain of light.

"Aurora Borealis," Casey said in wonderment, stunned at the ice-flame colors rippling through the sky above him, forgetting for a moment that he could no longer feel his fingers or toes, forgetting that he might die if he didn't get back to the boat and out of these wet clothes. "My God." he breathed in awe, feeling like a child getting its first glimpse of the world.

Beside him, Olie stirred slightly, breath a translucent white in the blue air. "Do you think there is a God?" Every word was a miniature battle against the limits of mortality.

Casey looked at the sky above, unravelling in streams of indigo and emerald, violet and a fierce penumbra of red. Below him, the ice, in its eternal impermanence, shifted slightly. The world seemed all water and sky, fragile and ever changing. And there amongst the violent colors that streamed and billowed, adrift on a chancy element, at the complete mercy of nature, he found his faith and knew that he'd never really lost it.

"Yes," he said softly, as much to the heavens as to the man beside him, "yes I do."

"Pull it out," Olie said.

"What?"

"The harpoon, pull it out."

"Ye'll die."

"I know."

Casey swallowed, the ice crystals in the air giving the whole scene before him a dreadful clarity.

"First reach into the pocket of my coat—on the inside," Olie gasped.

Casey frowned, but did as the man asked, his hand clumsy with cold. He emerged with a plastic bag, inside of which was a roll of money—American dollars—several thousands from the look of things.

"What is this?"

"The money, Love Hagerty paid me to kill ye. Take it. Think of it...as reparation."

"I don't want it."

Olie shook his head slowly, the movement exaggeratedly slow. "Just take it."

The words were slurred, and the blue eyes were closing for long seconds at a time now.

"It hurts. Please...pull...the fucking thing...out."

Casey looked Olie full in the eyes, and was surprised to see a smile spreading across the ruddy, weathered face.

"No... hard feelings...boy?"

"No hard feelings," Casey whispered in reply. And then he grabbed the steel bar tight, pulling it out in one hard move. It came free with a black upswell of blood in its wake, the scent of copper heavy in the air. The blue eyes blinked slowly, and an odd smile spread across Olie's face.

"Thank you," he said, voice barely more than a slipstream of oxygen. Against his arm, numbed with cold, Casey felt a change, as though life, in leaving, sought a last touch of that which it had been, but no longer was.

He crossed himself quickly, knowing he had to move before the lethargy from the fierce cold set in and rendered him as helpless as the man next to him.

Time blurred along with his flesh after that. And he felt a vague sense of surprise when he arrived back at the boat, with three wounded men in the dory—two able to get on *Jeannie* with the assistance of the Captain and two other crewmen. The third was badly burned and had died sometime during the crawl across the deadly ice field.

Back on the relative warmth of *Jeannie's Star*, all was pandemonium. Lengths of bandage were strewn about, blood and the smell of burned flesh were thick on the air and the sound of men in great pain resounded off the thick planking of the ship.

Captain Jack, looking more like a demented leprechaun than ever, gave Casey a cursory glance as he came aboard.

"Got all your bits and bobs boy? Nothing frostbitten?"

"No, I'll do," Casey said, for though his extremities were still numb, there was a painful tingle setting up in his fingertips, toes, and thighs that told him he'd not suffered frostbite.

"Good, we're heading back for th'island, can't take anymore on and there's two more ships waiting to take back wounded. I'll be damned if I lose one of my men out here. So back we go. Lost thirty-three from the sealer, and there's still twenty-odd missing, but we're hauling back over a hundred men."

Hallbjörn stepped on board then, having thriftily retrieved his harpoon, Casey saw with a queasy shift in his stomach.

Captain Jack eyed the two of them shrewdly. "Where's the Norwegian?"

"He fell into sea," Hallbjörn said, face blank and tone neutral. "He," he pointed at Casey with the harpoon, "try to save him." Hallbjörn shrugged, "too cold, sink too fast."

"Oh Christ, have mercy." Captain Jack didn't look as if he entirely believed the big Icelander. But at present he had to get his boat back to Newfoundland, and didn't have time to dispute Hallbjörn's story.

Though Casey knew there would be no evidence with which to dispute the story. For Hallbjörn hadn't gone back to merely retrieve the harpoon, but to sink the body and all its traces into the black and frigid sea. The sea which would welcome the still warm body back to its salty bosom, where it would never be found.

Hallbjörn gestured to Casey to follow him down the hatchway. He left him sitting in the galley where hot coffee waited on the counter. He returned moments later with a big fuzzy sweater and two murky brown bottles.

"You wear," he tossed the sweater onto Casey's lap and busied himself with taking the lids off the two bottles.

The man was so huge that the sweater fell halfway to Casey's knees. But it was warm and dry and, at present, that was all Casey required in the universe.

Hallbjörn held the smaller bottle to Casey's lips and Casey took it gratefully, thinking a nip of whiskey would not come amiss right now. He took a hearty slug and immediately gagged. Whiskey it wasn't. Hallbjörn was grinning, hairy face split like a whiskered moon.

"That's revoltin'," Casey said, throat still convulsing from the slimy taste.

"Cod liver oil—is human antifreeze. It's how we survive Iceland winter."

Suppressing the desire to scrub his tongue off with the hairy sweater sleeve, Casey said, "I thank ye, ye saved my life out there."

Hallbjörn shrugged, blueberry eyes hard as marble. "*Ja, þú ert velkominn. I did not like him.*"

"No?" Casey said, feeling the fine tremors of shock begin to jump along his skin.

"No. He talk too much."

Hallbjörn stuck another bottle under his nose, laughing when Casey shook his head and pulled away from the vapors issuing forth from its neck.

"Not cod liver oil—is *svarti dauði*—you drink."

Casey, not wanting to commit some breach of Icelandic courtesies, drank. Though he manfully refrained from gagging this time, his eyes were streaming after two swallows.

"What the hell is that?"

Hallbjörn grinned again, "Is *svarti dauði*—how to say?" He furrowed his massive brow. "Ah in English, is Black Death."

"I believe it," Casey said fervently, and took another swig.

🦐 🦐 🦐

JEANNIE'S STAR CAME TO REST in one of the wee outland ports. Mab's Harbor was the name of the hamlet, and though Casey was too tired to pay much attention to his surroundings he knew the ripe reek of a herring village when he smelled one. Compared to the smell of burned human flesh however, it was positively flower-like.

He took a deep breath in of the fishy scent, grateful to be alive. Beyond that all he wanted was to sleep until the resurrection. The small harbor was awash with people and bobbing lights, but he couldn't seem to make sense of anything and the faces were blurring in front of his eyes even as he stood.

"You need a bed?" A hand touched his elbow and he turned. A homely face, long and careworn, emerged out of the babble of light and sound. It was one of the men he'd brought back with him, off the ice.

"Aye, I do."

"Come with me then."

Casey followed the man up the steep hill from the harbor. It was well past dawn and though there was fog sifting up from the sea, he could make out snow upon great granite headlands that loomed dark and threatening towards the morning sky. The harbor had been built in the crevice between two jutting promontories and thus was protected from the worst of the sea's wrath. On top of the headlands was another matter altogether. There the winds had scoured the rock bare, and yet there was a spare, chill beauty to the tiny cluster of houses and shops that perched upon these bleak surroundings.

"Name's John," the man said as they rounded the twisting main street, which ran right to the foot of a small house with a peaked roof and a brightly painted blue door.

"Mine's Casey."

"Irishman?"

"Aye."

And that was the extent of the conversation, until Casey found himself sitting on the edge of a bed, fingers too stiff to unlace the overly large boots Hallbjörn had lent him.

"Here man, I'll get those."

He'd a vague sense of relief when the boots were removed and then there was the touch of rough yet gentle hands laying him down to rest, and a blanket being tucked up high over his shoulders. Then all was darkness, warm and shrouding. He fell into it gratefully.

HE SLEPT A FULL DAY, waking once in the long hours, and then only to turn over and sink back into unconsciousness with barely a glimmer of thought.

He awoke to a little room, walls painted the color of corroded copper. The fog had cleared and he could, when he sat up, see the bleak headlands, and beyond, the gray water, calm today. He lowered his legs stiffly to the floor, every inch of his body complaining of bruises and cuts.

He dressed slowly, washing in the cold water left in a basin on a brass-bound chest which sat in the corner of the room.

He found his way to the kitchen down a narrow hall, decorated with sepia-toned portraits of hard-looking people. The man's ancestors no doubt, and no wonder at the hard look of them either, for this was a hard land.

John was in the kitchen, packing up a bag with sweaters and socks, boots and small, lumpy articles wrapped in newsprint.

"Wife's left tea a'brewin' an' there's a plate for ya in the oven. Eat yer fill."

"Thank ye," Casey said, retrieving the kettle and pouring the tea into a cracked white cup.

"I'll be off then, boat's leaving for the pack in an hour. I'd best get down an' see the captain before then."

"Ye're goin' back out there?" Casey said disbelievingly, watching the man hang his canvas bag over his shoulder.

The man nodded, shifting his wad of chew from the left cheek to the right. "I'm fit enough, got eight hungry mouths to feed. Growlin' bellies don't care 'bout the danger of the thing an' my fear ain't goin' to fill them up either, so I go an' do what needs doin'. 'Tain't much else to be done."

Casey nodded slowly, seeing an odd beauty in the man's homely face. "Then best of luck on yer travels man."

The man turned back in the doorway, the chill blue light framing his worn countenance. "An' on your own, man. Chance should find you again in Mab's Harbor one of these days, there'll always be an open door an' a place at the kitchen table."

"Thank ye, I'll keep it in mind should I happen this way," Casey replied softly.

The house was silent around him after the man left, other than the occasional creak and the sound of the fire crackling in the stove. The lady of the house had left him a good breakfast of ham, hotcakes, and partridge berry preserves.

The house was small, and the idea that ten people lived within its walls astounded him. He took in the cracked and faded linoleum, the peeling paint and the worn furniture. It was shabby but it exuded the warmth of a real home.

He ate the food quickly, clearing his dishes away after. Then he reached in his bag and withdrew the bloody fistful of dollars that Olie had forced into his hand as he was dying.

He peeled off the outer bills, the ones stained rusty with blood. The remainder he left on the table, tucked between the sugar bowl and the fat-bottomed creamer. Then slinging his bag over his shoulder he opened the door and turned toward the sea.

He was going home for good, and to hell with any man who stood in his way.

Chapter Fifteen

Caught in the Crosshairs

A GENT GUS HAD TOLD HER that if the tag in the book was ever red, it meant they had to meet right away because some unforeseen calamity had occurred. Though Pamela could plainly see the scarlet length of paper that lay in Gibbon's *Decline and Fall of the Roman Empire*, her mind wanted fiercely to deny it. Wanted to hope that some patron had left it behind. The mildewy smell that emanated off the pages told her otherwise, however. The only time this book was ever taken off the shelves was when agent Gus removed it to place that week's marker inside and when she retrieved it to see what color lay within the brittle yellow pages.

That little strip of scarlet had brought her here, to their agreed meeting spot. It had been three months since she had told him about the secret meetings held between Love Hagerty and Mark Ryan. Thus far that particular trail had led nowhere. It was as if the Agent had sensed that someone might be onto him and Hagerty, and neither, as far as she knew, had been near the other in all that time.

It was cold by the pond, a fine drizzle of rain rippling the surface of the water that still had a thin coating of ice upon it. Agent Gus was waiting there for her, wrapped in a gray trenchcoat, hair mussed and tie askew. He looked slightly ill. As she'd never seen him less than composed in his manner if not his dress, she got a sick feeling immediately. The news was going to be bad, and there was no way that could bode well for her and her part in this play.

"How are you?" he asked with a wobbly smile.

"Let's skip the small talk," she said, "you look like you've just swallowed a worm."

"I think maybe I have," he said and there was no mistaking the worry that radiated off the man like a doom-filled fog.

"What do you mean?" she asked, through lips that suddenly felt ice-cold.

"I think Love Hagerty has been brought in as an informant, so the boys here can take down the Bassarelli family."

"Could you say that again?" she said, praying that she'd heard him wrong.

"I think Love Hagerty is partnered up with someone above me in the field office. It was you telling me about seeing him and Mark Ryan together that got me looking into this. But now something else has happened that makes me certain you were right."

Oh sweet Jesus, she *had* heard him right.

"What?"

"Because my boss is trying to shut down your file, saying you're of no more use to us. Which is just feeb-speak meaning they've got bigger fish to fry and are trying to protect someone they consider a better asset. I can't see who else they'd be protecting if it's not Love Hagerty."

"That's not all there is to it, though, is it?" Pamela asked, the blood in her veins running very cold so that she could feel every movement of it under her skin.

"No. The agent I think is running Hagerty got a 'tip' about where to find the remains of an old girlfriend of Blackie's—Cassandra Neil, who has been missing for six years. The police had always pegged Blackie for the disappearance but they couldn't build the case well enough without the body."

"And you think Love told them where to find the body?"

"He wants Blackie gone. He's ready to move on. Thinks it's the right time to become respectable. I can't see why else they'd be trying to shut down your file. Odd that the remains of a girl who has been missing for six years suddenly conveniently turn up, when no one had a clue where to look before. The case had been cold for years. It hadn't been re-opened either."

"Blackie had her killed?"

"Yes," Agent Gus swallowed, "and that's not all. Diane Killian is missing as well. The staties called us two days back saying her mother was frantic, hadn't been able to get a hold of her in a few days. Usually Diane never missed Sunday dinner with her family and so when she didn't show up last Sunday she got worried. Went to the little apartment Diane shared with Blackie down in Dorchester and there's not a thing missing. Looks like she was interrupted in the middle of making dinner. There were onions shrivelling up on the chopping block but no sign of Diane."

Pamela shut her eyes, head whirling. Pretty curvaceous Diane, with her bright blonde hair and long manicured nails. She'd occasionally done temp secretarial work for Love in the Back Bay office. She was the sort who brought in fresh baked muffins a couple of times a week, and knew whose aunt was sick, whose kids were starting kindergarten and when everyone's birthday was. Pamela had liked her; she was easy to talk to and had never treated Pamela as Love's high-priced whore.

The wind suddenly felt terribly cold, and she wrapped her scarf tighter around her throat, knowing nothing was going to help the chill that now penetrated her very bones.

"Her mother was real worried in particular because Diane had been talking about a new man she'd met, a banker from downtown. She was going to make the move away from Blackie. Cassandra was going to leave him just before she disappeared too—seeing the pattern here?" he asked bleakly.

"Nobody leaves Blackie," Pamela replied, "unless they have his permission first."

What she didn't add was that nobody left Love either, including herself. That he and Blackie were two sides of the same coin, only both sides of the coin were black.

"What are the odds of this field agent telling Love I'm the one selling him out?" Pamela asked.

Agent Gus shook his head. "I don't think he knows yet, I think my boss figures if he shuts the file down now we'll be able to cut you loose without Hagerty ever having to know."

"But there are no guarantees, are there? I mean they could use the information to get Love to tell them more."

Agent Gus was positively gray at this point.

"They could, if they find out."

She put her head in her hands, thinking she might actually throw up.

"So everything I've done—prostituting myself, risking my marriage and my life, was all for nothing?!"

"No," Agent Gus said, and she was startled by the ferocity of his tone. "I won't let it be for nothing."

"How are you going to manage that?"

"I'm not completely without friends and resources myself. I'm not going to let them can my whole investigation because someone can't get over his boyhood worship of Hagerty."

"So it's not just any old agent," she said faintly, "it's Ryan, isn't it?"

Agent Gus nodded, face set like stone.

She felt as though all the air had been sucked from her lungs. It might be too late already; Ryan had seen her with Love a few times. She knew the agent had never trusted her, but that he was blinded by the old Southie loyalty, and the glamor that the mere mention of Love's name conjured up for people. If he found out the informer against Love was her, he'd tell Love right off to protect his asset and to preserve a friendship that had been forged in blood and the position of insiders to a closed neighborhood.

"I got a glimpse at the file they're building and the Riordan name cropped up fairly often, and it wasn't your name preceding it."

She felt a wave of rage sweep from the top of her head to bottom of her feet.

"He's still trying to get Casey out of the way."

"Yes, and I think you know he doesn't much care how he does it."

Yes, she knew that all too well, but thought Love had understood how the deal worked. If anything, even a minor accident happened to Casey, she was off limits. Though she'd underestimated his treachery, she knew she was the biggest weakness the man had. She could make his whole house of cards come burning down around his ears. Given time, which she no longer had.

"What do I do now?" she asked, the question rhetorical as she was in a disastrous quagmire with no rope in sight.

"You're not entirely without options," Agent Gus said, "but you are running out of time."

"What do you mean?" she asked, afraid to hear the answer as it half-formed itself in the pit of her stomach.

The agent looked at her, eyes cool and assessing as if once again taking her mettle.

"Look, you didn't hear this from me, but I'm of the opinion that Guilio Bassarelli would be very interested to hear what Love Hagerty's been up to."

"The Bassarellis would kill him," she said bluntly. Agent Gus looked down into the pond, where a bit of waterweed swayed gently beneath the paper-thin ice. "I'd be making murder happen."

Agent Gus shrugged. "I can make your husband's name disappear from the files. It's only a matter of time before they get the Bassarelli clan anyway. Love Hagerty is a bonus, but he's not essential to making a case."

"Are you certain about that?"

Agent Gus looked up, and she saw there the steel in the spine that had put him in the ranks of the Bureau in the first place.

"They know what they've done to you, and they don't care. They are jeopardizing your life and that of your husband. I made you a promise when we made this deal. I believe in keeping my word. Screw them, if they don't."

"You could lose your job—or worse," she said.

"Do you think I care at this point? I didn't sign on to work for a bunch of corrupt bastards. Besides," he smiled, "they've severely underestimated me, and I really don't like that."

"Neither," she said, "do I. How much time do you think I have before it blows wide open?"

"You're the one blind spot Hagerty has and that buys you a little time. He's going to want to believe it's anyone but you when he finds out. Still when he does find out he'll turn like a snake. Whatever you decide..." he trailed off, not wanting to say the words. "It has to be soon."

"There's a party at his house tomorrow night, but I'm not due to be alone with him until Tuesday."

Agent Gus nodded.

"That'll have to do then. You've got two days to decide."

Chapter Sixteen

All the Way Home

IN THE DARK, IT SEEMED, he could feel every sensation magnified
to its limits. Each flake of snow burning into his skin, the very shape of
it discernible to his fevered surface. The light from the windows fell in
hard distorted rectangles across the swiftly whitening grass. Though the glass
separated him from the party of elegantly dressed people, he could smell
the food, and was slightly nauseated by the spices and heavy sauces. And the
people themselves, milling about, flutes of pale liquid gold in their soft hands,
smelling of ambergris and oranges, cinnabar and sandalwood. He had never
belonged to such a world. He didn't speak the language, had never been able
to train his tongue around the elongated vowels and clipped consonants.

It was cold out here, in the night, but he stood fast as if paralyzed by
the sights before him, a child looking through the eternally locked doors of
a sweetshop. Though, if he were honest, he'd never tried. It wasn't his world
and he did not desire it.

All the rooms were lit for the party, soft, flickering, flattering light to gild
away the wrinkles or the telltale tucks and nips of the surgeon's knife. The
dining room, table massed with hothouse flowers, orchids and amaranth. The
ballroom, marble floor polished to an icy glitter, fragranced with topiary trees
of roses, pinked in the golden light. And through it moved the women, hair
bound up or spilling down over powdered white shoulders, lips painted in a
dazzling array of reds as though they'd all just risen from a feast of blood.
Blondes, brunettes, redheads but none with a wild spill of blue-black falling
across ivory skin. And yet he knew she was there, could sense her movement
amongst the sparkle and spun sugar of the crowd, as if the same blood pumped
beneath their respective skins.

He shivered and drew his coat tighter, its wool scratching his neck, the
stink of fish rising up into his nostrils. It hardly bothered him now.

He stretched his neck back, adjusting several cricks and caught sight of
Orion climbing up from the horizon. His own star, pulsating steadily, hot red
and dying with every throb of its overgrown heart. Betelgeuse. He whispered

the name to himself like a prayer, the odd Arabic syllables comforting him, seeming less foreign than the gilt-edged world inside the glass.

When he looked back he started, feeling that odd slippage of skin against flesh that fear caused. Love Hagerty, unrelentingly glamorous in evening wear, hair polished to a bluish sheen, was looking directly out the windows at him, a balloon glass of brandy in one hand, a cigar in the other. Shielded though he was by the light within and the dark without, Casey knew instinctively that the man saw him plain as a bug on a white sheet. Love had a criminal's backbone, he knew what was coming and which direction it was coming from before *it* knew. He'd developed this particular talent from long years of dishonesty, of having to have eyes in the back of his head, and a general distrust of all who surrounded him.

Casey stepped back further into the shadows, feeling the finger-like shape of pine branches sliding across his right-hand side. He never once took his eyes off the man in the window, while his mind tried to decipher the distance to the nearest exit off the estate.

In the window, Love raised his glass, tilted his head and gave an ominous smile in Casey's direction.

"Shit," he muttered, feeling chilled to his marrow. He'd only wanted to catch a glimpse of Pamela, just for a minute even.

And then he did see her, a dim ghostly shape at the library window. The light in there had been so weak in comparison to the other rooms that he'd not paid attention. Her silhouette, silver-white, was fractured against the diamond panes.

He took an involuntary step forward, instinct guiding him and then just as firmly stopping him. As much as he wanted to, he could not go to her now.

He moved behind the screen of trees carefully, stepping from shadow to shadow until he'd gained a good thirty feet and could see the long library windows much more clearly.

It was definitely her, hair a smudged nimbus of curls against bare shoulders. The dress was new, he didn't recognize it. It was white, its lines as pure as her own. Designed to make a beautiful woman stand out like a white rose in the midst of a nosegay of gaudy posies. He'd understood from the first that she was different somehow, that she held herself with dignity and pride as though she faced the world as an adventure, with a wonder that disappeared from most during adolescence. Her clothing always became an innate part of her. Rather than a shield between nakedness and the world, hers seemed an organic outgrowth of her personality, her mood, her very being.

And suddenly he was weary of the fear, weary of looking over his shoulder for the next shadow to slip out from the cluster. He moved out of the trees with long strides, ignoring the slippery feeling in his knees. When he reached the front door, he grabbed the bell pull and yanked it hard before he could reconsider the insanity of what he was doing.

The man who answered the door had one of those faces that seemed like a bit of dust carefully arranged over bones. He managed to separate the 'yes' that he gave Casey into four separate syllables.

"Tell Mrs. Riordan that her husband has come to fetch her home." He stepped past the stickman into the marble foyer. "On second thought, I'll just tell her myself," he added, spotting the muscle that was headed his way. The ballroom lay directly to his left, down a short corridor, sheathed in slick black marble. He heard the butler's prim 'excuse me' as well as the less polite expletives of the thugs who had been sent to eject him from the premises. He quickened his pace, the ebony walls seeming to briefly close in on him. His exhaustion was catching up to him swiftly.

When the ballroom doors flew open, Love was in the midst of a toast, his raised glass refracting the light in a dozen different directions. Even his well-schooled demeanor slipped a notch, a blaze of pure hatred lighting his features before he could manage to suppress it and resume his smooth façade. Before he could open his mouth, Casey spoke.

"I've come for my wife," he said, voice hoarse with the adrenaline that pumped through him madly, making his muscles tremble and his bones turn the consistency of rubber.

Love raised his eyebrows. "I'll see if someone can locate her, I'm not even certain she's here." Casey didn't miss the sharp movement Love made with his hand behind his back. Calling off the thugs, Casey almost smiled, the bastard was afraid. And well he should be.

"Ye damn well know she is," Casey said, the grip on his temper slipping swiftly. "Pamela!" he shouted. The gathering crowd bunched a little, the murmurs beginning in stifled whispers.

He'd a sudden notion of how he must appear to the assembled, a wild man in stinking clothes, claiming his woman like he was fresh from the cave. The surge of adrenaline was ebbing, exhaustion taking the upper hand. His fingers opened and the money, stiff and brown with Olie's blood, drifted across the gleaming floor. A woman near him in purple chiffon fainted dead away, head clipping an antique spittoon on the way down. He didn't so much as blink though, he didn't dare. If he'd recognized his exhaustion then surely Love had seen it too.

"Where," Love asked, voice still civilized, "did you get that?"

"Out of the pocket of the man ye paid to kill me," Casey returned, and heard the low murmurs turn to gasps of disbelief. Where the hell was Pamela anyway?

"Perhaps," Love said, syllables clipped off murderously, "you'd like to join me in the library?"

"I just want my wife," he said, before collapsing to the floor in a faint.

HE AWOKE TO FIND HIMSELF on an ornate sofa, a pillow under his head and a fire crackling at his feet. All things considered, it was a much pleasanter atmosphere than he'd expected to awaken to.

"Pamela?" he croaked, aware suddenly of a sharp pain in the side of his face.

"Right here," she hovered into view above him, face drawn tight with worry, eyes the heavy bottle green they always turned when she was upset.

Love stood over her shoulder, features arranged into a mask of concern. But Casey would never again be fooled by the veneer. He saw clearly through to the murderous rage that smoldered right beneath the skin. He was beyond fear himself now, though, and matched Love's look. The man actually had the grace to blink.

Casey turned his gaze back to the matter at hand.

"Don't fuss darlin'. I'm fine, just got a bit lightheaded, I daresay a bite or two will set me right soon enough."

"Lightheaded," she said, sounding slightly hysterical. "*Lightheaded,* you bastard! I thought you might be dead this last week. Until I got the call three days ago, I thought you *were* dead."

"I'm sorry for that," he took her face in his hands and drew her down into his arms, ignoring the presence of Love Hagerty for the moment. She deserved that much comfort before he tore into the bastard. She was cold and shaking in his arms, and he felt a surge of protectiveness. He would never let this filthy, murdering whoreson near her again.

For a moment, the fear and fury of the last weeks fell away, and he was grateful to just be able to hold her, as he had feared he might never again. He breathed deeply of her scent and then drew away, looking her deep in the eyes. Then kissed her forehead gently.

"Will ye go an' get yer wrap, darlin'? For I'm goin' to take ye home now." This was uttered not in the tone of a suggestion, but rather a command. Pamela took one look at the set of his jaw, and went in search of her wrap.

"You simply don't know when to call it a day, do you?" Love had barely waited until Pamela had cleared the doorway, and Casey realized the man had allowed his hatred to push him into reckless behavior.

Casey laughed, a harsh sound without any humor in it.

"I'm not afraid of ye."

"That's very unwise," Love said, the smooth tones and charming smile completely gone. Here was the face of the cobra that everyone spoke of in hesitant whispers.

"Unwise it may be," Casey spoke calmly, and only one who knew him well would understand the deadly undertone to his words, "but I find myself not caring a great deal for wisdom these days."

"That's too bad, could be injurious to your health. I'm rather surprised you didn't mention your suspicions in front of your wife."

"I saw no need for it, this matter is between yerself and I."

"You goddamn Irish punk, you still don't understand who I am. My word is law in this town. My rule is absolute. You are only alive because that damn fisherman was so inadequate to the task of killing you."

"Outside this town you are nothing. An' yer rule is not absolute. Ye don't rule me, ye never did, only ye were too big of a fool to understand that not all men are for sale."

Love smiled, a smug expression that set off an alarm bell deep in Casey's psyche.

"Oh yes they are, one way or another all men are for sale, women too for that matter."

"No, they are not." Casey's voice was quiet, but carried with the force of a blade.

Love shrugged. "Believe what you like, it makes no difference to me. Just know that next time I'll hire someone who's much better at their job."

"Not if I kill you first."

Focussed on each other with such deadly intent, neither man noticed Pamela standing in the shadow of the doorway.

Chapter Seventeen

Into the Mystic

THE CHURCH OF THE ASSUMPTION was empty of worshippers, the spring air exerting a more forceful pull than the dark, quiet interior of the church. She had expected to find Father Kevin in his quarters, putting the finishing touches on Sunday's sermon or on the basketball court, even priests being not immune to the lure of soft spring winds.

However, the basketball court was occupied only by two raggedy looking youths who wolf-whistled at her and then flushed when she asked if they knew where Father Kevin was. Her knocks at the private entrance went unanswered as well, so she entered the main body of the church and found him there, bowed over in the front pew, as if he were in great pain.

"Father Kevin, are you alright?" she asked, her quiet question sounding like a shout in the vast silence of the church.

He gave a barely perceptible nod. She touched his shoulder lightly, worried by his stance and his silence. He started as if she'd laid a brand to his shoulder, head snapping up. She stepped back in shock, his face was heavily flushed, pale lashes wet with tears.

"She's gone," he said, wiping at his eyes with one hand, the other hand fisted against his side.

"Gone?" Pamela echoed, frightened by his tone. "Who's gone?"

"Emma—she's dead," he replied bluntly.

"What...when?" she stuttered, feeling the starch go abruptly out of her knees as she dropped to the pew beside the priest.

"Some old drunk found her by the Mystic, enough heroin in her to kill an elephant. Overdose, the police say, but she hadn't touched the stuff in years, not since she got pregnant with Jake."

"I don't understand," she whispered, the sound swallowed up in the great dark cavern of the church.

"Don't you?" Father Kevin turned his head toward her, eyes glittering with unshed tears.

"Love," she said, feeling as though she had something very sharp caught in her throat.

"He thought she was talking to the FBI, thought she ratted him out. So she got the treatment snitches get in this neighborhood."

"Oh God," she whispered, stricken to the bone with a sudden cold that had nothing to do with the chill gloom of the chapel. She could feel the odd breathless tingling in her lips and fingers that accompanied shock.

"Where's her boy?"

"With Emma's mother, that's where he'll live now."

She clasped her hands together, squeezing them until they hurt, in an effort to stop the dizziness that threatened to engulf her. In her peripheral vision, she saw the ninth station of the cross—Christ crushed under the weight of the cross for the third time. She wondered how tired he'd been of the endless foolishness of men. How tired and pained by the cruelty and waste? Bent, broken and killed by it in the end. Maybe tired enough to turn His face and never look back?

"May the souls of the faithful departed," she murmured, speaking from memory, *"through the mercy of God, Rest in peace."*

"Amen," Father Kevin finished for her, the words as ingrained in him as they were in her.

She unclasped her hands with effort and it came to her there, clear, and with the force of epiphany. Unfortunately, Agent Gus had been right. There was only one way out of this mess.

"Of course," she murmured, "of course." She stood, forcing the trembling out of her body through sheer willpower. She felt the determination of the inevitable within her, but still there was a small voice inside crying *'why does it have to be this way?'*

"What are you going to do?" Father Kevin, alerted by her tone, rose to his feet, worry written clear on the transparent features.

"There's only one thing I can do now; there's only one way to end this for once and for all," she said with a grim determination, wondering why it had taken her so long to see what should have been clear to her from the start.

"Let the feds deal with it," Father Kevin said. "Whatever it is you're thinking of doing, will only be going from the frying pan into a huge fire. The feds will put Hagerty behind bars where he's always belonged."

"Prison isn't enough," she said quietly, "you've lived in this neighborhood a long time Father Kevin, long enough to know that. He'd have eyes and ears outside the prison walls to do his dirty work for him. How much longer would Casey have? A week? A month? Then there'd be an accident that wasn't so accidental." She shook her head. "No, I should have seen this before, I just didn't want to face the truth."

She took a deep breath and held a steady hand out to Father Kevin.

"It's not likely we'll see each other again."

"Don't do this," the priest was pale now, freckles stark against his fair Irish skin.

"Shake my hand Father and wish me well, then just forget we ever had this conversation."

He shook his head. "I can't do that. Surely you can see that this is pure madness."

"Consider it a last confession of sorts, then." She held his eyes steadily and he saw within the pure green depths of her own a strength that frightened him. "Anything I may have said or you may have guessed is sacrosanct."

He felt as if his dog collar were choking him suddenly. "That verges on blackmail."

"Then I guess you have to decide what you are, a fine upstanding citizen of Southie or a priest? Today I'm afraid you don't have the luxury of being both."

"Do you hear yourself, Pamela?"

She shook her head angrily, color flooding the hothouse skin. Even now, when he felt appalled and terrified by what she was capable of, he was astonished by her beauty. Beauty of such a price that men had, and were going to, die for it. Suddenly he had an instant's pity for Love Hagerty. The man had been outmatched from the moment he'd laid eyes on this woman, but had never had the wisdom to understand it. And now he was going to pay with his life.

"Men think they understand love, but they don't." Her eyes were fixed on some point beyond him, words uttered with a strange ferocity that only deepened the chill he felt. "Men will die for freedom, they'll sacrifice their last breath for something that's only a theory, but they won't do it for love. Men look at women and see soft creatures, but do you really think anyone who's been a mother is soft? The first time you hold your child in your arms, you suddenly understand the darkness you're capable of. Life becomes very black and white. You know you'd kill and do it without a second thought should someone even threaten your child. And sometimes if you're lucky, you love the father of that child enough to do the same for him."

"Lucky? You call that lucky?"

"Cursed or blessed—when it comes to love I think you'll find it's the same thing." She sighed. "Why waste your morals on a man who'd kill you for merely crossing him once, even if you never intended to?"

"Pamela, two wrongs don't make a right, you know that."

"Save your platitudes for someone who still believes in a system of checks and balances, Father. I don't care if this is wrong in the eyes of your God or even the world. It's simple, it's black and white, either he dies or my husband does. Normally I wouldn't get a choice in this, perhaps the fact that I do is the hand of your God. After all, He's a God of vengeance and justice, there's dozens of Bible verses to back me up on that score. *I come not in peace but with a sword'*, 'an eye for an eye' does that sound like a God who tolerates fools?"

He looked at her, saw features which had become familiar and knew he was seeing a complete stranger. The realization caused a hurt he'd not expected.

"I never knew you, did I? I wonder if Casey even half knows you." He laughed, a harsh, choked sound. "It's a certainty that Hagerty never knew what he was buying himself."

"Please Father, have the grace to call me a whore instead of implying it. It's only a name. Did you really think that if I could crawl into his bed to keep him from killing Casey that I'd shirk from finding a way to see him dead, should it come to it? It's easy compared to what I've already done. I told you a man wouldn't understand it."

"But Emma would have."

"Choose your arrows more carefully than that, Father."

"I'm sorry; that was unnecessary."

"Don't apologize. I can hardly blame you for your anger. I as good as killed her."

"And would again if it saved your husband's life," he said, tasting a horrible bitterness on his tongue.

"I won't apologize for loving him," she said softly, "but I wouldn't have wished Emma dead—not ever."

"Maybe I'm jealous," he said, more to himself, speaking of the man who seemed inextricable just now from the priest.

"Jealous?" She raised an eyebrow in question.

"To love someone that much, to the point of sacrificing everything right in order to preserve that love."

She held his look without flinching. "Shouldn't a priest love his God that much?"

"Pamela," his voice was gentle, "He's your God as well, that bears remembering right now."

"Not today He isn't," she responded in a flat voice. "You didn't answer my question, Father Kevin. Shouldn't a priest love his God enough to sacrifice all?"

"I suppose he should," Kevin said, feeling a surge of resentment towards this woman who seemed intent on extracting honesty at any price, "but I don't happen to."

"Then I'm sorry for you," she said softly, "I truly am."

"And who am I in this? The one who's left to mop up the blood?" he asked quietly.

She gave him an odd smile. "Isn't that what priests do? Clean up the messes of humanity. Now please, shake my hand and let me go."

He looked at the hand and suddenly realized that she needed him to touch her, and by doing so to tell her she wasn't untouchable. He felt a wave of pity but suppressed it quickly. He took the hand. It was cold but steady.

"Will you...will you," he stumbled briefly over his words, "tell him I said

Godspeed and blessings on the rest of his days?"

She nodded, "I think he'd say the same, in less poetic terms, but with much the same feeling. I think he'd also tell you he'll miss you terribly. You've been a good friend to him, Father Kevin."

"Have I?" he said, "Perhaps. But not to you, I've failed you totally, haven't I? A friend would have realized a lot earlier that some secrets are too dangerous to be kept."

"I'm doing what I must, so I can hardly ask less of you." She took a deep breath, "If you feel you must go to the police about this, will you at least give me enough time to get Casey out of here?"

"I can't break the seal of the confessional Pamela, you said it yourself, it's sacrosanct."

"I won't hold you to that; you'll have to do as your conscience dictates."

"I appreciate that," he said wryly. Then asked the one question he knew the answer to, but that must attend this ending.

"Where will you take him?"

She smiled wearily, and he could see the cost of the last few minutes written plainly in her eyes.

"To Ireland, of course."

"You know what that will mean."

"I do, but he'll never be whole anywhere else. He's not a man for a life half lived."

Father Kevin shook his head, admiring her courage and yet not understanding it in the least. "No, he's not." Suddenly he realized he still held her hand and was slowly crushing it in his own.

"You're wrong, you know."

"About what?" She tried to pull her hand from his, but he refused to let go.

"When you said men won't kill for love. He would kill to keep you safe."

The air between them suddenly seemed charged with ice-cold particles. Her nails dug into the flesh of his palm. He could feel tension singing through the bones that he held in his strong grasp. This time he had chosen his arrow well and could not, at present, find it within himself to regret it.

"How can you be certain?" she asked, body very still, as if by not moving she could prevent his answer.

"Because I wasn't only his priest," he replied, hearing the past tense in his words with pain, "I was also his friend." He let her hand go and felt the welling of blood in his own.

He turned from her, eyes alighting on the statue of Christ bleeding for the sins of man. The irony was almost unbearable. Not a God who tolerated fools gladly she had said, not a God of infinite love and understanding but an avenging spirit who had come, not in peace, but wielding a double-edged sword. For such a love would always cut both ways. Was she right? Had he based his entire life's work upon a fallacy?

Oh my Jesus, he cried silently, *you bore the weight of the world on your shoulders and I am bowed by the sins of a few, my own included. Is this how gall tastes in a man's mouth? Do I turn a blind eye to things I cannot prevent?*

Unbidden, an image came to his mind of the tiny finch Casey had carved for him last Christmas. He had been touched beyond measure by the simple gift, seeing in it the hand of a master craftsman, the hours of patience and love it had represented. And it seemed as if Emma were like that finch, something small, golden, and unable to sing. Broken by a God who knew how to bear too much.

He closed his eyes and turned from the sight of the body of Christ. His words were softly spoken but in the dark air, they carried with the force of a hammer blow.

"He eats at Papa Cuccione's on Monday nights."

The slender figure halted in its tracks, but didn't turn. The one word came back to him quietly.

"Who?"

"Guilio Bassarelli. They close the place down on Monday nights and he eats there alone—relatively speaking, as there are always guards with him. But it's your best chance to see him without being seen yourself."

"Kevin—"

"Do not thank me," the words exploded from his throat with the force of sickness, echoing harshly off the vaulted pillars and stone arches. "Because surely to God I've just helped you commit murder." He tore the dog collar from his neck, dragging in a ragged breath.

She paused a moment longer, pale linen form insubstantial as a moth in the gloom. Then she turned and he caught his breath at the sight of her face. For once, he knew, the masks were all down. A ceaseless cataract of tears poured down her face, making her appear terribly young and fragile.

"I'm sorry," she whispered and then fled down the length of the aisle, past the font and out the heavy doors.

"God have mercy on you," Father Kevin whispered in reply, and wasn't certain if he spoke for her or the man he'd believed himself to be only an hour ago.

IT WAS SNOWING WHEN SHE EMERGED from the back door of Papa Cuccione's. Big creamy flakes that melted the instant they landed on the glistening cobblestones. She took off her pumps and walked barefoot, the wet soaking her stockings before she'd gone ten steps.

It was quiet in the North End, families tucked away behind lace curtains through which soft lights bloomed above her head. The light dusting of snow was already muffling the noise of cars and trucks. She might have been the only person in the streets. It made it difficult to believe that right now there were men—many men—dispatched in cars to the pretty little apartment in Brookline. That within minutes they would pull their dark-colored sedans to the front and back entrances of the building and would alight from their stealth chariots well muffled against the chill, and looking entirely civilized, would draw their sabers against the man who even now waited for her key in the lock, her step in the hallway, the drift of her perfume in the bedroom doorway.

She walked on feeling light and empty, the way one feels at the beginning of a high fever. Her senses were heightened and she could smell bread baking and espresso brewing, and overlaying it all, the smell of snow falling into the Charles River.

She walked for what might have been a long time or no time at all. At one point a cabbie pulled up and asked if she was lost.

"No," she said, "I was, but I'm not anymore." He gave her a look that told her he clearly thought she was crazy and pulled off into the night, red lights a blur in the thickly falling snow.

Without realizing where she was walking she'd ended up here, behind the weathered spire of the Old North Church, beneath the upraised knees of Paul Revere's trusty steed. The square was empty, dimly lit by mock gas lamps and the odd luminescence of a snowy night.

The trees soared above her into the snow-burdened sky, flakes whorling down between bare, wet branches.

She stood, snow feathering in her lashes and hair, soaking through the wool of her coat and tilted her head back tasting the fresh flakes on lips and tongue. Above her, a soot-smeared Paul Revere cried his eternal warning. Had he understood that freedom always has a price attached? Would he have appreciated the coin she had just paid in?

It was so still that she thought she might have heard the hiss of a passing feather, or maybe in the distance, where the Charles began to narrow in its snaking path, maybe—if you listened very carefully—you might hear the rattle of drawn sabers, you might feel the anticipation of a lover, you might smell the ghost of lime-scented aftershave, or the hotter copperpenny tang of blood. You might know the breathless slice when betrayal was understood. You might taste the last breath of a man who had loved you, despite the tragic mistake of it. You might see very clearly that there were some things which were bought so dear, you would never finish paying for them.

In her pocket she could feel the smooth glowing surfaces of the emeralds Love had put around her neck six months ago. The clasp had broken when she tossed them on the table in front of old man Bassarelli. It was all she had of worth with which to barter.

The man, gray eyes narrow, had inspected the stones, declared them beautiful and told her he didn't take bribes from women. Then he had thanked her for the information she'd given him, asked her if she was certain she wouldn't take a ride home. After all it wasn't pleasant weather, perhaps a glass of the house red—he recommended it himself—to warm her blood before going out into the night? It had all been formality, for she could see that he no longer saw her in front of him, his mind had already moved to the red-brick building in Brookline to the man she had promised would be waiting. He was impatient to get on with the task at hand. So she had excused herself and taken her leave.

So civilized and that, perhaps, had been the hardest part.

"Do you understand?" she whispered to the silent stone man above her.

Paul however, under his feathery cap of snow, wasn't talking. But she thought she knew what his answer would have been had he spoken. He was a ghost, but had been a man in life and she thought there were, as she'd told Father Kevin, things about the nature of sacrifice that men did not understand.

And this after all was not freedom, but love.

Part Two

A Little Irish Homestead

Chapter Eighteen

Scotsman's Lament

THE CRACKED POT WAS ONE of the few pubs in Belfast that British soldiers felt fairly safe drinking in, not completely safe, for no man who wore the Queen's uniform on Irish soil was that foolish. In the Cracked Pot, however, they could drink in relative peace in the overly warm, smoke-laden fug that wrapped itself around a man like a blanket of comfort.

Sandy McCrorey had been drinking there since the beginning of his tenure in Northern Ireland. Tonight, he'd come reluctantly, dragged along in the wake of friends. It had been a long day, though every day in Belfast seemed like a week. It was the tension; it spread time out like a hand pushing on a pile of sand. Just this morning they'd had some bastard take a snipe at them from the top of a bakery. The gunman hadn't hit them and though they'd returned fire, he'd disappeared into the warren of chimney pots and slated roofs that grew in tightly packed, mushroom-like clusters. And then there'd been the sweetly smiling young matron pushing an oddly silent baby in a pram. He hadn't even wanted to look. He knew the Provos had any number of tricks up their sleeves when it came to running weapons in and out of the neighborhoods.

Tonight he wanted nothing more than to be home, with the cobblestones of familiar streets beneath his feet and the lights of Inverness glowing about him. If he were home, he'd pick Fiona up around seven. She'd tuck her arm into his and look up at him with shy adoration shining from her eyes. She'd smell of lemon polish and beeswax as Wednesday was her day to clean the church. Maybe they'd go to the pictures, maybe they'd just walk until they were up in the hills surrounding the city and the stars seemed so close a man would almost believe he could grab a fistful and give them to his sweetheart. Barring these things, Sandy just wanted a drink, something strong and quick.

The pub was full, only a couple of tables unoccupied, and the odd nod greeted them as they sat at a table in the far back left, regulars who were there for the drink and not concerned with the politics of the man on the stool next to them.

Neil went up to the bar and came back moments later with two pints of black ale for himself and Donny, a nineteen year old redhead who looked all of twelve and had only been in Belfast a week. For Sandy he brought a whiskey.

"Here's something for the aches then, fast an' to the point like ye asked."

"Thanks, Neil," Sandy said, tipping his glass towards the boy with the thatch of blond curls, ruddy cheeks, and merry blue eyes. Neil was on his second month of duty in Belfast, and thus far his cheery disposition seemed unimpaired by the bleakness of the place.

Denny, the publican, gave a two finger wave from behind the bar. He was a nice fellow, a hard-working Protestant who kept his views to himself. Adorning the wall behind the bar was his collection of license plates from the United States. It was Denny's grand ambition to have all fifty states of the union represented on his wall. So far he had thirty-nine. Sandy, who had family in the US, had managed to procure a Maine plate for Denny, and had drunk free for a week afterwards as a result.

Sandy smiled and waved back, only to see the stout publican return the smile and have it freeze in place just as quickly. There was a breath of chill air behind Sandy that told him the door to the street had opened. His spine, from training and experience, went rigid. He turned slowly, so as not to seem obvious and glanced at the newcomers. Three men in work clothes, lads out for a pint after dinner, escaping the wife and kids for an hour or two. Two on the smallish side, one with a tweed cap pulled low over his eyes, another unbuttoning a navy pea coat, the third shaking droplets of rain from a chestnut thatch of hair. The third was taller and younger than the other two and good-looking in a feral sort of way. The sort that had luck with the ladies. Sandy knew it had something to do with the aura of danger such men projected, though he'd never really understood the appeal.

Though Denny was more friendly to some and less so to others, Sandy had never seen him less than cordial to a customer in his pub. But the normally cheerful publican had a stone face on him at present and his lips were held tight against his teeth as he served the three now lounging against the counter.

Sandy gave them a closer look, while appearing to peer down into the amber depths of his whiskey. They didn't appear so different from the regular clientele, Belfast toughs, though the youngest had an air about him. As if feeling Sandy's thoughts on him he raised his head, tilting it up as a cat would to scent the air. Even at a distance, his eyes stood out against his face as though lined in fine pen—pretty eyes, the lavender blue of forget-me-nots. The eyes met his own without warning and Sandy started from the impact and the embarrassment of having been caught staring. The man smiled, tipping his head in a friendly manner, except that Sandy felt even such a simple gesture held a wealth of unspoken threat.

He took a shaky breath and reapplied himself to his whiskey. Christ, this city made a man paranoid, where the simplest acknowledgement of one's presence caused such chilling thought. He'd once said to another soldier—a Glaswegian on his way home after a year in Northern Ireland—that the man must be glad to leave the place behind. The soldier had considered him for a moment, taking in, Sandy had suspected, his youth and inexperience.

"Ye'll know the saying about the beauty of things bein' in the backside an' not in the face, endearing more by their departure than their arrival. Well Belfast has got both an ugly arse an' face, an' I'd be a fool to think I'll not carry her with me the rest of my days," the Glaswegian had said, and then left Sandy to the untender mercies of youth, inexperience and a city with too much history.

A bit of corduroy jacket brushed past his shoulder then, and he realized to his chagrin that the only empty spot in the pub was the table directly behind the three of them.

"Evenin' to ye lads," said the young one as he passed, a flash of teeth and eyes and rain-wet hair.

"Evening," the three of them murmured politely, the mood at their table suddenly as damp as the streets outside.

The tables were bunched tightly, the Cracked Pot being a small establishment. Sandy could smell the wet wool and tobacco scent of the men's clothes as they sat, as well as a sharp whiff of some expensive aftershave.

"Yon laddies are a quiet bunch," Sandy heard a voice behind him say, and knew the man was referring to the three of them. A tendril of cigarette smoke, translucent blue, curled around his neck, making his eyes water and his throat itch. He sneezed, three times in quick succession. Behind him he heard the rustle of cloth as the man turned around.

"Smoke botherin' ye?"

"No, it's fine," Sandy said hastily, burying his face in his whiskey glass, the fumes making his eyes water once again.

The man rose and Sandy had to strain his neck to see his face. The Cracked Pot had been built in 1768 and its ceiling was of a height to accommodate the stature of the human species at the time. These, however, were different times and the man's thick thatch of chestnut hair brushed the low, smoke-blackened beams.

The man made to move past them, his pint in one hand, the half-smoked cigarette in the other.

"Got to piss," he said apologetically, flashing a mouthful of perfect, startlingly white teeth at the three of them. The space between tables was practically non-existent and the man seemed slightly unsteady on his feet. Odd, Sandy thought, he'd not seemed drunk when he and his companions had entered the pub. Likely this was not their first stop of the evening though. Therefore it wasn't surprising when the man slopped most of his remaining drink on Donny's shoulder while trying to negotiate the narrow space between chairs.

Donny jumped out of his chair with an audible curse, knocking into the man who stumbled back slightly, sending the drinks on the table behind him flying.

Two rather sturdy looking, red-faced men jumped up, obviously deep in their cups with fists at the ready. The man with the forget-me-not eyes smiled with distinct pleasure.

"Are yez lookin' for a fight, boys?" he asked in an amiable tone, then threw his empty pint glass to the floor. There wasn't even time to hear it smash when all hell, in the form of several drunken Irishmen, broke loose.

Sandy had the impression of several things happening all at once. Fists thunking solid against flesh, chairs being pushed back and then used as weapons, the air ripe with the smell of wet wool, spilled ale and smoke and filled with the triumphal roars of men in the joyous state of a full-fledged donnybrook. A glancing blow off the side of his head brought him stumbling to his feet.

The big man stood dead center of the room, eyes sparking with blue flame, flinging men off right and left as if they were no more than kittens. Which of course only caused more fools to charge him.

Sandy dodged several merrily flying fists, only to feel a chair leg make firm contact with the back of his head. The floor came up at an astonishingly fast rate towards his face. The next thing he knew someone had grabbed him by the shoulder and threw him towards the wall, wedging his head between table legs and wall.

It took a few minutes for constellations to quit wheeling in front of his eyes, and in those few minutes Sandy decided a Scotsman's pride could only take so much and then it was time to weigh in and damn the consequences. Besides, Irish or not, one man against twenty simply wasn't fair.

Two minutes later, caught in the midst of a heaving, grunting mass of wild, majorly pissed Irishmen, he wondered if he hadn't made a serious error in judgement. Pinned facedown on the pub floor, which was less than pristine, he could only sense rather than see the flailing limbs and hear the grunts and curses of men having a rollicking good time. He caught a flash of red hair out of the corner of one eye and knew Donny had joined the fray. He gave an almighty heave, managing to extract himself from under several thrashing bodies, only to catch a hob-nailed boot directly under his chin. The constellations came whirling back and the salty taste of blood filled his mouth. He crawled back to the scant protection of the wall, blinking through a haze of pain.

The blue-eyed man was still on his feet, apparently unfazed by the fists, feet and furniture coming at him full bore. He was a fighter by nature, that much was apparent. A man who'd known his size and face would bring him trouble all his days and so had learned the skills necessary to deal with such trouble. Barbarians, the Irish, his captain said, didn't understand the rules of civility, of where and when to make a stand. The man before him certainly fit the description, his entire being a lit fuse of raw, radiant savagery. And yet somehow his movements were deliberate, instinctual, each thrust and parry of other men's hands, legs and bodies effortless, graceful as a dance.

From mid-air, the man caught a bottle and tossed it away again. He might have used it to his advantage, but his strength had not yet begun to recede and he was in the throttle of the beast that coursed swiftly through his blood. He had no need as yet for helpful implements.

Sandy found his feet a moment later and got on top of them with only a slight wobble. The air was now so thick with blood, sweat, and liquor that it trundled into his lungs like a dozy creature. He squeezed as much of it as he could into him and then waded back into the battle.

The fight had become an entity unto itself with too many limbs, teeth, fists, and drink-addled brains. The blue-eyed man, still miraculously standing, was the central nervous system of the whole mass. When he moved they all did. When he ducked they accordingly rippled.

The whole lot of them surged as one body toward the back end of the pub. A narrow entrance hall fed down to a back door, passing a tiny washroom on the way. The doorway of the washroom flew open under the duress of straining, heaving bodies, giving all and sundry a view of an abundant bare backside liberally adorned with gray, curling hair. Sandy caught a glimpse of shaking, indignant flesh before sailing onward with the melee.

He caught up hard on the wall opposite the washroom, tossed like flotsam off a thundering wave. Down the wall he slid, looking dizzily upward, uncertain of where he'd ended, only to see a huge white face spinning out of the murk at him.

The bastard slammed into him with a force that rattled the teeth in his head. Sandy thought he could hear his skull crack. At first nothing moved and then the world spun in a dark circle, flipping his stomach over. His shoulders were jammed tight in a small alcove. It afforded some small sanctuary from the violence that had moved back into the main room of the pub. That didn't explain who'd hit him in the head with the force of a cannon though and now, judging from the weight resting on his head, was passed out on him.

Once big black petals of pain stopped blossoming behind his eyes, Sandy ventured moving his head and found, to his immense relief, that his neck was not broken, nor was his skull mashed to a pulp. He chanced a look sideways and found a familiar face. King Billy of Orange, done in white marble, tipped over in the fight and saved from smashing his lugubrious face on the floor by landing instead on Sandy's skull.

Sandy tried to move his right arm out to push the statue away only to meet with several hundred pounds of marble resistance. He was, for all intents and purposes, stuck fast and helpless. Just then he caught a glint of something sharp from the corner of his left eye. He turned his head slowly, the pain in his head still making him dizzy.

Directly in front of him, not more than a few inches from his throat, was the broken end of a bottle held firm in a dense meaty hand. Whiskey still dripped from its squared off edges, a whiff of it serving as smelling salts to his brain. He swallowed, feeling the surge of blood in his neck and how close the veins and arteries ran to the surface of the skin. He looked up the arm and into the eyes of his attacker.

The man was barrel-chested, a sheen of sweat gleaming on his ruddy face, brown eyes filmed by alcohol and bloodlust. Sandy knew men could kill with very little feeling in such a state. He also knew that he was younger, stronger, and quicker and that if he'd an inch of room to maneuver he could disarm the man swiftly. It was part of his training and by now as ingrained as the sound of his own name. But his elbows were pinned hard to his sides by the wall on one side and the statue on the other. His throat bobbed involuntarily, thick with panic. He was, he knew, about to be gutted like a fish.

The sound of his attacker's wrist snapping was as sharp and hard as the shriek that accompanied it. The man's face turned pale green and then he slid into a boneless faint, crumpling slowly onto the floor. Sandy half-choked on the acid flooding his mouth, his abrupt salvation surprising him.

"Grab yer pals," the blue-eyed man said, tipping the statue back into place by levering one broad shoulder under it, his words a terse command, "an' head out the back." Sandy obeyed what seemed the most sensible suggestion he'd heard all night. It was likely the police would be here soon, and then there'd be more explaining to do back on base than even a man of tender years had time for. He rounded up Donny and Neil, by grabbing the arm of one and yelling in the face of the other. They ran, each with unique bumps and bruises, to the back entrance over the inert forms of the first fallen, through a hedge of woolly chests, and a veritable steaming forest of gashed, cut, contused, broken and bloodied flesh.

Outside, the night was cold, their breath making long curling streams on the air.

"Car's this way," Sandy's defender said, emerging from the dark to their left and pointing to a Cortina that sat wedged between a garage and another car. He paused a moment to light a cigarette, the glowing tip throwing a red cast over his face. The effect was particularly demonic.

"What about your friends?" Sandy asked, noting the two other men were nowhere to be seen.

"Joe's got his own car; they'll follow where we lead." Seeing their hesitation he added, "I'll drive ye back to base, ye'll not want to be out an' about. Those haircuts are a dead giveaway an' word on the street is the Republicans are lookin' for someone to pay for Martin Diggin's death."

The car was blue; the front end slightly dented, but immaculately clean and polished. It seemed this Belfast working tough was a man who cared

about his vehicle.

Neil got in the front, Donny sat behind him, and Sandy slid in directly behind the Irishman, who gave himself a once-over in the rearview mirror before putting the keys in the ignition.

"What's yer names, boys?" their driver asked, raising one large hand to wipe some of the steam off the windshield, while giving a quick glance about at the soldiers who surrounded him.

"I'm Donny," the youngest spoke first, still high on adrenaline and ale.

'Donald, eh?" The man grinned as he shifted the car into drive, "As in 'I've just come down from the Isle of Skye, I'm no' very big an' I'm awf'ly shy.'"

The short Scot lurched forward, face flushed as red as his hair with temper.

"Ach, Donny, sit back," Neil said, then turned back to the dark-haired man. "If he'd a copper for ev'ry time someone sung that he'd be a rich lad would our Donny. It devils him somethin' fierce to hear it."

"An' what's yer name, laddie?" The man fixed his gaze in the rear view mirror, meeting Sandy's eyes directly. Sandy had remained silent to this point, trying to assess the extent of his injuries.

"Alexander," he said carefully, wary of giving out his name and yet not knowing how to withhold it without seeming rude. Alexander McCrorey had been raised to be polite to a fault. After all, the man had just saved him from a bloody end.

"Do they call ye Sandy then?"

"My friends do," Sandy replied in a polite tone that could not be mistaken for chumminess.

"And mine," the man said, with another of those quick, flashing grins into the mirror, "call me Robin, as in 'for bonny, sweet Robin is all my joy.' At least," he gave a wolfish grin, "that's what the lassies tell me. Now Neil if ye'd be so kind as to reach under the seat there, there's a bit of somethin' to keep the blood warm while we drive."

Neil emerged with a bottle that glinted darkly in the faint glow of the dashboard.

"Have a drink then pass it along Neil, it's guaranteed to cure all that ails ye."

Neil took a drink and began to cough immediately. "Holy Christ," he gasped, passing the bottle onto Robin, who took a long, smooth drink without so much as blinking.

"What the hell is that?" Neil asked, wiping his forearm across his eyes.

"Poteen, an old Irish recipe, me mam could drink it like 'twas honeyed milk," Robin said, swinging the car smoothly around and down a dark back lane. Behind them the lights of the other car swung swiftly around the corner as well.

"Tastes like bloody diesel fuel," Neil said, as Robin passed it into the back seat. Not wanting to appear unmanly Donny took a polite swallow, eyes bugging out as he did so. He shoved the bottle under Sandy's nose and Sandy smelled an aroma that cut his breath off at the top of his throat. Not being beyond the issues of male pride himself, though, he took a tentative sip and thought he might lose use of his taste buds permanently. Neil was right—it did taste like bloody diesel fuel. An uneasy feeling uncoiled in his stomach along with the poteen, which could have had everything to do with the inedible mess rations he'd had that evening, or nothing at all.

Twenty minutes and a few more swallows of whiskey later, and the feeling was considerably eased. The man named Robin chatted amiably as he drove through sleeping neighborhoods. He seemed nice enough, just another working-class swell from the streets of East Belfast. His dad, he said, was a member of the local Orange Lodge, marched in the parades and beat the drums, but himself, he didn't go in for that sort of thing. Live and let live was his motto.

"Would ye boys would be interested in a party?" Robin asked, lighting a new cigarette off the remains of the old one. "I've a friend lives out Ballymena way. The place'll be hoppin', plenty of girls, three to an arm if ye've the inclination."

"Ach, don't be tryin' to tempt Sandy with girls," Neil said, "he's got himself a sweetheart back home, he's devoted is our Sandy."

"Are ye then, Sandy? It's a lucky man who finds a good woman to love him." Drunk as he was Sandy didn't miss the slightly sneering undertone in the man's voice. He didn't let it bother him, the man had likely had a few bad experiences with women and now thought none were to be trusted. But he'd known Fiona all his life and had loved her for half that. He trusted her with his very existence.

Fog was beginning to settle into the streets, long floating tendrils of it, the lights coming fewer and far between as they reached the outer perimeters of the city.

Robin slowed the car slightly. "Look up there will ye, lads? It's quite the sight isn't it?"

The three soldiers obligingly looked up to the left where Robin's eyes were trained. Sandy had seen it before; one could hardly miss it, nor help but hear the legends that surrounded it and the man who lived within it. Kirkpatrick's Folly, lit like a brace of candles against the dark sky, on its lonely hill.

"I used to gaze at it when I was a boy, an' wonder what it was like to live in such a world," Robin said, a strange note in his voice, an emotion closely related to unquenched yearning, but somehow darker. He shifted the car down, reducing their speed to a near crawl. Sandy had the odd sense of drifting, like a ship lost at sea without anchor. As if the whole world were no more than liquid black sky, with nothing solid to gain purchase upon.

"Is he as handsome as they say?" Donny asked, neck cricked into an unnatural position in an effort to see the house more clearly.

"Aye," Robin laughed, a stream of smoke accompanying his words, "most bloody gorgeous bastard yer likely to see in yer lifetime."

"You've seen him then?" Neil asked, and Sandy wondered rather fuzzily when he'd started smoking.

"Aye, I've seen him," Robin said, but there was no laughter in his voice this time. Sandy shivered at the tone, even though he was having difficulty keeping his eyes open. He felt the car shift up to a higher gear, was blurrily aware of their speed picking up and the fairy lights of the Kirkpatrick house melting into a brilliant, stinging stream.

He'd one last twinging thought, as the night swallowed the lights of the house on the hill—that he was past the point in his consumption of alcohol where a man was capable of making decent judgements.

Within a minute he was fast asleep.

INSIDE THE PUB, Denny cracked one last skull for good measure then surveyed the wreckage in front of him. Broken glass, cracked table legs, blood and ale mixed in gruesome pools, and plenty of groaning and moaning amidst the carnage.

"Billy," he said sharply to his son.

Billy looked up from where he was neatly piling glass in a dustpan.

"Where'd the three young soldiers go?"

"They left with the punter that started this damn mess."

"What? When?"

"Don't know," Billy replied, "maybe twenty minutes ago, not much more."

"Oh Jaysus," his father said, bat sliding to the floor, "I should ha' known."

Billy cocked a sandy eyebrow. "Known what Da?"

"The whole thing," he gestured helplessly at the mess that surrounded him, "'twas done on purpose."

Billy looked at his father quizzically. "Don't worry Da we'll find the bastard an' make him pay for the damage."

Denny shook his head. "Send the bill to the local Sinn Fein office then, I hear that's where the IRA is pickin' up their mail these days."

"Ye think he was IRA?" Billy asked, the full ramifications of the situation suddenly dawning on him.

"Aye, an' those poor lads went with him. May God have mercy on their souls."

SANDY WOKE TO THE DARKEST night he'd ever known, bladder uncomfortably full, mouth feeling as though it was filled with damp cotton and the smell of cigarette smoke strong in his nostrils. It took a moment or two to clear the fog in his head, to realize where he was and how he'd gotten there.

Ahead of him, the tip of a cigarette glowed hot red, like a coal in a cave. The car was going slowly through a series of large potholes.

Where the hell were they? The thought was accompanied by a surge of nausea and he had to swallow back a hot stream of bile that bit at the back of his throat. Behind them the headlights of the other men had disappeared.

"Where are we?" he asked, the words emerging in a dry croak. Beside him Donny's head lolled against the seat, his red hair visible even in the dark.

"Shortcut to Ballymena," their driver replied, swerving abruptly to avoid something in the roadway. He must have the eyes of a cat on him to see anything in this light, Sandy thought, putting a hand out to steady himself against the swaying car.

"Pull over would ye, man?" Neil said from his position in the front passenger seat, "I've got to piss somethin' terrible."

"Are ye certain ye can't wait? My friend's place is just up head of the lane here." Robin said, casting a quick smile across one broad shoulder at the inebriated Scot directly to his left.

"No, I can't wait." Neil grunted slightly to emphasize his point.

"All right then, if ye say so." Robin stopped the car and as the engine died, the uneasy coil slipped its knot in Sandy's belly once again, for the night seemed terribly quiet. Still he'd a cramp in his bladder that was only going to depart along with the water and whiskey he'd consumed. Donny slid across the seat and out the door, catching his boot on the frame and lurching forward into a ditch.

Sandy's first impression was that it was considerably colder outside than had been the cramped quarters in the car's back seat. His second was that it was black as the devil's thoughts out here away from the city lights. Dark and silent. A shiver pressed itself like a spasm of quicksilver up his spine, and spread frost-like out along the sheathes covering his nerves. The primal brain telling the conscious mind what it should have known all along. That something was very, very wrong with this situation.

It was then that he saw the other two men; the two he'd thought had given up following and gone home. The men who stood now, in the dark, mere shadows, rifles slung taut over shoulders, leveled at waist height, fingers blunt on the triggers.

Robin had gotten out of the car. Sandy could see the flash of his teeth in the dark and hear Neil's zipper grate as he fumbled it down. The taste of fear, hot and bitter as scorched iron, flooded his mouth. The three of them were unarmed, their senses dulled by drink. He thought he might be sick and then swallowed the nausea. He didn't want to be found covered in his own vomit. His parents deserved better and so did Fiona.

He gave his last thoughts to her, even as he heard the slick hiss of a pistol emerging from cloth. He hoped she'd find a good man to marry, someone solid in a low-risk profession, not, please God, another soldier. Then he remembered the way the hair at the nape of her neck was like duck down and smelled softly of the scent she wore.

The first report from the pistol was muffled and Sandy felt the air beside him crumple as Neil fell first to his knees, then face forward into the brittle heather that covered the ditch. He'd given Fiona an armful of the summer's first heather only last July, how many months ago was that?

Donny was screaming now. Poor kid, he was only eighteen. Just a baby. They shouldn't let babies into the army—they didn't understand the risk. Then just as suddenly Donny stopped, mid-scream, his last words on earth ones of piteous terror. That left only himself. Sandy swallowed hard and straightened his back.

The barrel of the pistol slid cold into the soft and fragile hollow where the spine, with its ropes of blood and spiralled strings of vessels, exploded into ten thousand million nerve cells. But Alexander didn't scream, nor beg for mercy. There would be none to witness it, but for his own sake he would die as a soldier, asking no quarter, knowing there would be none granted.

He waited for the click of the trigger, wondering if he'd hear it, or if the bullet would do its work first. And then realized somewhere through the terror which had jumbled his senses that the man behind him was singing. The song came to him slowly, confused as he was by the odd turn of events.

> *'The breeze of the bens*
> *Is gently blowing,*
> *The brooks in the glens*
> *Are softly flowing;*
> *Where boughs*
> *Their darkest shades are throwing,*
> *Birds mourn for thee*
> *Who ne'er returnest.'*

"Come Sandy, do ye not know the songs of yer homeland? Sing the chorus with me man, for sure ye know it."

The man's compatriots had seemingly melted back into the night, for he knew without being able to look that they were alone and that the cat had, for some unaccountable reason, decided to play with the mouse. Sandy knew he was not dealing with an ordinary madman, but one who enjoyed the kill for its own sake and not just the political statement.

"I said sing with me. Sandy. Ye know we can make this hard or we can make it quick. It's yer own choice. Die standin' with yer dignity intact, or die beggin' for mercy in a pool of yer own blood. I'm inclined to the former as

I've other places to be, but if ye'd prefer it the other way I'll spare the time."

If Sandy had no one to consider but himself he thought he would have taken the second option just to inconvenience the bastard, but for the sake of his mum and dad and Fiona he'd take the quick death. He didn't want them to carry the double burden of knowing his death had been long, drawn-out, and painful. And so he sang.

> *'No more, no more,*
> *No more returning,*
> *In peace nor in war*
> *Is he returning;*
> *Till dawns the great Day*
> *Of Doom and burning,*
> *MacCrimmon is home*
> *No more returning.'*

> *Its dirges of woe*
> *The sea is sighing,*
> *The boat under sail*
> *Unmoved is lying;*
> *The voice of the waves*
> *In sadness dying,*
> *Say, thou are away*
> *And ne'er returnest.*

"One more time Sandy for the chorus, ye've a decent voice for the music. If ye'd been born on Irish soil we might have made somethin' of ye."

Sandy swallowed hard over the bile in his throat, willing it to keep working, willing himself to keep standing.

Above him the night was bitter and black with not a star to be found. Inside his boots his feet were aching with cold, toes already numb. Cold toes were an odd thing to worry about, he thought, when he knew he'd be dead within seconds.

> *'We'll see no more*
> *MacCrimmon's returning,*
> *Nor in peace nor in war*
> *Is he returning;*
> *Till dawns the great day*
> *Of woe and burning-,'*

Alexander McCrorey, a lieutenant in Her Majesty's Royal Highland Fusiliers, did not hear the shot, nor did he hear Robin Temple, voice arcing sweet and aching into the night, finish the song they had sung together.

'For him, for him
There's no returning.'

Turning back toward the road the man with the forget-me-not eyes crossed himself and walked away from the still warm bodies of the three young Scots behind him. He did not look back.

Chapter Nineteen

Home Again, Home Again

THE WEST BELFAST YOUTH CENTER, which admittedly only existed in a theoretical sense, stood on the fringes of the Beechmount Housing Estates. In previous incarnations the building had housed a cobbler shop, a grocery and, most recently, a storage facility for repossessed furniture and electronics. It was rundown, bought for a song, and needed more repair work than the Coliseum. It did, however, possess the benefits of a wee apartment above stairs and was, for the foreseeable future, the place Pamela and Casey called home.

Casey was, at present, cursing volubly at the doorframe leading into the tiny kitchen, having just hit his head on it for the second time that morning.

"Jaysus Murphy, did a midget build this damn place? Last night I got tangled up in my damp shirts." He fixed his wife with an affronted glare. "Anyway woman what possessed ye to hang them over the stove?"

"There isn't anywhere else to hang them," she said, kissing his bare shoulder as he squeezed past her to the table, where eggs, sausage, and toast were awaiting his attention.

Pamela waited for the tea to finish steeping before joining him. Under the tiny table their knees bumped. Casey sighed. "It's like bein' friggin' Gulliver in the land of the Lilliputians. I don't know how much longer I can manage this. I'm bruised from head to toe."

The table, where they sat eating their breakfast, was flush to the wall and next to the only window that graced the north side of the flat. It was a small window, likely the original from when the building was constructed. Despite its squatness, and a peculiar wavy quality to the glass, it provided an unobstructed view of Kirkpatrick's Folly, the ancestral home of James Kirkpatrick, so named for its hodgepodge of architecture. A Georgian front and Victorian rear, not to mention the Edwardian study; it was the result of a marital dispute several generations previous, over design. Casey had merely given the view a gimlet eye. Pamela took this as her cue to leave the topic of Jamie alone, though she found herself stealing surreptitious glances out the window several times a day.

The morning was particularly clear and she could see the western corner of the house, where Jamie's study sat. From this vantage point she could only see the spire that adorned its roof, but could picture the entirety of it plainly in her mind. Built completely of glass and wrought iron, in the fresh morning light it would sparkle like a trapped star.

She poured out Casey's tea, and pushed the cream jug toward him. "Drink your tea man, it'll restore your spirits."

"Will it then? I don't think there's room for them in here."

Despite damp spirits, Casey set to his breakfast with a hearty appetite. He'd found a temporary job on a construction site and was working long hours.

She munched absently on her toast, watching the morning sun gild the topmost chimney of Jamie's house a soft gold. The grounds would be fully awakened from their winter sleep now, and everything would have that shimmery green mist of spring about it.

"Are we goin' to talk about it then, or are we goin' to pretend the man doesn't exist?" Casey asked suddenly, breaking in on her reverie.

"What?" she asked, startled into slopping her tea onto her plate.

He gave her a pointed look from under dark brows.

"I'm not blind, an' there's only the one house on that hill."

"Sorry," she said ruefully, "it's only I feel awkward not having gone to see him yet."

"Ye needn't worry on that score," Casey said, helping himself to more eggs. "He's only just come back the three days ago. Pat said he was going up to see him night before last."

"Oh...well then perhaps I ought to wait."

"For what?" Casey asked practically. "Ye're the nearest thing to family the man has. I think he'd be insulted if ye stood on ceremony. It'd be rude not to go an' see him, Jewel. I understand that. I might not particularly like it, but I understand it. He must know we're here by now, he and Pat are pretty tight these days. Why don't ye do it today, ye've no other plans do ye?"

"Not as such." She looked around the flat, which she'd planned to tidy into some semblance of order. If escape was being offered she was more than happy to take it.

"Then go."

She eyed him as he stood and retrieved a shirt from the clean stack near the radiator. He neatly avoided her gaze though, shrugging into his shirt and buttoning it up. Jamie wasn't quite the point of tension he'd been early in their marriage, but the mention of him could still make the air vibrate with the words that weren't being spoken.

She stood and skirted the table to where he stood. Sliding her hands down the front of his shirt, she savored the smell of his freshly bathed skin.

"Does it bother you that Pat and he have become good friends?"

"Mmmhpmm. Well, I'd be a liar if I said no—but he's kept an eye out for the wee bugger these last years, an' I appreciate that."

"You're going to have to accept the fact that Pat's a grown man, entitled to get into trouble if he wants to."

"Aye well, even when he's gray as a goose he'll still be my little brother. He's our daddy's stubbornness. Has to right wrongs whenever he sees them."

"Oh, and you wouldn't have any experience with that yourself?"

Casey made a derisive noise deep in this throat as he tucked his shirt into his jeans and reached for his coat. He took a last long slug of tea from the cracked mug he favored, and then bent over to kiss her.

"I'll be back late tonight. I promised Pat I'd go to the meeting with him—so I can get a better idea of the plans for the drop-in center."

In exchange for the use of the tiny flat, Casey had agreed to run the drop-in center on a temporary basis. Or it might be more accurately stated that Pat coerced him into it, after plying him with several glasses of Connemara Mist the third night they'd been back in Belfast.

"I think Jamie gave him a case for purposes of bribery," Casey had said the next day as they stood contemplating the low-ceilinged, dingy bargain he'd struck. "He provided the lion's share of funding for this venture, though my brother's not so much said so; but Pat seems to have his way with most of the decisions an' only Jamie would give him that much leeway."

Despite his initial misgivings, Casey had begun to show signs of enthusiasm for the project as Pat laid out his plans for eventually reviving this entire portion of the city.

"Well he's maybe a wee bit optimistic, but the lad has a dream an' he's chasin' it, can't fault him there. It's nice to feel I might be doin' somethin' that makes a bit of difference to someone else. An' I'll not come home reeking of fish." He sniffed his hands, wrinkling his nose up, convinced that he still hadn't rid himself of the smell of the cod he'd pulled, filleted and gutted over the last eleven months.

After Casey left, Pamela loitered about a little in her robe, drinking another two cups of tea and contemplating the Belfast horizon. Kirkpatrick's Folly had been her home when she'd first come to Belfast and the man who lived in it the only friend she'd possessed in the world at the time. He'd also been her first love, unattainable as gold at the end of the rainbow but nevertheless the man to whom she'd first lost her heart. The man she'd gone away with, ostensibly as friends, the first summer she'd known Casey. The man to which Casey thought he'd lost her. Much had changed since then, for all of them. Her correspondence with Jamie over the last two years in Boston had been sporadic at best.

Jamie's life, what the papers and magazines didn't splash about, was very private. And very complicated. Though there were precious few who knew the truth of just *how* complicated. She was one, and even she had no idea what he was up to at present, nor how far into the fire he had his irons. Politically or personally.

Being back in Belfast provided more than one complication in her life. More than anything that fear was centered around Casey—despite his intentions to the contrary—getting sucked back into the vortex of the Provisional IRA.

The Provos had become *the* IRA since the split within the ranks of the Official Army in late '69. The Belfast Republicans had long felt disenfranchised from the 'lads in the South'. When Catholic Belfast burned during the riots in August of '69 and the South neglected to send help of any kind, it only confirmed what the Northerners had always suspected—they were on their own. During a December meeting in Dublin the Army voted to recognize the two Irish governments and Westminster. To many this was a slap in the face to the core of Republicanism which had never recognized the separation of Ireland into Republic and Ulster. By the time of the Ard Fheis on January 10, 1970, the writing was on the wall. When the vote to drop abstentionism was passed, 257 delegates walked out and met at a pre-hired hall and thus the Provisional Army was born. A split Casey had predicted and prepared for during their last months in Ulster, before their home had burned to the ground and he had, for a night, believed her dead.

The realization that GHQ had no arms, no real plan, and had—in the view of many Republicans—abandoned the principals of the 1916 Rising, had caused the movement in the north to turn to the physical-force men. The ones who had fought in the forties and fifties. The men that Brian Riordan had come of age with, fought with, and been interned with. Men who had inherited the legacy of such luminaries as Michael Collins, Padraig Pearse, James Connolly and Casey's own grandfather, Brendan Riordan. Men like Casey himself who were neither philosophers nor socialists, but men of action. Men who often died well before old age could lay claim to them.

Pamela touched the St. Jude's medal she'd worn around her neck from the time she was twelve years old. The words were worn smooth from handling but she knew them by heart. *Ora pro nobis.* Pray for us. St. Jude, the patron saint of lost causes. A saint she hoped she would not have to offer up many prayers to on behalf of her husband, now that they were back in this hard little corner of the world.

"Watch over him, deliver him from danger," she said, fingers moving slowly over the medallion in a rhythmic pattern. She closed her eyes, willing the cold fear in her belly to go away. "And may thy grace be with him always. Amen," she finished softly and turned away from the window.

Chapter Twenty
Kirkpatrick's Folly

PAMELA PARKED PAT'S CAR down by the cypress gate. The same gate where Casey had waited for her during their courtship. Above her head two golden cypresses swayed and murmured in the spring wind. Between the trees was the ancient gate, weathered smooth and silver-gray through many seasons. She put her hand to the latch, and with that small action came a rush of memory of long, quiet evenings, and conversations that went into the wee hours. Talk of ships and shoes and sealing wax, and cabbages and kings.

Beyond the cypresses was the oak wood, heavily under-storied with dark green holly bushes. In Ireland the old folk called holly the 'gentle tree' and it had long been believed to be a favorite of the fairies. In the stories her father had told her when she was small, hollies were always the trees that covered the roads to the Fairy country, guarding that world from this. That it grew so heavily along the boundaries of the Kirkpatrick land seemed appropriate, for she always felt a sense of stepping out of time while she was here.

Further up the path the house rose out of the surrounding woods, amber and misted from its gardens and gates, the sound of the sea a lullaby in the distance. The front of the house was built along dignified lines. Georgian, long-windowed, a widow who remembered the beauty of her youth with a quiet satisfaction. The back half of the house, however, was pure Victorian fancy. Small half-moon portholes, round towers, fanciful cupolas and an air of whimsy spoke of barefoot, moonlit meanderings in dewy gardens, boating down gently currented rivers, and bowtie and straw boater picnics.

The air was smoky with the scent of freshly turned earth, the roses shimmering a pale green with new growth. By June there would be a cascade of pink, white and red all the way up to the house, climbing on long limbs around the glass walls of the study and winding their way up the amber stones.

Pamela paused for a moment to collect herself. She hadn't seen Jamie for two years, and now her stomach was knotted with nerves. She took the path

which led around to the back of the house and the service entrance into the kitchen. Fragrant heaps of pine needles, the last of winter's detritus, lay in along the pathway, releasing a sharp tang as her shoes pressed down on them.

It was quiet in the watery light, a certain lack of animation in the very air telling her Jamie was not home. Pamela tried to squelch the disappointment that flooded her at the knowledge of his absence.

She rang the bell at the service entrance and after a few minutes of suspenseful silence heard the huffling tread of Maggie.

"Well it's past time ye showed up—" the housekeeper began indignantly and then stopped, vinegared words falling away from the round 'O' of her mouth.

Then Maggie smiled and opened the warm expanse of her amply fleshed arms. "Well if it isn't Herself then, come home."

Pamela sank into her embrace gratefully, smelling the comfort of flour and cinnamon and butter. "Scones?" she asked, lighter of heart than she had been only seconds before. This coupled with an odd sensation that she had indeed, come home.

"Himself's not here," Maggie said releasing Pamela and then dabbing her face with a damp teacloth.

"I didn't think so. Is he gone for long?" she asked, trying to keep her voice casual, as if Jamie's whereabouts were of little concern to her.

Maggie raised an eyebrow at her. "No, he ran up the coast this morning but he'll be back this afternoon. Bishop's comin' round for dinner tonight. I thought you were the butcher, I expect I'll have to call down an' see what's happened to the poor sheep that's to be the man's dinner tonight. That delivery boy they've hired is far too fond of takin' the drink despite the time of day. Come an' sit, I'll make ye a cup of tea an' a bite."

"Don't go to any trouble, I only came to say hello and let Jamie know we were back."

Maggie raised the other eyebrow. "An' ye think he's not aware that yer home. Ye know the man better, no?"

"Yes, I suppose I do."

"Now sit ye down. When the day comes that a cup of tea an' a liddle biscuit is any trouble I'll no longer be fit to work in this kitchen. Besides ye look as though ye could use some feedin', ye're barely more than bones with the skin stretched tight."

Pamela sat down gratefully, the scents and warmth of Maggie's kitchen wrapping about her like an echo of their mistress's embrace.

Only moments later, Maggie set a cup of tea before her and a plate of sugar-dusted scones. Beside these she placed a tray of milk and sugar, clotted cream and strawberry preserves. Two scones, and well into her third cup of tea, Pamela felt the knot in her chest loosen a little and a sense of well-being descend that she hadn't experienced in a very long time.

"So have ye come on holiday then?" Maggie asked, peeling carrots into the sink, while keeping half an eye on the clock and muttering distinctly uncomplimentary things about the butcher's boy under her breath.

Pamela felt her ephemeral sense of well-being begin to slide like sand out of an hourglass. "No," she answered quietly, "we're not visiting. We've come back to stay."

Maggie didn't so much as hesitate in her carrot peeling. "Have ye now?"

"Aye, we have," Pamela said dispiritedly.

"An' how is the boy?" Maggie asked, as if Pamela's news was of no surprise to her. Which it likely wasn't, considering just who was master of this house.

"He's fine. He's already found a job on a building site."

"Fine, hmm?" Maggie asked, managing to convey a world of disapproval in one syllable. "Didn't find Boston to his likin', did he?"

"No, not entirely."

"An' yerself?"

"I liked it fine," she replied softly.

"I thought ye might have," Maggie said, throwing a sprinkling of salt into a steaming pot on the stove.

"How is Jamie?"

Maggie gave her a sharp look over one plump shoulder. It was a loaded question at best. At worst, there were likely to be answers she didn't want to hear.

"There's a woman been hangin' about—seems a mite more determined to stay than he is to have her, but I think she's startin' to wear the laddie down a bit."

"You sound as though you disapprove."

"Well the boy needs his female company. 'Tisn't natural to live as he has though Lord knows he's no monk—" Maggie stopped short, realizing perhaps she was saying more than was entirely appropriate. "But this one has designs on him. Wants to be the lady of this house she does."

"Perhaps," Pamela said gently, "that would be no bad thing. It's to be expected that he should marry again at some point."

Maggie shook her head. "Aye agreed, but not this one." She eyed Pamela shrewdly, who in turn fastened her gaze on the china pattern, though a flush crept up from her neckline. "Time was I thought it'd be yerself that the man took to wife. He'd no notion of divorce until ye came along."

Pamela shook her head. "Jamie and I have never had our timing down. I'm not right for him."

"Well once yer fine Casey started hangin' about the back door I knew ye were done for. Took Jamie a little longer to see it, though."

"Casey's charms are a little less obvious when you're not female," Pamela said with a grin.

Maggie returned the grin with interest. "Aye that's likely so. The charms aren't lost on the women at all, at all though. De'il's tongue in that head. Never felt as compelled to feed a man as I did with that one."

"Be glad that's all you were compelled to do," Pamela said, with a solemn wink.

Maggie laughed. "I'd likely be more than even that laddie was willin' to take on."

She sighed then and heaved her bulk away from the sink. "Well that sheep is not goin' to deliver itself, though the wee butcher's boy goin' to wish it damn well had once I get hold of his ear."

"You go on then, I'll clear up the tea things."

Maggie cast a grateful eye at her before walking stiffly to where her coat had hung everyday for the last thirty years, on a simple hook beside the kitchen door. Pamela watched, feeling a pang in her chest. Maggie's arthritis had advanced quickly since Pamela had last seen her. Through Jamie's letters Pamela knew he had tried to hire extra help to remove the bulk of the physical work from Maggie's shoulders, and had been roundly chastised, in words, he'd said, that would have made an ironmonger blush for shame. The day that Maggie couldn't rule over the Kirkpatrick household with an iron fist and razor tongue would be a tragic day indeed.

A few minutes later she'd seen Maggie off, feeling a deep sympathy for the butcher's boy. If the lad had sense he'd take to his heels the minute he saw Maggie's broad form darken the shop door.

Jamie still hadn't returned when the tea things were done so she wandered idly about the main floor of the house, reacquainting herself with its quirks and beauties. The checkerboard pattern of the main hall, done on the diagonal in black and white marble, had always made her feel as if she ought to pull out a pocketwatch and start running, all the while muttering *'Oh dear! Oh dear! I shall be too late...'*

She paused at the bottom of the stairs, laying a hand on the purple heartwood banister. Up the spiralling stairs were the bedrooms—all twelve of them. Fitted out with the finest of furniture and linens, all fit for royalty, which in a sense the Kirkpatricks had once been in these parts. The master suite, twice as large and opulent as the rest, was where the current prince of this castle laid his head when he was in town.

Gilt-framed portraits lined the wall to the reaches of the upper floor. Portraits that had survived the fire, the oldest of these being one Silken James. Who, it was rumored, had once enjoyed the favor of Queen Elizabeth I.

He looked alarmingly like the present Lord Kirkpatrick; the thick silky gold hair, the sharp green eyes that brimmed with suppressed amusement, and the air, even in this old picture, of a glittering febrile tension that infected all those around.

Along the shining expanse of hall were several doors leading off to formal sitting rooms, a small ballroom, and an expansive oak-panelled library which housed a collection that had been passed down through eight generations. All the books had survived the fire in the original house, as the library had been under repairs at the time with its contents stored elsewhere.

Her favorite room lay at the far end of the hall, though, where a narrow corridor branched off. Here the floor turned to stone flagging, and a heavy wooden door guarded the entrance to the study. It was a rare visitor who ever crossed this particular threshold, but Jamie had never barred its door to her. The door creaked slightly as she pushed against it, the smell of peat ash and sandalwood filling her senses as the portal to this particular cave of wonders opened.

Soft spring light filtered through the newly budded rose canes that twined about the glass walls, bathing the room with a pale green tint. Small treasures lay cast about, as though they'd been brought in by the tide and deposited on the shore of carpet.

An ancient chest, stained with saltwater and piled high with crumbling leatherbound books, stood squat and disheveled at the ends of the two large rump-sprung sofas. A cashmere blanket, the color of rubies, was tossed over the back of one sofa, a pile of sapphire and emerald cushions heaped within the cozy depths. A troop of squash-faced fairies, made from what looked like petrified toadstools, capered across the mantelpiece of the huge stone fireplace. A Victorian black silk top hat lay on its side on a whatnot table, a long pipe with a curly cherrywood stem peeking out from beside it. A teapot, cracked and covered with a jumble of nursery rhyme characters, was filled to overflowing with chestnuts.

All these things were caught within the reflection of an old crystal ball, its surface clouded with age, giving the impression that the whole room was slightly off-kilter and filled with fog. Jamie claimed the thing gave him the heebie-jeebies, but as it was a gift from his godmother—who was a Russian Gypsy—he was more afraid to cast it out than to live with any possible evil eye.

Of all the rooms in the house, it was the one Pamela thought of as being the most essentially his: the room where he collected his thoughts or let them unwind, the room where he allowed himself the occasional luxury of emotion. It was the room he felt most intimately toward. It was here he'd told her he loved her, one miserable spring day. Here that he had held her for hours the night after she'd been raped. Here that she'd left the letter that told him goodbye, when she could not find the courage to tell him herself.

On his desk lay a hodgepodge of things. Even here there was no reading his mind or character in an easy fashion. The articulated skeleton of a puffin, a small pile of seeds, a wilted flower that looked as though it might have had a previous incarnation as a dusty blue forget-me-not. Two stacks of books, bindings worn and well loved, their titles ranging from Wilkie Collins' *The Woman in White* to a heavy tome on astrophysics. Papers, a jumble of pens, a tidy stack of correspondence and a pile of disregarded invitations, still sealed in their thick, creamy envelopes.

She wandered idly around the room, eyes following the titles on the shelves waiting for something to catch her fancy. She passed by first editions of Ruskin and Dickens, Carroll and Trollope, until her eye lit upon a battered red bound book with a tattered golden ribbon hanging out. It was a nature journal Jamie's grandfather had kept and that Jamie's father and Jamie himself had added to over the years. She carefully turned to the flyleaf, the smell of dust and green things long dead catching in her throat. There was an inscription in faded ink—*For my darling James, endless summer skies—Yours, Abigail.*

She took the book with her to the smaller of the two sofas and sank down into the garnet and paisley depths with a weary sigh. She turned the pages of the fragile book slowly, careful not to disturb the bit of thistle enclosed beside the delicate sketches of catkins and shrews, the faded violets cheek-by-jowl with watercolor periwinkles and blue-speckled thrush eggs. She read in random snatches, the words soothing her like a warm bath.

Glorious day. Went for a stroll along the hedgerows this morning and was rewarded with a find of sweet violets... Went to Murlough Bay where the woods run clear down to the shore and gathered an armful of wild hyacinth, pale butter yellow primroses, red campion, and ferns. Visited the oakwood this evening, where the rhododendrons are in full misty purple bloom, I gathered some...

As she read, the sun moved slowly across the glass walls, dancing through the ivy and newly leafed roses. The sun soon made her drowsy, the heat penetrating down to her bones. She drifted off to sleep reading about some *wonderfully fine specimens with hairy blue-green leaves...*, the crumbling petals of a rose held gently in her hand.

JAMES STUART KIRKPATRICK, Lord of Ballywick and Tragheda, had been home for three days and in that time had been to five meetings, made roughly fifty decisions, had fourteen children over for dinner the previous evening, had played an impromptu game of rugby on the back lawn with said children and had the bruises to prove it. The children were part of the outreach program in his constituency and the dinner at his house had become a monthly event. It was also an informal venue for their parents to voice concerns and opinions over education, housing, and safety issues in their community. At first he had wondered what he'd let himself in for with anywhere from eight to twenty ragamuffins running amuck in his house, but had soon come to look forward to the visits.

He'd also had his hair trimmed, mulched the roses around the study—a job he always tended to himself—and been properly seduced by his neighbor. Who just happened to be his girlfriend.

Tonight he was having the Bishop of Armagh to dinner, which should complete his list of immediate commitments. Tomorrow, Pat Riordan was due to come by to finalize decisions around the planned youth center. No doubt the man was going to ask if he could install his brother as the chief, cook, and bottle washer of that establishment. Which Jamie had no qualms about. There weren't many men who'd a better grasp of the lay of the land in that neighborhood, nor many as capable of keeping a stern hand on the tiller. Whether Casey would be able to swallow his pay coming from Jamie's pocket was another matter altogether.

While making tea he found a note from Maggie pinned to the corkboard and spared an inward wince for the hapless butcher's boy. He furrowed his brow at the last line of her note, '...*someone waiting in the study for you.*' He sighed. In his experience surprises were often nasty little occurrences that made one long for unbroken mundanity. Maggie herself was nowhere to be found, but she had been in the kitchen recently, for the kettle was still warm. She had taken, of late, to naps in the afternoon, an act she would not admit to and he pretended to ignore.

He pondered a variety of possibilities as he put tea things on a tray. Had Monty sired pups upon some innocent female of the canine variety and an irate neighbor had come to demand financial remuneration? Perhaps Belinda lay in wait? He grinned. Last night she'd shown up wearing a raincoat with nothing but bare skin beneath it. He was sure she had a charity committee meeting this afternoon however. Such was the fate of rich widows on spring afternoons.

It couldn't be the Bishop, as there was no way on God's green earth Maggie would have left him alone. Jamie glanced at his wristwatch. No, he'd three hours grace still before the Bishop was due.

He picked up his tray and headed for the study.

At first he could see nothing out of the ordinary. The sun had moved behind the oaks leaving the study dim and he could only make out the softened outlines of objects. Peering through the gloom he saw, hanging off the edge of his sofa, one narrow, delicately arched foot.

He caught his breath and just managed to miss dropping the tea tray. He crossed the floor and set the tray on his desk then turned and found his surprise—the lost girl come home.

She was fast asleep, skeins of hair tangled in her lashes, cheeks flushed like late summer peonies. A blanket was draped over her, bunched in rich folds around her shoulders. Jamie took a deep breath and allowed himself a moment, only that, to quench a thirst that had plagued him for two years now.

The skin around her eyes was bruised with exhaustion, her hands fisted beneath her chin, as if even in sleep she felt the need for defense.

"Oh, dear girl," he said softly, "what have you come running from this time?"

She stirred slightly at his words, quietly spoken as they were and he drew back, not quite ready to relinquish his minute. She looked terribly young in the half-light—still a girl, though he knew full well she'd passed her twenty-second birthday only days ago and that the circumstances of her life had forced her to leave girlhood behind many years ago.

With a light hand he smoothed the hair back from her face and watched as a small smile creased the corner of her mouth at his touch. Her eyes fluttered once, twice and then opened slowly, confusion blinkering her initial moment.

"Jamie?" she asked, as if his name came naturally, even in semi-consciousness.

"Here and accounted for," he replied, his hand now relaxed at his side.

Green eyes looked up and met their like and his moment was gone like a bubble burst upon a thorn. There had always been too much truth in her eyes for either comfort or illusion.

"I'm sorry." She sat up slowly. "I was waiting for you and I fell asleep reading." She gauged the light and alarm crossed her face.

"What time is it?"

"Three o'clock. Time for afternoon tea."

"Oh," she rubbed her face with her hands, "good."

Jamie turned on a lamp and she looked at him fully then.

"Still annoyingly beautiful I see," she said, with a touch of her old impertinence.

"Likewise," Jamie said and they smiled at each other, the moment's awkwardness dissipating as though she had left this room only yesterday. Which Jamie supposed, if one counted the ghosts of memory, she had.

"To what do I owe the pleasure?" Jamie asked, now leaning against his desk, hand moving lightly amongst the objects on it.

She shook her head. "We've moved back, though it's likely you know that already. I understand Pat sees a lot of you."

"Yes, he did mention it."

"I thought it was time to come and say hello." She curled her toes into the plush rug beneath her feet.

"Hello then," he replied softly. There was a vast no man's land of unspoken thought between them, even in the simplest of words. Things that neither could say for numerous reasons, feelings both suppressed and denied.

"Hello," she said, the tension once again thick in the air. She'd left this house without a proper goodbye. "I'm sorry for barging in this way, but I...I..."

"Don't be a fool, Pamela, my home is always open to you. You ought to know that by now."

"Are you angry with me?" she asked.

"When you left I could have sworn I'd never see you in this city again," Jamie said quietly, "and now I must admit to wondering why you've come back?"

Her voice, when she answered, was little more than a whisper, her shoulders bowed as if the question alone were a terrible weight upon her. "I really didn't have a choice Jamie. Living away from this godforsaken country was killing Casey. It was like he hadn't drawn a proper breath since we'd left. I only hope I'm not killing him by bringing him back."

"And what if you are?" Jamie asked, shocked by the honesty that seemed to present itself to her when it wouldn't for anyone else.

"Tell me Jamie, is a short life with meaning better than a long life with none?"

"Has it come to that so soon?" he asked.

"It's like an illness for him. When he's here he's whole, when he's not..." she shrugged, "he isn't."

"What about you?" he asked.

"I'm not whole without him. I go where he goes, it's that simple, Jamie. Not very progressive of me I know, but it makes my decisions easy. I just pray he can avoid any trouble."

Easy was, he knew, the last thing her decisions had been. He also knew for now it was best to let it lie. Casey's desire may have been the largest part of what brought them back to Belfast, but he still had a sense that she'd run as much as relinquished in order to find herself here.

"It'll be hard for him to avoid it altogether. His presence rarely goes unnoticed," Jamie said dryly.

"But surely if he minds his own business—" She broke off under Jamie's raised eyebrows. "Oh I know I'm being willfully naïve thinking he can come back here and not stir things up, but I'd hoped we could stay under the IRA's radar for a bit."

Jamie shook his head. "Pamela, a hamster can't sneeze in that neighborhood without it being reported to Joe Doherty."

She looked down at her hands. "Do you know so much about him then?"

Jamie folded his arms across his chest and sighed. "More than I'd like, actually. He's from the old school. You know, shoot first, talk later. There's been a complete cessation of any kind of talks since he took over the Belfast command."

"Will he see Casey as a threat?"

Jamie cocked a golden eyebrow at her. "Of course he will. Your husband, despite his lengthy absence, is still thought of quite highly by some in that circle. Mostly the men who were under his command before he left. There's been a lot of in-fighting, though Joe Doherty tends to silence any opposition with a well-placed bullet. Seamus, for instance, disappeared about six months ago and has been neither heard from nor seen by anyone questioned in the matter. Everyone suspects. Few know what actually happened. But the silence in those circles is deafening at present."

Pamela swallowed, peony flush faded to a stark white.

"Less honesty perhaps?" Jamie said, turning to pour tea into the shamrock Belleek that was the everyday china of the Kirkpatrick household.

"A little less," she agreed, trying to summon up a wan smile. He handed her the cup and she wrapped her chilled hands around it gratefully. He sat down on the sofa beside her, watching as she inhaled the steam from her cup.

"Drink up," he said sternly. He noted how thin she was and how exhausted. This close to her he could smell her scent, still like a freshly bitten strawberry and yet something more and something less. Despair, disillusion, loss? He didn't know the details of the last two years, but he knew enough to be certain it hadn't been an easy road for either Casey or herself. What had happened in Boston to make Belfast desirable?

He switched to neutral topics as she drank her tea. Where did she and Casey plan to live, Casey's construction work, the plans he and Pat had for the drop-in center. He caught her up on the doings of mutual acquaintances. She in turn told him about her photography and the few pictures that had been bought by magazines. It was the stories she didn't tell, though, that spoke most loudly. She never once mentioned Casey's foray into fishing or her own work for Love Hagerty. Yet she had to know he was aware of these things.

Just before five she looked ruefully at the clock. "I swear you have some sort of enchantment on this house Jamie. I never can account for time here. I'd best get home."

Jamie walked down to the gate with her. She turned to face him as he opened it for her.

"Thank you for the tea and the talk. It helped me put things in perspective."

He nodded. "Don't be a stranger then."

For a long moment their eyes met and he saw a dark fear move deep in hers like a frightened creature huddled at the bottom of a lake.

"I've missed you." The words were said with such simple honesty that a small raw pain flashed across his chest.

He'd an odd sense of time stopping just for a second, of being poised on the cusp of something that would vault them both forward or back in time and place. Where they would be able to speak of past and present without constraint. He opened his mouth to respond to her admission. Then his heart resumed its normal pace and so did time, and he did not speak.

A sea breeze, faintly salted, slipped past them leaving an echo of brine in its wake. She closed her eyes, drawing a deep breath. "I'd forgotten how much I love it here," she said softly.

Jamie stood at the gate for a long time after the car had disappeared down the road. He needed to get back to the house and change his clothes before the Bishop arrived, but still he stood, watching the April dusk fill up the hollows, smudging the outlines of the trees and hedgerows lining the long road down the hill.

Finally he turned toward the house and began the walk back. The house blazed with light, the long windows laying their golden rectangles on the grass. A strange sensation gripped him as he sighted the first star of the evening above the inky pines.

His nerves felt raw, as if they had been exposed to a cold wind. Jamie couldn't remember the last time he'd felt so unprotected.

It annoyed him as he realized just what it was. He felt vulnerable.

Chapter Twenty-one

Deuces Wild

WITH A SIGH OF RELIEF, CASEY LOCKED THE DOOR of the youth center behind him. It had been a long day of it. He'd had no less than eight boys come through, looking for food, advice, cash. One of the little beggars had pulled a knife on him and demanded all his money. Casey had merely raised an eyebrow and slapped the knife out of the boy's hand, after which the child became intensely apologetic. Still, that sort of thing tensed a man up. He was of a mind to go for a wee walk, complemented by a wee drink, before coming back to the cramped quarters they called home. Pamela was off with Sylvie until late evening, so she wouldn't miss him.

He walked eastwards, toward the city center, flipping his collar up to keep the rain off. Ground fog rose from the streets, mist clinging to the air as the rain drizzled down. The city, in the waning light, looked bleak and depressing.

It was, he knew, prime fodder for all the media that flew in and out for their sound bites and their shots from the top of the Europa Hotel. On camera, Belfast looked like a mean little town, its bleak terraced housing more reminiscent of Dickens than Yeats. Admittedly, it looked different to him as well, after his time in America. Smaller somehow, when it had once been the breadth of his world. The worn doorsteps and narrow laneways had taken on an appearance of shabbiness in his absence and even the evening mist couldn't soften the harsh rubble and distrustful faces.

Only so much could be blamed on this unofficial war, for he knew that long before the troubles began, Belfast was in decline. The demand for her goods—the ships she'd built, the linen she'd woven—had diminished, turning Belfast into an industrial slum for workers without prospects. It was an old city full of old houses, extinguished dreams, and roads not taken.

What *was* new were the military posts, the observation towers, the reinforced RUC stations that looked like jungle outposts, draped as they were in netting, surrounded by wire and guarded by young, pink-cheeked English boys. His city was now as weighted with trouble as it was shy on resources.

Turning off the corner of Fountain Street and onto the top of Commercial he saw a young boy struggling with someone who remained invisible inside a white car. The boy was half in the car, feet coming off the pavement when Casey started to run. The child was yelling something that sounded fairly obscene, but he was obviously terrified, long stork-like legs flailing ineffectually in an effort to wrest himself from his would-be abductor.

The car was starting a slow roll, the boy in almost to his knees when Casey got to him and reached in, grabbing the boy around the waist. Putting his other hand on his jacket collar, he yanked him out. The movement knocked them both flat on their backs as the car squealed away in sudden haste.

Casey lay stunned for a moment. He'd caught the back of the boy's head full in his face. His lip was bleeding and red stars were dancing merrily in the air, compliments of the hot pain in his nose.

"Are ye alright, lad?" Casey asked as the boy rolled off him, one hand clutched to his head, the other pushing himself off the pavement.

"Ya, no thanks to youse I'm sure. What the feck did ye think ye were up to there?"

Casey sat up, putting a hand to his stinging lip. "Saving yer arse, or were ye wantin' to go with whoever the hell was in that car?"

"No, but I'd have got away. Didn't need youse interferin'."

"Well," Casey said, voice ripe with sarcasm, "ye'll forgive me, but ye didn't look to be managin' yer escape very well."

The boy stood now to his full height. In the dim light, Casey could just make out that his shirt was ripped down the front revealing a skinny, hairless chest. He'd put his age at about fourteen maybe. A baby. He put a hand to his throbbing nose, and gave it a ginger squeeze, bleeding but not broken. Fucking Belfast.

"Did he hurt ye?" Casey asked, getting to his feet and wincing at the sharp pain in his ankle.

The boy glared out from under a loose fringe of ginger hair, one grubby hand rubbing beneath a leaky nose. "Mind yer own feckin' business next time then, would ye? I can manage meself."

"Ye're welcome," Casey said, slightly shocked at the child's hostility.

The boy just shook his head as if to say, 'ye've not a clue' and then turned on his heel and sprinted off down the dark laneway, ginger hair a small bobbing spot of light that winked out as he turned a corner.

"Jaysus Murphy an' the little green men," Casey muttered angrily, the movement causing his lip to bleed afresh. He made his way to the head of the alley and turned back onto the street, needing the drink more than the walk now. There was a place he'd drank often as a lad that was only another block up. Hopefully it hadn't been bombed or shot up in his absence, as he didn't feel like traversing much further for his medicine.

It was still there, though parts of the street farther along had taken some recent hits from the look of things. A faded brown sign hung askew on the pitted brick wall, and the heavy oak door was now plated with steel. Other than that it looked like the same hole it had always been. Fucking Belfast, he thought wearily, and opened the door.

The pub was low-roofed and shabby, the long counter worn from countless elbows tucking in for a long night of it. The air reeked of stale Sweet Aftons and spilled drink, but it was warm and dry, and there was ale on tap. Sometimes a man required little else of the universe.

The pub was empty other than a couple of old men at the bar and a table of five snugged at the back, near the gas fire. The two old-timers at the bar were silent; glum faces hanging over their half-empty glasses, they'd barely glanced up at his entrance. Regulars then. The men in the corner were an oddly lot, two on the smallish side, one with a face hidden under his cloth cap, the other missing two fingers from the first joint on his left hand. Another with the face of a priest, but he recognized him as Sweet Bill, a down-on-his-luck-bookie. The fourth man was the one who'd drawn his glance though. He was a big lad with a shock of glossy brown hair, and a pair of blue eyes that sliced through the wreath of smoke about their table.

The man had taken his measure as soon as he'd come in the door. Casey didn't take offence; a lifetime of assessing every room he walked into for unfriendlies had accustomed him to being given the once over himself.

"Thanks," he said as the publican set his Guinness on the bar. The barman nodded, then slid his watery blue eyes back to the flickering telly that burbled to itself in a corner behind the counter.

Casey took a long swallow of his drink, then turned on the rickety stool to watch the game in progress. They were playing poker; five card draw from the look of it. The man with the cloth cap had just thrown down his cards with a sound of disgust and stood, saying he was done for the night. Casey smiled; the drink had rinsed the day's sour taste from his tongue and he was in the mood for a bit of fun.

He waited until the capped man had left, before he stood and walked over to the table. The men looked up at his approach, but he knew it was the blue-eyed man he'd need to address. He fixed him with his most genial smile.

"I see ye've an empty chair," he said. "Will ye mind if I take it?"

The big man looked up, fixing him with a cold blue glare. "Are ye askin' to play?"

"An' if I am?" Casey said, returning the blue glare with a very black one.

"Then ye'd best take the plug out an' sit down," the man responded, though his tone was still frigid.

Casey took the chair, which was directly across the table from the blue-eyed man. He nodded to the other men, who returned his greeting with grunts and curt nods of their own.

"Name's Robin Temple," the man said, dealing Casey in, "what's yer own?"

"Casey Riordan," he replied, taking his seat between the old man and the young one who was missing the two fingers. "What are we playin'?"

"Five card draw," Robin replied coolly, flicking the fifth card onto Casey's stack. Casey waited until everyone else had picked up their cards, before touching his own. It was his own bit of superstition, like wearing certain socks on game days had been back when he'd played team rugby. It also gave him time to assess the other player's tells, expressions on their faces, sniffing, tapping fingers, etc. Most people had them, and sure enough the men around him began fidgeting. Right off he knew the two-fingered boy thought he'd a winning hand, the bookie had nothing, and Robin—well he remained inscrutable, face revealing nothing, cards neatly splayed in a hand that wore a curious looking ring. It was silver and heavy, with the outline of a phoenix, its rising mouth open to swallow a blood red ruby.

"Are ye goin' to pick up yer hand or not?" Robin asked, voice openly hostile.

"Aye," Casey replied mildly. He took his time fanning the cards out, arranging them to suit and then smiling about the table. "There, I think I'm ready now."

Robin smiled suddenly, but the feral parting of lip held no friendliness. Casey had a decent hand, with a good card or two he could likely win, but he'd lose a few, make some blunders, and put the men at their ease. When he did win, he'd make a show of crowing, which would lull them all into thinking he'd not played with men of their caliber before.

As things went they were a fairly easy lot to read. Two Fingers touched the tip of his tongue to his upper lip when he'd more than a pair. The bookie tapped his foot under the table when he thought his luck was on the rise.

Robin won the first round with three nines, Two Fingers trailing him with three eights, the bookie taking third with two pairs and Casey bringing up the rump with a pair of fours.

Casey did modestly well in the next three rounds with two pairs, three of a kind and another set of pairs. He remained amiable throughout, asking the odd novice question.

The deal came back round to Robin on the last game. Casey eyed his hand, three of spades and diamonds, jack, king and ace of hearts. He rubbed his chin thoughtfully, furrowing his brow as though stymied by the hand.

In the first throwdown he discarded his three of spades and picked up the queen of hearts. His own heart started to speed up a little, though he sighed lightly and gave his head the faintest of shakes. He watched the other discards and based his guesses on what they held accordingly. He was fairly certain that Two Fingers was working on a couple of pairs, a decent hand and often a winning one in other situations, but likely not so lucky for the laddie today. The bookie was going to go out on his turn; he'd no more than a pair and knew it wasn't going to be enough.

"I'll take one," Casey said, throwing down the five he'd been dealt in the last round.

Robin dealt him the final card, his index finger pushing it across the table to Casey, eyes never leaving his face.

"Thank ye," Casey said politely, waiting until the other man blinked first before turning his attention to the card that lay now under his own hand.

He didn't pick it up until everyone had been dealt their cards.

"Bets, lads?" Robin asked.

The bookie shook his head and put his cards down. Robin threw another fiver onto the pile with a flash of white teeth.

Casey sighed heavily and took the last bit of money he had, if it went higher he'd have to fold. "I'll see yer fiver an' raise ye another."

Robin eyed him speculatively over the top of his own cards, still as stone and, if Casey was any judge of these things, sober as a judge.

"I'll see yer five," he said finally, putting a crumpled note on the table that was the bottom of his own fund. "Gentlemen?"

Two Fingers sighed in disgust and threw his cards down, "That's me done then."

It was down to the two of them now. Casey didn't so much as blink, but merely held Robin's gaze with his own. Any sign of weakness would be exploited without mercy. He wasn't about to give Robin an opening.

No one breathed; the tension was high enough to walk clear across. Robin laid his cards down one at a time, clearly enjoying his moment.

On the table lay the five cards of a flush, ace of spades, nine of spades, four of spades followed by another four and nicely rounded off with a ten.

"Now do ye know of many hands that can beat that, gentlemen?" Robin asked, blue eyes gleaming triumphantly.

"I suppose a royal flush would do it," Casey said mildly and laid his cards on the table. The ten, jack, queen, king, and ace of hearts met three sets of incredulous eyes.

The two-fingered boy slammed his complete fist into the table, causing a cascade of coins to spill onto the floor, "He's cheated, do ye know the odds of such a thing?"

"About one in two an' a half million," Robin said, a reluctant smile playing with the corners of his mouth. "But I know a cheat when I see one, an' I'd wager a hundred pound the man didn't cheat. Do ye care to oppose me on that?"

The boy looked up and saw something beyond the lazy smile that cautioned him in his answer.

"No," he said, "If ye think he didn't cheat, I'll take yer word on it."

"Aye well then *sin sin*, man."

Wisely the two other men vacated their chairs and, within minutes, the pub as well, leaving the two big men opposite each other at the table.

Robin idly shuffled the cards, narrowing his eyes in assessment of the man across from him. He knocked the cards on the table, placed them face down and toward Casey.

"Double or nothin'?" he asked, dark blue eyes meeting the black of his opponent's.

"You call it," Casey said, not so much as blinking.

"Right, kings are high and deuces are wild. Cut."

Casey obliged, spinning the top half of the deck neatly to one side, and fanning them out in a perfect line.

"Nice trick," Robin observed, taking the top card, glancing at it and smiling like a cat with too much cream around its whiskers. "Yer turn," he said cutting the deck a second time and letting the cards splay in an arc, before coming to rest one after another in a very tidy pile.

"Impressive," Casey commented, taking his own card with a deft flick of the wrist.

"Time to hold 'em or fold 'em," Robin said with a lovely show of teeth.

"You first," Casey said politely.

Robin flipped his card over with a delicate movement of his middle finger, making it land on his wrist.

"King of hearts," he crowed triumphantly.

"Glad to see some things never change," Casey said with a grin, "but I believe," he flicked his card with the thumb of his right hand causing it to flip over twice before landing, sweet as a whisper, on the balance of the tips of his index finger and thumb, "that ye did say twos took all. Two of hearts makes me the winner."

Robin glared at him. "Ye black Irish bastard, where'd ye hide it—up yer sleeve, or down yer trousers?"

Casey winked. "I'll never tell."

"Goddamn it, Casey Riordan," Robin said, smile splitting wide, "it's good to see ye. Can ye be persuaded to take a drink with me?"

"Maybe just the one."

"Just the one," Robin said disbelievingly, "have ye gone an' joined the Temperance League whilst I was away?"

Casey shook his head. "No but it's more than my life's worth to stumble home drunk."

"Ah, she's strict is she?"

Casey grinned. "Not so much, but she knows which privileges to deny to keep me in line."

"The power of the female, eh? Whatever damn fool said they were the weaker sex obviously didn't have much dealins' with them."

Casey cleared his throat. "I'd heard ye married, Pat wrote me in prison to tell me of it."

"Aye, I married her," Robin said ruefully, thumb tracing the rim of the bottle that sat between them, "knowin' all the time that it was a damned mistake. I was no more than a pet monkey to her, her rebel Irishman that she could show off at parties with her society friends. I'm afraid I was bought for my shock value an' little else."

"I'm sorry to hear it, man," Casey said sincerely.

"Are ye?" Robin cut him a look, "I wouldn't be if I were you, it's me who should be apologizin'. Though I paid the price, she never forgot ye an' never let me forget it either."

"I never loved her proper," Casey said, "though maybe I didn't know it entirely then."

"Aye, when did ye figure it out, then?"

Casey met his look with one of his own. "When I met my own wife."

"I noticed the ring, how long will it have been then?"

"Just the two years this April, though I don't remember any life before her if ye'll know what I mean."

"Ye love her a great deal then."

"Oh aye." Casey smiled. "I love her to distraction an' beyond."

"She's a looker?"

"Doesn't even begin to describe her," Casey said, "she still takes my breath away. First time I saw her I felt like someone had hit me hard in the stomach, I could barely keep to my feet."

"How'd ye meet?"

"She was sittin' half-naked in my brother's kitchen, if ye can countenance it, the very day I arrived home from prison."

"Jaysus," Robin said, leaning forward over the table, a flicker of the sixteen-year-old he'd once been in his face. "Ye're never tellin' the truth man."

"No, 'tis true, she was posin' in the altogether for a drawing that Pat was doin'."

"Christ." Robin grinned. "Ye always did have the damnedest luck with women."

"Aye well," Casey shrugged, "Pamela was different right from the first; I knew there was no playin' with her."

"Good Irish Catholic girl?" Robin asked, re-filling his glass and Casey's own half-empty one.

"She's a Yank from New York originally, an' she darkens the door of a church about once a year."

"O-ho did ye marry yer American heiress after all?"

"No, when we first met we'd not even the two pennies to rub together."

"Have ye a passel of babies then?"

"No," Casey's face was tight as he contemplated his whiskey with sudden intensity, "we had a stillborn daughter October past an' haven't had luck in getting pregnant since then."

"I'm sorry man, tongue got ahead of my brain as usual."

"Not to worry, ye couldn't know," Casey downed his whiskey in one swallow.

"So what brought ye back here? Tim Newsome said ye'd packed up an' gone off to Boston a couple years back."

Casey shook his head. "This country, it's a wee bit like an addiction, ye know. Ye know it's not good for ye, that it may kill ye in the end, an' yet ye can't resist it at the same time."

Robin nodded in agreement. "I swore I'd left the dust of these streets behind for good, an' yet after Melissa an' I divorced I didn't see where else I was to go. Wandered out west for a bit, Nevada, California an' such. Then one day I find myself in the airport in Los Angeles bookin' passage for a flight to Dublin. An' I knew I was always bound back here, like a lemming to the fockin' cliff."

Casey laughed, despite the serious tone. "Aye, all things considered it's a wee bit suicidal I suppose."

"Aye," Robin said and now there was no trace of laughter in his face, "but I've made my peace with Joe. I don't suppose ye can say the same of yerself."

"I've no need to, I'm not part of that world anymore," Casey said.

"Aye well, the man remembers ye, so ye'd best watch how ye step."

"Is that a threat?" Casey asked, hands stilled around his drink.

Robin shook his head. "Jaysus man, have ye been gone so long as to think that little of me?"

"We'll both be changed by the time that's passed, no?"

"Aye," Robin replied softly, "we will at that."

Casey dug in his pocket, emerging with a pack of cigarettes and two pound notes.

"Yer money's no good here tonight, ye'll let me get it," Robin said.

Casey nodded his thanks as he shrugged his coat on. "It's been good to see ye," he said. "Ye should come by an' meet my wife one of these days; we're livin' over the Beechmount Youth Center."

"I'll do that."

"FRIEND OF YERS?" the publican asked, as the door closed behind Casey.

Robin smiled, a fleeting wistfulness gracing his features. "Aye, once upon a time he was. Best friend I ever had, like a brother really." He stubbed the remains of his cigarette out in the ashtray, smile vaporizing along with the smoke.

"Times change though," he said, and though his tone was mild, the barman stepped back a bit, a chill fixing itself in the back of his neck. "And ye know what they say."

"No, what's that?" the barman asked, thinking he'd not feel safe until the door was locked behind this man's back.

Robin threw some money on the counter, settling up the night's accounts. *"Ni dhiolann dearmad fiacha,"* he said, then whistled himself out the door.

The barman shivered and locked the door, there were enough lingerings of the Gaelic his grandmother had spoken to translate the man's statement.

A debt is still unpaid, even if forgotten.

Chapter Twenty-two

The Boys of Summer

IN THE SPRING THE POSTMAN brought Pamela an unexpected gift. "Package from New York," he said with a tip of his cap, after handing her the smooth manila envelope which had a pleasant heft to it. She didn't recognize the return address, but knew who it had come from as soon as the contents spilled onto the kitchen table where she'd sat to open the package. She picked them up, hands trembling a little, itching as they had not in months for the feel of a camera.

Image after image of their life in Boston came back to her—the streets, the people—Father Kevin, the Cardinal, Charlie, Desmond, Siobhan and Pat from the last Christmas they'd spent. Plenty of Casey, many where he looked harassed at being subjected to the aim of his wife's camera once again, but many natural shots that she'd had great fun taking. At the bottom there was a picture of Love Hagerty, a publicity still she'd taken, during the last campaign of him in a crowd, cuffs rolled up, tie askew, trying to make believe he was a man of the people. She dropped the photo as if it were poison, mouth suddenly dry and stomach flipping over.

There was a note inside, written in a firm, squared-away hand. Written, she saw smiling, with Lucas' usual economy of expression.

'You forgot these. You captured Hagerty nicely—the smug bastard.'
Lucas

She picked the photo of Love up again and slowly tore it into strips, ripping it again and again until there was no way of recognizing the face in the photo anymore. Until the blue eyes, which seemed to mock her even on paper, could no longer look out from their celluloid world.

"Pamela, what are ye doin'?"

She jumped up in startlement, scattering the torn strips of photograph onto the floor. She stood on them hastily, hand to her chest.

"What am *I* doing? What the hell are you doing, walking in here silent as a ghost in the middle of the afternoon?"

"It's near on four o'clock," he said raising his eyebrows and stepping out of the kitchen entryway to set his lunch kit on the counter.

"Get off the floor!" Her voice escalated into panic. Casey frowned in puzzlement. "I just washed them, they may be slippery," she finished lamely.

"Alright," he said, "I'll go take my boots off."

She swept the strips quickly into the dustpan, throwing them into the garbage and then adding in the day's tea leaves as a deterrent to curious eyes.

"Can I come in now?" Casey popped his head around the doorway. "Or are ye goin' to yell at me a bit more first?"

"No I won't yell and of course you can come in, it's your home after all. Sit down, I'll make you tea."

"My home," he said, "just not my floor though, eh?" He sniffed the air. "Is there somethin' burnin'?"

"Oh no, the biscuits," she said with a groan, wondering if they were to ever have a meal made by her hands that wasn't burned to a crisp.

"Medium brown, not even close to black," Casey said, eyeing the biscuits as she took them from the oven, "things are improvin'. Ouch," he snatched his hand back where it had just been smartly slapped in the act of taking one of the steaming biscuits. "Feelin' a bit prickly today, are ye?"

She pointed at the table with the flipper, "Go sit, I'll get the tea."

He held his hands up in surrender, settling at the table with a deep sigh.

"Busy day?" she asked, setting the kettle to boil on the stove before putting biscuits and butter on a plate and setting it down in front of him.

"Aye, more than usual. Gibbons has got a real press on to get the buildin' done; I think his little German friends must be gettin' impatient to move in."

"And how's his secretary?"

Casey gave her a gimlet glance from under dark brows, "The same as always, don't give me grief Jewel, I cannot be blamed if the woman looks at me as if I were breakfast, lunch an' dinner. Poor thing likely hasn't had a leg-over in a few decades."

"Casey Riordan, what a terrible thing to say!"

"Why? It's true, women get a pinched look about them when they've not had sex in a long while an' she's a face on her like a wee puckered prune. While you," he grinned impudently, grabbing her backside in one large hand, "have skin smooth as cream."

"Vain sot," she said uncharitably, turning back to take the whistling kettle off the stove. She poured the bubbling water over the tea ball, inhaling the fragrance of bergamot and lavender, giving the clock above the plate rack a cursory glance, six and one half minutes she had learned, neither less nor more, made the perfect pot of tea.

She turned back to find her husband with a peculiar and unidentifiable look on his face.

"It's the biscuits." She sighed in defeat, "They're inedible, aren't they?"

"No," he manfully swallowed, "they're actually not so bad."

"Then what's wrong? You've the oddest expression on your face."

"It's only that I never knew ye thought me vain."

"Casey Riordan, for heaven's sake..." she began, trailing off as she realized he was serious." I was only teasing."

He gave a half-hearted smile. "I know that. It's only I'm a wee bit thin-skinned when it comes to ye, Jewel, an' my da always said a man should know his worth but not let it go to his head."

"Casey, you're the least vain man I know."

"Ah, now ye're just tryin' to soothe my ego, woman."

"No, I'm not," she said earnestly, setting the teapot on the table and putting a cup in front of Casey and one in her own place. "You're completely unaware of yourself and your effect on other people, particularly women."

"Now, that's not true." He poured the first cup of tea for himself, as he liked the slight bitterness of it and she preferred the more mellow flavor that the second pouring provided. "I've noticed the wee prune-faced secretary gazin' at me, have I not?"

"It'd be hard to miss," she passed him the milk, spooning out the half teaspoon of sugar he always took in his tea, "she looks as though she wants to devour you whole."

"Aye well she puts the hair up the back of my neck, I'll admit. I'm not comfortable, I suppose, with that sort of attention."

"That," she said, getting up to scrape at the remnants of petrified biscuit in the pan, "is not what Pat told me."

"No?" Casey gave her a look of complete innocence. "What did my brother tell ye?"

"That the two of you, yourself and Robin, that is, left a swathe of broken hearts in Belfast a mile wide during the years you ran together."

"Ach, ye know Pat exaggerates somethin' terrible, 'twas maybe half a mile wide, the streets in Belfast bein' a bit on the narrow side." He grinned, winking at her before returning his attention to his food. She turned back to wipe at the floury counter, nervously aware of the brown manila envelope sitting next to his wrist.

Behind her Casey made a noise that fell somewhere between horror and amusement. She looked out of the corner of her eye, knowing he'd found the pictures.

In his hand he held a photo she'd taken of him one morning shortly before they'd left Boston. In it he was only half-awake, darkly stubbled, hair mussed, his attire the sheet, which covered very little, and in his hand a cup of morning tea. It was the most erotic photo she'd ever taken and she was very proud and not a little nervous about him seeing it for the first time.

"Jaysus, woman," he said in tones of shock, "is it not a little indecent to be takin' pictures of yer husband in the altogether?"

"I see you in the altogether all the time," she said equably.

"Aye, but generally speakin' ye're not tryin' to catch it on film. How'd ye take such a thing without me knowin'?"

"Hid in the linen closet," she said, "there was enough light that I didn't need the flash and there was a garbage truck below that hid the sound of the shutter whirring."

"Sneaky wee devil," he said half admiringly. He looked at the photo again, a reluctant smile beginning to play about his lips.

"Christ, do I really look like that?" He seemed uncomfortably pleased.

"Yes, you do." She came around the back of his chair and looked past his shoulder to the photo that he held with ginger fingers. "Do you like it?"

"Yes an' no," he said. "I mean I feel as if ye've caught my soul somehow here on paper, Jewel, an' it's a bit eerie lookin' at myself the way ye must see me in order to take such a picture. It's like seein' through yer eyes instead of my own."

"I don't see you through my eyes, Casey." She slipped her arms around him from behind, feeling the comforting expanse of his back against her. "I see you through my heart; I have for a very long time."

"Aye well, yer heart must wear rose-colored glasses."

"You're a handsome man, don't you realize that?" She rubbed her cheek against the fine cotton of his shirt.

"Ye tell me often enough, but I think it's love that makes ye see me in that light," he said gruffly.

"Maybe now," she acquiesced, "but at first it was something else."

"Aye, like what?"

"It was a purely physical reaction to the way you looked, to your presence. If I remember correctly I felt rather feverish and dizzy."

"Feverish an' dizzy, eh?" He sounded rather pleased.

"Mmhm," she breathed in his scent contentedly, "pure unadulterated lust. Right from the very first moment."

"An' now?"

"And now it's the same, only it's sweeter and deeper because I love you. It's more than wanting. It's—" she hesitated looking for a word that would match what she felt.

"Everything," Casey supplied quietly.

"Everything," she agreed. "I can't believe that you didn't see your appeal to the opposite sex, though," she put her face to the side of his neck, savoring the warmth and his scent.

"I think it was because I had no mother about. I think a young man or woman sees themselves as beautiful through their parent's eyes first an' if ye see that approval there ye thrive an' if ye don't then ye can never quite believe what stranger's eyes will tell ye."

"Pat told me the girls were mad for you when you were in your teens, said there was always some silly female trying to get your attention."

"Aye," he admitted reluctantly, "it's true. Daddy used to say I was like a sugar bowl to a bunch of hormone addled flies."

"Didn't that make you realize you were attractive to the opposite sex?"

"Not altogether, I mean I was a big boy but I spent a lot of awkward years gettin' there an' I was under the impression that it was my size they were particularly attracted to. The girls seemed to think that if I was big in stature..." he turned faintly pink on the back of his neck.

"That you'd be correspondingly large elsewhere," she finished dryly.

"Aye."

"And did you oblige their curiosity?" she asked.

He stood and turned in her arms, dark eyes creased with amusement. "Aye, I did, an' before ye wrinkle yer nose up in disapproval, it's not a period of my life I'm proud of. An' ye can believe my da saw to it that I paid for my sins. An' besides, I never loved a one of them," he drew her closer and kissed her softly, "until you."

"Mmphm," she attempted a disapproving noise that ended up in a sigh as his hands stroked her back and he kissed her again.

"You and your Irish tongue," she said rather breathlessly a few minutes later.

"As far as I'm aware," he murmured in her ear, "all my bits are Irish."

"Stop," she batted his hands away from her shirt buttons, "trying to distract me. Now tell me about these women."

He crooked an eyebrow at her. "Ye really want to know this?"

"I do."

He sighed, an extravagant and thoroughly Irish sigh. "I don't ask ye to dredge up the lurid details of yer own past, now do I?"

"Because I don't have one as you and I both know."

"Aye well then, if ye insist, but come here to me an' get comfortable first." He led her to the big, battered chair he favored and sat, pulling her into his lap, tucking her neatly against his chest. She settled against him with a contented breath, enjoying the heat of his body against her side, the comfort and security of his arms about her.

"Ye know that swathe Pat was tellin' ye about, well 'twas such an incident that got us banished from Belfast one summer. Robin had gotten a girl in trouble an' her daddy was lookin' for him an' it wasn't to congratulate him, if ye take my meanin'. I was consortin' with a rough crowd from the Unity Flats area an' daddy thought it wouldn't be a bad notion to get the both of us out of town for a bit.

"He sent us up to stay with Desmond an' Siobhan, knowin' they'd keep a tight eye on the two of us an' work us hard enough to make us grateful to get to bed early at night. It worked well enough to start but then Siobhan's sister died in New York an' they had to go over. Desmond checked with my da to see if he wanted us scuttled back to Belfast, but Daddy said no, that the two of us could earn our keep better up there by takin' care of the bed an' breakfast for the two of them.

"I think they were a little leery of leavin' the safekeeping of their livelihood in our hands but they were in a rush an' we assured them we'd take the responsibility seriously. Not to mention that Desmond had described at least a dozen inventive an' lengthy ways he'd kill us if we screwed up.

"'Twas hard work an' at first we enjoyed it, but after two weeks of gettin' up at the crack of dawn an' cookin' sausage for guests who complained that the food was scorched an' the tea too strong an' the sheets wrinkled an' so forth, the charm was pretty much gone. Robin had been walkin' out with a local girl an' she was real soft on him, so we hired her an' her sister to take over for us an' swore them to secrecy."

"She must have been soft-headed," Pamela said, "to work like a dog so the two of you could run about the country philandering."

"Well she thought we were on—" Casey cleared his throat, a chagrined smile playing across his lips, "a mission."

"A mission? The two of you? Granted I don't know Robin well but I don't think any woman would ever mistake you for a man with Godly intentions."

Casey managed to look as though his honor had been seriously impugned. "Now here I am barin' my soul to ye woman an' ye insult me, an' as for the Godly bit they do say as we're made in His image."

"Some," Pamela retorted smartly, "more than others."

"Well the lass could be forgiven for it wasn't that sort of mission we were meant to be on. 'Twas a covert operation, with code words an' all, I tell ye we'd a fine evenin' of it, makin' up the story."

She snorted. "Covert operation. She *was* soft-headed if she fell for that."

"Don't be so hard on the girl, Robin was handy with makin' the lassies believe the grass was blue an' the moon made of cheese if he so wished."

"I'm starting to see why the two of you got on so well."

Casey wisely chose to ignore this remark and continued on with his story. "We decided we'd have a bit of a lark down the countryside. We'd time, we figured—Dez an' Siobhan were likely to be some weeks longer as there were problems with the will, an' fightin' relations Stateside. Then Dez figured as long as he was over there he might as well have a gander about the country. Once we'd decided to go it was only a matter of figurin' out how to keep food in our bellies an' the occasional roof over our heads on rainy nights."

"And that was?" She asked, giving him an accusing look.

"Music of course," he replied, returning her look with a black one of his own. "We'd pretty voices the two of us, Robin with the face to match, an' no one can play the fiddle like Bobbie when the mood is on him."

"Bobbie?" she enquired lightly, smoothing back the hair around his ear.

"Aye," he smiled, slightly nostalgic, "I suppose even after all this time the name comes natural to me. I was the only one who ever called him that, everyone else called him Robin."

"He was your best friend, wasn't he?"

Casey nodded. "Aye, he was. We went through all those things together that bond ye, the girls, the fightin', the troubles at home, the awkwardness of bein' adolescent. We told each other everything, our hopes an' fears an' dreams. An' we watched one another's backs. There was no one I was closer to other than Pat an' daddy. Bobbie though, he only had me. An' there's somethin' that's open in those years, inside, that closes up later, so the friends ye make then are different, ye never make ties like that again. Did ye have friends like that, Jewel?"

"No," she said, "I didn't, I'm afraid I wasn't very approachable. And my father died when other girls were buying their first pair of high heels and going out on dates."

"Ye must have been terrible lonely," he said softly, hand cupping her face.

"I suppose I was. I just didn't realize it until I met you," she said. "But you were telling me about Robin."

He cocked an eyebrow at her. "Someday woman ye're goin' to tell me about those years whether ye like it or no. Understand?"

"Understood," she agreed, "now go on, tell me about the singing and seducing you two ran about doing."

"Singin' an' seducin', is it?" He gave a wry smile, "I suppose that does sum it up rather well, though it seems a little prettier in memory than that. Well we liked a bit of a fight now an' then, ye see. An' if there was no one willin' to fight, we'd stage one between the two of us."

"What on earth for?"

"Well ye see, women bein' of a rather sympathetic nature, we'd found—"

"That bumps and bruises got you sympathy," she finished for him.

"We were adolescent, an' were runnin' more on hormones than brain power, admittedly. Though it did come as a shock to find out just how aroused women were by blood an' sweat. Ye're odd creatures at times."

"I suppose it's bred in the bone, after all you men have been fighting for thousands of years and expecting a certain welcome when you arrived home from battle, stinking and blood-soaked. I imagine we got used to it, and learned to like it."

"Ye like it when I come home all sweaty?" He eyed her dubiously, as if this were a perversion that had never occurred to him.

She flushed slightly. "Well not always, but sometimes—well like last week when you were working on the cupboards downstairs and you were up the ladder and...and...well you know what happened."

"Aye," he smiled broadly, "I did wonder what had gotten into ye."

"It was the whole working man thing, the hammer, the t-shirt, the way you smelled of wood shavings, it was very—will you stop looking at me that way—it was very erotic."

"Was it then?" He gave her a knowing look that deepened her blush considerably. "I love that ye know, ye can behave like a complete wanton, rollin' me around on the floor of the kitchen an' yet ye blush like a virgin schoolgirl to talk about it. Now *that's* erotic."

"Can we please," she said, furious at the heat in her face, "get back to the subject at hand?"

"Well," he said, "we spent most of the summer havin' great craic altogether, singin' in every little out of the way pub all down the west coast an' along the southern shore."

"How'd you find gigs all the time?"

"Well we worked cheap, sang for our supper mostly, a meal an' a couple of pints to keep the pipes workin' was all we asked. An' we loved singin', we'd keep the place goin' all night, sang ourselves hoarse on a few occasions. Sometimes we'd even bring the dawn in, the landlord would lock the door at closin' an' keep the drink flowin', lots of times they'd put us up on their own couches."

"And the other nights?"

"Well there was always a patch of grass an' the stars overhead."

"And," she prodded.

"An' there were the women."

"And women," she said tartly, "are notoriously weak-willed when it comes to musicians."

"Aye, we'd noticed the phenomenon ourselves, an' certainly saw no need to question the reasons behind it too deeply. I could see the attraction to Robin, a fiddle wasn't without its appeal after all, but the squeezebox was altogether different."

"The squeezebox?"

"Aye, an accordion, that's what I played believe it or not, that an' the bodhran some nights. We took turns singin', though some nights we'd sing together, two part harmonies an' the like."

"You loved it, didn't you?"

"Oh aye, singin', fightin', an' beddin' willin' women, wasn't much like work at all, at all."

"Sounds like a young man's idea of heaven."

"Seemed like it at the time, though I think if either of us could have seen where it was headin' we'd have been a bit more restrained. Oh aye," he acknowledged her skeptical look, "I know restraint is not one of my larger virtues an' it was less so when I was young."

"Sounds like you had great fun together, what happened?"

"We fell out over a woman if ye can believe it."

"I thought," she said with a smile, "that I was the only woman you'd ever loved."

"Ye are," he said gruffly, arms tightening around her, "only a boy'll not know the difference sometimes between lust an' love, an' when yer hormones are rampagin' one will look a great deal like the other.

"She was an American, I seem," he wiggled an eyebrow at her, "to have a weakness in that area. An' she seemed dreadful glamorous to the two of us, city boys though we thought we were. Couple of provincials an' most definitely not in her league, but lookin' back I think we were a novelty to her. Rough lads from the wrong side of the tracks, who'd the blarney to glib their way through a lot of situations. We thought we were pretty hot stuff. Truth bein' that we were more than ready to be picked off like the jackasses we were. Neither of us had ever met anyone like Melissa."

"Melissa?"

They had been singing in a wee pub on the coast of Clare. The day had been a wet one and the place was steaming and stinking with wet clothes. When the girl walked in she struck the room silent, and even Robin, normally unflappable, missed a beat or two in the verse he was singing. For she was a beauty, with skin on her like a ripe peach and platinum hair that swung like a cape about her shoulders. She sat down, cool as you please, ordered a drink paying little mind to the musicians tucked in the corner. Robin had launched into a particularly slow sad song about a lad who died of a broken heart. He had the talent of making his audience believe he had lived every song he sang, and it generally melted women straight into the floor at his feet.

Robin had sung his heart out, bent on seducing the girl. He was on the top of his game that night, looking like the stereotypical romantic version of an Irishman with his dark hair and blue eyes set off by a cream-colored fisherman's sweater. The man possessed a voice to make angels weep with envy. All of it was apparently wasted on the girl though, for at the end of his set she clapped politely and turned back to her drink. Robin was so stunned, he might have been knocked down with a feather. Such things didn't happen to bonny, sweet Robin. It only made him that much more determined to have her, or to die trying.

"On the break between sets he went an' ordered a pint for the both of us, stood right beside her tryin' to make small talk, he'd a tongue glib as the devil when he wanted to an' he laid it out thick an' sweet for her. She gave him polite, one-word answers an' no more. Had him puzzled, he came back with our pints, the face on him like curdled cream an' says, 'maybe she's the sort prefers girls.'"

"No dents in his ego," Pamela said.

"Well no, but then ye'd have to understand his charm had never failed him before an' he was a bit bewildered by rejection. He was a little glum then an' told me to take my turn singin' for he'd lost the taste for it that evenin'. Someone asked me to sing *Captain Wedderburn*—do ye know the song? No? Well it's a bit on the suggestive side an' is really meant to be sung by a male an' female together in the two parts. But I, lackin' female accompaniment, always sang both parts myself. I'd got to the end of the male's part an' Robin was pickin' his way through the musical interlude on the guitar. I was just takin' a sip of my ale when this voice starts in on the female part, high an' sweet an' just a bit saucy, the way the song was designed to be sung."

"'Twas her of course, an' ye could have knocked me over with a feather, an' Bobbie looked as though he needed even less inducement to lay him out."

It was the girl. The song was an old English one where the male proposed a tumble in the hay and the female responded by asking six virtually unanswerable questions, with her virtue as reward, should the man be able to answer. Both Robin and Casey had been stunned, Robin forgetting to play in his shock. After the song was over the girl had come over and said, politely to Casey, that as he had answered all her questions he was now entitled to her own virtue, questionable as that commodity might be.

"Wanted to kiss more than your bruises, did she?"

"In a manner of speakin', I was in a bit of shock, for all my supposed experience, I was still a bit innocent."

"It's hard to imagine," she said dryly.

"The girls we knew were mostly girls we'd grown up about, hard mouths to be sure, but good Catholic girls for all that without much experience. My first encounter of that sort happened behind the local high school, an' I got my face slapped smartly for bein' a bit too bold."

"I suppose Melissa liked her men bold, though," Pamela said, voice a trifle cynical.

"She was a bold lassie herself; the summer was an education to say the least. Now, Jewel," he pulled her tighter to him as her body stiffened, "ye did say as ye wanted to hear this, have ye changed yer mind? An' besides I wasn't just talkin' about the beddin', she exposed me to all sorts of things I'd not known about before. Like what sort of power money wielded. How simply wearin' different clothes an' havin' yer hair cut right made people treat ye differently. She was generous with her money, an' she knew how to spend it. Bought me an Italian-made suit, pale gray it was, an' fit to me like a glove. Thought I was quite the spiff, sleepin' on silk sheets—"

"Silk sheets?"

"Aye she only slept on silk imported from China, said it was better for the complexion."

"I can't imagine your father was impressed by this situation."

"Well no he wasn't entirely but he tried to keep out of my affairs unless he thought I was headed for disaster. Earlier that summer he'd had Desmond lock me up in the pottin' shed to teach me a lesson."

"What on earth had you done?"

"Nothin', though I was plannin' on it. Donegal is Republican territory. My da said ye couldn't throw a stone up there without hittin' a dozen rebels. The place has always been a hotbed for the IRA. Bobbie an' I thought the whole idea of revolution was terribly glamorous an' we were tired of watchin' from the sidelines."

There was to be a meeting that May up the coast, out in the countryside near Killybegs. The men who'd been in the IRA in the Fifties were convening to see if they could reorganize and build a new structure on the foundation of the old. Casey had been angry with his father because he refused to have anything to do with it. It was a sore point between he and Desmond that they never did reconcile on. Desmond had thought it high time for Casey to understand his family history and what such a thing meant in the life of a man. Casey's own father thought the past a dangerous thing in the Riordan family and disagreed. Desmond hadn't liked it but had to respect Brian's decision. Casey had his own opinion on the matter and was very annoyed to find out no one gave a tinker's damn for what he thought.

"Their insistence on treatin' me like a child made me all the more determined to go to this meetin'. Lookin' back I think either Bobbie an' I had the balls of brass monkeys or were entirely stupid. Oh aye, keep the wicked eye to yerself woman, I know ye're thinkin' the two things are not so far apart.

"I never did know how, but Daddy got wind of our plan an' decided to give it a firm nip in the bud. I suppose we ought to have been suspicious when Dez asked us to come into the pottin' shed an' help him separate the spring bulbs. Well he got us in there—miserable dark little hole 'twas too—an' then slipped out an' padlocked the door. We pounded on the door 'til we both had splinters an' were bleedin', then we checked every corner of the buildin'. Problem was Desmond wasn't a great builder but when he did go to the bother of makin' somethin', it was made solid, 'so ugly it scared the crows,' Siobhan would say, but made to stand for a good long time."

They had sat in the shed for a full hour, before Casey had the inspired notion to knock the hinges out. They had loosened them up and then bided their time. Desmond had come back a while later to inquire after their well-being and to say he had left them a bit of food in a bag in a corner of the shed. They had thanked him meekly, and assured him they had no notion of even attempting the meeting now, if he would just let them out.

"Well now, lads,' he says, 'ye know I can't do that for all that I'm sorry to lock yez up. Yer Daddy made me promise to keep ye away from this meetin', Casey, an' ye know I can't go against yer da's wishes, boy.' We said we understood, even while I seethed in the dark that my da was tryin' to interfere in my life in such a way. 'Twas maybe an hour later we heard Dez's car start up. We gave it another five minutes an' then Robin popped the hinges out with his Swiss Army knife, an' we were on our way."

It had been pitch black by the time they got up near Killybegs. They realized they couldn't boldface their way into the meeting, not with Desmond in attendance, but had thought they could maybe listen in without being seen.

"What's the matter, darlin', are ye cold?" he asked, for Pamela had shuddered visibly.

"No, I'm just cringing in sympathy, I've a feeling this bit of the story doesn't end well."

"Well if we'd paid attention to our feelins' half as much that night we'd have saved ourselves a heap of grief."

"I knew it. What happened?"

"At first things went smooth, we found the place without a great deal of difficulty. We'd caught up with Dez on the outskirts of town for he'd stopped to put petrol in the car. We kept back just far enough so he wouldn't get suspicious but we could still see his tail lights. That alone should have tipped us off that somethin' wasn't right, but the one brain cell the two of us seemed to be sharin' that night wasn't workin' real well."

Desmond had turned down a narrow strip of country road. The two boys had hidden Robin's car in the hedges and proceeded forward on foot. They had crept through the scrub pine feeling a bit like James Bond without the good clothes. The house itself presented them with a bit of a problem. The perimeter had been carefully cleared and they didn't dare creep close enough to hear through the windows. They had sat in the brush for a few minutes, mulling over their limited options and getting chewed to death by the bugs. Then Robin had noticed that the windows were upside down with the opening at the top rather than the bottom. He had then come up with the inspired notion that if they were to scale onto the roof and lay themselves flat, they should be able to hear everything that went on inside. As the voices inside were already raised, there had seemed little chance of anyone hearing them, as long as they exercised due caution in their climb. Casey had boosted Robin on his shoulders, and Robin had gained the rooftop with little effort. Then it had been Casey's turn. Robin pulled from above, but as he had little leverage Casey had to resort to footholds and swinging his leg up and over, hoping the momentum would land him firmly on the roof.

"Did you make it?"

Casey rubbed the bridge of his nose ruefully. "Well in a manner of speakin' yes, the place was old though an' the roof, had we known it, rotted almost through. Bobbie could move like a cat, an' I suppose that's the only reason 'twasn't him that fell arse over teakettle right through."

"Oh Lord, you didn't?" She put her hand over her mouth, face red with suppressed laughter.

"Oh aye, ye may as well laugh, ye won't be the first nor the last, I'll warrant."

Casey had landed right on the table, knocking everyone's tea over and sending piles of papers flying. He had been lucky in that the roof was low and the only physical damage he suffered was popping his shoulder out.

"If I hadn't been in such pain I might have been able to see the humor in the situation. All these hard men starin' at me like I'd dropped from the sky into the midst of a garden party, an' Robin's face dead white, eyes big as saucers starin' over the rim of the hole in the roof. But as it was I was tryin' too hard not to scream an' sayin' the 'Hail Mary' over an' over, religion havin' returned to me rather swiftly. Dez was standin' at the end of the table, lookin' like the ten furies of Hell, his mouth all tight against his teeth. Then this man comes over an' looks down at me, a countryman with one of those big raw-boned faces that tells ye a man has spent most of his life outdoors in unkind weather. Well he hits my shoulder with the flat of his palm an' it felt like lightnin' had ripped straight through my chest.

"'There now,' he says, 'I've popped yer shoulder in fer ye, ye can quit mewlin' like a drownin' kitten, an' you,' he looked up, straight into Robin's face, 'ye can come down nice an' easy or we'll bring ye down an' there'll be nothin' nice nor easy about it.' Needless to say Robin came down off the roof, landin' somewhat more gracefully than myself, but bringin' down a good portion of what was left of the roof anyway."

"'Well Desmond, I believe ye know these two gentlemen,' says this man with the hard face, 'will ye want to have the decision of what's to be done with them?' Dez just shook his head an' said, 'It'll not be for me to decide, Jim, we can't let personal feelins' interfere with the settlin' of this matter.

"I tell ye, Jewel, my innards turned to water there on the spot an' I knew we were had; what had started out as a lark of sorts had turned deadly serious on us. 'Twas then I noticed the rifles sittin' near the door. A stack of them, some ancient, an' some with the dirt still clingin' to them in spots from the holes they'd been buried in. The men started to file out, stoppin' to pick up their guns on the way. Four stayed back, one to a side for both Robin an' me. Mind ye, even had our minds been workin' clearly it would have been foolhardy to make a break for it; such men have little compunction about shootin' a man in the back if he's tryin' to make a run for it."

The men had loaded the two boys into the back of an ancient farm lorry, which had a good thick crush of manure on its bed. They were made to lay facedown in the muck, with four guards sitting on the rails. Casey had no idea where they might take them for that area of Donegal was wild and he knew a man could disappear easily enough in any number of spots. He had spent the journey worrying for what his father and Pat would go through as a result of his vanishing in such a manner. And then had become rather maudlin about the woman, theoretical at that point, who had been meant for his wife and the children he would not have and had generally worked himself into a very unhappy state by the time the lorry stopped.

Robin tried to speak to him once on the ride, but had been kicked in the ribs for his efforts and so both boys had kept their silence after that.

Casey heard the sea before he saw it and it was then he knew there would be no worry about their bodies turning up somewhere inconvenient. His only satisfaction had been how difficult it would be for Desmond to come up with a plausible explanation for Brian.

The irony of dying in the sea had not been lost on him. The men had followed one of the old coastal paths and brought the boys out on top of Slieve League. The south side of the mountain had been eroded away by the ceaseless movement of the ocean and it was a precipitous drop straight down a sheer face. Under less trying circumstances it would have been a glorious sight, but Casey, viewing the waves crashing against the deadly sharp quartzite boulders below, had not been instilled with an appreciation of God's handiwork just then.

The moon was three-quarters full that night and so every rock and twig on the pathway was visible. During the day it would have been a dicey walk, but at night, with his knees knocking together, Casey was inclined to view it as purely suicidal. Not that it seemed to matter much at that point.

They had climbed all the way to the summit and then the men made the two boys lay down on their stomachs, noses hanging out into the void. Casey could feel bits of earth crumbling beneath him and falling away to the sea. The men, seemingly relaxed, were talking behind them, but it had been hard to hear over the sound of the waves. The sea seemed like a ravenous beast that was just waiting to devour a wee tender morsel such as himself. He no longer had the presence of mind to pray or spare a thought for anyone; he was in the grip of a sheer, mindless terror. Robin had managed to wiggle a hand over and clasp his own, and he had found that of some small comfort.

"I've been told that joy outlines moments in life an' makes them clear, but myself I think it's terror that works with the sharpest pencil. When I look back on my happiest moments they seem a bit hazy-like; the day I married you is all gilt-edged an' soft in my memory. But that night 'twas like some demon hand had carved every feature, down to the smallest grain of dirt, with a razor line of black ink. Everything was distinct, rock, sea, dirt, even the wee plants that had managed a foothold in the cliff-face."

"For Christ's sake, Casey," she burst out, "what happened then?"

"Well I'm here an' whole, aren't I?"

"Yes," she squeezed his hand tightly as though to reassure herself of this fact, "though I don't see how."

The boys had lain there waiting to hear the hammers click on the rifles, Casey hoping they would, indeed, have the mercy to shoot him before hurling him into the sea. He had wondered if there would be time to feel the pain, or if it would be so fast it would only be like a light turning off. By this time his hand and Robin's were welded together like two ice chunks, each the other's only link to the planet. Then a voice spoke in Casey's left ear.

"Have the two of ye had enough, then?' it says. My heart started to thump even harder an' I thought for certain I was hearin' things, ye know the voice of God or somethin', I figured maybe we'd already been shot an' were passin' over to the other side. Though it seemed an odd question for God to ask, an' what was even more disturbin' is that He sounded exactly like my father."

"I don't know how long I might have laid there, thinkin' myself Moses with God Himself chattin' in my ear, but then a hand that I well knew the feel of, gripped me by the collar an' pulled me back from the cliff an' said, nice and calm, that perhaps now I'd be a bit more cautious about nosin' in on events I didn't have an invitation to. 'Twas my da of course an' knowin' me as he did, he had anticipated Bobbie an' me doin' exactly what we did."

"So the whole thing was a setup?"

"Oh aye, though certainly no one planned on me plungin' through the roof an' landin' on the table. Had themselves a right good laugh, said they hadn't enjoyed any time as much since they'd all been young lads in the Border Wars. 'Twas entirely humiliatin'; they lit a fire an' sat about tellin' stories from the old days, passin' the whiskey from lip to lip, an' directin' a funny remark in our direction now an' again. Dez sayin' he thought the two of us lunkheads would never think of the hinges an' him wonderin' if he'd have to have Siobhan come whisper instructions through the door to us."

"Weren't the two of you angry at what they'd done?"

"Not so much, more like relieved to be alive. An' we'd deserved it; we'd no business followin' Dez up there in the first place.

"We behaved ourselves after that, acted like Jesuits for the next two weeks, was no wonder once Dez an' Siobhan left for New York we went pure barmy." Casey paused, sniffing the air suspiciously.

"Are ye makin' dinner, Jewel?"

"Oh God, the stew!" She flew off his lap and into the wee kitchen. She pulled the lid off the simmering pot and a puff of smoke emerged.

Casey peered dubiously over her shoulder. "Stew, is it?"

"Stew it was," she said mournfully. "Do you fancy fish and chips tonight?"

AFTER THEY RETURNED FROM DINNER, refreshed, fed and slightly damp with rain, Casey took out his carving tools, unfolding the leather pouch carefully upon the table. Each tool was tucked in its own grouping and wrapped in a clean flannel cloth. The tools had been a gift from his father, and he cherished them accordingly.

He pulled out a gouging tool and set to work on the pair of mating doves he had been carving these last few weeks.

Pamela sighed and surveyed her knitting basket. In a misguided attempt at domesticity, she was teaching herself how to knit. Thus far her efforts had resulted in a spectacular increase in both the variety and quantity of her personal store of curse words, and a small red square of wool, which looked as though it had been to the wars. She poked the ball of wool disconsolately and then gave it up to watch Casey detail the tail feathers.

"Did your daddy ever meet Melissa?"

Casey looked up, a smile of amusement creasing his whiskers. "I did wonder when ye'd get back round to Melissa. Didn't suppose ye were goin' to let me off that easy."

"Well did he?" she asked impatiently.

"Only the once. He was charmin' an' polite to her as he was to any woman, an' he never said a word to me after other than to mention she reminded him of one of those Siamese cats, which I knew meant he'd no likin' for her."

"Because she reminded him of a *cat?*"

"Well my da had no great fondness for cats bein' that he was allergic to them, made him sneeze like pepper'd been flung up his nose, though 'twas the Siamese bit that said it. Pretty to look at but temperamental as hell an' spoiled as all get out. I remembered him sayin' once that those creatures were fit for little but sleepin' on silk cushions an' eatin' from wee crystal dishes."

"Ouch," Pamela said sympathetically.

Casey nodded. "He'd the wisdom to let me figure it out for myself though, knowin' that was the only way I'd believe it. So for the most part he let me have my fun, even after I came back to Belfast partway through the summer an' she followed, takin' up residence in a posh hotel that was miles away from my neighborhood in all senses. 'Course I knew the scales wouldn't stay on such an even keel with my da for long, an' I kept waitin' for the boot to drop."

"So what was the thing that finally tipped the balance for him?"

"Well, 'twas the car, I suppose, that was the final straw."

"She bought you a car?"

"Mmhmm," he nodded, "she did, an' not just any car either, but a real sleek little Porsche. Half the people in our neighborhood didn't have a car; some didn't even have a relative with one. A car was a luxury not a necessity in those streets. 'Twas red, like them candy apples we had at Coney Island that one time." Casey sighed dreamily, "The thing moved like water over stones, smooth an' sweet. I thought I was somethin' in that car, everyone an' his dog stared as I went by. I took it home, parked it right in the street, and strutted round it callin' Pat an' Daddy out into the lane to see it. Pat oohed an' aahed appropriately an' at first I didn't notice that Daddy was more quiet even than usual. Finally though he says to me, 'Casey, a word if ye please' an' indicated that I was to follow him into the house. I followed but not before takin' a glance back to see if the neighbors were out lookin', an' tellin' Pat loudly to keep an eye on my car."

He paused to lay down his knife and blew the fine-grained sawdust from the long, delicate tail feathers which had miraculously emerged from the wood in the last few minutes. He eyed it critically before returning to his narrative.

"I was feelin' a mite too cocky, as ye may imagine, an' asked Daddy how he liked my new wheels. Well the man put the humility back into me right quick. Said I was no more than a gigolo, takin' Melissa's money, though I tried to explain that it was her choice to give me the gifts an' I was only bein' polite in acceptin' them. Well I tell ye Jewel he gave me a look that froze the blood in my veins an' said that my definition of politeness had rather broad an' dubious borders an' that he'd not raised me up by hand himself to have me plyin' my wares on the streets of Belfast for the tourists."

"He was fairly straight with his words, wasn't he?" she asked, firmly suppressing the desire to laugh.

"Oh aye, Daddy never left ye in doubt as to what he meant, an' if he thought the words weren't achievin' results he made certain the feel of his hand on yer backside would get his point across. Dear God," he closed his eyes suddenly, and she could feel the surge of emotion that shook him, "but I miss the man."

She took his hand, giving what comfort she could, knowing it was small in the face of the grief that lingered for a lifetime from the loss of a parent. Especially one who had meant as much to his sons as Brian Riordan. Casey opened his eyes and smiled at her.

"It was the first time I saw real disappointment in his eyes. I'd exasperated the man often enough, bein' somewhat stubborn in nature, an' even made him sore angry at me on several occasions, but I'd never seen anything like that in his eyes before. It hurt in a way I'd never known to be possible."

"Did you break it off then?"

Casey bit his lower lip, "Well not exactly..."

"Shame didn't run quite *that* deep, eh?"

"I gave back the gifts, even the car, which I tell ye hurt as few things had in my life at that point, but I can't say I gave up the silk sheets altogether."

"What did your daddy have to say about that?"

"Not so much, it was more the way he looked at me. He'd a way of makin' a man sweat that was purely unnatural. He'd sit at the dinner table an' be pleasant as a honey-lipped calf, too pleasant by half if ye'll take my meanin'. 'Will ye have a bit more of the potatoes Casey? Another glass of milk maybe?' An' I tell ye the sweat would start to bead on my forehead for I knew he only got that pleasant when he was entirely furious with me. Generally speakin' it would only last until the end of the meal an' then he'd light into ye but good. This time he was polite for two months, an' the more civil he got, the more stubborn I got. Pat said 'twas like livin' in a refrigerator, cold an' silent as things were. It got to the place that I more or less moved out, livin' rough with Bobbie or stayin' at Melissa's hotel, comin' home to change clothes in the day when I knew my daddy wouldn't be about."

Round about the end of September things had come to a head. Melissa's vacation was coming to a close and she had asked Casey to go back to the States with her.

"I'd not given her an answer as yet, but I was home one day, talkin' with Pat, tryin' to pretend that I wasn't half crazy with missin' him an' daddy, when my da came home. He said hello real stiff like an' then told Pat to get off his rear-end an' help him with the dinner. 'Twas somethin' about the way he said it, there was love in the words, an' I got angry, wishin' he'd say somethin' gruff to me. So I said, 'Patrick, will ye come an' visit with Melissa an' me next summer in Texas?' I only wanted a reaction, but I didn't get the one I was lookin' for."

"What happened?"

"Well Da turned to Pat real calm-like an' said 'tell yer brother that he can go straight to hell an' take up permanent residence for all I care, but under no circumstances will you be joinin' him there', an' then he started peelin' potatoes, cool as ye please, whistlin' the theme song from *Brigadoon*."

"What did you do?" Pamela asked, breath held, the tension of the story having caught her entirely.

"Well I got mad, as angry as I'd ever been, an' I said I'd rather roast in hell than stay another minute under his roof where I wasn't welcome. Then I packed all my things that were still there an' left. Pat ran out after me, tried to talk sense into me, said Daddy was just hurt, but I was so angry I wouldn't have known sense if it'd knocked me in the face. I was still angry when I got back to the hotel, it got me through tellin' Melissa I'd come with her an' packin' up all my things, but then I was listenin' to her make the reservations for the flight the next day, an' the anger just melted away, leavin' me with nothin' but a belly full of fear. But I thought I'd backed myself into a tight corner an' would have to brazen it out."

"All the way to Texas?" she asked, well knowing the full extent of his stubbornness.

"Most likely I'd have gone through with it. I tell ye I had a night I'll never forget, though. Couldn't sleep a wink, sat in the bathroom feelin' sick an' shakin' with cold, unwillin' to admit what it was my body was tryin' to tell me. 'Twas definitely one of those long, dark nights of the soul. Round about three o'clock there's a knock at the door, so I tug on some jeans an' go to answer it, shirtless an' shoeless, half hopin' it was someone come to shoot me an' put me out of my misery. The coward's way out was lookin' mighty attractive at that point."

It had been his father. Casey had never seen the man look the way he did that night, standing there in that posh hotel. There was an aura to him that Casey was not to understand until a long time later. Brian had been calm and had asked his son nicely if he could have a word. Casey had stepped into the hall, not wanting to wake Melissa, knowing if she did he would have a real scene on his hands.

"Da asks me point blank if I love her, an' I stood there on that red carpet, half naked, with the occasional passerby starin' at the two of us an' knew I couldn't answer him. Lookin' back I see that he knew it too. I remember it as bein' one of the worst silences of my life. I wanted to say yes, I wanted to love her, it seemed I'd never wanted anything as much for if I didn't love her, what did that mean about me an' what I'd been doin' for the last four months?"

"He said if I couldn't answer the question then an' there it wasn't goin' to change itself to suit me, an' that gold, given time, tasted as bitter as an iron bit in a man's mouth. Well I got the point, an' I knew I'd have to make the break, an' the sooner the better.

"I asked him if that was all he had to say, an' he replied 'yes' and started walking away down the hall, then he turned back an' said 'Ye're a stubborn bloody goat son, but I love ye'."

"I went back in the room then, not likin' what I was about to face, but mightily relieved at the same time. I got dressed an' then I woke up Melissa. Told her I couldn't go, that the both of us knew it wasn't right, an' it had only been meant as a summer thing." He winced at the memory. "She didn't take the news real cordial-like."

"No," Pamela said, feeling a twinge of sympathy for the girl, "I don't imagine she would have."

Melissa had yelled, cried and broken furniture once she realized Casey had truly decided against leaving with her. He had finally managed to leave, realizing his presence wasn't going to lend itself to calming her. He snuck out a side door, not wanting to face the stares of the staff in the hotel lobby.

It was still night as he stood in the alleyway, though the dark was of a quality to make him know dawn was near. He stayed there for a moment realizing he didn't know where he was going. Should he go home, could he? While he was standing there wondering his father had pulled up in his car and said, 'D'ye need a lift home, boy?' Casey's knees had almost buckled in relief. He got in the car, but his father just sat there, not moving and so he had turned to see what the delay was.

Casey shook his head, voice thick with emotion.

"Daddy's hand was shakin' on the gear shift, an' I could see in the reflection of the rearview mirror that he'd tears in his eyes. I'd never seen my father cry an' it scared me that I'd been the cause of finally witnessin' the man break in that way. He didn't so much as turn his head just said real soft, "Don't ye ever scare me like that again son, I thought I'd lost ye for certain.""

"I took his hand so," Casey put his large calloused hand over the top of hers, 'an' said, 'I'm sorry, Da, I never meant to hurt ye.' We sat there in that street for a bit an' if I live to be a hundred, darlin', I'll not forget the color of the mornin' sky an' how my daddy's hand felt beneath my own."

He looked down, hand still tight over Pamela's. "There's been many an hour I've regretted those two months when we didn't speak, I didn't have him for very long after that. I wasted a lot of time bein' angry over somethin' that didn't matter in the end."

She didn't say anything, just leaned across the table and kissed him gently on the forehead, knowing it was a thing he'd have to forgive himself for.

"Now where does Robin fit into this picture?

"Well I'm just gettin' to that bit. Melissa called me a couple of days later, was real sweet on the phone, said she was leavin' an' wanted to say goodbye proper, not leave things as we'd done, angry an' cryin'. I was a bit foolish, thought it'd relieve my conscience some to go an' smooth things over. No one answered to my knock but the door wasn't locked an' I thought perhaps she'd only stepped out for a minute or was in the bath. An' so I walked in an' there they were the two of them—Melissa an' Robin—bare-assed naked, wrapped around each other like a couple of snakes."

Casey knew he ought to leave, but he couldn't move, the sight of the two of them had paralyzed him. Seeing Melissa with another man hurt his pride and little more, but that the man should be Robin cut him to the bone. There wasn't anyone he trusted more and he felt as if he couldn't breathe much less turn and walk out of that room. He managed finally, though he bumped into walls a time or two. It was shock he supposed, making him clumsy. Robin had come flying down the hall behind him, wrapped in a sheet, but Casey couldn't make out anything he was saying, for he was that upset. He had finally looked at Robin and realized the man was stricken, begging for forgiveness. Casey had not been in the mood for apologies, though, and had shoved him so that he fell down in a tangle of sheets and bare skin. Then Casey had run, not wanting Robin to catch up with him.

The nearest pub was only half a block away and he had gone and swiftly gotten pig drunk, picked a fight and soon found himself lying outside the pub door, head ringing and rain falling in his open mouth. He would have laid there until he sobered up or drowned, if one of the girls from his neighborhood hadn't happened by and dragged his ungrateful arse home.

"Woke up with the filthiest hangover I'd ever known, feelin' mighty sorry for myself in any number of ways, felt used an' dirty, an' when I made the mistake of sayin' so Daddy said 'that's a mixture of yer cock an' yer pride talkin' boy, an' neither has the sense of a goose.' The man never had any sympathy for a hangover an' he made my life miserable that day."

Casey carried a head about with him which day that felt like an anvil that had been smacked one too many times. When Robin showed up at his door, he wasn't in the best frame of mind to deal with him. Robin had wanted to explain, but Casey had said there was no explanation he could give that would justify what he'd done.

"I remember standin' there in the doorway," Casey said quietly, "rain pissin' down in sheets an' half the neighborhood tryin' to cock their ears through their curtains an' I'm feelin' this terrible pain in my chest, an actual physical pain. The man was my best friend an' he'd broke my heart an' I hated him for it. He wouldn't go, though, had tears in his eyes sayin' if he thought I really loved her he'd never have done it. There seemed nothin' I could say to that so I spit at his feet. 'Twas what my Granny Murphy used to do when she broke with someone permanently. Robin had lived in Belfast all his life an' knew what it meant. He went a little white around the mouth but still he just stood there an' he seemed to get smaller, as if the rain pourin' off him were shrinkin' him somehow. I was beginnin' to think I'd have to hit him to get rid of him when Da came to the door an' said, in this real gentle tone like he was talkin' to a frightened an' confused child, that it was probably best if Robin left."

Casey's eyes were distant with the memory, and yet she knew he saw the eighteen-year-old friend he'd broken with as if it were yesterday.

"He turned an' walked down the path real slow, shoulders hunched against the rain. 'Twas the last time I saw him until that night in the pub playin' poker. I didn't know how I'd missed him until I saw him again."

"Where did he go?"

"He moved to America an' married her."

"He *married* her?"

"Aye, an' was miserable the whole time, to hear him tell it."

"Have you forgiven him?"

Casey shrugged. "It's of no matter now, he had a miserable marriage to a woman I never loved anyhow, an' I," he lifted a hand to her face and ran a thumb along her cheekbone, eyes dark and sweet as a summer night, "found you. It's hard to feel bitter under those circumstances. Robin came from a different place than I did, though he only lived but the two streets over. As a boy I didn't understand what his life at home must be like, but Daddy sat me down when he thought I was capable of listenin' an' told me not to take the betrayal so deeply, an' to try an' understand why Robin might have done as he had. At the time I was insulted that he'd even suggest it, but later I came to understand the wisdom of what he was sayin'. It's always that way, it seems, with the things our parents tell us—takes years to understand what they were really sayin'. D'ye suppose it'll be that way with our children?"

She heard the note of hope in his voice and gave him the reassurance he sought.

"Of course it will, they'll be as stubborn and unmanageable as you were and they'll drive us completely crazy, but we'll realize many years later that we wouldn't have had them any other way. Likely our son will run about the country leading poor, innocent girls astray."

Casey snorted. "There was nothin' innocent about Melissa, I was the naïve one in that relationship."

"Well I," she batted her lashes, "was an innocent when I fell into your nefarious clutches and look at me now, a complete wanton by your own admission."

"If ye remember correctly," he said sternly, "'twas yerself that asked me. Now considerin' that I was half-wild with lust for ye as it was an' just fresh from five years in prison, I think I can be forgiven for not exercisin' the strictest of morals. An' rememberin' further, ye didn't so much ask as tell me that we would be makin' love, an' my opinion of not much matter in the situation."

He pulled her up from her chair and around the table, tumbling her into his lap.

"I don't remember a great deal of protest on your part," she said, poking his midsection with an indignant finger.

"Well lass, a man will have his weaknesses an' ye know full well yer mine."

"Even if I don't have skin like a peach?" she said, only half in jest.

"More like white roses," he murmured huskily against her ear, "wet with rain." He ran his hands over the skin in question, making it apparent that, for all intents and purposes, story time was over. "Come on, ye wanton woman, an' take yer husband to bed."

"Wait a minute," she said, albeit slightly breathlessly, "you haven't finished the story."

Casey gave her a decidedly impatient look. "Aye I have, there's no footnotes nor epilogue to be had, ye know life is never tied up as neatly as those novels ye're so fond of readin'."

"No happily ever after?"

"Now I never," he ran his teeth lightly down the side of her neck, "said that. That's the part I'm working on right now—the happily ever after bit."

"You're doing...quite a good job...on that... part," she said, eyes closing in bliss, joints melting to liquid under his sure touch.

"Oh, but that's not the end of it."

"It's not?" she cracked one eye open to find him looking at her very tenderly.

"No, it's not."

"Then what is?"

"First," he said putting her hand palm up to his lips, "let's see what we can do about makin' one of them unmanageable an' pigheaded children ye mentioned, an' I'll tell ye the end of the story afterwards."

"Promise?" she said faintly, powers of speech rapidly deserting her.

"Promise."

Chapter Twenty-three

The Travellers

LIKE SMALL PLANETS PLACED WITHIN the vicinity of Jupiter, everyone in Jamie's orbit seemed to get pulled into his philanthropical galaxy. Pamela was no exception. A mere two days after visiting him, he called to ask if she was interested in taking pictures for a project of his.

"I understand you've the eye, so I thought perhaps you'd use it for a little project of mine."

With Jamie, *little project* could be a euphemism for anything from ensuring a child received adequate dental care to overthrowing the existing government. With this in mind she said yes, with just enough hesitation to make Jamie laugh.

"Don't worry, it's not armed rebellion, it's just a pictorial for your brother-in-law's housing project. He wants to get some booklets done up before he takes his case to the city councilors. He occasionally asks for my help in an advisory capacity, so I said I'd handle the making of the booklets. I thought you might like the work."

"I'll have to run it past Casey first."

She approached Casey with some trepidation, but with the thought firmly in mind she was a grown woman, and she didn't plan to confine her life to the dingy walls of their flat waiting for him to come home each night.

Casey heard her out and then said exactly what was on his mind.

"Ye know I believe strongly in yer talent with the wee box. I saw proof enough with the bits of weddin' work ye did in Boston, an' I don't doubt Pat needs the booklets done up. I'm just less certain of yon man's intentions. It's convenient for him, no? He's an excuse to spend time with ye an' it all looks perfectly above board an' innocent."

"It *is* all perfectly above board and innocent," she said calmly, "and the fact is I won't be working with Jamie at all. Pat has final approval on the photos and I'll be on my own other than that."

She could see the strain in his expression as his emotions fought for primacy. Jealousy of Jamie wasn't a new theme in their relationship, and Casey's feelings were not without foundation.

Finally he sighed in capitulation. "I can see by yer face there's no dissuadin' ye anyway. Just mind that the man has always had feelins' for ye and likely still does."

She took his face in her hands and looked him directly in the eyes. "I love *you* man, can you just remember that?"

He smiled, his one dimple creasing in his dark whiskers. "I'll try, but perhaps ye could remind me of it a few times a day, just so's I won't forget when himself on the hill is around."

She kissed his forehead and nose. "Now that I can do."

THERE WAS A DEFINITE DEMARCATION LINE in Belfast housing. After the riots in August of '69, those lines became glaringly evident. Near to six thousand families had begun an exodus out of their neighborhoods, out of fear or through intimidation. Adequate housing to accommodate these people simply did not exist and so gave rise to people camping out with relatives and friends or squatting illegally as they sought shelter where they would feel safe. The end result being that the two communities became more polarized than ever.

Pat firmly believed that as long as Protestants and Catholics lived behind their own lines, the strife and violence was only going to grow worse. Though he knew it would be naïve to think full integration of the two cultures was possible in the short term, he thought that small inroads were crucial. In theory it should have been fairly simple, in practice it was anything but. He'd understood that going in, and knew that his victories would be small ones, and often only temporary, but if one out of every ten relocations worked, then it was gain enough for him to keep persevering.

It was a tough go, though. As the violence in the city had escalated, the divide had grown into a chasm that was very dangerous to straddle. More than one threat had been delivered to his doorstep and he knew he was on the security forces watch list. If the rumors of impending internment amounted to anything, he knew he could fully expect to be lifted.

He had spearheaded the allocation of a small chunk of land to the west of the city, where he thought a community of detached houses could be built. This community could serve, he felt, as a model for integration of the two cross cultures. It was still in the drafting stages, but already the problems were mounting. Paramilitary organizations, whatever their affiliation, were wont to intimidate building contractors if they couldn't graft off them. Then there was the sectarian divide within some of the trades. A Protestant electrician wasn't likely to do the job if his union had advised him not to.

As to himself, the Loyalists saw him as a Republican agitator and the Republicans as a traitor to his own, one who was trying to force them to live with the enemy. There really was no winning that war, so he kept his head down and pushed ahead one step at a time. He felt akin to Prometheus laboring up the endless mountain with the rock blocking his view to the top. He wasn't entirely alone though, any push that money and time could provide, Jamie had willingly given him. The man was funding all the advertising and promotional costs out of his own pocket.

It had been with some reservation that Pat had suggested using Pamela as a photographer. But Jamie had merely said, 'Why not? I'm sure she could use the work.' And that had been that. If Pat had expected to read some sort of tale in the man's features he'd been sadly disappointed. Not that he suspected Jamie of still harboring a latent passion for Pamela.

Over the two years that his brother and Pamela had been gone, Pat had developed a friendship with Jamie that included, but was in no way exclusive to, their business together. It was a rare week that Sylvie and himself didn't have dinner at least twice at the Kirkpatrick table. He had come to care a great deal for the man. It would have taken an extremely strong will *not* to succumb to the charm, but when one got past it to see that there was a very fine, intelligent, compassionate human being beyond the façade, then it was next to impossible. He wasn't entirely certain what his brother would make of this friendship. If anyone was likely to be immune to Jamie's charms, it was Casey. Though, even he admitted to a grudging respect for the man—granted that had been when there was an ocean between the two men. Belfast was a small town as such things went, and Pat only hoped it was big enough to contain the both of them. He was a little surprised that Pamela had agreed to take on this assignment, being that her paycheque would be coming out of the Kirkpatrick coffers.

What he wanted from Pamela was a pictorial essay on the housing situation that could be used both for publicity purposes and so that he could present more than cold facts and figures when dealing with the city council. He needed to put a human face on the crisis, because getting the real flesh and blood humans to come and speak to their need was proving very difficult. Many were outright afraid of dealing with anyone that they perceived as being in power.

For better or worse, he was the link between those with all the power, and those with none. He only hoped he would prove equal to the task.

PAMELA WAS READY AND WAITING outside the doors of the youth center for him. The building was a squat utilitarian piece of real estate, which hadn't been chosen for its aesthetic appeal, but rather its location and bargain price. It was near the always volatile Falls Road area but was effectively in neutral enough territory that the disenfranchised young of both tribes should feel safe enough to come through its doors.

She slid into the passenger's seat with a smile, and the smell of strawberries and green things flooded his senses. He smiled back with a sudden sense of complicity; they had shared many adventures in the past and it was natural to feel that sense of expectation whenever he spent time with her. He pulled away from the curb, navigating the narrow streets without thought.

Pamela glanced at his profile as he drove. In the two years that Casey and herself had been in Boston, Patrick had come into his own. He was a man now, with only traces of the boy who had been her first friend here in Belfast. A fine-looking man, who resembled his father Brian, more and more with the passing of time.

"So where are we going?" she asked, adjusting the camera bag between her feet.

"A young couple, both raised as Travellers, but she's due to have a baby any day and I think I may have found a place for them—it's not grand, but it's a sight better than a trailer without water or heat."

South of Belfast the country unfurled in neatly farmed squares, ribboned with narrow, twisting rivers. Out here one saw the country of legend—misty, verdant, with swift sweeping rains that were often followed by a soft pour of sunlight which bejeweled the grass and trees, fence posts, and the empty milk cans left at the gate. The decay of the cities had not bled to the countryside, though by Western standards, most farmers were living on the fine edge of poverty.

Not the sort of poverty that the Travellers were accustomed to, however. Pamela wasn't sure what they'd be facing, but having lived at Jamie's for some time, was used to the comings and goings of the Travellers that he hosted every spring on his land.

The nomadic lifestyle was an ingrained part of Traveller culture, but it often left these people on the fringes of society without adequate access to medical care, education or housing, whether it was land to park their wee trailers on, or a chance for a more permanent situation. Pat was taking a risk in setting these people up in permanent housing, as many often found it too confining and were back on the roads within the month.

Pat sketched out the details for her as they drove, the countryside streaming past the car windows in brilliant green and lesser shades of brown, with the occasional flashes of scarlet where the first fuchsia of the season had begun to bloom amongst the hedges.

"There's a farmer who's let them park for the last few weeks on the edge of his land, but he's impatient to have them gone now and Victor—that's the husband—wants to be settled before the baby arrives. Impending fatherhood is makin' him nervous. I was a wee bit surprised that he wanted permanent housin' to be honest, but it's all I can manage for them. Ideally there should be sites set up across the country with electrical hookups, an' access to water, but I don't see that happenin' for a good while yet. These two came to me out of pure desperation."

Pat was quiet then, navigating the narrow twisty roads of South Armagh. It was a county of unparalleled beauty—of green rolling hills and isolated stone farmhouses whose pastures were thickly banded with high hedges. Every now and again a tiny, quaint village would emerge from the green, a small clump of houses gathered like chicks about the breasts of church and pub. And yet something about the area had always chilled her soul. It was a bit too isolated somehow, as though you could disappear into one of those high hedges and never be found again.

It was to the edge of one such farm that Pat drove them, the road narrow and pocked, ending in a copse of thick oak that ringed a small clearing. Within it sat a small caravan that had seen better years and two mongrel dogs that were scrounging in the dirt for stray food.

A thin-faced man sat outside the caravan on a stump, arms crossed against his chest, head down. He didn't seem to register the sound of the car pulling up, nor the two of them opening and shutting the car doors.

Pamela glanced about the small clearing. Things looked normal enough. A line of clothes moved idly in the cold breeze, a cast-iron pot swayed gently over the dead ashes in the firepit, and a baby cot lay tipped over by the steps. Yet the stillness was unnatural, as if the energy had been pulled out of the air, leaving a leaden atmosphere in its wake.

"Victor," Pat said quietly.

The man raised his head slowly. A blank gaze greeted them, as if he couldn't quite take in the sight of them.

"Where's Emily?"

"Inside," the man said dully, his gaze having returned to the ground.

"All right then," Pat took a deep breath. "In I go."

He opened the door and stepped up into the dark interior. She heard him let out a breath, "Oh Christ."

Her heart dipped to the vicinity of her toes; she knew that tone and that it didn't bode well for what was to be found inside the dank trailer.

"Pamela, could ye come inside?"

She stepped up, following him into the narrow interior. The smell of soured food assaulted her nose at once. She stifled a gag and blinked rapidly, trying to adjust her eyes to the dim light. The terrible stillness was even more palpable than it had been outside.

Ratty shades were pulled down over the tiny windows, and flies buzzed irritably in the folds. There was a rank undernote to the miasma that she recognized immediately. It was the particular scent of recent death.

When her eyes made the shift from light to dark, she saw Pat leaning over the form of a woman in a tangle of dirty sheets. Lank brown hair hid a narrow face. She appeared to be clutching a dirty bundle of laundry in her thin arms. Pamela didn't need to look any closer to know the woman was dead, and that whatever she clutched so tightly in her lifeless arms wasn't laundry, but was equally lifeless.

Pat felt the woman's wrist and then turned back the rumpled blanket in her arms.

The baby was a delicate mottled blue, as still and perfect as though it had been carved from lichen-filmed marble. Breath held, she leaned forward and touched a finger to the still form. The soft flesh was cold to the touch. The baby had been dead for some time, the kind of chill it emanated took hours to set in.

Pat reflexively crossed himself. "It's a wee laddie," he said, voice low with shock.

Pamela drew the dirty blanket back around the tiny infant, leaving it to the shelter of its mother's arms, then retreated outside. The fitful sunlight which had characterized the day seemed suddenly overly bright and harsh. Pat followed her a moment later. The man sat in the same position, though now he was rocking back and forth, a low keening coming from his mouth.

"Victor," Pat said gently, "we're goin' to have to find ye some help here. Ye can't leave Emily an' the babe there any longer. Do ye understand what I'm sayin'?"

The man nodded, a barely perceptible movement of his head, but an affirmation, nevertheless.

"Is there anyone in particular ye'd like us to call?"

Victor nodded again, somewhat more vigorously this time. "Emily's parents—they're settled people. Didn't want her to marry me, an' I guess they were right."

"Can ye give us the number then?"

The man dug a grubby square of paper from his shirt pocket and handed it to Pat.

"Looks like a Cork exchange. Are they in Cork?"

Victor nodded, his face resuming the blank stare it had worn upon their arrival.

Pat turned to Pamela. "Down the lane is a wee village, stop at O'Brien's pub an' call from there. An' when I say O'Brien's I bloody mean O'Brien's," he said sternly, "don't go into the Arms, it's not a friendly place for a Catholic. I'll sit with Victor an' see if I can get him to make a few decisions here. Christ," he sighed, "we'll have to get the police out here as well, otherwise it might look as though we're colluding in some sort of cover-up."

The village was only a five-minute drive along the bent-back road, and O'Brien's a comely little building that sat in the shadow of the tall-spired church.

The publican greeted her as she entered with a wave of his polishing cloth and a hearty hello. When she explained the situation, he was properly sympathetic and pointed her to the phone, an ancient wooden-boxed relic that hung on the wall beside the bar.

"Jaysus, the poor woman," the publican said, "she'd been in here to use the phone a week back. I'd no notion she was so close to havin' the baby, though. Thin as a reed, an' a mite anemic lookin'. You call the parents, lass, an' I'll call the RUC station for ye. My brother-in-law is the one token Catholic hereabouts on the force. If he comes out, ye'll get less hassle altogether."

The phone call to the woman's parents wasn't terribly pleasant, and once it was done Pamela felt completely drained.

"Sit a minute lass, I've poured ye a small whiskey to put the blood back in yer veins. Drink it down before ye go, 'tis on the house."

Pamela sat and took the whiskey in three grateful swallows. It went down smoothly and set to building a small fire in her core right away. It also went some way toward restoring her equilibrium, and taking the bloody edge from the picture in her mind.

She arrived back in the small clearing, with the police car right behind her. The coroner arrived a minute later and the system swiftly took over.

"Constable Flanagan," said the tall, slightly weedy looking man that emerged from the low car. "Did you two find the bodies?"

Pat quickly explained what had taken place.

The coroner was in and out within twenty minutes, having determined both time and cause of death. He was as round as he was high, and looked like one of those wobble bottom dolls that were made for very young children.

"Where's the husband?" he asked in a brisk, matter-of-fact tone.

"Gone," Pat said, his own tone rather brisk. Pamela gave him a sidelong glance, puzzled at his shift in temper.

The coroner harrumphed at this one word answer and turned to Constable Flanagan.

"Looks like they've both been dead the two days now. Mother died from blood loss and the babby from strangling on the cord. There's nothin' the man could have done to save either, they should have been in hospital."

"By the time he knew the baby was coming it was too late," Pat said quietly. "He told me that much before he left."

"Ye should have held him here, even if it meant ye had to knock him out. He'd no right leaving the scene of a death; it makes him look guilty."

"Of what? Being a bereaved husband and father?" Pat asked.

The man's face tightened like a balloon blown too far. "Ye should speak with respect to your elders and betters, young man."

"When I find a better I will," Pat said coolly, his eyes locked to the man's pale blue ones.

"Gentlemen," Pamela interjected, "it hardly seems appropriate to stand here exchanging insults when there's a mother and child dead inside that trailer."

Pat flushed guiltily and the coroner harrumphed again. It was enough to defuse the situation. Though she didn't have the slightest idea what about the man had provoked Pat in the first place.

Within a half hour the bodies had been bundled out of the trailer, the baby a small round under the sheet that covered both he and his mother. The coroner had finished off and was making notes inside his car while Constable Flanagan had a smoke by the remnants of the fire.

"May we go now?" Pat asked.

"I see no reason why not," Constable Flanagan said agreeably. "I've yer numbers should I need to ask any follow-up questions. The parents will be here by tomorrow to claim the bodies. Thanks for yer help here today." He shook their hands, his grip firm and dry.

Once in the car, Pat just sat there, hand holding the keys in the ignition, staring over the steering wheel.

"What is it?"

He turned, dark eyes pained. "I'm sorry. I'd no idea what I was taking you to face." She shook her head, the vision of the dead baby so clear in her mind that she thought she might never be rid of it.

"You didn't know, and it's fortunate we did turn up—he desperately needed help." She smiled to ease his worry.

"Aye, but did we give it to him? He's gone off in a terrible state, but it didn't seem right to stop him. Besides, all he cared about in the world is gone, 'tisn't as though he were leaving anything behind."

Clouds were scudding across the early evening sky, a dull gold permeating their pewter centers so that the odd ray peeked out here and there. They had the road to themselves excepting the odd farm lorry coming back empty from Belfast. They were about halfway back to the city when Pat pulled off on the rise of a hill and parked the car where its lights cast long beams into a freshly furrowed potato field. The soil ribboned away black and rich into the dusky horizon.

"There's a thermos of coffee in the back. I could use the fortification, I think it's just hit me what's happened. Do ye mind?"

"Of course not."

Pat poured them each a cup and Pamela clutched hers tightly, grateful for the small warmth it provided.

"You seemed very edgy with the coroner."

Pat took a swallow of his coffee and grimaced. "Christ that's strong, it needs more sugar." She handed him two lumps along with a pointed look.

"Alright, Nosey Parker," he said, "I did remember him, though I don't think he remembered me. Last summer durin' the marchin' season—well ye know how it gets round Belfast when the Orange parades are gearin' up—there was a group of Prods that went on a rampage through the streets, an' beat up an old man who was stumblin' home drunk. Set fire to a couple of the buildins' along the street where my old office was. I went down there, but all I could do was watch from a distance as the place went up. There was still a group of them millin' about and had I tried to interfere, I'd have lost a great deal more than an office. They started to drift off when they heard the sirens wailin', but one man stayed. I could see him clear as he was lit up by the fires, an' I was back in the shadows. He was standin' there, face all aglow, watchin' the buildins' burn, as though the fire were givin' him intense pleasure. It chilled me to the bone that look, an' I knew I'd not forget it in a hurry, an' then I saw him today—'twas the wee round ball of a coroner, I'd swear to it."

"He looked so starchy and respectable."

"Aye, didn't he, though? Hatred wears a thousand faces in this country, though, an' some of the worst of it is in the most respectable places ye can imagine."

"It's getting worse, isn't it? The trouble."

Pat took a moment before answering. "Aye, I suppose it is. There's a tension building, an' I'm afraid when the dam of it breaks, many are goin' to drown in the flood. There's pockets of peace, but they're small and the violence only seems worse as each one passes."

They finished off the thermos, watching as twilight threw a thick blanket over the surrounding fields and woods. It was cozy in the car, with the heater blowing and the coffee thawing both hands and stomachs.

"It may be that I am a selfish man, but I'm glad ye've come home," Pat said quietly. "An' that ye brought my big brother with ye," he added with a grin.

"I am too," she said, surprised to find the words were true. In some way she did feel at home here, despite the worry and fear.

Pat shifted the car into reverse. "Home then?"

"Aye, home."

Chapter Twenty-four

Nine Tenths of the Law

IN AND ABOUT THE TWO-POTTED CHIMNEYS, snow swirled in delicate eddies like lacewings caught in a vortex. The snow, fine and airy, laid a pretty blue-tinged blanket over the whole city, smudging its lines and rounding out the sharper corners. Even Napoleon's Nose had lost its beakiness and surrendered into a soft star-spangled hump.

Pamela leaned out the dormer window and took a breath of the wet, fresh air. The snow had washed the pollution away for the moment and the air had the quality of crystal, clean and thin, ringing with purity. In the east she could vaguely see the prehistoric shapes, like dinosaurs risen from stone, that soared against the night sky, of the Harland and Wolff Cranes, nicknamed Samson and Goliath. To the west the whitened slopes of Black Mountain, to the south, which lay behind her, were the long elm-garlanded expanses of Knockdene and Malone Park and the broken-down palace otherwise known as Stormont, Ulster's parliament. To the north, glittering against an indigo-streaked sky, the fairytale outlines of Kirkpatrick's Folly. At this distance it was an indistinct blur, but her mind filled out the details.

She had always felt that the artwork which appealed to a person said something very definitive about that person's soul. Jamie's collection was eclectic to say the least—from a moody, blue Degas canvas in the formal sitting room to the Jack Yeats with its definitive thick flowing lines to the Turner with its soft illumination that hung in his bedroom. He collected modern artists as well, mostly Americans such as Hockney, Pollack and Rauschenberg. In his study there hung only one painting, a Vermeer. It was this painting which best reflected the essence of Jamie. It was the work of an artist who'd shed the concerns of the world, who'd left his personal darkness behind and emerged to paint with a light-ridden brush—the work of a man who was, after a long and painful struggle, free. She thought that, for Jamie, it represented the promise of light after a long and arduous journey.

She was just beginning to doze, nose grazing the frosted windowpane, when she heard the sound of a key in the downstairs door. She started awake, shivering in the insubstantial nightgown. She had—rather optimistically—donned it hours ago in anticipation of her husband's arrival home. The room was freezing, and her nose and feet were most unromantically numb. The sound below went on for several minutes so she cracked the window slightly, hiking up her trailing silks and clambering onto the window seat in an effort to see the door below.

The night, awash with snow and streetlights, was almost as bright as midday. He was clearly outlined, the white of the ground throwing his darkness into sharp relief. She saw him fumble with the lock, curse, drop the keys into the snow, and then, uttering a rather impressive stream of invectives, go down on his knees in an attempt to find the keys. She opened the window wider, her skin immediately rippling into goosebumps at the invasion of freakishly cold March air.

"Need help?" she asked tartly.

"No, I'm just makin' snow angels out here an' will be in as soon as I've finished with Gabriel an' his wee trumpet," he replied, in broad and slightly slurred tones. Rather witty, she thought, considering he was gloriously, supremely drunk. She snapped the window shut, of half a mind to leave him until he could locate the missing keys. However, considering the state he was in, he was likely to freeze to death before he managed to find said keys.

When she opened the door he was laying on his back, a last few flakes of snow drifting down from a spent sky and landing daintily on his outstretched tongue.

"What do you think you're doing?"

"Tryin' to sober up," he replied cheerfully.

"By catching snowflakes on your tongue?"

"Aye, drinkin' water is the only way not to wake up with a godawful hangover in the mornin'. An' as I'd given up on findin' the keys an' ye seemed uncertain as to whether or not to open the door to me, I thought I'd best drink what was to hand."

He was even drunker, she realized, than she'd originally thought.

"If you've a mind to crawl in out of the snow," she said uncharitably, "I'll leave the door unlocked." She turned back towards the entry, silk fluttering around her calves, only to feel a strong, broad hand clamp itself around her ankle.

"Stay with me, the night is fine," Casey said, voice suddenly amorous.

"Are you mad? It's freezing out here and I'm not exactly dressed for the weather."

Casey grinned, snow spangling his lashes and hair. "I noticed. I can see all ye own. I take it ye didn't choose the garment for its warmth?"

"No, it was intended for other purposes, but now I'm going upstairs to change into flannel and rub myself down with mentholatum so I don't catch a chill."

"The tone of yer voice is startin' to make the snow look warm darlin', are ye angry at me?"

She glared down at him, a stinging retort on her tongue and then suddenly laughed. He looked ridiculous, arms and legs asprawl in the snow, fine whorls of frost forming in his curls. Arcing around him was the shape of an angel, with outspread wings and billowing skirts that were ever so slightly askew. Eyes a tad unfocussed, Casey appeared as harmless as a curly black lamb left to the elements.

The hand on her ankle inched its way upward. So much, she thought, arching her eyebrows at him, for the innocence of lambs.

"As much as I'd like to follow ye into the house," he said, closing his right eye, as if he'd only the strength to focus one at a time, "I don't think I can manage it as I can't feel m'legs just yet."

The hand had found the back of her knee and the index finger, well versed in her vulnerabilities, pressed into an especially sensitive spot.

"*Oof*—"he exclaimed, as she dropped onto his chest. "Felt that, must be regainin' my faculties."

She slapped his ear lightly and made to move off his chest. But he pulled her back down and kissed her in a manner rather impressive for a man so severely incapacitated. She felt slightly drunk when she pulled away, likely from the whiskey fumes that rose off him like steam from a sulfur bath.

"Casey Riordan, you're drunk," she said, trying to wriggle out of his grip and succeeding only in pulling her skirts up so that her legs were fully exposed to the night air.

"Mmphm, ye may be right, though ye know they say that an Irishman is never drunk as long as he can hold onto a blade of grass an' not fall off the face of the earth. Granted," he paused to blink a melting snowflake out of his lashes, "I can't even find the keys, much less a blade of grass at present. "Goodness," he blinked again, a slow smile spreading across his face, creasing his lone dimple, "ye're a wee bit scantily dressed for a winter evenin', Mrs. Riordan."

She gasped as his hands, rimed with snow, slid up the back of her thighs coming to rest firmly on her bare backside. He gave her a stern look, the effect of which was slightly marred by the fact that he had begun to hiccough. "An' I thought ye were a respectable married woman, with yer wee flat an' all in such an upscale part of town. Ye'll be after scandalizin' the neighbors, woman."

"If indeed," she said, batting ineffectually at his hands, "we had any neighbors to scandalize, my reputation would hardly be helped by my husband attempting to compromise me on the doorstep."

"*Attemptin'* is it? I've no intention of *attemptin'* anything," he said, managing to grin lecherously and hiccough at the same time. "I've every intention of compromisin' ye, Jewel, an' no attemptin' about it." His hands slid surely round the dipping arch of her ribs, fingers falling just short of his goal as his hands became tangled in the folds of silk.

"For such an insubstantial garment," he said irritably, "it's got the helluva lot of material." He focused then with new determination on the tiny buttons that ran from neckline to waist, eyes slightly crossed with the effort.

"A moment ago you couldn't feel your legs," she let out an undignified yelp, as his hands, wet with melted snow, found the rounded curve of her breasts. "And now you're up for making love in the snow in subzero temperatures?"

"Aye, darlin'," his voice was slightly muffled as he took a mouthful of silk, "not all my bits are numb." As if to back up his bold statement he pressed a rather substantial bit against her that was obviously not feeling the effects of the cold at all.

"Casey, what are you trying to do?" she asked, a pulsing warmth spreading through her center even while her extremities were beginning to sting with cold.

"Undo yer buttons," he said, pausing to gasp for breath.

"With what?" she asked as his face once again disappeared into a swathe of silk.

"My teeth," he said, just as a flash of blinding light caught her directly in the eyes. Instinctively she dove for the ground, cracking her nose against Casey's forehead in her haste. The pain was immediate and nauseating.

"Are ye alright, Jewel?" Casey asked in remarkably calm tones.

"Mmphmm," she mumbled, refusing to move her face from his chest.

"Good evenin' to ye, Harvey," she heard Casey say, and groaned inwardly. She'd entirely forgotten about Harvey, the one-armed security guard that had been hired to patrol the area after a rash of vandalism. Generally she left a thermos of something hot out for him each evening, or Casey would come down and have a cigarette and a chat with him on the man's tea break.

"Good evenin' to yerself as well, Mr. Riordan, an' to yer missus."

"It'll be a fine night, won't it then, Harvey?" Casey asked as though they were merely passing the time on a street corner. She had the annoying feeling he was thoroughly enjoying himself.

"Oh 'twill indeed be, 'twill indeed. The snow has cleaned everythin' up right pretty." The security guard cleared his throat and Pamela could feel his discomfort even at three yards. "Will everthin' be alright here then, Mr. Riordan?"

"Aye 'twill be fine, only ye'll have to make allowances for my wife, as ye've caught us in a wee bit of a compromisin' situation." His hand drifted down discreetly and flicked at the waves of silk that were rucked up on her back. She felt it drift chill and sheer over her bottom and bare thighs and bit him sharply on the nearest piece that was handy. He muffled a yelp and tightened his hold on her.

"Well I'll be off on my rounds then, sir, ye enjoy the rest of the night."

"I'll certainly try," Casey responded, a rumble of suppressed laughter sounding in his chest.

"Well good night to ye then, Mr. Riordan, Mrs. Riordan."

"Good night, Harvey," Casey managed before dissolving into laughter.

"In the house," Pamela managed through gritted teeth.

"Right then," Casey said and in one fluid move, stood, heaving her none too gently over his shoulder.

"Put-me-down, you bastard," she said, beating ineffectually at his back with her fists.

He nipped her neatly on her left buttock, effectively silencing her struggle, and headed toward the stairs leading to the open door.

"Settle down, woman, we can't have ye walkin' barefoot in the snow, ye might catch cold."

"Casey Riordan," she said, closing her eyes against a world of spinning white, "if it's the last thing I do in this world, I'll get you for this."

"Aye," Casey said with a certain relish as he stepped over the threshold, "I'm countin' on it, woman."

"I'D FORGOTTEN ALL ABOUT HARVEY. I tell ye Jewel, the look on the poor man's face—" Casey, still wiping tears of laughter from his eyes, underwent yet another paroxysm of mirth.

"Yes, poor Harvey," she said bitingly, "he'll likely have nightmares for months, watching us roll about in the snow with your head down my nightgown."

"Ah, now about that nightgown..."

"What about it?" she asked, digging in the top drawer of her nightstand for the mentholatum.

"Woman," he said, tones coddling with charm, "come here to me."

"You can save the Irish charm for someone who doesn't know you quite so well," she said huffily, turning away from the drawer in a flurry of skirts, only to feel a broad forearm catch her round the waist and tumble her backwards onto the bed.

"Now," Casey said, putting a knee on either side of her as one hand pinned her wrists above her head, "are ye goin' to tell me what the matter is, or are we goin' to not speak to one another for three days like the last time? 'Cause I'm tellin' ye darlin', if it's the latter I'll go sleep happily in the snow. It'll be a deal warmer altogether."

"Where were you tonight?"

"I had a few too many drinks with the lads, an' I know I should have been home hours ago—"

"Were you with Joe Doherty?" she asked. His whole body stiffened at the question.

"Are ye askin' because ye want to know, or are ye askin' because ye already know?" His eyes had gone an impenetrable black. He seemed suddenly sober.

"You were, weren't you?"

"Aye I was, though I'm a little more interested at present in how ye know that particular fact. Don't tell me it was a lucky guess for I can tell by the look on yer face, 'twas no such thing."

"I just knew," she said carefully, wishing the light in the room wasn't quite so revealing.

"Just knew because Jamie told ye? Would that be it?"

"I think," she said, squirming under his iron grip, "I liked you better when you were drunk."

"It seems, then, we both have our secrets." With his free hand he drew a line down her jaw, across the hollow beneath her throat and further down, pushing slightly until the first button popped under the pressure. Her body, turned traitor, arched toward the hand it knew, the hand it had succumbed to time and again.

"Casey," she said, trying to infuse calm into the situation, "we can't do this, it won't solve anything."

"Won't it?" he asked, breath soft against her skin, her nipples rising hard at the mere suggestion of his mouth nearby. "It's the language you an' I know best, darlin', an' all the words in the world can't come near that. We can talk an' then we'll fight, an' it'll be cold enough to freeze the balls off an ox in here, an' we'll not have solved a thing. Or we can mend things now."

"How," she said distractedly, as teeth caught her nipple through the silk and tugged it gently, causing her hips to rise in invitation, "will this mend things?"

"Because it does," he said simply, free hand slowly pushing her nightgown up, "it may not make any sense, but then it's not meant to, is it?"

She could feel the heat begin, in a slow rush before the wake of his hand, fingers as delicate as if they were tuning a violin. He knew her weaknesses well and played them like a virtuoso, losing himself in the passion of the performance. His fingers were still slightly cold and she half-gasped, half-cried aloud as he touched the center of her heat.

"Don't tell me ye don't want me, I can feel that ye do," he whispered, drawing his hand down from her wrists to push the silk away from her body. She could feel the leather of his coat, wet with drops of melted snow, press against her breasts. The unfamiliarity of the feeling was oddly arousing. Only this morning she'd told him he looked a right thug in that coat, while privately thinking he looked dark, dangerous and sexy. The sort of thug one could fully imagine taking one up against a brick wall in some fetid alleyway. Or on one's marriage bed, she supposed, if one happened to be married to said thug.

She heard the grate of a zipper being pulled and then in one quick, hard move he was inside her, making her arch and cry out. It was a possession, clean and simple. His body telling hers in no uncertain terms just whom it belonged to.

Rational thinking was no match for hormones apparently, she thought hazily, as her legs wrapped around his waist, arching and taking him deeper, making him groan as she felt the chafe of denim on the inside of her thighs.

He pulled back, taking her with him, so that they faced each other upright. She bit her bottom lip, nails digging into leather clad shoulders. He put his hands, broad and certain, on her hips, pressing her down firmly until she cried out, "No, Casey don't—I can't-please—"

"Yes, ye can. Jewel look at me," she did, and then closed her eyes just as quickly, frightened by the naked scorch of his gaze. "Jewel," his voice commanded, "look at me."

She opened her eyes, regretting the action instantly. His eyes, dark as obsidian, unfathomable as smoke, laid her bare as if every corner of her soul were open to his view.

"This here now, is what matters, this," he moved slightly, making her gasp and curl her fingers tightly into the front of his coat, "is our truth, our language."

He moved again taking her beyond pleasure, to the fine line that bordered pain, hands gentle but firm on her hips, allowing no escape from the sensations that knew nothing of logic or sanity.

She gave herself over to him, crying his name softly, head falling back on her neck as he took her mouth, his tongue thrusting against hers in delicate imitation of their more intimate connection.

All the world condensed into a diamond hard point of light, blackness swirling at its edges, dizzying, a maelstrom threatening to pull her in and dissolve her very bones. He thrust harder and she screamed, the sound lost against the rasp of his beard and the brutal assault of his tongue.

He seemed to be everywhere, under her, inside her, around her, in the cool slip of denim under her thighs, in the smoky taste of whiskey in her mouth, at her very core like a hot, hard brand, searing her soul with demand.

"*A liomsa*," she heard him whisper and then again, "*a liomsa*," as her mind translated it automatically to English, 'mine,' he said and again, 'mine' around the soft heat of his tongue. 'Mine'.

She pushed her hands hard into his hair, felt the curls crumple like damp silk in the creases of her fingers, looked into his eyes, burning like black fire, and felt the last barrier fall from between them.

"Yes, you bastard," she said, breathless against his mouth, "yours."

And then the diamond point of light burst wide, obliterating the darkness, carrying them both over the edge and down into the consuming heart of the maelstrom.

"SO ARE YOU FEELING LIKE MASTER of your domain again?" Pamela asked, warming herself against the long expanse of her husband's body.

"That obvious am I?" Casey asked ruefully, "I suppose I could just take up pissin' on yer shoes before ye leave the house."

"Granted, that would be fairly effective for keeping me in my place, but not nearly so enjoyable," she said stretching blissfully, every muscle and bone feeling like melted butter.

"I don't mean to be such a brute, ye know, it's only that I still have my moments of disbelief that ye're mine to keep. On the day we married I kept waitin' for ye to bolt, an' mutterin' a little prayer to God, sayin' if ye'd taken leave of yer senses altogether could He see His way to keepin' ye in that state for a bit."

"I've no intention," she tilted her head back and kissed the soft skin under his jaw, "of coming to my senses where you're concerned."

"Good," he replied, and returned her kiss with a thorough one of his own.

"Now are you going to tell me why you were with Joe Doherty tonight?" she asked.

He sighed melodically. "Where have my cigarettes gone? I've a feelin' I'm goin' to need them." He sat up on the bed, reaching for his coat, the pinkish glow from the window catching his torso and left arm.

"Casey Riordan," she said in tones of shock, "what the hell have you done to your arm?"

He froze in place, hand in the pocket of his coat, the line of his back and arm bold against the fuzzy light.

"Um, well, I've gotten a tattoo," he said as if uncertain as to how said tattoo had found its way onto his arm.

"I can see that." She leaned forward to have a better look at the dark band that encircled the girth of his upper bicep. "Is that writing? Turn the light on."

"Now darlin'—" Casey began in protest, as she reached across the bed for the little bead-fringed night light.

She flicked the light on, eyes narrowing in disbelief, "*Erin Go Bragh? ERIN GO BRAGH?!*"

"Aye, it means *Ireland Forever.*" Casey flicked the light back off.

"I know what it means," she said, "what I'm rather more interested in is why you've decided to have it permanently carved into your arm."

"Well..." Casey drew the word out rather reluctantly, "it was on a bit of a dare actually."

"A dare?" she said, eyebrows arched in inquiry.

"Robin dared me. I think he was tryin' to see how far I'd go before I backed down." Casey looked down at his arm, where a Celtic band with interlocking weave spanned a fair two inches of arm, the words Erin Go Bragh, artistically woven within the band. He grinned suddenly. "It could be worse, darlin', Robin's got *Up the Republic* an' it's nowhere near his arm."

"Robin was there too?"

"Aye," Casey said reluctantly, clearly aware that the presence of Robin wasn't going to be in his favor.

"A pissing match then, that's what all this is about, who's got the thicker skull and the least amount of common sense?"

"It's only a silly, wee tattoo—" Casey began, a slight edge of defensiveness in his voice.

"A silly wee tattoo is it? Should I inspect the rest of your body for signs of male ritual bonding? A bone through the upper lip, a ring through the nose? Just what the hell happened tonight, Casey? You tell me I'm supposed to avoid the man at all costs, that he's dangerous, and then you go out and get matching tattoos with him?"

Casey shifted uncomfortably and she could feel him trying to form the thoughts in his head into some form of coherency. The soft pinkish glow from the snow-drained sky fell across his back, turning old scars the color of new pearls. She touched his back and he shivered slightly, his skin responding with expectation even at her merest touch.

"Just tell me," she said gently, fingers resting at the top of his spine, where the first of the cervical vertebrae met with the occipital crest. One of the most fragile places on the human body and the point just below where the primitive brain sat. She could feel, as if through transparent material, the pulse of his blood and the rhythm of his heart.

"It'll seem foolish in the tellin'," he said, head tilted down like that of a small boy suddenly ashamed of his actions.

"It doesn't matter," she replied, for suddenly here in the half-light, the scent of their two bodies still heavy on the sheets and the feel of Casey's skin under her hand, it didn't matter. Only that he was here and safe.

"Ye see," he began tentatively, hand rubbing over the stubble that coated his chin darkly, "the whole evenin' was designed as a sort of test, for Joe to take my measure an' test my mettle so that he might best decide how to solve the problem of me."

"The problem of you?" she echoed, an uneasy thrum settling low in her stomach.

"Aye," he cast her a quick grin over one scarred shoulder, "I thought ye might be able to sympathize with the sentiment, if not the method."

She merely arched an eyebrow at him and he cleared his throat before resuming his story.

"Well Bobbie had come to me some days ago, askin' would I meet with Joe, somewhere that might be considered neutral ground, for he desired to have a wee chat with me. Well," he paused to take a deep breath, "I didn't like the sound of it, but I didn't think Bobbie'd lead me into a trap, at least not willingly, so I agreed."

"You knew about this for *days?*"

"Aye, an' before ye give me both sides of yer tongue woman, I want ye to know that I felt sick with guilt over not tellin' ye, but I also knew ye'd be upset an' worry yerself needlessly over this meetin', or maybe even try to prevent me from goin'. But, not growin' up in this city, nor in my neighborhood, there'll be some things that ye don't understand. If I'd not faced the man it'd be taken as pure bad manners an' a challenge to his authority."

"Yes, heaven forbid that we should appear to have bad manners towards Joe Doherty," she said acidly, "though I believe, even in Ireland, politeness doesn't extend to having to end an evening in the tattoo parlor."

"Well how that happened is a tad bit more complicated." Casey, having located his cigarettes, blew out a steady stream of smoke with his words.

"How complicated exactly?"

"Well it began with a game of darts, if ye can believe it," he said, tone apologetic.

"I can believe it," she replied grimly, thinking little was out of the range of possibility where her husband was concerned.

"I let him have the first three games but then my ego got the best of me an' I had enough of the drink in me to start feelin' slightly competitive. So I suggested we move on to the Republican club where they've the pool tables."

"Did you then?" she asked, thinking of the ruby earrings he'd bought her one Christmas, paid for entirely by hustling men with too much drink and too little sense in them. If he ever wanted a change of career he could have tried out for Olympic billiards.

"Well ye know I'm a dab hand with the pool cue, so I couldn't let the man have his way altogether."

"How many games did you let him win first?" she asked, sternly suppressing a smile.

"Five," Casey said, not bothering to suppress his own grin. "An' then I took him down nice an' slow in the sixth game, vain bastard didn't even see it comin', took twenty pounds off him as well."

"Casey, do you think that was wise?"

"Likely not, but when is a man wise when his pride's at stake?"

"Never in the recorded history of mankind, apparently," she said tartly. "Now can we move along to the part where you found yourself in a tattoo parlor?"

"All right," he said, turning to the side to stub out his cigarette, "it's likely ye won't want to hear the bit about the prostitutes anyway."

"*What?*" She snatched her hand away from the nape of his neck, as if it had suddenly become a flaming coal.

Casey sighed. "Aye, must be my Catholic upbringin' but I'm feelin' the need to confess all. Are ye certain ye weren't a priest in a former life, darlin'?"

She pulled the sheets up to her neck, aware that it was a little late for such measures, and treated him to an icy green glare. "You'll think I ran the Inquisition single-handedly if you don't explain yourself quickly."

"Now darlin', don't go jumpin' to any conclusions, Joe had invited a couple of ladies to join us for the evenin', an' I suppose if I'd proved to be susceptible to their charms, it would have been somethin' to use against me later."

"Ladies?" Pamela said acidly, determined to stick to what she saw as the salient point.

"Aye well, admittedly I'm applyin' the term loosely, no pun intended," he added, seeing the thunderclouds gathering on her brow.

She sniffed the air delicately, eyes narrowing and nostrils flaring as she picked up a thread of cheap perfume. "Just how unsusceptible were you?" she asked, striving for a light tone and failing miserably.

Casey turned sideways to face her fully, eye to eye.

"I'm a man, an' I've the weaknesses of the flesh as certain as any other, but I made marriage vows to ye, woman, an' I've never broken them."

"But you've wanted to?" she said tersely, feeling an unpleasant throbbing start in her temples.

He gave her a hard look and she was uncomfortably aware of his nakedness and her own. "If I tell ye that I've felt base lust for another woman, but not in any way that matters to what there is between the two of us, will ye understand it?"

"No," she said, knowing even as she said it that her answer was purely reactionary, for she did understand what he meant. Desire was a thing of little space, and when it had no basis other than the purely physical its fire was quickly doused. At present, however, she found herself in no mood to give him the benefit of the philosophical doubt.

"Do ye think so little of me, then?" he asked, his own anger quick to rise and darken his face. "That I'd lust after anything in a skirt?"

"Would you?"

"What would ye like me to say," he asked, grabbing her firmly by the upper arm, "that I feel no desire for any but you?"

She made a vain effort to twist herself out of his grasp but he only hung on tighter.

"Not if it's a lie," she gasped angrily, casting a narrow glance at his more vulnerable parts and judging the distance between them and her free hand.

"Don't even think it," he said firmly. "I'd have ye flat on yer arse before ye could get yer hand on them."

"You've already had me there once tonight," she said.

"I'm thinkin'," he said ominously, "ye'll not enjoy the method I've in mind this time." He was breathing heavily through his nose, eyes narrowed and lit with a pure black flame. "My da always used to say that people who live in glass houses ought not to throw stones." His voice was mild as fresh-combed honey, but having heard the tone before, she knew it meant he was beyond fury and was feeling calmly homicidal.

"What the hell is that supposed to mean?" She was tight in the grip of a seething fury herself.

"There's a mighty big glass house up on the hill an' even a blind man can see through some walls. Can ye say ye haven't desired him?"

The air between them was so deeply charged that it seemed as if every atom were separate and visible, proton and electron doing their age-old dance limned in blue fire. In that turbulent whirl there seemed no space for lies.

"No, I'll not say I haven't," she said, holding his eyes steady, though a hot flush crept along her cheekbones.

Casey flinched, his grip on her arm loosening considerably.

"I'm sorry," she said quietly, "but you did ask."

"Aye, I asked," he agreed wearily and took his hand from her altogether, the anger between them swiftly deflating. "But it's one thing to think it an' quite another to have it boldly stated to ye."

"So I guess," she said, hand tentatively touching his forearm, "we've established that we're both human."

"Can't say I'm thrilled with the results of that conclusion," Casey said, though he didn't make any effort to dislodge her hand from his arm.

"Casey," she said, voice tight around the lump that had suddenly formed in her throat, "do you regret marrying me?"

He closed his eyes and took a breath, face tight with emotion. "How can ye even ask such a question, Pamela?"

"It's only that I know it's—I can be difficult."

He shook his head, opening his eyes to search her face and, she suspected, her heart. There was nothing, it seemed, that the damn man didn't see when he really looked. And then, gently, he spoke.

"Do ye not know what a wonder ye are to me woman? That ye should love me the way that ye do, that ye should forgive as ye have time an' again. When ye come to me without reservation an' lie in my arms it's like holdin' a miracle. It restores my faith just to be allowed to love you. There's not a thing in this world that I'd risk that for. Not a thing, d'ye understand?"

She nodded, unable to speak, feeling as thin-skinned and fragile as a soap bubble.

"Let's get some sleep," he said, voice suddenly weary, "ye may not be so difficult but ye do wear a man out at times." He rubbed his temples with both hands and sighed. "I'm goin' to have a powerful hangover in the mornin', an' I've a feelin'," he smiled ruefully, "I'm goin' to get very little sympathy in the matter."

She leaned over kissing him gently on each temple before sliding down between the crumpled sheets, realizing just how exhausted she was herself. "I'll bring you tea and aspirin first thing in the morning," she promised, "and I won't look reprovingly at you once."

"Don't be after makin' promises ye can't keep, Jewel," he said, pulling the quilt up over the both of them as he settled against her spoon-fashion, skin to skin, his warmth radiating out over her immediately, cocooning her against the chill of the room.

"Casey," she said softly, "you don't have to worry about Jamie."

"Aye well," he said sleepily, left arm firm around her, "ye know what they say."

"No what do they say?" she asked quietly, watching the soft pink light lay its glow on their entwined hands, the two silver bands, Casey's slightly wider, side by side. Outside the snow had begun to fall again, flakes of it hissed softly against the window, melting into translucence at once.

"That possession is nine-tenths of the law."

Mine, he had said, *mine* and had meant it.

Chapter Twenty-five

Hollow of Flowers

ASAGGING, UNUSED LITTLE GATE HUNG between two elm trees. From there the land dropped sharply away from the main road, with steps cut into the hillside leading down to a small hollow.

A straggling, weather-beaten stone wall banded the property and was all but smothered in rambling rose canes and dark, gloss green ivy. In the base of the hollow sat an old neglected farmhouse. The roof was partially caved in, the thatch wearing a frowsy look like a woman with a bad permanent. The walls still stood straight, though all the windows were cracked or shattered. The chimney, which canted up the western wall of the house, was a crumbling ruin, sprouting luminous green ferns from its every crack.

Casey took Pamela's hand and led her down the steps with an air of barely suppressed excitement. Crocuses grew in golden abundance in the sunken ground, a cheery flash amongst the delicately mottled lichens.

She heard a sound like that of someone whispering and then laughing softly to themselves.

"What's that noise?" she asked, wondering how far they were in actual distance from civilization. Metaphysically speaking it seemed thousands of miles and at least as many years.

"'Tis a brook that cuts across the back corner of the property, it's not very wide," Casey gestured slightly more than a shoulder's width, "but it's a good-natured bit of water."

Pamela, belatedly, began to suspect there was more to this walk than stretching the legs. "So you've been here before?"

"Aye," he replied, "a time or two, out ramblin' about an' stumbled across the place. Literally, the first time, it was dark an' I fell over the stones there." He nodded toward the crumbled foundation of an ancient outbuilding. He tugged her hand. "What I want to show ye is over this way, Jewel."

He led her down an overgrown path, a barely discernible thread in the tall grass, which was knotted with tree roots cracking the skein of the soil. The path faded into a heavy carpet of needles, springy and sharp-scented beneath their feet. The undergrowth was sparse here, the evergreen branches overhead like softly up-tilted umbrellas.

"Here," Casey said, halting in front of a huge tree, "is what I wanted to show ye."

In front of her stood a tree that soared above the others, its bottom-most branches far above the tops of the surrounding trees. "What in heavens name is that?" Pamela asked, craning her head back as far as it would go.

"A sequoia," Casey answered, the sound of a discoverer's triumph in his words.

"A sequoia? Isn't that impossible?" Above her, eighty feet high, stretched the proof of his words though.

"Well that's what I thought too," Casey said, one hand running down the rough bark of the tree. "So I asked Dacy's brother-in-law, who belongs to the Belfast Naturalist Society, to come out an' have a look. He'd a theory that seems to make it very possible. Ye see, Jewel, Belfast is a city on stilts, which is something I did know. It's also been at a much higher elevation in years gone past, an' been swamped by the sea as well. About thirty feet down there's a layer of peat bog that shows where the level of the land once lay. There'd have been forests of Scotch pine, alders, willows an' hazel with Finn MacCool's red deer roamin' through the thickets." He made a broad sweeping gesture with his hand as though the ancient landscape were entirely visible around them.

"When the last ice age retreated it cleared the Lagan valley, but choked off the Lough, so the entire area of Belfast would have been a huge lake. It would have been there for a good long time, with streams feedin' layers of sediment into it, mostly red sand or red clay, which is where Belfast gets its penchant for red brick buildins'. I suppose. Then the land began to sink an' all of what's the city today was undersea an' for thousands of years layers of sleech—'tis a fine blue clay—built up. The blue clay is an adequate foundation for smaller buildins' but when they started to put up larger ones they had to provide a good solid underpinnin' an' so they drove huge balks of timber down through the softer layers 'til they hit the red sands or harder clay."

A suspicion was forming in Pamela's mind as Casey waxed in his enthusiasm for Belfast's geography, a subject for which he'd never before revealed a great passion. He was pointing to a drop in the land just beyond the tree now, where the earth had been sheared off sometime in the past.

'If ye look at the lay of the land, ye'll note that there's jagged escarpments here an' there at the side of a broad, level plain. That would have been where the ancient seas hit the shore an' left their mark. So if ye'd a bit of land that was high enough, it's possible it would have escaped the floodin'. Effectively ye'd be standin' on a wee bit of ground that was thousands of years older than what surrounded it even at a distance of a few feet. An' the soil might be of a different consistency altogether, bein' that sequoias prefer well-drained areas."

"So you're saying this tree has been here for thousands of years?"

"Well either that or some intrepid Californian dropped a seed out of his pocket several hundred years ago, which seems a little more far-fetched than my original thesis."

He took her hand and led her to the low stone wall. They sat on the crumbling stone, the damp of the moss instantly penetrating their clothing. Casey, however, warming to his subject, seemed oblivious to the elements.

"There's a strip of serpentine that shows up in the mountains of Scotland an' then again in Ireland, an' then picks up on the other side of the Atlantic in Newfoundland before runnin' a strip down the eastern seaboard into the Appalachians. There's a lot of controversy about the original landmass before the continents broke apart, but it makes sense in a romantic sort of a way, don't ye think? That Ireland was part of what's now the eastern North American coastline. Which would certainly explain why the Irish fled there like 'twas the Hibernian version of Zion."

"Either that or it was the first place the boat docked," she said dryly.

"Ah, have ye no romance in yer soul, Jewel? Sometimes I have serious doubts about yer Irish blood. I think that Yankee practicality takes a high hand with it at times. Then ye give me a severe tongue lashin' an' I've no doubt that ye're descended from the wild men that used to roam these hills."

"You're waxing rather romantic yourself tonight."

"Aye," a wistful note had crept into his voice. "'Tis this wee bit of land that does it. Stirs somethin' in me that's purely sentimental, I'll admit. First night I came here it made me think of this man, Robert Praeger, who wrote a book called *The Way That I Went*, many years ago. He was a field botanist who'd spent a lifetime wanderin' the hills an' bogs, pokin' into the burial mounds, swimmin' in flooded caverns an' diggin' up fossils. Seemed a grand life. I wanted to do the same, just wander the ground for all my days. I could imagine him, the first time I saw this place, walkin' through, stoppin' for a pipe by the old chimney. It was almost as if I could see traces of a life I might have lived, here."

Pamela felt slightly nonplussed, Casey was generally very practical when it came to jobs, taking up whatever was to hand. He'd never expressed any unfulfilled dreams in this vein before. And yet land was his natural element, just as water was hers. It satisfied something primitive in him, that needed no expression other than the pure joy of having a stretch of it to himself.

"Da read Praeger's book to us when I was about eight years old," Casey continued, "an' I remember becomin' obsessed by the fanciful notion the man had of a prehistoric Belfast under the foundations of the present one. That there'd be primitive forests down there, with Neolithic men runnin' through them in skins. I thought it'd be upside down though, a mirror image to the one I lived in, with the roots of their trees minglin' with the roots of our own, an' that if ye could find a wee hollow space by the roots of such a tree ye'd be able to wiggle through into this other world."

He laughed. "Well I scared myself half witless, thinkin' somethin' truly awful was goin' to creep up past those roots an' come straight for me. I think my brain must have mixed a few stories together an' then couldn't separate fact from fiction. My Granny Murphy used to tell us terrible tales about these wee red men called the Fir Deargs, an' then Da had told us about the Firbolgs, which as ye know were the dark people that populated Ireland before the Celts came. Somehow I'd mixed the two together an' come up with a nasty brew."

"Red leprechauns?" She raised an eyebrow, keeping a firm grip on her bottom lip with her teeth.

"Aye," Casey responded, looking blackly at her, "it may sound amusin' but I assure ye it was anything but to an eight year old. An' they weren't leprechauns," he added with some dignity, "but only cousins."

"Leprechaun cousins?" Her lips were twitching uncontrollably.

"Aye, leprechauns have all sorts of relations—piskies, brownies, coblynaus, redcaps, boggarts an' the like."

"Boggarts?"

"Aye," he said, in the tone of a reasonable man, "they're brownies gone bad."

She took a deep breath through her nose, knowing that to laugh would insult him. For a man whose pragmatism, at times, bordered on hardness, superstition seemed an inexplicable anomaly. Yet, she'd seen him eye small hummocks of earth with a deeply suspicious eye. And she knew he never walked the hills at night without his St. Christopher's medal tucked between chest and shirt.

"Did ye not have strange fears yerself as a child?"

"UFOs," she said.

"UFOs? Where'd ye get such a notion?"

"I read an article in a magazine that interviewed people who swore they'd been kidnapped by aliens and tortured in all sorts of unspeakable ways. I remember hardly being able to breathe while I read it, yet I couldn't put it down. I was struck by this absolute conviction that aliens were coming for me and I'd lay in bed at night rigid, waiting for them to show up. It was awful. My father had a terrible time getting me to sleep for months afterwards."

"Ye must have been a sweet little thing, all green eyes an' black curls."

She snorted. "Hardly, I'd a terrible temper, got in fights with the neighborhood boys all the time."

"Had a quarrelsome tongue, did ye?"

"Fist fights," she said with some dignity.

"Fist fights?"

"Oh yes, defender of the small and weak, friend to the underdog, that was me."

He cocked his head, perused her face for a moment, and then nodded as if he'd found the answer to a question that had been puzzling him for months.

"What?" she asked, narrowing her eyes suspiciously at him.

"It's just that I can imagine it. Well, I've seen it myself, haven't I? Ye've a righteous anger about ye to be certain. Ye'll not compromise on a point if ye really believe it, an' I've reason to know the truth of it."

She eyed him shrewdly, taking in the air of barely contained excitement, and the way he looked about, as if this ramshackle little hollow was his own personal Camelot. Suspicion began to turn to misgiving. He jumped down off the wall and turned, placing his hands on the wall on either side of her.

"Casey—" she began, but he cut her off, voice eager, but tender with feeling.

"Do ye ever think of it? There we were an ocean apart, havin' our own experiences, dreams an' fears, not aware of the existence of the other an' yet every decision, every fork in our separate paths was bringin' us closer together. The first time I saw ye," his voice was very low, and she could feel the touch of his eyes, soft on her face in the deepening twilight, "I felt as if all that time I'd been waitin' for somethin', only I didn't know it until I saw yer face. An' that," he swallowed as if suddenly nervous, "is how I felt when I saw this wee bit of land, an' the tree that had survived eons of time. It was as though I'd come home, and this place had simply been waitin' for us to find it."

"You want to buy this?" she asked, aware suddenly of the emerald gloom that had descended into the hollow.

"Aye, well..." he swallowed again, an odd half-smile playing about his lips, "as a matter of fact I *have* bought it."

"What?!"

"Now, Jewel—" he began in a wheedling tone, hands out in a supplicating gesture that was designed to sooth.

"You can save the sweet talk, you silver-tongued Hibernian bastard," she said, hands on hips. "And explain to me how long you've been up to this."

He attempted a weak grin. "I'm feelin' a real kinship here to those neighborhood boys ye spoke of before."

"*You're* not bleeding," she said grimly, "*yet.*"

He winced slightly and sighed, face sobering suddenly. "It's only when I found the place I could see us here, growin' old together, watchin' our children play amongst the trees. I wanted more than anything to rebuild the house here on this spot, to feel it shape an' form beneath my hands and rise up on a foundation that was more than just mortar an' bricks. Maybe it sounds foolish to ye, but can ye honestly tell me Jewel that ye don't feel it? This spot, this wee bit of earth is special. It's consecrated."

She did feel it, had from the minute he took her hand and led her down the stairs. She sighed, knowing he had her over a barrel. He saw the capitulation in her face and just barely restrained a grin of satisfaction. He took her hands, pulling her off the damp stone.

"I want to give ye a home, Jewel, will ye allow me to build ye one? Will ye accept the work of my two hands an' know that every board an' nail is fastened with love?"

She looked about her, seeing it with an unromantic eye, being that it was now connected to the balance in their bank account for several years to come.

There was no denying that the hollow held great charm. Bottle green shadows clustered at the foot of trees and gathered amid the tall grass. The gate, once white, was furred with moss and tiny purple flowers. In this hour, between light and dark, it might have been the portal from the real world to a place of timeless enchantment. However, she could see the house would need a great deal of work, as would the outbuildings, which would have to be re-constructed from the foundation up. On the other hand, the house, appearances notwithstanding, looked solid enough. The hollow was ringed in trees, a veritable forest of pine and elm, with a lone ash tree spreading its strong branches over the laneway. Yes, a good place to retreat from the world. To raise children and grow old, watching generations come and go.

"The wee village just down the lane is called Coomnablath, it means the hollow of the flowers. I thought it suited. That I should like to build ye a home in a hollow filled with flowers."

His words held the unmistakable ring of sincerity, and the sound of a man who'd found his bit of earth and wasn't to be moved from it.

"Where you go, Casey Riordan," she said quietly, moving into the circle of his arms, "I follow."

"Will I build ye a house then, Jewel?" he asked softly, though she could detect the tremble of pure happiness beneath his words.

"Aye, build me a home," she replied, and heard the echo of joy in her own words.

"I told ye I'd provide ye with better than stars for a roof an' leaves for a pillow someday."

"Casey," she pointed out practically, "there is no roof on that house."

"Aye, well I did say someday, did I not?"

She laid her head against his arm, the smell of crushed fern and tobacco rising from the weave of his sweater. In the hollow the little house, neglected as it was at present, glowed softly, as though it saw a glimpse of its own redemption.

"Welcome home, Jewel," Casey said, and the words, said with such love, seemed a blessing on this venture.

Above the first evening star winked into life, right upon the dark crest of a pine. And suddenly she felt an upwelling of joy flood her entire being.

Casey was right, this house, this bit of land had been waiting for the two of them to come and make it a home.

A home. Their home.

With the moon for light, the stars for a roof and the scent of roses all around.

Chapter Twenty-six

The Boy

THE FREAK FALL OF SNOW was the last they saw of winter. The weather had turned quickly after that, the day's hours stretching out noticeably and a fine haze of green wrapping itself around Belfast's shoulders.

Casey had begun work on the house; the foundation had been re-poured and the lumber delivered for repairs to the framework. He'd also undertaken repairs on the crumbling stone fireplace.

"I didn't know you could do stonework," Pamela commented, when he'd shown her the plans he'd drawn for renovations to their home.

"Aye, spent a year apprenticed out to a master mason, an' learned my lessons well enough that I can manage something like a fireplace. It'll not be an elegant thing, but if it draws the smoke upwards an' throws a bit of heat into the room, I'll not complain."

"You were apprenticed to a mason?"

"When I was fourteen. I'd quit school an' Da figured a good dose of manual labor would cure me of my longin' to be part of the work force. Didn't work though, turned out I'd a bit of talent for it an' I enjoyed the work."

Things were progressing fairly well at the youth center as well, though he'd not as much time as he'd have liked to get the inside of the old building fixed up. Both boys and girls had begun to drop by, and as he was the chief, cook and bottle washer as well as bookkeeper and counselor, there wasn't a great deal of time left over to play carpenter. He'd managed a patch and paint job as well as a few shelves and repairs to an old table that someone had donated.

This morning he planned to get a start on fixing the myriad leaks the ceiling was perforated with right after breakfast, but had to go out and get the plaster and a few other things for repairs. He was juggling cans and attempting to open the door when his keys dropped into the grating in the sidewalk.

"Jaysus Murphy," he muttered in frustration. The grate was ancient and weighed as much as he did. He sighed and got down on all fours, setting the plaster cans to the side.

He peered through the grate, unable to catch a glimpse of the key in the muck that lined the hole. He swore softly. Pamela was off taking pictures out Ballymena way so his only option was to go to Pat's work, and hope his brother had the spare keys on him. It meant at least an hour's delay on his own work day.

"I can pick the lock for ye."

He straightened up slowly, hardly breathing. He'd helped a lad out of a scrape with some Republican toughs three days before. He hoped he wasn't about to face the consequences of that action. But when he stood to his full height, he discovered a gangly, awkward boy with a black eye and swollen lip adorning his fair-skinned face. A shock of ginger hair fell over blue eyes, and the end of one long finger was being chewed nervously. He narrowed his own eyes in recognition; it was the boy he'd just missed rescuing from the silver car two weeks before.

"Can ye?" He knew he shouldn't be furthering the child's criminal career by taking him up on the offer, but on the other hand he didn't relish the trip to get the spare keys.

"Aye, I can, but then ye have to let me have a word with ye."

Casey sighed, watching his quiet morning swiftly disappear. "Ye can have a word, if ye can get us inside." He twitched his nose towards the building across the way. "There are ears listenin', if ye take my meanin'."

The boy nodded, and then dug about in his pockets. He came up with a professional lock pick. The ancient doorknob was no match for his expertise, the door swung open within thirty seconds.

"Come in then," Casey said, opening the door and flicking the lights on.

He took off his coat, throwing it over a chair before shuffling through the previous day's mail, all the while keeping an eye on the boy to judge his demeanor.

He still stood in the narrow entry, though he'd been swift to shut the door behind him. He took in his surroundings with suspicious eyes, as though he expected someone to leap out at any moment and throw a gunnysack over his head.

"It's not so much to look at just yet," Casey commented casually, "but it'll be decent enough when we're done. We've the small lending library," he nodded toward the shelf of worn paperbacks, with a smattering of ancient hardbacks that constituted their library. "Do ye read?"

"Nah," the boy said, "readin' is a waste of time. It's all pretend isn't it, words? Don't mean much on the streets."

"It depends on yer situation, I suppose."

"How d'ye mean?" The question was asked in a harsh tone; the child certainly seemed a native of Belfast's streets.

"Well if ye have a deal of time on yer hands, ye might be grateful for books. I know I read plenty when I was in prison." The boy's eyes widened slightly at this pronouncement. That ought to go some way toward establishing his own street credibility, Casey thought with satisfaction.

"Now what is it ye want to talk about?"

"Johnny McGuire said ye're a good man in a spot of trouble."

"Did he then? An' what else did our fine Mr. McGuire tell ye?"

"That ye were a mite hard at times, but that ye'd not a hypocritical bone in yer body. He said ye always play fair." And that, thought Casey, was about as kind a character assessment as he was likely to ever have bestowed upon him.

"What is this spot of trouble Johnny thought I could assist ye with?"

"I'd like to have someone rubbed out," the boy said, face dead white, but determined beneath his freckles.

Casey's eyebrows shot up toward his hairline. "I think ye've been watchin' too many American gangster movies. I'm not in the business of takin' care of people in that manner."

"Look, if ye're not interested I can take my case elsewhere."

Casey took a deep breath and reached into the reservoir of patience this boy was rapidly depleting.

"I'm interested in helpin' ye, man, but by help I don't mean haulin' dead bodies about in the boot of my car. However, if there's somethin' short of murder I can do to assist ye, I'll be more than happy to do so."

The boy wrapped his arms around himself tighter, pale pointed face decidedly unhealthy under its bruising. "Just fockin' forget it, alright? The lads up at the home said you were different, but ye're just like everyone else—ye won't see what ye don't want to."

"What home?" Casey asked sharply.

"Kincora," the boy said defensively, "the boy's home."

"Come to the kitchen," Casey said. "I'll make ye a cup of tea an' find somethin' for ye to eat. Then I think ye'd best start at the beginning."

The boy followed him to the kitchen, arms still crossed defensively over his thin chest. He sat at the newly finished table and eyed Casey with fervent suspicion. Feeling a tad suspicious himself, Casey kept the boy in his peripheral vision as he fired up the stove, cracking eggs one-handed while taking the sausage out of its brown butcher paper.

He put the kettle on to boil, measured tea out into the pot and rolled the sausages over onto their sides as they began to sizzle in the pan. Generally he'd no trouble talking to anyone, but was at a bit of a loss as to where one picked up the conversation after being asked to kill someone. Thus the room remained quiet, other than the pop of the eggs frying in butter, and the low hum of the kettle as the water began to roll inside of it.

When the food was ready, Casey added two slices of bread to the plate for good measure and set it in front of the boy.

He hesitated over the food, though he was only too obviously teetering on the fine edge of starvation.

"Eat up," Casey said gruffly, putting the pot of tea on the table between the two of them. "I'm not interested in a thing ye have to say until ye fill yer stomach."

The boy accordingly ate, with one eye on the door and one flicking up and down from his plate to Casey. A bloody street rat, who trusted no one and likely wasn't very trustworthy himself. Casey knew he'd have to take anything the boy said with a generous serving of salt.

Casey poured himself a cup of tea, added the sugar and milk, and then in an offhand tone asked, "Ye want to tell me who the man was tryin' to push ye into the car two weeks back?"

The boy hesitated halfway through swallowing half of a sausage, lashes sweeping down to cover his eyes. "Just someone I know."

"Didn't seem over fond of the man," Casey said calmly, noting the nervous tick which had set up in the boy's left eyelid. "Here have some more tea, are ye full then?" The boy had pushed the plate away, as clean and free of traces of food as a starving mongrel would have left it.

"Full as I'm likely to get," the boy said matter-of-factly, "can't seem to make food last for more than an hour or two an' then I'm starvin' again."

"Aye well," Casey poured a generous dollop of cream into the tea, "ye're tall. My da claimed I ate twice my own weight everyday when I was yer age. Have ye been on the streets long?" He tacked the question on casually, as if it were a query about the weather.

"Long as my memory goes back," the boy said, then gave him a sharp glance as if he'd been tricked into revealing a dark secret.

"Now that ye've eaten, do ye want to tell me what ye think I can do for ye?" Casey asked, fervently hoped the subject of contract killing wasn't going to resurface.

"Johnny McGuire said he dropped in here, said ye were easy to talk with an' that ye'd helped him out of a..." here the boy's tongue faltered slightly, "situation."

"Aye, I did," Casey said dryly.

The situation had been trouble with the lad's local chapter of the IRA. Johnny had been stealing bicycles for a fence who operated out of Dublin. The IRA had verbally expressed their disapproval of this particular manner of making a living, and had warned a non-verbal admonition would follow it up. Casey had intervened on the boy's behalf, the OC of those streets being someone he'd chummed with in grammar school. It had taken a little arm-twisting, a great deal of charm and promises he'd rather not have made, but in the end Johnny, while no longer in possession of contraband cycles, was still the owner of two unblemished kneecaps. Word being what it was on the streets, he'd had a steadily increasing stream of boys popping in to see if he could help them out. Quite often it consisted of little more than a meal and if they were sufficiently relaxed, a listening ear.

"Ye were sayin' ye'd come from the boy's home?" He had heard rumors about the things that went on behind the walls of the school and none of them were good.

"I did. What do ye know of the place?"

"Enough," Casey said, "to know it's not a place ye'll be longin' to get back to."

"The man ye saw me with t'other day, he's the governor of the Home. I'd run off a few weeks back, can't live there no more. 'Twas sheer bad luck he saw me that day."

"Ye're afraid of him."

The boy nodded, and seemed to make up his mind to something. The words came in a rush after that. "Bastard's a flaming nance, everyone knows it but no one's brave enough to say so, 'cause he runs with some pretty tough people, an' even most of them are afraid of him. He's got a gang, though they like to call themselves a 'paramilitary organization', like that makes rape an' murder okay. Can I have a fag? Don't worry," he said sarcastically, in response to Casey's look of disapproval, "ye'll hardly be adding to my corruption."

Casey sighed and handed over the cigarette, reaching across to light it for the boy. The boy wrapped one thin hand around Casey's broad wrist, putting the cigarette to the flame and fluttering his eyelashes in an unnervingly feminine manner. The boy then rubbed his thumb suggestively across the inside of Casey's wrist. Casey merely raised a brow and shot a black look at the fluttering lashes.

"Don't play me, boyo, or ye'll not get an ounce of help from my direction."

The boy took a long drag off the cigarette, slowly releasing Casey's wrist. Then he shrugged. "Had to be certain ye were playin' it straight."

"Don't do it again," Casey said firmly, leaving no doubt that the consequences would be dire should the boy not take him seriously on this matter. "Now how 'bout tellin' me yer name?"

"Name's Flip."

"Flip? I meant yer Christian name."

Flip laughed, "Flip is the name I goes by, don't hardly remember any other name now."

Casey sighed and lit a cigarette for himself. "What did yer mam call ye?"

"Don't remember my mam. Someone told me once she was on the game." Flip shrugged as if it were an everyday occurrence to find out one's mother was a prostitute.

"How long have ye been at the home?"

"Last three years, give or take a few months on the streets here an' there. Thought it wouldn't be so bad, hot meals, a bed at night." He shook his head.

"Ought to have known better, nothin' is ever free, is it then?"

"Not much," Casey replied, wondering if the boy's cynicism was earned or merely a façade to appear tough. Most likely a little of both. The street was no place for a child, the streets of Belfast even less so.

"An' how old are ye now?"

"Sixteen," the boy answered smoothly.

Casey fixed him with a gimlet glare.

"Alright, I'm fourteen, but ye can't tell anyone, I'll be thrown into some orphanage or somethin' an' I can't do that again."

"I can find ye a place to stay if ye like." Casey said, the words surprising him as they left his tongue, for he wasn't sure he trusted this child. "But I'd best be clear about what I'm dealin' with, before I find ye a bed to sleep in."

"Nah, I've a place to kip when I need it," he said. Then he cleared his throat as though giving himself time to assess just how much to say, and how much to keep back. "The man who was chasin' me?"

"Aye."

"His name is Morris Jones an' he runs with an organization called the Redhand Democracy. Heard of them?"

Casey nodded. The Redhand Democracy was a fanatical splinter group that claimed its roots within Loyalist conclaves. However, some of the things they'd claimed responsibility for made even hardline Loyalists look like cherubic choirboys. They were not a group a man could afford to come to the attention of. Particularly a man who was in a rather tenuous position with his own tribe.

"There's things," Flip paused to butt his cigarette out, pale brow knotted, "I've seen, that'd be better if I'd not. Morris knows I seen 'em, an' he's not thrilled about my bein' where he can't keep an eye on me. I'm not safe either way though, so's I'd just as soon take my chances on the street. Short of havin' the man shot," with this he looked hopefully at Casey, who gave him a vehement shake of his head, "I don't see many options."

Casey knew the child was right; his options were limited if he knew things that could potentially damage Morris or any of the crew of murderers, rapists and thieves that he surrounded himself with. Belfast wasn't really big enough for effective hiding, though the boy hadn't done too badly thus far.

"Maybe," the lad said quietly, "it'd interest ye to know that he meets with Joe Doherty, regular-like but always on the sly. Not sure which of them is tryin' to keep it secret, but they never meet durin' daylight, an' they pick a different place every time."

Now that was interesting, Casey thought to himself, while outwardly displaying no reaction. Until he knew exactly who this boy was, he needed to exercise caution with what he himself revealed. "What is it that ye know of Joe Doherty?" he asked quietly, though with a thread of steel to his words.

"Other than what I've just told ye, only what everyone on the streets seems to know. That he sees ye as a threat to the new IRA he's buildin', because ye're not corrupt an' he's not found the method to go about corruptin' ye. If Joe doesn't have ye in his debt, he's afraid of ye. An' fear in such a man is no good thing."

"Aye, like yer own situation with Morris."

Flip nodded, "I thought as we're in a similar boat..."

"We might as well go down together?"

"Or paddle ourselves out of it," Flip replied, blue eyes candid. For the first time he seemed like a frightened child, looking for an ally. Or, Casey thought cynically, a solid body to hide behind when the bullets started to fly.

Though not a man given to signs or portents, it was hard to ignore the fact that this boy was in a situation similar to the one he'd very recently been in himself. Had the Bassarelli family not conveniently taken out Love Hagerty, Casey knew he wouldn't be sitting here. And so maybe this moment here—this child—was his opportunity to square himself with the universe.

He sighed; his decision had been made for him. He had only to submit to it.

"Did ye happen to bring a set of oars with ye laddie?"

CASEY AWOKE TO THE SOUND of voices downstairs. He frowned, reaching down for the pants he'd shucked off in exhaustion the previous night. He could hear Pamela moving about the kitchen and the heady aroma of frying ham drifted up the stairs. He eyed the clock, then blinked and looked again. It was only five o'clock. Who on earth could be here at such an unholy hour, looking for a bite?

He pulled his pants on and then grabbed a shirt, shrugging into it on his way down the stairs. He padded barefoot and yawning into the kitchen, only to stop abruptly, halfway through the yawn, to exclaim, "Jaysus Murphy, what the hell are ye doin' here? An' in my wife's bathrobe no less!"

Flip, having just bitten off half a slice of toast was saved from answering. Pamela turned from forking ham onto a plate and said, "He showed up late last night, you were dead to the world and he was half-drowned and frozen from the rain. So I invited him to stay."

"Have ye completely lost yer mind, woman?" Casey demanded, "Ye don't know this child from Adam, we could have been murdered in our bed!"

"Well we weren't and he's not deaf, so I suggest you keep your lecture for later." Having said her piece, she proceeded to heap ham on the boy's plate and refill his glass with milk. "More toast, Lawrence?" she asked, as though it were an everyday occurrence to take in total strangers and feed them.

"Lawrence?" Casey queried, feeling like Alice stumbling into the midst of the mad tea party.

"'Tis my name," Flip said equably, nodding his thanks to Pamela for a second helping of toast. "Named after the meteor shower, ye know—the Tears of saint Lawrence. Bit of a joke on God mind, me bein' named after a saint. 'Course the story goes that Lawrence was grilled on a spit by that Roman Emperor, Dy—Dee—"

"Decius," Pamela supplied helpfully from her position by the kettle.

"An' that when he was sufficiently toasted he said to the emperor, 'flip me over I'm done on this side'. That's how I came up with me street name."

"Ye told me yesterday ye hardly remembered yer name, much less used it."

"Aye, well I had to be sure of ye, before I started givin' out personal information then, didn't I?"

"Casey," Pamela said, "your mouth is hanging open. Sit down and I'll feed you."

Casey shot Pamela a thunderous look. But she, well used to such things, merely began filling a plate for him. He turned to Flip, aka Lawrence, and fixed him with the same look. Unfortunately it seemed to have little more effect than it had on his wife.

"I offered to find ye lodgin' an' ye turned me down cold, ye said ye had it covered. So why've ye turned up on my doorstep in the wee hours?" Casey ignored the glare of outrage Pamela was sending his way and fixed the boy with a look of his own.

Lawrence looked down at his plate, long-lashed blue eyes hidden from view. "I was scared, all right," he said defensively. "I've been sleepin' behind the buildin' in that wee lean-to cross the alley, but it got powerful cold an' I saw a light on," he shrugged his thin shoulders, "so I knocked an yer wife was kind enough to let me in an' offer me a bed to sleep in."

The boy's tone indicated that although Casey was lacking in manners, his wife had made up the shortfall. In the morning light, minus his denim and leather, a mint green robe wrapped securely around him, he looked very fragile. Casey wondered if fourteen hadn't been a bit of an exaggeration on Lawrence's part. The child appeared little more than twelve, despite his gangly height. His translucent skin was smattered with ginger freckles, from his narrow forehead down to his pale stalk of a neck, his wrists and ankles bony under their milky covering.

"Ye're safe from him here, I'll not let anything happen to ye," Casey said gently.

Lawrence shook his head, the blue eyes shuttering tight. Morris Jones obviously had the child in a thrall of terror. Casey had been around fear often enough to know when someone was running for his or her life. Which told him that whatever the boy had seen, it was the sort of thing that could destroy Morris and his associates. That meant the man would be looking for him, and wouldn't stop looking until the child was dead. The boy needed his protection, or at least what he could provide, considering his own situation. He didn't want the problems this could bring to his doorstep, and yet it seemed too late to prevent it.

"Thank ye for the food," Lawrence said to Pamela, "an' the bed, it was kind of ye. Now I'd really best be on my way." He pushed back from the table, rising awkwardly to his full height. He looked like a prematurely hatched stork, all arms and neck with too much leg to manage gracefully.

Casey sighed from the depths of his toes, Pamela was glaring daggers across the table at him, and he knew defeat when he saw it.

"Sit back down boyo, an' finish yer breakfast. Then ye'll have yerself a good hot bath an' afterwards we'll talk about yer situation. Fair enough?" he asked, addressing the boy but looking at Pamela. Lawrence sat back down with a gruff, "we'll see" and Pamela beamed a smile of victory his way.

"Now can I have my breakfast, woman? If I'm to be murdered in my bed I'd like to go on a full stomach."

Chapter Twenty-seven

When the Evening Falls

AGAINST THE VIOLET EDGES OF NIGHT the bones of the structure rose stark and clear, the wood ivory-pale in the gathering shadows. Casey felt a warmth in his chest and a feeling of deep and utter peace, which was partly the satisfaction of using his muscles and bones until they were the consistency of gelled lead, and partly, he realized in surprise, a contentment that went to the very core of his being. He was a man with a woman he loved, building a shelter for the two of them. A place where they could leave the cold and dark at the door and retreat to the sanctuary of home.

It occurred to him that he'd been building this home in his mind from the day he'd met Pamela. He grinned to himself in the thickening dusk. There'd been a time when he'd have seen such a notion as romantic nonsense, but no longer. Well he'd gone soft, no doubt of that. It'd please his daddy, were he here to see it, to no end.

If someone had told him what pleasure he'd derive from walking through the bare bones of each room, of imagining the flesh of plaster, paint, rugs, pictures and furniture filling out the shell of the structure, he'd have thought they were barmy. But as he worked and shaped their home he saw before him, abstractedly, the moments that would come, the memories that would be formed and lived here between these walls, under this roof. He could feel the heat of the fire in the hearth, the smell of food cooking on the stove, the warmth and snug of the upstairs bedroom, with its window to the stars.

Right now it was only a framework of struts and stone, some twelve hundred square feet in size, but walking its boards, the wood sound and solid beneath his feet, he felt like a king. Within this shelter decisions large and small would be made, friends would come to visit, laughter would be shared, tears would be shed, love would be made and God willing, there would someday be the sound of children's feet pattering, and children's voices ringing. It was a castle indeed.

He walked down the sparse outline of a hallway, the evening clear in his view. He had knocked the back wall of the kitchen out two days before, so now the stairs rose up, making clear right angles against the outlines of trees and field and sky. He paused where the cut of stairs and wall made a small hollow. If he were a king, then here was the gem he'd present his queen. At present it was no more than the space behind the stairs, but when the house was done it would be a fully functioning darkroom. He felt the excitement of a child at the thought of Pamela's face when he presented her with it.

"Thought I might find ye here," a voice said from the edge of the house's skeleton.

Casey turned from twilight dreams to find Robin, hands shoved in his pockets, leaning against the casing of the half-built chimney. The harled stone was softly luminous against the dark thatch of his hair.

"Evenin', boyo," Casey said quietly, the spell of half-light still thick about him.

"An' yerself, boyo," Robin replied, his own voice low, as if he too felt the magic of one of those indefinable moments, where nothing mattered other than the light and air and the pure, clean fact of one's existence. They'd had times like this as boys, where they seemed to breathe in tune with the turn of the earth beneath their feet and they knew, wisely, that there was no need for words.

"Nature's church, isn't that what yer daddy called such moments?"

Casey nodded, feeling a rush of gratitude for the shared memory. "Aye, I'd forgotten him sayin' that."

"He was a good man, yer daddy, ye must miss him terrible now that ye're a man yerself, with a wife an' all."

"I do," Casey replied, the tone of Robin's voice speaking to some deeper part of himself that he kept buried most of the time.

"Ye've got the blue tint in yer talk tonight," Casey turned from the future darkroom, "is the melancholy on ye?"

Robin shrugged lightly. "I'm feelin' restless, got the itch of spring in the soles of my feet an' they don't know which way to turn."

"Ye used to think foreign soil was the only way to cure that." Casey walked over to the back wall of the house and leaned against the rough comfort of a two-by-four.

"Learned my lesson the hard way on that one, 'tisn't so much a man's environment on the outside, it's the one inside his head that matters. Still," Robin ran a hand along the unfinished mortar line of the chimney, "sometimes a man gets restless an' there's no cure except to wait for it to pass." He glanced up quickly and Casey saw a crack in the smooth veneer, something that was still bleeding down deep after all these years.

"Bobbie—" he began, reverting to the familiar form of Robin's name, the one only he had ever used. The line of Robin's body stiffened perceptibly, the crack in his seams closing over as fast as the word could be said, held together more tightly than the stones that rested beneath his hand.

"Do ye ever speak of it, man?" Casey asked, aware he was scratching at a wound that had never likely healed.

"No I don't, an' I don't speak of him either." Robin's voice was harsh, his stance that of a stubborn little boy, shoulders hunched in defiance against a cold night and an even colder world.

"It's only," Casey hesitated, knowing Robin was as likely to knock his block off as to admit to what was really bothering him tonight, "when the itch got into ye before 'twas about what ye were runnin' from, not runnin' to."

"Aye, well the two of us are old enough to know there are things no boy or man can outrun, as many miles an' years as he may put between him an' what he's tryin' to escape." Robin's hand was hard against the stone, white with a terrible tension that spoke volumes about how close the demons of the past hovered about him tonight. Casey, wiser perhaps than he'd been at seventeen, smoothly changed the tracks of the conversation, looking up at the sky, where the smoky twilight had deepened to a crystalline blue, the stars delineated by their unearthly fire as if they looked down on a planet newly born.

"Look at that star will ye, it seems as if ye could climb a tree an' catch it in yer hand."

"Arcturus?" Robin asked, the relief evident in his tone as he pointed to the twinkling silver-red light above the thick fringe of the pines which sheltered the back of the house.

"Aldebaran. It's too early in the season an' the evenin' for Arcturus," Casey corrected, fishing two cigarettes out of the pack at his side and handing one to Robin without thinking. There was a comfort to be found in old friends that could not be found in the new. The movements and words of it were not thought out, nor formulated to please, they just were. It was instinctive, he supposed, when the comfort of another's presence went this deep. Like an old song whose words never left your mind nor your heart, even when you hadn't sung it in years.

"Never could keep my star seasons straight," Robin said, taking a deep drag on the cigarette, the tip glowing hot in the cool air, "never bloody knew how you an' yer brother an' daddy did. Christ," he said, a stillborn laugh choking off in his throat, "I didn't even know the stars had names until I met ye. Remember how we used to lay up on the roof, an' ye'd name the constellations for me an' tell me the myths that went along with them. I think," he paused to scratch the back of the hand which still lay against the stones and Casey bit down on his tongue as the smell of scorched hair reached his nose, "I think that was the first time I thought there were possibilities in this world. I'd never seen it before."

"I know, Bobbie," he replied gently, wondering how fierce the hurt was to drive Robin to making such an admission.

"He's dead ye know," Robin's words were clipped as though he'd had to force them out.

"No, I didn't know man, when?"

"Five years ago now, though he was dead six months before I found out. Went to visit my Auntie Min, she lived in the Murph, ye remember?"

Casey nodded, not wanting to interrupt whatever it was Robin needed to say.

"She gave me tea an' a stale biscuit an' told me flat that he'd died after some pub brawl, choked on his own vomit layin' in the street, where they'd thrown him. Dignified, eh? Fittin' though." Robin took a jerky puff on his cigarette and then ground it viciously against the stone, as if he could grind the ashes of the past out of existence along with it.

"Christ, Bobbie, I'm sorry," Casey said, knowing the words to be of little impact on the tangle of emotions Robin had always had to deal with concerning his father.

Robin shrugged. "It's of no matter really, it shouldn't bother me, all things considered, aye? Should have felt like dancin' in the street when I heard the news."

"'Tisn't so simple, man."

"Why can't it be?" Robin asked, his voice as full of as much mute misery as it had been, at times, during childhood. "Why can't I just wash my hands of the bastard, the way he did me an' the rest of my family? Why do I still feel like I'm five goddamn years old when it comes to him?"

"Because he was yer father, an' there's never anything simple about blood."

A fleeting smile touched Robin's lips and then was gone. "How is it ye can take a few words an' make clear what's so tangled up in my mind?"

Casey shrugged. "Maybe it's only that I'm standin' on the outside an' can see more clearly. It didn't seem anywhere near so simple when my own father died."

"I was sorry to hear of it. I couldn't believe it when I did hear," Robin met Casey's eyes clearly, "didn't seem possible that a man with that much life force an' compassion could be gone. He was good to me, ye know, when no one else could find the patience nor the want, he did."

Casey merely nodded, feeling an uncomfortable tightness in his throat. He leaned forward to stub his cigarette out in a small tin can he kept handy for the purpose.

"Casey, I came here tonight because I wanted to say that I'm sorry for all those years ago."

"I've told ye it's of no matter," Casey said gruffly, busying himself with gathering his tools.

"Is that why ye won't look me in the face when I speak of it?" Robin asked, a sharp edge of desperation in his voice.

Casey dropped the electrical cord he'd been wrapping around his hand, standing abruptly. "Why the hell do ye want to dredge this up, Robin? I said it's the past, now can we just let it lie there?"

"No, because I need ye to forgive me," Robin said, fine lines of tension spreading out from his mouth.

"All right I forgive ye, now can we stop talkin' about this?" Casey said impatiently, drawing up to his full height instinctively.

"I need ye to mean it." Robin too had squared his shoulders. Once as teenagers they'd gone toe to toe over a minor quarrel, both too stubborn to admit they were wrong. Neither had come out of the resulting scuffle looking pretty.

Casey sighed, wishing he could absolve the man's guilt with a healthy swipe to his jaw, but knew things were not so simple between the two of them anymore.

"Why the hell is this so important to ye?"

"Because ye were the only person other than Jo who ever really mattered in my life." Robin replied, "Didn't know that, did ye? My parents were both drunks an' didn't care for me. My father was handy with his belt an' his fists an' little else. Ye knew what my life at home was like better than anyone, but I was too humiliated to tell even you the full truth. Do ye remember how we met?"

Casey snorted. "Not likely to forget, am I? Went home with a loose tooth an' two black eyes an' then Da let me have it for brawlin' in the streets."

"Aye well I had the eyes to match, a nose that bled on an' off for a week, an' a rib that's bent to this day. What I'm referrin' to is the end of the fight, though, ye'd have won fair an' square but ye helped me up off the ground instead an' shook my hand. No one had ever dealt fairly with me before, not teachers—Christ I'd already been given up at school for a lost cause—not the neighbors who always gave me the eye an' called me that little no good Temple boy from the house on the corner. Then ye asked me to come an' play rugby with ye the next afternoon, said ye could use someone with a head as thick as mine appeared to be."

Casey smiled ruefully. "Sounds like somethin' my daddy would have said."

"Ye're a great deal like him. Ye likely don't see it, but I remember him clear, an' I see it."

"Thanks," Casey said gruffly, feeling a flush of pleasure come over him.

"Aye well," Robin grinned suddenly, "ye're still an ugly bastard an' make no mistake of it."

"Ah well, not all of us can be pretty as the north end of a south-runnin' mule."

"'Tis true," Robin said pinching out the remains of his cigarette between thumb and forefinger, "but it'd hardly be fair to the lassies otherwise."

"So many women," Casey began—

"An' so little time," Robin finished. "Though some of us get less time than others." In a twinkling he'd gone from joking to somber. His moods had always been that way, changing on a dime, laughing one minute and dark as the devil the next. "Does it seem like that to ye, man, as if time just runs like sand through yer fingers an' ye can't account for the years?"

"Aye it does."

"How can it be that she's eleven years gone, when I can still see her face as though it were yesterday?" His voice cracked and Casey stepped closer, not needing to be told who Robin was speaking of, what ghost lingered more closely than any other. He knew, old friends always did.

"Bobbie," he said softly, wrapping his arms around the other man, feeling as though he were taking a broken-winged bird into the shelter of his embrace. Robin was a big man, but Casey stood taller by a good two inches and was slightly broader of shoulder. "It'll be alright boyo, ye'll see."

And knew even as he said it that neither he nor Robin believed a word of it.

"EVERYTHING ALL RIGHT?" Pamela muttered sleepily, one eye half open, as Casey sat on the edge of the bed.

"Aye, all's fine, Jewel, go back to sleep."

She yawned and half turned, brushing sleep-tangled hair out of her eyes. "I tried to wait up but it got so late and I couldn't," she yawned again, stretching toward him in welcome, "keep my eyes open."

"I'm sorry," he bent down and kissed her, "I'd no intention of bein' so late. Robin showed up at the house, though, an' wanted to talk. I'd no notion of how much time had passed."

"Robin?" she said, the question clear in the two syllables.

He nodded. "Aye. He was feelin' a bit blue an' needed to talk to someone who knew him from the old days."

"You mean," she said, sitting up, "he needed to talk to *you*."

"Well, I suppose. There'll be things that I understand without it bein' necessary for him to spell it out, an' that makes it simpler for him. Not havin' to put it all into words." He bent forward to take off his socks, depositing them neatly by the bed as he did each night.

"You're a good listener. Not so many people are, you know."

"Hmmph," he grunted as he did when pleased by something, "when a person speaks, ye listen, I don't think it's a matter of bein' good at it or not. I see little choice in the matter unless a man is deaf. Ye've ears—ye hear."

"But you hear all the things a person is trying to say under the actual words, most people don't. You also make a person feel as if ye can take any burden they've a need to rest from."

"There are some burdens," he said, swinging his legs under the quilts, instinctively seeking her warmth, "a man cannot carry for another, though, no matter how much he might like to."

"*Eeeagh*," she squeaked, trying to scuttle away from him, "you're half frozen."

"Aye, an' it's yer duty as my wife to warm me up," he replied, wrapping one arm around her and pulling her tight to him, relishing the sleepy heat of her.

"I do not remember anything of that nature being in our vows," she said, giving up her struggle, half-hearted as it had been, and snuggling tightly along his length.

"Don't ye? 'Twas right after the bit about keepin' me happy in bed an' always havin' a hot meal on the table—ow!" He tightened his grip in response to the sharp pinch he'd received on his thigh.

She nestled back into her pillows, with every intention of going straight back to sleep. Casey was fidgeting, though, and his restlessness communicated itself directly to her. She sighed, knowing she'd not sleep until he was easy in both mind and body.

"What's wrong?" She propped herself up on one elbow and peered down at him in the dim light.

"Nothin'," he said, trying to inflect a sleepy tone into his voice.

"Do you have a bridge to sell me as well?" Her voice was crisply sarcastic.

"Taken up mind readin' have ye?" It perturbed him that the woman always knew when something was niggling at him.

"Casey Riordan, I'd be a sad excuse of a wife if I didn't know you well enough to see when something is clearly bothering you. Now tell me what's wrong."

He turned over on his back, eyeing the ceiling with a contemplative frown. "Ye know how there are things that ye just know, but ye don't speak of them, because it would be wrong to put words to certain things. Like it would trivialize them somehow?"

"Yes," she replied, and he knew it wasn't just a word but that she really did understand. It was one of the first things he'd loved about her, that she didn't expect everything to be said, she knew that sometimes a silent understanding was enough.

"I suppose that's how Robin an' I were about his da, I knew an' he sure as hell knew, but we rarely spoke of it. I think he was humiliated that the man was his father to begin with."

"Why?"

"Well in the first place 'twas said rather freely about the neighborhood that Manny Temple'd not drawn a sober breath in twenty years. He'd go on binges for days at a stretch, an' Robin's mam would have no idea where he'd gone nor when he might come back. He'd leave them without a scrap in the cupboard to eat, an' drink up the few wages he managed to earn. The neighbors had little enough themselves but they took turns providin' for Ginny Temple an' her kids, though some of the women considered her nothin' but a charity case an' made sure she felt the shame of it. She'd refuse food for herself, but she'd not allow the kids to starve."

"Robin has siblings?"

"Had," Casey corrected, "Bobbie was the oldest, an' then there was wee Jo, his sister. She was three years younger, no more than a scrap of bones an' skin, with a mop of hair like her brother, an' a pinched little face that had never known much more than unremittin' misery. Bobbie adored her, tried his damnedest to protect her, but for all she'd been beaten down by the conditions of her life she'd still a spark in her, an' it got her into trouble with her da a great deal. Bobbie would take her punishment for her when he could, but his da cottoned on to this an' realized 'twas harder on Robin to see the skin peeled off his sister's back than have it taken off his own."

"What happened to her?"

"Disappeared when she was twelve, no one knew it for a bit though. Ginny told people she'd gone to stay with relatives in the South."

"But she hadn't?"

"No, but at first there was no way of knowin' any different. Robin an' I were away playin' rugby down in Wicklow at the time, an' when he came home his mam told him Jo'd been sent to stay with his Aunt Rita in Dublin for a bit. He was relieved, thought it'd be the savin' of her. He even talked about sendin' money for her keep so as his Aunt would let her stay with her an' not send her back to that house. A month goes by though an' there's no word from Dublin, the aunt's got no phone an' he's gettin' a little worried. Then one day all the letters that he's written his sister come back in an envelope an' he knows somethin' is very wrong. So he an' I hitchhike down to Dublin an' pay a visit to his aunt. She's shocked by our turnin' up on her doorstep, an' says Jo's not there an' never was. Robin's goin' clean out of his mind by then. He knew somethin' very bad had happened, but he wasn't ready to admit it. I think his body knew though, he got dreadful sick right off, throwin' up an' runnin' a fever. We found a ride out of the city, headin' north in the back of a truck. He was next to unconscious at that point an' I started to get real scared, wonderin' if he was goin' to die on me. I didn't understand 'twas the shock, his mind couldn't handle what it knew, so his body took the force of it. Poor bugger, there was nothin' he could do, but of course he had to try."

"What happened?" Pamela asked, feeling slightly sick at the mere idea of such an enormous betrayal.

"I don't know. Even Robin never knew the entire truth of it. All he knew was that his sister was gone, an' his parents didn't seem to care where or why. Rumors started to float round, as such things will, that Manny'd finally beaten the life right out of her. Robin went mad, goin' from house to house, poundin' on doors askin' if anyone had seen her or might have any notion of where she'd gone, but of course no one did. The police, to give them due credit, tried to help him out, but there was no sign of her an' nothin' to lead to her whereabouts, dead or alive. Of course they had their suspicions, but they could no more prove them than Robin could. His mam said she'd put Jo on a bus for Dublin an' had presumed she'd made it to her aunt's safe an' sound. Bobbie was only fourteen years old an' it wasn't long after that his father disappeared as well."

"Didn't their mother care?"

"She was a timid thing, Ginny was, didn't hang onto the backbone God gave her more'n a minute, an' she drank like a fish. She was one of those women who are just victims from the minute they're born, and men like Manny Temple can smell that sort of thing a mile off. If Jo's da had killed her, Ginny'd likely stood by an' allowed it to happen, maybe not realizin' until it was too late but still not stoppin' it. Have ye ever seen a rabbit, Jewel, that's about to be killed?"

"No, I can't say I have."

"Well they get all glassy-eyed an' paralyzed, as though they'll just lay down an' give their throat over to the knife. That's what Ginny Temple looked like, as if she'd always felt the shadow of that knife an' saw no way to avoid it. She just let things happen to her, if ye know what I mean, an' I guess she let the knife fall on her daughter in the end."

"So even now he doesn't know what happened to his sister?"

"No, he doesn't. 'Twas a horrible time, seemed as if the whole neighborhood had a black cloud hangin' over it, people talked less an' hurried past one another in the streets. There was a sinister feel even to the air, an' I think people were ashamed that they'd not paid more attention to wee Jo Temple. Truth be told, I felt wretched myself. She'd just been Bobbie's kid sister to me, an' I'd not paid her much mind beyond rufflin' her hair or givin' her candy."

"You were just a child yourself," she said soothingly, feeling the strung tension that ran through his muscles as he spoke of Robin's doomed sister.

"That doesn't excuse me from doin' something about it though."

"And what exactly could you have done? Confronted his father and gotten yourself hurt in the process? You were a boy, Casey; don't try to put the burden of a man on the shoulders of a child. It was up to the adults in the neighborhood and you know as well as I do that many people think other's children are none of their concern. Surely people knew."

"Well I knew, an' I suppose most in the neighborhood had some notion of it, but 'twasn't unusual for any parent to raise a hand to their child, an' maybe some thought 'twas only a matter of degree. I didn't really know the extent of it, I didn't bring it up with Bobbie. I figured if he wanted to tell me he would, an' if he didn't it was hardly my place to mention it. Things like that have a way of puttin' up walls between friends. Some secrets are better kept, aye?"

"I don't know," she said slowly, "wouldn't it have been better if he'd told someone?"

"He was too humiliated. Bein' male has its drawbacks ye know, pride bein' one of the biggest stumblin' blocks. Even though he was a wee boy he still thought he ought to have been able to stop his da, or to take the beatins' without fear. I know it makes little sense to ye, Jewel, but it's how a boy will feel, particularly if he's made to be the man of the house in every other respect."

"Obviously it came out at some point between the two of you."

"Was durin' one of them fights we'd provoked, lookin' for feminine sympathy an' such. He'd got the shirt ripped off his back, right down the middle in two pieces. Afterwards he was real stiff, goin' to great pains to keep his front towards me as if there was somethin' he didn't want me to see. So I asked him if he was hurt, an' he said no, just a wee bit bruised in the ribs. I nipped round him when he wasn't lookin' an' then I saw it. It was a triangle, with its edges curved out, wide as the palm of my hand across an' puckered on the edges. Inside of it the skin was real shiny an' not the right color. Well I guess I must have gasped or somethin' because he whirled round an' I could tell right off he was mad, his eyes were like a gas flame, fairly blazin' out of his head an' he asked me what the hell I thought I was doin'. There seemed little point in denyin' what I'd seen, so I just asked him what had happened to his back. He was real quiet for a minute an' I could see he was thinkin' of maybe lyin' about it but then he said 'my da took an iron to my back.'"

"Dear God," she whispered in horror.

"Aye," Casey agreed, "an' that wasn't the worst of it. The man was a bloody sadist. He'd tortured the kids for years, an' Ginny as well when the mood struck him. My da said such men were in the business of breakin' those closest to them an' there was little to be done about it short of killin' them."

Pamela, thinking of the Temple children and all they'd endured at the hands of the one who was supposed to protect them from the harsh realities of the world, was inclined to agree with Casey's father.

"Was he angry that you made him tell you?"

"No, once Bobbie'd made up his mind to a thing he didn't go back on it, an' he'd not use the fact that he'd shared it against ye. In that way he was honest in his dealins'."

"What on earth did you say when he told you?"

"I said I was sorry to hear it an' handed him his shirt."

"That's it?" she said disbelievingly, aware—for not the first time in her life—that the ways of men were mysterious. Casey squeezed her hand.

"We were boys, Jewel, an' so we dealt with it in a boy's manner, went straight to the nearest pub an' got completely legless. Mind ye, Bobbie had some odd behavior that reminded me now an' again of what he'd told me that night."

"Such as?" she asked softly, as he traced the outline of her hand against his chest.

"He'd burn himself with cigarettes, back of his hands, inside of his elbow an' such. I brought it up once, thinkin' I could maybe help but he just brazened it out, acted like he'd no notion of what of I was talkin' about. So I let it lie. I've often wondered since then if I should have pushed him on it, found a way to stop him."

"You can't be responsible for everyone you know," she said, stroking the side of his face.

"It's a weakness of mine," he said gruffly, "tryin' to make everyone behave as I see fit. My da always said I meddled where I was most likely to get hurt. Damn man was always right."

"Are you going to get hurt this time?" she asked, worried that it was already too late for such questions.

He looked at her in the dim light, expression rueful. "Ye're not a woman for comfortable questions, are ye, Jewel?"

"Don't sidestep me Casey, are you?" she insisted.

"And ye're pushy too," he added, "an' the answer is no, I'm a big boy now an' I learned my lesson with Robin a long time ago."

"That's your head speaking, what does your heart say?"

He sighed. "That I still love the man like he was a long lost brother."

"That's what I was afraid of."

He brought her hand to his mouth and kissed it, then yawned. "Don't be frettin' on my behalf, Jewel, I can take care of myself." He turned, punching up his pillow, making all the small motions she'd come to know as his pre-sleep ritual.

A moment later his breathing was deep and even and she thought him asleep when he spoke quietly, voice as soft as the dark which enfolded them.

"D'ye think, Jewel, that a man can haunt ye even though he's alive an' breathin'?"

"Yes," she said, speaking both to his pain and her fear, "yes, I do."

Chapter Twenty-eight

Lucky You, Lucky Me

AS MOVING DAY APPROACHED, Pamela became increasingly aware that the issue of Lawrence would have to be settled. He'd taken over the small room off the kitchen downstairs, took his meals with them, and even obeyed the strict curfew laws Casey had laid down early in his tenure. In short, he'd made himself quite comfortable.

From the little she could gather, Lawrence had been on the street for the last six months. Sleeping in doorways through all sorts of weather. Before that he'd spent an unspecified amount of time in the boy's home, a subject on which he maintained a guarded silence.

"If Kincora is where he went for sanctuary, then it was like leapin' from the fryin' pan into the fire," Casey said when she spoke to him about the boy's refusal to talk about his recent past. "There's whispers about what goes on up at that place, an' most rumors have a whiff of fact to them. If even a fraction of what I've heard is true, then it's little more than a stable of young boys for men with a taste for such things."

"What? But he was there for two years, surely..." her protest died on her lips at Casey's raised brow.

"He'll not know any different, Pamela, he'd been sellin' himself before Kincora, an' at least it came with guaranteed meals an' a bed at night. That was more than he could be certain of on the streets. It's what he knows, aye, an' humans are likely to do what they know an' understand even if it's threatenin' their life. If he decides to live with us, I'll not allow him to go about as he pleases. I won't have him falling back into that life."

"If he decides to live with us?" she echoed, glad that she wasn't going to have to broach the subject herself.

"Well," Casey said, avoiding her eyes, "it's only that it's occurred to me that God meant for us to take him in because we're not to have children of our own."

His words opened up the hollow place beneath her ribs that she managed to ignore most days. Hearing him give voice to her own fears, however, made them harder to discount.

"That can't be the only reason we offer him a home, though."

"I know that, Jewel, an' mayhap the main reason is because it's the right thing to do. I'd never sleep another sound hour were the boy to take to the streets again. I'd just as soon be able to check an' make certain he's in his bed at night. He needs us an' I think that's reason enough to do it."

"Then ask him," she said. "He needs to hear it from you to know that we really mean it."

"Aye, I'll ask, are ye certain yer up for this? Teenagers aren't the most charmin' of creatures at the best of times."

"I don't think we could separate him from you without surgery at this point."

Casey took her hands. "All jestin' aside woman, it's a big responsibility an' just because the lad has taken a shine to us doesn't lessen that burden. I wouldn't blame ye at all if ye didn't want to do this."

"We can't *not* offer him a home. Besides the right thing is rarely the easy thing, we both know that."

"Well it's rare that want an' right come together, but despite my nerves I'm feelin' the both things at present."

"Good, then it's settled." She stood, her mind already moving on to what to make for dinner. But Casey still held her hands firmly in his own.

"And what of yer own wants? What is it that *you* want, Jewel?"

"You," she said simply, "and a baby or two. To occasionally take a picture that means something."

"Well ye've got me, an' ye've a rare talent with the wee box." He smiled, an expression that didn't reach his eyes.

"Don't give up hope," she squeezed his hands in return. "I still believe we'll have a child."

He brought her hands up and kissed them. He laid his cheek against her palms, stubble plush and soft on her skin.

"And what about you, Casey Riordan, what is that you want man?"

"Just you, darlin'. As long as ye love me, the rest will sort itself out."

Outside it was full dark, the one functioning streetlight having given up the ghost the previous night. She and Casey were reflected in the window, the outline of the two of them slightly misty with condensation. It was like looking down a long hallway where time ran in both directions, a place where they were eternally young or caught in the clasp of old age. In such moments it struck her that she could not remember a time that she had not loved this man. Nor a time when she was not loved by him. The awareness of this both soothed and frightened her.

Casey turned his head and the reflection wavered. He kissed the palm of her hand. "Either way we're lucky," he said.

"Yes," she replied softly, not needing to ask what he meant, "we are."

Chapter Twenty-nine

Paddy's Lament

ROBIN HAD DEVELOPED THE HABIT of coming by of an evening and helping Casey with wichever task occupied him on the house. They'd slipped rather naturally back into their old friendship, though there was a reserve built up through years apart and secrets that they both kept. Casey was still wary, but relaxed a certain amount into the comfort of a shared past.

Tonight he was framing the upstairs hallway, which he'd opened up from its original state, as well as enlarging the landing at the top of the stairs. Robin, at present, was sitting on said landing, having a smoke and continuing his rundown of all the Republican news.

"Second battalion's OC just got five years in Long Kesh. They could use a good man to take his place—that'd leave ye responsible for the majority of the Catholic housin' estates. It'd dovetail well with what yer brother is tryin' to do."

This theme was not a new one, Robin had it down chorus and verse and was apt to sing it at least once every visit.

"I'll give ye the answer I've given ye the last six times ye've mentioned it—no, I'm not interested. Besides Pat would never speak to me, much less work with me, if he thought I was within a mile of that battalion."

His protests had the usual effect—absolutely none whatsoever.

"There's a lot of talk within the battalions. The lads aren't entirely satisfied with the present leadership."

"Mayhap not, but they're all scared of him, an' that's all he needs to keep control. Pass me that square, would ye?"

"Fear is not the right way to control, yer da taught us both that—d'ye remember the time he raked us over for usin' our size to intimidate Gus Bradley?"

"Aye, if I remember correctly he used his own size to put us neatly in our places, though."

Robin laughed, stubbing his cigarette out in the empty tin can that was kept about for that exact purpose. "He said a physical demonstration, with a dose of our own medicine, was the best preventative he knew."

Casey eyed the ceiling line owlishly. The damn thing would not come out perfectly level, try as he might. Apparently trying to square the roof wasn't going to square with trying to maintain the original integrity of the outside walls.

"So what is it ye think Joe cannot provide?"

"Well for starters he's not got a great deal of organizational skill," Robin said. "And he's no sense of history—an' that's not something anyone could ever accuse you of, man. There's no sense of what we're to be about; it's chaos from top to bottom."

"Bobbie," he sighed in frustration, both at Robin and at the roof. "Let it be, man."

Robin however, was not one to be gainsaid. "If I didn't know better man I'd say ye're afraid; ye never had fear when we were lads."

"I'm not that boy anymore, Robin."

"Then who the hell is it that ye think ye are?"

Casey sat and poured two cups of tea out of the flask he'd brought along. "Give me a cigarette."

Robin pulled one from his pack and gave it to him. He held out a lit match, and Casey took a sweet, lung filling drag that made his head swim with pleasure.

"Only the second one I've had today, I'm tryin' to cut back."

Robin merely quirked a dubious brow at him and continued doggedly on his previous track. "I asked ye a question man, who is it that ye think ye are these days?"

Casey gave him a black look, then relented on a long exhalation of smoke.

"I don't always know, Robin, but I'm tryin' to remember who it was my father taught me to be, an' that wasn't a man of hate, nor violence, but a man who worked hard an' looked after those around him. That's who I want to be, Bobbie—that man my father wanted me to be, the one he believed I could be."

Robin sighed theatrically. "When ye start talkin' about yer da in such a manner, I know I'm defeated. But perhaps we could use ye in an advisory manner, that way ye could salve yer conscience about bein' counted as one of us, but still use yer brain in the manner for which it was designed."

Casey took a deep breath through his nose and turned over a sheet of paper on which he'd been making rough plans for a pantry. He fished a pencil from his pocket and drew three broad strokes on the page.

"Look, it's simple really. The movement has always run on the holy trinity of the army, the party an' the paper. Never forget how important ink is to the revolution." Below his hand, he'd drawn a rough triangle of the three eternal supports of the Irish revolutionary movement. "Ye need a paper to support your ideas an' to unify all those that are on the fringes an' maybe feelin' a bit disenfranchised by the movement. Ye ought to publish both an English version an' an Irish one. Talk to Rory Callahan, he's a fourth generation printer. He'll know the costs an' difficulties of startin' up a paper."

He stroked a line out to the side. "Ye'll need to put a support system in place as well, for the families of the men who will inevitably find themselves in prison or on the run at some point. Ye talk to the women about that, they know who's in need of tea an' comfort an' has no groceries in the cupboard. Supply them with a stable fund of petty cash, they can come to ye direct for larger sums when there's need an' they'll put the supports in place."

Robin nodded, the beginnings of a smile playing about his mouth. Casey merely rolled his eyes and continued.

"Now the party is a bit of a different matter. Ye need to organize from the bottom up, youth clubs are yer first level of indoctrination as ye know. They're also handy for recruitment purposes, ye can skim the wheat from the chaff in that manner. Now about the women, the Officials I think are a bit out of date with the Cumann na mBan. The world is movin' forward an' ye'll have to accept that women are part of that movement. They'll want an active role, some will likely want to be on active service an' if ye know how to use what they offer, it's a good thing."

"As for Sinn Fein, open contact is out of the question. Publicly ye divorce the army an' the party; it's not good for the ballot box if ye take my meanin'. Ye let the local constituency offices deal with the neighborhood issues, they've got their own boys who can keep order on the streets. No hard men in the party, no one wants to take their complaints to a man who looks like he'd have little compunction about shootin' them at close range. Ye need the talkers, a man who can speak well is the best asset—an' he'd best be someone who's dog stubborn to push bills through an' stay the course, despite the discouragement he's goin' to come against. The further apart the party an' the army can be seen to be, the better. In fact if ye can get the politicos to publicly castigate the army an' its policy of armed force all the better. Even a man with the devil's own tongue in his head can't make much progress if the voters see him as supportin' a force that uses violence to make their point."

He stopped to take a swig of his tepid tea. "Now the army. What I see as yer biggest problem here is what has always been the stickin' point. Arms. Where do ye get the money an' where do ye get the weapons once ye have the money? Seems simple enough to say it, but ye know it's never been easy. There's never any bloody money, an' British intelligence is keepin' their eyes peeled for guns or ammo of any sort. Ye need money from outside, not just the annual contribution from skint farmers up north." He rubbed his forehead, leaving a smudge of lead in the wake of his fingers.

"Ye need to get somethin' organized over the pond. I know of a few men who could handle it. Ye need to beat the drum a bit—play on Irish American sympathies, the Mother country an' all that. With luck ye'll be able to count on a steady if small flow of cash, it'll be enough to keep things goin' once everything is established but it won't be enough for a large haul of arms, which ye'll need. Don't look to America for the arms either, it's too traceable, an' the Brits are keepin' a tight eye on those channels right now. If ye have the money, look to the Middle East. They've got access to Russian weaponry, which isn't the best quality but it's a sight better than a few rusty old Lee-Enfields an' pistols that have been buried in some farmer's field since the Civil War. I know a man in Germany who's got contacts. I'll leave his numbers with ye. Get yer boys in London to set up the deal, it's likely ye're bein' watched with a gimlet eye right now an' any call ye make, especially at the public phones, is goin' to be highly suspect."

"Ye need a good, solid man in the offices, someone with patience for all that are goin' to wander through—the journalists, the radical students, the man whose granddaddy fought the Tans fifty years ago, an' the dreamers; for some reason, which I can't always fathom, we always attract the bloody dreamers."

Robin leaned back against the staircase railing, folding his arms in a relaxed manner across his chest. "As I remember it, ye were a bit of a dreamer yerself, man. 'Twas you that taught me what the struggle was really about."

"Aye well, I was a boy an' now I'm a man, an' the direction of my dreams has changed a bit."

"Love her that much, do ye?"

"I do," Casey replied soberly, "I made a choice some time back, an' I'll stick to the course I've chosen."

"Despite all the bumps in the road?"

"'Tis the bumps that make a man appreciate the ride," Casey replied, but there was no levity in his face or tone and Robin took the hint that this particular subject was closed to him.

Robin took his tea from the floor, swirled the lukewarm depths and then peered into the cup as though searching for an answer in the scummy liquid. "Ye should be runnin' things," he said, tone light, eyes still fixed to his cup. "Joe'll never be the sort of leader you were an' could be again for us."

Casey shook his head resolutely. "Bobbie, I'm not interested. I've a good job, a nice home an' a marriage that I'll not risk for anything."

Robin shrugged. "It's only a wee bit sad, ye know. It's as if ye've completely avoided ye're destiny."

Casey made a derisive noise. "What destiny? An early grave or several decades spent behind bars? A grand fate, surely, but one I can live without. Besides there'd be a bloodbath the likes of which I've no wish to ever see."

"Still," Robin continued stubbornly, "I think ye'd be the best man for it."

"Why?" Casey asked, tone exasperated.

"For all the obvious reasons, the Riordan name is legendary, ye've experience of leadin' men. Ye've done yer prison stint, an' that always commands respect. An' then there's some more subtle reasons that ye're maybe not thinkin' about."

"Such as?" Casey asked, brow cocked quizzically.

"Because ye're such a fine upstandin' citizen," Robin said, with a flash of impudent teeth.

"Don't take the mickey on me," Casey growled.

"Seriously, ye daft bastard, think about it—ye're gamely employed, ye're respectably married, ye don't drink on Sundays, ye're well-spoken an' still know all the prayers on yer rosary beads. An' when the mood is on ye, ye're about as readable as a big stone wall. Those are all good qualities in a commander. Ye add those to yer name an' yer natural ability to lead, an' it's so obvious ye could trip over it in the street."

"Aye well it's of no matter man, for I'm not takin' the job, even were it offered an' I think we both know it won't be. I'm not Joe Doherty's favorite man."

"Ye were always the leader in everything when we were lads, the role came natural to ye."

"I think ye've a rose-colored version of who I was, an' the truth of it is, we were only boys an' everything seemed a grand lark then."

"I remember fine who ye were. I'd have followed ye to the ends of the earth, man, still would, come to that," Robin replied.

"Well follow me to puttin' up this damn frame then," Casey said brusquely. Robin merely cocked an eyebrow at him and helped him knock the frame into place.

Later when Robin left, Casey found himself restless. There were a thousand things to do but he couldn't still his mind enough to start on any of them. The talk had stirred something in him he managed to keep firmly tamped most days.

There were things, he knew, that were instinctual to his neighborhood, to his race. Things he could not expect Pamela to understand. A geography that was mapped in genetic code, in the sights and smells that you'd known from birth, and before, in all the things that your ancestors had known and done and been. A bit from here and a piece from there, melded together to make a whole. A way of viewing the universe and your own corner in it, a way of loving, of hating, of fighting. Things you weren't even aware of knowing until you needed them, and then suddenly the ability was there.

The Irish, through necessity, had perfected the art of guerilla warfare. From fog and bog went the old saying. Materializing from mist and ground to strike and then disappearing back into the elements just as swiftly as they'd emerged.

He remembered a story about his granddad, hiding from the British, going 'underground' as it were, literally in this case. Brendan had spent a full week hiding in a claustrophobically small hole in the ground that he'd dug with his bare hands, carefully arranging peat sods over his head so the ground appeared undisturbed. Seven days in a hellish hole, with the feet of the Black and Tans that hunted him passing overhead more than once.

Casey's father had told this particular story with pride, illustrating as it did the strength and perseverance his own father had exercised in most areas of his life. Casey had always identified strongly with the grandfather who'd been known to him only through pictures and stories. His grandfather had understood the Irish marriage of the ballot box and the gun. Casey did as well, though he was less certain these days of what the boys thought they were going to achieve by killing Irish civilians in Irish streets. Belief in a cause or creed was easy until you saw what the cost of a life was. Then belief cost a man something, and Casey was no longer certain he could afford the price. And yet...

It seemed that he could change his outward behaviors, but not the beliefs he'd held most deeply since he'd been able to draw together his own opinions. The belief that men were born with equality in their souls, that some rights were intrinsic to the human condition. These were the foundation of his spirit, and as such could no more be abandoned than the color of his eyes, or the set of his jaw. Somehow this stubborn defiance in the face of terrible odds, this feeling that a man could rise above the circumstances of his birth, his streets, his tribe, was inherent to his very ability to get up and face the world each day. These things were like a dark tide that raced in his blood, making him long for and believe in things that, to another man, might seem pure madness. Could such things be genetic? He looked down to where his hands lay braced against the windowsill. In the shape of them he could feel his father's touch, the strength that could both cradle and kill. He sighed and shut the window, then made his way down the stairs to where the kitchen's wood floors and new sinks glowed dully in the fading light.

He checked that the windows and back door were locked up. He'd a busy stretch of days ahead of him at the center and it wasn't likely he'd get back until the weekend. He paused on the doorstep, the serenity of the landscape stirring a quiet melancholy that sometimes caught him unawares.

He stood for a long time watching the soft smoke of twilight drift over the yard. In the dim the outlines of the buildings were muted, blending into the grasses and trees which surrounded them. Over the hill that crested up and away from the house, he could hear a cow lowing plaintively and the cawing of a lonely crow somewhere in the trees.

The first few stars were visible above the pines when he closed the door behind him and took the path that led home.

THE GENESIS OF THE IRISH REPUBLICAN ARMY could never be pinpointed to a particular place on the map, nor an exact date in the history books. It had been the culmination of disparate ribbons of movement which had spread across the country in the

eighteenth century, each ribbon eventually crossing the path of another and slowly forming a braid of cohesive movement.

Many felt the movement stemmed from the tragedy of the 1916 rising, in which poets and teachers and labor leaders had been shot down in the flower of their manhood, thus reaffirming the wheel of blood sacrifice on which the Republican movement ran. Casey felt the roots ran back much further though, certainly to the time of Theobold Wolfe Tone.

Wolfe Tone was an Irish Protestant, and the first man to marry the poor to the ideal of a Republic of equality in Ireland. Like many who would follow in his footsteps he ended his life in shame and disgrace in a filthy prison cell. The seeds had been planted though, and the harvest could not be prevented from coming to bloody fruition. Though it seemed at times that both man and nature had conspired to prevent anything from taking root in the soil of independence. For where man failed, the famine had almost succeeded in wiping out Ireland's hopes for freedom.

In a country where seven out of every eight people were entirely dependent on the potato for survival, three seasons of blight meant a doom that was incomprehensible. In the summer of 1845 the fields of Ireland were lush and filled with the dark green leaves of an abundant crop. People looked forward to a quiet winter in which rents would be paid, children fed and the pig nicely fattened. Doom came quietly, a silent fog stealing over the land, within weeks the crop of potatoes was destroyed.

The tenant farmers held short-term leases that were payable every six months in arrears. If the tenants failed to make their rent they were jailed or evicted, their homes burned to the ground to prevent them from attempting to shelter there.

Starving men with dying children didn't have the means to make rent, and yet the evictions just kept coming. The hills were aswarm with the hungry, whose wee homes had been tumbled to the muck by the landlord's battering rams. Then came disease to join its black hand with the spectral one of hunger. What hunger alone could not accomplish, typhus and cholera swiftly did. Death seemed to fly in the very molecules of the air the people breathed, stealing across lake and land with an ominous silence.

The roads were adrift with beggars and vagabonds, men, women and children who already resembled the ghosts they would soon become. The entire country had become a living illustration of the Book of Revelation, with the black horse of Famine running neck to neck with the white horse of Death. For indeed it seemed that the very stars of heaven itself must fall to the ground in witness to such a catastrophe, just as the book of Revelation had said they must. But they didn't.

The carcasses of bled livestock littered the ground, skeletons picked clean of the little meat which had been left on their bones. Such sites would carry the taint of so much slaughter for decades to come, and would be known as the hollows or moors of blood. The beaches too would yield up bones for many years, of those who in their hunger had eaten food which was poison when raw, or when eaten in the amounts that a desperate man would take.

Hunger lent fuel to the underground movements, hunger and the impotent rage of seeing food leave the harbors for a country that viewed the Irish as subhuman at best, as illiterate beasts at worst. Landlords who chose to pay their debts rather than save the lives of the peasant tenantry upon whose backs their fortunes had been built. To flee seemed the only way to avoid a certain and painful death. And so the Irish fled to England and to the Americas, in one last desperate bid for salvation. If they survived the perilous journey, they found themselves in nations that resented them and the disease and poverty, which trailed in their wake.

Most Irish had never been further from their homes than the next village, many had not even ventured that far. Now they were on the other side of the wide world in the role of reviled strangers, caricatures for the newspapers and society who saw them as a burden on the taxpayer. Many men who'd managed to escape the violence that rode the hills and dales of Ireland, were conscripted fresh off the boat to fight in the American civil war and would die on the bloody fields of the country where they had sought salvation.

In Ireland a new crop was rising, for starvation had sown hatred with a bountiful hand and the harvest of it would last more than a hundred seasons.

Wolfe Tone's rebellion of 1798; Robert Emmet's insurrection of 1803; the Young Irelander's Outbreak of 1848; and the failed Fenian uprising of 1867. Then came Easter of 1916 and a handful of men who knew they could not possibly win and yet sought to declare Ireland a free nation despite the odds against them. They stood on the steps of the General Post Office that fateful Easter morning and proclaimed the Republic in the face of intractable British might.

'We declare the right of the people of Ireland to the ownership of Ireland and to the unfettered control of Irish destinies, to be sovereign and indefeasible. The long usurpation of that right by a foreign people and government has not extinguished the right, nor can it ever be extinguished except by the destruction of the Irish people. In every generation the Irish people have asserted their right to national freedom and sovereignty: six times during the past three hundred years have they asserted it in arms. Standing on that fundamental right and again asserting it in arms in the face of the world, we hereby proclaim the Irish Republic as a Sovereign Independent State, and we pledge our lives and the lives of our comrades-in-arms to the cause of its freedom, of its welfare and of its exaltation among the nations.'

The nation did not immediately rise to their cause, in fact they were the focus of much derision and laughter, until the British executed sixteen of them, one—James Connolly—so badly wounded that they had to tie him to a chair to kill him. The executions were a fatal mistake for it aroused the ire of the country and made of the motley crew of poets and politicians, martyrs in the blood tide of Ireland's history. The terrible beauty, that would keep the hatred and the IRA alive for another century, had been born.

The British rule in Ireland would always show a complete lack of understanding for the Irish character. That men would continue to rise, without the support of country, without the hope of victory, without often the support of friends and family for an ideal that seemed destined to fail again and again, was beyond the realm of conventional thought.

Such ideas were illogical, insupportable and furthermore, unconstitutional. And it was in these assumptions that England would always underestimate and misunderstand Ireland. It was a mistake they kept making, time and again.

Revolution is always a dicey business, especially when a war lasts close to a millennium and both the British and the IRA would have done well to heed the words of Yeats,

'Too long a sacrifice, can make a stone of the heart.'

Chapter Thirty

A Little Irish Homestead

JAMIE'S HOUSEWARMING GIFT CONSISTED of an eight place setting of Belleek China smattered with pale green shamrocks, and a matching set of Waterford vases. For Casey there was a case of Connemara Mist. Lawrence's gift was, at present, soundly and justly asleep under the kitchen table, having disposed of a boot, an umbrella and having been indicted in the knocking over a pail of hot water. The lad had christened the knobby-kneed, puff-cloud gray pup, Finbar, and the two had fallen as desperately and unequivocally in love as only a boy and a puppy can. Knowing that Casey viewed any overture of Jamie's with a jaundiced eye, Pamela had worried that the dog wouldn't be welcome.

"'Tis all right," Casey said gruffly, "the man asked if I minded first. I think the whiskey was by way of a sweetener, though."

"You don't mind?"

"No, a dog will do the lad good. He's a bit closed off like, havin' a dog will teach him about love and caring."

It was their first evening in their new home and though she stood in a welter of boxes, tired, grimy and with a sneaking suspicion that Lawrence was currently out stealing a forbidden smoke behind the shed, she surveyed her surroundings with great satisfaction.

Upstairs, their bedroom was ready for the first night in their new home. Casey had presented her with the bed for their anniversary in April, and though at the time the ancient four-poster had looked rather rickety and worm-eaten, he'd somehow managed to find the time to restore it. It was a lovely cherry-wood red and was piled deep and snug with a featherbed and three handmade quilts. As the chimney ran up through the bedroom Casey had built them a small fireplace there as well, which would be very welcome on chill winter nights.

Presently she stood in the kitchen where, despite her lack of talent in that area, Casey had gone to special pains to make a warm and inviting space. There was a large work area, big windows that caught the morning and early afternoon sun, open beams to hang pots and herbs from, and broad windowsills for all the greenery she insisted on growing year round. The lefthand wall was dominated by the fireplace, built from smooth round fieldstone which held a warm umber glow. The floors were broad laid pine planking, stained to a ruddy gold that was slightly paler than the cabinets.

One morning a week earlier, they had come with paint buckets in hand to put the finishing touches on the upstairs bedroom. On the front stoop they'd found a solid mahogany sideboard that had been painstakingly restored. A tiny scrap of blue paper had a short message, '*For the lady of the house*'.

"That'll be from Mr. Guderson, I expect," Casey had said, "Owen says the man has a rare hand with furniture. Will be his way of welcomin' ye to the place."

Pamela had raised her eyebrows at this. She'd only had two encounters with the taciturn Mr. Guderson and both had been largely silent, other than her own 'hello' and his curt lift of an extremely grubby cap.

The sideboard stood now opposite the fireplace, adorned with their everyday blue delft plates and mismatched teacups. Pride of place, however, was held by Pamela's Neptune tea set, a gift from her father on the last Christmas he'd been alive. The translucent china was the same color as the interior of an oyster shell, delicate pinks and grays, with opaline tints of rose, lavender and green. It was, other than a few books and some oddments, the only thing she'd brought with her when she'd come to Ireland. No house was a home to her until the tea set was unpacked, and the first pot of tea brewed in any new home was always made in it. After that they went back to the brown betty which served for their everyday use.

Casey came in just then, bringing with him the lush green smell of an early summer night. "That's the last of the boxes then. I put yer books in the bedroom, near to killed my back with that last lot." He sat down and sighed, stretching his legs out in front of him.

"Do you want a bite of something?" she asked.

"No—too tired, though a cup of tea in the quiet would be nice."

"I'll put the kettle on," she said, stepping over boxes to light the new range.

"Will I light the fire then?" he asked, "It's a wee bit damp in here."

She shook her head resolutely. "No, it's my job to light the fire, that much I do know."

She set the kettle to boil, wiped her hands on a tea towel and went to kneel before the hearth, a feeling of reverence settling inside her. It had to be done right, this first fire in their home. It was both the center and the welcome of the place, where the young were brought to cradle and the old to warm their aching bones. It was where the singing and storytelling would be done.

She laid the peat in three lines, placing each with an invocation that she couldn't remember knowing before this moment.

"In the name of the God of Life
In the name of the God of Peace
And in the name of the God of Grace.

She closed her eyes and stretched her hand forth intoning these words softly;

I will build the hearth
As Mary would build it.
The encirclement of Bride and of Mary
Guarding the hearth, guarding the floor,
Guarding the household all...'

She finished quietly, "Bless this hearth in the name of Saint Brigit, the radiant flame, goddess of fire."

She opened her eyes and touched the flame to the dry peat, watching as it caught and held, spreading into a soft glow. Casey watched narrow-eyed, to see if the repaired chimney would draw well. He sighed with satisfaction when it became apparent that they weren't going to be smoked out.

She turned to find him smiling at her, a bemused expression on his face. "What is it?" she asked.

"You. Every time I think I've a grasp on the essence of you, ye manage to surprise me."

"I think Rose must have taught me this when I was little. I don't remember learning it and yet I knew it."

"A radiant flame is how ye look right now, with the fire behind ye an' yer face aglow." He crossed the floor to where she stood and wrapped his arms around her from behind. She leaned against him gratefully, savoring his warmth.

"Do ye like yer new home then, Jewel?" He sounded half eager for the answer, and half afraid. She saw suddenly how much this all mattered to him. For years he'd only known transitory places of abode. The first home they'd shared had been a two-up, two-down in the Ardoyne that had been burned to the ground during the riots in the summer of '69. Then the walkup in Southie and the narrow confines of the rooms over the youth center. Before that it had been a five-year stretch inside prison walls for him.

And yet, despite the years together and the shared experiences, she knew that to him this was their first home, the one that mattered, because he'd given it to her with his own two hands, because it had been formed, every nail and board and stone of it, with love.

"It's the home I've been waiting for all my life," she replied softly, and knew that it was true.

"Wishing you always...
Walls for the wind,

> *A roof for the rain*
> *And tea beside the fire.*
> *Laughter to cheer you,*
> *Those you love near you,*
> *And all that your heart may desire."*

Casey said, reading from the cross-stitch sampler that Peg had made for them shortly after their marriage. Pamela had placed it on the mantel, alongside a set of pewter candlesticks and a pair of doves Casey had carved.

"You seem happy," she said.

"Aye," she could feel his smile against her neck, "I suppose I am. I've a house, a wife and," he looked over the lit yard where Finbar had ambled out and was nosing around a guilty looking Lawrence, who was surreptitiously trying to roll his illicit tobacco up his sleeve, "a family. I guess ye could say I'm a man who has everything he wants."

"Everything?" she asked quietly, taking his calloused palm and placing it over the still flat plane of her stomach.

"Aye," she could feel the smile stretch further, "everything."

Chapter Thirty-one

... And Everywhere that Mary Went

THE VILLAGE OF COOMNABLATH CONSISTED of some one hundred souls, five pubs, several hundred sheep and a Catholic Church the spires of which could be seen poking above the tops of the existing trees. It also boasted a hardware store, a post office and a defunct railway station which had shut down service some twenty years earlier.

In true Irish fashion Casey had quickly established which pub was the one he would frequent on a regular basis. Upon first glance, Pamela had not seen the charm of the place. The front end was a grocery and newsstand, and a small snug at the back was the limit of the licensed premises. The seating admitted no more than six patrons at a go, but after meeting Owen and his wife Gert, Pamela quickly understood why Casey was so comfortable there.

Owen was roughly the size and shape of a gnome, with a slow amiable manner that put his patrons at ease. Gert, in true Mutt and Jeff fashion, was the epitome of the large German housefrau, though her wit was nimble and her tongue unsparing of those who mistook Owen's mannerism for a debility of mind. Both grocery and pub were simply called Gallagher's, that being the surname of Owen and Gert.

When she'd queried Casey about the lack of picturesque names on Irish pubs—for one rarely ran across a Green Dragon or Pig and Poke in the plethora of pubs that dotted the country, as one would every other half mile in England—he ruminated for a moment before replying.

"I've never given it much thought, but I suppose it's because when ye've had most everything stripped from ye an' ye finally manage to get something to call yer own, ye want to stamp it with yer name. If it couldn't be the land then at least it could be on the buildings. It's a way I would think of sayin' 'this here is mine, my property an' make no mistake of it.'"

For a city boy Casey had settled into the countryside without apparent effort, as if he'd spent his entire life digging gardens, building sheds and hoeing lazy beds in the dusk of summer nights. He came to bed at night smelling of wood shavings, freshly dug earth and the peppermint soap he favored for bathing. He slept soundly, awoke energized for the day's tasks and all in all was a man at one with his surroundings.

His contentment was contagious it seemed, for she herself, despite a frisson of underlying tension about her pregnancy, was happy. All the time in Boston she'd been like strung wire, ready to sing with tension at the slightest touch. But now she could feel herself relaxing, with a soft bubbling well of happiness at her core. She found herself lost in small moments, realizing she'd been standing in place for twenty minutes watching Casey work. Watching the look of concentration on his face as he shaved long creamy curls of wood off of a plank that would become a door.

He'd a touch with the wood that was magical, within a pile of it he could pick out the one piece that would form itself to his hand and knife and become a wee bird, a puzzle box, a tiny boat made to float on childhood seas. She knew the entire shape of the house was there in his mind, translating itself to his hands as he worked his way through the plans. He wore an absentminded look, always had a pencil tucked behind his ear and often muttered to himself as he scribbled things on bits of grubby paper. In short, he was a man in a state of bliss.

Lawrence, on the contrary, seemed to think the countryside something specifically designed to either terrify or bore him to death. He escaped to Belfast at every opportunity, even taking a job with Pat after school running errands and helping paint the tiny office space that was the entirety of the Fair Housing Council. And where Lawrence went, so went Finbar—down the lanes, in the car, through the narrow Belfast streets, leaving a path of toppling paint cans, muddy paw prints and disgruntled humans in his wake. Happily, both he and his boy were oblivious to these worldly concerns.

Casey had only a few rules where Lawrence was concerned, but on these few points he was adamant—he would be home before dark, or would be lodged in town with Pat, who would make certain there was no crawling out of windows past bedtime. He would attend the local school on weekdays when it resumed in the fall and would only be allowed into town with either himself or Pamela on weeknights. He would respect those whose roof he lived under and do his chores with minimal complaint. And he would be honest at all times about his whereabouts and activities. Casey also reserved the right to say no to any of the above activities and all whereabouts were subject to prior approval. Lawrence submitted to these conditions with a grace so meek as to arouse Casey's immediate suspicions. For now they were living in a good-humored détente, with each keeping a wary eye upon the other.

Casey's weekdays were still divided between his construction job and the youth center. Weekends, however, when he wasn't picking up extra shifts or sorting out ruffian boys, were completely absorbed into the simple routine of home repairs and yard work.

This morning he'd been up with the sun and out working on a small shed he wanted to convert into a workshop for his tools and garden implements. Pamela had heard him humming on his way out, his step light on the stairs, and had smiled to herself before falling back into a heavy sleep, one of the side effects of early pregnancy.

It was possible that his early rising was due in some small part to the cat that had set up house on their front porch, and who howled most mornings from the time dawn cracked the sky until Casey—with curses and imprecations both dark and threatening—went out with the bowl of cream that was the only thing that silenced the howls. They had named him Rusty, due to the rather dirty and unattractive reddish hue he sported. He was also missing half an ear, generally had at least one swollen eye from his latest brawl, and his whiskers sported a terminally singed look.

It wasn't uncommon to see this ragged-arsed creature—as Casey called Rusty's appearance—following Casey about the yard as he did his chores. Casey, despite vehemently insisting that he'd no use for cats, had developed the habit of talking to the cat and conferring with him on various aspects of their work. She could have sworn that only the other morning she'd heard him reciting *Pangur Ban* whilst Rusty sat on top of the lumber pile, blinking out of his one good eye at Casey.

Saturdays had acquired their own rhythm for her as well. She generally had tea and breakfast with Casey and Lawrence, though mostly she just watched them eat of late, being that nausea had taken a strong hold and didn't seem inclined to leave. Then if she didn't have to drive Lawrence into the city, she would venture down to the small farmer's market that was set up near the church. Here there were always treasures to be found and brought away for the week ahead—fresh vegetables and country bread, honey taken from the combs only days before, home brewed jugs of cider, and if one knew where to ask, poteen—though other than as a disinfectant or a swift method of blinding oneself, Pamela didn't see its charms. The wee market was also the hub of village gossip, and a way of quickly summarizing the past week's events in the moil of one hundred and some odd lives.

People had kept their distance at first. She was a stranger to their world with an even stranger accent. But slowly, as she showed up each Saturday, the women began to chat with her and enquire after the well-being of her family. The men would tip their caps and mutter a brief salutation, which is how they greeted everyone.

She had found an immediate friend in the gruff old Swede whose land bordered their own. Shortly after moving in she'd gone in person to thank him for the gift of the sideboard. The thanks he'd shrugged off, but had invited her in for tea. The ancient farmhouse was alarmingly cluttered, not terribly clean and rather strong with the smell of the four wet dogs that trailed them in and then flopped down beside the fire. However the tea was strong and hot, even if the biscuits didn't bear contemplation—and the company surprisingly good. Though he wasn't possessed of a glib tongue, Mr. Guderson was a kind man in his own homely way and was happy to show her about his farm, introduce her to his many sheep and his small shaggy donkey. As well as showing her the bits of furniture he was restoring in what she supposed was meant to be the parlor of the farmhouse.

When she'd left he had given her a small wheel of goat cheese, which he'd made himself, and silently patted her hand. Now on Saturdays she would drop by with a loaf of bread, some freshly baked scones and a pot of jam and he would be out in the yard, or the outbuildings, but always near enough to stop and take tea with her. Today he had a gift for her, and while she hadn't seen a way to refuse it, she wasn't looking forward to Casey's reaction to said offering.

The gift reposed in a large, smelly box in the back seat of the secondhand Citroen that Casey had found at a farm auction. It was, at present, still and quiet, though her ears were still ringing with the noise the box had made all the way home.

She dug the box out of the back seat with great trepidation. It shifted alarmingly in her arms and Finbar came galloping across the yard, long legs getting knotted halfway there and bowling him over in his excitement. His outraged woofs drowned out the plaintive noises the box was now emitting.

She struggled up the front stair, shifting the box to one hip in order to have a free hand with the door. The door however swung open, Casey on the other side of it, a tea towel slung over his shoulder and a hammer in hand.

Pamela smiled weakly and opened her mouth to speak, only to be pre-empted by the box letting out a startlingly loud, "MEEEHHHH!"

"Ye've been at Guderson's place, haven't ye?" Casey asked, in what seemed to Pamela, a rather accusatory fashion.

"I have and before you say anything, just let me explain—he's an orphan."

Casey raised a sarcastic brow. "Well of course he is. Do we have any other sort about here?"

Pamela sat the quaking box down near the hearth. A small black face emerged from the top, followed by a skinny, wrinkly neck. Then came a set of long gangly legs with great knobby knees. The owner of these abundant charms let go of another "MEEEEHHHH!" Only this one sounded distinctly distressed.

"He's hungry," Pamela said.

"Who the hell *is* he?" Casey asked.

"He's not got a name just yet. Lewis thought we might like to name him ourselves."

"Is this his idea of a housewarming gift?"

"No, the poor thing's been orphaned. Lewis tried to foster him with the other ewes, but they showed no interest. So he thought we might like to take him in."

"He did, did he? And how are we to feed the little beggar?"

"Bottles, I've got the milk replacement powder." She went to the sink and quickly whisked the powder into warm water.

"They need their feed the same temperature as blood," she said over the rapidly escalating cries of the hungry lamb.

She turned, bottle in hand, testing the temperature against the inside of her wrist. The lamb, recognizing salvation when he saw it, tipped the box over in his panic to get out of it. He spilled across the floor, hooves clacking as he scrambled and slid his way over to the bottle. He butted his nose against the nipple, sending a warm spray of milk over his tiny black face. Then he settled to sucking with the desperation of all newborn creatures.

Casey shook his head. "I see I'll not be able to let ye roam about freely here, ye'll bring every disreputable abandoned creature ye stumble across back with ye."

"Lewis said he'd die without anyone to look after him, what could I do?"

"*Pah*," Casey infused the one syllable with a great deal of scorn. "He knew a soft touch when he saw one. He'd not have let the wee thing die. Ye just happened along at a fortuitous moment for the man, Jewel."

"I've been had, haven't I?" she said ruefully.

"Afraid so." He sighed, "I suppose I'll need to build a pen now, won't I?"

Lawrence shambled past smelling rather strongly of Polo mints and Casey grabbed him by his grubby shirtsleeve.

"Ye might," he said plucking the cigarette from the boy's rolled cuff, "try hiding them a little better. Ye'd one behind yer ear when ye came in with the dog last night."

"I'll quit when youse do," Lawrence said boldly, and Pamela had to bite her cheek to keep from laughing. This was the one place he had Casey over the turnstile and the lad knew it well, though he'd not dared to challenge him with it before. Which she took as a healthy sign he was getting comfortable and secure in the knowledge that he had a home.

Finbar, the following wave to Lawrence's riptide, was now nose-to-nose with the lamb, both wagging their respective tails vigorously, despite the furrow of hair that stood high upon the dog's back.

"Who's that?" Lawrence asked, with the suspicion of one who viewed farm animals as merely cutlets, shanks and ribs.

"That would be the sheep that yerself an' I are buildin' a pen for this afternoon," Casey replied gloomily. "Come on lad, an' bring yer cigarettes with ye. I've a feelin' I'll need them before the afternoon is out."

Chapter Thirty-two

The Tears of Saint Lawrence

CASEY'S BIRTHDAY DAWNED in a breathless heat. Pamela woke when he rose from the bed. The night hadn't cooled off much and so the blankets lay on the floor, except for the one thin sheet that lay lightly over her bare skin. She stretched luxuriantly, feeling like a contented cat in a patch of sunlight. She turned her head to the side and encountered a twig, as well as the strong scent of greenery on the linens. She smiled to herself, and blushed at the memory of the previous night.

She'd awakened in the middle of the night to find Casey standing at the window naked, a soft glow of moonlight turning him silver. Despite the still of his body, she could feel his restlessness as though it were a separate entity pacing the room.

"What's the matter?"

"Mmm," he turned from the window. "I couldn't sleep. I woke up wantin' ye, but ye were so peaceful it didn't seem right to rouse ye."

"Come back to bed then," she said, raising a hand in invitation. Due to the nausea of early pregnancy and his own fears of endangering the baby or herself, Casey had been enduring a state of deprivation which didn't suit either of them.

He shook his head. "The night is fine, come outside with me where we'll not wake anyone."

"Are you planning on there being a great deal of noise?"

"Aye," Casey replied and there was no mistaking the gleam in his eye, "I mean to make ye scream, an' I'd just as soon the dog an' the sheep an' the boy didn't come to investigate the reason why."

"Think you can make me scream, do you?" she asked, arching a challenging brow at him.

He grinned smugly. "Ye know I can, Jewel. But if ye've doubts about my current ability to do so, perhaps ye'd like to accompany me outside."

The air was still thick with heat and as warm as bathwater on their skin as they stepped over the doorsill and into the night. Even the moonlight fell in a balmy cascade over the trees, pouring a sleepy light onto the path they took down to the water.

The ground was warm beneath her as Casey laid her back amongst the soft mosses.

Heat sprang up on her skin at the touch of his hands. Night was the only time she was completely free of the nausea that plagued her during the day. Her breasts were swollen and extra sensitive to touch and when he touched his lips to one she shuddered, desire flooding her entire body, mouth dry with want.

There was restraint in his body, she could feel it in the way he held himself above her, upper arms trembling visibly.

"It's okay," she whispered, wrapping her legs around him to pull him close. Too close for hesitation. "You're not going to hurt us."

He slid inside her, with a sighing breath that sounded very much like the relief of a starving man. Consciousness of her surroundings slid away, the moon a soft blur of melted opal above her. He moved inside her with slow deliberation, careful and yet determined to push her to the limits of her desire. Which he did again and again, only to draw back at the crucial moment, leaving her panting, nails biting through the dark band of his tattoo.

"Have mercy, man," she managed to gasp out, entire body slick with a fine dew of sweat.

"Aye," he said, grazing his teeth along the arch of her neck, "I'll have mercy—when ye scream for it."

The smell of water and earth was heavy in her nostrils. Above her Casey moved one last time, his shoulders blocking out the moon. The last thrust took her beyond thought, to where everything seemed to rush away like flotsam before floodwater. She came back to her senses slowly to feel Casey removing his hand from her mouth.

"Happy?" she asked, suddenly embarrassed, thinking of how often Mr. Guderson walked the hills at night. Hopefully his rheumatism had kept him indoors tonight.

"Aye," he said, and there was no mistaking the purely male satisfaction in his tone. "Though it wasn't so loud, I just didn't want ye wakin' anyone else's sheep." She could see the flash of his grin in the dark.

"You're lucky I've not the strength to hit you."

"Ungrateful wench," he said, then rolled off her landing neatly on his stomach in the moss. The night around them was thick with quiet, as though even the birds and bugs had been defeated by the heat.

"Was it this hot the day you were born?"

"Aye, enough to melt tar. Though I've had plenty of rainy birthdays as well."

"Were you born in the morning?"

He nodded. "Just as the sun came up, how'd ye know that, Jewel?"

"Makes sense, you're always up with the birds. I imagine you were just as impatient that day to get started on things as you are every other morning."

He laughed softly. "My da didn't hold much with superstition nor things such as birth signs, but he said it was fittin' that I was born under the sign of the lion as I'd come out roarin' an' mad, with the sun fit to boil out of the sky."

She thought of the pictures she'd seen of him as a small boy, always tousle-haired, the camera catching him on the run, as though he'd never had the patience to stand for a snapshot.

"How long did you stay mad?"

"Da said I wasn't happy until I got up on my legs and could run. Had scrapes an' bruises all over me from tumblin' over my feet 'til I was about fifteen. How about yerself? What time of day were ye born?"

"Early evening, Rose used to say that was why I was secretive and quiet, that I had a twilight soul."

"Twilight soul, I like that, it suits ye. I've always loved that time of day—not day, not night—just balanced there between the two worlds. Something so perfect that no matter how many times ye see it ye still can't take it for granted. Like yerself."

"Don't make me cry man, or I'll not give you your gift."

"Thought I'd already had it," he said, cocking an eyebrow at her.

"If you consider that a gift, then we've celebrated your birthday on an almost daily basis this year."

He grinned. "Don't worry yerself woman. I'll love it, whatever it is, ye know I will."

She sighed. "Gifts always seem inadequate. I want to give you intangible things, things that have no name but will keep you warm and safe everyday. I want to take all your troubles away from you and give you a quiet calm whenever you need it."

"Ye do, Jewel, yer love gives me all those things. This—us—is the best gift. I grow stronger the minute ye lay hands upon me. An' yet that's the time I'm more vulnerable than any other."

He traced the fine bridge of her collarbone with one hand, eyes dark as the night around them.

"It's this too," she shivered as he ran his fingers down the length of her back, still damp with their combined heat. "The way that ye trust me. It makes me feel protective as hell, an' yet it makes me want to cry at the same time. I feel a fool sayin' these things but I know ye won't laugh at me for speakin' them, clumsy as my tongue might be." His hand had come to rest over the slight round of her stomach, where the beginnings of their child floated in a primordial sea of blood and salt.

"Happy birthday," she said softly.

He smiled, a sweet curve with a flash of dimple. "It already is."

CASEY WAS LATE FOR DINNER. The day had been a long one, the heat close to unbearable, wearing upon everyone's nerves, until even Paudeen's half-hearted bleats seemed churlish and designed to annoy.

Pamela's nausea was heightened by the still heavy air, and she paid for her night time adventures with a thick lethargy that made her feel as though she was moving through syrup for much of the day. Cooking all of Casey's favorite foods did little to improve the heat in the kitchen, nor did the fact that the dishes were alternatively dried out or partially scorched by the time the man of the hour made his appearance over the doorstep.

He found his family in various stages of mutiny. The dog and the lamb in a tussle over a length of twine outside the doorway, Lawrence indulging in a forbidden cigarette behind the half-constructed shed, Pamela—flushed and miserable looking—taking something out of the oven that looked as though it had spent a season in the desert. He sighed, for better or worse *that* appeared to be dinner. Being that it was his birthday, he'd have to eat it and smile while doing so.

He kissed Pamela's shoulder and sniffed at the thing that was dinner. "Smells divine," he said, stifling a cough. The kitchen was noticeably smoky.

She merely glared at him and thumped the thing that was dinner down upon the counter.

"The lot of ye ought to be down by the water, it's likely to be a sight cooler."

"You think?" Pamela retorted sarcastically, dropping into a chair and fanning her face with a church circular.

"We," Lawrence said, coming in the open door, "were waitin' for youse to come home." He popped a Polo mint into his mouth and set to chewing it vigorously.

"Hand over the cigarettes," Casey said, sticking a hand under the boy's nose.

"Don't see why ye can puff away as ye please an' I'm treated like a criminal for havin' the one in five days," Lawrence grumbled, digging two lumpy hand-rolls out of his pocket.

"I'm grown, an' if ye don't quit smokin' these—" Casey shook one of the cigarettes under his nose, "ye never will be."

Lawrence opened his mouth to protest, but a shake of Casey's head was enough to silence him. The boy was a quick learner. He dug in his other pocket and emerged with a small roughly wrapped box, festooned with a yard of red ribbon.

"Will I give ye yer present, then?" he asked, face bright with anticipation though his hands shook slightly.

Casey raised an eyebrow at Pamela in question. She nodded, "Dinner won't suffer by waiting another minute or two."

Lawrence handed him the small box.

"Ye didn't need to do this, laddie," Casey said, voice rough as it always was when he was particularly touched.

Lawrence, eyes glued to the package, didn't respond.

Casey opened it quickly, noting the boy's impatience. There was a heavy silence as he gazed down into the box.

"Well what is it?" Pamela asked, impatient to see what Lawrence had been so excited about.

"It's a watch," Casey said, voice curiously flat.

It was a pocket watch, the fleur-de-lis design on its lid slightly worn with rubbing. Casey still hadn't moved, so she took it from him and touched a finger to the tiny button. The lid sprang up, as though freshly oiled, to reveal a face with dark Roman numerals and four tiny diamonds at each cardinal point. A delicate, one note version of *The Faerie's Lament* stepped out upon the still air.

"It's beautiful Lawrence."

Lawrence didn't respond, his gaze was riveted to Casey, who had placed his hands flat upon the table and was now looking at Lawrence with eyes the color of smoke.

"Did ye not understand me the other week, when I talked to ye about stealin'?" Casey still spoke in the flat tone he only used when he was very angry.

The color flooded up Lawrence's pale face, right to the fringe of ginger hair.

"Are ye sayin' I stole it?"

"I'm askin' where ye got it."

"Casey" Pamela interjected, "don't—"

"Pamela this is between myself an' the boy," he said, eyes still fixed on Lawrence, who stood still as a statue, the anticipatory shine wiped from his face.

"I just had it," Lawrence said in a sullen tone.

Pamela flinched inwardly, while still fuming at Casey. Lawrence's unwillingness to explain was only going to exacerbate the situation.

"I'll ask ye again where ye got it, but I'll not ask a third time."

"Youse aren't goin' to believe a word I say to ye anyway, so why should I tell ye?"

"Give me an explanation that sounds real an' I'll believe ye innocent."

"Ye don't want me to be innocent of it!" Lawrence yelled, pale skin scarlet with agitation. His eyes were suspiciously bright. He knocked the edge of the table, sending a glass of lemonade to the floor in a spray of sticky liquid and bright shards of glass. He ran out kitchen door, slamming the door behind him with enough force to rattle the remaining dishes on the table.

"Now look what you've done," she said in frustration.

"Look what I've done?!" Casey glared at her in righteous indignation. "What I've done—I suppose ye'll find a way to blame me for the crucifixion next!"

"You're being ridiculous," she responded.

"Right then," he said stiffly, "I'll take my ridiculous self out of here."

"Fine."

She felt guilt prick her the minute he left. It was the man's birthday after all, and she had her own doubts about where the lad had procured such an expensive gift. The look on Lawrence's face, though, as he'd presented Casey with the small gaily-wrapped box, had brought tears to her eyes. She sighed heavily and got to her feet, the taste of pennies still strong in her mouth.

Casey would have gone out to the shed to smoke or down to Owen's for a couple of pints, in an effort to take the edge off his anger. The door still hummed with the force of Lawrence's slam. Bloody men.

She surveyed her kitchen with a jaundiced eye. The dinner she'd so lovingly prepared was a heap of charred ashes. The smoke still drifted in lazy tendrils near the heavy beams and small bright bits of glass sparkled in the puddle of spilled lemonade. She gathered up the glass gingerly and threw it in the garbage, then sopped up the sticky liquid with the mop. She wiped a hand across her forehead in irritation. It was hot in the kitchen; the heat of the entire long day had built to a still, close fug.

She turned to clearing the plates and glasses from the table, feeling a prickle of tears, which only increased her irritability, at the back of her throat.

The icing had melted down the side of the cake, puddling like burned butter on the plate. She sighed, picking the wilted pansies off the top and throwing them in the sink.

"Bastard," she muttered under her breath, knowing the minute she spoke the word that Casey was behind her.

"I imagine ye're not talkin' about the dog," he said, voice still tight with tension. "If yer goin' to call me filthy names, ye could at least look me in the eye to do so."

She turned to look him straight in the eye, "Bastard."

"Christ yer an unreasonable bloody woman at times."

"Me?" she said in disbelief. "I'm not the one who started making wild accusations."

"They weren't wild accusations, have ye forgotten the wallet full of money he stole last week?"

She turned back to the ruined dinner, scraping the food into the sink, too angry to do it properly. She heard a long sigh behind her, as though it was *his* patience that had been taxed to the limit.

"Will ye at least turn around so I can look at ye while I grovel?"

"It's not me who needs groveling to," she said shortly, making more noise than was strictly necessary as she dropped the assorted knives, spoons and forks into a mug.

"Will ye please look at me?" he asked, and despite the words his tone was considerably less conciliatory than it had been a moment before.

She turned, having to pry her foot off the patch of stickiness where some lemonade had splashed. "Yes?" she said as though he were a brush salesman interrupting her cleaning.

"I'm sorry, ye planned a nice dinner for me an' I ruined it."

"You did," she returned, finding it difficult to keep her dignity with a foot that felt as though it had been dipped in melted taffy.

Casey tapped his nose. "Ye've a bit of icin' on yer nose," he reached over to remove it and just as swiftly retracted his hand at the look in her eyes.

"You might have thanked him before you assumed he'd stolen it."

"Look at the bloody thing, woman, it's got four diamonds in it, there's no way the lad could have paid for it."

"Maybe," she admitted reluctantly, "but he did it with the best of intentions."

"Woman," both Casey's tone and aspect were blackly thunderous, "I'll not tolerate thievery under my own roof, I don't care what the motive behind it is."

"Casey," she said firmly, "his world is not black and white, that child has known nothing but shades of gray from the day he was born. You're going to have to expect mistakes on a fairly regular basis."

"Ye call this a mistake? Stealin' is stealin' woman an' there's none of yer gray shades in there!" He added unnecessary emphasis to his words by hitting the blunt of his fist on the corner of the table, causing the cake to fall to the floor. Pamela glared daggers and Casey had the grace, albeit too little and far too late, too look abashed.

"You are the most thick-skulled, mule-headed ass I've ever met!"

"Well thank you," he said shortly.

"It wasn't," she replied tartly, "intended as a compliment."

"I'll take it as I like," he replied. At that juncture Finbar trotted in the still open door and gave a long, deep growl in Casey's direction before hopefully sniffing the spilled cake. This he gingerly picked up before turning a stiff back on them both and trotting back out the door and down the path Lawrence had run.

Casey threw up his hands. "Jaysus, I give up altogether, even the damn dog has taken against me."

She sighed in exasperation. "No one's taken against you. You're the one who went off like a firecracker. He's frightened, Casey, and he's trying to find his spot in this household of ours. The two of you are going to have to learn to accommodate each other. Maybe," she added hopefully, "you could go talk to him now?"

Casey shook his head. "I can't talk to the lad yet, I'd say something I'd regret. Ye're goin' to have to deal out a bit of patience my way too, Pamela."

"Fair enough, but *I* am going out to talk to him, he needs to know we're not going to desert him every time he screws up."

Outside she took a deep breath of the silky warm summer night. The day of blue and gold had gone down in a blaze of crimson sunset that left a clear twilight in its wake.

As frustrated as she was with Casey she understood his anger. The world he came from was bounded by a moral code that few outsiders could ever really understand. Including, at times, her. In his world, if you were caught stealing, you often lost the use of your kneecaps. You were expected from a very young age to know what to turn a blind eye to and what not. The IRA did not suffer fools gladly. And it was they who ruled the Catholic neighborhoods with an iron fist. Understanding the unspoken rules was a matter of life and death in the world in which he'd grown up. In Casey's view Lawrence had only added insult to injury by presenting stolen goods to him as a present.

She listened for a moment to the night sounds—small birds twittering down to sleep, the brook chuckling softly to itself, the dark settling in soft gray-tinged clouds into dips and hollows. Like her the boy seemed to need water for comfort, so she moved off towards the sound of it, some of her weariness lifting with the cool night air.

She found him facedown amongst the mosses that glowed acid green in the twilight. Finbar lay quietly beside him, long nose tucked neatly between his big feet.

She sat beside both boy and dog, knowing better than to touch Lawrence or give any comfort. The child only ever saw it as pity and nothing more. The bit of pride his life had left him could bear many things, but not pity.

"Lawrence, sit up, we need to talk."

It was several minutes before he reluctantly sat up, hands and face stained with dirt and tears. Finbar's head came up, his melancholy gaze searching Lawrence's face. He wiggled slightly closer to lay his head on the boy's thin sunburned leg. Lawrence put a reassuring hand on his head and the dog sighed, relieved for the moment.

"I s'pose ye'll want me to pack up an' go then." Lawrence said, defiance written on the narrow brow as he rubbed tears away with the grubby heels of his hands.

"No," she said softly, "but I do think if you've decided to stay here with us, we're going to have to learn to talk."

A tear-bright eye peeked over a narrow shoulder at her. "Stay?" he said, tone three parts suspicion and one part hope.

"Yes," she replied, "did you think we were going to put you out on the streets or send you back to that hellhole you were living in?"

"I...I," he stuttered, "I never thought ye'd want me to stay. I figured on bein' back on the streets. It's home after all. No one's ever cared if I'd a place to lay my head or food in my belly, why should you?"

"Why shouldn't I?"

The question silenced the boy for a moment, his ginger eyebrows rising up to meet the tuft of hair that always hung over his forehead. He looked away before answering. "Because of what I am."

"And what would that be? A young boy? A smart-mouthed kid?"

There was an angry flash of light from his eyes. "Ye know what I'm sayin'."

Yes, she knew what he was saying and knew there weren't words to fix it or heal it. Time would, or would not, perform its miracles. Beneath the press of her palm, the moss exhaled a breath of evening air, throated by generations of dead leaves. The thick, earthy smell seemed to catch on her tongue, leaving a faintly bitter taste.

"Yes," she said softly, "I do know."

"But ye can't understand," he retorted bitterly. "Ye can't know what it was like. You've likely always been wanted, he," he gestured toward the house, unwilling yet to say Casey's name, "adores you."

"Oh Lawrence," she smiled, "you've a lot to learn. Sometimes the way things look on the outside bears very little resemblance to the truth on the inside."

He furrowed his ginger brows at her. "I'm only fourteen but I'm not barmy, I see how he looks at you."

"I'm not talking about Casey. I was raped," she said, finding it wasn't as difficult to say as she'd feared it would be.

"You?" he sniffed, suspicion wrinkling the bridge of his nose.

"Yes me," she replied, "by a group of men on a train."

"How many?"

"Four."

He tapped his fingers rapidly against his thigh, the way he always did when he was particularly bothered. "I'm sorry then," he said.

"Yes, so was I," she replied, "it took me a long time to feel clean again, to not feel that I'd somehow provoked it, to not be sick with shame. But eventually I did. And he," she tilted her head toward the house, where Casey's outline could be seen moving about the kitchen, "had a lot to do with that."

"He knew?" Lawrence asked, swiping a thin hand under his leaky nose. She arched a brow at him and handed him a tissue.

"He found out, yes."

"An' he wasn't angry at ye? Didn't he see ye different?"

"No, he wasn't angry, at least not at me. He was careful with me for a long time, and sad I think, but no he never made me feel that I was any less to him than I'd been before. In fact he married me a few days after he found out."

Lawrence blinked several times. "I guess I always thought people could tell just by lookin' at me, what I was, what I'd done."

She nodded. "I know what you're saying but no one can see inside, though it's likely to take a long time before you truly feel that you're not see-through."

His head dropped to his knees, the line of his of shinbone shining like a length of pearl, emphasizing how little flesh there was to him.

"I never understood why it excited them," he said, voice subdued with the exhaustion that followed an emotional storm. "To hurt someone that way, to have someone completely unwillin' an' terrified beneath yer hand and have that make ye...make ye..."

"Aroused," she supplied for the sake of his faltering tongue.

"Aye, though it's a tame word for what those men seemed to feel."

"Who were they, Lawrence, the men who did these things?"

He shook his head vehemently, "I can't tell ye that, I wish I could fergit it myself. They'd have parties, sometimes take a bunch of us over to England for them." Lawrence had laid his head on his knees again, drawing in tight around the hurt his thin frame seemed too fragile to contain. "Ye'd be shocked if I told ye some of the names of the men, muckers in government, the sort ye see on the telly advising everyone else of their high moral standin'." His voice had slipped into a fugue-like cadence, his eyes fixed on the glistening waterweed that coated the banks of the stream. Pamela knew he saw nothing of his surroundings, though.

"I think you'll find, Lawrence, that I'm not easily shocked," she said dryly.

"I've never talked about it, 'cept to joke with the other lads, an' that only made all of us feel the worse. Seemed like we couldn't talk about it normal-like, though, it'd be admittin' that there was somethin' wrong, an' ye can't survive doin' that."

Over the water, a dragonfly flashed silver, carrying the last of the day's light off on its wings. She took one of his hands carefully, as gentle in her movements as she would have been with a half-broken horse. His skin was clammy with tears, skin that was still baby fine and unbearably soft. She gave the long fingers a small squeeze and then merely allowed him the time and silence in which he could choose to speak or not.

"Mostly it hurt, though I got used to it after awhile, ye learn tricks to make it bearable. It was worse, somehow, when I did feel somethin'. I'd feel sick later an' wonder if—" He stopped abruptly in his monologue as if he'd only just realized what he was saying.

"If it meant that you were homosexual?" she finished for him.

He nodded, freckles stark against his pale skin even in the dusk.

"That's something you shouldn't have had to think about until much later."

He sniffed. "Life's not so convenient that way is it though? Least that's what himself in there says."

"Himself," she said wryly, "often has the annoying habit of being right."

"I've noticed that." One corner of Lawrence's mouth turned up in a wobbly smile. The smile disappeared with his next words though. "If I were—an' I'm not sayin' that I am—but if I were he'd not want me under his roof anymore."

She was silent for a moment, weighing her answer, realizing that she really wasn't entirely certain of how Casey would react to such an admission. But she also knew that when he loved someone he did it with a ferocity and loyalty that overlooked almost all forms of behavior.

"He loves you, Lawrence, and he doesn't give his love lightly. I don't think there's much you could do to change that."

"But if he knew what I'd done, he'd think it unnatural an' then he'd not see me the same."

"Lawrence he does know. He also knows it was a matter of survival."

Lawrence's face had gone so white that his freckles stood out like stark points on his thin face. "How long has he known?"

"Always," she smiled gently, "the man is no fool, you know that well enough yourself. Did you really think he'd take you under his roof without knowing where you'd come from?"

"An' he doesn't..." Lawrence swallowed, unable to finish his sentence, eyes bright with a terrible tension.

"No, he doesn't," she replied firmly, knowing that Casey had put what he knew about the boy in a firmly locked compartment, aware of it, but not letting it color his daily perception of this child he'd become protector of.

"I wish I could forget, ye know, an' not have the memory of it on my skin."

Under the thick gloom of the pines, harebells and ragged robins looked like small patches of fairy light. She could picture Casey's evil leprechauns picking their way through, red-capped and gimlet eyed. She hadn't believed in fairies, neither good nor evil, for a very long time. She doubted Lawrence had ever had such luxury at all.

"A body is just a vehicle, Lawrence, something to pack our soul around in for this part of the journey. When someone violates that vehicle it's awful because the vehicle is how we give love. But you, the thing that makes you Lawrence, lives in there," she tapped his clear, narrow brow, "and there." She put her fingers to his heart and felt him flinch. It would be a very long time before he could allow anyone to touch him and know they meant him no harm. But he didn't move away from her hand and she knew that in itself said much about how far he'd come since moving into their home.

"I want ye to know, I didn't steal the watch. I'd never give him something stolen. It was all I had when I first went to Kincora. I think maybe my mam left it for me. Maybe it belonged to my father, I don't know. It was the only thing I had from before," the sincere gaze faltered for a moment, "I wanted to say thank you an'," his voice had dropped to a whisper, "the watch was the only way I could think of to say it."

"Tell him that," she said, "exactly as you just told me. He's not entirely unreasonable." This statement was met with a snort of derision and a great deal of eye-white on Lawrence's part.

"All right," she amended, "when he's not in the grip of his temper he can be reasoned with."

"I'm *not* speakin' first," Lawrence said, a mutinous quality to his tone that reminded her of how very young he was.

"Well until one of you decides to be less mulish, you might as well go in and get some sleep. It's very late," she said, feeling exhausted by all the male pigheadedness she was subjected to.

He nodded, rising to his full gangling height, the dog his echo in canine silhouette. He turned to the path, hesitating for a moment as though he'd a mind to say something, but couldn't quite decide how to word it.

"What is it?"

"Thank ye for...for the talk, it helped," he said awkwardly, poised on the balls of his feet, ready to flee.

"You're welcome," she replied, then started as he bent down and kissed the side of her face. He darted away immediately, slim form quickly disappearing under the gloom of the pines, like a sprite whisked into a barrow. She heard the faint *whush* of the door opening and closing after him, and felt the wash of relief that came with knowing he was safe for another night.

She sat for some time after Lawrence left. The night sky above her was uncommonly clear, pale and luminous against the long-fingered pines. She could smell the sharp tang of crushed mint in the air; Lawrence must have trod upon it on his way up the path.

Lawrence's words had made present thoughts she generally brushed off as if they were no more than an annoying fly. But to speak the words he needed to hear she'd had to let the shape and substance of her own rape become distinct, to remember the hurt and the shame and the sheer terror she'd felt. She'd been certain both she and Pat were going to die and indeed, Pat had come very close to doing just that. And though she'd boxed and sealed the memories of that night, the body had a recall of its own. The skin and cells remembering what the mind could turn away, then the violation would return, churning her stomach, dirtying her skin. But many days, more often now than not, it was distant—kept so by a love that had become sanctuary and in a deeper sense, the home she had sought all her life.

She rose, skirt damp and speckled with bits of the glowing moss. The night air was still warm, though with a hint of cooling like a tepid bath. She took a deep breath and let it out slowly, feeling the painful tingle of tension from her toes on up. She allowed the spectre of the blond man's face to rise in her mind, saw the hard hazel eyes, felt the shape of his bones beneath her hands and the brute intrusion of his flesh within her own. The other men did not haunt her, she had banished them long ago, but still the blonde man remained. She shuddered, a wash of nausea passing through her and leaving her empty and cold. Then she invoked her husband's face, the touch of his hands, sure and large, the scent of his skin both primal and secure. He was her anchor in the midst of every storm.

She opened her eyes, the house a warm sturdy shape on the horizon and felt the tension drain away, leaving her sleepy and whole.

No, Lawrence would not forget, but he might, given time, find forgiveness for himself and with that a peace that would grow into something strong, allowing him to bend but not break.

She walked up the path, brushing against the roses and releasing their heady scent. Globe flowers, petals cupped around their fragile hearts, glowed like small stemmed moons, lighting the way to the door. Casey had turned on the light over the stove, a beacon to guide her in from the night.

She opened her hands in supplication, or perhaps surrender and whispered the words that lay foremost in her heart. "Dear God, allow us to do right by this child."

Above, the stars meandered along on the billowing river of the Milky Way. She chose a small green one, almost obscured by the bright giants that surrounded it, and made a wish for Lawrence.

Maybe she no longer believed in fairies or wishes that came true but it didn't hurt to hedge one's bets. Then she opened the garden gate and stepped through it, leaving the night and its ghosts behind her.

SHE FOUND CASEY SITTING UP in bed reading, Paudeen tucked in the crook of one arm blissfully asleep. One hoof bobbed lightly over the book, the woolly head lolling over Casey's forearm. Casey flicked her a brief glance over the top of his glasses then returned to his reading.

"Did you feed Paudeen?" she asked, picking up her brush off the bureau and snapping it quickly through her hair.

"Aye, two bottles an' the wee bastard had the nerve to kick me in the chin three times while I was doin' so. I'll be glad when he starts eatin' grass instead of nibblin' the hair off my arms."

"Good book?"

He laid the book down. "Couldn't tell ye, I've read the same page over five times an' still haven't the slightest notion what it's about." He cleared his throat, rubbing one of Paudeen's big ears. "Is the laddie alright then?"

"He'll do for now," she said, "but you're going to have to talk to him. He didn't steal the watch by the way."

"I don't suppose," Casey took in the rather stern look on his wife's face, "this talk will wait 'til morning?"

"If your conscience allows it, then I suppose it can wait."

He kicked the blankets back, rising quickly enough that Paudeen let out a semi-conscious bleat of protest. "Ye've a wicked streak in ye at times woman, do ye know that?"

Pamela merely raised an eyebrow at him and continued to brush her hair. He sighed, Paudeen's heavy, milky breath tickling the bare skin of his chest. There was a trickle of moonlight coming through the little octagonal window at the top of the stairs, enough to guide him down into the dark of the lower floor.

He settled Paudeen into the basket on the hearth, the lamb no more than stirring at this change of environment. He headed for the foot of the stairs, then turned back with a sigh. He hesitated by the boy's door, not wanting to wake him, hearing the low growl of Finbar from the vicinity of the bed.

"Are ye goin' to say somethin', or just stare at the back of me head all night?" asked a defensive voice that sounded less than threatening, coming as it did from a heap of blankets.

"Didn't want to wake ye."

"Well ye didn't."

"Can I come in for a minute?" he asked, determined not to let the boy's tone rankle at him.

"It's yer house, do as ye like," came the less than convivial reply.

Casey uttered a silent prayer to whatever saint might be handy to give him some patience and then went to sit on the edge of the bed.

"Down," he said sternly to the dog, who'd emitted a low rumble of protest at this intrusion on the limited bed space.

"Don't get mad at him, *he's* not stolen anything."

"Nor have you," Casey said gently, "I've come to say that I'm sorry laddie, I jumped to a conclusion an' it wasn't warranted nor fair."

A disdainful sniff was the only reply Lawrence deigned to give him. Casey supposed he didn't deserve to have it made simple. The boy's back was still turned to him, stiff with reproach and Finbar had taken up his post right next to the bed, emitting the occasional disapproving *whuff* in Casey's direction. He ordered his thoughts and tried to imagine what his father would have said in such a situation. However none of Brian's words of comfort or wisdom made themselves immediately available to his memory. He was on his own here, without the knowledge of how to heal the damage he'd done. He would just have to fumble through it.

"Fact of the matter is," he said, pausing to clear his throat nervously, "I don't know much about bein' anyone's father, so ye'll have to give me a bit of time an' expect that I'll mess it up occasionally. Do ye think ye can do that?"

Lawrence turned on his back, face pale in the wash of moonlight. "Father?" he said, eyes riveted on Casey's face.

"Aye, I'm makin' certain there's food in yer belly, a roof over yer head, an' that ye're gettin' yer schoolin'. What would ye call it?"

"Ye're a bit young to be my da," the boy said doubtfully.

"An' I think ye're not really in a position to be picky about how old the man lookin' after ye is."

"True enough," Lawrence admitted pragmatically, though his brow was furrowed in a knot.

"What is it then?" Casey asked.

"Well it's only that..." Lawrence trailed off reluctantly, long fingers plucking at the sheets.

"Only what?" Casey coaxed.

The boy didn't respond at once, but took a shaky breath, then let it out in a stream of nervous words. "It's only that a father is someone that ought to care for ye more than anyone else does. An' he ought to trust ye," this last was uttered with a defiant edge.

"Do ye think I've taken ye in off the streets for the good of my health, man?" Casey said, shaking his head. "An' as to trust, it's earned laddie—even between father and son. Now I was wrong about the watch, but I wasn't wrong about the wallet two weeks back, was I?"

Lawrence shook his head reluctantly.

"Now as to the other bit of what ye said," he laid a hand on the boy's forehead and stroked the ginger hair back from the clammy skin. "I love ye, boyo, an' don't think that doesn't surprise me, but still there it is, I do."

Lawrence turned his head to the side, mouth tight and frowning. A long silence ensued.

"Have I said somethin' wrong?" Casey asked, feeling absurdly uncomfortable.

"No ye've not. It's only that I'm afraid ye'll be sorry ye said what ye have come mornin'," the words were spoken in a flat monotone, though Casey could see the tension in the boy's neck and shoulders as he fought to keep back his tears. It caused him a pain different from any other he'd known to see Lawrence's life had been such that he believed love was something that could only be given in the dark, and easily recanted in the morning.

"Once I love someone, I don't take it back," he replied gruffly, "it's simply there an' ye'll need to remember it in case I don't think to say it all the time. An' there'll be times that ye think I don't because I'm angry or disappointed in something ye've done, but it'll still be there. Ye'll have to learn to trust that. I imagine," he added softly, "that we'll both stumble a good bit before we learn how this is done, but I believe we'll manage it in the end."

A single tear slid down the boy's pale cheek. "Do ye think it would be alright if I hugged ye?"

The uncertainty in Lawrence's tone caused Casey's throat to tighten. "I think it'd be right, a fresh start for the both of us."

It was awkward at first, as though neither of them understood where to put their arms, but then Casey gathered him tightly, hoping to convey some security to the child through his strength. Held close, he seemed more fragile then ever, long slender bones and translucent skin holding together this creature built of pain, suspicion and a newly born hope. He'd been given a sacred trust, now he only hoped he could meet the challenge of it.

He carried the sight of the one tear the boy had shed up the stairs with him. He stopped for a moment on the landing, looking out through the eight-sided window. The night was still and hushed, the air on his bare skin the consistency of warm milk. Vega rode the horizon, blazing blue-white across the vastness of years.

"Am I doin' alright, Da?" he asked quietly, feeling, as he occasionally did, his father's presence within him.

Back in his own bed, Pamela held stiffly to her side of the mattress, pretending sleep though he could feel her wakefulness clear across the room. It appeared he'd another fence to mend before he'd get any rest.

"I'm sorry I was rough on the boy, I'm just...I don't..." he let go a heavy breath of exasperation. "I've an idea what he's been through an' I want to help him but I don't know what's right or wrong, I don't know what the child needs."

She turned in the bed and put her hand on his chest. "He needs you, not just anyone, but you. I suspect he's never trusted a single soul in his whole life, but he trusts you. Maybe you need to see that for the gift it is."

"I feel bad enough woman, ye don't need to spoon salt on the wounds as well." His voice was gruff, but she knew he was feeling guilty all around.

"You've just finally met someone as stubborn as yourself, Casey Riordan, and you don't know what to do with him."

"What *am* I to do with him?" he asked, tone half-amused and fully desperate.

"It's simple."

"Oh is it then? There's nothin' simple about this. Two months ago I was mindin' my own business, doin' my job, buildin' myself a nice uncomplicated life. Now I've got a handful of orphans in my home, who've no intention of leavin' an' all lookin' at me as if I've every answer God ever saw fit to give. Not to mention the damage they do to the pantry on a daily basis. Now what's yer simple answer to that?"

"Just love them," she said, "that's all they want."

He pulled her tight to his chest, dropping a kiss on her head. "Lord, woman, how do ye always manage to do that?"

"What?" she asked, mystified.

"Cut straight to the heart of the matter an' put me firmly in my place."

She rubbed her cheek against his chest and sighed contentedly. "You smell like milk replacement and wool," she said.

He snorted. "An' to think they say marriage kills the romance."

From downstairs he could hear the rustle of animals and children. Lawrence coaxing Finbar onto the bed most likely, the small bleat of Paudeen dreaming whatever it was lambs dreamed of. Fields of alfalfa and clover unending? On the porch Rusty began his nightly serenading of the moon. Casey laughed, then closed his eyes and breathed in the scent of his wife's hair. He felt much like a man who'd been given a lopsided and not altogether unwelcome benediction.

"Jewel?"

"Mmhm," she mumbled sleepily, lulled by the stroke of his hand across her head.

"It's all I ever wanted too. Thank you for lovin' me, despite my bein' the most mule-headed ass ye've ever met."

She took his hand and kissed the calloused palm. "Any time."

Part Three

Nothing Sacred

Chapter Thirty-three
With Extreme Prejudice

THE SMALL SEISMIC TREMORS of impending trouble weren't as noticeable out in the countryside, but they were felt all the same. Even Pamela, happily sorting out her new home, could not ignore what was coming.

"Will you be safe, do you think?" she asked Casey late one night, as they lay in bed thoroughly exhausted from a day filled with working on the house.

"Mmphmm," Casey mumbled, nearly asleep though they'd only got into the bed two minutes before. "I should think so, I can't be much of a worry. Bein' away the last two years may have kept me off the lists."

"I don't know," she said worriedly, "the rumor is that the lists include anyone who's been seen as trouble in the last several years. Pat says he's certain to be on it, because of the Young Socialists."

"Did I not warn the two of ye then that organization was goin' to lead ye to trouble?"

She snorted. "I think that's more than a bit of the pot calling the kettle black."

"Aye, I suppose ye might say so," he responded, "but I've not given them much cause for concern of late, unless ye count all the wee rabble-rousers I deal with on a daily basis. Now if ye don't mind Jewel, I've not the brainpower left to string more'n a word or two together, so goodnight."

Within minutes he was asleep. Pamela, however, was not so easy in mind. Pat seemed to think Casey was likely to be fairly high on the list of those to be lifted.

"There's granddads on the bloody thing that haven't done anything more rebellious than take a pint on Sundays for years. I'd say he'd best be on the move when the sweep comes."

This begged the question of where, exactly, they were to move. One man on the run was one thing, but one man, a pregnant wife, a juvenile delinquent, a dog, a sheep and a recalcitrant cat was another matter altogether. Casey tended to be a wee bit stubborn on the issue of being there to look after his family, and wasn't likely to think the risk of being lifted great enough to leave them alone.

"Even if the Army doesn't have him in their sights, he'd best watch for what Joe Doherty may have up his sleeve. Things get confused enough, an' it's an opportunity for tryin' things on ye'd not otherwise dare to do."

Casey's mind wasn't quite so easeful a few days later.

"I want ye to pack a bag an' have it ready should we need to go at a moment's notice. I've arranged for Lewis to look after the animals should something happen. Ye'll have to call him; it's not likely I'll have the chance."

"You're scaring me, Casey," she said.

"I'm sorry Jewel, I don't mean to. It's just that I'll not leave ye here on yer own to face a bunch of gun happy soldiers. The laddie needs to have a bag at the ready too."

She nodded, knowing the queasy feeling that had suddenly overwhelmed her had little to do with the incipient nausea of pregnancy.

The bags were packed and placed in the downstairs closet. There they sat for two weeks, a grim reminder that their new domesticity was a fragile and uncertain thing.

Then on the night of Sunday, August the 8th, the uncertainty became a certainty. Republicans all over Belfast were on the move, keeping well away from familiar haunts in an effort to elude the raid that was said to be imminent.

"It's only a precaution," Casey said, but there was no mistaking the grim set of his mouth as he loaded their bags into the Citroen. In the yard, Mr. Guderson was putting a violently protesting Paudeen in his truck. Rusty was nowhere to be found and Finbar was glued mutinously to Lawrence's left leg.

Lawrence, who seemed to feel the proceedings were of enormous excitement, kept bobbing up and down like an addlepated stork, until Casey gave him a sharp word and he subsided glumly on a stump in the yard.

They left after dark, the entire drive one of fraught silence, even Lawrence's normally agile tongue completely stilled by the tension that emanated off the adults in the car.

"Where are we going?" Pamela asked finally, her voice startling all of them.

"A safe house I arranged a couple of weeks back."

She could tell from the grim set of his face that that was all the information she was going to get out of him.

"What changed your mind about leaving the house?" she asked, hoping that the suspicion at the back of her mind, that he was still keeping loose contact with his old friends in the IRA, was unfounded.

"Pamela," he said with some impatience, "I'll answer all yer questions later. For now, though, I can't see a foot beyond the headlights, an' I'm not entirely certain how to find this place in the dark."

That it seemed highly unlikely that a man who knew the streets of this city like the back of his own hand would have trouble navigating, even in the dark, was a comment she knew it was best to stifle for the present time.

The countryside slid by in the complete anonymity of darkness. From the backseat a soft buzz emanated from Lawrence, who had fallen asleep a mile beyond the village.

"Did ye bring yer camera?" Casey asked.

"You put it in the boot yourself," she said. "Casey, are you expecting to get lifted?"

"No, but it doesn't do to be too certain of anything in this town. Should I be taken," he threw a quick glance over his shoulder to be certain Lawrence was still asleep. "I want ye to take pictures. It's important to record what happens."

"I...how can I do that?"

"I wouldn't ask it of ye, if I didn't think it important. They'll try to whitewash this situation when it's all done, we have to take what measures we can to ensure that some truth survives. Just promise me ye'll do it."

"Yes, I'll do it."

The rest of the drive was accomplished in a strained quiet. There was no way to make sense of what was happening around them, not on a personal level, nor on a communal one.

Casey at last turned into the snaky curve of an exceedingly narrow laneway, and then abruptly turned again. It wasn't an area of Belfast with which she was familiar. Nor one, at first glance, that she was eager to make a closer acquaintance with.

The house was a faint smudge against the fingernail slice of moon that hovered above the roofline. Not a great deal of light was needed to observe that it was past its prime. On the sidewalk was an ancient rusted Russian Lada up on blocks, stripped of its tires and what little dignity it had once possessed.

A narrow wedge of light managed to escape through heavy curtains, small puffs of smoke lofting from a mossy, crooked chimney. All in all, the house looked anything but safe. In fact, it seemed miraculous that it hadn't toppled down about its occupants' ears long before now.

The front door opened as they got out of the car, Lawrence's snores still whistling round the back seat. A slight man stood framed in the faint light.

"Liam," Casey said, nodding tersely as he grabbed their bags. "I appreciate this, man."

The man nodded. "Ye know ye're welcome under any number of roofs, we're flattered that ye chose our home to shelter in."

Pamela stood blinking in the entry, as Casey went back out to retrieve Lawrence.

A tired looking woman shuffled out from the kitchen, her belly a huge mound under a threadbare nightgown, a tatty cardigan clutched tightly about her narrow shoulders. Her face was pinched with exhaustion, but she managed a weary smile.

"Ye must be Pamela," she said, and extended a hand. "I'm Mary."

"Pleased to meet you. I wish it was under less strained circumstances," Pamela said, feeling awkward to be standing in a stranger's house, knowing she had to bed down here because of conditions that were completely out of her own control.

"Not certain less strained circumstances exist here," Mary said.

Casey entered then, Lawrence half stumbling on his arm, eyes still closed.

"Christ he doesn't look like much, but he feels like the fattened calf," he said with a grunt, depositing the boy's gangly frame on the couch.

"We've put the two of ye upstairs," Mary said, rubbing her hands in the small of her back.

"When are you due?"

She grimaced. "Two weeks, though it seems like two years at this point."

Pamela's hand went unconsciously to her own belly. It was an act of reassurance as well as one of protection. Mary smiled, a look of female complicity that was aeons old.

"An' yerself?"

"Not until February."

"First one?"

"No," she replied quietly. Casey's hand took hers and gave it a squeeze. For both of them, Deirdre would always be their first child.

Mary nodded. "We lost our second, though I was only the three months along. Still ye wonder who they might have been, no?"

"Yes, you do."

"Well, good night then." Mary waddled off in Liam's wake, the curved mound of her belly like the prow of a ship.

"Come on woman," Casey said softly, "let's go to bed."

They started up the narrow staircase, but she hesitated halfway, glancing back at Lawrence. He was still snoring, an afghan tucked securely around his thin-bladed shoulders.

"Will he be alright down here?"

"He'll do," Casey said, and gave her a gentle push up the stairs.

The room was a little one, set darkly under damp-stained eaves. The bed, in accordance, was narrow. Casey eyed it, one eyebrow cocked dubiously, even as he yawned.

"We've slept tighter before," Pamela said, shucking off her sweater and jeans, and sliding between the musty smelling sheets with a shiver.

"Aye, so we have, but I'm thinkin' sleep had little to do with it at the time." He yawned again and rubbing his face with one hand, followed her into the narrow bed. His body was hot against the chill of her own, and she snuggled gratefully into his length.

"Do you think we're safe here?" she asked, knowing from the rhythm of his breathing that he was still awake.

"Aye, safe as can be managed at this point. Can't see what the bastards would want with me anyhow—I've only just come home."

"Have they ever needed a reason before?" she asked pointedly.

"Mmphmm," Casey grunted wearily, "no I suppose they haven't. Now darlin' let's get some sleep, it's been a long day an' unless I miss my guess, tomorrow will be longer still." He kissed her shoulder, punched up his pillow a bit, and settled with a sigh. Two years of sharing his bed told her he'd be asleep in seconds. She hadn't even counted to twenty before she felt the deep, even rise and fall of his chest behind her.

She herself was tired, but her eyelids refused to close. When she forced them shut, knowing she desperately needed the rest, the image of Casey being manhandled by soldiers seemed to be imprinted on the back of them.

She rolled onto her back, careful not to disturb him. The tiny garret room was sliced in two by moonlight. The wash of it fell half on Casey, leaving his other half in darkness. He was peaceful in his sleep, face soft in a way it never was during the daylight hours. At moments such as this, she didn't regret bringing him back. Despite circumstances, he seemed to have found an odd sort of peace.

His left arm lay down the side of his body, hand loose and relaxed on his hip, each hair delineated, fine as a whisper, in the silver light. He seemed suddenly fragile, as if a breath would scatter him, that if she were to merely blow out gently, he'd disperse in moonlight and shadow like powder.

She rolled another quarter turn, put her ear to the solid wall of his chest, and holding her own breath, listened. His heart was steady, slowed by sleep. She let her breath go carefully, in pieces, a bit at a time until the ache in her chest eased, and then closing her eyes, fell asleep.

She awoke hours later to him above her, moonlight gone, his body moving against hers in need and urgency. She opened wordlessly, wrapping her comfort around him, answering him in kind with need of her own. It was quick and ungentle, an act of reassurance in the dark. As if each of them singly was necessary to the survival of the other.

They fell back to sleep without having uttered a word. When they next awoke there were soldiers on the stairs.

IT HAPPENED SO QUICKLY that she was never able to piece it together coherently in her mind later on.

She snapped out of sleep to the sound of shouts, a deep rumble on the stairs and Casey bolting out of the bed as if he'd been shot. He threw the sheet back over her body, grabbed his pants and shoved his legs into them rapidly, casting a desperate glance at the window as he yanked up his zip.

"Fock, fock, *fock,*" he said as his fingers refused to cooperate. Someone started to pound on the door then with the heavy ominous thud of steel against wood.

Their eyes met over the sound of splintering as the door began to cave in to the demands of a rifle butt.

"Take the boy an' go to Jamie," he said bluntly. "I'll get word to ye as soon as I can."

She began to protest but the words died on her lips as the door flew open and the small space became a whirlwind of violent movement.

They took him as he stood, shirtless and shoeless, thumb bleeding where he'd caught it in his zipper. Hands cuffed behind him, rendering him as defenseless as possible.

"May I be so rude as to enquire why yer doin' this?" Casey asked with, all things considered, an enviable amount of cool.

"We don't have to explain anything to you, you Fenian bastard, we're entitled under the Special Powers Act," said the soldier, who was busily yanking on the handcuffs to ensure they were tight enough. And who then stuck his gun roughly under Casey's nose as an added point of emphasis.

Pamela sat frozen on the bed, sheet clutched to her chest, and watched as they dragged her husband down the stairs and away from her. Once they cleared the stairs, though, and the last soldier had turned away and down, she moved solely on instinct, letting its swift hand guide her to her abandoned clothes and then to the smooth black box she'd hidden under the bed the night before. She grabbed Casey's shirt and coat and ran down the stairs, where khaki backs were only now funneling their way out the door.

Lawrence was yelling, and she could hear a scuffle begin at the bottom of the stairs.

"Lawrence don't," she heard Casey say in a sharp tone. There was a thump and then the soldiers pulled Casey out through the door.

Time shifted, its focus narrowed, the aperture she always sought in these adrenalized moments outlining the morning with a sharp finger. The camera was loaded with fresh film, ready to go, ready to aim and shoot, ready for its defining moment, this moment—even if she wasn't.

In the narrow street dawn was beginning its soft-shoe crawl, mellowing the cracked pavement, the shabby row houses, and the tiny patched gardens with their fading blooms. A muddy-colored lorry straddled the width of the lane, chuffing like an out-of-breath hippopotamus, a giant child's toy set down in a space too confined and dangerous for its girth.

Automatically, as it had begun to do in these situations, her brain separated itself, like taking a box out of a box, leaving the original in its place and moving the latter over parallel to the original, though slightly askew. Photographer versus wife, picture taker versus the woman who wanted to scream in the street, who wanted to take the rifles these olive-clad boys wore slung so casually over shoulders and narrow hips and turn them on their owners. And so the entire scene, (five minutes in real time, eternity on celluloid) laid itself out for her in freeze frame. *Click,* Casey cuffed now to the side of the lorry, morning light washing him over rose and silver and gold, half-naked and barefoot in the street; an Irish man in an Irish street in the twentieth century, hard to countenance and yet there for the *clicking,* there for the taking. Take the shot, take the picture, leave the pain, it interferes with the work, work now, bleed on the weekends, in the nights, in the quiet, that's what Lucas had taught her.

Click, British boy in uniform, scared stiff, because you can't trust the Irish, bastards have always been so goddamn unpredictable, they'll kill you as soon as look at you, feed you tea in one hand and poison in the other. He scares her, this one, fear makes him nervy and he keeps glaring at Casey who looks back with one of those impenetrable black looks she knows only too well. It was like running into a brick wall, full tilt, one of those looks—a point of no return 'this might be your game now but someday we'll be in no man's land and then the field is wide open' kind of a look.

Click. Another soldier, tramping through the garden of some horticulturally avid old age pensioner, crushing forget-me-nots underfoot, snapping hollyhocks with the stem of his gun, just another jungle boy in the jungle. A hard northern face, a Geordie from up near the line, couldn't predict these ones, sometimes they were nearly as disenchanted and disenfranchised as the Northern Irishman and sometimes they knew how to hate just like the Irishman, so they were much more dangerous than their southern cousins.

"Get the fuck back in the house," he said to her, voice low but carrying like a poison-tipped arrow in the morning. Hard man, hard voice. He'd chosen the right occupation.

Click. Another man being dragged into the stillness, half-asleep, confused, yelling and thrashing, getting a hard kick for his pains and subsiding retching on his knees as the soldiers cuffed him to the lorry.

"Mornin', Liam," Casey said as calmly as if they were merely passing in the street. And yet there was a steely undercurrent, a tone that made the man, cuffs biting hard into his wrists, stand up slowly, take control of his breathing and face his captors calmly.

Click. Liam's wife, Mary, standing in the street, clutching a threadbare housecoat about her soft frame, nine months gone with their fourth child, her mouth a round 'O' of silent tears.

Don't ever project your own emotion into the frame, Lucas had told her, don't become a part of it. When you take a shot with your emotions entangled, you cloud the clarity of your subject, you see them from a limited perspective. Our job is to get the story, he'd said, not become a part of it. Otherwise what we see is a mirror reflection, not the subject as they really are.

Click. Casey's face, unsheltered for a moment, a look meant only for her, a private communication here in the street, with tense uneasy soldiers standing all round. She lowered the camera and walked towards him with neither haste nor deliberation.

"I'd say goodbye to ye," he said low as she approached, "I don't know when—"

She shook her head slowly. "I know."

How many of these personal communications had passed between them before? A hundred? A thousand? A turn of the hand, a slant of the head, the flicker of an eyelash, a torrent of words in an instant, all without sound.

She stretched up on her toes, her cheek meeting his just as a blistering orange sun hissed above the horizon. She could feel his heat, even in the chill of morning, the dull burn of his unshaven cheek against her own. Then she drew back slightly, put her mouth to his, biting down on his lower lip.

"Open yer mouth," he said in a low voice, and she did as bid, as if it were the most natural intimacy in the world to kiss one's husband open-mouthed in the street while he stood cuffed to an army vehicle, with soldiers pointing guns in their direction.

"Hey there, break it apart," said a gruff voice to her side.

She pressed her face harder against Casey's in response, feeling the bone beneath the skin, and the blood that flew on its well-ordered way between the two. Then pulled back to meet his eyes. They were dark, fathoms deep, and soft. And for a moment, only a flash, she could feel him against her as he had felt that first time they'd made love, a private universe of two, blood to bone, two restless objects made of the stuff of stars. Then the long cold oiled barrel of a rifle inserted itself between them and Casey's face changed imperceptibly, and without a flicker of muscle or betrayal of skin he was once again the hard man in the street. And she the abandoned wife.

Then, all at once, they loaded them into the truck, Casey, Liam, and four dazed looking young men who appeared half asleep. Stunned by the shouting, the guns in their backs while the warmth of their beds still evaporated from their skins. She stood with Lawrence, arm wrapped securely around his shoulders, as much to detain him as to comfort him.

Casey looked back only once, the morning sun gilding him with liquid fire, a stray breeze ruffling the ends of his hair. His eyes met hers across air and light, and it seemed as if the whole world moved in slow motion as his head tilted to the side and he blinked once, a small smile lifting the left-hand corner of his mouth. And then he was gone.

"Where are you taking them?" she asked through gritted teeth, aware of the soldier beside her, the Geordie with the hard jungle face.

He smiled, revealing pointy teeth in a sharp face. "To hell."

Then he walked off whistling a jaunty tune, swung himself up onto the tail end of the lorry, slapped its side sharply, and yelled to the driver.

The vehicle rumbled in a higher pitch, as if protesting this early morning duty, and then with a grinding of gears and a lurch, they were gone.

She swallowed hard over a throat thick with fear, and felt the small flat plastic-wrapped packet bite hard into the roof of her mouth, where Casey had pushed it during their kiss, the taste of his tongue still on it. She knew before she spit it out into her waiting hand what she would find.

Under the plastic wrap, a sheet of thin paper, folded again and again until it was no more than an inch square. And upon it, etched in Casey's bold, decisive hand was the address of where it was intended to go, one letter, two strokes. A falling curve, and an up tilted slash.

A simple, black-inked 'J'.

Chapter Thirty-four
And Justice For None

THIRTY-ONE HOURS AFTER he'd left on a mission of futility, Jamie returned home. He was red-eyed, exhausted, and gripped in the claw of a fury unlike anything he'd before experienced. Internment had been expected, the streets rife with rumor for weeks, but as with many of life's uglier events, the reality had turned out to be a bit of a shock. He'd run into so many metaphorical brick walls in the last twenty-four hours that he felt physically bruised.

Three hundred and forty-two men lifted out of a list of four hundred and fifty. Three hundred forty-two, and Catholic to a man. That had been a tactical blunder, he supposed, made in the smug arrogance of the Orange inner circle. Somewhere in that number the two Riordan men had been swallowed up. And, at present, he'd no bloody idea where they might be spit out. He'd managed to trace Pat as far as Girdwood Barracks, but had met with an unnerving silence on any information beyond that. Casey, on the other hand, seemed to have disappeared into the ether, so insubstantial was any intelligence he'd managed to gather concerning the older of the Riordan brothers.

He climbed the stairs wearily, legs the consistency of gelled lead. He needed sleep desperately but knew that even a few hours of rest were a luxury he could not afford.

He stripped down in the bath off his bedroom, turned the taps up until the ancient pipes shrieked in protest, and then stepped into the scalding hot water. He scrubbed down quickly, wishing he could rinse his mind clean along with his body.

He leaned against the tiled wall for a moment, closing his eyes. Behind the lids he could see the streets, burned into his retina by fire and rage. His ears still rang with the cries of children suddenly fatherless, the screams and curses of women whose men had been yanked, without mercy, from their arms. And underlying the howls of human misery; was the flat, metallic keen of the dustbin lids, banging the cobblestones as they had done so many times before in his demon-haunted city.

After his shower, he toweled down, chose a simple blue shirt and charcoal dress pants and dressed quickly, mind running over the myriad phone calls he would have to make, the bereft and terrified families he'd promised to look in on today and the promises he'd no idea how he was going to keep.

In the kitchen, where a pot of hot coffee was brewing and the scent of fresh rolls fragranced the air, he looked out over the city. Thick, black coils of smoke rose against a brittle blue sky, the imperial domes of the city smudged in the haze.

Standing there, the sound of coffee drizzling in the background, he was suddenly overcome by a stab of despair so sharp he couldn't breathe around it. It came to him bluntly, the way such epiphanies often did, that he was, after all, only one man. One man, with all the frailties that the human condition came carelessly packaged with.

His hand sought a chair blindly and he found himself guided and pushed gently downwards by a pair of hands that, though not often felt, were recognized instantly.

"Sit down before you pass out," she said tartly.

He sat, the wave of weakness abating slightly, and looked up.

"You look worse than I feel," he said shortly, "and that's saying something."

"Compliments so early in the morning, Jamie?" she retorted, and then sat down heavily across from him, as though her bones had suddenly telescoped down into her knees.

"What happened to your face?"

"Belfast confetti," she said with a weak smile, flinching as he touched her left cheek, which was turning a vivid and Stygian black.

"Rock or bottle?" he asked, rising to get the coffee, legs still slightly wobbly.

"Paving stone," she said ruefully, "fortunately it just glanced off."

Jamie looked at the blackness that bloomed around the sharp edges of her scar, the one she'd sustained in yet another battle that hadn't been hers to fight, and thought he'd define fortunate in different terms than she'd become accustomed to.

"Where's Lawrence?"

"Outside with Finbar. He's like a little powder keg right now, thinks he can somehow avenge Casey and set him free all in one go. If we knew where he was, that is."

Jamie set coffee down in front of her and a roll still warm from the oven.

"You have to eat," he said, as she pushed the plate away from her and shook her head.

"Can't," she said wearily.

"Can," he said and shoved the plate back. "You won't do him any favors if you get sick. He needs you whole and well."

Her head came up swiftly, eyes lit with hope. "You know where he is?"

she asked with a sharp intake of breath.

He shook his head regretfully. "No, not yet. Pat's in Girdwood Barracks. Have you seen Sylvie?"

She shook her head mutely, eyes dropping to stare at the tabletop as she bit her bottom lip in disappointment.

"Have you even cried yet?" he asked, tone softer.

"No," she whispered, and he could hear the control beginning to slip in her voice. "He asked me not to. Told me not to give the bastards the pleasure of my tears. So I didn't. I stood in the street, Jamie," her head came up and he saw her eyes were glittery with unshed tears, "and took pictures like I was composing some storybook; I took pictures while they chained my husband like a savage to a truck. My husband," she gasped, as if only now the enormity of the last twenty-four hours had caught up with her, "barefoot, half-naked and chained and I...I took pictures. Oh God, I'm sorry Jamie, but I think I'm going to be sick."

"No you're not," he said briskly, wondering whose very sensible voice was speaking through him, "just stick your head down between your knees and breathe slowly, the shock has finally caught you up is all."

"Better?" he asked a moment later as her head re-emerged above the table, strands of hair glued by tears into the battered mess on the left-hand side of her face.

She nodded weakly.

"Right then, do you think you could manage some tea? Maybe a bit of bread?"

He didn't wait for her acquiescence, but put the kettle on to boil and set the bread to toast. Coffee was a good eye opener, but it was useless in a crisis. There were times, as any Irishman worth his salt knew, when only tea would do.

He watched her carefully while she ate, more to humor him than anything else, he suspected, and drank down the entire cup of tea.

"We're going to have to have your face looked at," he said as she gingerly wiped her face with a napkin, "your cheekbone could be fractured. Is it hurting you a great deal?"

She shook her head, "No, it'll be fine, I don't need a doctor."

"We'll see," he said sternly and then added, "you need to go upstairs and get some rest."

"No." Her brow was set in a stubborn line he'd become well acquainted with over time. "I have to find out where Casey is being held, I have to talk to Pat—"

"There's no way to get near Pat right now."

"If Pat's there, then it's likely Casey—"

He shook his head, hating himself even as he did so, but he couldn't provide her with false hope.

"He's not."

She shook her head in denial. "You can't be certain of that."

"He's not. I don't know where he is Pamela, but I do know for certain it's not there."

"No, you don't know for certain, you can't. Some were taken to Crumlin Road and...and..."

He shook his head again, feeling as if he were kicking a defenseless creature.

"He wasn't. Liam Connelly is in Girdwood, so is Thomas O'Faolin and Jimmy McGurty and the other men who were put in that truck yesterday morning. But Casey isn't with them."

"You're not God, Jamie Kirkpatrick, you can't know everything," she said pushing back her chair and lurching to her feet, the smell of fear beginning to pulse off her in rapid beats. "I have to go," she dragged the back of a sweater sleeve across her eyes.

"And where will you go?" he asked gently.

"I...I don't know, but I have to find him, Jamie."

"What did he tell you, what did he ask you to do?" he asked, tone still gentle, but now insistent, pushing her memory.

She shook her head and dug in the front left-hand pocket of her jeans. "He left this for you, told me to go to you." Her face twisted slightly, tears still standing in trembling pools above her bruised cheeks. "Did the two of you plan this in advance? Did you know? Did he know?" she asked, voice rising in agitation.

"Everyone knew this was coming, it's hardly a surprise," he said calmly and saw the answering spark of frustration in her stance. He sighed, rubbing the vertical crease between his eyebrows. As practiced as he was at the art of lying, he didn't quite feel up to the challenge of it this morning.

"Yes, he came to me some weeks ago, asked me to see that you were safe. We both knew there was a possibility that no house was going to be a safe house. He knew someone was betraying him to Joe Doherty, now he's got a better notion of who that is."

"What?" she asked in a hoarse whisper, disbelief stark against her pale skin and under it something uncertain, a flicker of doubt, a hesitation that told him more about the state of her marriage than he was comfortable knowing. "Are you saying this was all a game, a ruse to smoke some rat out of hiding?"

"No, not at all. He really was worried they'd come for him at home. I don't think he wanted that sort of trouble to touch your house."

"Well it's touched us now," she said angrily.

"Pamela, he never wanted this to happen."

She slumped down in the chair again, tears slipping the dam of anger and sliding down her bruised skin.

"I know," she whispered. "I just feel so angry and helpless."

"So do I," he said.

The clatter of a boy and dog sounded just then in the hall. Pamela hastily wiped her tears away.

Maggie entered the kitchen, followed by Lawrence and Finbar, both rather disheveled from the events of the last twelve hours.

"Found this one behind the barn, smoking."

Lawrence had the grace to look slightly shamefaced, as Pamela raised a brow at him.

"We need to find the lad a bed," Jamie said, rising to his feet, every muscle feeling like it had been beaten with a large stick.

"He's to be fed first," Maggie said firmly, already filling a pot with water and measuring out steel cut oats into a bowl. She nodded over her shoulder at Jamie, "Ye'd best find yer own bed, before ye drop on the spot."

"I'll get to it soon enough," Jamie said, knowing he wasn't fooling Maggie for a second.

The kitchen around them was warm and quiet, sunlight glowing in the surface of the granite counters, and gleaming off the tile above them. One might almost think that below them the city too still slept, though the sound of sporadic gunfire in the distance cured one quickly of such imaginings.

Once Lawrence was occupied with his oats and a small lake of cream, Finbar happily and noisily chewing a soup bone under the table, Pamela turned to Jamie.

"Why did he send me to you?"

"Because other than his brother, it appears I'm one of the few people he trusts."

"What are we going to do now, Jamie?"

Jamie shook his head, feeling unutterably fatigued.

"*We* are not going to do anything. I have an idea or two—but you're going to have to trust me to do this alone. Can you do that—trust me?"

"You know I trust you, Jamie."

"Yes, I suppose I do know that."

"What now? Not just for us," she indicated the city below, "but for everyone."

"I imagine the violence will be fairly bad for the next while," Jamie replied, "and the government, whether it realizes it or not, is finished, they've signed their own death warrant. The road back is closed forever, all we can do now is look ahead and pray."

At present, that seemed very little.

Chapter Thirty-five

Pat

ON THE FLOOR OF THE GIRDWOOD BARRACKS gymnasium, in the midst of what he estimated was close to two hundred men, Patrick Riordan sat, slightly bruised, and clad only in a hastily grabbed undershirt and grubby jeans. He hadn't even had time to stick his feet in a pair of shoes.

He shivered, pulling his arms as tight to his sides as his manacled hands would allow. Internment came as no great surprise to him, but he'd thought he might escape the sweep. Hindsight, however new, made that assumption look very foolish.

If the government was desperate enough to kidnap unarmed socialists, it was highly unlikely Casey, with his past IRA associations, was going to escape the net.

They'd been here since early morning, and he guessed it was some time in the afternoon now, heading toward tea time. Not that he was likely to get his tea today.

Thus far he'd had his particulars taken down, been photographed, and his personal effects, which consisted only of the Celtic cross he wore around his neck, removed from him. Then he'd been led down a long corridor and into a small holding room, where he'd been confronted by two Special Branch RUC men who had questioned him extensively about IRA doings (of which he knew nothing), his ties with local Communists (it had taken him a bit to realize they meant the Young Socialists) and then he'd been accused of pretty much every crime from petty vandalism to attempts to blow up the Queen. He'd also been kicked and punched in the stomach, and slapped hard enough across his left ear that it was still ringing.

He had yet to have so much as a drink of water, which might be a blessing of sorts, because so far no bathroom privileges had been offered to any of the lifted men.

Next to him, half lying on the floor, was an elderly man who was obviously hard of hearing. He'd been kicked for his inattention to orders roughly a half dozen times.

"Do ye think they'd allow me to go to the latrine if I asked?"

Pat turned, slightly startled by the man's voice.

"I don't know drawin' their attention may not be wise."

The man let out a small whimper, obviously in a great deal of discomfort.

"I've the weak kidneys, had them since the War," he said piteously, "I'd not complain otherwise, but I'm like to go all over the floor if they don't let me to the toilet."

Pat gestured to the closest MP, a grommet-faced specimen that he'd have given a wide berth to on the street. However, here he couldn't be quite so picky.

"What d'ya want?"

"This gentleman," he jerked his head toward the old man, "needs to use the facilities. He'd not ask only it's got to the point where it's an emergency."

"He can piss his pants for all I care."

This bit of speech drew forth a groan from the old man.

"Christ, can't ye have a grain of compassion? The man's in dire agony here."

"Who the hell do you think you are? Telling *me* my business, fucking IRA dog."

Pat sighed, there was no use protesting this particular insult.

"I'm just askin' ye to show a little mercy to an old man, whose only crime is bein' Irish at the wrong time an' in the wrong place. An' while we're at it, when are ye goin' to allow us access to legal representation?" He couldn't resist this last bit of sarcasm, knowing that seeing a lawyer was about as likely as a trip to the moon at present, but needing to use the one weapon he had—his tongue.

The soldier gave him an ugly sneer.

"Listen you stupid fuck, under the Special Powers Act we can keep you here as long as we like. You can't see anyone. No one knows where you are and we don't have to charge you with anything to keep you here. If you happen to get shot there won't even be an inquest. You're at our mercy, and mercy's a fickle thing."

It was pretty much what he'd expected, yet he could still feel the ice water turn to shards in his intestines.

"Please..." it was all the old man could gasp out in his desperation.

The MP looked at him for a second and Pat could feel the movement before it actually cracked through the air; he got a half yell out just as the butt of the boy's rifle caught the old man hard in the side of the head. The blow knocked him flat to the floor, his teeth making contact with the filthy cement. The next blow hit him hard in the ribs and the man screamed on an explosion of breath.

"Jaysus, ye're goin' to kill him—stop it!" Pat yelled horrified into the outburst, even though he knew it wasn't wise under the circumstances.

This earned him a sharp smack with the butt of the man's rifle, but he managed to twist quickly to the side so that it glanced off his shoulder, leaving a burning pain in its wake, but an intact collarbone.

He could feel his hold on any kind of composure slipping rapidly, as though he'd mentally iced up and couldn't melt it off with meaningless reassurances. How did you tell yourself you were going to come out of this unscathed when someone was cheerfully beating an old man in front of your eyes?

The soldier had backed off after hitting Pat, looking slightly disgusted with what he'd just found himself capable of. Pat knew only too well that good men often found they were capable of all manner of unpleasant actions when under pressure, and the constraints of their normal workaday society were loosened. They would all soon learn there was no such thing in Ulster.

He took a breath, eyes still gauging the tension in the young soldier. The boy flicked one last glance at him. Pat held his look without blinking, not in challenge, but merely standing his little portion of ground.

Beside him, the old man was curled up on his side in a pool of urine, crying softly to himself. Pat looked away; he couldn't help him, but he could at least give him the dignity of not staring as the man came unglued.

The rest of the day was a blur of impressions. At some point they were given a bowl of stew and a piece of bread to eat. Tea was offered, but as there were only a dozen cups to share amongst all of them, he passed on it. Near nightfall he was interrogated again. This time he wasn't hit, but the screaming his questioner indulged in was almost more painful.

The light was blurring in his eyes, and sounds were starting to seem as if they had traveled a long tunnel before reaching his ears, when he was finally returned to the gym where the men were all bedding down for the night. There was no way of knowing the time, as everyone had had their watches confiscated under the heading of 'personal effects'.

He lay down on the thin blanket, too tired and disoriented to bother pulling its fragile shelter over him. He hurt in a vague numb way, as though his body were a separate entity.

His eyes burned with a thousand pinwheeling shapes when he closed them. Both interrogations had taken place under hot solar-bright lights, and his retinas felt seared.

He wondered where his brother was right now, how Pamela was faring, how long he was going to be held without charges and how many more beatings he might have to endure before they believed that he really didn't have any special information for them.

For a single agonizing second his mind lit on Sylvie and the panic in her face as they'd dragged him out into the half-light of dawn that morning.

His mind swerved away from Sylvie, there lay his break point and he knew he'd have to avoid that to get through what the days ahead of him were likely to hold.

Pure exhaustion took hold of him and bore him down past worry and pain into the dark embrace of Lethe.

HE DIDN'T KNOW HOW LONG he'd slept but when he awoke it was purely black and something was moving across his face like the brush of wingtips. He raised his hand to push it off and then realized the something was being pulled down over his head. Hard on the heels of that realization came a pair of hands, rough and bruising, hauling him to his feet.

He stumbled, earning him a harsh curse from the man, as he tried to peel away the layers of confusion with which sleep had shrouded his conscious mind. The pain was the first thing to come back. He tried to take a breath and felt as though someone had stabbed him hard in the stomach. Cracked ribs, he thought, trying not to panic as the shroud over his head was tightened around his neck like a noose. They'd hooded him, which could mean any number of things, none of them pleasant.

He heard the grind of the door opening a second later as his captor yanked him towards the rush of air, using the knot end of the noose as a lead. Then there were only impressions, hard, scorching and gone as quickly as they'd come. The feel of night air on his skin, and then a flash that cut through his hood and stung his eyes. Searchlights. And then he heard a noise, heavy in the night, that turned the trickle of ice water in his intestines to a glacier-fed stream. A sound that was both soft and hard at the same time, the dull *thunk-slice, thunk-slice* of a helicopter's blades. Were they moving him again? Already he was disoriented, out of time and place, with no notion of how this game might play itself out.

The tarmac was freezing under his feet as he stumbled along, pushed by a baton poking hard into his back. They were putting him in the helicopter, transporting him God only knew where. The tarmac was scattered with bits of glass, barbed wire, and sharp stones. Every step caused a new puncture in his soles. Batons smacked at the back of his knees, causing him to stumble every other step, without hands to catch him if he fell on his face.

The entire world was this—pain everywhere, noise, cursing, laughter and hands that wanted to hurt, to maim, to damage, hitting out at him from every direction.

He felt the bottom drop out of his stomach as the helicopter lurched into the air. They didn't allow him to sit and so he had to stand wide-legged to maintain any sort of purchase on the swaying floor.

They seemed to be flying in ever widening circles and he thought he caught a whiff of salt air through the oily smell of the hood. He'd tried to gauge the distance roughly in his mind, but panic and flying blind made it next to impossible to even guess how far they'd traveled.

He thought there were four soldiers, not counting the pilots. Four soldiers for one unarmed Irishman. He'd be flattered if he wasn't so busy being scared out of his mind.

"Jump time ya' fecker," the voice closest to his ear said.

"What?"

"Are ya deaf? I said it's time to *jump.*"

"But I'll die," he said, knowing he was stating the obvious, but unable to stop himself from uttering the words.

"Christ this one's a thickie—that's the point ya IRA bastard scum."

"You won't get away with this; ye can't murder a man an' not pay for it."

That one made them all laugh for a good long time. And with good reason, for he knew only too well what had happened in Cyprus and Palestine and Kenya, not to mention the myriad violations of basic law that were committed every day here in his own country.

"We're out over the Irish Sea, ye daft fucker—no one'll know where to look for ya. Couple hundred feet, hear it's the same as hitting concrete when ye land—SPLAT!" The soldiers laughed at this apparently funny fact.

Pat found himself repeating the Act of Contrition over and over to himself. *'Oh my God, I am heartily sorry for having offended you—'* Christ that was an understatement, Pat thought, and if he knew just *how* he'd offended, he would gladly take it back. *'and I detest all my sins—'* well the one that had landed him here anyway, *'because of Your just punishments,'* the *just* seemed up for strenuous debate at present. The words streamed from rote memory, a form of comfort in the face of incomprehensible actions.

'I firmly resolve... to sin no more and to avoid the near occasion of sin...'

Though it seemed likely that where he was going there wasn't going to be much occasion for the committing of sins. Because it was clear that the only place they were intent on transporting him to was directly into his grave.

He was on the precipice of the helicopter, with the sick feeling in his gut that they were going to push him if he didn't jump. Damn them if he'd jump though, they were going to have to shove him out the door to kill him.

Someone put a boot directly in the middle of his stomach and left it there for a moment so he could fully taste the fear that flooded his mouth and then the foot pushed him out into the void. He knew a split second of sheer dropped stomach terror and then he hit the ground hard. His shoulder gave a sickening crunch as he rolled over landing finally on his face on wet asphalt.

The fall had been one of about five feet. He could still hear the soldiers laughing above him.

"Fuckin' paddy, that'll teach ye, next time we'll drop you from about a hundred feet higher."

He could feel rage, but it was a long way off. The most immediate sensation was relief, that for the moment he was still alive and relatively whole.

Without time to catch his breath he was yanked to his feet, a soldier on either side of him dragging him along the rubble strewn tarmac.

They took him into a room and shoved him onto what felt like a mattress, before yanking the hood off his head. He simply lay there, eyes tightly shut, merely grateful that the world had stilled for a moment. They left him there, their voices fading and then abruptly ceasing as a door shut between him and them.

He lay there quietly and began assessing the damage to his body. Every inch of him throbbed, his feet were cut to shreds, the back of his neck burned where they'd put a cigarette out on him and one eye was swollen completely shut. He could feel blood drying in tight, itchy patches in a variety of places too numerous for his numbed mind to take inventory. And his shoulder, to put it mildly, felt like someone had stabbed it numerous times with a heated knife. He'd no longer any idea how long it had been since they'd dragged him out of his bed and into the street.

For all his exhaustion, sleep didn't come easily. Every position hurt, every shift of his muscles pointed out a new area of agony on his body. The mattress reeked of smoke and piss and it was cold and damp in the room. He tried to crack one eye and felt his eyebrow split and gush blood at the mere suggestion. He groaned, blinking to clear the red haze from the tiny slit he'd managed to open up in his eyelid. The shed appeared to be no more than a large culvert cut in half and turned over. The end walls were made of corrugated tin, amplifying the rain that was now falling. An off-kilter rectangle cut in the side, covered over with barbed wire, served as the only window. Even without the barbed wire the hole was too small to even consider as a means of escape. Even if he could squeeze through it, where would he go? He'd no notion of where he was, nor how much time had passed on the helicopter. Fifteen minutes? An hour? A lifetime.

Where was he? The question beat at the part of his brain not numbed nor panicked, a small corner for him to hide in, no bigger than a foxhole, but he'd take what he could get at present. And the larger question, he supposed, was what the hell did his captors propose to do with him now?

'Oh you've been reserved for a very special treat.' The oily voice of the corporal echoed through his head, causing a small surge of adrenaline to charge into his bloodstream, nauseating him as it rushed the hollow pit of his stomach.

Yet all that had happened, and all that would happen in the coming days, had about it the weighty feeling of inevitability. How could he have expected to remain unscathed in Belfast, as a Catholic man? As a human being, for that matter?

His father had raised them to hope for the best, but to prepare oneself for the realities of living in a country which had been at war with an enemy, but mostly with itself, for close to a millennium. He would need the lessons of his father through the next weeks and perhaps months.

He only hoped that whatever lay in store for him, he had the will to survive it.

Chapter Thirty-six

The Devil and Mr. Jones

IT WAS A SMALL HOUSE, well kept compared to its neighbors. Walkways swept, flowers neatly trimmed, windows sparkling. Jamie paused, with his hand on the wrought iron gate. Some of his happiest hours had been spent here. It seemed a lifetime ago. In many ways it was.

The front door, painted a vivid red, opened as he placed a foot on the bottom stair leading up to it.

Staring at him with a fierce silver glare was a tiny woman, with a head of hair the color of new pennies. She sat, crook-shouldered, hands laid lightly round the grip of a bat. Minus the armor of her chair she was no more substantial than an eight-year-old child.

"Joan," Jamie said, nerves flickering along his hands despite his exhaustion.

"Remember my name, do ye? Thought it had slipped yer mind completely." The voice was pure Protestant Belfast, tough as nails and about as subtle as a sharp cuff to the ear. Jamie held to the first step, neither retreating nor advancing.

"Well are ye goin' to stand in the stair all day?" she asked. "Sure an' the rumors'll be flyin' up an' down the street as it is." She nipped her head to the side sharply, where a suspicious face had poked out through the curtains next door. "Can I do somethin' for ye, Mrs. Mac?" Her voice was all ironclad politeness.

The head popped back in and a window was heard to shut with an irritated snap.

"Bloody old gossip, told ye to get yer arse inside quick-like. Come on then, man," she backed her chair deftly into the wide entryway, the bat balanced across her knees.

"Will it cause you trouble?" Jamie asked, slipping in behind her and shutting the door.

"Ah, that one's tongue flaps like a sheet in the wind, people don't pay her a great deal of mind. Ye know I'm not one to care what others say, Jamie."

The chair swiveled about abruptly, the sharp silvery eyes piercing him across the expanse of well-scrubbed flooring and gleaming furniture.

"How are you, Joan?" he asked gently, meeting her gaze with one of his own.

"As well as can be expected an' no better than I ought to be," she replied tartly. "Twasn't for the papers an' the telly I'd have thought ye'd died an' been buried without notice years ago," she said without preamble. Joan had never held with small talk or the protocol of polite conversation. Even if she hadn't seen you for over a year.

"When did you take to answering the door with a bat in your hands?" Jamie asked.

"Since my brother has been keepin' the sort of company he holds truck with these days. I imagine it's him ye've come to see."

Jamie nodded. "I do need to speak with Thrawny, do you know when he'll be back?"

"How's yer memory Jamie? 'Tis only the two days past his pay; he'll not be sober 'til Sunday. An' then he'll come creepin' in, tail tucked 'tween his legs an' crawl into a corner, not fit for the cat to chew on."

"Where is he?" Jamie persisted, fixing her with his prettiest smile.

He got a cocked brow and a silver glare in return, then unable to help herself she smiled in return. "Ach, ye fair-faced devil, ye'll be the ruin of the women yet, won't ye? He's up Little Bombay way, Black Mary's," she smiled, less civilly, "ye'll know the address I believe?"

"I'll know it," Jamie said, then with a wink he knelt down in front of the wheelchair, reached inside his coat and then held forth his cupped hands. Joan edged forward almost gingerly, from long experience she knew the man was never predictable. She held her breath and then let it out all at once.

"Do ye never forget a woman's weaknesses?"

"I'd never be so foolish," he said and opened his hands into her own. In her work-rough palms, frilled and lucent as a new lime, head tucked under a ruffled wing, was a baby myna bird.

"An' wee Mountbatten dead the month only, damned bird, I've missed him sorely. Ah, but who's a duck then, darlin'," she said cooing to the shivering ball of feathers in her palm. "Wherever did ye find him?"

"A certain Mr. Sukhar in Dublin," Jamie said, happy in Joan's obvious pleasure. "There's a bag of food on the steps for him."

"Can ye spare the time for a cup of tea?" Joan asked, surreptitiously swiping her eyes across her shoulder.

Jamie shook his head regretfully. "Not this time, I'm sorry. I've got business to attend to that cannot wait."

"Is it bad trouble then?"

Jamie glanced up sharply, finger stilled on one downy wing of the tiny bird. "Trouble?"

"Jamie, I'm neither deaf nor a fool," Joan replied tartly, drawing her twisted frame as upright as she could. "I know what my brother is, an' I know how many times ye've pulled his irons out of the fire. I'm thinkin' maybe the time for collection on those debts has come. Am I right?"

The green eyes that she'd always found so disarming never faltered under the sharp question of her own. "In a manner of speaking."

"It's all right Jamie. Ye don't need to spare my delicate sensibilities; sittin' in this chair half my life has left me plenty of time for thinkin' and questionin' situations that don't seem right."

"I'm sorry, Joan," he said simply, but she understood the wealth of feeling that was disguised in the three short words.

"How's Colleen?" he asked, eyes averted for the first time in the conversation.

"She was up this Easter past," Joan said reluctantly.

"It's alright, Joan," Jamie said quietly, "I never expected that she would cut all ties. You're her family."

"An' what of yerself man, what do you do for family?"

"I manage."

"Which means ye go it alone, an' ye drink when ye canna stand the pain no more. Am I right?"

"Roughly speaking."

"She asks about ye, always, but I never have an answer for her. I tell her that ye don't come around anymore an' she says she thought ye were wise enough to understand that we were still yer family too."

In answer Jamie merely touched the side of her face lightly. "I see Michael when I look at you Joan. He'd the gray eyes and the ha' penny hair."

"Do ye think I don't remember?" she said roughly. "I bathed the wee laddie afore ye put him in his lace."

"I was always grateful that he only knew loving hands, even if he wasn't alive to feel them."

Joan shook her head, lips in a tight line that spoke eloquently of dammed tears. "He was family."

Jamie bowed his head, fighting the desire to fall asleep where he was. Joan put a hand to the sun-bright hair, stroking it with a tenderness she usually reserved only for her beloved birds.

"I know it's hard, but do ye think once in a rare while ye might stop by an' say hello?"

"I will," he said, head coming up with the mercurial smile firmly in place. It only served to highlight the exhaustion that hung about his edges like a smoky aura.

"If it were anyone else I'd know that for a lie, but I know ye always keep yer word, man." She grasped his hand in one of her own cracked, red ones.

"Make certain it doesn't get ye killed."

"I'll do my best." He stood on legs that trembled with exhaustion, knowing he didn't fool her for a second. It was a relief somehow.

In the street he paused for a moment, thinking he felt the brush of eyes on the back of his neck. He took a deep breath, shrugged it off, and got in his car.

Behind him a curtain twitched shut, the person behind it smiling grimly to themselves.

BLACK MARY'S ESTABLISHMENT took up a block of six row houses just beyond the fringes of the Little Bombay area of Belfast. The outside of the two-up two-downs looked pretty much the same as every other building of the type. Inside, though, it was a revelation of silk walls that rose two stories high, a great cavern of a kitchen where some of the best meals in Belfast were known to be partaken of—for the freshest vegetables and choicest cuts of meat always made their way to Mary's kitchen. Upstairs narrow hallways led to equally discreet and well-appointed rooms. For those weary in spirit, in body, in mind, Black Mary's provided succor and rest, as well as other activities designed to fill the soft hours when the planet turned its face from the sun. No one really knew where Black Mary originated from, it just seemed that she'd always been there. Olive-skinned and raven-haired as an Indian princess and just as regal, she was a fixture to the environs. Whether one approved of her sort or not was irrelevant.

Jamie's polite knock at the back door which led, as he well knew, into the kitchen, was answered by a woman of indefinable years, who'd the face of a cherub and the body of the Venus Willendorf. Surprise re-aligned her features from boredom to unfeigned delight. "Well ye pretty golden bastard, we thought ye'd gone an' left us for good."

Before Jamie could get his mouth open to make protestations, he was engulfed by dimpled pink arms smelling sweetly of talc, and kissed soundly on the mouth.

"What," she asked, blue eyes sparkling like aquamarine, "have ye no pearls in yer mouth this time?"

"Pearls?" Jamie queried, with a look of innocence. He stepped into the kitchen to the homey smells of frying sausage and eggs, toast browning lightly and fresh squeezed oranges. Around the kitchen women stood in various states of morning *deshabille*. Some faces he was familiar with, some not. It had been a time since he'd visited Mary's premises. Suddenly the troubled streets seemed a world away and he could feel a little of the tension leave his neck and shoulders.

The cherub-faced Venus, who went by the rather prosaic moniker of Winnie, led him into the kitchen by the hand, seating him at one of the baronial chairs around the big wooden table. Then she sat in his lap, surrounding him in sweet, silk wrapped flesh and put her arms comfortably around his neck.

"Don't tell me ye've forgotten the pearls, Jamie?" She ruffled his hair with one plump, beringed hand. The other women in the kitchen were staring with undisguised interest now. Winnie made a mock moue of protest. "Ye used to put them in that flowered vodka ye liked so well back then—the one that sounded like a sneeze?"

"Hyacinth," Jamie supplied.

"Aye, that'll be the one," Winnie agreed, "then ye'd drink off the vodka an' store the pearls in your mouth."

"An' then what did he do?" asked a fresh-faced girl, with a mop of red ringlets and a smattering of ginger freckles across her nose, her rosebud mouth an 'O' of fascination.

"An' then," Winnie said with obvious pleasure, "he'd take his tongue an'—"

This intriguing tale was brought to an end by the appearance in the kitchen doorway of a tall, elegantly boned lady, with one jet braid flowing down the front of her white silk robe.

"Despite your obvious charms, Winnie, I don't think our friend is here to see you. Jenny, you're dripping bacon grease on the floor; there's a small bucket of sand under the sink, sprinkle some on it." Having dispatched her orders with a firm tongue, she turned her gaze on Jamie and smiled, the mere act transforming her face into that of a young girl.

"It's been a very long time, Jamie."

"It has," he agreed, as Winnie, flushed with pique, delivered her pretty pink self from his lap.

"Have you come looking for himself?" she asked, and Jamie remembered suddenly why she was so good at her chosen profession. She anticipated a man's requests and wants often before he was aware of having them.

"He's here?" Jamie asked, rising to his feet and flashing a smile of regret in Winnie's direction.

"Where else would he be, two days past pay? He's still halfway down the bottle neck though and not inclined towards company. Come on," she turned on bare elegant feet, "I'll lead you to him, but then you're on your own."

Jamie followed in Mary's wake, the clean smell of shampoo and soap wafting back to him.

"He's going to be sore-headed and miserable as a bear."

"It won't be the first time I've had to sober him up."

"Why today?" Mary asked and stopped abruptly in front of a door painted a bright red, which stood in harsh contrast to the other muted tones that graced the hallway. "It's the only way he can find the right door at night," she said noting Jamie's enquiring look. "Why Jamie?" she asked. "I'd think you'd have more important business than this today."

Jamie smiled, gracefully avoiding the question. "Do I need to sign a waiver for damages before I go in?"

Mary gave him a hard look then opened the door and waved him in. "It's your neck you're risking; I'll not take responsibility for what happens to you in there."

Jamie nodded. "I'll take my chances."

"If you can sober him up you're a better man than I am," Mary said, flicking the end of her black braid over her shoulder as she turned on her heel. "I wish you the joy of him."

The room was dark as the bowels of purgatory and Jamie took a moment to adjust his vision. The furniture was much the same as he remembered; heavy, ornate Victorian, the centerpiece being a monstrous four-poster that would have looked more at home in Buckingham Palace than a Belfast brothel.

On the bed something stirred, emitting a series of loud popping farts before settling itself back into paralytic sleep. Jamie stepped forward and surveyed the smelly heap on the bed with a bemused look. He then retraced his steps down the hall to the bathroom. The taps were cast in bronze and depicted two of the more acrobatic positions from the *Kama Sutra*. He only had need of the one on the right though. He set the plug in the drain and turned the tap to its furthest reaches, rolled up his sleeves and bracing his shoulders, returned to the dark room.

He took hold of the extremely grubby collar of the heap and twisted it, yanking the heap onto its feet. The heap exploded into vociferous cursing, limbs flailing in all directions, even as it was dragged, ungently, down the hall.

Jamie had the advantage of surprise, his wits, and a strength few would have suspected of him. The heap had its abnormal size and a temper to go with its flaming hair and beard. The heap, however, having been intimate over the last forty-eight hours with several bottles of spirit, was at a distinct disadvantage and found itself head first in a tub of water that was only slightly above the freezing mark.

Thrust in and out of the water like a clog of rags, the heap found full consciousness and with it, the return of all five senses. They were not welcome. "You," he wheezily intoned, between dunkings, "are," *splutter,* "a dead," *cough, splutter,* "man."

"Tsk, tsk," said a honeyed voice above him, "threats so early in the morning? You'll poison your spleen along with your liver."

The heap, now fully cognizant of whose clutches he was in, described five fascinating, if circuitous, routes by which his captor could take himself indirectly to hell. For this information he received another dunking.

"Well my little poppet, have you had enough yet?" Jamie asked, hand like a vise in the man's hair.

"Get ye back to the gates of hell where ye came from, spawn of Satan," the heap roared in reply, water streaming through a thick beard the color of Chinese poppies. One eye, the mottled texture of a fresh-nipped prairie oyster, cracked open, glaring things best left unuttered. Utter them he did, though—in five languages, a ripe polyglot of syllables and vowels that geographically straddled the linguistic divide from pole to pole.

"How colorful," Jamie said pleasantly, "if my ear serves, you've just called me a stinking, fresh-lipped whoreson mothered by two-headed yaks, fathered by Lebanese sodomites."

The mottled eye cracked again. "Aye, an' ye deserved it, 'twas you taught me to curse in every known language."

"Those being the only words you showed any proficiency for, I hardly had a choice."

The heap, commonly called Thrawny, collapsed against the tub and ruffled two big hands through his beard, a great laugh rolling up from the pit of his abundant belly.

"Ach, never could stay mad at ye, ye daisy-headed bastard. Sit will ye? My head is spinnin' fit to kill."

Jamie put down the lid of a cherub festooned toilet and sat. "You owe me a new pair of shoes you poppy-faced souse. These," he looked distastefully at the dripping buttery leather on his feet, "are completely ruined."

Thrawny cast a bleary eye on the shoes. "Made by a blind cobbler in a tin shack in Calcutta, formed to yer royal little bones no doubt."

"His name's Badeesh and he only works from dawn 'til dusk, so you'd best get your grains of rice together and put the order in now and," Jamie said with dignity, "he's only blind in the one eye as the other was lost to leprosy two years past."

Both oyster blue eyes were open now, the flaming beard dripping a pool into the hollow where belly rounded over into massive chest. "Ye're an evil man, Jimsy, an' make no mistake of it. Now help me to my feet, will ye?"

Jamie gave him an arm and levered Thrawny onto his feet. Thrawny shook his massive head like a Saint Bernard flinging off fleas, then cocked it towards the doorway, around which curious heads bobbed like loosed apples from time to time.

"Mary," Thrawny roared, "make us a pot of coffee will ye, now there's a girl."

Mary said something distinctly uncomplimentary about the state of her bathroom and then headed off toward the kitchen. The scent of extremely strong coffee drifted down the hallway to the parlor where Thrawny plunged into a deep wingback chair that dwarfed even his mammoth proportions.

"I take it," he said, peering at his visitor through slitted eyes, "that this is not a social call?"

Jamie sat opposite him and came swiftly to the point. "Yesterday a man was lifted out of a safehouse in the Murph. There were eight men in the army lorry that took them away, only seven made it to Girdwood Barracks. I want to know where the eighth went. His name is Casey Riordan."

Thrawny gave him a narrow eye. "An' why d'ye think I might have that sort of information?"

"If you don't, you certainly know who does," Jamie said coolly, hands laid lightly on the damask arms of the chair he sat in.

"Jesus, I'm too hungover for this conversation," Thrawny sighed. "Colleen always said ye were a chilly bastard when ye wanted to be."

"*You*," Jamie said, "are the one with the bleeding eyeballs, don't try distracting *me*."

Thrawny looked at him, curiosity flaring like pinpricks in his eyes. "Hundreds of men were lifted this mornin', why's this one so important?"

"That's my business."

"Ye're a mite prickly, this a personal matter?"

Jamie merely raised his eyebrows and delivered a chill green look.

"All right, all right, the name's familiar he's a 'Ra boy, isn't he?"

"He was, but he's not any longer."

"An' he's still got use of both legs? Jesus they must be gettin' slack in the ranks."

Jamie folded his arms, placed them on his knees and leaned toward Thrawny. "Stop avoiding the question."

"Jamie ye know this sort of information never comes without a price for somebody."

Jamie didn't so much as blink. "You owe me this, Alexander, just answer the question."

Thrawny winced. "Lower yer voice, Joan an' yerself are the only ones that know my Christian name." He shifted his bulk uncomfortably, sunlight threading in the nutmeg tufts of hair on his forearms. He pursed his lips and took a reluctant breath. "There was some money changed hands, lot of it actually, to make sure that boy didn't make it to Girdwood. Truck was paid to go down a side road an' stop. Someone was waitin' to take him off there. That's all I know, I swear to ye, Jamie. If I was found to be talkin' to ye my life'd be worth no more than a peckerless snake."

"There were seven other men in that truck, why him?"

There was no mistaking the look Thrawny gave in response to his question. "Well as ye're here askin' the question I imagine ye know better than I do, why someone wanted him bad enough to pay that sort of money."

"What sort of money?"

Thrawny drew his eyebrows down and began to give off distinct emanations of discontent. "Never miss a goddamn beat, do ye?"

"I've been up roughly forty-eight hours and I've a house filled to its gilded ceiling with refugees so you'll have to forgive me if my patience is wearing a little thin."

Thrawny named a figure, which gave Jamie a moment's pause.

"I'll need a name."

Protest formed in Thrawny's face immediately. Jamie heard the excuses, could have recited them verbatim before they crossed the man's lips, but he allowed him to finish his litany of the rain of curses that was likely to land on both their heads for this one name.

"Are you quite done then?" Jamie asked politely when Thrawny came to the end of his hellfire monologue.

"This is no bloody joke Jamie," Thrawny leaned forward until there was no more than an inch between their faces, his breath a fog of stale whiskey. "Have ye heard of the Trustees?"

Jamie gave the slightest nod.

"All right, well they've got their own hired guns. Assassins who go in an' out of the Catholic neighborhoods an' kill who they're told." He pressed a meaty hand to his head, wincing slightly. "I'm goin' to need a drink if ye want me to continue."

Never a man to arrive unprepared Jamie took a bottle of Connemara Mist out from under his coat. Thrawny took the cap off and drank a long steady stream of the golden fire before returning to his story. "Boy," he said emerging for air, eyes streaming, "that's powerful potent stuff."

"The name," Jamie repeated calmly.

"The lawyer that was killed with the car bomb, that was their doin'."

"These Trustees?"

"Aye, though ye'd be hard pressed to prove it."

"Then how'd you come by this information?"

"There's four assassins that I know of all right. Two are drones, do what they're told to, pick up the envelope of money an' go home. 'Tis neither here nor there to them who's killed nor why. The other two are a bit of a different story." Thrawny's eyes darted quickly about the room as if he expected the faded wallpaper to have sprouted ears. "One's got a mouth on him, gets liquored up an' brags a bit. Times he's partnered with the fourth man an' this is where the story gets really frightenin'."

"This fourth man?"

Thrawny nodded, tongue flicking around his lips nervously. "Two months back there was a murder, ye'll remember—body was found in an alleyway off Wimbledon Street. Some poor sod stumblin' home drunk got beat real bad, teeth'd been pulled, fingers broke, face cut up fierce from a knife?"

"I remember," Jamie said curtly, the vertical crease between his eyes deepening.

"'Twas the fourth man that did it. Word is there's no political motivation behind most of his murders, he just kills for the sheer joy of it. Name's Kenny Murray an' he killed a man in prison as well. Poisoned him before the poor bugger could take the witness stand against him."

"Are you telling me this Murray is the man I want?" Jamie asked.

"Aye," Thrawny clutched the bottle of whiskey tight to his belly, "unfortunately it is."

"And how do I find him?"

Thrawny shook his head violently. "Ye don't man, don't even think it. This man is psychotic, he's not just some Shankill tough, he'd slaughter ye for a lock of yer hair. Besides no one knows where he lives or what he does."

"I imagine his partner does," Jamie said quietly.

"Oh no, no, no, no," Thrawny said agitatedly, "ye'd not get near him either."

"You have."

"Only when I've ended up in the same drinkin' establishment an' that's The Club. Ye'd never get past the door an' if ye did, ye'd not come back out it."

"Not if I went with someone who's known there."

"Are ye feckin' nuts?" Thrawny said, a slight squeak in his rumble. "Everyone an' his dog knows who ye are man. That club is sacred Loyalist ground, they'd roast ye an' eat ye an' use me for toothpicks once they were done."

"Can you be sober enough by—" Jamie glanced at his watch, "eight o'clock?"

"No," Thrawny shook his head so hard that whiskey slopped over the neck of the bottle and trickled in a stream over the hummock of his belly. "No, you may have some crazed death wish, but I don't. I'll not go an' ye've no way to make me." He thumped the bottle against his knee for emphasis.

"You won't?" Jamie asked lightly, and Thrawny felt the short hairs on the back of his neck stand straight up. He'd a miserable feeling that old debts were about to be called in.

"Now Jimsy," he began in a conciliatory tone, but was cut off by Jamie's raised hand.

"No, don't waste your breath, I can see you've your reasons." He stood as if to leave and Thrawny relaxed slightly, which was his mistake.

"Oh by the way Joan said not to forget to pick up milk before you drag your useless corpse back home."

Thrawny, already an unhealthy gray, blanched visibly, "Ye went to see Joan first?"

"Did I forget to mention that?" Jamie smiled sweetly. "Odd that it should slip my mind. She worries about you a great deal, doesn't she?"

"She's my sister, ye know our family is tight man, or at least ye knew it well once."

Jamie turned and came across the room, putting his face in Thrawny's, hands on the arms of the chair. Despite the fact that he outweighed Jamie by a good eighty pounds he shrank back as far as the chair allowed.

"She worries too much, hardly seems fair does it? But even Joan doesn't know the extent of your troubles, does she?"

Thrawny went deathly still, suddenly understanding where the conversation was heading. And knew the man wasn't even going to give him the illusion of choice.

"I don't know what ye're talkin' about," he said, attempting to bluff it out.

"What I'm talking about, Alex, is gambling debt. Joan doesn't know how shaky the floor under her feet is, does she? What do you think she'd do if she realized the house is mortgaged to a loan shark, who has every intention of kicking her out in another month."

"I was goin' to find the money..." Thrawny began in protest but Jamie merely raised an eyebrow.

"You've got thirty thousand pounds up your sleeve?"

"I had twenty," he said angrily before he could stop to think what he was letting slip.

"*Had* being the operative word in that sentence," Jamie said. "All gone on the horses. Twenty to win on Balmoral's Whelp, am I right? Blew all twenty grand in an afternoon didn't you? I find it interesting that you could come up with it in the first place. No overtime hours at the shipyard, no extra job and yet you had it certain enough."

"Look man—"

"No you look," Jamie grabbed him hard under the chin, "I know, do you understand? I know where that money came from. Couldn't believe it at first, said to myself you couldn't do that sort of thing, wouldn't get mixed up with those kind of people. Not the Thrawny I knew. But the facts kept piling up and I, not being given to blind faith, saw the picture. It made me sick, actually physically ill, Alexander. Realized I didn't know you anymore."

"Jamie please, ye don't understand, ye don't know how desperate I was."

"I don't care how desperate you were, nothing excuses what you've done. You could have come to me, did you even consider that? I'd have lent you the money, Christ, I would have given it to you, you had only to ask. Or is Catholic money tainted?"

Thrawny shook his head slowly, tears moistening the pale oyster eyes.

"Ye know better than that. How long since ye been by, Jamie?"

"That has no bearing on this situation."

"Oh but it does, we were family Jamie, we loved ye as our own, we wept when ye lost the bairns, we died a little when Colleen left ye. We loved ye an' you abandoned us."

Jamie took a deep breath and stood. "I couldn't be there Alex. I just couldn't."

"Well neither could I anymore," Thrawny said through gritted teeth. "An' if ye bear me any fondness at all man ye won't go to that club. Ye don't understand how deep this thing goes."

"I have to find this man, Alex, do you understand? I have to find him now, alive and well."

"Jamie, I can't."

Jamie sighed, wanting only his bed and oblivion. Thrawny had left him little choice but to make this last desperate move in the game. "The mortgage on the house is paid. Joan will never know the difference, she can go on believing her drunken brother is still capable of taking care of her."

He watched as Thrawny's shoulders slumped in relief and knew he'd broken a man as surely as if he'd sliced him in half.

"Are ye blackmailin' me, Jamie?" Thrawny asked, though there was little question in the words.

"Yes," Jamie replied coolly, "I suppose I am. Eight o'clock, be here and be sober—understand?"

"Aye, I understand," Thrawny said, glaring out of bloodshot eyes, "ye're not the devil, ye're his master."

In the street Jamie took a deep breath of the smoky air and shut his eyes for a second, banishing the memory of Thrawny with tears in his eyes.

Right now, he could not afford anyone's tears.

Chapter Thirty-seven
Zorba and Company

"C HRIST ON A PIECE OF TOAST, I don't know how ye expect me to get through this sober." Thrawny eyed the oddity before him with a great deal of worried skepticism.

"I'll keep quiet and follow your lead," said the vision in front of him, nimbly adjusting its greasy leather cap and bouncing down off the wall like an acrobatic Pan spotting a nymph.

"What in the name of all that's holy is that?" Thrawny asked a moment later when confronted with their transportation.

"A chip van as you no doubt can see," Jamie replied, blithely swinging up onto the driver's seat and waving impatiently at the passenger's seat.

Thrawny reluctantly took it, knowing he'd no choice in the matter. The lack of options, however, didn't make this scenario more appetizing. He'd been in on escapades with Jamie before, had even been known to orchestrate a few, but the prey they were hunting tonight played for keeps and had the meanest set of teeth he'd ever seen.

The Club was a nameless establishment that was known only to those who drank and played billiards there. Like a secret society, you had to earn your way in through a process of initiation. Wedged at the end of a brick laneway that was accessed through a narrow crack between two buildings, it was a low-ceilinged, nondescript building with no sign above its door. The barred windows and metal door made certain that no hapless tourist ever made the mistake of wandering in to slake his thirst.

Standing in a hard rectangle of barred light, Thrawny thought there were likely very few doors in the world he'd less like to step through at the moment.

"How will we know the man?" Jamie asked, smoothing down the corners of a dense, oily mustache.

"There'll be a space about him of two seats to a side, an' he's a face on him like a Netterjack toad. In fact he's called the Toad, though no one's fool enough to say it to his face."

The place was harshly lit and about as inviting as a medieval dungeon.

Cinderblock walls had been painted an institutional shade of green and were a perfect match for the dour expressions that were to be seen on each and every face as they entered the building.

"Friendly crew," the Greek muttered out of the side of his mouth.

Thrawny hitched up his pants with a deep breath, "Don't say I didn't warn ye."

The Greek threw him a sideways smile, causing his moustache—large, black and oily—to twitch alarmingly. Thrawny felt a jolt of worry; in the aftermath of previous excursions with Jamie his primary emotion was a fervent gratitude to still be in possession of his life.

The man called The Toad was obvious at once. There were the two empty spaces to either side of him that Thrawny had said there would be. And he did, most assuredly, bear a strong and unfortunate resemblance to a small brown amphibian.

The Greek, ignoring the societal rules of the club, went and hopped onto a stool adjacent to the Toad.

The Toad turned slowly, menace apparent in his every move. Several sets of eyes were trained on them now, unblinking and tense with the expectation of violence. The Greek seemed unaware of the heavy currents running toward him and smiled cheerfully at the stubby man, a gold tooth winking insolently under the heavy moustache.

Thrawny, a shade of pale that looked distinctly greenish, gave a nod to the Toad.

"E's with me."

"Is he?" The Toad's eyes narrowed. "An' who the feck is he when he's not at home eh?"

"Coo-zan," the Greek said with the wide-eyed innocence of one who found the complexities of English entirely beyond him.

"Yer cousin?" The Toad lifted his tufted shelf of a brow. "Doesn't look like no relation of yers."

"Aye, well," Thrawny shot a heavy look in the Greek's direction, "he's distant—second cousin, three times removed."

"An' does yer cousin have a name?" The Toad asked, eyes flat as stagnant water.

"Uh, his name," Thrawny swallowed, corner of his mouth twitching in nervous hilarity, "is um, Zorba."

"Zorba the Greek," the Toad snickered, "is this some kind of fockin' joke?"

"You think is funny?" said the Greek, thick brows lowering ominously, "I think not is funny."

"Yeh, I think is funny," the Toad replied with a sneer.

"*Koutoc*," the Greek said and spat distastefully to one side.

"What the hell did he say?" the Toad asked, rising on springy legs off his stool, blunt pocked hands fisted up and ready to knock the insult, for the tone was clear, back down the foreigner's throat.

"Ees Greek for stupid," the dark man replied heatedly, oily mustache bristling in indignation.

The Toad eyed him for a long moment. "Well ye get points for stupidity anyhow. But maybe ye don't understand how things work about here. That's what's wrong with this country, lettin' greasy foreigners come an' go as they like. Get him out of here, Thrawny, before ye're short one coo-zan." The Toad laughed at his own hilarity and sat back on his stool, dismissing the Greek's presence in a most insulting manner, or at least that was how the Greek seemed to see it.

"*Seenoeteekos proveeos*," the Greek said haughtily, arms crossed high on his chest, a dark look aimed down his nose.

The Toad cocked his head and blinked. "What's he said now?"

"My Greek is no' so good," Thrawny cleared his throat delicately, "but chancin' a translation, I think he's called ye—roughly speakin' ye understand—a sodomizer of sheep."

The signal was subtle, fore and middle fingers lightly tapping the seam of his pants as he hopped off the stool. It would have, and had, passed without notice under many a set of ordinary eyes. The Greek, however, not possessing such mundane orbs, swung quickly into action.

"*Yia va zoee!*" the Greek bellowed and with a tornado like swipe, dismembered the counter of its contents. Glass and bottle alike, flew, spirit-winged, flinging liquid jewels in their wake. They arced, they tumbled, they head-over-heeled, landing with a glorious smash, one upon the next, in the glowing bed of peat.

For a shocked heartbeat, there was silence.

Then chaos, with a chuckling hiss, loosed itself upon the room in the form of thick clouds of creamy blue smoke. It spread quickly, like a fungus, invading throats, eyes and noses with impunity. Like moles under the summer sun, all were blind and stumbling. Profanity, of a wide and astounding range, vented the air as men fell one over the other, upended tables and chairs, upset bottles and barrels, knocked heads and knees.

Thrawny, as sightless and choking as any man present, felt himself to be in the midst of a hurricane. Furniture whirled past his head, the pungent smoke filled his senses with an oily reek, and over it all he heard a voice, distinctly lacking in Mediterranean nuance, declaim,

> '*...as a bear, encompassed round with dogs,*
> *Who having pinch'd a few and made them cry,*
> *The rest stand all aloof and bark at him.*'

The bastard, Thrawny thought to himself, *the sodding sadistic bastard* was enjoying himself! He tried to make his way towards the voice, but found that it seemed to move about in the smoke, as if it were the disembodied organ of a phantom. His ears, he knew, must be playing tricks on him, for the last line seemed to issue straight down from the rafters. Then suddenly he felt a charge and whirl of scented air at his shoulder.

"The devil," said a honeyed tongue, sweet in the midst of chaos, "is betaking himself back to hell."

And then the charge, the whirl, the devil were all gone and the smoke began to dissipate, rolling in no great hurry out the door that someone had left open in their departure. Thrawny looked about wildly. The Toad's stool was empty, the Toad himself conspicuously absent in the milling, coughing crowd.

"—the hell's that?" said a man who was emerging rodent like from behind an overturned table. Thrawny followed the man's puzzled gaze onto the top of the only upright piece of furniture in the place.

Left behind, side by side, were two water-stained shoes, with a heavy, oily mustache arranged, very neatly, amidst the laces.

TRUSSED TIGHT AS A CHRISTMAS GOOSE, but without the benefit of trimmings, the Toad chewed furiously on the gag in his mouth. In his nose hung the heavy smell of deep fried potatoes. On his back was an ungiving weight that seemed to have a finger on each of his nerve endings.

Suddenly the gag was unceremoniously ripped from his mouth.

"Who the hell are ye?" the Toad managed to gasp out with a great deal of blood-specked spittle.

"Your worst nightmare," said the devil on his back, whose grip was still ungiving as iron. "One you won't wake up from if you don't give me the information I want."

"I can't tell ye—owww—a thing," these last two words started low and ended in a sort of piercing yowl. "Stop! Stop, will ye! I heard a bone snap!"

"It hasn't broken just yet," said the demon, who gave the arm another sharp prod, eliciting a high-pitched swarm of profanity from his captive, "but it will soon if you don't give me what I'm asking for." The Toad heard an alarming creak issue from the twisted arm. He was gasping in agony, sweat running freely down his brow.

Thrawny, watching from the front of the van, noted that in contrast to his captive Jamie was entirely cool, only the white set of his face any indication that he found the situation stressful. Thrawny loved the man as dearly as a brother, but the man knew well enough how ruthless he could be when threatened.

"I can't—Christ that hurts—tell you—AAHHH!" the bone snapped clean through, the sound causing the bile to rise in Thrawny's throat.

Jamie got up off the man's back, crouching to the side, green eyes sharp as a scalpel blade on the Toad's face.

"Why the hell d'ye have to break my arm?" the Toad whined, tears running down his face along with the sweat now.

"I figured you'd understand me better if I spoke in your language."

"Ye're sure as hell no Greek."

"Brilliant deduction," Jamie replied dryly. "Now if you don't want me to break the other one, you'd best tell me what you know."

"Boy's good as dead," the Toad wiped his blood-speckled mouth against a dirty sack that lay under it, "if Kenny's got 'im."

The momentary relief the Toad had felt when the devil climbed off his back, was shattered by the feel of a pistol being slid neatly into his ear, the hammer click like a reverberation of thunder against the drum.

"And where would Kenny take him to kill him?"

The Toad tried to breathe, but panic was tying his lungs in knots. "There's any number of places, I don't know, I—" he gasped as the man dug a knee into his spine again.

"I don't know is not on my list of acceptable answers, you had best try again."

"There's an old burial mound, looks like a hump under a green carpet, down Ardglass way, on the Lough. Near that old wreck of a fort."

"Dun Siog?"

"Aye."

"Are you certain?"

"Yes." The one word was a faint hiss. Sweat was streaming into the Toad's eyes now and he wished he could just pass out and awaken in a different country under an assumed name. Anything less and Kenny was going to find him and make sure he'd a long drawn out death. If this bastard didn't kill him first. Which might, he thought, be a mercy, all things considered.

He got the first part of his wish a second later, as the butt of the pistol clipped him neatly behind the ear, rendering the world a deep and welcome black.

DUN SIOG, OR THE FAIRIES FORT, was a crumbled ruin that lay at the southernmost end of Strangford Lough. Originally an earthen stronghold built—local lore had it—by the people who'd come before the Druids, it now held the remains of an old Norman castle constructed by a warlord for the Knights Templar. To reach it one had to wind one's way along a cart trail which hadn't been used with any frequency since people had ridden about on horses.

Shrubs and wild vines had long ago covered most of the ruins, though the topmost tower of the blackened hulk still loomed up spectrally out of the surrounding wild.

Thrawny, eyeing the chill landscape, where the mist seemed to ooze out of the ground, shivered uncontrollably.

"I'll wait here," he said, not even bothering to control the chattering of his teeth. "Keep an eye out like, in case anyone should come along."

"If someone comes along," Jamie said, coolly tucking the pistol into the waistband at his back, "you'll be a sitting duck out here and it'll be too late for the both of us. Come on, man, buck up, the stories about this place aren't true." He grinned, a flash of impudent white. "At least not entirely."

The moon was a gibbous sickle, hanging low along the eastern horizon, casting an odd surreal mist through the skeleton of the castle. Thrawny could feel the damp of it in his bones.

"Do ye not remember the night we ran away an' stayed here when we was lads?"

"I remember," Jamie said shortly, putting a flask of something into his righthand pocket. "Just at present, though, I've not the inclination to reminisce."

"We swore we'd never come here again, Jamie," Thrawny said, trying to shrink his bulk into the crack between seat and door.

"I believe we were about twelve years old at the time. I'm much older now and so are you. I don't believe in evil fairies."

"Lower yer voice man," Thrawny whispered through gritted teeth.

"There's a man in there that desperately needs our help, Alexander. I'm not about to let him die because we hallucinated a few ghosts once upon a time. Now get out of the van, before I drag you out."

"How the hell do you expect to get in there undetected?" Thrawny asked when they were standing in the long grass that obscured the old pathway.

"There's a secondary route into the burial mound. I'm hoping the bastard doesn't know about it, it's the only thing we've got on our side right now."

To the right a chimney rose a good fifty feet into the air, slanted at an alarming angle into the tumble down stones of the exterior wall of the old castle.

From underfoot rose the scents of crushed plants and dank earth.

There were legends about this place, and none of them were pleasant. Some land was never meant to belong to people; some land had been claimed before people were even a twinkle in the creator's eye.

Thrawny cast one last look over his shoulder. Behind them the lough was glassily calm, its myriad drumlins rising like hunchbacked hobgoblins under the still silver light. Bladderwrack beckoned across the water's skin like boneless fingers, glowing an odd milky green. He shivered and hurried to catch up to Jamie's swiftly disappearing form.

Jamie's memory had served him well. There was another entrance, overgrown with rank weeds and partially obscured by fallen stone, but once these were cleared out of the way the ancient doorway stood high enough that Jamie barely had to duck to clear the huge beam that supported the enormous weight of earth above.

Thrawny stepped inside. The darkness was profound and suffocating. He heard the click of a torch and suddenly Jamie was there in front of him, face lit from below, cat eyes sparked with an unearthly glow. Bastard probably saw better in the dark anyway; most demons did, Thrawny thought, feeling distinctly annoyed at the turn his life had taken tonight.

The flickering torchlight did little to ease his fears. It gave him, in random glimpses, the sight of things he felt sure no man was meant to see. He was certain he could feel evil faces leering out of the dark at him. The great damp earthen walls seemed to be breathing in and out, emitting an eerie blue ooze. The smell was literally that of the grave. Thrawny could feel a clutch of panic in his chest, squeezing his lungs tight and hard, as though they were turning to stone.

Above he could sense the very weight of the earth, the great heaviness like a pregnant body ready to separate itself from its burden. He swallowed and fought to catch his breath, succeeding only in making himself lightheaded. There was no light, not even a pencil thin wedge of it. He'd suffocate in here, his lungs seizing, seemed to know the truth of it, even if his brain was not yet willing to acknowledge defeat.

Ahead of him, Jamie's golden head winked out of sight. He had the distinct impression he was following Hades directly into the Underworld. He took one last glance at the upper world and shivered. The mist was getting thicker, obscuring both water and land, as though it were dissolving and would cease to exist as soon as he looked away.

Given the choice of turning back—well—he took a deep breath and put his feet to the path Jamie had gone down. Better the devil you knew than the one you did not.

THE BURIAL MOUND was a huge passage tomb, more than five thousand years old. Jamie felt his way down, torch casting flitting shadows amongst the long roots and dripping earth. The tunnel would end, provided there were no blockages, in the central chamber, which is where he felt certain Casey must be. Along with the men who had taken him off the lorry.

There was no way to know how many of them there might be, but Jamie suspected and hoped that their number would be few. He couldn't count on Casey for help, as he wasn't likely to be in any shape to do battle.

"Just let him be alive," he mumbled grimly to himself. The sound echoed off the spongy walls and Thrawny uttered a nervous yelp behind him.

"Quiet," Jamie hissed. "I'm going to have to turn the torch off, so grab hold of my shirt and just follow."

The entry to the tomb yawned in front of them through a high, narrow door with a flat lintel stone crowning it. On the lintel stone a stubby candle flickered, under-lighting a hideous face. Jamie felt a thin shiver, like a spasm of quicksilver, pass down his spine. The stone face was ancient, that of a *sheela-na-gig*, this one with prominent ribs, horizontal scars across the flat cheekbones and the protruding genitals that made many associate these figures with fertility. She was the crone in the Celtic Trinity of maiden-mother-crone, and as such was an invitation to young heroes to enter back into her womb in death. The original womb, that of the Earth herself. Here the symbolism of the squat stone figure seemed all too hideously apt.

He stepped under the lintel and into the inner chamber of the tomb. A sense of yawning space engulfed him after the claustrophobia of the tunnel. Light soaked into the walls, reflecting back the dimmest of glows. Above, the ceiling soared several feet above their heads, spiralling up in steps of huge stone.

Candles, stuck into cavities in the walls, hissed uncertainly in the fetid air, casting faint pools of light that only served to intensify the darkness that lay between them. In one of these murky pools were three men; two with their backs to him and the other with his head being held firmly in what looked like an ancient cistern. Casey.

At this point, both caution and the element of surprise seemed like superfluous luxuries. Jamie simply cleared his throat.

The two men spun about, and Casey slid boneless to the floor, water trickling from his mouth.

The man to Jamie's right brought a pistol up, cocked. In the half-second between heartbeat and thought, Jamie knew he didn't have time to aim and at this range was looking his death square in the barrel. A solid *crack* rent the air, and the man dropped to the floor.

The other man launched himself at Jamie, in a flurry of curses and wet corduroy. Jamie, though, had read the intention in his eyes before the movement, and halted the ill-guided missile by the simple expedient of shooting him in the foot.

He dropped to the mucky ground howling, the ruckus causing a shower of dirt pellets to rain down from the roots above.

"Watch him," he said shortly to Thrawny, who still hovered in the doorway to the chamber.

Jamie knelt on one knee at Casey's side, assessing him for damage. Casey's eyes were closed. In the murk of candlelight, he was a trout blue, with the darker notation of a knot swelling on his forehead. Jamie felt for a pulse and heaved a heartfelt, "Thank Christ," when he found it. It was thready, but it was there.

He ran his hands along Casey's ribs; if anything was broken he didn't want to risk puncturing a lung. Satisfied that it was safe to proceed, he compressed the chest. A plume of water spouted up from Casey's mouth, but the man himself was still unconscious.

Jamie compressed the chest twice more and then bent to clear the airway and to breathe into Casey's mouth. Compression, breathing, compression, breathing. Jamie began to lose count, as a trickle of dirt rained on the back of his head.

Finally Casey sputtered violently, the force of it dragging him up from his prone position and causing him to vomit a stream of brackish water out.

He cracked an eye open and peered at Jamie.

"You," he said, and fell back to the ground again.

"No time for chat," Jamie said rather wildly, having felt a vague tremor beneath his feet that he found more than mildly worrisome. "Come on man, we need to get the hell out of here before this place collapses." Jamie pulled the gasping Casey to his feet and half dragged, half pushed him towards the tunnel opening.

"Run!" he shouted at Thrawny, who stood still over the thug with the bloody foot.

Thrawny snatched up the torch, nodding curtly at Jamie. "You an' him first, I'll bring up the rear. GO!"

Casey stumbled, dragging heavily on Jamie's shoulder, but at last found his footing well enough to keep up. Root branches whipped their faces as they ran, the steady shower of dirt that poured down on them swiftly becoming a storm. Behind them there was an ominous rumble, that of angry earth rushing and heaving.

"*It's goin'?*" Thrawny yelled.

Clots of dirt were falling now, big as a man's fists, striking their heads and shoulders. Thrawny had taken up a steady stream of cursing, and Jamie was finding it harder and harder to guess how much farther they had to go before the tunnel entryway.

"*Please dear God, let it be close,*" he said under his breath. The earth above their heads was roaring like a mighty beast, ready to gorge itself on their all too tender carcasses.

A waft of air swept past his face at the same time that the roaring abruptly ceased, and Jamie felt a moment of complete panic. The silence, he knew, was tonnes of earth letting go entirely.

It went with a great lung-collapsing *whoosh*, just as Jamie shoved Casey face first with all his might out into the night. A huge chunk of earth knocked Jamie to the ground, flattening the air out of his lungs with a suffocating weight.

He tried to scrabble forward, hands dug deep in the ground beneath him, but he could not get purchase, the weight on his back was far too great.

And then redemption came in the form of two big hands grabbing his shoulders and yanking him with tremendous force clear of the killing earth. He gasped, mouth filled with grainy soil and bits of grass and rock. Casey reached past him and dragged Thrawny out with a great heave.

Covered in muck and sucking in great lungfuls of the misty night air, all three men collapsed in the tall grass, chests heaving, the euphoria of having survived sweeping through them.

The mound, now a shattered heap, was distinctly quiet. As if it had lain thus in ruin for the last thousand years.

Beneath Jamie the world was thrumming and he thought he could feel the rotation of the planet itself as it spun endlessly in space. He drew a shaky breath and lifted his head, once he could manage, looking over to where Thrawny lay hummock-like.

"What did you throw at the man?"

"I grabbed the wee witch off the lintel, likely cracked the bastard's skull, though that's of small worry to him now," Thrawny replied.

"Thanks. That was quick thinking on your part."

"Well I figured after all was said an' done tonight, if anyone was goin' to have the pleasure of killin' ye, it was goin' to be me."

Jamie gave him a wry look. "Thanks anyway."

"Aye, ye're welcome."

Thrawny heaved himself to his feet, small balls of dirt showering off him as he stood. "I'm goin' to the van to find a blanket for the laddie," he nodded toward Casey. "I'll be back shortly."

"Come on," Jamie said, "let's get out of the open. There's cover over there." He nodded toward a small stand of trees, looming inkily through the mist.

It was a narrow hollow ringed in rowan trees, the ground thick with decayed leaves and the debris of many years. The trunks of the trees were furred with moss and thick with tangled ivy.

Casey managed the short walk on his own power, though Jamie noticed that it wasn't with his usual long strides.

"Are you injured?" he asked, casting an assessing eye over the man as he sat down on the heavy carpet of leaves, shivering.

"No, I don't think so. One of my ribs is maybe cracked, but that's it. They seemed much more intent on drownin' me than doin' me bodily harm."

"Any notion of why they plucked you off that lorry?" Jamie asked, as he set out building a fire. He'd matches in his pocket and had found enough pieces of dead wood to build the flames to a cheery blaze that Casey was only too grateful to huddle near.

Thrawny returned then with two heavy blankets in hand. They reeked copiously of fried potato, but Casey wasn't in a position to complain.

"Thank ye," he said, grasping the edges of the blanket as though it were a life preserver. "And I'm not talkin' about the blanket. The two of ye saved my life, another minute or two an' I'd have been dead. How the hell did ye know to find me?"

Jamie smiled. "I bent a few ears, twisted a few arms."

Thrawny grunted in affirmation, pulling a flask of whiskey from his pocket. "Here, swig this back laddie, ye're still lookin' like a fish belly, day after it's been gutted."

Casey quirked a brow at him but took the proffered flask. The whiskey was strong, the fumes making his eyes water, but the long trail of fire it left on the path to his stomach went some ways toward thawing his bones.

He cast his eyes around the ring of trees. "My gran always called these witch trees, because the berry has a wee pentagram where they join to the stems. She was a great one for the old ways, planted rowans on her parent's grave, said 'twould keep the haunts away." He shuddered under his cloak of blankets. "Hope it holds true in this realm as well." He looked in the direction of the collapsed mound, though it wasn't visible through the undergrowth of young holly.

"There was no way to save them," Jamie said bluntly, taking a sip off the flask himself. "I shouldn't think you'd have any grief over their death as they just about succeeded in killing you."

Casey shifted, looking suddenly uncomfortable. "They weren't the only ones there at first." His eyes shifted toward Thrawny, and he cleared his throat.

Thrawny, never slow on the uptake, heaved himself to his feet, "Finish the flask off lad, ye need the heat of it."

He stretched his shoulders, the fire kindling his beard and hair to flaming copper. In the night he looked like a Viking berserker.

"I'm goin' for a walk, need to piss somethin' fierce, an' then I'm goin' back to the van where there's a heater. I'll be there when the two of yez decide it's time to move along."

Jamie nodded, watching as the massive bulk lumbered off through the trees.

"I imagine that's meant to give us a chance to talk privately," Casey said, glancing in the direction Thrawny had taken, his eyes hooded.

"Did you know the third man?" Jamie asked.

"No. Maybe," Casey shook his head, "that's the odd thing, they had me blindfolded from the time they took me off the truck. Wasn't much of a battle for them, bein' that I was handcuffed an' all. The third one was waitin' in the mound for me. It had all been pre-planned like, or so it seemed. He'd a voice that was different than the other two. More posh, like yer own. Though maybe not quite so cultured as yerself."

"Jade instead of pearls?" Jamie quipped lightly, though Casey's statement had set off an alarm bell deep within his subconscious.

"Aye, so to speak, an' I thought perhaps I'd heard the voice before, but what with them kickin' me an' plungin' my head in the water every other minute, it was a bit hard to get a fix on things." Casey looked directly at Jamie across the fire. "But I'm certain of one thing, the man wanted me dead."

Jamie added more pieces of wood to the fire. The two of them watched it blaze up into the night, smoke blending with the mist like ghosts moving through fog.

"Someone in league with Joe Doherty?"

"That was my first thought, an' I know Joe sees a bullseye on my chest every time he chances to meet me—but no, I don't believe 'twas him, this time."

"This time?" Jamie echoed.

Casey nodded, drawing the blanket tighter. "Aye, there's been a couple of things that have happened out of the way since I've been home. I kept it to myself, because I didn't want to scare Pamela."

"She's nobody's fool, man, she's been worried sick since you came home."

"Aye, I know, the woman is *my* wife after all."

"I'm aware," Jamie said dryly.

"Well," Casey went on, "I had a near miss on the construction site one day, thought my line was secured when I was up on the beams. But the link was next to breakin', sawed through. Another night I was closin' up the center an' a car came by slow. Ye know that's always a worry in Belfast. They came round again, but I'd ducked into a doorway across an' up the street. Man got out of the car, had a rifle tucked under his arm. Took a look around for me, an' thank the Lord didn't see me."

"Christ man, why didn't you tell me sooner? It's not just yourself you have to worry about these days."

"I'm aware," Casey replied, with no little sarcasm. "I didn't come home plannin' on gettin' myself killed. An' frankly ye're not the first name on my list when I need assistance."

"But you're asking now?"

"Aye, I'm askin' now. Because I know ye'll watch out for her as well as I would myself. She's stubborn as a goat an' doesn't take kindly to bein' told where to go an' what to do. But she's still a wee bit naïve about Ulster. I know ye understand her nature." Casey swallowed as if he'd a bone in his throat. "An' if I don't make it home any time soon, will ye tell her I'm sorry?"

"I will."

PAMELA CAME UPON JAMIE pulling his head out of the rain barrel which sat outside the stable doors. His hair was streaked translucent and streaming, skin flinching from the icy water.

She handed him a towel wordlessly, earning her a weary quirk of his eyebrow before he took the towel and buried his head in it, vigorously scrubbing at his numbed scalp.

"Get any sleep?" he asked, noting that the house was still quiet in the faint morning light.

"A little more than you, I imagine," she said, voice sharp with strain.

He emerged blinking from the towel, in the midst of an extravagant yawn, to find her looking at him in chin-up resignation. "He's dead then?" she said and he saw that she'd no more slept than he had, but rather had used her hours to prepare for what uncertainties her life with Casey had always held.

"No, not dead," he said, bracing his hands on each side of the barrel in an effort to stay upright.

"Not dead," she echoed, voice a mere whisper in the vast silence of dawn. "There's a '*but*' at the end of those words, Jamie."

He admired her strength in the midst of terror. She always wanted her truth undiluted. Some would think such bravery foolhardy, but he knew well enough to respect it. He also knew that she wasn't going to be happy with what he had to tell her.

Behind her where the hill dropped away and gave onto the city, the sun rose through a haze of smoke and the dull glow of dying fires. An occasional pop signalled the fact that bullets were still being exchanged. Exhaustion had put a delineating edge around everything he saw, so that it appeared magnified.

The city seemed no more than a toy set up for imminent destruction. The roads annexing off the wedges of neighborhood, small tribal enclaves wrapped tight around themselves and their pain, breathing the stilted air of violence. Today people would emerge from their hidey holes, exhausted, injured, confused, and for a moment—perhaps a mere second—would pause to wonder what any of it meant. And then they would stoop to pick up the stone that would continue the war.

He sighed, one last moment of strength, and then even he was due a rest. "Casey's fine, a little banged, a little bruised, but I managed to find him before any serious damage was done."

He saw the swift intake of breath, the light that sprang to her face as she began to look about wildly.

"He's not here, Pamela."

"Then where is he? Somewhere safe? Can I go to him?"

"Safe as can be at present," Jamie said grimly.

"Jamie?" The fear returned swiftly to her face.

"There's only one place that's beyond the reach of the men who paid to have him taken off that truck. It's ironic really."

"What is?"

"Last I knew he was headed for a ship anchored in the Lough called the Maidstone."

"Jamie, what have you done?" she asked, voice sharp with fear.

Jamie, gone beyond the bounds of exhaustion and sense, laughed without humor.

"I've handed him over to the British Army."

Chapter Thirty-eight

The Maidstone

AS PRISON SHIPS WENT, the Maidstone, anchored in Belfast Lough, was totally unsuitable. Built in 1937, she had been used as an emergency billet for troops in 1969. For the latest round of troubles she'd been hastily converted into a prison ship to lodge close to 150 men.

Moored twenty feet from solid land, the ship was berthed at the only wharf in Belfast equipped for unloading pitch and tar. Pipes for tankers to unload ran through the ship's sides. Entry to the jetty was guarded by a sandbagged army emplacement. Short Brother's airfield overlooked the ship on the pier side, and on the starboard lay a 300 foot stretch of water leading to a huge coal yard.

The ship was cramped, stuffy, and overcrowded. The prison itself was at the stern and consisted of two bunkhouses, one up and one down, and two mess rooms. Above these were the quarters of the governor and his staff, and above them was the deck, used twice a day for exercise and surrounded by ten-foot high barbed wire. Forward were the army quarters, separated from the prisoners by a high mesh fence and a solid gate.

It was here that Casey had landed. The irony that he was locked up in the only Belfast prison that sat upon water was not lost on him, nor was it greatly appreciated.

An army jeep had been waiting at the head of the road leading away from Dun Siog. It seemed unlikely that the soldiers had been driving by coincidentally. It seemed more like insurance against his possible survival.

For Casey and most of the men who also found themselves at the mercy of God, England and the RUC, this was not the first time they'd been incarcerated, and so they settled quickly.

Routines were established swiftly, leaders rising to the head of small motley groups through a natural and instinctive pecking order. The ship had a committee that was comprised of four Provos and two Officials under the chairmanship of an old Derry Republican, Matty Loughlin, a man Casey knew from his boyhood as he'd been a compatriot of his father Brian.

The committee set up rotas of men to take care of the food serving and latrine duty. There was a great deal of grumbling over this, as many of the men saw no purpose in doing what they termed 'lackey' work. They felt their captors should do the work that came of illegally imprisoning 142 men.

While Casey understood their attitude, he knew the real reason for the rotas was to prevent the apathy and depression that inevitably befell imprisoned men. Particularly ones who had no clear idea when or if they might hope for release. Cooped up for twenty hours a day, or more if the weather was foul, with only two thousand square feet of deck and that liberally coated with gull excrement, it was imperative that the men have some sense of order if they weren't all to sink into complete anarchy.

Casey's own small crew consisted of some six men. Matty, who never slept in a bunk, but curled up on an old couch every night. Declan Roy, who'd a sarcastic tongue, a mane of black hair that he kept tied back, and who stayed up from dark to dawn playing rounds of chess, solitaire and bridge. Roland Dempsey, who was fanatically religious, had a wife and four sons on the outside, and possessed an enormous talent for getting directly on the one nerve Declan had left.

And then there was young Shane McCann. It was the first time he'd been incarcerated and therefore he was the hardest hit of the lot of them. He was frightened and jumpy, a bad combination what with the frequent 'raids' and 'reprisals' the troops subjected the internees to. Detainees were locked up for three hours while troops plundered their quarters, destroying many of their scant belongings as well as the small crafts many men did to pass the time—matchstick crosses, hand-painted handkerchiefs and the like. They also stole their cigarettes, not the wisest move on a ship where morale was lower than a snake's belly and the tension as high as a kite in a gale.

Arrangements for visitors were next to non-existent. Permits, without which no one could visit, were arriving after the date fixed for the visit. Frustration both within and without the ship was mounting.

Thus far, two weeks into his time aboard the ship, Casey had received two messages. The first a tersely worded and heavily coded message from Jamie letting him know that Pat was being held at Girdwood Barracks. The other was from Pamela, telling him that she was doing everything in her power to get a visitors pass; that she and the boy had returned home; and that all was as well as could be hoped for in his absence. The first message he had burned to ash and flushed down the latrine. The second he kept in his shirt pocket, unable to bear parting with the small bit of familiarity and home her few words provided him. Other than a briefly worded missive saying that he wasn't being maltreated, he'd sent no other message back. He knew full well that every word in and out of the ship was being scrutinized for any bit of information that could serve in the end to incriminate the lot of them. Pamela knew enough of Ulster to understand that he could not reveal anything of either the true conditions of the ship, nor the true condition of his heart. Both of which were less than golden.

His heart she knew, the ship he didn't want her to know in any way.

Ostensibly the governor, a hard-faced Ulsterman named Norman McDonough, was supposed to be in charge. But it was the volatile Sergeant commanding the British troops that was really in charge, and every manjack of them knew it.

Sergeant Boyce was a regular bastard with a penchant for screaming until his eyes bugged from his head, and a hatred of Irishmen that Casey had experienced once or twice in his lifetime, but never with the fervency that Sergeant Boyce evidently felt. He wasn't averse to inflicting pain on anyone who looked sideways at him, either. During the first week there'd been a scuffle between troops and a man named Alan Kelly, who had felt it was his right—as well as that of all the prisoners—to bombard the governor and the Ministry for Home Affairs daily with protests about their arrest, treatment, and conditions aboard ship. For his pains, Kelly had been tricked into believing his lawyer was waiting for him in an interview room. Who was really waiting was Sergeant Boyce.

Kelly emerged from the interview room an hour later, staggering, bleeding and closemouthed. He'd maintained his silence from then until now and hadn't demanded nor complained in any of the intervening days. Nor had any of his visitors received their passes, and his mail had mysteriously dried up. In the outside world Kelly was a solicitor who'd been charged with *'scandalizing a court, and preventing the course of justice',* for successfully defending a client. Word also came back through Kelly's bunkmate that Kelly's younger brother had been badly beaten and Kelly's home ransacked while his wife stood crying in the front garden. Every man on the ship understood the message. Nothing was safe, not your wife at home in her bed, not your brothers and sisters, nor your mam and da.

After the incident with Kelly, an uneasy rhythm set itself in motion on the Maidstone. The men retreated into their small enclaves, did their duties, and obeyed the command that came down from the committee of Republicans that were the only authority they recognized. The others they ignored, averted their eyes from, kept their heads down and their mouths shut within the hearing of the soldiers, RUC and governor.

However, an incident occurred during afternoon exercise three weeks into their incarceration that put Casey directly in the sights of the sadistic Sergeant Boyce.

It started simply enough, with Roland and Declan indulging in one of their endless spates of bickering about Roland's habit of praying wherever and whenever he was seized with the desire to commune with God. The crowded, gull shit laden deck was no exception.

Roland often claimed to see visions of the Holy Mother's face in windows, in the air and on one memorable occasion on the front of Declan's Dubliners t-shirt. Today she apparently was peering out of a rather dirty porthole at him, because he dropped mid-stride while Shane was passing a ball to him, directly onto Declan, who was attempting to have a quiet walk and smoke simultaneously.

"Jaysus Christ!" Declan exploded. "Get off my goddamn foot."

Casey turned toward the men, knowing the tension between them had been at break point for a good three days. For Roland his religion was his safe haven, for Declan it was his innate cynicism that kept his sanity intact. The two were mixing about as well as oil and water.

"Don't blaspheme," Roland said calmly, returning to fingering over the rosary beads that never left the sanctity of his scarecrow thin chest.

Casey winced, knowing that Roland's very calmness was going to be the thing that drove Declan over the line. It was.

Declan simply went to shove Roland off his foot, but as fate would have it caught the clasp of Roland's rosary on his finger. The chain, worn from years of usage, snapped, and the beads exploded out from Roland's neck in a spray of jet.

"What have ye done?" All things considered, Roland's tone was beautifully calm.

"I've broken yer wee necklace," Declan said, and Casey groaned inwardly, seeing the apologetic route wasn't about to be taken.

"'Tisn't a wee necklace, 'tis a rosary," Roland said stiffly, the red mounting his face in a tidal surge that put Casey on full alert.

"It's just a bunch of beads an' superstition," Declan said, his own temper still well and truly stoked.

"Jaysus, the fool should have apologized," Matty muttered.

Casey only had the time to get out an, "Aye but since when has Declan done as he should?" —before Roland came round off his knees with whip-crack speed, the glint of something silver in his hand. Before Casey could clearly understand what was happening, Roland had Declan's ponytail firmly in hand and was holding a knife to the base of it.

"Oh shit," Casey and Matty said in unison.

"Superstition is it?" Roland said, as Declan twisted ineffectually, batting at Roland with fists cuffed. "I'll scalp ye and then we'll see who's superstitious."

"Oh Christ," Matty muttered. Declan was as certain as Samson had been that his luck lay entirely within his refusal to cut his hair. He was convinced that was what had kept him alive and relatively unharmed through years of imprisonment and interrogations.

"Get yer fuckin' hands off me hair," Declan howled, scrabbling for purchase on the slick deck beneath his feet.

The young soldiers standing watch had tensed up, their guns now up and pointing toward the huddle of men. It was only the glut of men on the deck that made it impossible for the soldiers to discern what was actually happening.

Casey pushed his way through the other men toward the two furious combatants. He placed a large hand lightly on the back of Roland's scrawny neck, the implied threat unmistakable.

"Roland, stop it now, before someone gets hurt."

He risked a glance at the observation post, casting a reassuring smile at the tense soldiers, as if to say 'all's fine here, lads.' What he saw in the window though made his intestines clench. The Sergeant's rawboned face had appeared and was trained directly on the three of them.

"Fockin' give over the knife," Casey whispered tersely, "the Sergeant is watchin' the both of yez. Roland, I'll see that ye get a new rosary."

"That one was blessed by the pope," Roland said, the light of real murder still in his eyes.

"I can't make promises there, but I think I can get one blessed by the Bishop of Armagh," Casey said, thinking Jamie was going to be scratching his head over this particular request.

"That and an apology will do."

"Declan," Casey said in the tone of a man who still had hold of his reason, "apologize to the man before the lot of us get shot."

"Not to me," Roland said primly, "to the Blessed Mary, for interruptin' our conversation."

Casey sighed, trying to keep a rein on his own rather frayed nerves.

"I'll not do it," Declan said through gritted teeth.

Casey leaned down into his face, "Ye'll do it, or I'll cut yer fockin' hair off meself." He gave Declan a long dark look that communicated volumes.

Declan swallowed, chest heaving with an angry breath, but when his lips parted, a surprisingly humble, "Holy Mary Mother of God, I am extremely sorry to have offended you," came out.

Roland's long nostrils flared briefly, the red slowly fading to patches, leaving him looking like he'd a bad case of nettle rash. He let the haft of the knife go and Casey took it with shaking hands.

The entire deck had stilled, the milling, tense crowd suddenly frozen in place. And Casey knew without even looking up, that the cat had come amongst the pigeons.

"It's my understanding that even cockroaches have some base understanding of the rules by which the universe functions," the Sergeant said, each word punctuated by the snap of the riding crop he carried hitting his leg. "So I would think that even you Irish would understand that to be in possession of a weapon on this ship, which is *my* universe, is a very, very bad thing."

Casey felt the blood drop down below his knees as he realized he was still holding the weapon in question. He'd that horrible feeling he'd had once as a child when his father had taken him on a ferris wheel and the thing had paused at the top before starting the spinning rush downward. As though he'd lost his grip on the planet, and the bottom of his stomach along with it.

The Sergeant had fixed his ghostly pale eyes on Casey.

"I believe you have a weapon in your hands, Mr. Riordan?"

His stomach lurched a little further with the knowledge that the man knew his name. If he knew his name, he likely knew a great deal more, including his address, the names and locations of all his nearest and dearest, and what brand of briefs he wore.

"Hands up and out, Mr. Riordan."

Casey felt the knife slip from his fingers, taken by a silent hand. The bottom of his stomach seemed to reassert itself a little. He put his hands palm up for the Sergeant's inspection.

The cold blue eyes met his own, but Casey neither blinked nor looked away.

"What have you done with it, Riordan?"

"Done with what?"

"Clear back from him now!"

No one moved. The universe was stilled to this single point, here and now, and Casey knew his very existence could well depend on how the next few seconds played out.

"I said clear back NOW!"

The Sergeant's eyes were next to bugging out of his head and the riding crop had assumed a staccato beat that didn't bode well for anyone.

"Do as he says," Casey said, tone quiet but carrying with enough force to make the men move back so the deck could be inspected. The knife was likely sinking to the bottom of the lough at this point. At the very least it had been kicked down off the deck, for Casey knew there was a small gap in the fencing in the northernmost corner. He was certain the knife had made its way swiftly to that gap.

"You will not order these men. This ship is under my command and as such so are all those under it. You will mind that you are a prisoner."

"The ship may well be yours, but these are not your men," Casey said.

"Neither are they yours," the Sergeant replied, with a tiny smile that pinched the corners of his eyes.

A rustle began amongst the men on the deck, a quiet stepping back to clear the deck for searching, even as somehow it became clear that their ranks had closed around Casey. The deck was searched, but it did not yield up the knife. Every man was patted down, most none too gently, but the knife, as Casey had suspected, was well and truly gone.

After they were searched, the men, one by one, came back and took their places beside and behind Casey. The Sergeant watched this proceeding with a look of mounting fury on his countenance.

"Ah, I see. Is that how it is, Mr. Riordan?"

"Aye," Casey replied, "that's how it is."

The Sergeant nodded, the small smile still tucked firmly in place. There was something obscene about it. Casey fought the desire to shiver. He knew he had to hold his ground at all costs, though. Any sign of weakness would give the man what he sought.

"Until later then, Mr. Riordan."

Casey didn't respond, merely stood tall and firm as oak in the midst of the men who surrounded him. They had given him their support and he had to face this man down on their account. Or they would all pay.

The Sergeant walked away, bending down to whisper something in the ear of a young Scots soldier called Campbell.

Once he'd disappeared into the stairwell leading to the officer's quarters, a collective breath was released around Casey. It sounded like the sighing of a thousand leaves in an autumn wind. Slowly the men began to mill away, many stopping to touch Casey's shoulder in passing, or to give him a nod.

"Christ, man," Declan said, face still a starchy white, "that was a mite too close for my likin'."

Casey gave Declan a smile of reassurance, but the bottom of his stomach had fallen out again.

"Couldn't ye have buckled, man?" Matty said in a low voice, his own countenance distinctly worried. And so Casey knew he wasn't alone in his understanding—that today he'd made an enemy he could not afford to have.

Chapter Thirty-nine

The Music Room

WITHIN THE WALLS OF THE JAIL, time held no meaning. Day blurred into night, one minute could have been an hour, or an hour an entire week. Pat had no idea whether it was night or day as he'd been hooded continuously since the brutal helicopter ride. The hood was rudely shoved up above his nose, but no higher, when he was given his paltry meals. A sort of watery stew that he was expected to eat with his fingers. He was continually dizzy, as though his head were miles away from his body and there was a continual ringing in his ears. He knew that he and all the other men were on a deprivation diet, a tactic to keep them weak and off balance along with the interrupted sleep and regular visits to the 'music room'.

It was what he called the room they put him in for hours on end, bombarding his senses with white noise of a variety that was designed to make a man want to blow his ears off. Which was likely the general idea. It was also ungodly hot in the room.

He'd been issued a boiler suit right after his helicopter ride. It was far too large and this too was purposeful. As was the hood, which hadn't been removed since he'd first been beaten. The air he managed to pull in was stale and fetid and seemed lacking in the oxygen he so desperately longed to take in in great gulping lungfuls.

He understood the theory behind sensory deprivation. Take away the enormous stream of information the brain was used to processing and the brain would start to malfunction. Knowing it in theory, however, didn't help a man greatly in practice. Particularly after being made to stand against a wall, legs spread, forehead not quite touching, hands splayed and arced against the damp concrete.

The last time they'd stood him there for what might have been a few hours or a few days, he no longer knew. There was no light, only darkness.

He eventually collapsed to the floor, no longer able to stand the pain in his legs. A doctor had been brought in to ascertain if he was fit enough to withstand more interrogation. The doctor obviously felt he was because they'd propped him back up against the wall and continued with their questions, which were screamed from close range into his tortured ears.

He didn't respond to their questions—couldn't have even if he'd wanted to. He didn't know anything about the things they asked him. Was the IRA planning a large scale campaign? Where were the 2nd Belfast Battalion's weapons cached? Where were the safe houses along the border? He had no clue, but his captors either didn't believe him, or they just enjoyed inflicting a lot of pain.

He couldn't even remember what proper sleep felt like. Every time he managed to lose consciousness here, he was slapped awake, had bright lights beamed in his eyes or someone shout in his ear. All of it designed to keep him off balance, to make adrenaline stream through his body, keeping him in a constant state of panic.

Pat lay now where he'd collapsed some time ago. He didn't know how long, nor did he care. They'd threatened him with any number of things if he didn't get back up, but he simply couldn't, in fact if they'd said they were going to kill him, he'd have seen it as a means of escape. Finally after several threats and a few kicks to his ribs they'd abandoned him in the wee shed, where he lay grateful for the cessation of noise and freshly inflicted pain.

He wasn't aware of having fallen asleep until he heard a voice.

"Here man, have a drink." The voice seemed to come from a very great distance, muffled and fuzzy. Pat turned away from it, wanting only to sink back into unconsciousness. It was the one safe place in this unending nightmare. But the voice persisted. "Come on, we've only a few minutes, you need the water."

He'd the vague sensation of the cord being loosened around his neck and then the hood was pushed up to just below his nose and the cool rim of a canteen was pressed to his split lower lip. He found, to his consternation, that despite his ravening thirst, he couldn't open his mouth. His jaw, tensed for days, was locked tight.

The man seemed to sense his difficulty, for a hand, smooth and warm, touched the knotted muscle, then pushed into it with increasing pressure until it gave.

The water tasted like rain directly from heaven, sweet and chill, it trickled down the back of his tongue causing his throat to spasm in shock. Much of it spilled back out onto his coveralls, but eventually some made it past the bruised constriction of his throat.

"Th—thank you," he managed to stutter out, vocal chords protesting even the one small word.

"You're welcome," the voice was soft, gentle, and undeniably British. The double-layered hood was as effective as complete blindness, and Pat had learned in a few short days to rely on his other four senses. His hearing had heightened considerably, and he was able to sort noises out, separating them, categorizing—dangerous or not dangerous, immediate threat or postponed agony. He knew one soldier from another. The one with the clipped upper class accent had a mean kick on him, the harsh Geordie accent belonged to the one who specialized in squeezing testicles, the Cockney voice belonged to the one with a penchant for putting out cigarettes on any bare bit of skin that was handy. But this one wasn't familiar, there were no telltale regional epiglottal stops and starts or lilts to his words, just a smoothness as though it had been carefully trained to be free of such clues.

"Could ye take th-the h-hood off?" he asked, tongue stumbling still over small syllables.

A long stretch of silence greeted his question and then the voice, still soft and calm, said, "I'm not supposed to...if someone were to come in...I...well just for a minute, all right, and then you can't resist when I have to put it back on."

"I w-won't," Pat promised, his whole body trembling in anticipation of this small bit of freedom.

The man loosened the knot further, the hood slipping with no more than a passing sigh against Pat's face and then all was light—blinding, consuming, agonizing light. His eyes throbbed and burned with it, felt as if they might burst from his head with it but he forced himself to keep them open, to absorb the dazzling brilliance for as long as he might.

"Are you all right?" the man asked, no more than an indistinct blur in front of him, outlined in a hazy blue aura. Pat blinked several times and then squinted his eyes down to narrow slits in order to achieve some sort of focus. It worked.

The man was not as young as Pat had thought. Though with his slight build, soft brown eyes and fine blond hair, he retained a boyish aura. Still he was at least in his twenties, possibly early thirties.

"Hello," the man said, smiling. "I've brought you some tea, strong with lots of sugar. We need to get it down you quickly before someone comes along."

"Why?" Pat asked stupidly, feeling like a stunned owl knocked from its perch and left to the mercies of the sun.

"Because you're not allowed sugar, it's all part of the program. The brain needs three things to function properly—oxygen, sensory stimulation, and sugar. So drink up."

Pat gulped the hot, sweet tea that the man held to his mouth, scalding his tongue in the process and not giving a damn. He could feel it go all the way down through his esophagus and into his stomach, burning a path through the chill that seemed to have settled permanently in his center.

"Good man." The man didn't take the tea away until Pat had drained every last drop. Then from a satchel on the floor he produced a sandwich, cookies and an orange.

He unwrapped the sandwich and Pat, sense of smell painfully acute, caught the scent of ham, his stomach contracting painfully at the idea of food.

The man held the sandwich to his mouth but as much as he longed to take a bite, to devour the thing whole without even bothering to chew, he turned his head away.

"Why are you doing this?" he asked, watching the man out of the corner of his eye.

The man colored slightly, he'd very fine skin that flushed easily.

"You don't have to worry you know," he smiled faintly, "last time I checked neither pork nor tea was on the list of brainwashing tools approved by the British government."

Pat, too hungry to care, too tired to second guess what seemed a random act of kindness took a bite and then another and another.

"Go slowly," the young man advised, "your stomach, much as it needs it, won't be inclined to treat the food gently."

"I don't suppose ye'd consider takin' the handcuffs off so I could feed myself?"

"No, I don't suppose I would," the man replied, "I saw what you did to Johns and Diddy the last time you were out of handcuffs. Being that I'm somewhat smaller than them I imagine you'd make short work of me."

Pat smiled ruefully, face stinging as several half healed cuts re-opened, and looked the man directly in the eyes. "How did ye know what I was thinkin'?"

"I didn't," he replied calmly, "but nor am I a complete fool either." He neatly peeled the orange, segmented it, and held a piece out to Pat. It was an oddly intimate act, to be fed by a stranger's hand.

"David," said the man, peeling off another segment of orange.

"Mmgghpm?" Pat enquired around a mouthful of sweet, tart fruit, juice leaking into the split lip and stinging like fire.

"My name is David Kendall," he reiterated, retrieving a napkin from his satchel and dabbing Pat's lip with it.

Pat eyed him warily. "Is this some sort of new torture the Army's instituted, death by table manners?"

"No, I was just raised well."

"Oh," Pat said, feeling suddenly awkward. The hate, the violence—these things he could handle summarily, retreating into a corner in his mind and holding that small part safe. Simple kindness, though, disarmed him and left him feeling terribly vulnerable.

"It's all right, I wouldn't trust me either if I'd been in your shoes for the last two weeks, but I really mean no harm."

"Won't ye get into trouble if they find ye feedin' me?"

"Yes I would, a great deal I imagine, but I'm willing to take that chance."

"Why?"

David sighed and looked Pat directly in the face. His eyes were hazel, brown around the center, then ringed with green and flecks of gold. Pat found himself oddly mesmerized by the colors.

"I did it because I'm absolutely appalled at the tactics being used over here and cannot sleep as a result. I know feeding one man doesn't balance the scales out but I thought perhaps it would help me to rest at night. So you see," he broke off a piece of one cookie and held it out to Pat, "it's really a rather selfish act."

Pat took the bite between his lips and felt the brush of the man's finger, warm and dry, against his bottom lip. He hesitated, oddly frightened by the first gentle touch he'd known from another human in days. David's hand smelled of rifle oil, ham and something far softer, not sweet but warm and comforting. His own smell.

"Why me?" Pat asked quietly. David drew his hand away slowly, dropping his eyes down to Pat's bare feet. There was an odd tension in the air and Pat wished he hadn't asked the question, for somehow it had brought down his own barriers a bit, put a chink in the brick wall that he needed to keep impenetrable in order to survive what had happened and what was likely still to come.

"Because you have a good face and—," he glanced up, giving Pat a glimpse of flushed cheeks, "you remind me of someone."

"I see," Pat said, thinking he'd seen altogether more than he was comfortable with. "I'm not...you...it's just that—" he closed his mouth in frustration knowing there was no polite way to string together the words that he'd been about to say.

David looked at him candidly, eyebrows raised and an amused smile playing about his mouth. "It's all right; I don't want anything in return."

Far down the corridor came the faint sound of clomping boots headed in their direction.

"We'd best get the hood back on," David said, businesslike once again.

"What were you supposed to be doing in here with me?"

David laughed. "If anyone asks I grilled you brutally about the mythical arms dump at Toome, to which you, being stubbornly Irish, refused to give an answer. At which point I beat you mercilessly about the head and face with my fists. You're so bruised up that it'll be difficult for them to prove otherwise."

Pat nodded, and then took his last glimpse of light in the form of David Kendall's eyes.

"Thank you," he said, then surrendered to darkness.

Chapter Forty

Nothing Sacred

PAMELA STOOD IN THE STREET OUTSIDE Pat and Sylvie's wee house, horror-struck. She had awakened that morning to the sound of someone pounding on the door, Finbar barking like a mad thing, and Lawrence sleeping straight through it all.

She'd opened the door with adrenaline racing through her, disorienting the normal waking process and jumbling her usual precautionary nature, now that she and the boy were living alone in the house.

Jamie stood outside, face grim.

"You shouldn't open the door without being certain you know who is on the other side first," he said in an admonitory tone.

"It's five AM, what on earth are you doing here?" she asked, ignoring his statement.

"Can I come in?" he asked, a trifle impatiently, considering he'd just woken her from the soundest sleep she'd had in weeks.

She stepped aside and he came in, bringing with him the smell of morning rain, which lay in crystals upon his coat and hair.

Since the morning Jamie had told her just what had happened with Casey, their relationship had danced on the most fragile of eggshells. In fact if she looked closely enough, she could still see the trace of blue beneath his left eye, where she'd slapped him hard enough that she'd shocked them both into a stunned silence. But then Jamie had regained his equilibrium and said, "You've a helluva right hook on you."

Since then they'd been wary as cornered cats around each other, though Jamie had done his best to explain the events of the night that had led to Casey being incarcerated on the Maidstone, a prison ship of which she'd heard little good.

"They were waiting at the top of road leading out from the mounds. Four soliders in a jeep Someone had gone to a bit of trouble to make certain that Casey wasn't going to get away, if they didn't manage to kill him. We would have made a run for it, but they were fairly persuasive with their guns held to our heads. Otherwise, I would have found him a safehouse in which to ride out the time."

Instinctively she knew that there was a great deal more going on in the interstices of events than either Jamie or her husband thought she needed to know.

She'd left his home that day and hadn't seen him for a week until one morning he'd shown up, tools in hand and set to finishing the roof on her and Casey's home.

When she'd gone outside in her nightgown to protest, he'd merely said, "It needs doing. Would you prefer to have the rain falling on your head and belongings?"

Grudgingly she'd allowed him to finish it. When he came down the ladder several hours later, she invited him in for dinner. A dinner that he ate with a good appetite, considering Lawrence glared daggers across the table at him and made comments about people showing up where they were neither welcome, nor invited.

Jamie merely arched a golden brow at him and took another helping of potatoes. He really could be the most implacable bastard at times, she thought, banging the teapot down on the table and slopping hot liquid onto Jamie's sleeve.

He had looked at her then, green eyes candid, and said, "I would never cause you deliberate hurt, nor, I believe, would Casey."

While she doubted that their definitions on what constituted deliberate hurt matched up, she knew his words were not uttered lightly, and so they had mended their fence as best they might. The air still hummed with tension, but she had advanced to a cool civility, despite her inability to get a visitor's pass to see her husband. Knowing where Casey was and that he was relatively unharmed had gone some way to softening her attitude, a crumpled and terse note from Casey, somehow smuggled off the ship under the guard's noses, had gone another stretch towards relieving Jamie of blame.

"What's wrong?" she asked, as Jamie shook the droplets from his hair. There was always a heart-stopping moment for her when she awaited news.

"It's not Casey," he said, relieving her of her initial and foremost fear. "I heard on the radio that soldiers ransacked the Ardoyne last night. I think it's likely Pat and Sylvie's place has been hit. I stopped to bring you with me, I think Sylvie may well need your sympathy right now."

She turned toward the stairs, heading up to get dressed and then halted and turned back. Jamie looked at her enquiringly.

"Why didn't you go directly to her?" she asked. "This is a very roundabout route to their house."

Jamie flushed, looking slightly guilty. "I was on my way past. I had business in Armagh yesterday and it went later than expected, so I stayed over and set out early this morning. I heard the news on the car radio."

"Really?" she said politely, but knew the doubt was clear in her voice.

She dressed, roused Lawrence and sent him down the lane to Mr. Guderson's, and got in Jamie's car. So that they now stood, speechless with shock, on the narrow pathway that led to Pat and Sylvie's front door. Or rather, had.

Wisps of tear gas still floated on the air, and both she and Jamie were breathing through their coats which they had put up over their faces before even opening the car doors. A pall hung over the entire street, which looked like a war zone. Shell casings littered the narrow sidewalks, traces of the soldiers who had rampaged through the lanes and small homes. Broken glass traced glittering paths through the rubble—remnants of shattered windows and petrol bombs that would have been one of the weapons employed in retaliation. Both armies, the ostensibly legal one and the outlawed one, had been here and left behind their particular calling cards.

Jamie blinked through eyes that were tearing up, and walked up the path. There was no need to knock, for there was no longer a door to knock upon. He put a restraining hand on Pamela's arm as she came up behind him.

"Let me go in first." He stepped through the doorway, beyond which lay a silence that didn't bode well.

A minute later his golden head appeared in the gloom of the entryway. He beckoned to her, his face grim.

She followed him to where Sylvie was sitting at the little kitchen table, head in hands, while around her lay the wreckage of the soldiers' foray into her home.

The devastation was complete; there wasn't an inch that hadn't been torn up, defiled, broken, or smashed. It must have taken some special effort to smash the porcelain of the kitchen sink, but it had been done so thoroughly that there were only broken off chunks remaining—hanging precariously off the pipe which had been pulled away from its mooring, rendering it also, quite useless. Water was an inch deep on the floor, broken dishes, bent utensils, and shredded linens littered throughout it.

"Dear God," Jamie breathed out and Sylvie's head jerked up from the table, her expression a distillation of the ruin that surrounded her. Her face crumpled further when she saw the two of them standing in what had once been her kitchen.

Pamela went to her and put her arms around her. She held her tightly, rocking her, knowing words were pointless. When Sylvie had quieted, and a measure of calm was restored to her, Pamela began to thread her way through the damage, picking up the odd bit of crockery and linen that she thought might be salvageable.

Sylvie gave a wan smile. "Well, I've the comfort of knowing there's nothing else for them to destroy. They've got my man and they've ruined the little we had here," she sighed, "what else can they take?"

"Don't even ask that question," Pamela said grimly, putting the head back on a figurine of the Virgin Mary. "I've a feeling they're only getting warmed up."

"We still hadn't finished cleaning up from the last time," Sylvie said wearily. "Guess it's just as well. They'll likely be back in a couple more months anyway."

"You won't be here if they do. You're coming out to live with Lawrence and I," Pamela said firmly, ignoring Jamie's look of surprise over Sylvie's head. "We'll pack up whatever isn't entirely ruined and bring it with us."

She handed Sylvie a tissue from her pocket, feeling a brisk determination sweep through her. It was only the thin edge of the fury that was boiling behind it, but she wasn't about to indulge her anger in front of Sylvie.

"Miracle these survived," she said, pointing at a small collection of china figurines on a bookshelf.

"They're glued down," Sylvie said. "We're learning our lessons in odd ways. Not that it matters now. They might as well have torn the walls down while they were at it."

"No," Pamela said firmly, "no, they don't get this too."

"Don't get what?" Sylvie asked, lifting her head up from her hand.

"This," Pamela indicated the wreckage around her with a sweeping gesture of her arm. "They don't get to have your home."

"There's no home left," Sylvie said bleakly, "and if Pat doesn't come back—" her sentence was cut off in mid-stream by Pamela's hand grabbing her chin none too gently.

"Don't you dare say it Sylvie, don't you dare. Our men are coming home if we have to go break them out of whatever hellhole the British have dragged them off to."

She released Sylvie's chin and began to pick up shattered bits of china and glass, piling them onto a half-broken picture frame whose missing photo Sylvie had found razored to bits and thrown in the toilet.

"We'll glue together what we can and put the rest in the dustbin. Did the bastards leave any of the cleaning stuff?"

Sylvie didn't answer, just watched dazedly as Pamela stuck her head into cupboards and under the sink, emerging triumphantly some moments later with a cracked bucket and mop, a container of bleach and some matches.

"What are the matches for?" Sylvie asked, a glimmer of worry at the determination in Pamela's face.

"What we can scrub clean we do, what we can't remove their filth from— we burn."

"Burn?" That had gotten her attention. "We can't just burn things in the back garden there's laws..." she trailed off at the look Pamela gave her.

"Laws, Sylvie? Do you really think there are any laws after what happened today? We are the only law, Sylvie, we will decide what's to be done and what's not. It's that simple."

Pamela became a one-woman hurricane after that. Sylvie helped half-heartedly, but the tears that she now could not hold back, made it hard to see what she was doing and Jamie finally pushed her firmly toward the couch and made her sit.

"Let her do it, she always cleans when she's upset," he said.

"She looks soft, but she's tough as nails," Sylvie said half resentfully, half admiringly.

It took several hours but between them Pamela, Jamie, and Sylvie were able to get the small home back into a semblance of order. It wasn't pretty, but it was liveable. Jamie had called in a favor and a plumber was coming to replace the sinks later that day. A locksmith was already replacing the smashed locks.

There were the things that could be fixed—sinks, floors, walls and cupboards. Things that could be replaced—china, utensils, picture frames, a mattress that a soldier had urinated on, and clothing that had been torn out of drawers and off hangers. But what, Pamela thought, placing the few plates and cups that had survived in a cupboard, of the things that could not be replaced nor fixed—the fear, the sense of violation, and the knowledge that as an Irish person on an Irish street in an ostensibly Irish city, you were not safe nor did you have rights, even within the walls of your own home.

"Ready to go?" Jamie asked.

"If you don't mind," Sylvie squared her shoulders and took a deep breath, "I think I'm going to stay here. When Pat comes back I want his home to be waiting for him. And if I leave now I'll feel as if they've won, and I won't have that."

"Good girl," Jamie said, "just don't be foolhardy, if they come back get out right away. Come to my house."

"I will, I promise," she said, fighting to keep the tremble out of her voice. She stood in the doorway, small and fair, appearing even tinier by virtue of an old sweater of Pat's that she wore wrapped about her. As if she could keep some ghost of his strength beside her by wearing his clothes. Pamela understood the act, the attempt to keep the fear at bay, and to move forward for yourself as well as the absent man. She, after all, slept in an old jersey of Casey's every night.

Sylvie waved, backbone straight and a defiant smile on her face. Maybe there was, Pamela thought, a way through the fear and violation after all. The strength of the human spirit never ceased to surprise her. It was the one thing no enemy had ever been able to flog out of the Irish.

The total arms haul secured by the army came to some 100 weapons, a similar number of homemade bombs, about 250lbs of explosive waiting to be made into bombs, 21,000 rounds of ammunition, and eight two-way radios. Thus the search had, in the army's purview, been justified, regardless of the means to that end.

Arms, though, had not been the only intent of the search. It was a rough-handed sack and pillage operation meant to scare the natives into behaving themselves. It didn't quite have the intended effect, for the horror and anger it would leave in the Catholic community would exact a far greater price upon the occupying force. The stain of it would bleed forward into the years ahead, creating bitterness where once had existed a guarded tolerance.

Though the British would not officially admit it, they were now openly and brazenly at war in their own province.

Unofficial wars by definition are messy things and none more so than the war that had existed in Ulster for eight hundred years. It was updated occasionally with new players on the stage, many of the old cast having died or simply faded into the oblivion that endless fighting creates. New props were introduced from time to time in the form of anti-tank rockets, surface-to-air missiles and bigger, tougher tanks that rumbled through the narrow streets like behemoths in a nightmare landscape.

Chaos reigned all that autumn. The travesty of internment meant all bets were off, it was now clear that the British were not going to play fair. All the talk of peace and political solutions was just what it had always been, talk. The IRA, returning to its militant roots with the phoenix-like rise of the Provos, was taking no prisoners and asking no quarter. Neither was there any granted for the civilian in the streets, merely trying to survive such a society. A society where police were murdered in their own homes or on the job with frightening regularity. A society where banks were robbed at gunpoint, arson was commonplace and riots were an after school activity every weekday.

It was a society that was freefalling into anarchy, where the only coin of worth was that of brute force. The government sat upon its emerald hill, isolated from the city, paralyzed within the knots of their own tribal biases.

Soldiers patrolled Catholic neighborhoods amidst the hollow clang of bin lids, ball bearings shot with deadly skill from slingshots and a miasma of hatred so thick that it could be smelled above the reek of cordite and tear gas.

No one could pinpoint where it had begun, or what the latest battle was about, nor how in the name of God, it might end. What no one really seemed to understand was that it was not a war anyone could win.

Chapter Forty-one

Traveller's Prayer

JAMIE PARKED THE CAR AT THE BOTTOM of his estate, and they walked up through the woods that spread out behind the house. He'd convinced her to stay to dinner. In an effort to elude the press he had chosen this way as the path of greatest avoidance.

The walk was a silent one. It was very still when they entered the woods that skirted the Kirkpatrick estate. Late afternoon sun slanted through the leaves creating a soft haze in the air, which was enhanced by the bone-deep exhaustion felt by the both of them. Pamela followed behind Jamie, as he cut a path through the heavy undergrowth. Under her feet she could feel the pungent release of the half-decayed berries twhich hat had fallen from their stems.

Jamie stopped so suddenly that she knocked into the back of him. She half stumbled, but Jamie reached back and caught her by the elbow, steadying her before she could fall.

"What is it?"

He shook his head and moved toward the small creek that cut across the northwest corner of his land. She looked in the direction his eyes were fixed and put a hand to her throat.

The woman lay on her back, completely submerged, staring sightless into the vault of heaven. The odd bronze light of the day, muted here by the leaves into amber, cast a mask across her features. The current hadn't been strong enough to pull her along, but had only stranded her here; the vee of one arm crooked about a rock that rose above the water's surface.

There was no need to ask if she was dead, the expression of surprise on her features spoke eloquently enough.

Pamela's vision was slightly hazed with exhaustion and so she saw as if through a vapor the waterweeds that waved gently between the woman's fingers, the glint of a worn wedding band, and the faded pink flowers that were scattered across the print of her dress. Her photographer's mind took note of other details; the woman was barefoot, a bruise the color of gentians flowering up her left shin, her face tinged blue under the rippling gold of the shadows. Her hands were rough, small transparent bubbles of air had affixed themselves to the ridges of skin, the way they would a worn piece of wood. The woman's hair, a faded copper, waved in the tug of the current.

Blown by the wind, small bits of dandelion fluff skimmed across the surface of the water, creating the illusion of movement across the still face. Pamela shivered, clasped by a clammy dread.

She realized suddenly that Jamie stood beside her, gazing down upon the face of the dead woman.

"There's a bullet wound just under her right ear," he said. She bent down and looked closely, and certain enough there was a small neat hole, long since stopped bleeding, behind the woman's ear. Jamie's vision, even through the exhaustion, was preternaturally sharp.

"Why?" she asked, the question seeming to encompass the weeks that lay behind them and the uncertain future they were moving towards. Jamie, as always, understood the myriad meanings in the one word.

"A thousand reasons and not a one that makes any sense."

The wind moved through the trees, causing the dry leaves to rustle against one another. It was a stark reminder that autumn was approaching swiftly, with its cold nights and chill dawns. The presence of death seemed to linger everywhere, biting into the marrow of her bones, reminding her of the fragility of life. It struck her suddenly that one could die even when needed by a husband, by children, by the very weft of the world around them. Much as Casey was needed—by herself, by his brother, by Lawrence. Fear clenched her suddenly, sharp claws in her chest, like a frantic animal. It took her this way sometimes without warning; the terror that Casey would be plucked from the weave of his own life, that days might pass before she knew of it.

She turned, realizing Jamie was speaking and that she'd missed most of what he'd said.

> *The Maiden be with you in every pass,*
> *The Mother be with you on every hill*
> *The Crone be with you on every stream,*
> *Headland and ridge and lawn.*
> *Each sea and land, each moor and meadow*
> *Each lying down, each rising up,*
> *In the trough of the waves, on the crest of the billows*
> *Each step of the journey thou goest.*

"It's an old Celtic prayer for travellers," Jamie said quietly. "Death being a journey into the greatest mystery of all, I thought it appropriate." His words had served as some sort of incantation, it seemed, for the wind died back, though the fresh chill of the air remained. The icy claws of fear had retracted from her heart, but they'd left a tenderness behind that would remain.

Jamie took her by the elbow and wordless, led her away under the trees, over moss and stone, the prayer lingering in the air behind them.

Chapter Forty-two

In the Watches of the Night

THE BEECHMOUNT YOUTH CENTER had become a strangely calm center to Pamela's universe. In Casey's absence she had done what she could to keep it open, knowing it was what he would want. He had succeeded in making small inroads into the youth of both communities, though for the life of her she didn't know how he had managed such a balancing act. The footing was precarious at best and the job itself required the juggling of politics both public and private and an innate knowledge of not just the city, but the neighborhoods and even the various streets. Casey had managed this balancing and juggling act with a calm precision which awed her now that she stood in his overlarge shoes, feeling wholly inadequate.

Lawrence, as it turned out, was her most valuable asset. He understood, almost as well as Casey, the lay of the land. "Ye can't let any of those bastards from the Boyne Boys Brigade in here. All they are is a breeding ground for the Loyalists. They'll make bad trouble for ye."

"And how am I to know who they are?" she asked, pausing from her task of re-filling the small larder.

"They're the ones with the tattoo of a fist crumplin' up an Irish flag. They have them on their forearms, can't miss it."

Between the center and the odd photography job, she was spending the vast majority of her time in the city, a place she was both horrified and fascinated by. Despite unceasing violence and disruption, people still married and had babies, attended weddings and christenings, and it was here she picked up her photography work. Through the offices of Father Jim, a fellow American who had come to Belfast a few years back on sabbatical and never left, she was alerted to all the social functions which might require her services within his parish. She somewhat cynically thought that it was his way of getting her through the church doors, and then plying her with work once she was there, in an effort to reignite the dim glow of her Catholicism.

Some nights she didn't make it home at all, and she and Lawrence would bed down for the night in the small apartment above stairs at the center. Mr.

Guderson had taken to checking on her place each day, and if he noted they were absent would feed and tend to the animals for them.

It was on one such night, exhausted by feeding no less than fourteen boys—all of whom regarded her with a guarded suspicion merely for not being Himself, but also an inadequate, not to mention female, fill-in—that she had dragged herself up the stairs just past midnight and collapsed on the lumpy bed, too tired to remove more than her shoes.

When she was small, she'd often woken in the middle of the night, gripped tight in fear with the shadowy vision of a dark creature standing horribly still at the foot of her bed. It always turned out to be one of those odd moments between sleep and wakefulness, where the subconscious still held sway and presented up its demons for viewing.

At first she thought the specter at the end of her bed was just that, a figment of a sleep-addled brain. Then it moved, which wasn't something that had ever happened before. She screamed and shot straight up in the bed, heart pounding fit to come out of her chest.

The figure started but then moved up toward the head of the bed.

"Get back," she said, "I've a gun and I'll use it." She backed up into the headboard as tightly as she could, drawing the bed linens with her. The dark figure continued to advance though, and she wished fervently that she really did have the gun in her hands, and hadn't left it unloaded under the mattress.

"I'm sorry, but—" the figure began, in what was, all things considered, a very mild and polite tone, when a second man shot into the room attacking the original intruder with what appeared to be a large stick, and a bloodcurdling yell that would have terrified an entire legion of Roman soldiers, and didn't do much for the state of her own backbone.

Six to one, half dozen to the other, but it seemed the larger of the two wrestling, grappling figures was more likely to be on her side.

She grabbed the lamp, which had a solid marble base, and flung it at the smaller man. Aim having never been her forte however, the lamp connected solidly with the back of the larger man.

Her putative rescuer yelped, then exclaimed, "Jaysus woman, don't hit *me!*"

She paused, the voice was familiar but she didn't have time to place it before the narrow cot was thrown on its side and the blankets flew over her head. All sound was muffled, though the voluble curses and grunts were still audible from the two men careening about the room. She tore the blankets away from her face, eyes straining to see in the dark.

The smaller figure shot out onto the narrow landing and started pell-mell down the stairs. The larger gave chase, the sound of two men pounding down the stairs loud enough to shake the house to its seams.

She scrabbled under the mattress for the pistol, then in the bedside table for the bullets. She loaded it with shaking hands and made her way down the stairs on legs that felt like unset jelly.

She turned the light on in the kitchen, finger tight on the trigger. The building was quiet now, preternaturally so. The back door stood open, and in the distance she could hear someone yelling and then the report of a gun. Thank God Lawrence had gone to Derry with Sylvie and was staying the night there with her and her family. He'd likely have shot both intruders just for good measure.

She put her back to the sink and surveyed the kitchen. Beyond was the common room which lay in absolute darkness. There was no feeling of menace, though, she was certain she was alone now.

Footsteps fell on the walkway outside the door, a milk bottle chinking against the bricks.

"Who's there?" she called out, trying to sound hard and in control of the situation. "I've got a gun and I'll use it."

"It's me, Pamela—Robin Temple. I'm comin' in okay? Don't shoot."

"Give me one reason not to," she said, the familiar voice not comforting her.

"I mean ye no harm, lass," he said, and walked in across the doorstep. He was flushed and winded and she knew now who her rescuer had been. Gratitude didn't make her less wary, however. "I couldn't catch the bastard, tripped over somethin' in the street an' lost him. I'm sorry, it won't happen again."

"Who the hell was he?" she gasped, not loosening her grip on the gun at all. "And for that matter what the hell are you doing here in the middle of the night?"

Robin put his hands up in a gesture of surrender, careful to keep his expression neutral. "He," he gestured with one thumb to the back door that still stood open to the night, "was one of the lads that's been hangin' about the last week."

She narrowed her glance and put one thumb to the hammer of the gun.

"Just how the hell do you know who's been here this last week?"

Robin ventured a step forward, keeping his hands up in full view.

"Stay put," she said sharply, "I don't trust you any further than I can throw you."

"I've had a watch on the center since Casey was taken away. It's one thing for a man to run this sort of place an' another altogether for a bit of a woman to do it. I'd not feel right if I left my best friend's wife to the mercy of the wolves. Honest, it was my turn to watch tonight."

"Are you trying to tell me that the IRA has nothing better to do than mount nightly surveillance on a drop in center?" She tried to maintain a certain coolness to her tone, but it cracked slightly and she could feel her hands getting slick around the gun.

"It's not an IRA operation," he said patiently, "'tis myself an' a couple of lads I trust. No more than that I swear; now can ye be persuaded to lower the gun?"

She lowered it slightly, causing him to raise his eyebrows.

"Well if it's castration rather than killin' ye've in mind I'd just as soon the latter, if ye don't mind. Now come on, yer hands are slippery as glass an' ye're as like to hurt yerself as me with the damn thing." His tone was matter-of-fact rather than thick with charm and somehow that reassured her enough to ease her thumb off the hammer.

Robin wisely kept his hands up. "I'm goin' to sit down, all right, 'cause my knees are shakin' fit to drop me on my face here."

She nodded, watching as he put one arm out slowly and pulled one of the kitchen chairs towards himself. She was still ready for some lightning quick move, knowing he was as well versed as Casey in these things. But he sat, dropping the last couple of inches onto the chair as if indeed his legs would no longer hold him.

"Will ye sit?" Robin asked. "Ye're makin' me damn nervous with that thing."

"All right, but don't so much as twitch or I'll shoot you right where you sit."

"I don't doubt it," he said, and put his hands palm up on the table so she could see them plainly.

She eased back carefully, feeling the chair with her legs, not taking her eyes off of him for a second, knowing that' all he'd need to drop her on the floor and get the gun.

He waited until she sat, gun still leveled across the table at him, and then said, "I'm goin' to reach in my coat and get a flask, because I need a drink if I'm not to piss myself here. I'll get it slow an' easy, no false moves okay?"

She nodded and Robin did as promised. The flask was in the inside pocket of his coat and he brought it out slowly. He took the cap off and placed it on the table, then helped himself to a long and generous swallow. He put the flask down by the cap with a long exhalation. "There, I can feel my nerves returnin'. Did Casey get ye the gun?"

"Yes," she said bluntly, "and he taught me how to use it as well, so don't think I'll accidentally plug the stove when I'm aiming for your head."

Robin nodded. "I believe ye. The man said ye were fearsome when the mood was on ye to be so. I can see that he spoke the truth. Would ye like a drink?"

"No thanks, I'll pass," she said dryly.

"I promise I'll not do anything if ye put that gun down, I swear to ye on my wife's grave."

"Your wife," she said pointedly, "is neither dead nor is she any longer your wife."

Robin laughed aloud. "Ye're a hard one, Mrs. Riordan, but for all I'm a liar an' a cheat, do ye honestly think I'd hurt the wife of Casey Riordan? First of all the man'd hunt me to the ends of the earth did I dare it, an' have my balls for breakfast when he found me, an' in the second place I've nothin' to gain by hurtin' ye. Besides," he slanted a look sideways at the gun, "I've a feelin' ye're no slouch at takin' care of yerself."

Oddly enough, the man had a point, there really was nothing for him to gain by hurting her. In fact, he'd saved her from a potentially horrible incident. She lowered the gun, flipped the barrel over and took the bullets out, then put the empty shell on the table by the flask.

"Thank you," Robin said, and there was no mistaking the sincere relief in his voice.

"I'll have that drink now," she said, and took the flask, hoping he would not note how badly her hand shook. It wasn't likely, he didn't seem to miss much of anything. She could see clearly why he and Casey had been such good friends.

It was brandy, which she found surprising. It shot straight to her stomach and immediately found her veins, billowing out in warm waves through her bloodstream. The general effect was a swift and speedy comfort. She pushed the flask back at Robin, knowing too much comfort was a very dangerous thing at present.

"D'ye think perhaps one of us," he suggested carefully, "ought to shut the back door before we've the neighbors an' the army pokin' about wonderin' what's happened?"

"Go ahead," she said, knowing the brandy hadn't fortified her shaking knees just yet.

Robin rose and walked to the back door, shutting it against the interference of nosy neighbors and men with guns. He still wore his coat and boots and was as perfectly groomed and polished as ever. She wondered what it took to really ruffle the man and thought it was likely not something she wanted to find out.

"Tea?" he asked, coming back to the table.

"I'll make it," she said quickly, not quite ready to trust him with boiling water at her back. "Is there any crisis in which the Irish don't find tea applicable?"

"No," Robin said mildly, the sarcasm seemingly lost on him.

The oddness of the situation impressed itself upon her, making tea for a man who was either her husband's best friend or worst enemy, in the middle of the night.

The kettle was on the boil and the tea spooned into the pot before either of them spoke again.

"I suppose—"

"I have to apologize—" they both began at once.

"Go ahead," Robin said, taking another nip off the brandy bottle.

"Thank you. However it was you ended up here tonight, I'm grateful that you did. I've no idea why that man was in here, but I'm sure it wasn't to chat about the good we do for the community." She shuddered, realizing just how close she'd come to being assaulted. Her legs were shaking again, the brandy's fortification proving to be rather fleeting.

"Sit," Robin said in a firm tone, "I'll finish the tea."

She sat gratefully, goose bumps rising all along her skin as the fear she'd not had time for earlier came in a wave.

Robin placed the teapot on the table, adding two cups to the table before striding out into the entryway. He came back seconds later with a blanket which he handed to her.

"Wrap that around ye, ye're in shock, ye need to keep warm."

She did as she was told, though the blanket had burn holes in it and smelled rather strongly of the cigarettes that had contributed to its tatty state. Still it was warm and large enough to feel as though it provided shelter of a sort.

Robin poured out the tea and added a good quantity of brandy to hers.

"Drink it, ye'll not get tipsy on that amount, but it'll go a ways toward calmin' ye."

She sipped the hot liquid cautiously. He was right, it did go a ways toward calming her.

"Any idea why he felt the need to break in here?"

Robin cocked a dark brow at her. "I don't know, politically speakin' I suppose it's a bit of a target, but it seemed more personal than that. I think it'd be best if ye didn't stay here anymore at nights."

"You're a tad bossy," she said, the brandy having loosened her tongue.

Robin gave her an amused look, "Aye, well ye ought to be accustomed to it, yer husband used to think he knew what was best a great deal of the time."

"He *is* right a great deal of the time," she said primly.

"Annoyin' isn't it?"

She laughed, "It can be."

She finished her tea. The brandy had given her a warm glow, though she still kept the blanket wrapped tightly around her.

"I have to admit," she said, carefully watching Robin's face, "I did wonder if it wasn't someone sent by Joe Doherty?"

Robin quirked an eyebrow at her and she sighed. Casey always told her she wasn't terribly good at anything requiring subterfuge, and that her face could be read easier than a child's picture book. Robin, however, seemed to want to humor her.

"Joe's beef is with Casey, not yerself. Joe's many things, most of them not admirable, but I don't think he'd harm ye."

"He certainly seems to hate Casey," she said, realizing it was quite likely Robin knew the reason for that as well as Casey himself did.

"Aye, well the history there goes back some way, an' none of it friendly.

He's never told ye what happened?"

"No, he doesn't talk about the man, other than to tell me to keep clear of him."

Robin's lip quirked up. "Likely what he told ye about myself as well."

"He may have mentioned something in that vein," she smiled, but she wanted him to know she was wary of him. He needn't think he could make himself too comfortable around her.

"Joe's been aimin' to take over the leadership of the Army here since the split in '69. He's a hawk, aye, likes the fightin' an' the violence. He's not a brain nor an orator, nor does he instill a great deal of respect. What he has is the fear he stirs in others, an' it's a powerful enough weapon to have given him a great deal of authority. Casey's not afraid of him, an' Joe don't like that one little bit."

"The thing that started it, though, was a boy named Danny Greavey—every neighborhood has a Danny Greavey. Danny wasn't quite right in the head. He wasn't retarded as such, just a bit slow. We'd all looked after him in our own rough fashion, growin' up together as lads. Admittedly 'twas a bad mistake he'd made, stealin' on Joe's territory. But he'd not a real notion of right an' wrong, least not in the fashion you or I would. He was a bit like a crow, really, if he saw somethin' shiny he couldn't resist it. But one of us, or one of his brothers, would always return the thing, so that it was more borrowed than stolen. But Joe wasn't given to tolerance, not even for Danny, so when Danny made the mistake of stealin' the hubcaps off his car, Joe made it clear he wasn't goin' to make an exception for him, though Casey an' myself had put the hubcaps back, polished an' all."

He paused to take another swig off the flask.

"Joe said it was time someone taught Danny that he couldn't take as he liked. We knew what that meant, but Casey wasn't havin' any of it. Christ," Robin laughed, "we spent *days* shadowin' bloody Danny. Got in trouble with Casey's da after old lady McLeod called him sayin' we were lurkin' about her window near dark. She thought we were tryin' to get a peek at her naked. Seventy if she was a day," Robin laughed. "'Twas only that Brian was certain even a couple of teenaged boys couldn't be that hard up that saved us from a good hidin'."

"It's my impression neither of you had to look far for female companionship anyway," Pamela said, with a smile.

Robin grinned. "He'll have told ye a bit about how it was with the girls back then?"

"Oh aye," she replied dryly, "he'll have told me a bit about how it was."

Robin had the grace to blush. He swallowed the last of his own tea and brandy and continued on with his tale. "When the moment finally arrived it felt like a scene out of *High Noon* in the end. Middle of the day, right in the street, an' Joe had come upon Danny. Casey an' I were right behind him an' managed to catch up, an' then Casey just moves in between Joe an' Danny."

Pamela could well imagine it, Casey had never been one to stand by while any sort of inequity existed. He'd taken her to task over putting her own feet in the fire more than once, but paid no heed when it was his shoes in the flames.

"He just stood there in front of Danny an' wouldn't move—imagine it, fifteen years old an' standin' down this man thirteen years his senior. He never flinched, never blinked, an' so I came up an' flanked his side. Joe just looked at him an' said 'ye're makin' a very bad mistake here, boy.' Casey said 'twas his mistake to make. I can still see that day clear as if it happened last week, an' how I felt. I could hear my blood rushin' in my ears an' feel the wind like it was cuttin' right through me. I was terrified, an' yet I don't think I've ever felt more alive. Needless to say Joe blinked first an' walked away, though not before tellin' Casey that he'd best watch his back—fell a little flat after what Casey'd just done, though."

Robin shook his head. "I knew then that he was born to lead. Some men just are, ye know?"

"And if he doesn't want to lead?" she asked quietly.

"I think ye know it's got little to do with want."

She did know; she understood that men saw something in her husband that she often turned a blind eye to, because this thing they saw in him was a thing that would lead him away from her and into danger.

"It was what kept me goin'," Robin said softly, "knowin' he always had my back no matter the fight."

"You've missed him," she said.

"Aye, I will have missed him a good deal over the years, more I'm certain than he will have missed me."

"You were his best friend too."

"Didn't act much like a friend to him. Will he have told ye the story?"

"About Melissa? Yes, he told me."

"Well then ye'll know I'd not much honor as a friend."

While she agreed that he'd not exercised a great deal of integrity as a friend, still he'd been a boy. She could forgive that if Casey had. However, it remained to be seen if he'd honor as a man. She wondered, looking at him now across from her, blue eyes soft with memory, why she really hoped that he did. Likely because if he didn't, despite protestations to the contrary, Casey was going to get hurt.

"Ye'll be wantin' to get back to yer bed. I'll stay down here, if ye've no objections. I doubt the wee bastard will come back, but I'd as soon make certain of it."

Sleep came with the dawn, when the rigors of the previous day and night caught up with her. Before she drifted into unconsciousness, it occurred to her, matters of honor notwithstanding, that while she might have formed a grudging liking for Robin Temple, she didn't trust him in the least.

Chapter Forty-three

History Lessons

BY MID-SEPTEMBER DAVID KENDALL knew beyond a shadow of a doubt that he'd taken complete leave of his senses. For if he hadn't, there really wasn't any explanation for the insanity that had provoked him to sneak the big, black Irishman named Pat to the showers for a respite from the filth of his surroundings and the hellish shell of the overalls.

Taking the hood off and feeding him had merely become an accepted rite between the two of them. He could do no less, and it was little enough, considering what the man endured each and every day. Somewhere around the fourth meal they'd shared, David, against his own better judgement, took the man's cuffs off as well. He'd merely said 'thank you' in that polite manner that was quite disarming, and did not refer to it again.

Pat had mentioned casually two days before that he'd give a decade or so of his life for a hot bath and David had immediately begun to consider how he might arrange exactly that. Having spent all his adult years in the British military, David was nothing if not resourceful. Two carefully placed bribes, an extra shift, and a carton of cigarettes had gotten him all the averted eyes and closed lips he needed. And had gotten him here, closed in a small space with a man of whom he was half-afraid, and wholly attracted to. Not, David was wise enough to know, a good combination for anyone.

There was a sense of immediacy to the man that David had never encountered elsewhere. Of raw and barely leashed savagery, held in check by a gentle civility that was profound in its parameters.

He stood at the sink, back to David, which, David knew, was a sign of unprecedented trust. He'd not seen the man turn his back to anyone, unless forced, since he'd been brought in. Recent events considered, it was only natural that the man should be distrustful and yet here he stood, bare from the waist up, carefully and leisurely shaving his face. He was a dichotomy, that much was certain.

His stubble was blue-black and heavy, the bruises around his eyes fading from black to a deep purple. His hair, slick as an otter's pelt from his recent shower, gleamed in the same shade. And against all this darkness his shoulders and back seemed uncommonly fine, like ivory carved to fierce perfection; his backbone a deep line between smooth planes of muscle, falling from broad shoulders into a narrow waist, stomach flat and hard. The thoracic line well defined, ending in a fine strip of black hair that led down...David wrenched his thoughts back abruptly, aware that the other man was suddenly still, muscles like cut silk under the smooth expanse of skin, his gaze black and hard in the mirror. He flushed and glanced quickly away, cursing his fair English skin for the truth it always told. He'd broken too many rules tonight and the ground under his feet was becoming increasingly unstable.

"Your fiancée, what's her name?" he asked suddenly, wanting only to break the unbearable tension that hung in the air.

Pat's eyes narrowed, the separation between pupil and iris hardly discernible. "How d'ye know I have a fiancée?"

"I...well I," David realized his gaffe immediately, "you must have mentioned her in conversation."

"No, I don't think I have," Pat said quietly, body still as that of a predator smelling weakness. The air around him was charged, ready for the slice of sudden movement. But rather than attacking he turned back to the sink and resumed his careful shaving. "So they're keeping a file on me, are they? Must have made for a scintillatin' read." He tilted his head back, the razor beheading whiskers in a slow moving arc under his chin. "Ye must be more important than ye let on, Corporal Kendall, if they're allowin' ye access to such information." He glanced at David in the mirror, though David knew the man had never taken his eyes off of him. "Or did they allow ye?"

David could feel beads of sweat begin to form under his collar. How much did the man actually know and how much was lucky guesswork on his part?

"I'm a soldier," he said stiffly. "I do as commanded."

"Like tonight?" Pat said, and laughed, a soft menacing sound.

"I was simply trying to do a good turn for you," David said, hearing the uptight, upper class inflections of his background coating all the syllables.

"Don't do me any favors, Englishman," Pat said, wiping the cut whiskers off the grubby porcelain of the sink.

"Is that what I am to you, an Englishman?" David asked, aware his tone was inappropriate. He knew he was treading a fault line he could fall into permanently if he wasn't careful.

"Ye wear the uniform of a Queen's man, do ye not?"

"It's hardly that simple," David responded, the remark cutting into the thin skin of his emotions like a whip tipped with steel.

"It's a line, an' for all it's invisible, it's there an' ye cannot deny it."

David fought to control his temper, thinking the man might have shown some small hint of gratitude rather than being antagonistic.

"It all seems rather silly, don't you think? Hundreds of years of fighting and what have either of us got to show for it?"

"Perhaps," Pat said sharply, "you an' yer fellow countrymen ought to have read yer history before ye came here."

"Do you propose to give me a history lesson? You Irish," David said hotly, forgetting his vow not to rise to the man's bait, "seem to think you have a lock on the making of it."

"Ach, forget it," Pat said dismissively, packing the razor away after carefully rinsing and drying it. "We might have our feet on the earth of the same country, but we're speakin' different languages."

"Ha," David said triumphantly, "*you* don't even know what it's about, do you?"

Pat turned, face dark as a thundercloud. "Don't I then? Well I've a few bruises and bumps compliments of yer fine an' upstandin' British boys that go a fair way toward explainin' it."

"I'm sorry," David said, instantly repentant. He'd forgotten for a moment how the two of them had come to be here, together, in this room.

"Oh ye're sorry, are ye? Well doesn't that just make it all better? Eight hundred years of occupation an' subjection when all we wanted was to be left in peace. We never asked ye for anything, never exploited nor oppressed ye as others did. Never invaded ye, never stole yer land an' parcelled it out to our own people as war booty, never let yer people starve while food rotted in the harbors. We've never put yer women an' children to the sword, nor massacred or transported yer men to foreign lands where they'd no more notion of how to survive than a wee child, where everything was foreign, an' all ye were was another goddamn paddy, a mick, a fockin' bogtrottin' Fenian bastard.'

His breath was coming in uneven savage bursts and David saw the capability for quick, brutal murder deep in his eyes. "Ye took our language, our schools, our priests had to flee or die, ye took our culture, an' even after ye'd stripped us of everything we'd ever been or known, ye mocked us—stupid Paddy, with his backward ways. Oh aye, look away, there's a thousand Irish jokes an' don't tell me ye haven't laughed at them yerself. An' then when we've the temerity to stand up against ye, when we rise from the fire an' say enough, ye call us terrorists. The goddamn Irish, they say, all they know is hate. Well I ask ye, Corporal, who taught it to us, who made sure it was bred deep into the bone an' blood of us?"

"Do you hate me, then?" David asked quietly, frightened by how deeply the answer mattered to him.

Pat gave him a long look and shook his head. "No, I don't suppose I do, hardly matters in the broader picture here, though, does it?"

"It matters to me," David said, knowing his face showed all he was feeling and suddenly not giving a damn.

Pat braced his hands against the sink, lashes dark against the hollows under his eyes. Despair was evident in his lines. "All I wanted," he whispered as though he spoke only for himself, "was to do good work, to help find and provide housing for people who have come to see such a thing as not a right, but a luxury. I went about it as quietly as I could, I never wanted to stir up trouble. I'm a simple man with simple dreams, but history will not leave me be. That's the curse of bein' an Irishman who stays in his own country, though, history will not leave any of us be."

Emotion, David was to reflect later, always made him foolhardy. A fact his father had pointed out to him a number of times. Managing to infer that emotion was a particularly undesirable quality in a son. But his father was not present, and neither, apparently, was his own common sense. There was only the air, heavy with the last of night, and the soft light of the man's skin and the pain that seemed to reach across the space dividing them. He reached out and touched Pat just below the shoulder, in the shadowed groove of the backbone.

The man moved like lightning, there was no time for thought between the half second during which David touched his back and the next when he found himself smashed against the wall, arm halfway up his spine, his own gun pressed tight to the corner of his mouth.

David felt the muzzle of the gun click sharply against his teeth as hysterical laughter rose in the back of his throat, his commanding officer's words ringing in his head. 'Rule number one of any tour of duty in Northern Ireland is— don't let down your guard around the bastards.'

"Do they not teach ye to never to turn yer back, Englishman? Do they not say how unpredictable an' untrustworthy the lot of us are? How an Irishman will cut yer throat as soon as look at ye? Or were ye absent from psyops that day? Hmm, David?"

The muzzle had insinuated itself between his teeth, the gunmetal tasting oddly like blood against his tongue, sharp and salty. The man's forearm was like a bolt of steel across his throat, already things were going black and fuzzy about their edges. Despite several tricks he'd been taught, he knew he'd never be able to get the jump on him. There were worse ways to die, he knew for he'd seen many of them, than at the hands of a blackly murderous Irishman. He thought, in his proper British way, that he ought to pray, tried for the doxologist version of the Lord's Prayer and found he'd an incomplete recollection of it.

"Here's history for ye, Englishman, my daddy died because of this silly little eight hundred year war, my brother spent five years in one of yer prisons an' will never be the same because of it. My granddad was shot like a dog in the street in front of his own son, an' I've been ripped from my home an' my woman merely because I'm tryin' to change the status quo in a system that's kept me an' mine on our knees for centuries. That's Irish history." The hammer of the gun clicked neatly, reverberating with the force of thunder in David's ear. Then suddenly it was gone—gun, arm and man, the voice behind him no longer angry, just very weary. "Ye'll not touch me again."

David, gasping in equal parts oxygen and relief, slid to the floor, knees having turned the consistency of unset jelly.

"Oh Christ—Christ—I'm sorry man, I don't what possessed me. Oh God, what am I becomin'?" Beside him Pat slid to the floor, the pistol laying slick on the tile.

"It's o-kay," David managed to wheeze out.

"No it's not," Pat said wearily, "ye've shown me nothin' but kindness an' at great risk to yerself, an' this is how I repay ye."

David merely shook his head, too exhausted to even reach for his gun and not caring a great deal at the present moment. The silence between them was heavy, laden with the apologies for which neither knew the words. Feeling he'd little to lose, David put himself into the breach.

"What did you want," he swallowed, his throat swollen and thick, "before all this?"

Pat turned his head to the side, exhaustion pulling at the corners of his mouth and eyes.

"Sometimes I don't remember, the present seems so all occupyin'. But what I really wanted, I suppose, was to be an astronomer. Wanted to be somewhere that it didn't rain nine days out of ten, an' just study the sky at night. I wanted a quiet life, y'know, a wife an' kids an' a house with a bit of a yard."

"What happened to make that so impossible?" David asked gently, aware that outside the barred window, night was releasing its hold on the planet.

Pat shrugged. "My daddy died an' my brother went to prison for five years, an' I couldn't seem to dream proper for a long while after, if that makes any sense."

"It makes a great deal of sense," David responded quietly, Eddie's face swimming up, unbidden, in his consciousness. "My brother shot himself a few years back. Things seemed meaningless for a long time after that."

"I'm sorry," Pat said simply, surprising David with the calm sincerity of his words.

"An astronomer, is it? I've always thought they were rather romantic souls, spending their lives searching the heavens, leading an uncomplicated life."

"Told ye I was a simple man with simple dreams."

"I don't think," David said in a strained voice, still wiping blood off the corner of his mouth, "there's anything simple about you, Patrick Riordan."

Pat shrugged, as if to say the designs of his character were of little concern to him anymore.

They sat there for a moment, both weary, while morning gathered behind them in gray slipstreams of cloud and the faint whisper of rain against the window.

"It's gettin' light," Pat said finally, as the room around them turned the color of ashes.

"Yes it is," David said, trying for some modicum of dignity in his tone. "I suppose we'd best get you back to your cell before they realize you're gone." He took a deep breath, hoping his shaking legs would bear him up onto his feet. In front of him, however, broad and strong in the heavy light, a hand held itself out. He hesitated, uncertain of the meaning of it.

"Take it, ye're still shakin'," Pat said gruffly.

David took the hand, and allowed himself for a moment to rely upon the strength whose natural bent was to help not harm, and wished fervently they'd met in another time and another country.

Pat was clad again in the overalls, the hood held loosely in his other hand.

"I'm sorry," David said, not knowing clearly just what he was sorry for, just knowing that he was.

Pat nodded, dark eyes inscrutable as he turned again into the Irish prisoner who could not allow himself the weakness of human flaws. He put the hood back on himself, voice slightly muffled through the two layers of thick material.

"Tie it for me, will ye?" he asked, and by these words David knew he had been given a fragile gift, which must be held carefully.

Forgiveness.

Chapter Forty-four
An Examination of Conscience

IT HAD BEEN A LONG TIME since Pamela had sought the comfort of the church. In Boston she had been tempted, but had not felt worthy to seek solace in the arms of her childhood religion.

The prayers and articles of faith were so deeply ingrained in her that she knew she still, on a daily basis, lived as a Catholic. And someone raised Catholic could never quite shake the fear of Purgatory. Nor the knowledge that to commit such an act as she had those last days in Boston might well condemn her unequivocally to hell.

To cross the threshold of a church made her feel like a scarlet hypocrite and she was quite certain that all who saw her would see her sin writ large across her face.

Father Jim however, had made it easy, by asking her several times to come and help with various projects he was instituting in his parish neighborhood. The man wasn't above using guilt as an inducement either, for he'd remarked on more than one occasion that Lawrence could well use the moral ground which the church could provide, as an underpinning for his new life.

Thus many of their weekends were now spent here, within the building of the church itself where assistance was meted out to those most in need. Basic necessities such as food and clothing were attended to and for those in search of temporary shelter, be it of the temporal or spiritual variety, the church was a place to lay their heads.

Father Jim took his particular brand of spirituality to the streets as well, for he believed in walking amongst those to whom he preached. In living and working in understanding of their lives, loves, and circumstances, even those who might well consider themselves beyond the boundaries of salvation.

Over the weeks, the small parish had become a shelter to Pamela. The violence of the streets ceased at its doors. Inside was sanctuary in the finest sense, where the peace could be felt as a softness, as a quiet difficult to find outside its doors.

So she found herself in the dim confines of the church on a Saturday morning in early October, after a night of arguing herself near senseless—had she committed this sin in free will? Yes, and yet what other choice had she been given? It was Love or Casey. One life in exchange for another. So was her contrition perfect when she did not regret that the act had saved her husband's life? The Church might argue that she could not know that Love would kill to keep her, but of that one fact she was certain, he had meant to kill Casey in order to claim her for his own. These thoughts would give her no rest and she determined to find a way in which to broach the subject with Father Jim.

It took the entire morning, as the two of them sat putting together hygiene packages for the local orphanage, for her to gird up the courage to ask him the question that had burned within her for months now.

Father Jim had just held up a small bottle with a wry smile and said, "Seems a bit foolish to be handing out socks and tooth polish when the wee fiends are out stoning soldiers and lighting tanks on fire."

Then she simply blurted it out, as was often the way when she'd carefully planned what she would say.

"Do you believe there are sins that are unforgivable?"

Father Jim looked up sharply from the washrag he was tucking around a small pamphlet on the care of the adolescent body.

"I mean rather," she stuttered, "that what I'm asking is—is what if a person had felt they'd no choice but to commit a sin, that someone else was in grave danger had they not committed this sin. Do such circumstances expiate the need for perfect contrition?"

Father Jim placed a bar of soap in the box and put the lid on, putting it to one side with all the other completed boxes, before answering.

"It's a bit hard for me to give you an answer without knowing the exact circumstances around the commission of the sin. All I can tell you with surety is that there is no sin so great that it cannot be forgiven by God. You know that surely."

She trembled suddenly, afraid now that she had broached this subject that had been like a great stone sitting on her chest for months now.

"*If your sins be as scarlet, they shall be made white as snow; and if they be red as crimson, they shall be white as wool.*" Father Jim quoted, his brown eyes soft with compassion.

"Do you really believe that? I mean *really*. That there is no sin too grievous for God to forgive? You don't think He exacts some earthly price for sin? For mortal sin," she added, feeling a wave of panic as soon as the words left her lips.

Father Jim's brow furrowed into three distinct lines, as it did when he gave all his attention to a matter. She held his gaze, though it made her shake, it was too important to hear his answer, to know what he really thought, to look away now.

Her own pulse sounded loud and ragged in her ears. Minutes uncounted passed, a small eternity as she awaited his answer. In the distance she could hear the soft chatter of teacups meeting saucers, as the ladies who polished the oak pews took their break in the rectory.

"Perhaps, Pamela," Father Jim finally said, "it's more a matter of forgiving yourself, rather than needing God's forgiveness. The two things are, many times, one and the same."

"You don't think there are some sins that cannot be forgiven? Don't quote me Church doctrine, tell me what you yourself believe."

Again there was the searching gaze, and the wrinkled forehead. At long last, he shook his head.

"My thoughts and the Church's are one on this matter; a sin is only unforgivable if there's no repentance in your heart, and even then I don't presume to understand what the measure of God's forgiveness might be. Neither should you."

She nodded, and knew that he could see she remained unconvinced.

"Perhaps confession would help to unburden you of whatever it is that's haunting you."

"Haunting me?"

"Yes, haunting you. It would be good for you to lay it down, however terrible you think it is. I don't need to remind you that the confessional is sacrosanct."

"I know."

In the eyes of the Church, life was sacred, a gift from God to be used well, to be spent on good works and lived in faith. Did the fact that Love Hagerty had committed few good works, and had lived only by his faith in the ultimate corruptibility of man, make his life less sacred? And how could she ask Father Jim these things, without leading him to understand just what the demon was that haunted both her sleeping and waking hours?

"I—" she began, but Father Jim's eyes looked past her suddenly, and her skin prickled. Then a smile broke across his face, lighting the small space around him.

She turned, heart thumping painfully.

In the last pew he sat. Her heart picked up and she began to half run down the aisle. The dark head was bent down as though in prayer. Behind her she heard Sylvie emerge from the kitchen and give a small yelp of utter shock. Then she flew past Pamela down the aisle.

Not Casey then, but Pat. For which she was truly grateful, and yet she still felt as though she'd been punched in the stomach and winded.

She continued her walk down the aisle, limbs leaden with disappointment. She could hear Father Jim call softly after her, but she ignored him, unable to face anyone in this moment.

Sylvie was sobbing and Pat's arms were around her, speaking softly, words of comfort and reassurance. She slipped past them, feeling that she was intruding on a very private moment.

Jamie stood outside the vestibule doors.

She smiled, knowing she wasn't fooling him for a New York minute.

"It's wonderful that you got him out. That he's safe now."

"I'm sorry it wasn't Casey. You know I'd have moved heaven and earth—"

She shook her head. "Jamie you don't need to apologize...I...it's just that for a minute I thought it was Casey. If I hadn't mistaken them I would have been thrilled that Pat is out."

"I know," he said, "but nevertheless I am sorry."

His words, simple yet genuine, knocked her interior walls a little. Her face twisted, and she knew that she wasn't going to be able to hold the tears back for long. She wanted to run headlong down the church stairs before the storm overtook her.

But Jamie, knowing her despair only too well, opened his arms, though he did not move forward.

She stepped into his embrace. And felt an immediate sense of relief and exhaustion as though all her carefully constructed barriers had melted at his touch. That for the moment she was safe. The tension leaked out of her shoulders.

Suddenly she realized she was clinging to him as though he were a life preserver, but he did not move nor flinch from her touch, knowing, as he so often did, what was necessary to her.

"What is it?" he asked quietly.

"I'm afraid, Jamie," she said, eyes closed against his shoulder. As if here and now she could be blind to sin and the need to atone for it.

It was a mark of Jamie's understanding that he did not ask of what she was afraid, but rather responded simply to the fear itself.

"It's all right, whatever it is, we'll deal with it. You're not alone."

And suddenly she felt the shape of forgiveness, as insubstantial as a whisper in the dark and yet there all the same. Not forgiveness entire, but the possibility of it.

This, she knew, was as close to confession and the expiation of her sins as she was going to come just now.

"YOU'RE WORKING FOR WHOM?" Jamie asked, glasses slipping off the end of his nose in consternation.

Two weeks after Pat's release, Pamela stood across from Jamie in his study, informing him that she had been, for the last two weeks, employed as a photographer.

"The police," she replied, looking back steadily.

"They've hired you—with your bloody last name, they've hired..." a grim look crossed his face. "You didn't use Riordan, did you?"

She flushed, but tilted her chin up defiantly. "I can do good work for them, Jamie. I understand this work. I like it."

"What did you tell them your last name was?"

"I used my mother's maiden name—Vincente," she said. "It's my business what church I attend anyway."

"That is completely beside the point, as you well know," Jamie said flatly. "If your bosses ever find out who your family is, you'll be fired directly, and that's only if you're very lucky."

She knew Jamie wouldn't be impressed by her reasoning, and so did not explain to him that it was work or go mad at this point. She needed something to fill the empty hours spent waiting to hear about a husband from whom, since that first terse missive, she had heard little. Only rare, much handled missives that, by necessity, were short on information and emotion. Pamela knew it was unavoidable, and that Casey was very aware how many sets of eyes might look upon his words, and would be careful to compromise neither her nor himself. Still it made for a most unsatisfactory form of communication.

Legal recourse had thus far proved frustrating in the extreme. She was stonewalled at every juncture, the lawyer she'd hired telling her he'd twenty-five cases identical to her own and that none looked terribly hopeful.

Jamie would be even less impressed if he knew she'd been receiving anonymous notes tucked into her lunch or sometimes in her car about files that existed regarding Brian Riordan and his early demise. But Jamie was distracted, for he'd had police roaming his property in an effort to discover what had led to a dead body in his stream—so far the result of that investigation merely pointed to a woman that had gone missing two days before Jamie and Pamela had stumbled upon her. The police weren't entirely certain, but Jamie had told her all suspicions seemed to be aimed at an abusive husband who had merely used Jamie's land as a conveniently remote spot to dump the body.

The first note Pamela received had shown up at the end of a particularly long day, when she'd stayed behind to finish developing pictures of a crime scene that had been especially gruesome. The body had been dumped off a country road just over the border of County Armagh. And it had been different from her usual purview in that it was the body of a woman, and it looked as though the murder had been sexually, rather than politically, motivated.

"Bar slag," the constable who'd been with her had roughly said, and then gone and lit himself a cigarette while Pamela had started the process of photographing the body and the few small artifacts that surrounded it.

Though she strove to maintain a professional distance from her subjects, the woman had bothered her. In a week in which she'd photographed no less than six corpses in various states of torture and mutilation, this one had gotten under her skin.

Something about the woman's chipped red nails, her peroxided hair and short skirt had made Pamela feel a wave of pity for her. Had she gone out in hope that night of meeting at last that special someone? Had she thought he was the one? Or was he just another in a long line of faces and bodies that ultimately proved disappointing? Or perhaps it was the bottle of Tabu that had fallen out of her purse. Her old nanny Rose had always worn Tabu and the scent was a poignant memory note for Pamela.

By the end of day she had been exhausted, the trembling fatigue of early pregnancy catching up with her. She was also more than a little depressed, having been once again sent a visitor's pass to see Casey that had expired by the time it reached her.

The note was taped to the visor in her car. If the evening sun hadn't been directly in her eyes on the drive home, it might have taken her several days to find it. As it was she had locked the doors immediately, and driven a good ways home before pulling over and opening the note.

It was only one line, but the wording was guaranteed to catch her attention.

'I know what really happened to Brian Riordan.'

Other than that there was a small, crudely drawn symbol of two interlocking rings at the top of the paper.

More had come, sporadically, so that there was no pattern to their appearance. She never saw anyone near the car, though it chilled her to the core to know someone was getting in and out without being detected. This led her to the conclusion that it had to be one of the men she worked with. Whoever he was, he also knew of her relationship to Brian Riordan. All of which made her distinctly wary.

Yet the notes, which all seemed fragments of a much larger picture, did not frighten her. She had a sense that someone was merely trying to lead her to a conclusion and didn't intend her any harm. The latest had been slightly more alarming in that it would require some action on her part. It directed her to the file room of the station where she worked, stating that something of interest awaited her there.

On each and every one of the notes was the same sketch of the interlocking rings. She knew she'd seen the symbol elsewhere, but couldn't for the life of her remember where.

When she opened the latest note, a small heavy object had fallen into her lap. A tarnished key, which she felt quite certain would unlock the door of the file room. She only hoped she was ready for the Pandora 's Box this key would unlock and bring to light.

She told none of these things to Jamie, though. She even managed to keep a stoic face as he listed the one hundred and two disasters that could occur as a result of her foolhardy venturing into police work.

Nor did she tell him she believed that through cataloguing the dead, gathering the sad bits of evidence that told the story of their end, she could make up for causing the death of another. Could atone, and perhaps buy her way back out of the cold into grace or life.

Part Four

When the Dark Night Seems Endless...

Chapter Forty-five

Letter from Beyond

THERE WAS NO CHANCE OF GETTING into the file room until after lunch. The station was quieter then, the morning rush over and the evening one not yet begun. Outside it was raining again, and the station itself seemed as gray as the low skies beyond its barred windows. She spent some time fiddling about with the kettle, drinking unnecessary cups of tea, waiting until the hall outside the file room door was completely empty. The key seemed to be burning a hole through her pocket directly into the skin of her thigh.

Her chance came a half hour later. Most of the constables were out on calls and those left at the station were in a meeting about dealing with the post traumatic stress the city was overwhelmed with in the wake of the recent spate of bombings.

She unlocked the door, and after glancing both ways to be certain no one had popped into the hall, slipped into the file room. The room was cold and damp and the smell of mildew strong. The lights flickered and buzzed for several seconds before coming on. The light didn't help; the room was bleak, with cement floors and cobwebs drifting in the corners.

She still didn't understand exactly what the note writer wanted, nor what he'd been trying to communicate without actually saying anything directly.

She glanced around and sighed. Boxes were piled up to the ceiling and along steel shelving six layers deep. Every crime committed in Northern Ireland since Cromwell's departure must be detailed and filed in here. She walked slowly down two aisles, seeing nothing out of the ordinary and feeling more confused by the second, not to mention a tad annoyed at the note's cryptic words. Two more aisles yielded little in the way of inspiration, though she'd acquired goose bumps and a prickly feeling up the back of her neck. There were only three more aisles.

Midway down the first of these she saw a box hanging out, enough that it was set apart from the dozens of its fellows. It was on the second shelf from the top and just barely within her reach.

Her fingers just touched the bottom of the box. She stood on her toes and slowly levered it out from the shelf. It toppled, spewing dust and several pounds of paper onto her head. She froze. The noise was deafening, echoing off the stone walls and ringing tinnily from the shelving. The resulting dust cloud took several minutes to clear—time which she used to smother sneezes and clear her eyes of the grime. The noise didn't seem to have breached the walls or the door of the file room, for no one came bursting in accusing her of meddling in things that could get her killed.

She righted the box and picked up a handful of papers, tidying them before placing them to one side and reaching for another handful. They appeared to be copies of official documents; letters between RUC personnel and government officials. Her eyes skipped through several paragraphs filled with the over wordy lingo of government correspondence.

"Pursuant to the section titled Part C...the aforementioned party of the third part... buildings subject to the city code established in...' she sighed. Perhaps the note writer meant to kill her through sheer boredom. She picked up the next batch of papers and fanned them out. They all looked the same as the last batch. She bit her lip in frustration, wiping a grubby hand down the side of her jeans.

Then a sheet caught her eye, the logo of MI6 prominent on its heavy cream surface. It seemed oddly out of place in the midst of all this dry and dusty correspondence. She pulled it out of the pile. The name leaped out at her at once. *Brian Riordan* there in the middle of the few paragraphs. She steadied her gaze and started at the top of the letter.

Dear Terence;

Pursuant to your letter of March 12th in the matter of Mr. Griffin Waite, a former Senior Information Officer liased with the (here someone had taken a broad tipped felt and blacked out the words.)

In answer to your second question—at present no one knows the whereabouts of Mr. Waite, nor what his connection to the deceased—the Belfast Republican Brian Riordan—was. I think we must take the view in this matter that no news is good news, the longer Mr. Waite stays off the radar the better. It may be that he himself is deceased.

Grounds for a murder investigation were never fully established, and Mr. Waddell feels that no new evidence or any other consideration of substance has come to light that endangers this position. The matter is not worth pursuing. Should further questions arise, please deal with them in as summary a fashion as possible.

Again the black felt had slashed out a good two inches of print and despite holding it to the light, she couldn't make any of the words out. However two lines further down it appeared the pen had begun to run out of ink, by squinting and holding it up to the flickering light she made out the tail end of a sentence that made the fine hairs on her neck stand up.

...trust that any trail in the Riordan case has gone sufficiently cold.

Pamela re-read the line four times—the Riordan case, what case? And why in heaven's name was MI6 fielding questions about his death?

Unfortunately Terence I can only answer for decisions made during this Administration, these decisions you've inquired about were made under a previous Administration and therefore files or other information pertaining to this matter cannot be accessed by the current Administration.

Sincerely,

Arch Fielding

She flicked through the pages underneath but they bore no relation to the letter in her hand. She glanced over her shoulder at the door, it was still tightly shut but it was only a matter of time before someone came in for something and discovered her here.

She forced herself to go through the papers carefully, despite the shaking in her hands and the pounding in her ears that told her this was exactly what the note writer had wanted her to find. Why though? How could he know this? And what did the letter mean anyway? She bit her lip nervously and tasted blood. There had to be at least two thousand papers scattered on the floor around her, how on earth was she to peruse them before someone came upon her? She took a breath, she would have to try. She continued to leaf through them, laying each one face down and to the side as she finished scanning them. Half an hour passed in such a manner and she had found nothing, her fear of getting caught increasing by the minute.

A flick of blue had just caught her eye when she heard a key in the door behind her. She froze, paper cutting into her palms as she squeezed it tightly. Whoever was trying to unlock the door seemed to be having problems with the key as they were still fumbling with the knob. Her heart was threatening to come up through her throat when she heard Constable Frye's voice outside.

"Murray, the sarge wants to see ye—ye'd best nip right quick, he was in a temper about ye lettin' that girl go last night without questionin' her. Nip along lad."

Pamela let out the air she'd been holding and returned to the papers, knowing she only had another minute or two before she needed to be out of this room.

The flick of blue was a tab that had been attached to the top of the paper. The tag looked relatively new, the paper itself damp and reeking of mildew. The tag had been added recently. She picked it up and saw that it had a number in the top righthand corner. It was number six of ten, and looked to be part of a report. This particular page consisted of a list of names.

Thomas Jans- builder, Portadown
Desmond McMann- butcher, Markethill, Co. Armagh
Alice Robards- housewife, Belfast

The list went on to total up dozens of names. The one she was looking for was halfway down the page.

Brian Riordan- driver, Belfast

She'd known it would be there. This, after all, was what the note writer had wanted her to see. Yet something in her refused the knowledge the papers had given her. She laid the paper to the side on top of the heavy cream stationary of MI6. The rest of the papers she put back into the box, tapping, shuffling, and tamping them in until the whole lot fit. She returned the box to its place on the high shelf and turned back to where the two papers lay face-up with information she wasn't sure she wanted to possess.

She folded the two papers and put them inside the waistband of her jeans, feeling sick even as she did so. Apart the two letters were little more than innuendo and half-truths, together they were damning evidence.

Casey and Pat's father had been murdered.

Chapter Forty-six

Truth and Consequences

PAMELA ENTERED PAT'S SMALL OFFICE space on a gust of chill wind, brown and gold leaves caught fast in her hair and on her scarf. "It's like trying to get in to see the Wizard of Oz," she said, removing her navy pea coat and laying it over the back of a chair. "Though I didn't get the impression your gatekeepers were particularly enchanted with you. What are you doing?"

"Loadin' up pamphlets—finally got the results of that employment study, so we're goin' to blanket the city with it. Not that it contains any earth shatterin' information," he said wryly. "Catholics are three times as likely to be unemployed as Protestants," his tone mimicked those of a pompous politician, "and are disproportionately represented in the poorest paid, least skilled and most insecure jobs—well tell us something we *didn't* know." He kicked an empty box across the floor toward her.

"Give us a hand then."

She took the box and grabbed a stack of pamphlets. The paper was still warm and the ink fumes heady. Her hands were trembling and she suddenly found herself at a loss as to how to tell Pat about the papers she'd found. How did one begin? She couldn't just blurt out that she was certain his father had been murdered, and yet there was no delicate conversational gambit to open such a topic.

"Out with it," Pat said, shifting a full box onto the top of another.

"Pardon me?"

"Whatever it is ye've come here to tell me, ye'd best just say it. Ye look as though ye've a fishbone stuck sideways in yer throat an' won't breathe easy until it's out."

She took the papers out of her inside pocket, where they'd felt like a brand against her chest for the last two days. She'd briefly considered not telling Pat but in the end hadn't been able to live with the thought of keeping it secret from him. This was his father and he had a right to know.

He gave her a searching look as he took the papers from her hand and for a fleeting second she wondered if she'd just made a very grave mistake.

She watched him as he looked over the papers and read the letter again. His face was a blank slate, giving her no clue as to what was going on inside his head.

"This paper," he waved the list of names at her, "what do ye think it is?"

"A list of people that were designated as killing targets."

He sighed heavily. "Aye, I thought as much. Do ye have proof of it though?"

She nodded. "I've done some checking and found at least seven other people on that list that are dead. Most weren't made to look like accidents though. Some of the bodies have never been found, others were dumped in fields, another burned in a car. Some I simply couldn't track down and I had to be careful about when I was using the file room and how often."

He took a deep breath, dark eyes unreadable. "I never did think it was an accident."

His statement surprised her; neither he nor Casey had ever spoken about the circumstances surrounding their father's death. That in itself seemed odd enough, particularly when neither of them were men for avoiding the truth.

"I can see by the look on yer face that ye think it strange that I've never spoken of it before. Well I did, an' I thought Casey was actually goin' to take a literal strip off my hide for bringin' it up. I think he's always feared that Daddy did it on purpose an' that to look too closely at his death would present him with facts he couldn't bear."

"Your father didn't seem like a man who would take his own life."

"He wasn't," Pat said quietly, folding the papers over and then unfolding them to look again at the undeniable message they relayed. "Ye see, nothin' about this ever fit; he wasn't depressed an' the idea that it was accidental didn't wash either. My da had a rare steady hand, might have made a good surgeon in some other life. Ye'll have noticed Casey's the same, even when he's carvin' his wee birds ye'll never see him slip, nor tremble. So if I had trouble believin' the official version of my da's death—well," he shrugged, "ye can see why that might be hard to swallow."

"Then why didn't you go to the police?" She realized the naïveté of the question even as it left her lips. Even she had lived here long enough to know better.

"An' what do ye think might have been the outcome of that? Considerin' what ye've already found?"

"But you were both so young—you don't think..." she trailed off as he shot her a dark look that was more than vaguely similar to his brother's.

"Don't make the mistake of thinkin' that because they share their tea an' cakes with ye, that they are good people, Pamela. Granted some are, an' then there's plenty that aren't, an' ye'd best remember it. If ye don't think most of them would welcome a clear shot at Casey, then think again."

"I'm well aware that there is no black and white in this country, Pat, there's nothing but endless shades of gray. I'm more careful than you give me credit for."

"Aye, I suppose it's yer own business," he said grudgingly. "Casey does say ye're not a woman to be gainsaid when ye take a notion into yer head."

"Does he then?" she responded tartly.

Pat merely cocked a dark brow at her as if to say he was well acquainted with her stubbornness himself and hadn't needed his brother's confirmation of the fact.

"So you've just lived with this knowledge all these years?"

"Aye well, it wasn't what ye could call knowledge, an' I was very young when he died. Then Casey went off to prison an' I had other worries. Like survivin' from one day to the next. But it was always there in the back of my mind, that someone else must have done it—didn't make any sort of sense that he'd have had gelignite there where he died."

"Would he have known if someone other than him had been near," she paused wondering if there was a delicate way to say this, and concluded there wasn't, "the materials?"

"There are ways of tellin', an' my da was a careful man. He'd methods of makin' sure no one was tamperin' with his things. Sometimes it's as simple as placin' hairs in places where you'll see if anything has been removed. Had anything changed in the slightest since last he'd touched it, he'd have known an' not have made the mistake of dealin' with it himself. Truth is, though, he wasn't in the business of buildin' bombs anymore, hadn't been for a long time before he died. He'd distanced himself from the IRA. There was no reason for him to have explosives. Sure as hell he'd not have had it on the premises where one of us could have gotten to it, so ye see none of it made a damn bit of sense."

"He died at home?" she asked, shocked by what he was saying.

"No, at a garage where he fixed cars an' such on the side, but Casey an' I worked there with him on weekends often." Pat gave her a quizzical look, "Casey didn't talk to ye about any of this?"

"He's never spoken of it. He gets that granite face whenever I've asked. So I don't ask anymore."

Pat hefted the last of the boxes onto the pile by the door. "He's not likely to speak of it. I think he's tried to forget what he could, an' lock the rest up tight. 'Twas him that found daddy, or," Pat grimaced, "what was left of him."

"Oh," she said, and sat down feeling as though someone had taken the starch out of her knees. "I'd no idea."

Pat sat across from her, hands ink-stained, nails rimmed in indigo.

"Well, if he was to tell anyone it'd be you, but I don't think he could ever find words to describe what it was like, an' how it was for him afterwards."

"No, I don't imagine he could," she said faintly.

"I remember that night, ye know. He came in an' sat on the side of my bed. I think he sat there for a long time before he actually said anything. I woke up an' there was just this very still weight on the edge of the bed. I think I mumbled somethin' an' he said ''tis only yer brother'. The words seemed odd, an' I think I knew somethin' was very wrong just from his stillness an' those words. An' then he just said it, flat an' soft—'da's dead, Patrick.'" Pat shrugged. "It doesn't take many words to turn a world upside down, does it?"

She shook her head, not wanting to interrupt his narrative.

"An' then he told me what had happened, that da had been blown up," Pat took a deep breath, face oddly impassive. "An' I knew it wasn't the truth, that there was more to it, but I knew too that he wasn't able to talk about it. There was still blood on his hands, he smelled strong of soap, but the blood was there in the lines of his knuckles an' under his nails. Sometimes," Pat's long lashes swept down, covering his eyes, "I think, for him, it's still there, an' always will be." His voice was soft, but a chill swept over Pamela at his words. They bore too closely to her own thoughts at times, that she'd married a man of blood, who wouldn't be able to rest until he'd had vengeance. However, until now, vengeance hadn't been possible, one couldn't kill something that had neither form nor substance.

"He won't thank ye for the information. Ye're openin' a can of worms if ye do this, an' exposin' yerself to all sorts of danger as well. He'll do what he has to to protect ye, but he can't be with ye twenty-four hours a day. There are people who'll kill ye for lookin' in the wrong direction at the wrong moment. If someone gets wind that ye're pokin' into a ten year old murder, ye'll find yerself in more than one set of crosshairs."

A knock at the door brought his head up sharply, eyes narrowed in anger. "Bastards," he said wearily.

"Who is it?"

"Army—who else? File on me must be gettin' to the size of a small novella, they'll be splittin' it into installments soon. Considerin' the number of bodies you take pictures of every week, ye'd think they'd have somethin' more constructive to do."

The knocking was more demanding now, a command to open the door. Pat addressed a silent, but eloquent, finger to the escalating noise.

"Aren't you going to open it?"

He shook his head. "What for? There's nothin' new to go over. They've my address, license, car make, an' likely what I eat for breakfast. If I sneeze under my pillow at night, they ask how my cold is in the mornin'. What more can they want to know? It's a bloody waste of time, which I think is maybe the point. They didn't hurt ye, did they?"

"No," she replied hastily, seeing the look that had become common to his face since he'd been interned; it was the look of a man who needed very little provocation to lash out.

"They asked a lot of questions, but they were polite about it."

"Oh yes, the bloody English, polite even while they're hangin' ye."

"I managed a visit with Casey last Sunday," she said, thinking it wise to change the subject. "It was only twenty minutes mind you, but we managed to talk a bit. He says he's fine," she shrugged, the visit had been hard on both of them and Casey had discouraged her about attempting another.

"Did ye tell him what ye're doin' for a livin'?" Pat asked, dark brows drawn down.

"Yes, well no—maybe I made it sound a little more innocuous than it strictly is, but I don't think he needs the worry of it right now. He frets too much. I'm a grown woman but he still thinks I'm a child when it comes to Belfast."

"Well aren't ye a wee bit of a child to be naïve enough not to see what risks ye're takin'?"

"Are you angry at me, Patrick?"

He breathed out heavily through his nose, face like a thundercloud. "Aye I suppose I am a wee bit, though it's not yer fault. I...this news about my daddy has addled me."

"It's all right; I feel a little addled myself."

Pat gave her a considering look. "That doesn't mean I don't think ye're bein' a pigheaded fool with that job of yers, an' I know Casey'd be fit to be tied if he knew. Ye've not considered it from his angle maybe, an' I don't think ye can understand the risks he took merely to be with ye, can ye? To marry someone from away—someone who'd no past that was common knowledge, men have been killed for less in this city."

She shook her head. "No, at the time I didn't understand. I was so mad in love I couldn't fathom any impediments. I wanted him, that was all I knew. I didn't think beyond that for either of us. Now, though, I've a better appreciation of what it must have meant to marry someone who was a complete alien to this environment. Do you think he did the wrong thing?"

He gave her a queer look and then shook his head. "How can ye even ask that, Pamela? Once he'd seen ye, there was no turnin' back for him, I know it's somethin' ye're used to but perhaps ye'll also know that the way he loves ye is no common thing. People wait their whole lives to feel somethin' that would fill up a corner; when my brother looks at ye it's somethin' so large there's no space adequate to it. He knows he's blessed, an' I know it too. How could I feel that was the wrong thing? No one who cared for the man could be so foolish."

"But you feel this thing I want to do is foolish, don't you?"

"Aye," he nodded, "I do. It's not only yerself ye'll put in harm's way, it's him an' Jamie as well."

"Casey's safely behind bars and Jamie's more than capable of looking after himself."

"There's no such thing as 'safe' behind bars, Pamela, an' ye know it. As for Jamie, I'll agree that I've not met many a man more capable than him, but when it comes to lookin' after himself—where ye're concerned I'd say he's not very capable at all."

She looked away, Pat's eyes had always seen too much. "There isn't anything between Jamie and me anymore."

"I know neither of ye have ever acted on yer feelins', leastwise not since ye married my brother, but I see the way the man changes when ye're about. He's careful to cover it, but it's there in the air, make no mistake."

"I would think it would make you angry with the both of us," she said softly.

"No, were ye different people I'd not understand, but somehow the love ye bear him doesn't seem to affect what ye give my brother. If I felt it was takin' somethin' vital from him I'd be the first to complain, but somehow ye manage. I'll not say I'd like to be in Casey's shoes at times, though," he smiled, taking the sting from his words.

At this juncture the letter was looking like a less fraught topic. "What do you want me to do about this?" she asked.

The letter lay between them like an incendiary device, as though any minute it would ignite and blow the both of them—and all they'd grown familiar with—to kingdom come. Pat stared at the heavy cream stationary mutely, his face a mask that she could not decipher.

"He was your father too, Pat," she said quietly, feeling faintly giddy from the ink fumes that surrounded them. "Don't you want to know?"

Pat shook his head. "There's want an' then there's necessity—maybe I'd want to know, but do I need to?" he paused, and she noted his hands, blue-streaked, were tremoring slightly. "I've lived this long with my da's death, never certain of the truth, but able to bear it. Do I want to change that? Knowin' that the circumstances of his death were different than what I imagined won't bring him back, an' yet," his eyes fixed on hers, "an' yet how can I sleep proper if I turn my face from this? Damn it, Pamela," he slapped the top of the box he'd just sealed, "why couldn't ye leave well enough alone?"

She started slightly; it was so unlike Pat to lose his temper. The fact that he had only proved how badly this news disturbed him.

"I'm sorry, but I couldn't imagine just leaving it once I'd seen those papers."

"Aye, ye're right, an' I suppose I ought not to shoot the messenger." He sat down across from her again, face grim. "What do we do then?"

"We?" she echoed.

"Do ye suppose I'm goin' to let ye go about alone pokin' into this? An' I know ye will, so don't bother sayin' anything to the contrary."

There were times, she thought, biting her tongue, that the man was annoyingly like his brother. She also knew that Riordan obstinacy was not something she could prevail against. Besides, two heads were infinitely better than one in this case.

"It'll have to stay between us," she said, feeling a small flutter of conscience and quickly smothering it. Casey was, as she'd stated, tucked away in prison and couldn't be consulted.

Pat nodded. "Aye, we'll keep it to the two of us, but that means ye're not to go runnin' off on some wild goose chase on yer own. If ye find somethin' out ye have to come tell me first an' then we'll decide on the best course. Cool heads prevailin' an' all that, all right?"

"Scout's honor, I promise I'll tell you right off if I find anything out, and we'll decide together what to do about it."

He cocked a dark brow at her. "Were ye ever a Girl Scout?"

"Not officially," she admitted.

"Aye," his tone was resigned, "I thought not."

Chapter Forty-seven

All Hallowtide

AWAY FROM THE CITY LIGHTS, fall closed in quickly. A large moon sat upon the tops of the hills, only to find itself snared in the grasp of the ancient ash tree that looked like a ghost of its summer self. At dusk large flocks of crows skimmed in silence over the treetops. Mornings brought browning fields rimed with frost. The scent of smoke and peat drifted, phantomlike, down the roads.

Just that dawn, she'd awakened early and was treated to the sight of a neat vee of geese crossing the face of the moon. It was an hour she found herself keeping company with more often than not these days. She never had slept well when Casey wasn't in the bed, but rather drifted on the surface of sleep, with the occasional sinking under to a deeper state from which, of late, she would jerk awake with a pounding heart and sweaty palms. Then for the hours before dawn, she would exist in an uneasy state where she felt for a certainty that someone was watching her. Or at least watching the house.

The feeling had started about a week after she'd returned from Jamie's house. She'd tried to shake it off, read it away and curse herself for a superstitious fool, but the feeling persisted until she found herself wandering her home in the dark, like a ghost who could not rest.

Worry gnawed at her bones almost continually; worry for Casey, worry for the dark restlessness that had possessed Pat since his release, worry for Lawrence, and worry for the tiny life she sheltered within her body. Two days ago she had started spotting, and the blood was a bright red, not the normal and unalarming brown that often accompanied early pregnancy. Her doctor had reassured her that the baby was fine at present. But she had seen the unspoken words that hovered at the back of his eyes and knew that this baby wasn't on the most secure of ground.

Tonight, in an effort to banish the ghosts of anxiety she had invited Pat and Sylvie, as well as Jamie, to come share Hallowe'en with her.

It was a mild day, with a mellow sun lighting the great drifts of oak and ash leaves that lay about the yard. As early night swallowed the sun, the yard came to flickering light through the eyes of grinning jack o'lanterns that she and Lawrence had carved and placed on the front stairs, and in the crooked elbows of a gnarled oak. With the encroaching darkness, a crisp wind sprang up and set the leaves to whispering and scuttling in small eddies about the ground.

A great bonfire, heaped with fragrant apple wood, cast long tongues of violet and gold into the dusky night. Bathed in the heat, Pamela felt warm for the first time in weeks. The feeling of odd menace which had been her constant companion of late, fled in the wake of Jamie's arrival. For the moment, the home she'd grown to love, felt again like a safe warm harbor.

Going inside to prepare dessert, she took a deep breath of cider spices, pumpkin pie, and dried rosemary. The pine floors glowed in the soft, flickering candlelight, a basket of apples giving off stray gleams of ruddy ripeness. On the Aga, a large pot bubbled merrily as a witch's cauldron, the heady steam of hot cider warming her nose.

Pat, under the pretext of helping, followed her into the kitchen.

"Have ye received any more of the wee notes?" he asked, voice near to a whisper.

She cast a glance over her shoulder. Both Jamie and Sylvie were busily restuffing the scarecrow that Finbar had dragged around the back of the shed and de-stuffed. Lawrence was nowhere to be seen, but she thought she detected the faint glow of a cigarette lighter at the edge of the dark woods.

"Just one more, two days ago. He wants a meeting, but didn't say exactly when."

Pat's eyebrows rose in consternation. "A meeting? Ye're not to even think about goin' alone, understand?"

"Understood," she said in as meek a tone as she could manage, which only made Pat give her a very black look.

"I mean it, Pamela, ye're in no condition to be traipsin' about the countryside on yer own, meetin' God knows who, God knows where."

"I know that," she hissed, hearing the sound of a step on the porch.

"I mean it," he repeated ominously, glaring daggers at her just as Jamie came in the kitchen, trailing the scents of wood smoke and roasted potatoes.

"What are the two of you brewing up, anarchy with a pinch of mayhem?" Jamie asked lightly, a smile on his face that melted into a look of suspicion as he noted their still intensity.

They both laughed a little too heartily, and it was Jamie who had the raised eyebrow now.

Pat, never good at deception of any sort, fled back outside, causing Jamie's eyebrow to rise even higher.

Pamela quickly busied herself with refilling the heavy ceramic mugs with cider and laying out the plates for pie.

"How was your visit?" Jamie asked, rolling up his sleeves to wash forks for dessert.

"Not great," she replied, rooting through the fridge for cream. "I had all of twenty minutes with him."

"How is he?" Jamie had turned from the sink, tea towel in hand. He gave the forks a brisk polish as he waited for her answer.

She shrugged, determined not to give into the tears that prickled at the back of her throat. The visit with Casey had not gone at all as she had hoped.

"As well as might be expected. There was a guard in attendance the whole time. Made it a little awkward to talk. He told me he doesn't want me visiting anymore."

"Oh. Did he tell you why?"

"He said the visits compromise both him and myself and that he doesn't want me going through that. I think it's my decision. He doesn't agree."

"He knows they'll use you as leverage against him, he's trying to protect you and himself by doing this."

"Are you saying he's right?" she asked incredulously.

"Yes, as a matter of fact, I do agree with him on this point."

She sighed. "Why does everyone seem to have an opinion on this?"

"I take it Pat thinks you should stay away as well."

"He does," she admitted reluctantly.

"He understands the situation."

"And I don't?" she said in outrage. "It was my bed Casey was torn from, the man is *my* husband."

"A fact," Jamie said, tone dry, "of which I don't need reminding."

"Well, I don't understand. The other men have visitors. You know how hard it was to get that pass to see him."

"Yes, I know, and I understand your frustration, but you might try to see it from his side."

"Which would be what, exactly?" she asked, tea towel now fisted tightly at her hip.

"He's not some green internee, Pamela, he's been imprisoned before."

"I do know that," she said stiffly.

"Well perhaps then you need to think what it does to a man to realize his wife has been strip searched, considering what has happened to you in the past. Add to that the fact that they'll taunt him with it later, possibly talk about your body to him. Men who've beaten him, interrogated him, and can hold him indefinitely without charges."

"Damn it, Jamie!" she slammed the cream jug down on the counter, sending a wave of the thick liquid onto the floor. The tears, always hovering too close these days, spilled down her cheeks. "I understand how he feels. I do, but that ten minutes is all I've had to reassure me that he's all right in these last few months. I'm scared as hell every minute of every single day—" she shook her head, "I'm sorry. Maybe it's selfish of me, but I *needed* to see him."

"I know that," Jamie said. "I'm sorry, but I do think he has valid reasons for wanting you to stay away. I know your reasons for wanting to see him are equally valid. Perhaps—"

Whatever Jamie had been about to say was cut off by a terrible screech from outside. They looked at each other in startlement and then Jamie flew out the door, towards the pine coppice from which the horrible scream had sounded.

Finbar was barking madly as she ran down the stairs, Jamie's fair head already disappearing in the inky blackness of the wood.

Sylvie stood next to the fire staring at the coppice, face tight with fear. "What happened?"

"Lawrence was over near the trees—there was a cracking noise and Finbar shot off into the trees, and then Lawrence pelted after him. Then Pat and Jamie went off after him."

The two of them huddled closer to the fire, neither wanting to approach the woods. The entire mood of the night had shifted to one of menace, the trees seeming to crowd in upon them. The flickering flames, which had given her such content before, now seemed like writhing snakes, ready to strike.

It was a small eternity before Jamie emerged from the dark bank of pine, head a pale glow against the dark. Something in the way he moved, though, warned her.

She could smell the sharp edge of cold and pine needles as he approached. The vertical crease in his forehead was sharp as a knife cut.

"Where's Lawrence?" she asked, tremors shaking her from head to toe.

"Lawrence is fine. Come with me," he said grimly, "there's something I think you had better see. Do you have a torch handy?"

She nodded, throat thick with fear. "Bottom drawer, right of the fridge."

Jamie was back a second later, torch in hand. "Come," he said shortly to Pamela. "Sylvie, go in the house and go upstairs. Turn the light on in the master bedroom please, and then in a few minutes, start walking back and forth across the room."

Sylvie nodded, her pixie face ashen in the firelight.

Jamie turned and headed back toward the tree line, glancing back once to be certain Pamela followed.

The bobbing torchlight cast huge ghoulish shadows all around them, heightening the aura of menace. Her teeth were chattering uncontrollably, and she was freezing cold again, the small warmth of security that she'd felt earlier abruptly shattered.

It was dark and damp once they crossed from the fire-lit yard into the heavy undergrowth of the pines. She could feel the chill of her own breath as it misted onto the air. The set of Jamie's shoulders as he trod ahead of her told her that whatever he'd found had greatly disturbed him.

Pat stood at the edge of a small area that lay beneath the arms of a lone oak. Finbar was stiff-legged and pacing the area, nose to the ground, hackles still up, a low growl emanating from his throat.

"Where is Lawrence?" she asked, voice sounding small and weak to her own ears.

"Up here," came the muffled reply from above her head. She looked up to see the pale urchin face pop out from a network of black oak branches.

"Thought I heard somethin' in the wood, an' when I turned to look I saw someone movin' through the trees. I yelled at him, an' I must have startled him badly because he tripped over somethin' and broke a bunch of branches before settin' off runnin. He'd a bit of a head start, or I'd have caught him." The head retreated as quickly as it had emerged, and she could hear the sound of his long limbs scuttling back up the tree.

Pamela looked around the space. Even in the limited light of the torch she could see that someone had most definitely been living in amongst the small band of trees. The brush was completely flattened, and there was more than one sign of recent occupation—a heavy shirt, sodden with October damp, the coals of a small camp stove and a scrap of cellophane wrapping from a cigarette package. A neatly rolled sleeping bag lay on its side on the ground. It looked as though it had been tossed down from the tree, which had a good-sized hollow several feet off the ground that would allow a grown man to sit fairly comfortably.

"I went up the tree," Jamie said, "the view is quite astounding from there. Particularly when you use the binoculars I found stashed in the crux. I could practically make out the date stamp on your china. What do you see, lad?" Jamie called up.

"Light's on now. Ye can see all four corners of the bedroom even without the eyeglasses—" there was a brief scuffle and a muttered curse as Lawrence presumably adjusted the 'eyeglasses'. "With them—" there was a sudden silence from above.

"With them what?" Jamie prompted impatiently.

"I can see the stitchin' on the pillowcases. I can see everything." The boy's voice was small now, and afraid. The emphasis he'd placed on *everything* leaving none of them in any doubt as to just how complete the surveillance had been.

A feeling of violation swept over her. So none of it had been her imagination. Right now feeling like a hysterical female would have been a great comfort opposed to the notion that someone had been peering through the windows for weeks.

"Lawrence tells me you've been jumpy as a foxed hare these last several weeks." There was no mistaking the anger in Jamie's voice.

"What?" She looked up to where a long leg was feeling about for a sturdy branch. At her sharply uttered question, though, it recoiled like a yoyo back into the shelter of the tree.

She should have known better than to think she was hiding anything from the child, he'd lived most of his life looking over his shoulder and honing his primal instincts for survival to a fine and cutting edge. Those pale blue eyes saw a great deal.

"Why on earth didn't you tell me?"

She crossed her arms over her chest in a defiant attempt to stop shaking. "It was just a feeling. I thought I was imagining it. I can't run to you with every little problem that crops up. I'd no reason to think it was anything more than my imagination running rampant."

He shook his head, mouth set in a grim line. "Pamela, I told you to come to me with anything, no matter how trivial. This is hardly trivial, though."

She put her chin up, trying to summon a bravery she most certainly wasn't feeling. She couldn't shake the feeling that even now eyes were crawling all over her.

"I'll be sure to tell you if it happens again. In the meantime I'll keep the doors locked and curtains drawn."

The fine golden brows arched in surprise. "Are you mad? You're not staying here."

"Then what," she said, voice terse with fear, "do you suggest I do?"

"I suggest you pack up the boy, the dog, the sheep, yourself, and even that damned cat, and come home with me."

"I can't just leave the house empty," she protested, "and we can't all come huddle under your roof."

Jamie gave her a very straight look that told her he'd had about enough of her nonsense for one day. "I'll have someone out here to check the place everyday, and we'll get the police to have a look at the things in the woods. But you and Lawrence cannot stay here any longer."

"I don't want to run, this is my home," she said angrily. "For all we know whoever is in the woods means us no harm. It could be a Gypsy or a tramp."

"Neither scenario is comforting, and it seems unlikely to me that a Gypsy or tramp roams the woods with binoculars in hand," Jamie said grimly. "Be sensible, Pamela, this is your property, someone's trespassing and has been for awhile. It seems doubtful to me that it's for an innocent reason."

"We've got Finbar," she said, knowing it was a ludicrous statement even as she uttered it. As though to punctuate it, Finbar ambled over, tripping on his huge feet and ploughing, headfirst, into Jamie's knees.

"Yes," Jamie said, with no little sarcasm, "there is that."

"I'm not afraid, we'll lock ourselves down every night, and I've the pistol Casey left me. He made certain I know how to use it."

"Could you just once make a decision based on common sense rather than your monumental stubbornness?"

"He's right," Lawrence said, dropping suddenly at her elbow, looking like an underfed wood elf with dried leaves and twigs in his hair. "We'd be best elsewhere for a few days at least."

"*Et tu, Brute?*" she said acerbically.

"Yes, me too."

She was surprised by this sudden volte-face, wondering when Lawrence had decided he no longer wanted Jamie strung up and skewered.

"I've seen ye lookin' over yer shoulder when ye're out of an' evenin' tendin' to the sheep," Lawrence said. "I've felt it meself—hairs up on the back of me neck. An' there's no reason to think he'll not be back, once everyone else leaves an' it's just me an' yerself."

She turned toward Pat, grimly silent to this point, and saw that there would be no support there either. "It's the only thing that makes sense Pamela, Casey'd not want ye here with someone lurkin' through the woods. Ye know anyone doin' that doesn't have good intentions. None of us can stay here twenty-four hours a day; at least under Jamie's roof ye'll be safe. Or ye can come stay with Sylvie an' myself. It's yer choice, but stayin' here is not one of yer options."

She sighed. "All right, but only for a few days, whoever it is has probably been scared off. Come on, young man," she nodded at Lawrence, "you can pack up the animals, while I get our clothes and things together."

Pat stayed back with Jamie, eyes still moving from one item to the next.

"Who do ye think it is?" he asked when Pamela and Lawrence were well out of hearing, though they could still see their silhouettes as they approached the lights of the house.

"Were I a betting man," Jamie said, bending to pick up the small shred of cellophane. "I'd put every farthing I possess on Robin Temple."

"Aye," Pat rejoined darkly, "so would I. What next then?"

There was a certain grim anticipation in Jamie's voice when he responded, and Pat thought if he didn't dislike Robin so much, he might have found it in him to feel a bit of pity for what the man had set loose upon himself.

"I think we need to have a chat with our bonny Robin."

Chapter Forty-eight

If I Were a Blackbird

THE WARY PEACE LASTED ANOTHER FEW WEEKS and then was abruptly blown apart. Almost literally, as it turned out. Casey was out having a smoke by the wire with Declan, who was grumbling his usual litany of complaint about Roland's attempts to whitewash his soul, when Matty, fair hair on end, came rushing out.

"Christ, what's happened, Matty? Ye're white to the lips," Declan said, stubbing his cigarette out on the fencing that surrounded them.

"They've found the makins' of a bomb in our quarters. Stash of sugar an' some bleach under Shane's bunk."

Those two items were all that were needed, along with a bit of water, to rip a heavy-duty postbox in half. In large enough amounts it could do real damage on board the ship.

Casey swore softly under his breath. "What was the silly bastard thinkin' of?"

Matty shook his head, "I don't imagine thinkin' played a great part in what he did."

They went quiet then as the Sergeant strode out on deck, bony face suffused cherry with rage. Behind him came four soldiers, all blank-faced and sternly at attention. He began without preamble.

"It has come to my attention that someone among you is stockpiling explosives," the words were aimed at them all, but the Sergeant's pale eyes never left Shane's face. Explosives seemed a rather grand term for the bit of sugar and bleach that had been found, but Casey knew it was as bad as if they'd all been caught with ten pounds of Semtex each under their bunks.

"This is a very serious offense. The lives of many good men are reliant upon my vigilance in such situations, as such I cannot take this discovery lightly. It would be best for all concerned if the man responsible steps forward. Otherwise, all will be punished with extreme prejudice."

Casey didn't even want to contemplate what this man might mean by those terms. The riding crop was being drawn through and through the Sergeant's hand now, and despite himself Casey couldn't take his eyes from it.

"Shall I tell you what I'll do if none of you confesses?"

No answer from the small huddle of them.

"Well then, I'll tell you," he smiled luxuriantly, like a cream-fed cat. "To begin with there will be no more family visits, no mail, no parcels to make your miserable lives bearable. Each of you will be questioned separately at *length.*" His tongue lingered over length, suggesting all manner of pain and misery. "I'm authorized to use all means at my disposal to keep the soldiers of Her Majesty's army safe, and to ensure that safety at any cost. This ship is a world unto itself; the Geneva Conventions don't apply here."

None of them moved, though Shane was getting noticeably twitchy.

"Or perhaps we can keep the visits and make it—how shall I put this— very undesirable for your wives and sweethearts to come pay a call." The pale eyes were hooded now, but Casey could feel their gaze upon him.

Beside him he could feel Shane's entire body straining to move forward and held just as hard in place by the fear that had him firm in its grip. There was something very ugly in the Sergeant's face and even Shane wasn't naïve enough to miss it.

Casey took a deep breath and stepped forward. "'Twas me," he said firmly.

In his peripheral vision he saw Matty's head snap around, and heard Declan swear under his breath.

The sergeant stopped mid-stride, the cat-like smile spreading across his face. "Was it then?"

Casey swallowed, knowing he'd just handed the man what he'd wanted from the first. "Aye, it was."

The man slapped his palm smartly with the riding crop, an affectation that had caused the men no little amusement. Just at present, though, Casey didn't find the sight of it the least bit funny.

"Well, Mr. Riordan, that makes you a very silly boy, and as such you'll have to take the punishment of your actions." He turned toward the young Scot. "Private Campbell, you'll bring the prisoner to me in ten minutes. I refuse to have insubordination on this ship." He walked off with his goose-stepping walk, though Casey fancied there was a joy in the step that he'd not seen before.

The men started buzzing about him right off, excepting Shane who remained silent, dark eyes trained on his feet.

"They can't do this," Declan said firmly, as though merely saying it would make it fact.

"There aren't any rules out here, other than those of their makin'," Casey said dryly, "it's up to us how we manage to survive it."

"'Tisn't yer punishment to take," Roland said with a pointed look in Shane's direction. The boy looked completely miserable now. The men would go hard on him, Casey knew, but perhaps not as hard as the Sergeant.

"It's done, Roland, and that's an end to it, understood?" Casey's tone brooked no disagreement and Roland reluctantly nodded. "Now, if yez don't mind, I'd have a minute alone with Matty."

The men moved off with much muttering and dark looks in Shane's direction.

"Don't let them go too hard on the lad, will ye? I'm not takin' his punishment in order to have them be worse on him than the soldiers would have been."

Matty shook his head. "Are ye mad? That bastard's had it in for you since the day we came on this be-damned ship. They'd have batted the boy round a bit, but that man's really goin' to put the boots to you. Don't take Shane's punishment for him; he needs the lesson of it."

Casey shook his head, face impassive. "I've been in his shoes, Matty, an' I remember clear what it felt like to be young an' afraid in such a manner. It'll not be a pleasant way to achieve yer manhood. Besides, ye know how the man looks at the boy—he'll not damage me in that way."

Matty gave him a hard look and then sighed. "Christ, ye're a stubborn bastard, I see there's no swayin' ye from this. Aren't ye a wee bit frightened, though, man?"

Casey smiled ruefully. "Be a damned fool if I wasn't, aye? But not so afraid as I am of what it might do to the boy. I'll manage," he conveyed a confidence with his words that he didn't feel inside.

Matty gave him a speculative look, the stiffening breeze lifting strands of fair, thin hair from his pink scalp. "Ye're friggin' mad, ye know."

"Aye," Casey agreed, "so my wife says."

He hadn't lied, the thought of pain did not frighten him as it once had. Still there was a certain weakness in his knees that no amount of stern talk was going to shore up. He took a deep breath and braced his shoulders, after all he didn't have to enjoy it, just get through it. The young Scots soldier was standing in the doorway and gave him a curt nod, though the man's eyes were filled with a dread sympathy.

"I've been beat before, how much worse can it be?"

CASEY STOOD INSIDE THE SMALL ROOM the young Scot had brought him to, the question he'd posed Matty ringing in his head. He swallowed. It was much worse.

A heavy 4x4 post was bolted to the floor, a crossbeam shackled to its top. A leather neck brace was fitted to the post. They were going to flog him. The skin across his back rippled with dread.

Upon a small table to his left lay the whip. Five-stranded, it was tipped with small lead pellets. Such things had killed men before and were designed to strip a man down to his bones, and more importantly, to break his spirit.

The Sergeant entered just then, as polished and ironed as always. His pale eyes were agleam with a light which Casey had only seen twice before in his life. Neither had been happy occasions. This man enjoyed inflicting pain and planned to take a great deal of pleasure out of Casey in the next few minutes.

The Sergeant wore black gloves, which he tested the fit of before laying a loving stroke on the whip handle. It took everything Casey had not to visibly shudder. His insides had turned to liquid as it was.

"Twenty strokes seems fair enough for the possession of explosives. What say you, Mr. Riordan?"

Casey said nothing. He might have to hand over his pride and his dignity for the next little while, but he'd be damned if the man was getting his words. Twenty strokes though—twenty strokes *might* well kill him.

He removed his own shirt; he would not have them touch him until it was unavoidable.

They tied him with rope, arms spread-eagled to their limits, stretching the skin of his back taut. The leather collar was fastened about his neck, to prevent it from being snapped during the flogging. The splintered wood dug into his forehead. Good, it would help to keep him from fainting. He took as deep a breath as his restraints would allow.

It was much worse than he expected. The first blow would have dropped him to his knees had he not been so securely bound to the post. He closed his eyes, forcing himself to take deep breaths between the strokes. For a moment his wife's face came to mind, but he shoved the vision away. He would not have her here.

His skin didn't break at once, scarred as it was from past abuses. The pain was instant though, his cells flooding with the panicked memory of knives and acid. He needed to focus his mind elsewhere, needed to bring it to a fine point where the pain could not break him.

He began to sing.

> *'I'll tell you a story of a row in the town,*
> *When the green flag went up and the Crown rag came down,*
> *'Twas the neatest and sweetest thing you ever saw,*
> *And they played the best games in Erin Go Bragh.'*

"What the hell is he doing?" the enraged Sergeant demanded.

"I believe he's singing sir," the young Scotsman said.

The whip came down with renewed ferocity. Five. Six. Seven.

> *'One of our comrades was down at Ring's end,*
> *For the honor of Ireland to hold and defend...'*

Casey lost the last two lines of the chorus on the ninth and tenth stroke. Then picked the song back up on the third verse.

> *'Now here's to Tom Pearce and our comrades who died*
> *Tom Clark, McDunna, McDurmott, McBride...'*

"Stop singing, you stubborn bastard!" the Sergeant shrieked. Casey braced himself, knowing the next blow would be the worst.

The tip of the outside pellet came around and tore the skin across the bottom of his ribs, gouging its ounce of flesh out as the whip was snatched back. Passing out would be a mercy at this point. He was singing through gritted teeth now, the words barely more than a forced mumble. The refrain a black mist in his head that he fought to hold onto.

On the twelfth stroke he briefly lost consciousness until a soldier with frightened eyes hunkered down and looked up into his face.

"Throw water on his face if he's fainted," the sergeant barked out.

"Stop singing," the soldier hissed urgently, "for Christ's sake stop singing! You're goading him."

"Fuck off," Casey said with as much force as he could manage. Then with a great gathering of will continued his singing.

> *'One brave English captain was ranting that day,*
> *Saying, 'Give me one hour and I'll blow you away,''*

Thirteen.

> *But a big Mauser bullet got stuck in his craw,*
> *And he died of lead poisoning in Erin Go Bragh.'*

Fourteen.

> *'And our children will tell how their forefathers saw,*

Fifteen.

He pressed his head hard into the wood on the last line and shouted the last line, blood spraying out with the words from where he'd bit through his tongue on the fourth stroke.

> *The red blaze of freedom in Erin Go Bragh.'*

Sixteen.

The blood was warm where it ran in streams down his back.

Seventeen. Eighteen.

He was going to pass out again. Could feel it approaching and welcomed it.

Nineteen.

Twenty.

"Sir, you have to stop now, you have to."

He was still conscious, more's the pity. The soldier who'd spoken undid the leather collar around Casey's neck and he slumped against the post, head on the crossbeam. Then the boy began working on the ropes. It took a moment before it came loose, giving Casey a small reprieve in which to find his legs, which he couldn't feel. The last knot came free and he staggered slightly, then caught himself. He'd not collapse in front of the bastards.

"We're taking you to the infirmary," the guard with the frightened eyes said.

"Keep yer fuckin' hands off me," Casey snarled, making a controlled effort to reach the door. His legs were going to bear him about thirty steps at the absolute most and he intended to be back among his own before he let the weakness overtake him. The entire universe had distilled itself to these next few seconds. He would not, he *could* not show how badly they'd hurt him. However, the distance to the door seemed to be growing exponentially with every step he managed. Then he heard the oiled silk voice of the Sergeant behind him.

"And that, lads, is how you teach the Irish to come to heel."

Casey stopped and turned very slowly, very carefully, and met the pale blue eyes of the Sergeant. A great stillness filled the room.

"Englishman," he said. The other men backed away slightly from the Sergeant, eyes flicking nervously toward the exit door. "Ye'd best grow eyes in the back of yer head, for ye'll need them to see me coming. And I will come. *Tusa duine fear.*" Then with great precision, he spit at the man's feet. He saw through his rapidly shrinking vision that he'd sprayed a great quantity of blood on the man's highly polished boots and creased trousers.

"What did he say—you Campbell—do you know?"

"I believe," the young Scots soldier replied quietly, "he's called ye a dead man."

Casey staggered forward, the door within reach now. He pushed through and from a great distance heard Matty exclaim, "Jesus Mary an' the Saints, what have they done to ye!?"

Then, with a sense of vague relief, Casey passed out at Declan's feet.

AND THEN SUDDENLY, as startling as a sharp cry in the midst of a profound stillness, it was night. A night like slate, without reflection or redemption. A black that sat hard upon his shoulders, weighty and consuming.

"I'm lost," he said, voice hollow and small.

"No ye're not," came the impatient reply, "how can ye be lost inside yer own head? 'Tisn't as if ye can fall off the edge of the earth without noticin'. As long as there's ground beneath yer feet an' a sky above yer head ye're not lost."

"But it's so dark, I can't see the sky nor the ground," he retorted, feeling some small flicker of annoyance at the voice.

"Ye don't need to see to know there's sky an' earth. When did ye lose trust in every

sense but yer eyes? Can ye not feel?"

He was about to say 'no', when suddenly he did feel it. Stones, smooth and lucent beneath his feet, his bones curving gently to follow the round, hefted shape of them. A kinship through the soles of his feet, pure and unthinking, to the things of the earth. As a child he'd never worn shoes, couldn't stand the constriction of them. In the city, of course, he'd had to. But in the summers he'd discarded them in a heap and ignored them until his autumn return to pavement and gray, grassless spaces. He had understood as a child what he had forgotten as a man, that through the soles of one's feet one could feel a connection to the divine, to rock and dirt and water, to young, greening things only beginning, and to falling, tumbling browning things, sliding down into the darkness of ending. Through that bond of feet and earth he had known a wisdom beyond words, a knowing that lay on the far side of the bounds of language. So much he had forgotten, so much blurred in the blind complexities of adult emotion.

He closed his eyes against the suffocating darkness, it was easier to breathe with eyes sealed against night. His feet found stone upon stone—lichen-damped, salt-crusted, moss-furled—and then the scents of boyhood rose all about him, juices released by skin and sole. The smell of dirt, equal parts water and sunshine with an underlying hint of something far darker. How you could almost taste the iridescence of a bumblebee's gauzed wing, the skitter of a beetle's feet across dry leaves, the shimmer and flash of a trout in a brown stream.

And the feel of water, its chill so prescient that it was like needles pouring through and around his skin. He realized suddenly that the feeling was not memory, but that he stood, knee-deep in cold, rippling silver. He gasped, unable to remember the last time he'd felt something—any element, so deeply, so clearly. He opened his eyes, looked down, looked deep and saw something glimmer there, sparkle like a delicate trill of laughter. Instinctively he reached for it but it shattered and scattered in a thousand different directions beneath and between his fingers.

'Never could keep ye clean or dry for long, boy,'' said a voice that was part of his very cells.

'Da,' he tried to say, tongue dry as sand and working against a throat swollen with fear.

"Walk with me, boy. The night is fine for it."

"I can't, I'm hurt," he said.

"The rules don't apply here, son, just put one foot in front of the other, ye'll do fine."

And suddenly he was walking, a high road thick with the scent of late summer clover and a moist salt wind. It seemed to him as though they walked forever and the road did not end, and yet it also seemed only seconds before his father stopped.

They stood upon the crest of a hill, the road running off into the horizon, through mountain and stream, across field and wood.

"Do ye remember I once told ye that the sky above yer head an' the earth below yer feet were sometimes all ye would have, an' that it would have to be enough?"

"Aye, I remember all ye ever told me, Da."

"I was wrong to say that. The truth is, all ye'll ever need is in yer hands."

Casey looked down in startlement, realizing that some small weight was indeed cradled in his hands. A tiny seed, blue green in color, nestled there.

"As small as a seed, as large as the universe—call it love, call it spirit. None can take it from ye, an' ye don't allow it. An' that, boy, is sometimes all ye'll have, but it will always be enough."

Casey peered up through the darkness of the night, seeking his father's face, but a thick mist shrouded it and he could not see Brian well at all.

"I miss ye, Da," he said, sensing his presence even if he could not see him.

"And I you, Patrick as well," his father said simply. "Ye'll have been angry when I died. I left ye with a big burden to carry. It wasn't how I'd have chosen to have ye find yer manhood."

"Aye," Casey admitted, "I was angry for a long time, I didn't understand. I felt ye'd been careless."

Brian brushed a gentle thumb along his cheekbone. "I don't expect ye to understand, don't myself at times, but I think it's a bit like Van Gogh said."

"What do ye mean?"

"He wrote a letter to his brother Theo an' said that he thought disease was like a ticket on a train to the stars, to die of old age meant ye'd walked there on foot. Same destination, different speeds. I suppose what I'm sayin' is we're all meant to get there in our own time. My ticket came up long before I expected is all." His father's voice was beginning to drift apart like the smoke from a dying fire.

"Da, I can't hear ye well." Casey felt panic building in his chest, he didn't know the way back without his father's hand to guide him.

"Don't take yer life for granted, that's all."

"I don't, Da."

"Look down son, look at yer hands."

He looked down into his palms and saw light, innumerable and uncountable, light clear and swift, breathtaking in its purity.

"Ye're holdin' stardust laddie, be careful not to spill it," Brian said, words no more than a whisper, a sound of the sea in the great distance or the wind through the leaves on a summer night.

The light began to rise into the air, starring the night that surrounded them with a million fireflies...

"Daddy," he whispered, throat pained with all the words he couldn't seem to say. He took Brian's hand, wanting to feel safe, to know once again the broad strength and reassurance of it around his own. But it didn't feel right, the bones were too fine and short, not like his da's. He looked up quickly, panic already thick and clotting in his veins to find that he could no longer see Brian's face. "Daddy, don't go!" he screamed, but knew that there was no sound, only the clamoring inside his skull.

"It's all right, man, it's all right, ye're just havin' a bad dream—where's the damn cloth gone to?"

Casey tried to keep hold of the dark, of the dream, but it slid through his grasp like stars at dawn, fleeting and seemingly unreal. It wasn't his father's voice in his ear, nor his father's hand stroking the hair back from his face.

He tried to sit up but the pain was immediate and nauseating, causing him to collapse at once.

"Just lay still, man," the voice above him said, and he realized he'd been dreaming, his father gone like smoke against wind, as if he'd never existed. Something hot and scalding surged at the back of his throat.

"Christ get the pail, he's goin' to be sick," said Matty's voice.

Matty was right, he was sick, though there was little in his stomach to get rid of. Every heave started a ripple effect of pain. His ribs felt like they were being scraped with shards of glass and his back felt like one big raw wound. The nausea finally ebbed, leaving him weak as a newborn kitten. Matty wiped his face gently with the wet cloth.

"Thank Christ, man, we were worried ye were never goin' to wake."

Casey opened one eye, the effort sapping what little strength he had left. The room spun like a top and he abruptly shut the eye again. His back stung like a thousand fires, and he could feel the tightness of freshly wealed scars. He wanted nothing more than to pass back into oblivion for the foreseeable future.

"Don't move too much," Matty said, patting the back of his head gently. "Declan checked ye over an' two of yer ribs are broke. He strapped 'em as best he could, but he had to be careful of the open cuts on yer back. They made a right mess of ye, boy, but Declan says ye'll heal up nice an' be right as rain in a few weeks. Mayhap there'll be a few more scars but as ye're not a lassie, we didn't think it'd matter so much to ye."

From the way Matty was babbling Casey knew he must be in even worse shape than he himself had suspected.

"Quit cluckin' Matty, ye're makin' me dizzy. Be honest, how bad is it?"

"Pretty bad," Matty admitted.

Casey cracked an eye again; the room was wobbly but not spinning. "Where are we?"

"Infirmary," Matty said. "Declan an' Roland packed ye here an' Roland has slept across the door every night, refusin' to let the bastards in, an' Declan's not had more than a wink or two."

Declan hove into view. "Wasn't goin' to let the bastards touch ye if it could be helped. We demanded a doctor brought in from town."

"That's unprecedented," Casey said. "How long have I been out?"

"Three days," Declan answered, "we kept ye doped so ye'd not wake. Thought it best that way. Ye've a few stitches in yer back an' the rest is only skinned over, so ye'll have to stay still as best as ye can manage."

Casey drifted out again, hearing snatches of an argument between Declan and Roland over whether lapsed Catholics, after a suitable stint in purgatory, would be allowed into heaven. Matty was smoothing some kind of smelly ointment onto his back and the pain had settled to a low ebb. They must have given him something, he felt as though all his edges were blurred and even the long open channels in his back were undefined.

The next time he surfaced, he discovered the Sergeant had been 'removed' from the ship less than twenty-four hours after the flogging.

"Think the wee Scot had somethin' to do with that, what happened didn't seem to his taste." Declan said. "Mind we'd not have allowed the bastard near to ye again. Told them we weren't leavin' ye in the infirmary alone, not after what they'd done to ye. Once we got in here, they locked it down an' we've been here ever since. Could ye stand a cup of tea, laddie?"

Casey managed a weak nod, though when the tea arrived he had to drink it through a straw that the men had pulled from the medical supply cupboard. Even at that he only managed four sips before passing out again.

When next he woke it was night and only Matty was awake. He could hear the buzz saw of Roland snoring, and heard Declan muttering in his sleep. The noises made him feel oddly safe. Matty was reading, a small light hovering over the book.

"Thank ye for lookin' after me," Casey said, throat raspy and dry from the drugs and the three-day slumber. "I appreciate it, my da always said ye were a kind man."

"Did he then?" Matty said, sounding pleased. "Yer da was a kind man as well, always looked after anyone weaker than himself."

"He said it was a man's duty to look after those that couldn't do for themselves. He never questioned it, nor blamed them for their weakness; he just did what he felt necessary."

"Like his son that way, I'd say."

"I don't feel so strong right now," Casey said quietly.

"No, I don't imagine that ye do, lad, but ye're made of a finer mettle than I've seen in many a year. Yer da would be proud."

"No, he'd think me a pigheaded fool."

"Aye well, laddie, seems to me the two things are much the same at times."

The pages of Matty's book rustled as he leaned forward to hold a straw to Casey's lips. The water was fine as champagne on his tongue, but he drank it too quickly and began to cough. The pain was instant and fiery.

"Not so quick, lad," Matty admonished. "Yer body can't afford to cough just yet."

The bout of coughing left him weak and dizzy. He closed his eyes and found himself fighting tears, as broken down as he was physically he found his emotions equally fragile.

"Yer da once told me ye reminded him strong of his own da, an that he saw the same strengths in ye an' the same capacity of spirit."

"Did he?" Casey asked.

"He did."

"I hope I can be half the man he was someday, I'd not like to think I'd let him down too badly." Casey shivered, the skin of his back was so sensitive the slightest move in the air currents raised a sheathe of goosebumps on him.

"Are ye cold, lad?"

"Aye, a bit."

Matty laid a sheet of gauze over his back then drew a blanket carefully over top of it. "I think I'll take a wink or two, lad, do ye mind if I turn the light out?"

"No, I don't mind." The dark settled over the room like the touch of a mother's hand, soothing and peaceful.

Matty settled with a rustle into his own narrow cot and Casey could hear the quiet click of his rosary beads begin. The man always prayed before sleep. He began to pray himself, but kept losing the thread of what he wanted to say in the pull toward unconsciousness.

When Matty spoke, the words seemed to come from a great distance, though he could hear every one.

"Yer da was a rare man, an' I'll admit I was drawn to ye for the sake of his memory at first." Matty was quiet for a long space, and Casey thought he'd fallen asleep until his voice, quiet and soft, came once again through the dark. "But I've stayed near for the sake of the man I found in his son."

SHANE'S FACE WAS NOT MARKED, but the boy moved with a hesitant stiffness that told Casey he'd paid for the flogging in his own manner. Still, what had happened here with these men was less severe than what the boy would have suffered at the hands of the soldiers. Casey was glad to have spared him that. And now that he'd been taught his lesson in their own language, there was a chance they might forgive him.

On Casey's first night back in the hold with the other men, he was hard put to find sleep. All the men had greeted him jovially, faces tight with smiles they did not feel. They were afraid now, each man realizing he could be culled from the relative security of the group and broken on the wheel of isolation. He was the embodiment of their worst fears. It was silent, the men pretending to sleep, the nightly sharing of stories and life experiences bypassed in their discomfort. Only the occasional hiccoughing snuffle broke the quiet, coming from the vicinity of young Shane's bunk.

He could hear the men rustle in the dark, making unnecessary noise to cover the sound of the boy's crying. They would both hate and pity him, and yet knew the tears were of little use, for there would always be more to cry. Most of the men here had been incarcerated before and, though not fond of the situation, were wearily resigned to it. No Irish Republican was a stranger to the interior of a prison cell. But Casey remembered what it had been like as a boy, the fear that took you hard in the knees and belly, turning your intestines to water. There had been no one to comfort him and he'd never been more alone in his life. He sighed and sat up, pulling the threadbare blanket tight around his shoulders, and leaned against the wall, knobs of riveted steel cold and hard against his spine. There'd be no rest for him until the boy found some peace, and perhaps a bit of hope to hang onto.

His voice slipped a bit on the first few words and then found itself and continued on, gaining in strength as the notes slid off his tongue.

> *'I am a young sailor,*
> *My story is sad*
> *For once I was carefree*
> *And a bold sailor lad*
> *I courted a lassie*
> *By night and by day*
> *But now she has left me*
> *And gone far away.*

In the dark around him another voice joined, soft and tuneless, and then another low and rough, rising into the chill air like ghosts and memories unbound by the night.

> *Oh if I was a blackbird,*
> *Could whistle and sing*
> *I'd follow the vessel*
> *My true love sails in*
> *And in the top rigging*
> *I would there build my nest*
> *And I'd flutter my wings*
> *O'er her lily-white breast.*

Casey closed his eyes and allowed the music to work its magic, to feel as he had not allowed himself to in the many weeks past, since he'd been torn from his wife and home. Music had always allowed him release, the notes, pure as a thrush's warble, giving him permission to feel, a brief moment where he didn't have to count the cost against tomorrow.

The voices gathered around him in the dark, as good a promise as an oath. These men would stand by him, these men, for reasons he himself did not understand, had chosen him as their leader.

He finished the song alone, the notes singular and lonely, absorbed into the skin and breath of each man there.

Sleep came then for others, there was the rustle of men settling in, the faltering rumble of early sleep snores. Casey stayed awake for a long time after, watching the sky through the cracked porthole, feeling strangely at peace. In the music he'd felt the last lingering of his father's presence which had clung like smoke since the dream. In an odd way he knew his Daddy had said goodbye. Not goodbye forever, but for now.

He settled himself, drawing the blanket over his still tender shoulder and closing his eyes.

Chapter Forty-nine

Midnight Secrets

I T WAS THE MOANING OF THE WIND that woke her. A storm had been threatening all evening, black clouds boiling up over the hills and laying low across the city. It had finally broken near bedtime, though the wind had built considerably in fury since she'd fallen into her troubled sleep.

Pamela came to with a start, as though someone had clapped their hands by her ear. She was tangled up in the linens, heart pounding, an old jersey of Casey's rucked up above her waist.

At first she thought she was in her own bed and reached out instinctively to touch Casey. But the pillow beside her was empty, as it had been for months now.

She put her hand automatically to her stomach, a slight mound beneath the soothing of her cupped palm. It was tight now with the residual spasms of her dream. Christ, her whole body was thrumming, her skin taut and fevered, heart pounding and flesh still arching up toward a man who was not there. She blew out a breath of pure frustration, still feeling the smooth calloused touch of his big hands, floating along the surface of her body like water over smooth stone.

"Damn it!" She scrubbed her hands through her hair, pulling the sweaty strands away from her face, where it clung to her skin like seaweed, clammy and cold. The man, dream or no, might have had the good grace to finish things before she awoke to a bed empty of his presence.

She tugged the jersey down and untangled her legs from the sheets, remembering where she was. Jamie's house, with Lawrence only a door down the hall.

It was her old room, still with the same bed and luxuriant linens. Her fingers traced the graceful scrawling 'K' that denoted the House of Kirkpatrick upon the pillowcases.

Her stomach rippled again, this time with the movements of its occupant, though. She felt a wash of relief go through her. She was worried that the baby didn't seem to be growing as it should at this stage of pregnancy, so every movement was a reassurance that the child was still thriving. Still, the size of her belly hadn't increased markedly in the last month and a half, and it was scaring her.

She sighed and swung her legs over the side of the bed. It was becoming all too familiar, this hour of the night. She glanced at the clock, though she hardly needed to do so. It was just after two o'clock, a time she seemed incapable of sleeping through.

She stood. The room was warm enough to walk about bare-legged. The peat fire in the hearth had been built before she retired to bed, as it had been every night since she'd arrived here. Jamie, as always, saw to their every comfort and need.

She put her hand to the window and shivered. It was icy to the touch. Outside the sleet lashed at the trees, bending them over so that it seemed they must snap. Away from the muffling comfort of the bed, the wind was louder, the wail in the chimney chill and mournful like the screech of a banshee. She shuddered; all that was missing was a great black coach rumbling up the drive, pulled by six headless horses.

At least the spooky aura of the rain-lashed night had taken away the last remnants of her dream, the third such dream she'd had this week alone. Deprivation dreams—frustrating as heck, unfulfilling as all get out. And then she'd awaken guilty, wondering if Casey slept, was he warm, was he well? Did he too dream of her, in the crowded berth of the ship among men who also dreamed of absent girlfriends and wives? She half hoped he was as frustrated as she, that even dreams could not give him release, that he needed the tangible presence of her to find completion, as it seemed she did with him.

Not all people shared her current state, though. Some people were not lonely, it seemed, in the least.

Kirkpatrick's Folly, basking in the chill mists of late November, should have been a bastion of peace and quiet. Rather it seemed to be the crossroads of all Ulster at present. And at the center of the swarm of travelers, all looking for instruction, direction and comfort, stood his Lordship of Ballywick and Tragheda, James Kirkpatrick. There were many people who sought his attention, and to all of them he gave a courteous listening ear, rendered what help he could, and then politely showed them the door.

With children, however, he was pure magic. He understood how to talk to them, but more importantly how to listen, and he gave their concerns the same serious consideration he would give the MPs he sat with in the House. And to none did he accord more of his magic than small Nelson McGlory, for in this young boy Jamie had found the stalwart knight to his own role of king.

Nelson, whose father had been killed when the brakes on his milk truck had failed on a steep incline, had found the father figure of his dreams in Jamie. Nelson was small, with a leaky nose, messy brown hair and glasses that distorted his large brown eyes to mad scientist proportions. He was an intensely smart little boy, with a fiercely loyal heart that he had given in its entirety to Jamie. And Jamie, being who he was, treated Nelson with all the gentle respect that a true knight deserved, but did not make promises his heart was no longer capable of keeping. Three sons lay under the cold earth of the Kirkpatrick land, and with them lay a part of Jamie's very soul that he counted forever lost.

Nelson, though very young in body, seemed possessed of a much older spirit and only took what Jamie could manage to give. He was a half-permanent fixture in the house and was often underfoot in the stables, pestering the grooms. Or he could be found in the kitchen, tucking into one of Maggie's savory stews or the endless stream of baked goods that came from her oven at all hours of the day.

Twice weekly he played chess with Jamie, who accorded him the respect of never letting him win unless he'd done it fairly. Pamela had come upon them during one of their games just two nights ago. She'd been wanting something to read, and had gone to the study to browse Jamie's shelves. She had halted in the spilling light of the study doorway, transfixed by the scene before her.

Jamie's fair head was bent over the game, gleaming more brightly than the quartz-inlaid board. Nelson had said something and suddenly Jamie leaned back and laughed—loudly—with a complete abandonment that he rarely allowed himself. It lit the room, that sound, and pierced her heart through like a needle. She had fled back up the stairs without a book, unable to understand what had so bothered her about the scene in the study.

And then an unpleasant thought had struck her; it was because she was no longer part of his inner circle. He was always kind to her, caring and solicitous of her every need and want, and yet it was the care one took for a guest. Not the easy relationship she had once enjoyed with him when she had last lived under his roof. Not that it had *always* been easy. He'd disapproved of her relationship with Casey from the start and they had both, at different points, declared their love to each other only to have it thrown back in their respective faces. No, not always comfortable, nor easy, but still something had changed and she knew that she stood slightly outside the charmed circle of golden light that Jamie allowed only a very chosen few to enter.

With Lawrence, who was suspicious of anyone whose last name wasn't Riordan, it was a different kettle of fish altogether. Jamie, knowing this, was careful with the small inroads he made, and slowly but surely Pamela saw small signs that Lawrence was thawing in his attitude. That the boy could not trust easily was something Jamie respected. He also understood that Casey stood ten feet tall in Lawrence's eyes, and his current incarceration had served to make that estimation grow another foot or two. And so with Lawrence, Jamie trod very carefully. His method appeared to be working, for the frostbitten glares that Lawrence had once served to Jamie regularly were now warming to a grudging respect and liking.

With small Nelson McGlory attached like a limpet to his person, Jamie managed to sort out the household, directing things smoothly, leaving the nuts and bolts to Maggie who, after all these years, deferred to no one in either the kitchen or in her protectiveness of the master. Jamie understood what served him well in such matters.

Though Pamela had not forgotten his preternatural competence in dealing with twenty matters simultaneously, it was still a wonder to behold him in action. He was charged with an inner fire, had the energy of five men, and seemed to shed this light upon all in his wake. Somehow, though, that light, which had once warmed her, now left her only chilled and lonelier than ever.

And then, of course, there was the matter of Belinda.

There was, rather unfortunately, no denying that she was lovely. Possessed of flawless pink and white skin, dulcet blue eyes and hair of a burnished bronzey-gold, she also had ownership of charm, wit and a sense of humor, and she was entirely enamored of Jamie. It showed in the way she was always touching him, the way she watched him as he entered and exited from the room, and the low, throaty tone she most often used when speaking to him.

Pregnant, pale and dealing with a teenager with more than his normal share of angst, anger and general attitude, Pamela was predestined to find Belinda incredibly maddening. Not that Belinda was in any way charmed by her own presence in Jamie's house. In fact, it would be fair to say that the two of them had hated each other on first sight. Yes, Belinda was definitely a woman in love, and Pamela, having stood in her shoes, could hardly blame her. It was something else that bothered her. For Jamie had every appearance of being a man in love.

It was what she had wanted for Jamie, that he find someone to love who loved him in turn. And yet the emotion she felt every time the two of them were in a room with her didn't feel a great deal like happiness on Jamie's behalf. It felt rather a lot, unfortunately, like jealousy.

A flicker of movement in the grounds below caught her eye, snatching her from her ruminations. A man was moving through the shrubs near the house. She stepped back from the window, knowing the white stripes on the jersey would make her stand out against the darkness like a neon bumblebee.

Before she could think about what she was doing, she was in the dark hall outside her room heading toward the stairs. She hesitated on the landing, hearing the house breathe around her. It was quiet on the upper floor, but she'd the sense that below someone was still awake. Not that that was unusual; Jamie was a night owl and often read or did paperwork in his study until the wee hours of the morning.

She slipped down the stairs in the watery half-light that crept up from the bottom of the stairwell. There was a draft coming from the lower floor that chilled her instantly, peppering her legs with goosebumps. Though the house was old and large, normally it kept its heat well. The draft told her that someone had opened a door or a window, and the cold November air had rushed into the house.

So not an intruder then, but a guest? But what sort of guest showed up in the pre-dawn hours? One that couldn't risk being seen, or one with whom Jamie couldn't risk being seen.

The study door was oak, heavy and ancient, nothing short of a scream could be heard through it, except that it possessed a keyhole, that while narrow, was always kept carefully oiled and through some freak of acoustics, amplified the noise within the study.

She held her breath, wondering why she didn't just very sensibly go back up the stairs, get in her warm bed, and mind her own business. All the while positioning her ear toward the small stream of light that pooled through the arc of the keyhole.

Jamie was speaking, the flowing cadences of his voice instantly recognizable, spiked with the occasional sardonic or sharp note. She frowned when the other man spoke. Despite the heavy *thrump* of her pulse in her ears, she could make out his words more clearly than Jamie's. The voice was without a doubt British, upper class, and Oxford in its modulations, lacking only the rich buttery undertones of Jamie's vowels. Those vowels were the only thing that betrayed the Irish origin of Jamie's tongue.

And then two words were spoken that would have frozen her to the spot, were her feet not welded like chunks of ice to the flagstones already. The two words were spoken by Jamie, and it was then she understood just how dangerous a game he was playing.

"If you'll forgive my saying so Lord Kirkpatrick, you'd be a fool to attempt it."

She strained forward, hearing only a low laugh and a murmur from Jamie, but was frustratingly unable to make out his exact words. A fool to attempt what, exactly? What *was* the bloody man up to now? And with whom? These cogitations were rudely interrupted by the feel of tiny, freezing cold paws running across one of her feet. She jumped back, clapping a hand to her mouth to stem the shriek that rose instinctively.

She looked down and saw a small gray mouse up on his hind legs, looking inquisitively at her. She glared at him, silently cursing his timing. The mouse, however, merely blinked bright black eyes at her, and being obviously in possession of a wisdom far superior to her own, scurried off to his warm dark hole somewhere in the wainscoting.

After an exclamation from inside the study, a deadly silence filled the narrow keyhole along with the flickering firelight. She stepped back, not even daring to breathe. Jamie would be furious if he found her lurking out here in the hall.

"Nothing I'm sure," she heard Jamie's tone, soothing and reassuring the man in his study, "I've been having a wee problem with mice snooping about for crumbs—rather large mice."

She resisted the urge to stick her tongue out at the door, knowing that the last remark had been for her benefit and that Jamie was fully aware of her presence on the freezing flagstones.

She waited a moment for the conversation to resume inside the study, then she slowly crept back to the stairs, her legs numb with cold, feet aching from the bare stones.

She climbed partway up and sat in the curve of the stairs, where shadows clustered thick and deep enough to hide in.

The Trustees—those were the two words Jamie had spoken which had sent a shock through her system. Words that were enough to chill the very blood to ice in her veins. She had, of course, heard the rumors—a group of affluent and highly placed men, all Protestant, lawyers, bankers, accountants, clergy, and CEOs that funded and directed a Loyalist assassination squad in a campaign of terror and murder. Though it would now seem that it was more than a simple rumor. She was suddenly terrified for Jamie. He was walking on a knife-edge precipice where one misstep would result in certain death.

She tucked her arms tight around her body, as if she could quell the fear that welled up dark and cold from her depths by the mere act of doing so.

Her head was spinning with too many questions that didn't seem to have any easy answers—the mysterious notes with their dark-inked rings, the Trustees and all the other innumerable splinter groups that had split off from the main bodies of idealism, and its flip side—hatred. There were too many to keep track of, some half rumored, some acknowledged, some existing only in the hissed whispers and dark corners of seedy pubs and cold meetings in the empty countryside.

She shivered, thinking of the meeting she had agreed to two days hence, in a very lonely corner of countryside. She hadn't told Pat that it was on, as the low voice on the telephone had told her to come alone or there would be no meeting at all. Pat would be furious when he found out, but she would deal with that later.

A hand gripped her knee—hard. Her hand flew to her chest, heart going like a trip hammer. "Christ! You scared the bejesus out of me!"

Jamie, standing three stairs below her, lifted a sardonic eyebrow.

"You didn't do a great deal for me either. What the hell are you doing sleeping on the stairs?" His eyes raked over her, and she flushed hotly, aware suddenly that in her curiosity, she'd not paused to pull extra clothing on, and that the jersey rather inadequately covered her thighs, which were glowing milkily in the dim light of the stairwell.

She pulled the jersey down as much as possible, unable to meet Jamie's eyes. His sharp tone had not only startled her, but had rather hurt her feelings as well. Jamie rarely got annoyed with her, and so when he did it always came as an unpleasant surprise, like being flicked with a leather strap when you weren't expecting it. She looked up, meeting the chill green of his eyes, and realized suddenly that not only was he angry, he was also afraid.

"Your feet must be freezing," he said dryly, "the stones outside the study door get very cold this time of year."

"I—I—" she stuttered.

"Yes? You—you what?"

"I saw someone walking up to the back of the house. They seemed to be sneaking. At first I thought it was a burglar and then," she faltered under the green eyes, which were simmering with an anger he rarely displayed, but that could wither all in its path when let loose.

"And then what? You charged downstairs half-naked, not even stopping for socks to confront the burglar?"

"I'm not half-naked," she said indignantly, tugging angrily at the jersey to little avail.

Jamie merely raised a gull-winged brow.

"I'm going back to bed," she said, "I'm freezing and—"

"Oh no you're not," Jamie smoothly interrupted her. "You're going to come back to the study with me and tell me exactly what you were doing outside the study door, and how much you heard of the conversation."

She considered protesting his highhandedness, but taking a look at his expression, rather meekly followed him down the drafty hallway, the flagstones so cold that her feet ached.

The study by contrast was a haven of warmth and coziness. Jamie threw a blanket at her and shoved a pair of slippers across the carpet with his toes. "Cover up," he said curtly.

She could feel the hated flush flooding her skin to her hairline, but nevertheless put her icy feet in the slippers gratefully. The blanket had been draped over the chair by the fire and was hot to the touch. She wrapped it around her waist, the heated folds clinging to her chilled skin.

Jamie took the chair across from her, looking preternaturally alert for such an ungodly hour. Whatever had been the genesis of the meeting in the study, the result of it had obviously agitated him. The golden hair, falling uncharacteristically long over his collar, was disheveled, and the green eyes were hectically bright. His attic profile did not discharge its normal aloof elegance, but rather a febrile tension that pulsed in the very air, despite the cat-like stillness of his body.

She realized suddenly what it was that had disturbed her about his near manic energy. She had seen him so before, and knew that the glitter preceded a darkness that was so profound it could take months for him to find his way out of it.

"Exactly how much did you hear?" he asked, the tone deceptively mild, though the look in his eyes was anything but.

"Only snatches," she said, feeling like a guilty schoolgirl who'd been caught *en flagrante* with the gym master.

"Enough to gather exactly what we were talking about. I've warned you before what happens to nosy little girls who stick their face too close to the fire."

She ignored the sarcasm. "And who is likely to be burnt in this particular fire?"

"Me," Jamie said calmly. "And possibly the man you overheard, though I hope I can prevent that."

"Stealing government documents though," she said, "that seems an insane risk to take."

"When the stakes are this high, so are the risks."

"You really are an implacable bastard," she said in frustration.

"We're talking about government sponsored murder for hire here; I rather think an implacable bastard is exactly what's called for."

"It's true then?"

"It seems to be."

A needle of ice pricked at her heart. Every time she thought she had seen the worst this country had to offer, it inevitably surprised her by taking the game down to a more frightening and murderous level. Her husband and brother-in-law were in the category of highest risk—male and Catholic. Which included Jamie himself, a fact of which he was no doubt uncomfortably aware.

"If you knew I was out there the whole time, why didn't you say something?"

He closed his eyes and rubbed his fingers hard against the lids. "Because I didn't want my visitor to *know* you were out there. I trust you, him I'm not entirely certain of just yet."

"You trust me? Despite what you know about my past?" she asked softly.

"Shouldn't I? Besides I rather thought you'd given up spying on a professional level."

"I think you rather showed me up for a rank amateur last time I played Mata Hari. Besides, I would never intentionally do you harm, Jamie."

"Good."

"Will telling your contacts help?"

Jamie shook his head. "It might help, or it might open a can of worms that I'm not able to handle. They may be involved, I don't know. Half the time I don't know with whom I'm dealing on the other side."

"So you've chosen a side, then, Jamie?"

"The only side I'm on, Pamela, is that of peace. It's just that peace tends to make for some odd and fairly undesirable bedfellows in this strange little war of ours."

"The man tonight—he was one of those undesirables?"

Jamie shrugged, face inscrutable. "Perhaps, perhaps not. It remains to be seen."

"You're playing with fire here, Jamie."

"And you're not?" He had, with his usual maddening precision lobbed the ball straight back to her. "Investigating Brian Riordan's death?"

She could feel the blood rush out of her face to the vicinity of her midsection.

"Well aren't you?"

"Why don't *you* tell me?" she said tartly, "As you seem to be able to read my mind."

"Your mind," he smiled in an annoying manner, "is about as decipherable as the aperiodic crystals of Assyrian cuneiform."

"Which you've probably been decoding since your third birthday," she retorted, tongue tart as his own.

"Could you try for an instant not to be difficult? You don't understand what's at stake here. One false move, one misstep, and the whole house of cards is going to tumble down."

"Don't tell me to be careful, Jamie Kirkpatrick, don't tell me what I can and cannot do when you play with fire on a daily basis."

"What are you talking about?" he asked as if he'd no notion of what she referred to, but she'd seen the spark of fear in his eyes.

"When was the last time you took your medication, Jamie?" she asked, knowing it was insanity to be having this conversation with him. It wouldn't help the tension that was growing between them like a well-fueled fire.

"Pardon me?" he said, voice calm though the hand around the glass had tightened until the bones showed hard against his skin.

"Your medication, the little pills that are supposed to keep you on an even keel, the ones you're supposed to take every day without fail. How many bottles are sitting in your medicine cabinet unopened? Don't tell me to watch myself when you're risking everything with every day you leave the lid on those bottles."

"Have you been snooping through my things?" His eyes narrowed and elongated the way they always did when he was very, very angry. The firelight struck gold off his hair and glowed in miniature in the depths of his whiskey, lending him the aura of a fallen angel. She swallowed, thinking she might rather face one of the lesser castouts of heaven than James Kirkpatrick in the grip of a black temper.

"Yevgena told me to check," she said defensively, feeling the first tremor of doubt as to her motives.

"And as we know you always do exactly as you're told," he said, voice suddenly smooth as glass. She knew well enough to be alarmed by this.

"Only when it's this important."

"When what is this important?"

"You—your life," she replied, lips dry and tongue thick with panic.

"And why is my life of concern to you?"

"Because...because," she stumbled, "I care for you."

He smiled, though it did nothing to reassure her. "You care for me? How touching, and yet I fail to see how that gives you the right to pry into personal matters and rummage through my things."

This was patently unfair, Pamela thought fuming inwardly. He was the master of meddling in things that were not his affair. "If you can't be bothered to keep yourself back from the precipice, why shouldn't I?"

"Because, quite simply my dear, it's no longer your business."

"Oh," she said in a small voice, feeling that she had been put rather sharply in her place.

Jamie had the grace to look shamefaced. "I didn't mean that quite how it came out. I'm just a bit tired and my head is aching."

"What else is it?"

Jamie gave her a dry look, and then laughed. "I'd forgotten you always read between my lines."

She merely raised a sooty brow in his direction, making it clear he wasn't going to lead her off down a conversational side path.

"I'm maybe a wee bit discouraged. Despite everything I don't seem to be effecting any real change." He took off his glasses, rubbing the marks on his nose that they left behind.

"Jamie Kirkpatrick you're a fool. You've done more than anyone else could have for those people. We're all just caught up in events so much larger than ourselves right now, it's hard to see that making sure Nelson McGlory has new eyeglasses is still important."

This bought her a tepid smile. "It *has* stopped him from walking into telephone poles."

"It all matters, even the small things, and Jamie, you know how important your—," she paused, trying to decide how to most delicately phrase the next few words, "other work is. And I think things are changing, the world press is here in droves."

He gave her a weary look, as though he saw something in her face that made him profoundly sad. "American innocence, what a beautiful commodity and yet what a price it comes at."

"You don't think it helps, all this attention?" she asked, piqued by his comment on the state of her cynicism.

"No, I don't. We're just the latest stop on the atrocity tour, Pamela. They'll hang out at the Europa for a few more months, a few might get addicted to the story and even try to stay and develop an understanding for it, but most will move on as soon as they realize there are no easy answers, if indeed any at all, to the Irish question."

"Don't you believe that any change is possible?"

He paused for a moment before answering, fixing her with a weary look. "Change in increments perhaps. But not the sweeping reforms that those people in the streets are looking for. Unfortunately, after eight hundred years of waiting, nothing less than the world turning upside down and inside out is going to satisfy them. But there isn't going to be a happy ending, at least not anytime soon."

"Oh Jamie, how can you believe that?" she asked, realizing, even as she said it, that she was confirming his opinion as to her political naïveté.

"How many dead people did you photograph these last few weeks?"

"Touché."

"Pamela, you know as well as I do that in any country there are always two histories—that of the politicians and the privileged and that of the dispossessed. In no way do the two histories bear any resemblance to each other. One survives to make its way into textbooks and the annals of history, the other dies with the people who lived it. The journalists aren't here to tell the whole truth. They malign or cozy up to the IRA, depending how many atrocities they've committed in the last month, and when something comes along that's sexier in the business of unofficial war, they'll be gone. Ireland is but a season on the world stage," he shrugged eloquently, "and it plays well on American television. It's just that sometimes what my role is on that stage becomes a little unclear."

"Do you ever think of just leaving the stage and walking off into the sunset—maybe with Belinda?"

He eyed her shrewdly, the firelight casting his face half in shadow, so that his expression was unreadable, though the undercurrent of despair was evident in his words.

"All the time, and yet I'm afraid I'm as much a prisoner of this country as your husband. We've different lines, but we're playing much the same role."

"Except you don't seem to be illegally imprisoned at present," she said, somewhat more sourly than she had intended.

"Do you wish that I were?"

"No, I'm sorry, Jamie."

"Likewise. We both seem to be in less than congenial frames of mind this evening."

"Perhaps it's that we seem unable to be less than honest with one another."

He smiled. "Perhaps."

"I think I'd best get back to bed," she stood, the blanket no longer warm, but still a comfort against her bare legs.

"What you heard tonight—Pamela it goes without saying, you have to keep it to yourself. It's not just me who would be in danger should any of that information get out."

She looked him directly in the eye. "It does go without saying. It always has."

Chapter Fifty

Fire, Fleet and Candlelight

THE MOON CAME UP LOW AND SMOKY over the hills, lending a spectral cast to bony tree limbs and the hunched shoulders of the surrounding hills. The light hadn't managed to seep down to ground level; there shadows clustered thick as club moss. Pamela shivered. Despite several layers of wool and a stout pair of boots, the cold was insidious and seemed to have crept right into her marrow.

She'd parked the car some ways back, behind a hedgerow so tangled with drenched and withered fuchsia that there was no way anyone could spot it.

Now she crouched in a thick stand of wych elm, alternating between looking at her watch and forcing herself to not run back to the car as fast as her shaking legs would carry her. Underfoot, the papery seed discs of the majestic trees rustled ominously. Every little noise struck at her nerve endings like an ice pick.

Had something moved in the undergrowth? It was hard to see, but yes, there it was again. She held her breath and peered, eyes watering with the effort to make some shape of the formless thing that slithered along the ground. A snake? No, this was Ireland; a snake hadn't been seen here in hundreds of years. So not a snake. The movement flickered again and she leaned forward, hand going to the pistol she'd strapped to her ankle.

Just then, a hand came across her mouth from behind and an arm like an iron bar fixed itself across her back. She tried to twist out of the hold, but couldn't budge the grip on her more than a hair's breadth. The other hand slipped the pistol out of its holster.

She tried screaming but nothing more than a squeak managed to get past the cold leather against her lips. It was then she realized her captor's finger was lodged between said lips and took a deep breath through her nose before biting down hard.

A muffled *'ouch'* was the only reaction, though the one syllable managed, even through her panic, to sound familiar.

"Don't yowl, I'm letting you go now."

She whirled round as best she could from her undignified position. "You scared the hell out of me," she said, voice sounding more relieved than indignant, however.

"You little fool, what did you think you were doing, sneaking out here on your own?"

The tide swept back toward indignation. "It's my business what *I'm* doing here. What the hell are *you* doing here?"

"I believe you made a promise to Pat that you wouldn't go off on your own."

Damn Pat! He'd obviously told Jamie to keep an eye on her. She opened her mouth to protest and then closed it. She was actually quite grateful for his presence. It wasn't likely that anyone had seen him, Jamie was well versed in slipping in and out of places without arousing notice. When he wanted to, that is, at other times he seemed the epicenter of whatever universe he was moving through.

Like her, he was dressed in black from head to toe, the only spot of color on him the occasional flash of teeth as he spoke.

"Is he late?"

"Not yet," she said, struggling to keep her teeth from chattering. "Don't you even want to know why I'm meeting him?" she asked, feeling rather irritated at his smooth taking over of the situation.

"I assume it's the next mile on your wild goose chase."

There was really no response to *that*, Pamela thought, so she wouldn't deign to give him one.

"Are you certain he meant here?" Jamie asked, the vertical crease in his forehead matching the frown on his face. "I don't like this, it's terribly isolated. Something feels wrong."

She brushed spiderwebbing out of her face. "I'm not leaving. If this man knows anything I want to find out what it is."

"Then we need to be somewhere we can hear him coming before he sees us." Jamie eyed the byre in the quickly fading light. "There's a loft," he said speculatively, "that will have to do. Come on."

They ran low and quick across the open ground, though Jamie, who'd the senses of a hungry jungle cat, didn't sense anyone about.

The byre was a tall, narrow building with the loft high up and tucked toward the back. It was apparently used as a storage facility and not to house animals, for none of the usual ordure of sheep or other livestock tinted the air.

Jamie chose a small door at the side, with a large clump of lilac sheltering the opening. It opened easily and the two of them, after a last scan of the area, slipped in. The byre was built of gray fieldstone and was cold as the bowels of hell on this November night.

Jamie clicked on a narrow beam of light, casting it around, careful not to shine it near the small, thick-paned windows. There was no ladder, but large spikes stuck out at regular intervals from a beam which ran up the length of the wall to join with the roof joists.

"Up you go—test your weight with each one before you move on, though."

Jamie needn't have worried, the beam was stout and the spikes well fixed within it. She was up and over the lip of the loft in seconds. Jamie followed on her heels, clicking the light off as he came over the top, into the piles of hay.

The hay smelled relatively fresh and was peppered through with timothy and clover stalks that lent a sweetish aroma to the dank atmosphere. The chill moonlight crept through an opening at the far back of the loft. Individual stalks of hay were delineated in silver, giving the impression that the two of them had landed in a frosty field. An impression that was helped along by the small puffing clouds each of them emitted every time they took a breath.

Jamie settled in beside her, well back from the edge of the loft, but close enough that if they lay full length on their stomachs they'd have a good view of the barn below. He tucked his light into a pocket and removed a flask. He handed it to her and said, "For the cold. We may need it if we have to sit here any length of time."

They sat quietly, the small night sounds magnified in the hush. The bare branches of the lilac tree rubbed against the stones, creating an eerie moan that did nothing to calm Pamela's nerves. The entire night had been created for spooks and chills, even down to the smell of dead vegetation and the lonely hooting of a barn owl somewhere in the valley below.

Jamie rubbed his hands together and then blew on them. "We'll play a game. That should help pass the time."

"Didn't think to bring cards," she said, somewhat snippily. Jamie's coolness in the face of imminent danger had always been one of his less attractive qualities. Jamie wisely ignored her tone.

"Just a word game; here's the rules, neither less nor more than four syllables per line, each verse with four lines and each word beginning with the same letter, though we'll allow for is, and, A and I."

"Easier for some of us than others," she grumbled, tugging her cap down farther over her ears.

"It'll take your mind off your cold toes," Jamie said unsympathetically, "I'll even let you pick the letter."

"Heavens," she replied icily, "does your generosity know no bounds?"

"Cranky, aren't we?" he responded back sweetly. "Now are you going to pick the letter or shall I?"

"I will, you're likely to pick Z," she said firmly, "just for sheer bloody-mindedness."

"Alright then, give us a letter and a theme," he said, and she could see his grin even in the dim light.

" 'S' is my letter and our theme shall be—*The Seduction of Sally Scrimshaw.'* Your turn first," she said in a spirit of generosity.

"Stop batting your lashes at me," Jamie said dryly, "it's more effective by firelight." He gave it no more than a moment's thought and then let fly in a flurry of playfully enunciated tones.

> *'Sidney Shawshank*
> *Sorely sought sweet*
> *Sally Scrimshaw*
> *'Sweetling' said Sid—,"*

Jamie broke off abruptly, "Over to you."

She shot him a look that could be described as less than gracious, cleared her throat, and picked up where he had left off.

> *"Sagaciously speaking*
> *Savory Sal,*
> *Suitor-wise Sid*
> *A scorcher is.'*

"Too many syllables in the first line and I'll have to take issue with suitor wise." Jamie said with dubious scorn.

"Hyphenated," she said triumphantly.

"What," Jamie sighed, "would Dr. Johnson say?"

"I don't see why he should have all the fun, I like to contribute to the English language every now and again myself."

Jamie took a deep breath, flexed his fingers, and launched into the third verse.

> *'Said superbly*
> *Sauced Sally*
> *'Sweet Sir Shawshank,*
> *Simply stated—'*

"Oh not fair, feeding me half a line," Pamela said, tucking a stray curl up under the fisherman's cap she wore.

"Can't take the heat darling, stay out of the kitchen," Jamie replied blithely.

She arched a sooty eyebrow and launched into the next verse of their composition.

> *'Solicitous*
> *Syllables sir*
> *Stir some silly*
> *Sows to sighing,'*

"Your turn," she said gleefully, passing the flask back to Jamie as a welcome warmth began to bubble through her veins.

> *'Sober Sally*
> *Seeks solitaire*
> *Solemn scion*
> *Of solvency.'*

"Oh very good you rat, an alliterative want-ad," Pamela said laughing, taking the flask from Jamie's flourishing hand and helping herself to a small slug. She eyed the rafters owlishly, seeking inspiration.

> *'Scornful Sally*
> *Succulent sylph*
> *Scathing statements*
> *Swell my sabre.'*

Jamie took back the flask and pointedly put the lid on. "From glib to gutter in one small swallow," he said sternly, "no more for you."

> *'Sir Sidney' said*
> *Spirited Sal,*
> *Saddled supine*
> *I shall not be.'*

"O-ho," Pamela crowed, "you've broken your own rules, forfeit the game."

Jamie shook his head abruptly, index finger gone swiftly to his lips. Below there was movement. She couldn't hear it herself but knew that Jamie, with his preternatural radar, did. Following his lead, she slid down into the hay until she was half on her side, as flat as could be managed with the hard mound of her belly in the way. She was careful not to disturb the straw, fearful that some vagrant wisp floating down would announce their presence.

She heard voices, deep tones, two men it seemed, approaching from the rear of the byre. Her heart thumped hard against her ribs, the jollity and adventure of the last few hours suddenly lost in the prospect of serious danger.

Jamie held up two fingers, eyes narrowed in question. She shook her head very slightly and held up one finger. She was only expecting one man. Two men meant trouble. She could hear them clearly now, approaching the door, opening it and then a muffled oath as one of them stumbled over the threshold.

"*Hssht*," the other hissed.

Her heartbeat was threatening to come out her ears, and she'd a sick oily feeling in the pit of her stomach. Below, the men were checking the perimeter of the barn.

The ground outside was too hard for them to have left a trace and yet she was quite certain the two men below hadn't merely stumbled across this barn. She prayed they would stay below and wouldn't feel the necessity to search the loft. The men had halted now, and seemed to be listening for something. She only hoped it wasn't the sound of her pulse echoing off the stone walls.

An uneasy stillness descended. Jamie's hand had found hers in the straw and he kept a steady pressure on it, the touch of his skin calming her, despite the fraught circumstances in which they now found themselves. Below, the men shuffled slightly, though neither made so much as a murmur.

Then amongst all the held breath, she heard footsteps on the frosty ground outside. She closed her eyes, knowing there wasn't a thing they could do to warn him. The leaves were hissing under his shoes, the thin coating of ice magnifying the noise of his footfall. A sense of heightened expectation drew the air tight around them, and she knew the men had heard the footsteps as well.

The side door creaked open, and for a split second the universe held still, poised on the edge of chaos, and then all hell broke loose. There was a great deal of muffled thumping, a clear and querulous—"*What the fock?!*"—as well as other more colorful curses, as the man fought blind at the unexpected attack. There was a sickening thunk that Pamela instinctively knew was the sound of a revolver being cuffed upside the man's head.

A curious thud sounded in front of her and she peered through the dark, then heard the scrape of rope across wood. The bottom dropped out of her stomach as the rope fed out over the beam. She bit down on the hand that Jamie wasn't holding, stifling the exclamation that came with the realization of what the two men had come here to do. They were going to hang him. They weren't here to question him, they were here to make certain he didn't answer any questions ever again.

Apparently they weren't there to make conversation either, as only grunts and the occasional curse word were audible in the scuffle below.

"Where's the fockin' ring?"

Her ears ached in an effort to hear the muffled reply, which must have been in the negative because the man swore again and there was the dull thud of a fist impacting flesh.

What kind of ring was so important that these thugs felt the need to strip the man of it before they killed him? It had to be the rings drawn on every note, and the importance must lay in what they represented, not in their actual physical form.

She turned her head to Jamie. In the moonlight she could see his face clearly, and he had the look of set determination that she knew too well. He was going to do something, and get them all killed in the process. From his pant leg he produced a knife, which winked silver at her before he stuck it between his teeth. She looked along the beam in horror, as the realization struck of just what he meant to do.

She clutched his coat sleeve tightly, but he pulled it free and set out across the beam. She held her breath, ribs hurting with the pent up oxygen. It would be a miracle if the men didn't see him, despite the dark clothing and face paint. Like a slender spider on a single strand of webbing, the slightest breath would send him tumbling to the ground. To reach the rope he would need to be out over the center of the byre, completely in view should either man look up. She wanted to look away, but couldn't. It was like waiting for a train to crash right in front of you.

Jamie had reached the rope, his body balanced precariously where the beams met. He sawed through the rope, halting each time the men paused in their questioning. Endless moments passed with him braced on that thin wedge of wood.

She let a bit of her breath out when Jamie started to inch backward, barely visible in the shadows that clustered thickly around the beams. Though she couldn't see, she had the sense that the man in the noose looked upward, that he knew she was here, and about to witness his death. She closed her eyes, an incoherent prayer for deliverance whirling through her head. She could feel Jamie settle himself back into the hay beside her and she opened her eyes.

She'd never been consciously present at a killing and wondered if it was always this way; this unnatural awareness of one's own fragile being. She could feel every bit of air that her lungs took in, the dust of timothy and clover sticking in her throat, the feeling that her blood was running very close to the surface of her skin, the heat of Jamie's skin like an electric current along her hand. The extraordinary awareness elongated each sensation and gave it an odd and unfamiliar shape. Even sound seemed to slow to an odd arcing motion, as though she felt the support give way beneath the man's feet rather than heard it.

He dropped. And the rope held.

Jamie's hand came down hard on the back of her neck, forcing her to turn her face to the side so she wouldn't see the man who swung below them now, but in her mind's eye she could see his face turning from dusky to turgid.

Jamie's own face was only inches from hers, green eyes holding her own forcefully as he shook his head ever so slightly, hand tightening considerably on the back of her neck, warning her not to give in to the instinct to scream. Through the roaring in her head, she heard the barn door creak open, the low laugh of one of the men and the smell of cigarette smoke. She thought she might throw up.

"Sit up slowly and take a deep breath," Jamie said in a tone that brooked no disobedience. She did as he'd told her to, feeling the bile slowly retreat from her throat and the painful throb behind her eyes begin to fade. He rubbed her back, hand firm and unshaken. Christ, did nothing ruffle the man? They'd just witnessed a hanging, the beam still creaking from the weight of the dead man and Jamie'd not turned a hair.

The nausea slowly receded, though the tingle of shock still resounded in her bones, leaving them the consistency of rubber. She took as deep a breath as she could manage, her other senses returning with the intake of oxygen.

The barn was quiet, the only noise the rhythmic one of the rope creaking back and forth on the beam.

"Do you think they're really gone?" she asked in a whisper. Jamie opened his mouth to reply but a large *whoosh* from below answered her question.

"Damn—they've set the barn afire! Either they know we're up here or they want to destroy evidence of the murder."

"Either scenario isn't comforting," she said grimly, pushing herself up out of the hay. The barn below was no longer the depthless hollow it had been moments before. Now a dull glow licked at the walls, soft smoldering puff-heads of fire rising sleepily from the damp straw. As soon as the fire found some dry straw, the place was going to go up like an inferno. Jamie crawled across the loft and stuck his head over the opening into the barn below. When he turned back, his face was grim.

"We can't risk it, some of the straw is catching quite quickly. We could get stuck between the ladder and a wall of flame. We'll have to go out that way." He pointed to the square opening behind them. She shook her head, feeling suddenly the tugging sensation low in her pelvic region. She couldn't risk the jump. Jamie didn't heed her, though, and dragged her toward the opening. She peered over the edge, hearing the low chuckle of the fire as it got a good hold on the straw below. The ladder was no longer an option. Below her stretched a black abyss. She'd no idea how far the fall to the ground was. Any fall was likely to be too far, though.

"There's a pile of manure down there, it'll break the worst of the drop. I'll follow right behind you, so when you hit, roll away as fast as you can. Don't think about it—just do it."

"I can't," she said through lips gone stiff with fear.

"Jump," Jamie said grimly, "or I'll push you and then you'll break something for certain."

She turned to face him. The approaching inferno lit him from below, making a golden chiascuro of his face and hair. She had always trusted him to keep her safe, this time would be no different.

"Jamie, I'm pregnant," she said. The fall would kill the baby, if indeed it didn't kill all of them, and yet there was no way back through that wall of flame.

"Oh, Christ," he said softly, then wrapped his arms tightly about her and launched the two of them into the air. He twisted just before they hit the pile of manure, taking the brunt of their fall on his back with her still wrapped securely against his chest.

She lay there for a second, dazed by the impact. Jamie's arms fell away and she rolled off him, hands sinking in the muck.

"Jamie," she managed to croak out with the bit of breath still in her lungs.

"Here," he gasped, "I think I've cracked my collarbone. Are you alright?"

She moved her legs experimentally. "Everything seems to be working.

We'd better move," she added, for above their heads an ominous glow lit the opening they'd been poised in only a minute before. Even now, small bright, burning bits of straw were starring the dark night.

"Can you stand?"

She pushed herself up onto her elbows, still winded, bones jarred and tongue bleeding where she'd bit it. She sat back on her knees and then stood.

Jamie was sitting up, right arm held tightly to his chest.

"How bad does it hurt?"

"Enough, thanks. Help me up, we've got to get clear of here."

She helped him to his feet and they fled for the cover of darkness, beyond the long ribbons of light the fire was already throwing out. The brush was thick and dry with dead leaves, though the roar of the fire more than amply covered the sound of their stumbling into the wood.

They halted to catch their breath, Jamie leaning his forehead against the bark of the nearest tree trunk and examining his collarbone with ginger fingers.

"Is it broken?"

"Not sure, it's maybe just cracked."

Pamela, breathing into lungs that felt slightly scorched, looked back toward the barn and shuddered. Suddenly she clutched Jamie's torn sleeve.

"What is it?"

"I saw something move—in the byre—look there it is again!"

Jamie looked and cursed softly, for something was indeed moving just within the doorway.

"Christ. He's not dead, the rope must have finally broken."

"How could he have survived the hanging?"

"If the rope stretched enough it's possible," he said grimly. He turned to her and grabbed her by the arms, fixing her with a very stern gaze.

"Don't move from this spot until I come back, no matter what happens— do you understand? If I don't come back out within ten minutes then you need to go for help."

"Jamie, no you can't, you'll be killed in the fire and those men could still be around." She looked about in panic, certain suddenly that they were lying in wait, gun sights beaded, just waiting for that fair head to come into view.

Jamie, however, wasn't heeding any warning. "There's a monastery in the middle of the lake we passed coming in here—Pamela, are you listening?"

She nodded dumbly, thinking that if he didn't come back out of that barn it wasn't likely she'd have the strength to do anything other than crumple on the spot.

"Listen to me. The monastery is only twenty minutes on foot from here. Stay near the road but don't travel on it directly. You'll come across a sign at the first crossroads that points the way to the abbey. The abbey itself is on the island in the lake. There's a boat on shore that you can use to row across.

When you get there ask for Father O'Donnell, he'll help you if you tell him who you are. Understand?"

She nodded again.

"All right, good girl. I'll be back in a minute." He leaned forward, kissing her hard on the forehead, and then was gone into the hellish flame and shadow which danced around the small clearing.

In the dragging minutes that Jamie was gone, she took stock, as well as her bruised psyche and body would allow. She let her mind go down the pathways of bone and blood and found there an assortment of cuts and bruises and a slight winded feel that remained from the impact of the fall. The mind stopped short, however, of the small weight in her womb. Fear gathered in her throat, tasting like hot copper. She swallowed it back and then forced instinct to go where her mind refused to. No pain, no tenderness, only a feeling in the pelvic bones of jarring and a slight stretching.

She offered a wordless prayer of gratitude, while still focused with her entire being on the fiery opening Jamie had disappeared into. It seemed an eternity before he emerged, carrying the man on his back, the two of them silhouetted against the flames like some strange beast forged from the terrific heat.

Jamie was staggering under the burden of the man's weight. She rushed forward, uncaring if the woods were rife with cutthroats. He made it to the edge of the clearing before he collapsed to his knees and laid the man down on the ground as gracelessly as a sack of potatoes.

"He's still alive, though barely. His throat's badly swollen. We'll have to cut him."

"Cut him?"

"Tracheotomy," Jamie said curtly. "You're going to have to hold the neck firm for me and I'll make the cut. Do you have a pen on you?"

She dug in her pockets and came up with a ballpoint pen.

"Take the ink out and give me the tube," he said, already rolling his sleeves back and opening the blade on his pocketknife. "Christ, where's that flask?"

She patted down the pockets of his coat and came up with the flask, dented but with the contents intact. Jamie poured some over the skin of the man's abraded throat and then sloshed the remaining whiskey over the knife.

He placed his little finger directly below the man's Adam's apple, and his thumb into the groove at the top of the breastbone. He touched the tip of the knife to the smooth column in between, nodded to her, and then with a swift sure movement, cut. A flow of black blood erupted onto the bruised surface of the man's skin and then while they both held their own breath there was a wet gurgling wheeze, and the man's chest began to move beneath Jamie's hand.

Jamie took the pen tube and lodged it in the cut, providing an airway, albeit a small one, for the man's labored breath. Then he lifted him in his arms and started walking back towards the road that would—hopefully—lead them to sanctuary.

It was a long, hard slog as they couldn't risk walking directly on the road but had to stay in the heavy shadows that the thick hedging provided. Twice they had to stop to readjust the tube in the man's throat and to give Jamie's arms and collarbone a rest.

"His pulse is pretty thready," Jamie said on the second of these stops. They stood in the shelter of an enormous oak whose roots arced out of the ground at knee-height. "I don't think I can take him any further without help. There's a bend in the road just beyond that clump of rowan. If you cross the road there and take the path on the other side, it'll lead you straight down to the lake. The boat is tied to a tree there. Take it across and ask for Father O'Donnell like I told you. Ask them to send Brother Gilles back—he's their doctor in residence. You stay put there, you'll be safe."

"What about you?"

"I'll be fine. Those wideboys are well clear of here by now, they know the fire will draw attention. I wouldn't send you off over the road if I thought otherwise. Now go."

She was about to move off when she was started by the man, whom they'd both thought was unconscious. He had grabbed her hand and was struggling to speak.

She looked down into his face. Crooked tree branches shed flickering shadows over his skin, mingling eerily with the blood that was liberally smeared about his face and neck. His eyes were pleading with her to understand the words he could not speak.

He reached toward his chest, hand tugging at a leather thong. Pamela pulled it out from under his bloody shirt carefully. At the end of the thong was a small pouch and the man indicated that she should open it.

Inside was a ring. The same ring he had drawn on every one of his notes. She looked down at it, a cold fear stirring deep inside. The ring looked familiar, but not just from the notes, from somewhere else. A memory only half held, or half seen.

"He wants you to take it," Jamie said quietly, eyes intent on the man's face. As soon as Jamie uttered the words, the man closed his eyes, relaxing visibly. Pamela nodded, tucking it away in her pocket, frustrated that the man could not tell her what had made this ring worth nearly dying for.

"Go now," Jamie said, "he's passed out again." He gave her a small push in the direction of the road and she went, still slightly dazed and not entirely certain Jamie believed what he was saying about the men being well gone from the area.

A bit of autumn fog might have been nice she thought, creeping up to the road. The night however was cold and uncommonly clear. Visibility was remarkable, a fact that served her well, but would also serve the murderers from the barn.

She checked the pale ribbon of road that ran between the hedgerows. It stretched empty and silent on each side of her. Still she darted quickly across it onto the faint path on the other side. The ground was so hard with frost that her footsteps echoed loudly, startling her and making her look round with her heart in her mouth.

The boat was exactly where Jamie had said, tethered to the thin trunk of a young willow and bobbing lightly upon the skin of the lake. The thickly wooded island was no more than a hulk upon the water and from the perspective of her aching arms and shoulders, a vast distance off.

Here the night was very still and silent, so that her slightest movement or even the echo of her breathing seemed to carry a great distance. She untied the boat and pushed it out into the water, following it several steps before getting in and grabbing the oars from where they were tidily stowed in the flat bottom.

After that there was only the hiss of the marsh grasses against the boat as it passed over them toward deeper water, the dip of the oars and the occasional eerie cry of a night bird.

She soon found a cadence to her rowing, and set a swift pace despite the trembling which had seized her muscles. The island loomed larger and larger as the shore slipped further behind. As she moved closer she could see, here and there, the bobbing of lights like fireflies amid the trees. Did the monks have someone who watched for travelers on the lake?

The fireflies soon gathered in a narrow-throated clearing between the trees, which must be where the boat docked. She shifted her direction to the east so she would land where the lights had clustered and rowed with a strength fuelled by relief that help was near at hand.

And then she felt it—the low wrench deep inside that doubled her over the oars.

"Oh God, please no," she said, pulling hard at the oars in an effort to make the island's shore before it got much worse. But she felt the hot rush of blood between her thighs and knew it was too late.

A soft mist was encroaching on the edges of her vision, threatening unconsciousness. She gave two more pulls on the oars and then felt the soft scrape of earth against the boat's hull.

Several men stood in a cluster, a few with lanterns aloft. The mist was getting thicker and the faces before her were a blur. Out of the haze, though, a hand emerged toward her. She took it gratefully, stumbling with unsteady feet onto the shore. Around her the monks' voices buzzed like so many bees in a glade, but they sounded very distant. Firm dry hands grasped her own.

"Father O'Donnell," she managed to gasp out, before being dropped to her knees by a wave of pain so vast it temporarily blinded her. Around her were exclamations of shock and murmurs of worry. Then a very no-nonsense, unmistakably Gallic voice cut through the fog.

"Back away, let me at *le jeune fille*—stop clucking about like silly chickens, the child needs help."

"She asked for Father O'Donnell," a young voice said uncertainly.

"Then for heaven's sake go and fetch him," the Gallic tone replied with more than a grain of impatience.

A face swam into view out of the fog. A long nose and narrow lips gave it the appearance of a largish rat. Pamela blinked and the world receded back into fog.

"Help," she said and promptly passed out.

BRUISED AND ABRADED IN BOTH BODY AND SPIRIT, Pamela awoke in a shaft of weak November sunlight. The events of the night before came to her in pieces. The fire, the hanged man, the plunge through the woods and her flight across the lake...here she turned resolutely away from her thoughts and put her hand to her belly. She didn't need to really, she knew she was hollowed out, that there was no longer a child. But the touch was instinctive—to protect that which no longer existed.

"Jamie," she croaked, throat painfully dry.

"He's sleeping in the room next door," said the Gallic tones she vaguely remembered from the night before.

"They found him...Father O'Donnell..."

"*Oui.* Brother O'Donnell realized something was dreadfully wrong when he saw you, and so a small group of the brethren went back across the lake, and scouted the woods near the road."

"And the other man?"

The rat-like visage hovered into view. The resemblance to the rodent was unquestionable, but the eyes which sat above the drooping nose and thin lips were the warmest and most compassionate Pamela had ever seen. This must be the Brother Gilles Jamie had said was doctor in residence for the monastery.

His gaze assessed her swiftly. The shrewd observancy of the born physician sat comfortably on his features.

"I am sorry to say, *mam'selle,* that he died during the night. It was a quiet death, the damage he had suffered was too profound for man's paltry medicine."

Disappointment swamped her. Now there was no possibility of finding out what the man had wanted to tell her. The entire mission had been one of futility, and she had lost their child as a result. If Casey were to ever find out how reckless she'd been, he'd never forgive her. Which only added one more item to the list of things he'd find impossible to forgive.

"What time is it? Is Jamie all right?" she asked, attempting to sit up. It was like a heavy black blanket had been thrown over her head, though, and she collapsed back against the pillows immediately.

"*Mam'selle,*" the voice was gently chiding, "you are still very weak, you lost a great deal of blood. You must lay back and try to rest. James is fine, a little scratched and bruised and his collarbone—which I mended twice myself," here there was an impatient cluck of the tongue, "when he was a boy—is cracked, but otherwise he is fine. He stayed with you until morning. It is late afternoon now."

One of the warm dry hands was laid across her forehead. "No fever. That is good." The hand was joined by its companion and moved down to her neck, feeling the glands under her chin.

"Do you wish to ask of the child?"

She shut her eyes and shook her head, "I already know, I could feel the blood while I was still in the boat and then..." she stopped, throat aching with tears. "No, please I—"

The hands stilled on her neck. "Do not agitate yourself. We will not speak of it just now. I will have to check you, though, do you think you might manage that?"

She nodded dully, there was always this after the blood, checking the body over to make sure the bleeding wasn't worse than it should be, that the emptied womb was shrinking back to its non-pregnant size and consistency.

His hands were strong and efficient, yet gentle. The broad blunt fingers probed above pelvic bone and he nodded to himself, face wearing the inward look of a man who saw the body's structures as clearly with his hands as he would have on a chart. She winced as the hands outlined the edges of her uterus.

"Does it pain?" he asked.

"No, at least not in the sense you mean. It just feels," she took a shaky breath, "empty."

He nodded. "It is retracting well, but of course the emptiness you speak of is not a physical symptom."

He drew the sheet up over her and turned toward the counter where he began to take down a variety of bottles and deposit a little from each in a small bowl. When he turned back, his hands glimmered with pale gold oil.

"It's a mix especially prepared for miscarriages," he said. "Geranium, frankincense, grapefruit, and Roman Chamomile. It will take the edge from your nerves, and help you rest. Later, if you need it, I'll give you a sedative. Rest is most important."

The smell was heady but soothing. Exhaustion made her drowsy, but it was a surface coating, underneath which lay a bone-deep grief that was like a sore tooth; if she so much as touched it the pain would be electric and consuming.

She watched the monk from beneath half-shuttered eyelids. His touch was impersonal yet comforting; it was a talent found only in those who were born healers. He was no stranger to pregnant women either. It seemed an odd thing that a man who was sworn to celibacy would tend to issues of childbearing. There was about him, though, something suggestive of a man who'd seen much more of life than this little island.

"Have you been here many years?" she asked.

"Eighteen. I was new here when Brother O'Donnell brought James the first time. Before that, though, I was an obstetrician with a thriving practice in Paris. I had a wife and two healthy sons. It was a good life by any measure. I loved my family, loved my work, and then one night my wife and sons were coming back from Lyon—where my wife's family lived—and they were hit by a large truck. They were killed instantly. I lost faith for a time. Then one day I realized that any happiness we might achieve here in this world was a fleeting thing, and it would never come with guarantees. So I devoted the rest of my life to things beyond this existence. I work and live here, but I visit the nearby villages that are too small to have their own doctor and I do what I can for the people." He shrugged, a purely Gallic gesture that held a wealth of unspoken words. "It is enough."

"I'm sorry," she said quietly, "about your family."

The brown eyes met her own. "I too am sorry—that I could not help you."

"Was it the fall?"

"No mam'selle," he said, confirming her own suspicions, "the fall only hastened the inevitable. The placenta was insufficient and the child could not have been brought to term. How far along were you?"

"Almost six months," she said.

"The baby was *petite*." He indicated with his hands a length no more than a tiny doll.

"Was it a boy or a girl?" she asked, not wanting to know, and yet having to at the same time.

"A girl." The brown eyes regarded her gently, "You must not think it was anything you did. A month at most and then the pregnancy would have ended regardless. Now," he wiped his hands on a flannel cloth, "you must try to rest. Though perhaps a little company would be welcome first?"

She nodded, knowing he meant Jamie.

"The Brothers are preparing a room for you that will be more comfortable than this one. I'll be back to check on you in a few hours."

With a soft swish of his robes he was gone, the rich fragrance of frankincense lingering in the air behind him.

She took in her surroundings with a tired curiosity. The bed on which she lay was enormous, low, and as wide as it was long. It looked as though it had been brought back from the Crusades by a crew of sturdy knights. It took up an entire corner of the room. The room itself wasn't large, but it was bright despite the stone walls. It had been brought into the modern age with tall windows through which the pale autumn sunshine now fell in elongated rectangles. The stone had been whitewashed recently from the look of it. Long counters ran along the back wall of the room and down one side. There were a couple of covered trays of surgical instruments and a tidy cluster of mortars and pestles. The warm dusty smell of herbs permeated the air.

Shelving rose above the counters all the way to the ceiling. Upon them, glittering like ground jewels, were bottles and jars. The tall bottles had cut glass stoppers and were filled with dried herbs, some with the plants suspended in oils, some with bright powders, others with a variety of elixirs—teas and tisanes, unguents and salves. Squat jars that resembled toads with wide open mouths held more exotic substances—small, powdery balls, strips of bark, dark viscous strings of plant root, clumps of mosses, a wide variety of funguses, and even small acorns suspended within a slimy green substance.

Each jar and bottle was adorned with a plain white label on which, written in a spare, tidy hand, were both the Latin and English names of the plants. Thus chamomile was also *anthemis nobilis* and mugwort was *artemesia vulgaris*. A glutinous mass of what appeared to be frogs eggs in a yellowish liquid, bore the rather illustrious name of *oculus de lacerta*—someone had a dark sense of humor, or at least she hoped someone did.

There was a soft knock at the door, and a second later Jamie poked his head in.

"May I come in?" he asked quietly. She nodded, sitting up in the bed despite Brother Gille's admonitions to the contrary.

Jamie was freshly washed, gold hair still damp. He was dressed in a navy blue sweater and a pair of worn jeans, which fit him perfectly. The only signs of the events of the previous night were his neatly splinted collarbone, and a bruise of a very vivid blue peeking out from the collar of his sweater. The uninjured arm carried a tray loaded with a variety of heavy crockery.

He put the tray down on the counter and set about pouring tea with one hand. He handed her a mug and then with his own mugful in hand, sat beside the low-slung bed.

"How are you feeling?" he asked.

"I'll be okay, after all it's not the first time this has happened to me."

"I'm so sorry Pamela. If I'd thought for a minute there was any way back through that barn that wouldn't have burned us to a crisp, I would have taken it."

She shook her head. "No Jamie, it would have happened anyway—there were signs. I think I knew it even before Brother Gilles confirmed it. He said it was likely only a matter of a few more weeks at best, the fall just speeded things up."

"The inevitability of it doesn't make the loss easier to bear."

She turned her head away towards the long windows. Her eyes had filled with tears; somehow Jamie's presence made it harder to be strong.

His hand grasped her own and held it firmly. "You don't need to hide tears from me," he said. His words broke the small dam in her chest. The tears came in a hot salty rush without sound, the grief of them so deep that it seemed they came from an endless wellspring that she would never be able to stem.

Jamie simply leaned forward, took the mug from her shaking hand and then gathered her to him with his good arm and held her. His strength provided her a balance that allowed for both pain and guilt. When she was afraid to look down, he always seemed to provide ground for her to stand upon.

The storm of grief abated, dulling the edges of the pain and leaving a bone-deep weariness in its place. Jamie, feeling the lassitude in her body, eased her back onto the pillows.

"Do you want to get word to Casey?" he asked.

"No, he has enough to deal with. I won't add this to it."

"He'll have to know eventually," Jamie said gently.

"I know, but it's not something I can tell him in a message. He feels helpless as it is, this might make him do something crazy."

"He's a strong man; you don't need to protect him as much as you try to."

She shook her head. "I know his strength, but I also know his spirit and what internment is doing to it. I can't protect him, yet I can't seem to stop trying to do just that. The least I can do is tell him to his face."

"Drink your tea," Jamie said, handing her the mug. "Brother Gilles said you need to rest as much as possible; you've lost a great deal of blood."

She took a swallow of the tea, smelling the calming scent of passionflower and catnip. Herbs for soothing and sleeping, herbs for oblivion.

"Will you stay with me until I fall back to sleep?"

He nodded, taking the mug from her and readjusting the pillows more comfortably behind her head. He settled against the broad back of the bed, too tired to keep up the constructs of the walls he usually held fast around her. She settled her head in the crook of his shoulder, the way she had when he'd read to her as a child. And yet she was no longer a child, and he was not the man he'd been then.

"It was all for nothing—last night. Brother Gilles told me the man died."

"Yes, about two hours after we got here. His throat was too swollen to talk, so I'm afraid we didn't get any of the information he'd promised you."

"It may have been a wild goose chase anyway. He was very elusive with his messages. This whole thing seems that way, a fragment here and there, but it never amounts to even a corner of the picture, never mind the whole thing. Maybe I'm not supposed to find out what happened to Casey's father. At least it's starting to feel that way."

"I wish I believed that would be enough to stop you," Jamie said wryly.

"Somehow it seems even more important now. He's becoming real to me, not just as Casey and Patrick's father but as a man in his own right. All the stories and the way Casey and Pat live their lives tells me a lot about who he was. I feel I owe him this, because for some reason the information came to me."

"Truth won't always set you free, Pamela. I hope you bear that in mind while you pursue this. It won't set Casey free either."

"I know," she said quietly, "but I have to do this, despite everyone's fears, despite my own. I won't hide my head in the sand or look the other way. Jamie, I can't, surely of anyone you can understand that."

"Why do you think that I, in particular, should understand your inability to stay clear of trouble for more than a day or two at a time?"

"Jamie, I know your secret. You know I know it, so let's not play pretend with one another. I know what you risk on a daily basis and I think I've some small notion what it must cost you to maintain the charade."

"Do you?" he asked quietly. "I don't think I know myself what the cost is, or just what I'll do should the bill come due one of these days."

"It frightens me, Jamie, the thought of that. Of what could happen if someone other than myself and whoever it is you trust on the other end was to find out what you're up to."

"I can't look the other way either, Pamela, I've spent too many years doing just that."

"I know," she said softly, "but I still worry."

"So do I."

It was very quiet in the infirmary, with only the faintest echo of the monks going about their daily chores to remind them that they were not the only two people left in the world. Leaf shadows quivered in the sunlight laid down on the floor. He felt drowsy, the pull of sleep near to irresistible here where he knew himself warm and safe for the time being. Against the curve of his shoulder, he could feel the pulse in Pamela's neck slow and heavy, and wondered to himself why, even in the midst of crisis, he seemed destined to find his only moments of peace with this woman.

"Jamie, how do you keep hoping when this keeps happening?"

"I don't know," he replied honestly, "all I remember is the fear I felt. Father Lawrence told me in the boat on the way here what had happened, and it all came back to me—what it is to lose a child. It brought back the night my second son was born, it was much like last night, cold and clear, almost winter. He was born in the room you sleep in."

"Alexander," she said, not questioning for she held Jamie's memories as carefully as he held hers. "Tell me about him."

"There were a few minutes, after they took Colleen downstairs, when I was alone with him. I knew I didn't have much time, so I wrapped him up in the pillowcase. Then I took him and stood by the window. It was the middle of the night, the very darkest part, you know, when it seems as if morning will never come. It was forever, and yet no time at all, a few minutes of the most perfect love and the most hellish loss. I don't remember them coming to get us, but suddenly I was on the front drive and they were telling me I had to let him go. How long did they let you have your daughter?"

"A night," she said, "as you say, forever and no time at all."

He placed his hand over hers, a fleeting bitterness crossing his heart. Between them they had lost six children. It seemed a cruel joke to place them both upon such barren ground. And yet despite loss they were both still here, stumbling forward into an uncertain future in an unforgiving country.

"I think loving children is as close as we come to the love that Christ taught. My sons were strangers to me and yet I loved them all without restraint or condition. Given the choice I'd still trade my life for any of them, even if it meant I'd never know them or see their faces."

"I feel the same about Deirdre. She was so beautiful, Jamie, like the most perfect gift I could have imagined, but wasn't allowed to have. Sometimes I imagine she plays with your sons. That she's not alone. It only makes what I did in London—the abortion—seem that much worse. There are times that I still wonder if it was a mortal sin, if I committed murder. And maybe this is how God has chosen to punish me for it, by taking any children I might conceive away."

Jamie looked at her, startled. She was perfectly earnest, though, green eyes dark with pain. "No Pamela, it wasn't a sin, it was heartbreak but not sin."

"The Church says it's murder."

Jamie shook his head. As Catholic as his own conscience was, it enraged him that the Church had taught this woman that her tragedies were somehow of her own making. "Pamela, the Church is an imperfect institution. Many of the laws and mandates, and even systems of belief, are left over from the Middle Ages. God is timeless, though; He knows your heart better than you know it yourself. I believe that's enough, sometimes."

"I've never confessed it, though many times I've thought I should. I think…" she faltered briefly, "I'm afraid if I confess it, I will be admitting that I did something unforgivable, that I really was wrong."

"Confession isn't only about sin, there was a time it meant a profession of one's belief, the concession of an unavoidable truth. I used to believe it was a secret you would only share with God."

"An unavoidable truth," she said quietly, "is a confession of the soul."

As they spoke, shadows began to gather in the corners of the room, the lit rectangles on the floor stretching out, edges blurring with evening's encroach.

"Is the tea taking effect yet?" he asked, for she felt suddenly heavy against his arm.

She turned her head toward him. She was terribly pale; dark crescents bruised the skin beneath her eyes. "Yes, it's working."

"You need to sleep, Pamela."

She nodded, all movements slowed by the herbs that were stealing through her blood. Her eyes closed, the lids smooth as carved ivory. Her breathing took on a deep and regular pattern. He eased himself from her side, then drew a soft wool blanket from the foot of the bed up under her chin. He walked quietly across the floor, feeling the sticky residue of blood on the soles of his feet.

Her voice stopped him in the doorway.

"Jamie."

"Yes?"

"You're my dearest friend. That's my unavoidable truth."

For a heartbeat, time stopped, and he allowed himself the gift of her words. The only thing he could give back was his own confession.

"And you mine," he said softly, then stepped into the hall and closed the door between them.

Chapter Fifty-one

The White Doe

PAMELA, UNDER STERN ORDERS from both Father Gilles and Jamie, had been two days in bed. Both had stopped in at regular intervals with food that she had no appetite for, books that she couldn't concentrate on, and talk that she only half heard.

Tonight restlessness had seized her, despite the heaviness which had invaded her very bones. She couldn't bear the sight of the same stone walls and small arched window that looked inward toward the chapel. More than that, however, she could no longer bear to feel the small hollow in her womb which felt like a deep and permanent bruise.

She pulled a sweater over her nightdress, a white flannel shroud that looked like the sackcloth of a novice nun. Brother Gilles had left a pair of cloth slippers tucked under the bed in case she should rise. The monks would be at evening worship and there would be none to observe her walk in the night.

She glanced at herself in a basin of water that had been left for her to wash with. The candlelight cast odd shadows, both adding and taking away depth. Her face looked gaunt and strained and dreadfully white. She'd the odd sensation that one got when looking down a well, that at the bottom of that dark, unfathomed depth there was another world, a place where light did not exist and the small slippery things that populated the edges of nightmares did.

The water shivered, tiny ripples gathering at its edges and dispersing the white face, with its smoke cloud of hair, as though it had never been more than a momentary illusion.

> *The mirror crack'd from side to side,*
> *The curse is come upon me, cried*
> *The Lady of Shallot.*

The lines of Tennyson chilled her as they flitted through her head. She had always loved the poem and yet it seemed ominous now, as though she herself were the accursed Lady. Despite Jamie's words of reassurance there was still a sense that she had been punished by God, for the murder of an innocent.

Her mind could rationalize but her body could not. Inside was desolation, as though she were an autumn tree stripped bare of its leaves, but still able to hear the mournful tone of their papery rustle all about her.

She shivered, and gathering the bulky sweater tightly around her, stepped out through the door into the long corridor, off of which branched the guest rooms and small infirmary of the abbey.

The monastery had been built by the Cistercian order shortly after they landed in Ireland in 1142. The building and its grounds had largely escaped the pillage and plunder other religious orders had been subjected to when the Vikings had swept through Ireland like Greek fire, unquenchable and unstoppable. The thickly wooded isle, banded by water on all sides, had been too much trouble for invaders, it would seem, for the violence and burnings which had plagued the rest of the country had passed by this monastery. The site had been well chosen by the little band of monks, who had begun the order's long history with a series of small daub and wattle buildings. Cistercians sought the peace of isolation from the world, and thus this spot had seemed ideal. However, the sweeping changes of the Reformation spared none, and the White Monks of the order had been forced to leave Ireland behind. The forty abbeys they'd established by 1500 had largely disappeared one hundred years later. The Cistercians would not return until after the Catholic Emancipation in 1829.

The entire atmosphere was one of peaceful contemplation that some part of her could not help but succumb to. She contrasted it with the fuss and scurry of Father Jim's parish, and the madness the man was made to deal with on a daily basis. The day here was so simple; awake at dawn for the first vigil of prayer, then breakfast, then a time of quiet study, Lauds and mass, study again, Tierce, work, Sext, dinner, work... it gave the day a pleasing rotundness and she saw the appeal of it for these quiet, diligent men.

Along the east flank of the abbey ran a long open passageway. Here candles burned softly in the arms of the Gothic arches, lighting the way down to the path which ran along the perimeter of the lake. Beneath her slipper-clad feet, the stones were cool and mossy, smooth with the steps of the many pilgrims who had sojourned here over the last eight hundred years. The air was chill and smoky, like very fine whiskey, stinging her eyes and spreading a burn along the expanses of skin that were bare to the night.

Movement caught her eye along the shoreline of the lake. It startled her, as she thought all the monks were in the chapel for Compline. The flash of white was not one of the good Brothers, though, but rather a small white deer who was looking at her with some curiosity. In this world of men, perhaps a woman was an oddity. Though not, Pamela thought, as much an oddity as a white deer with translucent pink eyes.

The deer held her gaze for a time-stopped moment, and a small shiver passed along Pamela's spine as though some strange understanding had passed between the two of them. Suddenly something else caught the deer's attention, for her ears pricked and she stepped forward, scenting the air.

Jamie stood farther along the shore, the pale fire of his hair identifying him at once. The deer walked toward him without hesitation and took the berries he held in his outstretched hand, eating with a slow gravity that told of how well she trusted the man who fed her. Jamie murmured to the doe while she ate, and Pamela could hear the silky fragments of the Irish language as it slipped from his tongue.

She walked slowly down to join him, careful not to startle the deer, who seemed entirely unconcerned at her approach, though the large ear closest to Pamela flicked the air every few seconds.

Jamie wore a ridiculously big shearling coat that certainly must be the garment of the large and gentle Brother Aloysius, whose height and width would have made even Casey look positively boyish in comparison. In the high-collared coat with its ruff of sheepskin, Jamie looked like a Russian prince freshly returned from the hunt. The deer however, now nosing at his pockets, didn't seem to agree with this summation.

"Is she always so tame? Or is it just for you?"

Jamie shook his head. "There's nothing to harm her here, she knows that. She's known me since she was a baby. Even if she doesn't see a great deal of me these days; still she remembers. *Tcha*, Virginia," he gently admonished the deer, who'd poked her head entirely under his arm in an effort to see what the smell in his pockets was.

"She's yours?"

He laughed softly. "Well as far as a wild creature can belong to a man, I suppose you could say so. I found her on my land in Scotland, just up above the pond. Her mother had been killed and she'd either strayed from the herd or been rejected. Being albino isn't the most advantageous thing in either the human world or the wild, and I knew she wasn't likely to survive long without help. So I brought her here, where she'd be safe and sheltered from harm. She'll be ten years old this spring."

"Why'd you name her Virginia?"

"I named her Virginia Dare for the first English child born in North America," he answered, watching as the deer moved away from them to nose among the last of the green shoots at the lake's edge.

"I know who she was," Pamela said. "What made you name the deer after her?"

"For the Indian legend. You've never heard of it?"

"No. Will you tell it to me?"

He smiled above the ridiculous collar. "You always did like your stories. But it's perishing out here and you're not dressed for it. Take my coat."

She shivered, her feet beginning to feel very penitential in their thin coverings. Jamie took the ludicrously large coat off and folded it around her shoulders. She cuddled gratefully into the warmth he'd left in its depths. The thick collar smelled of balsam and smoke and earth.

"You'll freeze," she said, even as she stuck her hands deep into the pockets, fingers encountering the oddment of small treasures Jamie seemed to accumulate wherever he happened to be. A bit of rock that had caught his fancy, two of the little aniseed balls that he liked to roll around his tongue when he was deep in thought and a pen with a small scrap of paper attached to its clip.

He smiled, rubbing his own hands together. "It's good for the soul, or at least Brother Gilles would have me think so. I believe he intends to retrieve my soul for good and all before I leave here. Come, there's a wee shelter amongst that thick stand of oaks, it'll cut the chill from the wind."

The shelter was hewn of wooden planks, three-sided, its front supports built right into the lake, providing an unbroken view of moonlit water to the darkly forested opposite shore. One could be forgiven for thinking they had fallen into a crack in the seams of time, and landed smack-dab in the Middle Ages.

"Here, sit." Jamie pointed to the bench that ran along the back wall of the shelter, while he rooted underneath it.

"What are you looking for?" she asked, settling onto the worn wood.

"Blankets. Father Lawrence generally leaves a couple out here. He knows my habits well. Besides, Jesuits aren't big proponents of discomfort adding to one's spirituality, at least not in theory."

"But they are in practice?"

Jamie grimaced slightly. "What do you think?"

"I think they're probably the masters of it."

He came up with a heavy quilt that he spread across her lap, keeping half for himself where he sat down beside her.

"Do you remember that summer I read *Les Miserables* to you?"

She was startled by the question. Jamie rarely ever referred to their shared past.

"Of course I do," she responded, "as I was rather *miserable* myself that summer. I must have seemed a dreadful little ingrate, moody as I was, and you a complete stranger who had taken pity on me. I doubt it was too attractive for you, coming to see me everyday."

"Actually that summer saved me. You gave me something to focus on other than my own troubles. Colleen and I had just lost our first son and she'd withdrawn from me and gone to stay with friends in Spain. She was angry with me, and truth be told, I was angry with her. It was hurt and confusion more than anything. I'd gone to the Vineyard to sort myself out, an old friend from Oxford had a place there. And then there you were, a little ragamuffin with too much hair, a rebellious streak and a broken ankle. I felt a little like Galahad, coming to your rescue."

"I remember the night we danced on the shore," she said softly, "it was the first time I'd ever felt beautiful. I was so awkward and ungainly and yet somehow dancing there with you I felt as though I were someone else entirely."

"You *were* beautiful, anyone with half an eye could tell you'd be stunning in a few more years," he grinned, "once you started combing your hair that is."

"I waited for you to come back every summer," she said softly, remembering the terrible loneliness of those years, "but you never did."

He didn't respond directly. "The more things change the more they stay the same. Here we are and I'm still telling you tales."

"And my hair is still uncombed," she said, remembering the nimbus cloud which had floated around her white face in the water's reflection.

Jamie settled back against the rough planks with a sigh, and she knew that, for whatever reason, their trip down memory lane had made him uncomfortable. When he spoke again, his words curled upward from a slipstream of white breath, as though they were players preparing to take on the forms that existed within his tale.

"I first heard this story when I was staying on Martha's Vineyard. It was a night around the campfire on the beach, with a dark bluff overlooking the spot where we sat. An old Wampanoag told it, enacting it as he went. There was complete silence when he finished and everyone was looking over their shoulders at the trees. I can't possibly tell it as he did, it really did seem—watching him—that he was remembering something rather than just a tale he had inherited."

She smiled to herself, for Jamie was a born storyteller and could captivate an entire roomful of people with the simplest anecdotes. Had he been born a thousand years earlier he'd have sat by the fire, surrounded by shaggy-haired listeners, passing down the legends of creation and flood and fire.

"It's said that when the first child was born in the settlement of Roanoke the Indians called her White Fawn, and it was told that when this child died, her spirit would take the form of a frosted fawn whose face would always be turned to the Eastern sea, because that was where her people had come from. The story went on to say that if ever a hunter should catch the fawn after she had grown to a doe, and shoot her with an arrow whose head was tipped with silver, she would be restored to her mortal form.

"Many years later an Indian hunter named Little Oak came upon the ruins of log houses in the saw grass of the settlement of Roanoke. There were no pale people living there anymore; the brambles and rose hips had long grown up between the cracks of the logs. Slow autumn turtles lay amongst the abandoned hearths and the sea wind blew through the ashes that had been left behind many moons before. All the hunter could find was an old baby's rattle, clutched fast in the thorns of a rose bush. Then he spied a beautiful white doe picking her way amongst the ruins of the house just beyond the one he stood in. By instinct he drew his bow, but he couldn't find it within him to loose the arrow.

"Time passed and the white doe became well known to the hunters of Roanoke Island. Often she was seen browsing amongst a herd of brown deer that lived there, but she always stood apart, turning her head to the east, sad-eyed and dreaming in the direction of the distant sea. Those who hunted her said that their arrows, though well-aimed, fell harmless at her hooves, whereupon she would leap with the west wind, swift as milkweed down, bounding along the sand hills, driving the quick curlews and iron-winged cranes up into the cold gray sky.

Some feared the deer in her desolation, thinking she was a portent of death, others thought to catch a glimpse of her meant good fortune. Always in the legends, though, she remained apart, yearning for a land across the sea from whence her people had come.

"Then one early autumn the people of the islands decided to invite all the best bow hunters for a hunt. The plan was to hunt the milk-white doe. If any runner or hunter could bring her down then all would know if she were flesh or spirit and thereafter, if she should prevail, none would ever hunt her again. And so the hunt was on. The hunters spread out swift as a peat fire across dry ground. The best bows were drawn and the straightest arrows notched. Amongst their number was a hunter who carried about him a silver-tipped arrow that had come from the faraway isle called England. This arrow was reputed to have come from the icy queen who sat upon the throne in that land. Such a thing, it was said, could reach to the heart of even the most charmed lives."

Under the spell of Jamie's voice, Pamela shivered, seeing all too clearly the hunters swift along the ground, the scent of blood on the air, and the body's primal response to it.

"And so it happened that the doe was chased from the grasses of the land, through tangled wood and trail-less bog she flew swift and silver as the north wind, with the hiss of loosed arrows following in her wake. She plunged on through the billows of the sound, finally reaching the sand hills of Roanoke. Here she stopped and stood amongst the ruins of an old fort, winded and tired, breathing in the air of the Eastern sea.

"In the grass the hunter with the silver-tipped arrow loosed the fated bowstring. It seemed to hang in the salt air for an eternity, glimmering in the moonlight before plunging into the heart of the white doe. She sank to the ground and the hunter threw down his bow and ran to her side, lifting the snowy head to his lap. He looked into the creature's dying eyes and saw the face of a pretty, young woman who, through dry-bled lips, whispered her name,

Virginia Dare, and died."

With Jamie's last words the white doe looked up, flicked her ears, and with one quick leap was gone into the dark of the night wood.

Icy mice feet skittered up her spine. "Now that was a little spooky," Pamela said quietly.

"It's mostly atmosphere," Jamie said sensibly, "this place has a sense of being between realities. The first time I came here was practically the same time of year. About a week after I arrived it was All Soul's Night. They lit the traditional bonfires to warm the souls of the departed, but they also had candlelit lanterns that they set into little boats and put out upon the water. It was beautiful and yet frightening, because this is one of those places where the veil between worlds seems a bit thinner than most places. You know?"

She did know. There were gateways in this world, invisible to the naked eye and yet felt all the same. One sensed it when one strayed too close to them, for then the hair would go up along the skin and the primeval brain would feel eyes watching though none could be found. And there were times in the stillness, if one listened very closely, that the unlatching of those gates could be heard.

She shuddered, instinctively moving closer to Jamie on the bench.

"I thought the fire would draw them. Father Lawrence said that was the point, that the souls that were lost and forgotten could come to the fire and warm themselves, and know for that one night they might be lost but they weren't forgotten."

"Sounds pretty pagan for a bunch of monks."

"Irish Catholicism has always been a mix of both the old ways and the new. The monks here were so isolated that they pretty much worshipped as they liked."

"How old were you that first time?"

"Seventeen."

"Did Father Lawrence bring you here then?"

"Yes, on an enforced retreat."

"Why?" she asked, noting the underlying bitterness in his voice.

"Because Jesuits will do what they feel is best for you even if you don't agree with them. They're rather stubborn that way." The long gold lashes veiled his eyes.

"Must have seemed rather extreme to a boy of seventeen," she said.

"I wasn't entirely lucid to my surroundings at the time." The lashes flicked up and the green eyes were candid in a way they so rarely were these days. "It was my first plunge into the rabbit-hole of manic depression. Father Lawrence had found me passed out in a doorway in Rathcoole in Dublin. I'd gone on a tear for several days and finally crashed, and so he brought me here—unconscious, sick and mad—to see if he couldn't straighten me out."

"And did he?"

"Yes, it was exactly what I needed, though I didn't feel the least bit grateful at the time." He fell silent, profile still as finely carved marble, the touch of a master's hand evident in every line.

When Jamie resumed speaking his voice was very distant, ephemeral as the mist that was gathering upon the skin of the lake. The past seemed very close, as though all times might exist at once, and she felt instinctively that here Jamie was, in some part, still that anguished and confused seventeen-year-old boy.

"There were many nights when I did not think I'd live through to the morning; in fact I rather hoped I wouldn't. But he wouldn't let me go, every time I cried out, his hand would come out of the darkness and hold my own.

"I was terrified. I'd no idea what was happening to me, no memory of where I'd been or how I'd ended up in that doorway, filthy and bruised, reeking of stale alcohol. I thought I was going insane. In some strange way I had things so twisted in my head that I thought if I couldn't remember anything of those days, I'd somehow ceased to exist. That I was forgotten and alone in the longest night I'd ever known. Father Lawrence kept me here until he convinced me that none of us are ever, even in the darkest hours of our lives, alone. That to believe we were alone was a transgression against God and against those who loved us."

"Do you still believe that?" she asked, the small ache low in her belly suddenly bearable.

He didn't answer at once, but took her hand under the blanket and gently squeezed it.

"Some nights I do."

The soft lament of Compline had begun. Tendrils of the night prayer reached across the open courtyard and wound their peaceful notes amongst the flickering flames and the bare-branched oaks.

O God, come to my aid.
O Lord, make haste to help me.
Glory be to the Father and to the Son and to the Holy Spirit,
as it was in the beginning, is now, and ever shall be,
world without end.
Amen. Alleluia.

The final strains of the alleluia drifted out across the water and filled the night air with prayer. The notes drifted upward until it seemed they must touch the face of the stars.

"When the dark night seems endless..." Jamie said softly, eyes fixed on some invisible horizon in his memory.

She returned the warm pressure of his hand and finished the thought he'd begun.

"Remember me."

Chapter Fifty-two

Visiting Day

THE SHIP LOOMED OVERHEAD like a great steel leviathan that had crawled up onto the shore, to rest there breathing heavily. Pamela shivered in its shadow. Casey had been incarcerated for four months now and this was only the second time she'd managed to get through all the requisite red tape in order to see him. Or rather, Jamie had finally twisted enough arms, and promised enough favors—a fact that bothered her a great deal—to get the permission she needed to spend an hour with her husband.

Jamie had handed her the visitor's pass the morning before at breakfast. "You can take the Bentley," he said, "or Liam will drive you."

Holding the pass in her hand, she felt like Christmas had come early. Last night she had barely slept, excited at the thought of seeing Casey, yet knowing their meeting was likely to be fraught. Part of the reason Jamie had pushed so hard to get her the pass was that he thought it was past time to tell Casey about the loss of their child. She dreaded telling him, yet knew it had to be done.

Now she was here and had been led to a grille which had facing it another grille. Between lay twelve feet of no man's land. This was as close as they were going to allow her to her husband. Casey was brought in on the other side a few moments after the guard left her. His guard stepped back out of her line of vision, but she knew he would be well within hearing range.

"Sorry about the atmosphere, if I'd known ye were comin' I'd have tidied up a bit." He gave her a weak smile, but the tone didn't quite come off.

Across the space that separated them, she took quiet stock. He looked exhausted, grim lines carved down either side of his mouth. He'd been thin when he was lifted, but now he was hewn down to his muscles. Against the grille her hands shook with the need to reach across that space, to touch him, to find a way to keep him whole.

"How are you?" she asked, feeling absurdly awkward, uncertain of who might be listening, even more uncertain of what to say.

"I'll do," he said flatly, then his expression softened slightly. "How are things at home?"

"Fine," she said, and then told him as much as she could about Lawrence and his schooling, how much Finbar and Paudeen had grown in his absence. There was much she left out. Her job with the RUC, the fact that all of them were living with Jamie now and the reason they'd wound up under his roof. None of this information seemed designed to bring the man comfort. "But we all miss you something terrible."

His eyes looked her over and despite the loose sweater she wore, she knew he was noting the absence of a belly. "The baby?" he asked, his words barely audible over the clanking.

She shook her head mutely, hating that he'd asked, not wanting to take this from him right now. She couldn't lie, though.

"I'm sorry." The lines around his mouth were like knife cuts now.

"Me too," she said, uncertain of whether he heard her.

He rested his forehead against the bars and closed his eyes. He looked unutterably tired and grieved. "I don't want ye to come back here," he said, low enough so his words wouldn't carry to the guards, but strong enough to tell her he meant it.

"What?" the disbelief was evident and yet she wasn't surprised, this had been the main theme of the last visit.

"I said," he repeated firmly, eyes open and locked on her own, "I don't want ye comin' back here."

"I think you'd better tell me why."

"It's too hard," his voice barely carried over the muffled clanking above them, "havin' ye see me like this. Please, Jewel, don't come back."

"The hell I won't," she said angrily, not caring now who overheard. "What sort of wife do you think I am?"

He sighed deeply, as though wearied beyond reason. "The sort who might occasionally listen to reason."

She shook her head vehemently. "You can't stop me from coming. It's the only way I've got of being certain you're alright."

"Do ye think I don't know what ye've been through to get here?" he asked, the wire grille casting criss-cross shadows on his face. "It's a small ship as things go, Jewel. I know what they did to ye before ye got in. I can't be in here, helpless, knowin' that ye're bein' subjected to those sorts of humiliations an' there's not a thing I can do about it. All I can do is ask ye to stay away."

Part of her wanted to rage at him, tell him exactly what she had endured these few visits, how the guards had laughed as they fondled her in the name of searching her person for possible concealed weapons. But she couldn't, the man was obviously coping with enough. She knew he couldn't understand that she would endure much worse for a minute of time with him. Just to reassure herself for those few moments that he was whole and safe, for she could never really believe it until she saw him with her own eyes.

His eyes flicked to the side, as though he were watching for someone.

"Why are you doing this?" she asked, uncertain whether she wanted to cry or yell at him. He gave her an odd look she couldn't interpret and then he unbuttoned the shirt he wore and lowered it to his waist.

"Casey, what on earth are you doing?"

He didn't answer, merely turned his back toward her.

She stared in horror. His back was like one of Jackson Pollock's darker works. Long weals stood out against the older silvered scars, the edges of the new ones still tinged black, the old ones limned in blue. There was barely an inch of undamaged skin left. The thought of the pain he must have endured made her sick to her stomach. The nausea was followed by a wave of rage so huge she'd the sense of being lifted off her feet.

Injustice should not surprise her anymore. He'd been incarcerated now for four months without charges, without trial, without any form of due process. And yet, that they could also do this to him...it left her speechless with fury and the need to take the person who'd done it apart with her own two hands.

"Oh God," she breathed, "why? Who did this?"

He turned toward her, shrugging up his shirt, face turned away as he did up the buttons. "Doesn't matter, it's done. I showed ye so that ye might understand a bit why I don't want ye here."

She shook her head. "I just want to take you home." She wanted more than that, she wanted to rewind their lives to the place where things had started to spiral out of control. She wanted to find a safe place and hide there with him until their lives were done.

"Ye can't take me home, but ye can stay away. Please don't come back."

"Casey, please—"

"Time's up," the guard behind her said. Pamela fought the urge to smack him hard across his stern face. At the sound of the man's voice, Casey's expression had gone as smooth and blank as water. She knew she wouldn't get another word out of him.

He nodded curtly to someone out of her range of vision and with one last look, he was gone.

WHEN CASEY DIDN'T JOIN the rest of the men for evening exercise, Matty told them to leave the lad be. He knew the boy had received a visit from his wife that afternoon, and had not spoken a word since. Matty knew things had not gone well. He understood why and felt sympathy for both sides. There was no winning for either man or woman in a situation like this. She would come to visit thinking her presence and concern would help, not understanding that it only made her husband feel vulnerable and open to assault. Because he had something to lose. Something precious. The guards could and likely would find a way to use that against him. He knew that and she didn't.

Near to the end of their two hours on deck, Matty crept off from the other men and made his way back to the cramped quarters the five of them shared.

The lad had stewed long enough; he was still fragile physically, not to mention the psychic scars that would take much longer to heal. Action of some sort was what was needed. Even if he had to be pushed toward it.

Casey was lying on his bunk, his shoulders held stiffly, and his face turned to the wall.

"Are ye feelin' poorly, lad?" Matty asked quietly.

"No just thinkin'."

"About anythin' in particular?"

"Figurin' out how to get the fuck off this ship," Casey said, and though his tone was quiet, Matty heard the despair underneath. "They'll transfer me to the Kesh soon, I know my number's comin' up, can't shake the feelin' of it. I could be there for years, Matty. This is the only chance I've got."

Matty had been in prison many times and knew all about the superstitions that arose around feelings of impending doom. He'd heard it all before, nine times out of ten it came to nothing, but he'd a bad feeling himself about the lad's chances on the next rotation off the ship. Especially now.

"Well, son, if ye're serious, I think I might know how it can be done. If I tell ye my plan, will ye let me come with ye?"

Chapter Fifty-three

Phouka

I N THE WEE HOURS OF CHRISTMAS MORNING, Pamela awoke to the feel of someone gently shaking her shoulder. She opened her eyes groggily, to find Jamie, clad in a heavy sweater, jeans and gloves, exuding a fresh cold that said he'd only just come in from outdoors.

"Come with me, I've something to show you," he said, voice a low whisper. "Put something warm on, it's chilly outside."

She followed him down the long winding back stair, the smell of the Christmas trees scattered throughout the house reaching her nose at the first landing. The lights glowed softly throughout the downstairs, and she knew that Jamie likely hadn't yet slept.

It was hushed as they went out through the kitchen. It was too early even for Maggie. Jamie handed Pamela a heavy coat and wrapped a scarf around her neck before opening the door to the long sloping back lawn.

The air was cold but clear and a melting half moon sat low in the sky. The stars were only beginning to fade into the blue velvet background of a Christmas dawn.

On the great sweep of frosted lawn stood a horse. He looked as though he'd been set down in a shaft of moonlight, his coat a pure dappled silver, the arch of his back beautifully curved and gleaming. He was deep chested, with the rippling hindquarters of a racehorse. He must have stood sixteen hands high, and had legs as straight and delicate as carved ice.

Pamela clasped her hands together with pure delight.

"Oh Jamie, he's beautiful."

He smiled. "He's yours. Merry Christmas."

"What?" She turned toward him in surprise.

"He's yours, though you can leave him here if you like. Billy's already under his spell, though he says he's a moody bastard. Still, you've a touch with horses that's rare. Even Billy agreed that if he was likely to behave for anyone it was you."

"Oh Jamie, thank you!" She flung her arms around him, and hugged him tightly. Trust him to know that if anything could touch her in her current state, it would be horseflesh. She had not had a horse of her own since her father had died when she was sixteen.

"What's his name?" she asked.

"Phouka, I've got his papers in my study. He's a beauty isn't he?" Jamie stroked the horse's long gleaming neck and Phouka nosed at his coat pockets, looking for apples or sugar cubes no doubt.

"He's utterly glorious," she sighed and leaned her head into the horse's neck, breathing in the smell of his coat—hay and oats and a pure green smell that was simply young healthy horse. It was, for her, the scent of heaven.

Phouka breathed out heavily, snorting into her hair. She laughed and Jamie handed her an apple. "Here, he's hopelessly spoiled, so you'll have your work cut out with him."

Phouka took the apple between silky gray lips, munching fastidiously as the great brown eyes stared down a haughty length of nose at her. He blinked and stuck his cold nose in the lee of her neck, blowing out a great gust of apple-scented air.

"I knew it," Jamie said with satisfaction, "he's already taken to you. Been a complete SOB in the stable these last twelve hours, driving everyone to distraction—myself included—and he's putty for you. So what do you say? Do you want to put him through his paces?"

"Right now?" she asked, though the horse was saddled and edgy as a train ready to charge out of the station.

Jamie nodded, and helped her up onto the horse's back. It took her a moment to find her seat; it had been a long while since she'd ridden. Her hands flexed around the reins, thighs tensing against the horse's sides.

Jamie gave Phouka a gentle slap on the rear end and the two of them were off into the frost-gilded morning. The air was heady as chilled champagne, frost riming the gates and glittering in the boughs of trees. In the western sky, Orion was sinking into the horizon, his belt shining softly like arctic pearls.

Phouka had a high step even to his canter, and the suppressed power beneath her was evident in both his energy and the way he moved. She kept him reined in a bit, careful for ice and the slickness of frost on grass. When his hooves found the comfort of the old bridal path that ran down to the very edges of the Kirkpatrick estate, she let him out a little and Phouka took his head and ran with it.

They might have crossed the invisible boundary into Faerie Land, so otherworldly was the dawn. The trees, diamond-edged chiascuros against air, seemed dimensionless and without weight. Everything—trees, stars, and the very morning itself, hung high in the ringing crystal air. She laughed aloud with the pure perfection of the moment and Phouka, catching her excitement, ran faster.

She had no idea how much time had passed when she realized her surroundings were no longer familiar. Both the trees and underbrush looked foreign, the oaks having changed to thick growths of hazel, their smooth trunks black and misted, their roots spread with small milk-capped fungi. She slowed Phouka down to a canter and then to a walk, gazing about her in confusion.

The cottage was small, and so immured into its surroundings that she was almost on top of it before she realized it was there. It was only Phouka's stomach, which had detected some withered corn stalks in the garden, that stopped them before they collided with a stone wall, overgrown with masses of ivy.

She got down off the horse, looping his reins over the wooden gatepost that led into the garden. She frowned, trying to get her bearings. She had ridden that bridle path dozens of times, but had never before come across this small cottage and she had the eerie thought that it only existed in some alternate reality, and that she would wake shortly to find herself one hundred years older. She thought she well knew the borders of Jamie's land. She shivered. The morning felt suddenly cold.

The cottage was shuttered, and looked like it had been abandoned for the winter. The thatch on the roof was relatively fresh, though, and must have been replaced as recently as the spring.

Inside the wall was a garden. In it, the winter skeletons of lavender and rosemary stood stark and brown. Heads of dill weed were crowned with puffs of snow and the dry pods of poppies rattled in the chill December wind. Vines grew round the thatch-eaves, and apple trees with mossy trunks crowded up to the low and deep embrasure of the back door.

She approached the door and knocked on the heavy wood, painted a deep green that looked as though it, unlike the thatch, had seen many a season. There was no response.

A small window, thick-glassed and square, sat divided into four equal leaded panes in the upper half of the door. She rubbed away the frost crystals on one of the lower squares and peered in, cupping her hands to the sides of her face to block the outdoor light.

The cottage was simple and neat, composed of three small rooms. The main room that she looked in upon was both kitchen and parlor. The furniture was spartan and hand-hewn, bare of linens which would have been folded away to save it from damp and mildew. Small muslin bags hung suspended from the thatch, and she knew they would hold the dried contents of the garden. The counters were neat, no sign of occupation upon them. Saving for a long white envelope that looked as though it had sat waiting for some time for someone to come and open it. She narrowed her eyes, for there was writing on the envelope, just the one word stroked in a heavy, black hand. Five letters and a symbol. She tilted her head and squinted in an effort to bring the word into focus. Quite suddenly it did, and her heart began to thump painfully in her chest.

She stepped back, crushing the leaves of a comfrey plant that crept round about the doorstep. The hair on the back of her neck prickled unpleasantly, and though the silence was still complete beyond Phouka's nosing amongst dry-leaved plants, there was a sense of something having moved amongst the trees.

Most likely an animal she thought, trying to calm her pounding pulse. She turned and walked toward the horse, realizing that she was holding her breath, waiting for the sound that was no sound at all.

She had no reason to be poking about this cottage, other than the oddity of it being upon Kirkpatrick land and Jamie never having mentioned its existence. Even that, she admitted, did not give her the right to trespass. And that was what she was feeling now, a sense of trespass, despite what she had just seen in that cottage.

Phouka raised his head from the edges of the winter-shorn garden, his gaze bright and inquisitive. She hurried toward him, wanting nothing more than to be away from this place with its desolate garden and shuttered windows.

She gave Phouka his head once again, trusting that he would lead the way home without mistake. His ears pricked; the light was now clear and the sky above pale with full morning.

The forked path became plain as they approached it, the wood once again turned comfortingly to oak and ash. In the distance, she could hear the ringing of church bells greeting the morning of Christ's birth. When she turned back the path was no longer visible, though, and she could not see where it forked. She shivered and gave Phouka a nudge with her knees.

Within minutes they came up on the edge of the lawn. Christmas lights glowed comfortingly through the windows, and she hoped that she hadn't missed Lawrence waking.

Jamie was in the stable, rationing out the small, winter morning feed of oats and corn. She knew he often did this chore himself, relishing the quiet company of the horses in the early hours, when no one else was about and there were no immediate demands on his attention.

The stable was warm, smelling of fresh hay and well-oiled leather. The feeling of otherworldliness shed itself in such prosaic surroundings. Phouka followed her to his stall, where his breakfast waited.

"Well then," Jamie asked, looking up from the hay cube he'd just cut the twine from, "how was he?"

"He's perfect," she said softly, still entranced by the weird magic of the morning.

Jamie tossed her a currycomb as he unbuckled the saddle from Phouka and hung it over the stall gate. He grabbed another comb and set to work on Phouka's right hand side. Pamela worked her way from the silky mane, the color of polished pewter, to the gleaming sides as the horse breathed out in noisome content.

"Jamie, who lives in the cottage down at the bottom of your land?"

He looked up, clearly startled, a flash of fear rippling through his eyes, and then gone so that she wasn't certain if she had only imagined it.

"An old lady," he said, "whose family has been on this land for many generations."

"Is she a tenant then?" she asked, disturbed by the sharpness of his tone.

"No. In fact you might say I'm her tenant," he moved off to grab a soft cloth to finish Phouka's grooming, but she had the strong feeling the action was more to avoid her eyes than anything else.

"Her tenant? What on earth do you mean, Jamie?"

"Nothing—a silly joke—ignore me. Just don't venture down there again, all right? There's an old well or two that needs tending to and I'd rather you stayed away. The old woman doesn't welcome company, I've not spoken with her in years. She wasn't there, was she?"

"No, the cottage was empty."

"Well just stick to the horse path from now on."

"I thought I had, but I must have made a wrong turning somewhere along the way."

"Just stay away, it's not safe."

She nodded.

"I mean it Pamela, it's not safe. A fall down one of those old wells would kill you."

"I promise I won't go back there," she said with some exasperation, knowing instinctively that it was not ancient wells that had Jamie so troubled, but rather the idea that she'd stumbled across the cottage.

She watched him out of the corner of her eye, as she gave Phouka his final strokes with the comb. Much, she realized, as he had watched her now for the last weeks, worry over the miscarriage and its effect on her, clouding his eyes. This morning he had tried to take some of that pain away for her. For the last hour she had managed to forget the darkness inside, the echoing hollow at the center of her being filled instead with the pure physical pleasure of taking a horse through its paces. And she understood that Jamie had meant for the horse to do exactly that.

"Thank you, for the horse, but for everything else as well. Taking us in, caring for us. Mostly, though, I want to say thank you for being my friend."

Jamie paused, hands full of hay as he broke apart another cube for Grainne, who was awake and rumbling in her stall. "It's my pleasure." He smiled, one of those quicksilver flashes that was heart stopping, his green eyes faceted as emeralds in the half-light of the stable. "It always has been. Now," he continued brightly, "we should head back to the house. Lawrence will be up soon and Maggie will have my head if I'm not ready to cut the pudding when it comes off the stove."

Jamie chatted all the way up to the house, about the events that lay in the day ahead, conferring with her about the wine and food, and basically filling the questioning silence as fully as he could. She recognized the form of avoidance, and decided that for now she would respect it.

And so she did not ask him why a woman, to whom he'd not spoken in years, had left an envelope with his name written across it, along with two interlocking rings drawn in the same dark hand, in the topmost left hand corner.

Chapter Fifty-four

Christmas on Board

C HRISTMAS ON BOARD A PRISON SHIP wasn't likely high on the
list of how people would choose to celebrate the season but it wasn't,
Casey thought, the worst Christmas he'd experienced either.

He looked about him, neck still somewhat stiff but no longer painful.
Matty was building wee stickmen from yarn and matchsticks, between taking
nips off a bottle of cherry wine. Everyone had shared in his largesse earlier
in the day, and as a result a fug of mellow peace hung over them. Declan was
industriously knitting away at a puce colored balaclava—when ribbed about this
particular occupation he'd merely said 'twouldn't be his ears fallin' off when
the cold came.' Roland was still sleeping off the previous evening's rampage,
knobby shoulder blades just poking above the blanket, and Shane was re-
reading his wee pile of Christmas cards for about the hundredth time that day.

Despite his refusal to allow visits, Pamela had left a Christmas parcel earlier
in the week. Around Casey was arrayed the plunder. Declan who always found
the cold perishing, had a pair of football socks, tucked up over his jeans, their
broad green and white stripes finishing gaily at his knees. Matty his own bottle
of Connemara Mist, which he was wont to pat lovingly now and again. Roland
a book of the saints, and Shane the component parts (inventively smuggled
in in a fruitcake) of a small transistor radio.

For himself there was a letter from Pamela full of all the bits of news
she knew he'd long to hear, an array of goodies that he'd immediately shared
out amongst the men, and a bright red muffler she'd knit herself, which, were
he inclined to lay down and roll himself up in it, might have served nicely as
a blanket. It was warm, though, and smelled sweetly of her perfume. He'd
not removed it, other than to wash, since he'd opened the package. She'd also
included toothpaste and new brushes for everyone.

Lawrence had sent a scrawled note, full of misspellings and assurances
that he was 'looking after tings'. Pat had sent a letter and a book, Sylvie some
baking. From Jamie there was the requisite bottle, warm socks and a curtly
coded note that gave him the lay of the land, both politically and personally. The

thing he'd most wanted, though, had been at first conspicuous by its absence. However, realizing the bastard was never one to make things easy, he re-read the note several times, turning it round and perusing it from every angle. Still no joy though, he couldn't find anything beyond what he'd already deciphered.

He shifted his shoulders carefully against the bunk. The skin was freshly grown and still tender. He turned his attention back to the letter he was in the act of composing, re-reading what he'd written thus far.

Dear Pamela,

I imagine you all sitting snug about the tree. The first one we were to have in our new home. I'm sorry that I cannot be there to share the day. If I close my eyes, though, I'm almost there, I can smell the tree, feel you sitting beside me on that disreputable couch. Ah, what's that—the smell of goose burning, wafting in from the kitchen...sorry Jewel, but a man must have his wee bit of fun.

He paused in his writing for a moment, there was so much he couldn't tell her. For instance how the hold, for weeks, had reeked of fermenting apples. Matty had somehow gotten hold of enough apples, sugar and yeast to make *poitín*, and from the smell of it, were any man bold enough to imbibe it, it'd be likely to knock him permanently on his arse. Were the man to step up production, Jamie would have serious competition. How they'd all gone off their head with joy when Shane managed to tune in the BBC World for a half hour the previous night. Because there were moments, especially in the night, when it felt like this damned ship was all of the world that still existed.

We'd a bit of an adventure here last night, as Roland, normally a teatotaler as I've mentioned before, decided to indulge in a wee nip. No one thought much of it until Declan said he was up the main mast of the ship screaming obscenities down at the soldiers. Needless to say they weren't impressed with him, nor were we. We puzzled about for a bit, had a smoke, puzzled some more and tried to come to a consensus on how to get the bugger down. At last, having reviewed several scenarios and rejecting them for one reason and another, we sent Declan up to get him. By this point the soldiers were threatening to shoot him down and be done with his foul tongue.

Declan, being at present, the most nimble among us, was up like a shot and brought Roland down none too gently. While I don't think Roland enjoyed the method employed, Declan came down filled with holiday cheer.

He knew the portrait he'd painted was one of hilarity, and yet standing there with the sleet stinging their faces, watching Roland teeter out into the void, had been anything but funny. They were all on the brink of hysteria, thus the fights, the barbed teasing, the short tempers, and for himself, the silence he'd maintained since the whipping. He still felt the separation from the other men, and knew they felt it too. There was no point in sharing all this with Pamela, though, he didn't want her to worry anymore than she already did.

He lay the letter aside momentarily, and returned to the note Jamie had sent. It simply wished him best tidings of the season and ended with a quote from Robbie Burns.

> *Freedom and whiskey gang tegeither*
> *Tak aff your dram.*

Casey frowned down at it. He'd expected expertly coded notes done in iambic pentameter—something the bastard had actually done in his last missive. Was this simple sentiment merely that, or was it the clue he'd hoped for?

Then the light broke as though a bulb had been smashed over his head. He had to contain himself from slapping his forehead and shouting *Eureka*! He glanced about quickly at the other men. All were still absorbed in their various amusements, Roland now snoring loudly.

He picked up the whiskey. It was a bottle of the house reserve. This particular blend never left Ireland, unless it went in a suitcase. Never aged less than twelve years, its rich, peaty flavor was deservedly famous. He'd a different bottle than the other men, though he wasn't certain what the significance of that could be. Other than the label. He examined the edges of it closely, but it appeared to be tightly sealed to the bottle. The lettering the same, Celtic weave in scarlet and black, and the border—this he examined minutely, running his fingers along the raised interlocking weave. Christ, the man must have had hours of amusement devising this. Nothing seemed abnormal here either, until his fingers felt a slight bump, more of an oddness to the texture really. He held it as close to his face as he dared, and saw the tiny frayed end of a golden thread. He slid his thumbnail under it, then began to pull and felt its length running around the entire label.

The label peeled back easily, revealing three tiny squares of onionskin paper covered in spider-fine writing. Casey smiled and palmed the papers. The last piece was in place.

Three weeks earlier he'd stood by the rail, listening to Mattie outline his plan for escape. Had listened with mounting horror as he realized just what the man was proposing.

"Swim? Have ye done yer nut man?!"

Matty had calmly regarded the agitated man in front of him. Having had some experience with the father and his opinions on largish bodies of water, he was willing to let the son vent before he elaborated further. Casey had gone on at some length, detailing why this wasn't a good idea, but rather a suicide mission doomed to fail.

A day later, he listened grimly silent while Matty explained it to him once again. This time he watched while a silken head, the color of glossed pewter, bobbed in and out of the waves. Biting back the nausea that merely observing the movement caused, Casey counted the seconds off between each time the seal resurfaced. It was a way to gauge the waves and where the tide was likely to land them at a given point of the day.

His father, neither more nor less fond of the sea than he himself, had nevertheless taught both his boys to swim in it. 'Know the enemy, an' either figure out how to beat it, or work with it,' he'd said and then shown them how to do just that; swimming with the currents, resting before your strength ebbed too low, knowing that time and determination were the only things you had on your side with such a formidable foe. He didn't want to do it, but the fact was he *could* do it.

A few more days and they'd informed Declan, Roland and Shane of their plan. Declan, as was his wont, pointed out the flaws in the plan, and helped them take the wrinkles out. Thus on the next moonless night Casey found himself holding his breath and watching as a soldier's silhouette drew parallel with the porthole the five of them were clustered about.

"Now," he said urgently, and Declan and Roland heaved a large can over the side. It made a frightful noise when it hit the water, but the guard above never flinched in his stride. He'd neither heard nor seen a thing. A bubble of elation began to form in Casey's chest, this harebrained scheme might actually work. As men, they could likely hit the water much softer than the can had, but it was as wise to be certain that if one of them fell and hit the water, the noise wouldn't rouse the guns above them.

The plan was on for the second week of January. Christ help them all if it didn't come off as they hoped.

He drifted back to himself enough to hear that Roland had awakened and was having one of his escalating conversations with Declan.

"God or no God," Declan was saying heatedly, "ye'd not catch me walkin' through there alone at night."

"That is an indication," Roland said piously, "that yer faith isna strong enough then."

"Walkin' through where?" Casey asked, striving for a casual tone, though his heart still thumped madly.

"The Murph," they replied in unison, then glared at one another.

"Why ever not?"

"Because of that old man's dog, remember the big Shepherd that was killed by the Brits—"

"I don't think ye can fairly blame the Brits for that," Matty interjected, "the dog picked up a nail bomb, thinkin' it was a ball. A nail bomb that was thrown *at* the Brits, if ye remember correctly."

"Had the Brits not been there," Roland said, looking down his long nose, "there'd have been no need for the nail bomb to be present."

Matty, always one to pacify, replied, "True enough, lad, true enough."

"I was there," Declan said, "'twas tragic really, was a great beast of a dog, hated the Brits somethin' vicious. He comes runnin' up to Jim Scally— ye remember him—like he's somethin' grand to give him. Soon as everyone realized what was what, they took off like the devil was loosed, people were arse over teakettle into hedges an' over fences. An' Jim's runnin' hell bent fer leather up round Divismore Park, with the dog gallopin' merrily behind him an' Jim screamin' 'drop it Pansy, drop it!' Would have been comical if it hadn't ended so badly. Killed the dog, an' Jim lost the three toes. Oh Christ, I've lost me place in the pattern," he exclaimed, having abandoned construction on his balaclava in the excitement of the tale.

"I still don't see what the problem is with walkin' through the Murph," Casey said.

"It's because they," Roland aimed a gimlet glance from bloodshot eyes at Declan, "say that ye can hear the dog howlin' still, when someone from the Murph is about to die."

"'Tis true," young Shane said solemnly, looking up from his cards. "I heard it one night, when I was walkin' down the Glenalina Road, an' the next day Col Naylor was shot."

Roland merely appealed to the ceiling for divine intervention, rather than dignifying this with a response. Declan however, stirred by the story, continued on with a list of 'remember whens'.

"Do youse remember that big bull mastiff, name was somethin' funny— Amarbas? Amercan?"

"Amergin," Casey said quietly.

"Aye, Amergin—belonged to that Temple kid. Did anyone ever know what happened to his kid sister?"

"No, but the rumor was always that Hunchback Pete had taken her," Roland said, "he was always a mite shifty round the little ones, especially the girls. Do ye remember the summer he disappeared? Word was Joe Doherty had him taken out in a field beyond Ballymena an' tortured then shot him, let Robin do the shootin' was what I heard."

Matty cleared his throat and gave Roland a pointed look.

"What? It's not as though I'm tellin' secrets out of school; everyone knows what sort of—"

"Shut the feck up," Declan said, poking Roland in the shoulder with a knitting needle, "the man ran with our Casey here for years. If anyone's like to know the truth of the matter it's him."

Roland turned red in patches the way he was wont to in moments of great embarrassment.

"'Tis alright," Casey said, "ye didn't know, an' I've few illusions about Robin an' what he's capable of. I know for a fact though, that 'twasn't Robin who killed Hunchback Pete, he froze to death in Liverpool the next winter."

Roland changed the topic and soon he and Declan were in one of their laborious arguments about who was the greater man, Mick Collins or James Connolly.

Later, when quiet had resumed and the only noise to be heard was the clicking of Declan's needles and the occasional snap as Roland turned over another card in his game of solitaire, Casey noted that Shane had put his head down, his mail bunched under one gripped fist. The lad was having a hard day of it. Christmas tended to magnify loneliness and troubles until they blocked out the little light to be found. And on a ship such as this, light was in short supply already.

"Matty, how many years have ye been imprisoned?" Casey asked casually.

Matty served him a sharp glance, taking in the situation at once.

"Mmphmm, lad, ye'll have to give me a moment to add it up. There was those two years in the Curragh, when I met yer daddy, an' there'd been four years afore that, then the five in Brixton—bad years them, but then ye'll be no stranger to the Englishman's prison yerself an' then the seven months in Portlaise," Matty continued on, ticking off fingers. "When ye add it all up, I 'spose it amounts to about twenty-two years of my life."

"Roland?"

"Nine years all total, though times it seems more. I've missed the births of all my sons, excepting Luke. He's the second oldest."

"Declan?"

Declan finished his row of stitches before replying.

"Four years, my da died last time I was in. Didn't get to the funeral."

"I damn near missed my weddin' day," Matty said with a chuckle, "eluded the police by a hair, though they caught me the week later soon as we returned from our wee honeymoon."

"I didn't know ye'd been married Matty," Declan said, biting off a wool end with his teeth.

"Oh aye, though 'twill be a long time past. She left me when I was in England. Divorced me, married my younger brother an' emigrated over to New York."

"Yer brother!" Declan exclaimed, "I'd have killed the bastard."

"Ach no, he was the man that was there for her, made certain she had what she needed. Always put groceries in the cupboard an' made sure there was a roof over her head. I didn't blame either of them, life moves on without a man when he's locked up too long. It's a fact. She needed someone, he was there an' I wasn't. He's been a father to my daughter these many years."

"Ye have a daughter?" Casey asked, sitting up in surprise.

"Aye, she'd be nineteen last May," Matty replied. "She's been in America since she was three. She's the three sisters now, never did know that I was her da. I thought it best if I was just Uncle Matty to her same as her sisters."

The five of them fell silent as they digested the magnitude of such a loss.

Matty looked over at Casey. "An' what about yerself, laddie? How many Christmases have ye spent starin' at prison walls?"

"This'll be the sixth," Casey said, feeling a sudden slump in his spirits. He stood up off the bunk and stretched carefully, his skin protesting instantly. "I'm just goin' out for a wee breath of air."

"Mind how much air," Declan said with a stern look over his needles, "ye've a ways to go before ye're fully mended."

"Aye Declan, I'll not be long."

'Outside' merely consisted of a cracked porthole through which one could catch a bit of fresh air and on the odd night see a star or two.

The night was very still, the snow falling so lightly that he could discern the individual flakes. Even the big spotlights that swept the water seemed softer than they usually did.

Someone moved behind him, the hesitancy of the step told Casey that it was Shane.

He turned from watching the snow. "Do ye need somethin' lad?"

Shane smiled. "I just wanted to say thanks."

"For what?"

"For what ye did in there, getting them to talk about their time. It put things in perspective for me."

"Aye, well, do yerself a favor an' be certain ye're not someday their age, an' tellin' the same story to another lad."

"Merry Christmas, Casey."

"An' to yerself boyo," he said. Behind him he could hear the boy go back to join the others, leaving him alone with the night. He settled the scarf more tightly around his neck, the smell of strawberries and grass and vanilla rising from it. His wife's own particular scent, overlaid with a simple perfume.

In his mind's eye, he saw the night as it might have been at home. It would be quiet after the madness of the day, Lawrence finally gone to sleep. Christ, what he'd have given to see the lad's face this morning. He'd never had a Christmas before, at least not a real one with a tree and a family and love wrapped around you from morning until night. Hopefully the lad had had a good day despite his absence.

What he missed most, though, was the recounting of the day, beside Pamela in their bed, going over the details, tucking away the memories of another holiday, despite the fact that it would blur into the details of a dozen others. That, of course, was half the beauty of it. God and saints willing, he'd be there next year and every year after that.

The paper he'd crumpled up when Shane had joined him still lay damp within his hand, but he had taken a glimpse before the lad had come out and knew what it contained.

At the top, written in Jamie's firm, elegant hand were the words 'Merry Christmas' and under them was the one thing Casey had asked for that Christmas.

The tidal charts for the lough for the second and third weeks of January 1972.

Chapter Fifty-five

Moth to a Flame

I T HAD BEEN MANY YEARS SINCE the Kirkpatrick home had held such a party. Of course, it had been many years since Jamie had felt like celebrating in such a manner. That he did now had Pamela somewhat worried. Over the holidays the febrile glitter he'd developed through November had become a blinding aura with a terribly sharp edge to it. He was headed for a spectacular fall, the likes of which he'd not experienced in years. She didn't know how to stop it, however.

The scents of roasting beef and goose mingled festively with the exhaled breath of several bottles of decanted wine. Fires were lit in every downstairs hearth, the light reflecting off of bookbindings, polished floors, and stair rails. Maggie was ordering the catering staff about in fourteen different directions at once, and looked as thoroughly happy as only a woman in her element can. Fresh flowers floated in vases and bowls, glowing softly in dim corners.

The two hundred year old crystal had been dusted and polished until it glittered like diamonds on the long dining table. Above, the spun-sugar Venetian chandelier was ablaze with all two hundred candles lit. Guests milled through the rooms, glasses refilled at the slightest suggestion of emptiness. The women beautifully gowned, bejeweled and perfumed, the men in formal attire that made even the least fair of them look wonderfully elegant. Strains of Bach wafted over the assembly like a subtle fragrance misted onto the air.

Pamela watched the spectacle from the safety of a corner in the long drawing room, a glass of wine clutched tightly in her hand. Jamie, as always, was the consummate host; his head a gilded lily in the crowd, his voice smoothing all paths and any obstacles that stood in his way. All eyes gave themselves to him, following in the light-ridden wake. He was, of course, intelligent enough to know it and wise enough to ignore it. On his arm, dressed in a pleated column of pale green Chanel silk, was Belinda.

A long mirror held Pamela's reflection as though she were a painting, burning against the background of the long dimly lit hallway. The pale ivory skin of her shoulders in stark contrast to the blooded crimson she wore at her throat and ears, and in a snug velvet sheathe around her form. She wore her hair up, with long tendrils curling down around her neck. It had been a while since she'd dressed up, or felt like doing so, but Jamie had been so excited about the party that his mood had become contagious.

Suddenly, though, she felt deflated, as though her flesh had collapsed in on her bones along with her mood. These sudden feelings of despair had come upon her without warning several times since the loss of the baby. It seemed to her that her womb was an ash garden, where no child would ever survive to light and life. She wondered if it wouldn't simply be better to be barren. At least then she could stop hoping.

She glanced once more in the mirror, noting the dark hollows that were permanently carved beneath her eyes these days. Compared to Belinda's rose-gold charms, she looked positively ghostly. The absence of Casey was a constant ache in her chest, and so was the anger that he'd pushed her away. Yet right this moment she would have given up a year of her life just to rest in the secure strength of his arms. To know that he was safe.

Jamie caught her eye in the mirror, concern written clearly on his features. He raised one golden eyebrow almost imperceptibly, but she understood the implied question and managed a smile for him. She was aware that he was still watching her closely, and so she had endeavored to put a brave face on things. Some days it was exhausting, however.

Jamie turned away, and she let the smile go along with the pent up air in her chest. He had bent to talk to an elderly lady, and a blaze of light crowned his hair, his lithe form clad in a black dinner suit that managed to be less formal and more elegant than anyone else in the room. More than one woman in the room watched him with a slightly unfocused gaze.

A large sigh sounded in her ear, a breath that conceived itself slightly lower than the person's stomach and somewhat higher than his knees. "Oh Lucifer thou son of morning," a voice murmured. Pamela recognized the voice, and turned to look at its owner.

"Comparing his Lordship with Satan?" she asked tartly, the wine tasting bitter on her tongue, "others tend to think he sits much closer to the divine than that."

Small Davey of Armagh, so named because of his less than imposing stature, gave her an inquisitive look, one bristly eyebrow raised. "Only in looks," he replied imperturbably, "one could imagine even God being jealous of such a face and form."

She treated him to an owlish look, taking in the stocky body, the green and scarlet kilt, black velvet dress jacket and the wiry hair that poked out of his shirt collar and curled over the tops of his Argyll socks. He was a remarkably hairy creature, she thought uncharitably. Unfortunately for Davey, nary a wisp of it adorned his head, which was as round, shiny and hairless as a cannonball.

His abbreviated height put him at an eye level that would have made most men very happy. However it was common knowledge that Small Davey's appetites did not run to the curves and roundels of the female form.

His eyes, however, were a warm, sherry brown, and at present filled with empathy.

"Does it hurt very badly?"

Her instinct was to prevaricate but some other process, with a greater wisdom, chose honesty. "Like a knife in your soul that never stops twisting," she said baldly, feeling an odd relief in the admittance.

"Yes, I would imagine it does," Small Davey said, voice gentle, brown eyes still intent on her face. "Does he know?"

"No...I mean...I don't know," she stuttered, hot blood flushing along her skin. "I am married you know," she finished lamely.

"I had," Small Davey gave a small smile, "heard that. However, if you'll permit an observation by one who has never enjoyed the comforts of a legal union, it seems to me that one does not stop having inconvenient emotions once the rings are exchanged."

"I must be terribly transparent," she said, feeling as if the naked yearning that Jamie never failed to stir in her was printed in scarlet letters across her forehead.

"Perhaps only to one who takes the time to look," Small Davey said kindly. "Smile, dear girl, he's looking this way."

She glanced up, unerringly meeting Jamie's eyes across the whirl of small talk and social eddying that was moving about the room in a great undulating spiral. He raised a questioning eyebrow, as if he knew they'd been talking about him. Likely the bastard did, he'd the radar of a bat and the ability to listen to several conversations at once, all the while seeming to pay complete attention to whomever was in front of him.

Just then the dinner bell rang.

"Shall we?" Davey offered his arm, as much, she suspected, in support as in manners.

MAGGIE HAD WORKED HER USUAL MAGIC, so that despite the harried crew hustling to and from the kitchen, there was a feeling that the whole thing had been beautifully effortless. The food had been divine; the wine poured with a generous hand. Now the whiskey had replaced it, so that there was a feeling of soporific content that pervaded the entire length of the table. The candles were burning down, and the dining room was bathed in a soft golden haze. The young man Jamie had hired to play piano for the evening was sounding out the first notes of Cole Porter's *You Do Something To Me*. Even Pamela felt a slight thaw of the icy core which had sat in her chest for the last six weeks.

Conversation and laughter mixed agreeably with the tinkle of fine crystal and china. Pamela turned toward Jamie, and he flicked her a brief smile of complicity, as though to say "well it's not turned out so bad then, has it?"

From the corner of her eye, Pamela could see that Belinda had caught the exchange and had put a proprietary hand on Jamie's arm. A flicker of red-hot anger shot through her at the sight of that soft, white hand laying there in unmistakable possession. Though Belinda was ostensibly giving all her attention to the old gent beside her, there was look of a cat with too much cream around its whiskers on her face that Pamela knew was for her benefit alone.

"Damned fine bit of new horse James has gotten, will he be letting him race in the spring?" The neighbor was asking, the rough hand that held his whiskey glass testifying to his own years spent in and around stables.

Belinda smiled, tightening her fingers on Jamie's forearm to turn his attention away from Geordie Cohen, one of the managers from the linen mill with whom he'd been discussing flax prices for the last ten minutes.

"I don't know. James, will we be letting Phouka race?"

Pamela could feel the simmer in her blood begin a rolling boil. How dare this woman talk as though she made the decisions here, particularly when it came to Phouka.

"Phouka won't be racing this year because he's too young," Pamela said smoothly, "and because it's for me to say whether he races or not. He is, after all, mine."

"Yours?" Belinda enquired, politeness barely covering her animosity towards the woman opposite her.

"Yes," Pamela said, smile still firmly in place, though her eyes burned like wildfire. "Mine, my Christmas present actually."

"Phouka," Belinda narrowly missed choking on a swallow of wine, "Phouka was a Christmas present!"

"Er—yes," Jamie said, beginning to look mildly alarmed by the hostility that was very nearly palpable between the two women.

"Jamie never misses giving me a Christmas present—hasn't in years," Pamela said, in a tone that was a direct challenge to the woman who sat so smugly across the table from her.

"That damn horse is worth a quarter of a million pounds!" Belinda said, as if Phouka, by merely being, had committed a crime.

"Jamie," the two women said simultaneously, one in bewilderment and the other in outraged humiliation. Jamie noted that all his other guests had ceased even pretending to eat or attend to their own conversations and had turned raptly fascinated faces to the drama unfolding at the head of his table.

"You told me," Belinda said, no longer bothering to speak in low tones, "that you bought him as an investment."

"An investment?" Pamela said, turning her attention to Jamie as well. "An investment in what?"

"Yes, Jamie, an investment in what exactly?" Belinda asked, blue eyes hard as two points of cobalt. "The long-term future, wishful thinking? It seems the sort of present one would give a wife, or perhaps a beloved mistress."

"How dare you!" Pamela said, throwing her napkin down and rising from the table. Small Davey laid a restraining hand on her forearm which she abruptly flung off.

"How dare I?" Belinda queried coolly. "Tell me Pamela, does your husband know about Jamie's gifts to you?"

"That's none of your business," Pamela said through clenched teeth.

"No, I didn't think he knew. I doubt he'd be very pleased by the news, would he? Where is he now? Which prison, or internment camp as I understand you prefer to call it, is he gracing with his presence currently?"

"Belinda, please, not here," Jamie said in a low tone.

"Not here? Where better, darling? I think, Jamie, your money would have been better spent on bribing all the officials and paying out all the hush money her husband will need to see the light of day again. Or is that where the two of you prefer to have him? Safely behind bars so you can continue to play your little game with each other. White knight and damsel in distress. How touching," Belinda rose, slightly unsteady on her feet. "You're a fool Jamie, you could have had her for a fraction of the price. I understand whores in her neighborhood come cheap."

Pamela lifted her still full wineglass and flung its contents in Belinda's face. Jamie took her swiftly by the elbow, excusing himself grimly from the assembly.

He stopped by Belinda, who stood dripping wine onto pleated silk. "Are you all right?"

"No," she said quite calmly, all things considered, "I'm about as far from all right as one can get."

"Go upstairs," he said tersely, "I'll be with you as soon as I deal with Pamela and get rid of the rest of these damn people. Please," he added in a slightly more contrite tone.

She nodded numbly. She stood, wine still dripping from her face and hair, managing to avoid the shocked faces around the table. She collected her bag and wrap, then catching a glance of Jamie closing the study door on him and Pamela, walked directly out the front door.

"JUST WHAT THE HELL WAS THAT ABOUT?" Jamie asked, his breath still coming in quick, angry bursts.

"Why are you asking me? It was your girlfriend who called me a whore,"

Pamela replied truculently, eyes studiously on the carpet.

"Please," his tone was biting, "can we skip the accusations as to who said what first and cut to the part where you explain throwing wine on my dinner guest in front of dozen of witnesses? And, if it's not too much to ask, look me in the eye as you do it."

Her head came up reluctantly, her mouth still set in a mutinous line. "I'm sorry, I acted reprehensibly. I'll go out and apologize publicly to one and all, and then, if you don't mind, I'm going home."

"As it happens," Jamie said coolly, "I do mind. And if you think some lukewarm public display is going to reverse your actions out there, think again."

She shrugged her shoulders, knowing even as she did it how annoying he would find it.

"I don't know why I did it. She makes me angry with her lady of the manor airs, as if this house," she gestured angrily around the room, "and everything in it belongs to her."

"I see," Jamie said, one golden gull-winged eyebrow raised in skepticism. "Well the fact of the matter is, though she's a guest in my home, she does have more intimate claims than most visitors. If she feels at home here, it's perhaps excusable, all things considered."

"I suppose you are referring to her claims on your bed and yourself," she said before she could think to edit the conduit between thought and speech.

"I suppose I am," Jamie said, giving no quarter. Standing near the windows that caught and held the reflection of the fire, he looked like a medieval angel; straight-nosed, stern-lipped and capable of all manner of unpleasant punishments. "Though why that should cause you to throw a perfectly inoffensive little wine in her face is something that I'm less clear on."

Green eyes, suddenly without defense, held to green that simmered with anger.

"Well Jamie," she said, voice exhausted, "I suppose it's just plain old jealousy isn't it?"

"Jealousy?" he asked, face suddenly wary.

"Yes," she said, "I'm jealous of her. I'm jealous that she has claims on you that I don't. I'm jealous that you'll take her to your bed but you wouldn't take me when you had the chance. I'm jealous that she sits at your table as if she belongs there. That she shares all the little inside jokes and thoughts of someone who is half of a couple. I watch her touch your arm and the way she meets your eyes in one of those looks that make it clear you two are lovers and it takes every ounce of self-control I have not to slap her."

She shook her head and sat down suddenly in the overstuffed wing-back by the fireplace. "I know it's awful and unjustified, I know it's horribly selfish and ridiculous of me, but there you have it. And I will apologize to her, Jamie, I did behave like a furious child and I know it. But please," she said, face naked now without its shield of defiance, "don't ask me to be around the two of you together anymore. Pathetic or not, I don't really think I can stand it."

"Perhaps it bears remembering that you are the one with marriage vows here," Jamie said, still unmoving and lit by long shards of dying fire.

"I know that," she said, "and it only makes me all the more ashamed of my feelings. I'm married and I love my husband, and yet I still want to somehow be central to your life. Believe me, I know how that sounds." She drew a ragged breath, pushing her hair, now tumbling willy-nilly from its pins, behind her ears.

"And there," Jamie said quietly, voice drained of all emotion, "we come to the crux of the situation, don't we? You love your husband, while I am very fond of Belinda. I think we're both wise enough to recognize the insult in that."

"Perhaps, though, someday you'll feel more than fondness," she said softly, "and that's what I can't seem to breathe around."

"No, Pamela," he said in a flat tone. "I've had it both ways and I know the difference. I won't wake up one morning and suddenly find the woman beside me in the bed has become the love of my life."

"You don't even admit to the possibility of that? You weren't always such a cynic, Jamie."

"No, I don't admit to the possibility of that. The woman I love won't ever lie in my bed," he said, with only the tiniest trace of bitterness belying his defeat, "her affections are otherwise engaged. And so," he walked across the room, feet halting and hand coming to rest near the whiskey decanter, "I find ways to ease the pain of that. With work, with other women, with a friend who knows she can never be more and yet loves me enough to make such allowances."

"Jamie, I—"

He shook his head, putting a halt to her words. "Let's not say things that we'll devoutly wish unsaid in the morning."

She rose and went to where he stood, his long fingers now curved around the stopper of the decanter. She laid her own hand, cold and trembling, on top of his.

"I'm sorry, Jamie, truly I am. I wish," her voice broke slightly, "I wish a great many things but mostly, of late, I wish that someone would give me a key, or the recipe for a draught I could drink down, or would just tell me how to wake up one day and find myself simply not loving you anymore. Can you tell me how to do that, Jamie?"

"If," he said, and turned his face to her own, "I knew the answer to such things, we wouldn't be having this ridiculous conversation, would we?"

Of its own accord, her free hand came up and touched lightly the side of his face, traveling down until it lay, pulse to heavy pulse, against his neck. He closed his eyes for a moment, a small space where he allowed himself to feel the bitter sweetness of her hand upon his skin.

His lashes, red-gold in the fading light, fanned against his cheek and his face turned to her hand, his own coming up and capturing her fingers, pressing them against his lips. He breathed out against her skin, caught the crushed berry scent beneath his nose, and found himself trapped in a dizzying place where the house of cards he'd so carefully built, tethered together with the fine crystal bones of deception, subterfuge and regret, threatened to tumble down all in an instant.

A touch, a moment—no more, before he put her hand from him, gently but firmly, knowing that all he desired most in the world was open to him this moment. But knowing also where the root of her present weakness lay, found the strength to refuse that which was offered.

No more than inches separated them. He could feel her tremble across the air, now dimmed from red-gold to the ash of spent fire.

"And so," she said in a brittle voice, "I am still, it would seem, playing moth to your star."

Jamie stared unseeing at his own fingers, so tight around the crystal now that it cut into his palm; the nerves in his fingers still painfully unsheathed to the memory of her touch.

"Have you ever looked into the night sky, really looked, Pamela? There is no lonelier place than the firmaments, a beautiful hell and yet," he laughed, a small, strangled sound, "despite its jewels, hell all the same."

"I hate her," she said in a broken whisper. "I resent every look, every word, every touch she's ever had from you. I hate her as I have never hated anyone and yet I would wish her well enough that she might take care for you."

"Then perhaps you can understand," Jamie replied in a tightly controlled voice, "in some small measure, the nature of my feelings for your husband."

She closed her eyes, sensed the humming of an edge place which threatened to crack the foundation of her life, the air so sharp against her skin that she could feel its slice. To breathe seemed impossible, to step towards the door completely beyond her powers.

"Having said these words," Jamie spoke in measured and flavorless syllables, "we can now close the door to this room for once and for all, leaving our respective weapons inside."

"You once said that it seemed all of life was standing on the threshold in darkness, waiting for someone to open the door and bring you into warmth and light."

"Did I?" his tone was light, the mask taken up once again. "One of these days I must learn to still my tongue, I seem to have a ghastly habit of telling all my most imprudent thoughts to you."

She ignored the masquerade and replied at her own peril. "Sometimes when I look at you I feel as if I am twelve again, waiting at that door." She looked out through the glass walls of the study where the first small lights of Jamie's vaulted hell had begun to glitter.

He turned, eyes not green, but black with restrained emotion. "We neither of us have the ability nor the right to open that door, Pamela."

"I think," she said faintly, "perhaps, all things considered, it would be best if I gave Phouka back to you."

He nodded wordlessly, the scent of crushed berries still blistering his senses.

And so saying, she went, leaving in her wake a man who wondered how many times one could properly be expected to die within a lifetime.

Part Five

An Aran Idyll

Chapter Fifty-six

The Fabulous Five

THE NIGHT CHOSEN FOR THEIR ESCAPE came up dark and drizzly, the moon in sullen hiding amongst the drenched clouds. At five pm, they gathered, the five of them, jumpy as fleas and starting to feel the pressure of their plan.

"More polish, laddie," Matty said to Shane, tossing him another flat tin of the stuff. The boot polish would irritate the skin, causing it to heat in protest and the thick coat of butter would seal in the warmth and keep them 'right as ducks in a gale,' Matty claimed.

Over the last several days they'd acclimatized themselves with a series of brutally cold showers, standing naked under the streaming water until their bodies were blue.

After basting themselves liberally with both polish and butter they re-dressed, ready for the six o'clock head count. The warders were punctual to a fault and the head count never took more than a few minutes. They could be off the ship shortly after six, and easily make the rendezvous point by a quarter of seven, which was the agreed upon time for the land meet. A car would be waiting to whisk the five of them to safe houses in Andersontown, deep in Republican territory. Timing was all.

Disaster struck in the form of the six o'clock head count. One man was missing.

"Ker-ist," Declan muttered, "it's that friggin' Tom Hanigan, never can rouse the bastard when he's needed."

"Keep yer calm," Casey hissed, as rattled as Declan, but determined not to show it. "Fan out an' see if we can't find him."

Twenty minutes of fruitless searching did not turn up the feckless Tom Hanigan, and Casey, who could hear the threats Declan was muttering, thought it might be better for Tom if he was never found.

Another minute even and the plan would have to be scrapped, and then *sin sin*, it would all be over. There'd not be time for another chance before they were moved. He'd not much faith in the possibility of release, not with his name.

Just at the moment that he was considering how to endure the next twenty years in the Kesh, Tom Hanigan, foolish smile in place, wandered out from the bog with a book in hand. Casey strategically placed his broad shoulders between Declan and the oblivious Tom.

The head count went smooth as silk. The plan was back on.

It moved like ballet after that, the skiffle group took up position and started playing their assorted instruments. Men placed tables near the portholes, and then set about playing chess and draughts.

Casey nodded in approval; it looked like any other evening aboard the *Maidstone*. Not a thing appeared unusual or awry.

He gave the sign to Matty and a minute later the five of them were stripped down to their undershorts, faces blacked and buttered to match their bodies. The skiffle group took the music up a notch, all of them singing *The Rising of the Moon* at the top of their lungs.

Roland was already sawing away at the bar, tongue stuck out between his teeth in exertion.

Casey took a last look at his wee group. A pathetic looking bunch, near naked and filthy with boot polish, white patches glowing with butter. Roland and Declan on the verge of yet another of their series of unending arguments. Matty, looking for all the world like a contented garden gnome, with nothing more pressing than a stroll about the fields on his mind. Shane no longer able to swallow his nerves, jittering like a flea in a fry pan. Aye, pathetic as a picture, but he'd trust his life to any one of them.

Roland had stopped sawing, he gave the bar a push and to everyone's delight it snapped clean through on the top weld.

"Christ, that's luck," Declan said, white smile cutting a gleaming swathe in his boot blacked face.

Casey took the first decent breath he'd had in several hours. This bit of good fortune would buy them back ten of the twenty minutes they'd lost.

The porthole was open now to the dark and the freezing expanse of water beyond. He nodded. "Let's go, men."

Roland slipped through the porthole first, scrambling nimbly onto the hawser and then dropping swiftly out of sight. Declan followed, atypically silent, and grim looking.

Shane was next. Casey patted his shoulder. "Don't look back an' don't turn back unless they start shootin' at ye."

Shane nodded, eyes as big as saucers. They helped him through the porthole, keeping a grip on him until he'd a firm hold of the hawser. Casey peered down after him. "Christ ye could see the head of a pin out there, it's like high noon at the OK corral."

"Then get off with ye Gary Cooper," Matty said.

"No I'll go last, bring up the rear," Casey said, voice hoarse from all the whispering he'd been doing. The skiffle group had launched into a raucous version of *The Boys of the Old Brigade*.

"I'm goin' last, an' that's final," Matty said firmly. "I couldn't face yer da if I left ye to bring up the rear. I've got yer back, son—now go."

"My da is dead," Casey said in whisper, wondering if the man had taken leave of his senses at this crucial moment.

"Aye," Matty replied imperturbably, "but if I don't make it through this, I'll have to face the man at the pearly gates, an' I'd just as soon not have ye on my conscience should it come to that."

Casey knew to waste any more time arguing would be suicidal to the escape at this point, so he seized the hawser rope and swung himself out over the sea. The rope was surprisingly smooth and his journey down swift. He gasped when he hit the water; it was purely desperate. He felt as though he'd fallen into a patch of stinging nettles. The salt immediately stung his eyes and flooded up his nose. He stripped the sodden socks off his hands and abandoned them to their fate.

Matty had negotiated the steel rope and was in the water now, with only a small splash to remark upon his entry.

Casey took a deep breath and slid through the water, praying that none of them would get caught in the barbed wire. He negotiated his head and shoulders through without incident, grazed his chest on a barb and thought he'd made it free when a sharp stab to his leg told him he'd caught his thigh on the wire. It pulled him down, head just below the surface. He fought the desire to panic, the five of them had made a deal that if any of them tired or even began to drown the others would not turn back to help, as it would destroy everyone's chance at escape. He was on his own.

He needed to breathe soon, the pressure in his lungs was already next to unbearable. He'd have to risk the injury to his leg. He kicked hard at the wire and felt the barb pull loose, leaving a throbbing trail in its wake. Then suddenly he was free and swimming, the back of Declan's head bobbing up and down ahead of him, outlined by the searchlights that swept the dark water. It would be a miracle if they weren't caught; the stretch of water was as bright as a floodlit football pitch. The only thing they could hope for was that the guards had taken shelter from the rain and wouldn't be able to see clearly over the water. Or better yet, would believe the Army's contention that the Maidstone was inescapable, and wouldn't be paying attention at all.

Behind him he heard Matty clear the barbed wire, though not without injury from the sound of the soft expletives coming from him. That was the last of them then, they'd all cleared the wire and were on their way.

He swam forward expecting the sound of gunfire to explode around them, or for the alarm to sound, putting an end to the freedom that he could now taste in his mouth.

Each time his head came up he looked for the other men. Declan was about fifteen yards ahead swimming steadily, Roland just beyond him, head popping up and down like a cork on the waves, and Matty's breathing was audible behind him. Shane was unaccounted for.

Casey maintained a firm grip on his calm; he blinked the salt from his eyes and looked left on the first stroke, right on the second. Then he saw him, twenty yards out on the right. He was struggling, head going under for several seconds before emerging weakly and going directly back under. Despite Casey's dire threats to the rest of the men, he didn't hesitate, cutting cleanly through the water. When he arrived at the last spot he'd seen the boy's head go under he paddled in place. He was ready when the head emerged, barely breaking the surface.

He dove under, locked a forearm around Shane's chest, and pulled him to the surface. The lad started coughing immediately, spitting seawater out. Casey flipped him onto his back, floating him on the skin of the water.

"Can ye hear me, man? Ye're goin' to have to float for a minute, get yer strength back an' then get on yer stroke again. Do ye hear me?"

He shook the boy's arm, panic making him angry, knowing that every second upped the odds of being caught and foiling the escape for everyone. Finally, though, he got a weak 'yes' from Shane's lips. He paddled beside him, the water around them lit up so bright it pained his eyes. He ought to go and leave the boy to his own devices, but knew he couldn't live with himself if the lad drowned.

He floated on his own back, knowing he needed to conserve his energy. The cold would sap it quickly and they were still a long way out from shore.

The water lapped across his face, the night sky above dark and starless. A strange lethargy crept over him. The temptation to let go, to slip his hold on life and let the current take him, swept through him. His mind was drifting down through the layers of water below him, to a place where darkness was not the mere absence of light, but an absolution all its own. Where sunrise and sunset had never been and neither time nor tide had meaning. And for a moment he felt it, the lure his wife knew in the sea's embrace. The dark call to salt-matched blood, the return to a timeless origin. A mother that would rock you in the cradle of ancient leviathans and give your bones a soft bed of fine white privacy, undisturbed by the grasses of the upper world.

Sound exploded in his ear and he started, the water forming a shroud over his face. He came up sputtering to see Shane, wide-eyed above the canary diamonds the searchlights scattered over the wide water.

"What the hell—" he coughed, words tangled on a sputter of saltwater from his lungs.

"Was a seal," Shane said, "ye were goin' under an' he barked straight in yer ear. I could swear he knew."

"Knew what?"

"That ye were tryin' to drown," Shane replied, a queer look on his face, as though he were suddenly afraid.

Casey shook his head, clearing the salt pools from his eyes. "On yer stroke man, we've lost time."

He struck out, the shore lights a distant beacon. His muscles tremored with the fear of what they'd sensed in him. Beneath him, something slid slick as oil against his belly but solid with speed. The seal.

"Ye've an odd notion of guardian angels," he muttered to the sky, as the seal slid past him once more, a quiver of muscle and sleek hide against his leg.

He forced himself to keep his stroke even and measured, knowing a burst of speed might well sink him at this point. The seal stayed with him, its head appearing out of the waves every few strokes, never more than a few feet away. He focused on it instead of the ache in his muscles and the cold that now insisted itself through the wax of butter and shoe polish.

The seal didn't leave him until the pier loomed up in his vision. His muscles were dense as cement with exhaustion, the small distance seemingly insurmountable. He heaved a breath and put on one last burst of strength. A dozen more yards—eight, then six, then four and he was there, hands slicing on barnacles, weary beyond caring for pain. Then other hands reached for his own, and fastened his grip to land.

He glanced back once, before Declan and Roland pulled him up and onto the pier.

The seal was floating in the current, head a chimera in the confusion of light and dark. He'd the strong impression, however, of unblinking black eyes meeting his own unwaveringly. Maybe then only a trick of the moving water, for a second later the waves were empty other than Shane coming up, white arms churning the water.

For a moment Casey lay on the pier, letting the rain fall in his mouth, merely grateful to be alive and to have made it this far. They'd lost close to half an hour due to the screwed up head count, but gained ten on the porthole. Which still put them twenty minutes out, and after seven o'clock. Their pickup would have left thinking they weren't coming, that for one reason or another the escape hadn't come off.

"Christ where are they?" Declan echoed his thoughts, arms wrapped tightly around his chest, entire body shaking like a leaf.

"If they're wise, they're well clear of here by now," Casey said, feeling his heart sink to the vicinity of his toes. The dark would help them hide, but it was also going to make it harder for them to find their way. Especially now that they were going to have to find alternative transport into the city.

"What's the contingency plan, lad?" Matty asked, as all heads swiveled toward Casey.

He bought himself a bit of time by sneezing, for there was no contingency plan. He cast an eye about their surroundings. The Queens Road terminus was in the near vicinity. It seemed madness to emerge from cover, but the chance would have to be taken. It was all they had at present, unless they walked all the way back to Belfast, which didn't appeal greatly and would leave them open to being scooped up by the security forces.

"We'll have to get on a bus," he said. "The lads are long gone by now, it's the only option we've left."

"Are ye mad? With the five of us in shorts and pyjamas an' soaked to boot," Declan said. "They may have heard of the escape by now, the Army'll be on our heads in about five minutes flat."

"Do ye have a better idea, Declan?" Casey asked mildly.

"No."

"Anybody else have objections?"

The polish smeared faces gathered around him remained mute.

"Right then," Casey strove for a resolute tone, "best if one of us goes first an' takes the lay of the land." He sighed. "I suppose it might as well be me."

Before he could think better of what he was doing, he stepped out from cover and strode across the tarmac toward the bus terminus. A bus was just pulling in as he approached. He hesitated a moment, then walked over to the opening door. He knew he was a hell of a sight, hair plastered to his head, body covered with long streaks of boot polish and only a pair of undershorts between him and the big, cold world.

"Hello there," he called out. "Are ye headin' back into the city?"

The bus driver standing at the top of the stairs was short, bewhiskered, balding, and apparently unflappable. He eyed Casey dispassionately.

"Well laddie, ye'll have to wait as I'm just off on my tea break."

"Oh," said Casey, barely able to hear above the chattering of his teeth.

The bus driver stood, removed his coat, and laid it neatly over the back of his seat before descending the bus stairs with a smile and a tip of his hat.

"Good day to ye, lad. I'll be fifteen minutes or so if ye care to wait, though perhaps ye're in too much of a hurry to," he said and walked, without haste, to the small hut where the drivers took their tea.

Casey blinked dazedly at him before turning back to the bus, where the keys, bright and swaying a bit from the wind whipping in the open door, sat snugly in the ignition.

Never one to look a gift horse in the mouth Casey leaped up the stairs, seating himself swiftly behind the steering wheel. His hands were shaking so badly that it took three tries to turn the ignition.

He jumped up from the seat when the bus roared to life, certain he was done for, even if the man had meant for him to take the bus. Odds were there was a supervisor in the offices that wouldn't be quite so sympathetic to the plight of a half-naked, butter smeared escapee. He dared a glance at the small hut and saw that there was no sign of any furious office clerk coming to save the city's property. Now he could only hope there was enough air built up in the brakes for the engine to engage.

He thrust the clutch in, shifted gears and the bus lurched forward hard enough to jar the teeth in his head. Ahead of him, the gates swung to and fro in the wind, the drizzle of rain coming down harder now. He punched the gas to the floor, hands gripping the steering wheel with every ounce of forbearance he possessed.

The bus gave a clanging wheeze, sputtered a bit and then shot through the gates with the ease of sliced butter. Casey only had a disturbing impression of an open-mouthed guard with tea slopping out of his cup, shaking a fist at him and yelling what were no doubt great streams of obscenity and then he was on the road, gravel kicking out from beneath the back end as it fishtailed onto the narrow strip of pavement. He eyed the road ahead; there were no cars in sight.

"Thank the Lord for small mercies," he muttered grimly through gritted teeth, aware that the bus was not going as fast as one might expect it to, when one's foot was firmly gunning it to the floor. He allowed himself only a flickering glance up into the rearview mirror; there were no headlights behind him. So far, so good.

A hundred yards down the road, he brought the bus to a lurching halt, hoping to God his bearings were right and he was roughly in the vicinity of where he'd left the others.

A desperate glance where the headlights shone showed him nothing but leaves canting left, and showing their undersides to the wind that was increasing with every minute. Should he chance going further up the road, or had he already gone past them? Did he dare get out and look for them? He was exhausted and freezing and did not, in the least, relish the idea of a crawl through the thick and unforgiving branches of the rhododendron. But he had little choice; he couldn't risk leaving them behind.

Just then the bushes parted and a blackened face, topped with fair, thinning hair popped out, gave the bus a narrow eye and popped back in.

"Matty, it's me," Casey yelled hoarsely, hoping the wind would carry his words rather then rob them straight out of the air. The head popped out again followed by a bare shoulder and thin body, one arm gesturing madly behind to those still huddling in the vicious sanctuary of the bushes.

They scuttled up out of the ditch, a motley looking crew in the dim light, greased and blacked in their undershorts, twigs and leaves stuck all over them and falling from their heads. Christ have mercy but it'd be a miracle if they weren't all caught.

Declan ran aboard followed closely by Shane, then Roland, with a green-streaked Matty bringing up the rear.

"Have ye stolen the bloody thing?" Matty gasped as he flung himself down into the nearest seat, helped along by gravity as the bus, door still closing, resumed its precipitous flight down the road.

"Aye, I have," Casey responded shortly, senses acutely strained as if he could urge the bus to go faster by willing it so.

"Did I not tell ye," Roland said piously, "that the Lord provides in times of need?"

"The Lord," Declan gasped, pulling rhododendron twigs out of his undershorts, "by way of my hand, is goin' to provide ye with a swift cuff upside the head, if ye don't shut yer gob."

"He prayed for Declan's eternal soul the entire time in the bushes," Matty said, hunching over the back of Casey's seat. "Can ye not make the blasted thing go any faster?"

"No, I've about got my damn foot through the floorboards as it is," Casey responded in frustration. Feeling was beginning to return to his numbed extremities and his right leg, already bruised and cut, was now aching from the force he was applying, apparently in vain, to the gas pedal. "The needle's stuck at forty an' not budgin'."

"Will I drive the bus then, or pray over the needle?" Roland asked, with all the pleasant calm of a man out for a Sunday drive in the countryside.

"Will ye what?" Matty asked incredulously, turning back to look at Roland who sat bolt upright against the precarious swaying of the bus, rosary bouncing merrily against his thin chest.

"I drove bus for a living," Roland replied, "and on Saturdays I raced cars. Sundays of course I went to Church."

Everyone grabbed for seats and poles as Casey brought the bus to a sharp stop and jumped out of the driver's seat. He pointed a finger at Roland. "You drive, I'll pray," he said shortly.

Roland took the driver's seat, adjusting his stork-thin frame as if he'd all the time in the world. Then proceeded to bow his head and cross himself, "Lord bless us in our endeavors—" he began in an earnest tone.

"Jaysus, Mary an' Joseph, Roland, we've not the time for this," Declan said, face turning red under its mask of shoe polish and bruises.

"Ye'll not," Roland lobbed a dark look over his shoulder, "blaspheme while I'm behind the wheel."

"Roland," Casey said in as pleasant a tone as could be managed under the circumstances, "move the bus or I'll throttle ye here an' now."

"Right then, let's be off," Roland said and thrust the bus into gear, hands aligned at ten and two on the steering wheel. "Does anyone mind telling me where we're headed?"

Behind Roland, the four looked at each other nonplussed, the plan not having extended much beyond escape and providing no contingencies for stolen busses. "Gentlemen, we need a decision, as we've got someone on our tail."

The four turned their heads as one to see the beam of headlights in the distance, rapidly gaining ground on them.

"Roland," Casey said, taking command without hesitation, "keep on this way to the Queen's Bridge, then down Oxford an' we'll make a run for the Markets."

"Are ye mad? Ye propose to go through the heart of Belfast in this wheezin' clunker? We'll never make it," Declan exclaimed.

"It's the only chance we've got, that's an Army vehicle behind us. The one shot is to get into a Republican stronghold, they'll not dare follow us there, it'd be a suicide mission," Casey replied. "Roland, can ye do this?"

Roland coolly checked his rear and side mirrors, jacked the bus up into the next gear, and put his foot down on the gas pedal as far as it would go. "Hang on lads, it's goin' to be a bumpy ride," he said, something very much like sheer joy lighting the narrow, dour face. "The rest of youse better get yer heads down, in case they decide to shoot it out."

"Lord have mercy," Declan mumbled, "the fool thinks we're in the Wild West."

"He's a point," Casey said tersely, shimmying his large frame down between the seats and sticking his head out into the aisle to keep a clear view of the swiftly advancing jeep. His mind raced, the map of Republican Belfast laid out in his head.

Thought became impractical seconds later when the back window of the bus was blown out, most of it shattering onto the roadway behind them but a few rogue shards scattering in.

Casey muttered a terse prayer that consisted mostly of the words 'please' and 'one piece'. A moment later, it seemed God had heard him, and forgiven him the rather curt method of address. The bus, from somewhere in its beastly old guts, pulled up a last burst of speed. The jeep behind them started to lose ground and the few more shots that were loosed fell wide of their mark. The lights of the bridge illuminated the interior of the bus. Five mostly naked men, scratched, soaked, bleeding and on the run of their lives. If it hadn't been so deadly serious he might have laughed at the farce of it all.

He risked a peek out at the swiftly passing scenery. The Markets was within their reach. He took a breath; they were going to make it. It would buy them a few precious minutes, but not much more.

Despite the army's disinclination to enter hardcore Republican areas, he knew they'd call in the cavalry and have the area cordoned off in no time at all. Trying to hide in the Markets area would bring down the full wrath of the British Army on the heads of the locals. They'd have to move quickly.

Republican Belfast was a tightly woven web of interconnected lives, and word of their escape had spread quickly along the sticky lines of communication. When the bus finally came to a coughing, belching stop a crowd of people awaited them with cheers for their bold escape.

Casey was the last to stumble off the bus, still clad in the bus driver's coat, barefoot, unshaven, looking thoroughly disreputable but feeling lightheaded with relief. For a minute he could enjoy it, just a minute because he had to figure out how to get this ragtag lot of his across the border and safely down to Dublin, but for now he took the cup of hot tea someone shoved in his hands and the change of dry clothing. The five of them changed in the street, too tired to care for modesty. From somewhere in the cramped laneways a getaway car had been provided.

The five of them piled in the minute they were dressed, amidst admonitions of which streets to avoid and wishes for a speedy flight.

Roland took the wheel, carefully buckling himself in before looking questioningly at Casey.

"We'd best not tackle the border until dark," Casey said. "Question is where do we hole up 'til then?"

"My brother-in-law has a pub," Shane offered, "he'll shut it down if we want him to; no one but Republicans ever drinks there anyway. We'd be safe as houses until we're ready to cross the border."

Casey nodded. "All right lad, lead the way."

One hour later found them safely hidden in a dark pub, miles from where the Army still hunted in vain for them.

Matty, Declan and Shane sat round a table that was crowded with empty pint glasses. Roland was, from Casey's current vantage point, nowhere to be seen. Casey listened with growing frustration as the telephone in a house far from him, rang on without answer. It was likely to be his last chance to make contact.

"Damn it," he muttered under his breath, "someone answer."

There was a shout of laughter from the far side of the dim room. Casey turned. All the men were looking up at the fuzzy, wee screen of the television.

"They've caught us then, or are imminently about to do so," Declan said, grinning through the traces of boot polish that still smudged his thin face.

Casey shook his head in astonishment. The five of them had been in the Markets for all of about ten minutes and now the bastards had it surrounded, and were declaring that they had the situation entirely under their control.

He let the telephone ring twice more, then gently replaced it on the hook. "Where's Roland?"

"Here man," came the answer as Roland rose up off his knees, a look of beatific calm lighting his deep set eyes.

"Are we ready then?" Casey asked, pulling the too tight coat across his shoulders.

"Ready boss," Declan said taking one last long swallow that emptied his pint glass. He placed it by its fellows. Casey only hoped the men could hold their alcohol as well as they had their fear.

He looked regretfully at the telephone one last time.

"Let's go, lads," he said.

Five minutes later they were on the road to Dublin.

Chapter Fifty-seven

I Will Lead You Home

CASEY WAITED DAWN OUT PATIENTLY. The light, bottle green and heavy, pulled itself wearily over the horizon like a rheumatic old man rising on aching bones. In the gloom he checked the crumpled map, the one that had been palmed into his hand by the reporter, and hoped to God he hadn't fallen face first into a trap.

He sat, exhausted, stubbled and with the faint reek of rancid butter still clinging to him, back huddled against the knotted trunk of a black oak. It was cold this morning, the air thick and heavy with mist, a warning of rain in its purling drops. He shivered and fought to keep his eyes open and his senses alert to his environment. Above his head he heard the rustle of birds beginning to wake, the ruffle of sleepy wings, the first irritable cheeps of morning. He ached with cold and lack of sleep; the night had been a long one. He'd alternatively walked and hid through all of it, not daring to travel on the roads.

He'd found the grove of trees just before dawn, the black oak unmistakable. There weren't so many of the ancient trees left in Ireland, the armies of Elizabeth I had seen to that. The map in his hand was finely drawn, the instructions just explicit enough for him to understand, but not so clear that someone else could have followed it. It was this that made him think he knew where the map originated and that he was quite safe in following its directions.

He burrowed deeper into his heavy corduroy coat, its soft collar damp against his face and tried to not think of how badly he wanted a cigarette, a hot cup of tea and to see his wife's face. He'd an unhappy feeling that she was as angry with him as she was worried about him.

Like a genie sent direct from a golden bottle in answer to his unspoken wishes, Jamie emerged at his right arm in silence, one finger to his lips as Casey jumped slightly.

"I wasn't followed," Jamie said in a whisper, "but we'd best keep it as quiet as possible in case you were."

Casey choked back an indignant comment as Jamie placed a lumpy bag on the ground opening its neck and handing Casey a thermos of scalding hot tea before he said a word. Then seeing how badly Casey's hands shook, he took the thermos back and poured the tea into a plastic mug, and wrapped Casey's stiff fingers firmly around it.

"Drink up, you need the warmth badly."

Casey did as he was bid, gasping when the tea, heavily laced with sugar and brandy, burned down his throat. Jamie watched until he drank the whole thing, then refilled the cup and ordered him to drain it again. Casey did so and felt with relief the warmth spread out from his belly into his numb extremities.

Jamie continued to rummage in the bag, coming out with a heavy sweater, thick corduroy pants, dry socks, thermal underwear, and a sturdy pair of boots.

"Get changed," he said shortly, exchanging Casey's empty cup for the pile of clothing, "you're still blue about the gills."

Casey stripped down quickly; having been incarcerated so often in his life, he'd long ago lost any false sense of modesty.

"How is she?" Casey asked as soon as he could control the chattering of his teeth.

Jamie's eyes, dark green in the murky light, narrowed slightly. "As well as can be expected under the circumstances, which is to say frantic with worry, furious as ten demons and only slightly less dangerous than a lorry-load of Paras. Here," he put his hand in his pocket and withdrew a pack of cigarettes, "for the journey."

"Am I going somewhere?" Casey asked, feeling his spirit revive slightly under the influence of warm clothes and brandy.

"There's a car up on the road. In the bag you'll find food, money and a map. Take the back roads as much as possible. When you get to Doolin, you'll find a man there named Tommy who'll be dressed identically to you, he'll take the car on and you'll proceed on foot until you come to the place indicated on the map. There another gentleman will pick you up and take you out to a fishing boat, where it's anchored is also shown on the map. The fishing boat will take you to your destination where," Jamie gave him a hard green look, "you'll stay until further notice."

"But—" Casey protested, but Jamie shook his head, knowing the words before they were spoken.

"You can't, she's the first place they'll look. I believe that Joe Doherty has her shadowed twenty-four hours a day. It's likely she doesn't breathe without him being informed of it."

"Jaysus, I'd no idea. The fockin' bastard, when I lay hands on him he'll wish to Christ he'd never even been conceived, much less born."

"That's as may be," Jamie said acerbically, fine golden eyebrows raised slightly, "but you'll find it easier to accomplish your goal if you're actually alive, so for now Belfast is entirely off limits to you. Understood?"

Casey nodded, trying to contain the mulish stubbornness rising up in him, knowing it would show only too clearly on his face. "How long?" he asked, feeling his chest tighten at the thought of even another day without Pamela. He didn't feel as if he'd breathe proper again until she was in his arms and he could see and feel for himself that she was safe and whole.

"As long as it takes to straighten this mess out," Jamie said curtly, and then softened his tone slightly, "a few weeks at most, no longer." Casey noticed for the first time since the man had entered the glade how tired he looked. Though he was, as always, impeccably dressed, shaved and alert.

"Jamie, just how worried should I be about Joe Doherty?"

"Frightened out of your wits," Jamie answered sharply, "he wants you dead, you must have realized that by now."

"Aye," Casey answered wryly, "the attempted drownin' was a fairly clear hint. Though I can't see why my hide is worth any more to him than a number of others on the street."

"It goes higher than Mr. Doherty," Jamie said.

"I thought it might," Casey said, unable to suppress a shiver up his spine at this confirmation of his fears. "How high?"

"You've heard of an exclusive little club, I'm sure, its members culled from all walks of life. Government officials, corporate heads, industrialists, academics and all the way on down the line to career criminals."

"I'd heard rumors," Casey said uneasily, thinking he could use another shot of the brandy-laced tea. "But it's never been confirmed."

"There's thirty or forty of them," Jamie said, "at present. They've got hired assassins, so called death squads, which are soundly supported by certain policemen, who provide armed escort for them in and out of the target areas."

"Ye know this for a fact?" Casey asked harshly, feeling a trickle of ice run through his veins.

"I do."

"Jaysus, if they ever found out..."

"I'd be dead," Jamie bluntly finished the thought Casey had left hanging in the air, "however I've safeguards in place, even the man who reports to me doesn't know who I am."

"I'd heard there was a list," Casey said, lungs tight with held air.

"There is," Jamie replied calmly.

"Have ye seen it?"

"I have."

"Am I on it?"

"Yes, you are," Jamie said quietly.

Casey took a deep breath, searching for the courage to ask the next question. "An' my brother, is he on it?"

There was a long and dreadful silence that stretched across the space between them giving Casey his answer before Jamie spoke the words.

"He is."

"Oh God," Casey said, as his knees buckled and he sat gracelessly on the damp ground.

Jamie was beside him in an instant, placing a small flask in Casey's hands and saying in a harsh voice, "Take a drink. Only one, though, you've got to drive. I am doing everything in my power to ensure your safety but in return you have to keep a clear head and not do anything foolish. Pat's safe for now."

"Where is he?" Casey asked hoarsely, the aftertaste of the whiskey like hot blood on his tongue.

"He's home with Sylvie. I managed to get him a pardon for crimes he never committed, but nevertheless it constituted a get out of jail free card," Jamie said.

Casey nodded, knowing it was the best that could be managed under the situation. Had he thought it would have gotten him released, he too might have been tempted to confess to any number of crimes he had not committed.

"This little committee, ye say they've thirty or forty, do ye mind me askin' how many ye've got on yer own team?"

The pause that ensued was painfully long. Casey took another swallow off the flask before Jamie could stop him. "Christ man," Casey whispered grimly, "don't tell me ye're alone."

Jamie eyed him benignly.

"Would ye say somethin'?" Casey finished a little desperately.

"You said not to tell you," Jamie said in an annoyingly composed voice.

"Jaysus, Mary, Joseph an' the little green men, would ye give a man another drink?" Casey said in an explosion of breath.

"No," Jamie replied sternly, capping the whiskey firmly and sticking it in his own pocket. "Now up on your feet, you've got to get going," he helped Casey to his feet with more force than the dazed Casey thought was strictly necessary. He then held him by the elbows until Casey's knees stopped wobbling.

"Why are ye doin' this?" Casey asked, taking the bag and slinging it over his shoulder.

"Doing what?" Jamie asked, face suddenly a cool mask.

"All this," Casey gestured with one large hand, "savin' my skin, arrangin' cars an' boats an' hideaways when ye know," Casey tried to catch Jamie's eyes, "that a man in yer particular position can afford no mistakes. Is it for her?" he asked, though the question stuck in his craw like an indigestible lump.

Jamie's gaze shifted only slightly but it was enough to tell Casey what he wanted to know.

"You'd best go, you've a long day ahead of you," Jamie said, once again in perfect and enviable control of his expression and tone.

"Aye, thank ye man for all ye've done," Casey said awkwardly.

"Think nothing of it," Jamie quipped lightly as the morning's dull light gilded his hair a dark gold, painting an airy crown about his head.

"She once said ye were like a prince in a fairytale, a dream in the darkness."

"Did she? Well it's not the most unflattering comment I've been handed," Jamie said, and Casey saw he'd unnerved the man, even if only slightly.

He continued on as if Jamie hadn't spoken. "Ye're always runnin' about savin' everybody else, but ye can't save yer ownself, can ye? Do ye always do what's right even when the cost is so high, man?"

Jamie sighed and Casey saw he was considering one of his pretty obfuscations that he was so used to dealing out to the world, but then he smiled wearily, his mask dropping for the first time that morning.

"It's a character flaw; one rather gets into the habit of playing Prince Valiant after awhile even when one finds the role tiresome. Now you'd best go, time's a-wasting."

Casey started for the road, then turned, walked back, and put his hand out. "Thank ye," he looked directly into Jamie's eyes, "for everything."

"You won her fair and square Casey; you don't owe me thanks for that. She chose you."

Casey nodded. "Aye, she chose me, but only after you let her go. I think I've some small idea what that cost ye."

"Do you?" Jamie asked lightly, but his smile was more strained than it had been only a moment before.

"I do," Casey said, "an' I am thankful to ye for it."

"Then take better care of yourself, would you? In case," Jamie spoke softly but there was a steely thread ribboning under his words, "I'm not there to pick up the pieces next time."

"Aye, I'll try," Casey said turning and walking toward the rising day. He hesitated on the edge of the circle of trees and looked back, but Jamie was gone, disappearing into the mist like the prince of a long forgotten fairytale.

Nevertheless, Casey whispered the last words he'd not said, "Aye man, I do know, for I love her too."

INISHMORE, NORTHERNMOST OF THE ARAN ISLANDS, was by nightfall shrouded in the thick pea soup of Atlantic fog. But the little fishing boat knew every rock and crevice of her coastline and put to without incident in a sheltered cove.

Casey stood blind on the rocky shore, feeling a steep fall of rock above him and the icy breath of the Atlantic directly behind him. Between the devil and the deep blue sea, he thought, shouldering his bag purposefully, he'd take the devil every time. He began the treacherous climb up the rocky slope that he could only just make out in the heavy darkness.

Twenty minutes later he stood upon the barren sweeping plateau that was Inishmore. Two hours out of Galway Bay was a land beyond the point of memory, a land of stone and silence. Of wind and rock and the cry of birds caught forever between sky and sea.

Casey shivered. Even blinded by dark the island felt indescribably ancient, a land where the stone gods still ruled from their violent perch. The man on the boat had said to go directly up the cliff and he couldn't miss the cottage. Certain enough, ahead of him was a tiny flickering light, disappearing in and out of his wind-whipped vision. He walked quickly over the low rock walls that fragmented the land again and again into tiny plots, across a landscape as tree shorn as the moon, towards a dubious and fragile sanctuary.

He came round the back of the blasted stone walls, glowing dimly with whitewash, and in the salt-lashed air he tasted the faint tang of peat smoke. Someone had left a fire burning and he hugged his arms tight in the anticipation of the warmth and his first decent sleep in months.

The door was open, its black latch freshly oiled. He pushed it and went in. Low ceilinged and thick-walled, the cottage was snug, holding off the wind and rain. The roof was thatched with reeds set in wire, done in the traditional manner, but replaced recently. Small, thick-paned windows distorted his reflection and threw it back at him. There were two rooms, the larger one for both cooking and company, and the smaller for sleeping. A double bed, piled high with thick quilts took up most of the space in the smaller. He slid his bag off his shoulder and sat down on the bed with relief, feeling the incredible luxury of a thick mattress beneath him. He was suddenly overwhelmed with exhaustion and decided to worry about food in the morning. There'd been a good load of coal in the corner, he'd bank up the fire and it would keep the place snug until dawn.

He went back into the other room, knelt down on the floor, and smoored the fire securely, leaving enough space for the air to feed the flames. It threw a terrific heat and he considered just laying down beside it and passing out when a sudden gust of air pulled a ribbon of flame from the slumbering coals.

He turned quickly, hand automatically reaching for the nearest weapon even as he sprang upright. His right arm was raised, iron poker in hand, ready, poised to strike and then just as swiftly dropped as he saw who stood, framed by night, in the doorway.

"Jewel," he said hoarsely, in disbelief, in welcome, in uncertainty.

The door stayed open but she didn't move, her face beaded with rain, her hair wild with wind and water. A single glance told him she'd been out wandering the crumbling limestone cliffs with her usual disregard for safety and he wanted to shake her for it, even as he fought the urge to crawl across the floor on his knees to her.

"I...I didn't expect you for a few more days," she said, a vicious gust of wind blowing her hair about her face in a cloud of wet curls and pushing fretfully at her clothes.

Casey walked over, reached around her, and shut the door. "I didn't know ye were goin' to be here at all," he said quietly. Of its own accord, his hand reached out automatically to help her with her wet things, and then hesitated. Would she welcome his touch? He didn't, at present, think he could bear it if she flinched.

"It's all right," she said in a low voice, "you can touch me, I won't break."

"I might," Casey replied, feeling lightheaded and giddy suddenly, as if he were made of something clear and translucent that would shatter with the slightest breath or touch.

"You'd better sit down," she said, tone brisk as she stepped away from him and retrieved a rough wooden chair.

He sat and watched as she removed her coat, hung it on a peg behind the door beside his own and then, stepping back outside the door, filled the kettle from a pump in the front yard. She brought the kettle in and hung it on the cast-iron hook that was mortared over the fire.

"You need to eat," she said firmly, and began taking things down from the tiny cupboards—cup, plate, scones, cream, jam, sugar, milk, whisking back and forth from the table in a flurry of wet hair and damp clothing.

"How's the laddie?" he asked, swallowing over the hard lump that was forming up high in his throat.

"He's fine, he's with Jamie for now."

Casey nodded, the awkwardness between the two of them so palpable that it seemed an entity of its own in the room.

"I've got stew in the cold cupboard out back," she said, making once more for the door.

"Don't," he shook his head, "the scones will do, I only need a bite, I'm damn near too tired to chew."

"I'm sorry." She stood nervously by the door, looking like she wanted no more than to flee back into the night. "I should have thought. Do you just want to get to bed then?"

Casey smiled wryly. "Aye, I'd like nothin' better, but I don't want to go alone, an' I think ye're not ready even to lie beside me, much less anything else."

She looked down, away from him, her hands nervously twisting a tea towel between them.

"Darlin', can ye not even look at me? I've spent months imaginin' this moment an' now I can't even get ye to look me in the eye."

She glanced up quickly and he caught a quicksilver glitter of tears before she dashed them away with her hand.

"Ye cut yer hair off," he said softly.

"I had to. We used Jamie's secretary as a decoy and her hair only comes to her shoulders, so mine had to go."

"It looks well on ye," he said, for it did. Released from its weight it curled untamed up around her face, lending the glass bones and green eyes a wild beauty. He noticed other things, though he didn't mention them. She was too thin; her skin lay tight against her frame and she seemed older, not so much the girl he'd lost his mind over in another time and place, but the woman their life together and apart had made of her. 'These things—you did,' a little voice said accusingly in his head and yet still his body, every bone and cell and pulse of it, longed to touch her, to tumble her soft into the bed and tell her anything, any lie, no matter the cost, that would make her able to meet his eyes with faith again.

Small things impressed themselves upon his consciousness, the beginning rumble of the water boiling in the kettle, the lick and hiss of flames, the rosy bronze light that flickered and roiled about the room. The flecked Wedgwood blue of the cupboards, the pearled knobs of her wrist bones with the tiny blue veins shadowing them, the arcing line of her lashes held over the disillusion she did not want him to see. It seemed to him in the silence that he could smell the soul of her, the salt of all the tears, hot and dammed, that she held back for the both of them.

"I'm drownin' here, darlin'," he said, voice trembling, "an' I need ye to throw me a rope."

There was a long silence, terrible in its weight, that spread itself between them like a cloud of fine and cloying sand. Casey didn't even dare to breathe for fear he'd choke on it.

One step, and then another, her hand extended, red-gold in the shifting light and then the words of salvation.

"Let me take you home, Casey."

In the bed they had to relearn each other, gestures once familiar now made awkward by the anger and pain that insinuated itself between them even here, where words had no dominion. Limbs tangled and parted, breath came hard with frustration, bone met bone and found resistance.

Casey, poised at the brink of renewing their physical bond, stopped, resting his forehead against her own, feeling the tension under her skin as though the two of them were connected by fine and invisible wire.

"Let me in darlin', let me in so that I may go with ye."

Under him she took a small breath, a sound of struggle, of air drawn through tears.

"I'm trying," she said and he heard, with relief, the sound of anger in her voice.

"Be angry at me, rage if ye need to, but take me with ye," he said, and moved against her in question and felt her body rise in demand.

Her hands held his shoulders, nails digging into the soft skin. "For God's sake, Casey, just do it."

He moved his head, caught her face between his two hands, and held her eyes in the frail, flickering light with the force of his own, her ribcage heaving with frustration beneath him. "Ye promised me once," he said roughly, "that ye'd always take me with ye. I'm holdin'ye to it, just let me feel ye, Jewel, let me breathe one breath with ye. I want to feel all of ye—heart, mind, soul. It'll not be right any other way."

"You bastard," she said furiously, "why does it have to be all or nothing?"

"A starvin' man can't settle for half a loaf, it'll only take the edge off the ache in his belly. Ye said ye'd bring me home, darlin', don't leave me standin' outside a locked door."

Her eyes met his, shimmering with tears, and he saw there in the cut-glass depths, not anger but fear, and further down emotion so boundless that he understood again that love held no earthly parameters.

"Then come home," she said, as much in challenge as invitation.

And home he went with heart, mind, soul, and body and in rediscovering her, found himself as well. Broken down in the strong places, mortared in the weak, made whole in the fires of love.

"YOU'RE TERRIBLY THIN," SHE SAID QUIETLY, one hand gliding down his ribcage with careful fingers.

"Aye well," he yawned extravagantly, "my dietary requirements were not high on the list of the British Army's priorities."

He lay full length on his stomach, quilts thrown back to his waist; the grooves of his back a faint, quivering silver. One large hand rested gently on the side of her face, his thumb trailing soft as a moth's wing along her jaw.

"I could stay here forever," he said, eyes heavy-lidded, with only the soft glow of borrowed firelight reflected in his irises, to let her know he watched her.

"We've time," she said, "and I intend to feed you at every opportunity, make love to you after breakfast, lunch and dinner and watch you sleep the rest of the time, and somewhere in there give you a good hot bath."

"An' will ye peel my grapes before I eat them as well? I'll be after thinkin' I'm one of them sultans, be purely debauched by week's end."

"You look as though you could use a little debauchery," she said lightly, but her face was taut with worry.

"Ye're lookin' a little frayed around the edges yerself," he said softly, "an' even at that ye still take the breath from me, just to look at ye so."

"I was so afraid," she whispered quietly, "that they would kill you."

"Well they didn't," he said, then added dryly, "though it wasn't through lack of tryin'."

"There were terrible rumors floating through the neighborhood, things the men who'd been released were saying. About the torture—" she let go a shaky breath and with it the flood of tears he'd sensed in her.

He gathered her close, offering the comfort of his body, warm and sound against the darkness of her fear, his tongue making soft, soothing noises, his hands stroking her body as she shook uncontrollably in his arms.

She subsided slowly, her grief and anger bleeding down to snuffles and hiccoughs. "Y—you can t—tell me what happened," she said, "it might help to t—talk about it."

"Hush darlin', it'll keep for another day," he said gently, "tonight I just want to hold ye, an' sleep knowin' ye're there in the dark." He rested his cheek in her hair, smelling salt and wind and water trapped within its silken skeins. His wild Irish girl.

"I was so lonely," she said, voice the slightest bit bleary with exhaustion, "I'd wake in the middle of the night and there was no one to tell my dreams to, no one to chase my nightmares away."

He stroked her hair back from her face and kissed her softly on the forehead. "Sleep now, darlin', an' I'll keep watch over yer dreams. I'll chase yer demons away. When ye are lost an' afraid in the dark, take my hand an' I will lead ye home."

He watched her then as she fell slowly toward sleep, face flushed, eyelashes still glittering with tears, felt her breath come deeper and slower, as if she breathed in tune with some far greater force that lay beyond the night and the sea and the stars. Then felt himself begin his own slow, heavy tumble toward deep and anonymous sleep. And wished for a moment, before the darkness, vast and silent, claimed him, that he knew how to chase his own demons away.

Chapter Fifty-eight

The Morning After

IN THE MORNING THE COTTAGE was shrouded in a thick gauze of fog. Casey, walking out for a load of coal, couldn't see beyond the doorstep and had to feel his way along the whitewashed stone to the coal shed and creep back in the same manner.

Pamela was up when he came in, preparing a breakfast of oatmeal, leftover scones and piping hot tea.

"Fog's thick as cotton out there," Casey said, depositing the coal by the fire and wiping droplets of mist from his face.

"We were shut in a good part of yesterday as well," she said, giving the porridge a vigorous stir and wrinkling her nose over it. "Damn, I've scorched it."

"Drench it in cream an' a spoonful of sugar, I'll not notice the difference. I could eat a moldy sheep this mornin' an' not complain, I'm that famished." He gave his hands a quick wash then settled himself at the table.

She ladled him up a healthy serving, dropping a kiss on his head as she placed his bowl in front of him. "Speaking of moldy sheep," she said, "you'd best give me that sweater, it stinks to high heaven."

"'Tisn't the sweater," he said, pouring cream over the steaming oatmeal and adding a dollop to his mug for good measure. "It's me. Did my best to scrub the butter off but the damn stuff must of leaked into every crevice an' crease I've got. I've only had cold washes, in a couple of streams an' such. I think I need to steam it off."

"Butter?" she asked, pouring his tea and then her own.

"Aye, we all slathered ourselves with butter packets to keep from freezin' when we took our swim." He cut two scones, covered them both thickly with butter, and took a long swallow of tea.

"Ah, that's heaven, I could inhale the stuff. Ye may not be the world's greatest cook, darlin', but ye have a hand with tea like nobody else."

This compliment earned him an arched eyebrow. "Tell me how you all managed," she said, topping up his mug and tipping another scone onto his plate. "The radio was nonstop with the story, but the details weren't too clear."

She busied herself with spooning up porridge and refilling the cream jug, but Casey knew her well enough to understand that she was avoiding his eyes for fear he'd see what all those news reports had cost her.

"'Twas a bit mad, really," he said quietly, "the papers an' such made it sound a lark, but it wasn't. We were sittin' in a pub in the Murph when the report came down that the British had us in custody. We'd a bit of a laugh over that. I called ye from there but no one answered. After that we were on the run an' there was no opportunity to call, an' I was afraid to risk it; I'd no idea if they were watchin' ye or if the phone might be tapped." He reached across the table to take her hand, but she curled her fingers under, tight around the butter knife, head down over her untouched breakfast.

"Don't," she said, still staring fixedly at her plate, "just tell me what happened, don't make excuses for why I didn't know if you were dead or alive for the last two weeks."

He nodded, withdrawing his hand, knowing they'd lost whatever small ground they'd gained last night. How to explain to her what these last months had been like? How he'd been certain several times that he'd never see home, nor hold her in his arms again. How he'd written a phantom letter in his mind many nights, telling her goodbye, then written another to Jamie asking him to care for her and how much the thought of asking *that* of the man galled him. It was purely impossible and seemed slightly unreal, sitting here with food and hot tea, and her across from him in his shirt, hair tousled, skin still sleep flushed, like any normal morning.

So he told her the facts, without embellishment or embroidery. The capture, the beating, the arrest by the British soldiers, his time on the ship, the men who'd become friends over the dark, stagnant weeks. Under his tongue, bald as he tried to make it, the men came alive for her. Roland's religious fervor, Declan's taciturn nature, Matty's care of him after the beating, Shane's foolish innocence.

"How do you do that?" she asked quietly, after he'd finished telling her of the escape off the ship, the flight on the stolen bus and the heart stopping journey that had finally landed them all in Dublin.

"Do what?" he asked.

"Gather a bunch of ragtags around you and turn them into a cohesive group."

He shook his head. "All most people need is a little direction. Maybe I'm a bit more clearheaded in a crisis an' can see my way through things. That's all it is. My daddy taught both Pat and to think on our feet."

"Damn you," she said, tears bright in her eyes.

"What have I done now?" he said in bewilderment.

"Made it impossible to be angry or resentful with you."

"Well I don't know what I've said or done, but if it's made ye feel kindly towards me I'll not regret it."

She stood and walked to his side of the table, taking his head to her breast and laying her cheek upon his hair. "You break my heart, Casey Riordan, and the worst of it is you don't even know that you're doing it."

They stayed thus for several moments, grateful for the peace and warmth that surrounded them.

"I am sorry, Pamela." His hand came up and wrapped tightly around her own, "For all of it."

"I know," she replied, and found that in the morning light, with him here solid and real, it was enough. "Casey."

"Aye?"

"I love you."

"I love you too."

It was enough.

Chapter Fifty-nine

Nuala

THE WESTERN SHORE OF INISHMORE bore little resemblance to the eastern side. Worn limestone cliffs soared skyward, glistening blackly in the odd light of the sea. The light seemed possessed with a life of its own, breaking stone into rainbow parts, shattering the sea into infinite patterns that changed every second. It was an empty wind-scoured world, where one could not help but be completely aware of the elements.

Above was a glassy sky, and below, the ocean—snorting white sea horses galloping into shore from America, tossing their tangled red-brown manes of seaweed, slick and oily and deep as a man was high. On the sand, oystercatchers danced in awkward hops with the delicate-legged sandpipers. It was evening and the light was fading from the land, shadow filling up the hollows and dips, clustering near the foot of rock walls and gathering softly against the base of the monuments to drowned fishermen that dotted the island.

"It's going to storm," Pamela said, stooping to fish a length of shipboard out of the grasping seaweed. They had spent much of the day in a narrow cove that protected them from the worst of the wind, even if it had been a precipitous climb to reach the small haven of sand and rock.

"How can ye tell?" Casey asked, giving the rolling breakers a suspicious look, as though he suspected the waves of harboring a force ten gale.

"I always get a metallic taste in my mouth when it's going to storm. Right now my tongue tastes like iron."

An uneasy *mmphmm* was Casey's only reply. He was sitting on a large rock, intent on keeping his feet dry, casting mumbled aspersions at the water occasionally, and sketching the small shorebirds as they sorted amongst the grains of sand for avian treasure.

It was a rare day of fine weather and they were happy to leave the cottage, where the weather had confined them for the last four days. Casey had brought along paper and a pencil to make sketches of birds, from which he'd carve small figures so like that they would seem to be caught in the moment before flight, or in the cautious watchfulness they displayed around humans.

Pamela had occupied herself with the small wonders an ebb tide always left behind; the small, scuttling things, the diaphanous jellied creatures, the strange flotsam that was as foreign as vegetation from a distant planet. Now, tired but happy, lungs filled with briny air, lips tasting of salt, she watched Casey as he drew a solitary plover.

"Are you going to tell me what happened to your back?" she asked softly, resting her chin on his shoulder, fascinated as always by how he could render the essence of any bird in a few bold lines.

"Ye know what happened," he said, squinting at the black-bellied bird that regarded him with its soft, large eyes, uttering a inquisitive *pee-a-wee* every few seconds.

"I know what," she said, "but I don't know why."

"His name was Shane," he began.

"Ah," she said, beginning to see the *why* very clearly.

He paused to blow some warm air onto his fingers. "He was young an' stupid. Lord above knows I've been in that state myself, an' more than the once. I thought if I could spare him an experience of that sort it'd be no bad thing."

"It was an incredibly foolish and brave thing to do."

He shook his head, resuming the fine pencil strokes that conveyed the ephemeral quality of the bird in the half-light. "There's some that could take it an' be stronger for it an' then there's others it would break permanently. I knew the lad was of the latter school an' I'd not rest easy with myself if I let it happen."

"And you of the former school," she said, watching another timber make its way toward the foaming shore.

He gave an eloquent shrug. "A man is made how he is, an' there's only so much he can do about it."

"Don't you ever feel fear?"

"Aye, plenty, but ye can use it to yer advantage most times. It's when ye let it go to yer head that ye're in trouble. But I know the taste of it, to be certain," he said grimly.

"What does it taste like?"

"Tastes a wee bit like blood, actually," he said, rolling up his paper and tucking it along with the pencil inside of his coat. "Salty an' coppery. Bit like yer storm tongue. Speakin' of which we'd best head back, I don't like the look of those clouds." He nodded toward the western sky, which had gone from a soft, goosedown gray to an ominous ochre black. He jumped down from his perch. "Come on with ye woman, let's collect yer bits of wood an' go."

She'd left the planking neatly piled at one end of the small cove, knowing it would do nicely to keep the cottage warm, should the coal run out before the next boat was due in to the island.

"I can't help but think that our gain is someone's loss," she said, hefting three of the broken spars into Casey's outstretched arms.

"Sometimes I think that's the way of all life, Jewel," he replied seriously, "that a gain for one man is always a loss for another."

She looked down at the timber, flecks of green paint still visible in the grain. "Do you think they drowned or were rescued?"

Casey didn't answer, for just then the metallic taste on his wife's tongue bore itself out and a swathe of rain-filled wind smacked into them.

"We'd best move quick," he said, shouldering the timber and starting up the narrow ravine that led off the strand onto the stark headland above. She followed behind him, feet feeling for the worn grooves in the limestone, as the darkness had moved in with such startling suddenness that they couldn't see more than a couple of feet in front of them.

By the time they reached the top of the cliff the storm had trebled in intensity, the wind a vicious scour that turned the rain into stinging stones, their clothes a soaked mass that dragged at their limbs.

"We'll have to dump the wood," Casey yelled, "an' make a run for shelter."

They soon lost all sense of direction as the wind lashed ever harder, throwing the rain in vicious horizontal streams, visibility down to a scant few inches and the possibility of finding their cottage in the uproar quickly taking on the appearance of insanity.

The wind had become a living thing, a screaming legion of witches abroad on the night, kicking up sand and dirt and swirling it in a mad dance that choked the very breath from their lungs. Disaster and confusion loomed on all sides, and Pamela knew they wouldn't be the first to stumble off the cliffs to a sure death in such a storm. Panic clutched at her intestines, starting a shaking along her skin that she couldn't control. She stopped suddenly, causing Casey to lurch, his coat still clutched tight in her grasp.

He put his mouth to her ear and yelled, the force of the wind such that it was only half-intelligible, "—is it? We can't stop—or we—"

She shook her head mutely, terrified to move another step for fear they'd step out into nothing, blind and senseless. He wrapped his arms around her tightly, no doubt sensing her fear, giving her what small shelter his body could provide.

She saw them suddenly as if from above, two fragile creatures at the mercy of the elements, small and inconsequential within such an ancient landscape. And in the midst of all the darkness and fear, two words, "Trust me." She swallowed over the taste of fear and nodded. Casey must have felt her movement, for he took her hand tightly in his own and pulled her along as they continued on their perilous journey.

It might have been a minute or an hour later, when he halted abruptly and yelled over the clamor, "There's a light, at least I think it is, it keeps blinkin' in an' out. We'll head that way, best as I can manage. Don't let go of my hand whatever ye do!"

Pamela held on for dear life, stumbling across the stone strewn field behind him, wind shoving at their backs like an angry beast that would not be satisfied until it had driven them completely from the land.

They almost missed the cottage, and if Casey hadn't walked straight into the tiny outbuilding that lay behind it, they likely would have stumbled clear across to the eastern shore. They had to feel their way back to the main cottage. There were no windows in back and so no telltale light shone forth. There was merely an impression of something of substance and form looming in the dark ahead of them. They found the north wall and followed it around to the west face to be presented with a door.

"Thank Christ," Casey said with great sincerity. He knocked hard against the door. It flew back suddenly, startling them both, though hardly more than the apparition that stood beneath the lintel. She was eye level with Casey, long bony feet bare, iron streaked hair whipping about her face. Pamela recognized her from her own nightly walks. A ghostly figure that stood on the cliff tops looking out to sea each and every night. She had frightened Pamela half out of her wits the first time she saw her. Her voice however, acidic as over-steeped tea, soon banished any notion of pale seaweedy wraiths.

"Will ye stand there all night, or do ye intend to come in?" she asked, as if it were a mild Sunday and they'd been expected for tea hours ago. Casey pulled Pamela by the hand in over the doorstep.

The interior of the cottage was small, but its warmth and light was welcome to their thoroughly chilled skins. The wind still shrieked like a mad thing against the doors and windows, but the thick walls paid little mind.

"Come, yez had best get yer wet things off an' sit close in to the fire," the woman said, placing two reed-backed chairs in front of the roaring hearth. "Here, give me yer sweaters, I'll hang them to dry."

They handed over their sopping sweaters gratefully and sat in the proffered chairs. The fire was built high and bellowed heat into the tiny room. Their clothes began to let off wisps of steam immediately. Pamela chanced a look around the tiny room, curiosity about the old woman who walked the cliffs at night taking the upper hand over the receding fear.

Softly furred shapes moved in the corners, stretched and retracted to their nests on cushions and bits of furniture. One cat, missing both an eye and an ear, sat, orange fur puffed out, on the top of an upturned barrel. He winked his one big golden eye at Pamela, looking for all the world like a battered pirate king. The firelight threw wavering, distorted shadows on the walls, making the atmosphere fitting to a woman the villagers called witch. A china cabinet stood against one wall, filled with broken crockery and what looked like a wide variety of bent and rusted fish hooks.

"Ye'll take tea," the woman said emphatically, startling Pamela. "Ye'll need it to take the frost out yer bones. I'm Nuala," she added, as a kitten leaped from atop a highboy onto her shoulder, its yellow eyes gleaming out from the shanks of her hair.

"Aye, we'll take the tea an' be grateful for it. I'm Casey an' this is my wife Pamela. We're much obliged to ye for lettin' us in out of the storm."

"And what do be the name of yer people?"

Casey had barely opened his mouth to reply when Nuala fixed them with a hard gimlet eye, as though she suspected them of having come to thieve and pillage.

"Ye're not Bean people, are ye? I hold no truck with such folk."

Nuala must belong to the O'Bradaigh side of the island war, Pamela thought. It dated back more than a hundred years to the wreck of a Spanish galleon, and just who had the rights to the spoils. The two families had been in a mostly silent but deadly serious war since then. Pamela, having been filled in vigorously by Mrs. Sparks, whose two stout legs held firmly to the Bean side of the Island's divide, had told Casey the story in its entirety the night before. To which his reply had been, "Jaysus Murphy, an' they call us Northmen crazy." However, he chose to exercise more tact at present and replied in a tone that could leave no doubt upon the matter, "No, we are not."

"Well that's good then. I'd not let them as is drink from my cups, but as ye're not ye'll do." She rattled the kettle vigorously, as if to say that had they the grievous misfortune to be Bean people, she'd have finished them off here and now, with a good wallop from the copper-bottomed pot.

"Michael," she called out suddenly, "I'm puttin' on the tea, for we've company, will ye be wantin' a jot of something warmer in yer own, man?"

Pamela looked about bewildered, the cottage appeared empty but for the three of them. Casey bit his bottom lip and shook his head ever-so-slightly at her. This only served to mystify her further, but she held her tongue, not wanting to offend, nor ask questions that didn't seem likely to have a simple answer.

From the rear, Nuala looked like an angular and exotic bird, all flapping multi-colored cloth and sharp bones. Above her head, the light and shadow mingled like goblins dancing round about a bonfire. Pamela was reminded sharply of the image she'd always held of Yeats's Crazy Jane in her head.

The kettle was merrily upon the boil, but Nuala poured out a mugful of a suspiciously dark liquid from a pot occupying the other half of the stove. To this, she added the ingredients of two different bottles that lined the shelf above the ancient cooker.

"This one's yers," she said, presenting the brew to Pamela with an unyielding hand and firm look. Pamela gingerly took the mug and eyed it with deep misgiving; it looked like builder's tea, left to stew itself black and scummy the whole day.

"I've put a pinch of pepper in yers as well as a drop of the ginger," Nuala told Pamela, "ye look to takin' cold."

She drew forth a small bottle from her skirts, filled with a honey-bronze liquid. The green and gold label, with its band of Celtic knotwork, made it instantly recognizable as Connemara Mist. Casey looked like a man who'd just caught a glimpse of redemption.

"Michael is after wantin' a wee nip of the bold stuff in his tea, are ye so inclined yerself?" she asked. Casey, never one to look a gift horse in the mouth, held his cup forth. Pamela looked longingly at the whiskey bottle before taking a tentative sip out of her own mug. If possible, it actually tasted worse than it looked, and she bit down hard on the inside of her lip to stop herself from spitting it directly back out.

Nuala herself dispensed with tea entirely and filled her china cup with a good few ounces of the 'bold stuff'. She then put it to her lips and swallowed the entirety of it without flinching. Casey looked suitably impressed. Pamela heroically took another swallow of her tea and shot Casey a filthy look, which he replied to by saluting her with his mug before downing its contents, Nuala-fashion, in two neat swallows.

Nuala faced the mantel now and seemed to be speaking directly to a pair of skulls in a low murmur which had the rhythm of a crooning lullaby. When she turned back toward Casey and Pamela she cradled a skull delicately in each hand, held out towards them like a queen presenting her court.

"These do be my sons. Michael is on the left an' Colum to the right. 'Tisn't everyone I introduce to them," she said shortly, "but Michael likes the look of yez. Colum, ye understand, was never much of a talker even in life, an' he's less so in death."

Pamela swallowed the desire to laugh hysterically, uncertain of how one was expected to address a skull. Casey however took it in his unflappable stride, calling each skull by the name Nuala had told them, and adding a polite, "Nice to make yer acquaintance."

Nuala, after the pleasantries were through, returned each son to his proper place on the mantel. The fire flickered oddly in the hollow eye sockets, giving the illusion of something looking out over the room. Pamela shivered; suddenly the atmosphere in the crowded little cottage no longer seemed absurd.

"Yez may think me mad, but the bones lay closer to the spirit than does the flesh. You," she said to Pamela, "will understand this, no?"

Pamela nodded reluctantly, avoiding Casey's sharp glance sideways. She understood all too well the memory that bone held. The cradle of human fragility, the fretwork of a divine plan, it was aria to the flesh's libretto, holding the memory of what was and what might have been. The bones that haunted her, now buried in an unmarked grave in an undisclosed location, had told a tale of fury and violence, composed of words that could not be spoken aloud.

As if sensing the direction of her unspoken thoughts, Casey took her hand in his own and she felt with gratitude the strength of his fingers as they encircled hers, the warm security of flesh, the reassuring pulse of blood. His touch banished the smell of violets that had risen within her.

Nuala settled herself in the rocking chair, sheltering the delicate teacup in her rough hands, the fire striking sparks of hammered silver from the blaze in her hair. She gazed at the skulls, a distant smile on her face as she began to speak in a low voice.

"I saw the water in them all when they was born. An' I knew the sea would call her own, she always does. You," she pointed at Pamela, voice suddenly fierce, "you will know, for she calls you."

She turned to Casey, long white fingers snaking out to grip his wrist, until the tendons in her hand stood out taut. "Keep her from the sea, boy, if ye want to keep her at all. The sea does know its own an' will come for them. All the merpeople do be havin' the green eyes. An' tis told the O'Flaherty are descended from the sea peoples."

Pamela started and opened her mouth, but Nuala simply shook her head. "Ye can't be days on this island and not have people know yer business. I'd know you for an O'Flaherty anyway, ye've the way of them about you."

A slow smile that wasn't exactly pleasant spread across her mouth and she began to speak directly to Casey. The gaelic was too rapid and fluent for Pamela to comprehend, but she was afraid she understood the general gist when Casey grinned and nodded. She'd seen that particular grin before. She cocked an enquiring eyebrow at him.

"She says," Casey cleared his throat and she could have sworn he was blushing, "that the O'Flahertys were known for their talents in...er...the bedroom. She also says I'll always come hungry to yer bed, because I'm fire an' yer water. An' there's a great deal of heat in such a pairing."

"Oh," Pamela said, feeling rather flushed herself suddenly.

"An' she says that water people are harder to trust because ye can't always discern what lies beneath the skin."

Pamela glanced up sharply, but Nuala was staring fixedly at a spot in the air. It was impossible that the woman should know anything and yet there was something very odd about her. Her voice, when she spoke again, was soft as ether, sending chill tendrils out into the room.

"I did know them by their sweaters, aye. I knit them myself, an' there's not another pattern like it to be found on the whole of the Islands. After the sea has kept yer child for ten days ye may not know them by the face God gave them. 'Twas so with my Michael, but I knew him by the wee ivy leaves twined with thistle, that I'd knit into the pattern of his sweater. Colum washed up the very night he was drowned, looked peaceful, as if he slept. But the sea did not give me back my Sean, nor the son named after him. They say that in time the sea surrenders all her dead, but I think she likes to keep a few for herself." Her rocking slowed as she spoke, until the chair was only the softest grate against the floor.

"My Sean was a big man like yers," she said to Pamela. "He'd the red hair though, an' blue eyes an' a laugh that ye could hear clear up from the shingle. It'd be the sound I waited for all day, for then I knew my men were home an' safe as I could keep them for another night. Sometimes when the wind blows right from the west, I can hear it still." She shivered and drew her heavy shawl tighter about her shoulders. "He was a fine strap of a man an' he might have had his pick from the Island girls, but he chose me. There were those that muttered he'd live to regret it. But he never did. I always knew he was the only one for me, from the time I was a wee thing, but I still couldn't believe it when he picked me for his own.

"He'd been to sea from the time he was twelve, was mad for it, obsessed by it. We went on holiday to Athlone the one time, he'd relatives there, an' I thought he'd take sick from the lack of the sea. Said he couldn't breathe right an' felt as if the air were pressin' in upon him. I never took him away from it again.

"Each evening I'd wait on the cliffshead for him, so even far out he could see me. He said it was the best of his day, the sun behind him an' his wife before him, knowin' that he'd soon be home to a warm meal an' a warm bed. It was a good life for a very long time, we'd the three boys, all fine an' strong, handsome like their da." She looked up, piercing Pamela with her odd gaze.

"It's said the gods are angered by the joy of humans. That it never does to be too happy. I think that was my sin, I think my joy drew their attention an' they decided to punish me for it. For all the boys had their father's love of the sea. Sean more than the other two, but all infected by it. I'd hoped an' prayed one of them would choose somethin' different, would become a barrister in Dublin or a clerk in some wee town. But they didn't, an' though it worried me, I thought I'd made my peace with it.

"And then came that day. I'd ill thoughts from the start of it. Three men of the same name in that damned boat. My Sean, our son that was named so, an' Sean Cuddy from the other side of the island. 'Tis ill to have three men of the same name in the one boat, but my Sean laughed. He never held with the old superstitions, an' said they could use the extra hands. He knew the boy could use the money an' he was never one to turn back a man in need.

"I went early to the cliffs that night, for I'd not been easy at my work all day. 'Twas odd weather, the sky heavy an' low with clouds, but not a breath of wind to be had. The boats came in just afore twilight, but only a straggle an' twas then I knew somethin' had gone wrong. I could see it in the set of their shoulders as they came ashore.

"Five days an' nights I waited on those cliffs," she continued, hollow-voiced, "an' five mornins' did I see the men put out in their boats, an' the same come home at night. But never did I see the one I waited for. Finally the women came an' dragged me home. They say I yelled somethin' fierce an' fought them hard, but I've no memory of it at all. Ah," she shook her head, silver blaze a dull gleam now in the night of her hair, "it's a terrible place an' no mistake about it."

"And that's why you wander the cliffs at night," Pamela said softly, in the tone of one who knew what it was to wait for a ship to appear on the horizon.

Nuala nodded, a smile of shared understanding on her face. "Aye, I want him to know I still wait for him." The smile faded and she seemed suddenly very tired. "For I know someday, when the wind is right, he will come back to me." The story had cast a pall upon the room, the fire burning low during the telling, though the chill in the air seemed to have little to do with the dying embers.

Prodded most importunely by the peppery tea, Pamela sneezed three times in succession. It had the immediate effect of snapping them into the here and now.

Nuala nodded grimly after blessing her. "I knew ye'd a cold cloud hangin' about ye. Ye'll need somethin' stronger than the tea to ward it off."

Pamela shot a look of horror at Casey, who merely shrugged and wisely suppressed his laughter while Nuala rustled in the cupboard beneath the washstand.

"Ah, there we go, 'tis part of last year's batch." Nuala emerged triumphantly with a bottle in hand, which she then uncorked, breathing in the resulting fumes with a look of dreamy pleasure. "I make it meself, 'tis perhaps a bit stronger than poteen is meant to be, but it'll do ye no harm."

Pamela, catching a whiff of the brew, suspected there were few organisms that could survive such a cure. With luck, she might make it to morning. Administered with a fierce eye by Nuala, the poteen went down like living fire through her veins. Though she drank it meekly enough, knowing so much as a drop left in the copious mug would offend the woman.

The wind slapped the side of the cottage with a particularly vicious gust and Nuala's head turned sharply as though controlled by outside forces. The hair on Pamela's neck went up when she saw the wild light that entered the woman's eyes, turning them an odd murky green.

"Do ye hear him, then?" she asked, long fingers tight around Casey's forearm.

Casey took her hand and spoke gently. "No, I cannot hear him, but it could be I've not the ears for it."

"I must go," the woman said urgently, the tension in her fairly singing off her skin. "I can hear him call."

"Ye could die out there," Casey said in a patient tone.

"Do ye think I'd mind such a thing, boy?" she asked, releasing her grip on his arm. "What do ye think it is I seek on those cliffs? I must go," she turned abruptly, throwing her shawl over her head and putting her hand to the latch. She pressed it, releasing the hasp and then turned back, eyes riveting Pamela, even through the poteen haze that was beginning to cloud her senses. "You girl, you've the seawater in yer veins, tell me where will I find him?"

"I—I don't know, but I believe one night you will find what you seek."

Nuala nodded as if queerly satisfied by the answer and then with a swirl of skirts and a flash of one bare, dirty foot she was gone into the night and the storm.

Casey stood looking after her, rain lashing angrily against his face, but he did not follow the old woman.

> *Old Mad Meg stood by the sea*
> *A thousand years stood she*
> *Her skin flame, her touch burn*
> *A threnody sang she*

Pamela paraphrased the Jack Stuart poem to herself, the picture of the old woman with her ageless quest shining in her eyes, bringing the poet's madwoman back to mind.

"What did ye say, Jewel?" Casey asked, turning from the door after closing it firmly.

"Nothing, just a bit of poetry."

"Oh aye," he ran a hand over his face, rubbing his stubbled chin vigorously, "ye do feel the need to quote at the oddest moments."

"You look exhausted," she said, squinting at him in a vain effort to limit him to one solid image.

He laughed in reply. "Do I then? Which one of me would it be that looks so? Number two or four?"

She grimaced wryly. "There was enough drink in that mug for all five of you. I can't feel my face nor my toes."

"To bed with ye then," he said firmly, "before ye lose yer faculties altogether."

"We're going to stay?" Pamela said, stifling a sneeze with great effort.

"Do ye suggest we attempt the storm again? Listen to it, woman."

She fixed her wits and realized the storm had died back but little, and still railed with salted fists at the doors and windows. And within the immediate furor another noise, that of the sea building in upon itself and breaking in a towering temper that threatened to destroy with impunity. Casey was right, they'd be fools to even attempt a trip back on unfamiliar ground in such a tempest.

"Do you think she'll be all right?" Pamela asked, not at all happy about the thought of searching the storm for a mad witch.

"She knows all the dips an' hollows, besides ye heard her. She'd not let us drag her back. No use all of us lookin' for death out there. Here," he lifted the nightgown Nuala had left hanging off the rack by the stove, "ye'll put this on, yer clothes are still a wee bit damp, an' Nuala was right, ye look to takin' cold."

The nightgown was made of a fine wool that smelled strongly of camphored confinement. "It reeks," she said pushing it back towards him, unable to stifle the sneezes that came in a quick succession of three.

"Ye'll put it on or I'll sit on ye and force another mug of that peppered tea down yer throat."

"Sadist," she said, giving in with ill grace to having her clothing removed and the eye-watering woolen sack dropped over her head. Casey did the buttons up to her throat and then dispatched her onto the settle with a smart smack to her rear end.

"Ow," she muttered, navigating the neatly laid sheets and quilt with some difficulty.

"Quiet or I'll make ye a mustard plaster for yer chest like my da used to do when Pat took cold. I see there's a tin of the dried stuff on the shelf, so don't think I won't."

"Mustard plaster?" She squinted up at him, one eye closed as she'd discovered this cut his numbers nicely in half.

"Aye, it's a kill or cure. Only had it the once but it was more than enough, burned like the devil an' smelled even worse."

"I thought you'd never been sick."

"Wasn't," he replied, voice muffled as he drew his sweater off over his head, "was only pretendin' in an effort to miss school. Da saw through me from a mile off though, but he let me stay home an' plied me with home cures all day. Never did pretend sickness again, I tell ye."

The settle was old and solidly built. It was snug, but it fit the two of them comfortably enough. Pamela, flat on her back and feeling akin to molten lead that'd yet to gel, tried shifting to give him room and then gave up as the beams above her head spun in a dizzy circle.

"Have you enough room?" she asked blearily, lips fuzzy and warm.

"Aye," he mumbled, pulling her neatly under his chin, arm firm about her waist, "I'll do." He yawned, kissed her, and relaxed into the heavy, even breathing that told her he was already asleep.

Shrouded snugly in the woolen nightie, head reeling with drink, husband emitting heat like a well-stoked furnace, Pamela tipped over the edge of unconsciousness straight into the deeps of a heavy sleep.

NEAR DAWN, THE FURY WITHDREW from the storm, leaving only a

steady thrum of rain that soon spent itself.

Pamela, who'd slept through the rising and falling crescendos of the weather, woke to an ashen morning, the small noises of someone moving about having roused her. She yawned and blinked, taking a moment to recollect her surroundings. Casey was gone from the narrow settle, but three spots of cozy warmth lay firm upon the blanket. She peered down the length of the bed discerning a milky purring coil by her left knee and a coal black one by her right hip. The pirate king lay across her feet, great gold eye agleam with an unearthly light. She turned her head, dislodging a kitten from the nest it had made in her hair. It bit her scalp sharply and delivered a stinging smack to her ear, before stretching and jumping off the settle, tail twitching in indignation.

"Ouch!" she exclaimed.

"Mornin', Jewel," said Casey's voice. She raised her head and found him by the fire, poking it up into a steady blaze. By his feet, a heap of rags lay, steam rising from them. A closer look identified them as Nuala, a barely discernible lump beneath a heavy wool blanket.

Casey saw her look. "She came in when the storm began to die back. Said Sean was not comin' tonight, but he'd come soon. An' then she lay down an' fell direct to sleep. She's been so since an' not a stir out of her. I wanted to get the fire goin' well an' then bank it. It's likely she'll sleep the day away so I see no reason to stay."

The previous night's eerie atmosphere had banished with the light. Pamela maneuvered herself out from amidst the balls of sleeping fur, receiving little more than a slitted golden eye for her pains. The woolen nightgown was wound tightly around her waist, exposing her legs to the chill morning air. One thigh sported a blaze of whisker burn, the sight of it igniting her memory along with a deep flush.

Casey flicked her a glance from his position by the fire and grinned.

"We...um...did...?" She left the words hanging in the air, uncertain now what had been dream and what reality. For the cottage seemed to hang suspended between two entirely different worlds.

"Aye," Casey said, the grin broader now, "we did. Unmannerly, I suppose, in a stranger's home, but after five months of deprivation I'm none so concerned about my manners as I might otherwise be. Ye were fairly insistent yerself. Do ye not remember? I didn't think the poteen had gone to yer head quite so bad as all that."

Pamela wrestled the nightie into a semblance of propriety, cheeks burning as she remembered a little more clearly the events of several hours ago. Casey cocked a dark brow at her.

"She did say as there was a great deal of heat between the two of us. I'm sure she'd not mind." He winked, sparking another recollection of the previous night and what she had thought a dream of a merman with healthy appetites.

"Will ye be hungry, or shall we wait to eat?"

"Let's go home," she said, suddenly wanting nothing more than to be alone with him, to watch him breathe, to hear the thud of his heart beneath her ear, and the leap of his pulse to her fingers. And then a fig for the rain and wind. Casey seemed to sense her mood, for his gaze held hers a moment and when he spoke his voice was hoarse.

"Aye, we'll go home then."

She dressed quickly, clothing stiff and earthy with the smell of smoke and rain. Casey waited outside for her, facing toward the sea. She joined him after tidying up the sheets and blankets and checking to be certain Nuala was well. The woman still slept as though half-dead, face sunk in its mask of age. She touched the blaze of silver hair lightly, then stood and left the old woman to her dreams of men and boats that would never again crest the horizon.

"Ready?" she asked a moment later, touching a hand to Casey's arm. He turned and smiled, dark eyes abstracted.

"Oh, aye," he took her hand and they skirted the cottage together, each quiet in their thoughts.

They walked back along the landward side, where the shifting sand dunes lay in drifts of dull bronze in the morning air. Here the land gently sloped into Galway Bay, and the seabed shelved itself gradually toward the Connemara mainland.

"It's a new world," Casey said quietly, slowing as they neared the tiny, sand-clogged outlines of a church. She understood his meaning at once, despite the ancient ruins that lay so near. This morning bore no resemblance to the dark, storm-racked landscape of the previous night.

The sky was low, lit softly pink like the underbelly of a pearl. A great stillness gripped the world, as if the entire planet was exhausted from the previous night's dramatics. Even the gulls, fine white arches over the landless deeps, wheeled in silence. Casey stopped and drew her to him, slipping his arms around her waist.

"On a fine day, when the weather is calm, they say ye can see Tir na nOg, just there," he nodded towards the northwest, "along the horizon."

"On a clear day you can see forever," she said softly.

"Aye, just so, Jewel."

"Do you believe in that—in worlds we can't see?"

Casey shrugged. "I don't know. There's what ye can see, an' then there's what ye can sense but would feel daft to try an' explain."

"Like Nuala believing her husband waits beneath the waves for her."

"Aye well, I suppose in a sense he does."

She shivered and he held her tighter.

"If you'd been taken in such a way, I'd do the same," she said.

It was Casey's turn to shiver. "For God's sake, Jewel, don't be after lookin' in the waves, that's not where I'd wait for ye, ye can be damn certain of that."

"Where would you wait then?" Even as she asked the question, she curled her fingers tighter into the knit of his sweater. The thought of losing him again, even for a moment, was more than she could bear.

"Somewhere that was special to the two of us. The rock where we first made love, mayhap. I'd want to be certain that ye'd know where to come to me."

"And what if there is no after, no Tir na nOg, no Avalon in the mists? Would you still wait?"

He turned her face up towards his own. "After Parkhurst I didn't believe in much of anything except myself and what I could manage in this world. But then I met you an' it seemed that if someone as fine as you could love me, there must be a God. Darlin'," he lowered his head and kissed her forehead gently, "you are my hope of heaven."

She closed her eyes against the tears that seemed to hover so near these last days. "Bloody man."

She remembered the story her father had long ago told her about the land of Tir na nOg, and how Oisin, the leader of the warrior Fiannas, had followed the golden-haired Niave there to the land where time did not exist. The ground around her exuded that sense of timelessness, as if they might emerge on the mainland in another week only to find they were a thousand years behind the rest of the world.

"Maybe the Arans were the land under the sea where Oisin went."

"Maybe, most legends have their feet in the truth somewhere along the way. Did ye know these islands once belonged to yer people?"

"My *people*," she said, with an amused look, "the only people I have are yourself, Lawrence, Pat and Sylvie."

He gave her the look he always did when he felt she was being unnecessarily obtuse. "The O'Flahertys, I mean. They once held these islands along with the O'Briens. The clan split over whether or not they'd accept the English king as their overlord, an' the losin' half fled here."

She snorted. "The winning half only supported the king in an effort to grab land with his blessing."

"Ah, so ye do know yer history then."

"I know a bit about the people I'm descended from, and none of it flatters my blood."

"No, well there's times I see their ruthlessness in yer face." He ducked the hand aimed at his ear. "They weren't the first to claim these islands, though no one knows who the first people here were. I liked the story my da told us though."

"And what was that?"

"'Tis island folklore really. When the Firbolg were defeated on the mainland, legend has it they came here." He nodded toward the northwest shoulder of the island. "The big fort up there is called Dun Aengus after the prince of the Fir Bolgs. 'Tis said that he stood 'til the last with the blood of his people coloring the rocks around him, an' when there were none left to stand with him, he let the wind take him off the cliffs an' into the sea. These islands were their final chance for refuge, or maybe just their last stand against the coming of a world they couldn't understand. On winter nights they say ye can still hear Aengus' last battle cries among the rocks an' the cliffs on the western shores. Can ye imagine it? 'Twould have been like standin' on the very edge of the world and knowin' there was no escape."

In her mind's eye she could see the valiant warrior, sword in hand, defeated and yet still defiant enough to allow the wind and water to take him, rather than bow to the enemy's hand. Flesh and coursing blood one moment and then gone, a mere whisper on history's long roll call of saints and martyrs.

"All flesh is grass, and all the goodliness thereof is as the flower of the field: the grass withereth, the flower fadeth." Casey said, echoing her thoughts, the look of dark abstraction on his face once again.

"And thus passes away the glory of the world," she replied. "You know your bible verses well."

"Aye," Casey smiled ruefully, "don't be too impressed, Jewel, my da made me memorize ten verses every time I swore. I've a score of them I can quote on demand. Which gives ye an idea of what my mouth was like."

"I like your mouth just fine," she said, drawing his head down for a long kiss that demonstrated her appreciation rather well.

"Do ye then?" he asked, minutes later, slightly breathless.

"I do," she said, and heard in the tone of her simple declaration something which signified much more than the words spoken. She held him tightly, her head to his chest, feeling the strength in the arms that wrapped around her and kept the world at bay.

The sun slid over the horizon, a watery sliver that sent narrow tongues of pale gold to taste the edge of things.

"And if there is no after?" he asked, so softly she thought she might well have imagined the words.

The sun now streamed across the sea, turning it to a great blaze of moving diamonds. She looked away from it to the tiny church where sand poured, gold-throated, through the hourglass of the ancient stones.

"I would still wait," she said softly, not wanting to shatter the great hush that enfolded them.

"So would I."

Chapter Sixty

All That You Can't Leave Behind

IN THE MORNING, THE UNNATURAL STILLNESS of the previous day held, though a heavy fog had moved in blanking out the coastline and the hunchback of Hag's Head. The island felt like a ship adrift, as though given enough time and lead it would fetch up with a soft thud upon the shores of Newfoundland. It was time out of time, she knew, and as such could not last forever.

It was oddly warm, as sometimes happened on the islands in the winter, the gray green furze of lichens and brown mosses thick with morning dew. The warmth had brought on a faint mist of struggling ferns and small primroses in the cracks between the great limestone slabs.

She awakened alone, Casey having risen early to get down to the boats before they were entirely emptied of coal and oil and other provisions. After an abbreviated wash in the chill basin, she set out for the cliffs, a walk that Casey could not be prevailed upon to take. This morning, however, the solitary ramble brought her no comfort.

She stood upon the island's western shoulder where an enormous silence gripped the atmosphere, as if even the air were awaiting some event. Below, the sea gave off only the occasional murmur, and once she thought she heard the pale hiss of a gull gliding past through the fog. Other than that, the silence was complete and menacing.

She turned, shivering, and walked swiftly down the rocky path, wanting the comfort of a fire, a cup of tea and her husband's presence. She saw Casey as she rounded the small knob of a hill that brought her out just below the cottage's battered red door and felt a cold fist grip her throat at the sight of him.

He was on the rough bench that sat just left of the open door. He sat, elbows on knees, head bowed and in the language of cell and bone she understood at once that their time here was done.

"What's happened?" she asked, not wanting to utter the words and yet knowing they had to be spoken. Silence would no longer suspend reality.

"The army opened fire on the demonstrators in Derry," he said, voice soft and weary. Anger had not laid its hand upon him yet, but it soon would.

"How many—how—"

He shook his head. "Don't know yet, more than one, less than a hundred. Ye know how these things go, Jewel, there's no telling until some of the smoke has cleared."

"How did you hear?"

"News came over with the boat. When the coal came in this mornin' it was all the talk."

"We're leaving then?" she said, voice stiff.

For the first time since she'd turned to find him sitting so silently, he looked up. His face was drawn, mouth sharp cornered, stubble a deep violet against the white of his skin.

"Pat was there, Pamela."

"You can't be certain of that," she said, knowing her voice didn't quite carry the reassurance she sought to give him.

"Ye know he would be. He can never stay clear of trouble for more than a day or two. He'd have been there."

"But you don't..." the words died on her lips at the look in his eyes.

"They didn't know so much about what had happened, an' the news was all confused like, but one thing everyone seemed certain on an' that was it was mostly young men who had died. Maybe a few older ones, but the rest between 17 an' 27."

She put her hand to her mouth to stifle a cry of horror; he needed her to stay calm and clear-headed right now.

"There had to be hundreds of people there."

"I know, an' it's likely he's fine, holed up somewhere plannin' his latest insurrection, but until I see him with my own eyes, I'll not be certain. I have to go home, Jewel."

"And what if you're caught? If the army comes for you, what then?"

He gave her an apologetic look. "I'm sorry, darlin', but I'll have to risk it."

She nodded, mentally beginning the packing of their belongings, but found she was rooted to the spot, unable to move her feet, as if the conduit between thought and movement had temporarily suspended itself. They had to go back, that was clear. Casey would not rest until he was certain that Pat was whole and safe. Yet she dreaded it—the risk, the thought that soldiers could come and wrest her husband away from her yet again.

"Jewel."

She took a deep breath to steady herself. "Yes."

"I'm sorry. Given the choice I'd have kept the two of us here for as long as possible."

"I know," she said, but despite the firmness of her tone, could hear the doubt clearly expressed. She knelt down and took his hands in her own. "He will be fine, I know it."

"Aye," he said quietly. "I know it one minute an' then I don't the next. What if—"

"No," she put her fingers to his lips, "we're not going to ask that question."

He nodded, but the traces of fear and doubt still lingered in his eyes.

Inside she packed their few belongings, while outside Casey battened down the windows and put the sacks of coal under shelter to be used by the next occupant of this small safe house. She uttered up prayers as she moved about tidying; that Pat hadn't been in Derry, that if he had he was unharmed, while all the time a serpent of fear writhed in her belly.

The day slipped slowly away to the sea, strange minutes of silence and lukewarm mugs of tea. Neither of them could summon an appetite and Casey alternated between staring intently into the blue eye of the fire, and pacing relentlessly round the outside of the small cottage. By mid-afternoon the wind picked up, shredding the fog into spectral fingers and Casey's head turned toward the sea with tense expectation. It was then she heard the distant chug of a boat engine.

Before night fell, they were on their way back to the mainland.

Part Six

History's Prisoners

Chapter Sixty-one

Butcher's Dozen

THE WIND COMING OFF THE RIVER FOYLE that day was particularly cold. Pat, standing to the side of a rambunctious group of boys, dug his hands into the pockets of his coat and shivered. Despite the chill of the air there was a current that warmed the crowd, the sense of being in attendance at a moment in history that rests upon a pivotal fork in the road. Trouble was expected; after the events at Magilligan last week, it wasn't likely that the army would let another 'illegal' demonstration slide past.

Some three hundred soldiers had broken up the small anti-internment protest near the Magilligan camp the week earlier. Thus, today the Northern Ireland Civil Rights Association had put special emphasis on the need for a peaceful demonstration. Ivan Cooper, one of the local MPs, had stated that the IRA in Derry had agreed to withdraw from the area prior to today's demonstration, in the hopes that there would be no reason for any altercation with the army. Still, there was the frisson of edgy anticipation that had accompanied every public gathering in Ireland since the People's Democracy March in the fall of 1968. Pat still bore the scars of that march, compliments of several police batons to his head when he'd stuck an Irish flag in the Derry wall. However, he'd also met Sylvie as a direct result of that march, so felt the scars were a small price to have paid.

The previous evening he'd gone for a drink with a couple of friends to the Rocking Chair Bar, which was notorious as the place to pick up current information on both army and IRA activity. British intelligence being what it was, he'd left with many assurances that today was to be a peaceful day of it. Still he'd awakened that morning with a vaguely uneasy feeling, due in part, he knew, to the fact that the paratroopers were coming to Derry for the day.

The Paras were the elite corps of the British Army, hand-picked, trained to total discipline, with an infamous reputation for their combat ability. It didn't make sense to send such a crack bunch to a little demonstration in Derry. It was this that was at the root of his restless worry. In his experience, the Brits rarely did anything without some larger plan in mind. He just couldn't quite get a grasp on what piece of the puzzle the Paras were meant to fit.

On the other hand, he knew what to expect from the march itself. The stewards, like impatient shepherds, would harry everyone into shape, then all would march toward confrontation where there was likely to be some form of violence; CS gas, cracked skulls, rubber bullets, outrage at the expected and more grievances to nurse. Then the paper cup of lukewarm tea and the trudge home in the gloaming to live over the events of the day, and see if you and your mates had made the evening news. Part of him was repelled by it and part of him knew it was necessary. Yet another part, which had grown considerably during his time in Long Kesh, wondered if it made a damn blind bit of difference.

For a country that had been at war for eight hundred odd years there was little evidence to be found of a war zone, and yet, he supposed, if there was a flashpoint in the cradle of Ulster, wee Derry was it. Divided Derry had been the nexus for conflict since William of Orange's victory over the papist James II in 1690. Derry, which, despite a population comprised largely of working class Catholics, hadn't seen a Nationalist mayor in fifty years. Where blood had run in the streets over election results, and people had died for exercising their democratic rights.

For a minute, he saw all the blood that had been spilled in this tiny city, as though the dank walls and depressed streets were some mythical and priceless jewel that could restore a people to itself, if only the sacrifice were large enough.

The march started out much as he expected, the crowd, ragged about its edges, moving out from the large grassy area of Bishops Field which lay under the shadow of the vast Creggan housing estate. Banners flapped in the wind above hunched shoulders and ruffled hair—*Civil Rights for All, Release all Internees* and *End Special Powers Act* were just some among the many that furled and fluttered, giving the moving mass a festive air. Still the uneasy feeling grew stronger, spreading out through his stomach like slow moving ice water, as the crowd wended their way down toward Brandywell along the Lone Moor Road. Like some slow-moving beast eating all in its path, they gathered more marchers at every corner, the edges of the crowd shifting and absorbing the newcomers, while the stewards fought like collies on the fringes to keep the flock moving in a half-assed orderly fashion.

His eye was drawn to a little girl watching from the roadside as they passed. The January sunshine gilded her red hair with a watery glow. She raised a hand and waved to him, he waved back and she grinned, her gapped smile warm as fire, yet the ice in his belly resisted the thaw. He looked back once as they rounded the corner into Williams Street and saw that she was still up on tiptoe waving.

They were down the steep incline of the street now, and it was there that the first soldiers were seen. A large detachment on foot, flanked by Saracens.

Pat sighed and moved forward. There was never a more certain sign of a society's failure than the sight of soldiers and tanks in the streets. He looked up; the Guildhall Clock Tower was clearly visible. The time was three forty-five and the world was about to come open at the seams.

There were boys popping about like fleas on the rubble strewn barricades; ones who'd come out for trouble and the chance of knocking a soldier a good whack with a stone. Hands shoved in their pockets, high on the balls of their feet in anticipation of the uneven battle to come.

He scanned the area; the barricades that blocked Rossville Street, the main thoroughfare coming into the Bogside, putting the crowd's back to the Free Derry sign where Catholic Derry began and British rule held no sway. The uneasy shiver in his spine had grown considerably as the crowd progressed up from the Bogside. He eyed the horizon that wrapped chill and gray around city stone and grassy slopes. He thought he saw a shadowy figure high on an abandoned building, but when he turned his head, the shadow was gone.

On the platform, Bernadette Devlin was speaking, assuring everyone that it was a perfectly legal meeting and there was no need to panic, when a volley of shots erupted from behind the crowd.

The growl of armored cars filled the air and the sudden thump of soldier's feet as they poured out of the vehicles. There were at least twenty and they rushed forward, rifles up and cocked. Pat felt as though he were frozen in place while madness swirled around him. Then the air was rent in two with a series of sharp cracks. *Christ.* That wasn't the sound of rubber bullets, Pat thought. The ice water in his stomach rushed through his whole body and his legs unlocked, moving of their own accord.

"Those are real bullets!" someone screamed.

"Disperse, disperse, disperse!" came over the loudspeakers, panicking the crowd further as everyone rush pell-mell in a thousand different directions under the report of rifles that were shooting to kill, not control.

Blocked by troops releasing choking clouds of CS gas, rubber bullets and dye at the end of Williams Street, the crowd surged back toward the open area near Free Derry Corner. Between was the waste ground of the Rossville Flats car park and the open area behind. A huge mass of unarmed humanity now out in the open, whose flesh was all too vulnerable to the bullets that were flying down from the walls.

Moving through the crowd, Pat risked a quick glance up at the clogged artery of Rossville Street. People were still bunched like panicked cattle trying to make their way through to some sort of safety. The panic was in the Paras' favor, no one could tell where the shots were coming from, and so all were clear targets as they ran in complete panic. The only cover might come from the walls and rubble in the forecourt of the Rossville Flats. There were soldiers directly across in Glenfada Park, he'd seen them, rifles at the ready, eyes scoping the crowd, just waiting for an excuse.

He made his way across the street. It was like moving through a maelstrom of screaming, terrified souls who'd just discovered the gates of hell were opening beneath their feet. He made it, though, pushing as many as he could with him, yelling at them to find cover rather than running about in the open.

He yelled at a boy walking slowly across the open ground of the forecourt, in clear view of the rifles. He recognized him as one of the boys who'd been near the barricades, laughing as though they were on a grand lark.

"Come on man, move toward the wall!"

The boy turned, face a blank. "I think I've been hit, I...it hurts to breathe."

The front of the lad's sweater was soaked with blood; even now it dripped into the weave of his Sunday trousers. There was blood leaking from the corners of his mouth as well. Lung shot.

"Christ have mercy," Pat breathed, and then took the boy by the arm and pulled him toward the dubious safety offered by the high walls of the Flats. The boy collapsed twice, and Pat finally hooked an arm across his chest and pulled him, half running, half crawling as bullets singed the air blue around him.

He saw Father Jim standing up from the side of an injured man and took the boy directly to him.

"He's been hit in the chest," Pat said, laying his burden down against the brick wall. "Can you help him?"

Father Jim was already kneeling, peeling back the boy's sodden shirt. He shook his head. "I'll do what I can," the priest said grimly, "but he needs to get to hospital. I think the bullet's gone through his lung."

Pat knew the odds of getting the boy to the hospital in time weren't in their favor. Right now it looked as though the soldiers were preventing any aid from coming into the area. So he would have to get out to relay information, and to find a way to bring help in. It was impossible to go back down towards Williams Street. Gas was still heavy in the air, slight whiffs of it floating up to sting eyes and throats. The only possibility seemed to lie with getting out past the Free Derry wall. He was gauging the distance and trying to decide if he should make a run for it when he saw a flutter of white across the forecourt. A man was walking out slowly, white handkerchief aloft, trying to reach a boy who was lying wounded near the middle of the open ground. Some primal instinct must have warned him that he was caught in the crosshairs of a soldier's rifle, for he dropped to his knees and began to crawl, still heading for the wounded boy.

Movement at the corner of his peripheral vision caught Pat's attention. He looked up and time stopped, poised itself on the fulcrum of a pin, and then exploded outward into history; the burn of cordite in the air, the motion of the sniper rising over the wall as the man crawled as close to the ground as he could manage and still keep moving. These things became memory and event even as they happened. Something surged in Pat, blind animal rage, the taste of it red in his mouth, the smell hot on the wind.

"Christ have mercy," he breathed to himself before crawling out toward the man. The ground in front of him was instantly peppered with bullets, the dust blinding him as it kicked up into his face. Someone grabbed his ankle from behind jerking him back, scraping his knees in the process. He kicked his leg free and started forward again, blinking the grit from his eyes.

The man was still crawling, dazed, uncertain which direction might offer some safety. None did. The first bullet to hit him drove him to his chin, his mouth a round 'O' of shock. Still he pushed himself along, cheek scraping the ground, eyes unblinking with bewilderment. His body jerked one more time and then he fell full length against the cold stones.

Despite the futility of it, Pat had to try and reach him. He stretched out close to the ground, wriggling more than crawling. The man's face was turned toward him, mouth open, trying to form words, pale blue eyes wide with pain.

Bullets sprayed the ground in front of Pat again, dust choking him, eyes streaming from the smoke. He tucked his face into the collar of his coat and pushed forward. A bullet grazed past his ear with a high-pitched whine, singeing his skin in passing. He moved again, was within feet of the man when the pavement exploded in his face. A burning pain sliced across the side of his head, flattening him to the ground instantly. His vision filled with a haze of smoke and fire, then went black.

When he came to, he was lying, fingers just touching the scraped knuckles of the man he'd crawled out to save. A sudden silence had enveloped them, as though the chaos were very far away. Maybe, he thought dazedly, the bullets had temporarily deafened him. From somewhere a breeze blew across them, ruffling the man's thin pale hair, animating that which was no longer alive. For it was too late. The look of profound surprise had changed into something far more permanent.

Pat closed his eyes, willing himself to stay still, despite the overwhelming instinct to run and hide. He knew if he moved he was dead, it was that simple. Now all he could do was pray that no one was crazy enough to try and come after *him*.

Someone did try, though.

He heard the footsteps, careful and slow. His rescuer was a middle-aged man, wearing an anorak and a pair of navy trousers that he'd likely worn to church that morning. His dark hair was thinning in front, and his narrow face was anxious as he approached Pat and the dead man, his arms held up high in a gesture of peace to the soldiers. Pat willed him back, his mouth forming the word 'no' in silent desperation.

"Tis all right son, we'll get ye out of—"

The shot came from behind and spun the man around so that he faced the wall he'd left behind. The exit wound opened out into an arc of blood and bone as he fell to the side, his head only a few feet from where Pat lay. The blood was warm on Pat's face, the smell of copper so strong that it took all he had not to retch onto the slick rectangles of pavement beneath his face. The taste of it was leaking into his mouth and he could feel tiny fragments of bone cutting into the back of his left hand.

Behind him a wail rose, high and thin on the chill air, a keening for an entire people, for a nation shot down while trying to get up off their knees. He thought that if one cared to look, one would see hope rising, ghost-like, on that wail, abandoning all those that were lying below.

How long he was there on the pavement, the chill of the stone leeching into his body, the lifeblood of another drying tight on his skin, he never knew. It felt like forever, as though the world might have passed through an age, progressed a thousand years or fallen back a thousand, before he heard the voice of redemption in his ear.

"Come on, laddie, we've got to get you out of here."

"Father Jim?"

"It's me, all right. I'm goin' to have a look at your head before we move you."

"It's only a graze," Pat said, though the amount of blood that had flowed into his face since he'd been hit frightened him.

Father Jim probed around the wound, causing Pat to take a sharp breath.

"Does it hurt badly, then?"

"Stings like the devil. I'd be more worried if it didn't hurt though."

"You're right, it's a shallow graze, they always bleed the worst for some reason. We'll get you a stretcher.

"No, I can walk," Pat said, "I was only scared to move for fear they'd shoot again."

"I think they've stopped," Father Jim said, though he didn't sound entirely convinced that the carnage was over.

Pat pushed himself up onto legs that were the consistency of poorly set jelly. He leaned into the brick wall, dazed, the cut on the side of his head still trickling blood. He blinked, trying to take in what was before him, numb with incomprehension. A slight haze still hung over the courtyard, the wind unable to clear the bullet traceries out of the air. Around him, people kneeled, sat, stood dazed and horrified, some still half choking on the whiff of CS gas that had blown their way. From where he stood, he could see two bodies that were unmistakably dead, and more wounded. The young boy who'd been shot through the lung was now lying on a stretcher, with Father Jim praying over him.

Pat wiped a hand across his forehead, clearing the blood from his eyes, then limped over to the boy. He was on his back, a large dark pool of blood congealing beneath him. His eyes were a dark brown and stared sightlessly at the sky above. A fringe of brown hair, neatly trimmed, fell over his forehead. Christ, he was just a baby.

"Is he—"

Father Jim nodded, then drew a jacket up over the boy's face. "Yes, he's dead and about all of sixteen years if he was a day, God help us."

The priest stood, face gray and exhausted with shock. "You'd best let me look at your head again, lad, it's still bleeding."

"I'll do, there's people need your help more than I."

"Quit being such a stubborn bastard, and let me have a look."

He winced slightly as Father Jim parted his hair to have another look at the wound. "It's shallow enough that you won't need stitches. You were damn lucky, another millimetre to the right and you'd be dead."

Pat nodded numbly, wondering why he'd been spared. It had been *that* damn close, and he'd walked away with a cut in his scalp, nothing more. It made no sense, particularly not when he could still taste another man's mortality on his own tongue.

"I think the Paras have left," Father Jim said, eyeing the walls warily. "So we'd best get on with it."

For the next hour they assessed the wounded, patched them as best as they could with cloth torn from shirts and jackets, and got them into ambulances. The ones suffering from shock and fear they set on the road home, knowing there was little they could do for them in any case.

Finally they had cleared everyone off, and Father Jim was conferring with the last set of medics to leave the scene, his good wool coat long gone to cover an injured boy, his black shirt now three quarters red, hands and face smeared with dried blood.

Pat leaned against a post, eyes still smarting from the gas, throat raw and head thumping. How could this have happened? And why? Did the British establishment really hate the Irish so much that it would issue a shoot to kill order on a bunch of unarmed civilians? How could it be declared illegal for a man to have rights in his own country? He was so damn tired of questions that had no answers. Tired of not having the right to be a man who was allowed to walk free in the streets of his own land. The rage was still there, crimson as the blood that stained the streets in this wee town, and it frightened him, for he no longer knew of what he might be capable.

"Pat lad, are you coming? We've done all we can here."

Pat nodded and followed the blood-soaked form of the priest from the killing ground.

LATER, WHEN THE DEAD WERE TOTALLED, they numbered thirteen,

all male, all unarmed, all Catholic. They ranged in age from seventeen to forty-one, and left behind mothers, brothers, sisters, fathers, and wives and children that would never be able to make sense of that which had no reason. The wounded numbered eighteen and were, again, predominantly male, with the exception of Margaret Deery and Alana Burke, the lone women wounded that day. And then there were all the things seen by those who had escaped the bullets. A priest being led off at gunpoint, denied the right to give absolution to the dying. Boys with gun muzzles shoved to their foreheads, young men beaten to the ground and soldiers who stood by as people bled to death on the pavement.

As the news flowed out around the world, it became clear just how far apart the Irish and British were ideologically, politically and in basic understanding. This was apparent in the attitude, which manifested itself in one British military correspondent, who was in high spirits after the news came in and was heard to say of the Paras *"They shot well, didn't they?"*

For the Irish it was horror, a slaughter, a tragedy that was entirely senseless. For the British it was a regrettable mistake, but these things happened under pressure, civilians would just have to understand that. But what was portrayed as a technical disaster on British newscasts, flickering cheerily in British living rooms was, in Ireland, a crossing of the Rubicon from which there could be no turning back. The monster might hide behind smooth suits and plummy tones, gentleman's clubs and ancestral privilege, but its bloody teeth and claws had been felt and seen, and would not be forgotten.

In the House of Commons, Bernadette Devlin, the lone nationalist member in an alien Parliament, was denied the right to speak on Bloody Sunday, while wake was read over thirteen dead Irishmen by an Englishman who'd gone to the right schools, had the right accent and not a clue about the wee country across the water.

In England it was a minor event, unfortunate, but quickly swallowed by the business of crown and country. In Ireland, there were now few left who would say no to the men who preached physical force as the only medium that Britain could understand. And so the IRA flourished in the wake of a chill winter's massacre, their numbers swelling through city and field and even over the border in the sleepy Republic.

Rage, both righteous and dissolute, had raised its head from slumber and the roar would be heard down through the corridors of history for decades to come.

Chapter Sixty-two

No Place for Love or Dream at All...

THE POSTMORTEMS WERE BEING HELD at Altnagelvin Hospital. Father Jim explained this to Pat over an untouched breakfast and tea that was tepid in their cups. Neither could summon an appetite, nor had either slept since the horrific events of the previous day.

"The Archbishop wants me there as an observer. I've also been asked to help with the postmortem examinations. I'd like you to come and record the results. What I'm asking is a fairly serious task, as we cannot afford even one mistake. They are going to try and make it seem as if this was a provoked action, not the slaughter it really was. We need to make sure we have every fact straight and written down in duplicate. We can't allow emotion to taint anything we say or do in this investigation. We're going to have to play this out by rules they understand, despite the horror of the situation."

"What difference will it make?" Pat asked dully, the taint of shock still flattening his words.

"You're going to have to do something, or kill someone," the priest said dryly.

It was the first thing that had made any sort of sense to Pat in many, many hours and thus he found himself present at the postmortems, taking the careful notes that Father Jim had requested of him.

"Shot on his knees," the doctor said, the dry, medical matter-of-factness in his tone having a rather dreamy quality to Pat's ear, after the events of the day. "Bullet entered through the right chest, traveled in a slightly downward trajectory, and exited through the lower left chest."

"Amazing," Father Jim responded, "when he was apparently up on a roof in sniping position." The list continued on in much the same manner, a litany of atrocity that numbed minds could hardly comprehend.

"Age of deceased twenty-seven. Bullet entered through the left abdominal wall...bullet found lodged in the posterior chest wall. Bullet penetrated the aorta and inferior vena cava...age of deceased twenty-two...age of deceased seventeen...Christ have mercy..."

Pat recorded the results with a blank mind, knowing he'd collapse here and now if he allowed himself to really understand what had happened in the square and on the rubble-strewn barricades.

"Shot in the back while lying on his face on the ground....wounds consistent with his arms being held above his head in a position of surrender at the time of the bullet entry...wound consistent with the position of crawling on hands and knees...bullet entered left buttock and traveled through his body, exiting near his shoulder...subject killed by single shot to the head....shot at close range..."

The postmortem examinations took several hours, the early January dark having fallen long before they were finished. Father Jim touched Pat's shoulder. Pat blinked, feeling as though he'd just come up from under water.

"You ought to go home, boy," Father Jim said gruffly. "I can finish up with the doctor here."

Pat shook his head mutely, throat turned to stone. "No," he finally managed to rasp out. "I'll do for now."

"Not without food and sleep you won't," Father Jim said firmly. "I've only a couple more things to finish with here and then we'll find the both of us some hot food and a good stiff drink."

He knew Father Jim was right. He was so tired he was half-hallucinating now. Twice when he'd looked down at his hands today he could have sworn they were sheathed to the wrists in crimson, that the blood of those dead men was somehow, despite hot water and soap, still there and maybe always would be.

There was something inside his chest, something hot and red that threatened to overspill its boundaries and lay waste to all in its path. It had grown steadily larger over the last twenty-four hours.

He had always known, in a theoretical sort of way, that all men and women held within them the capability for violence. Any mother with a threatened child could tell you that. But to know it on another level, to feel the urge of it in your very veins, to fear that it would take you over, seize your rationality, conquer the very finest things in your soul—this, he found, was another thing altogether.

THE CHURCH'S SMALL CEMETERY was walled. Blowing snow had found its way in, banking in light drifts against the headstones and bringing a cold peace to the inhabitants. Pat stood in the lee of an oak tree whose roots and branches had mingled with the stone and stood sentinel over the dead for many generations. The late winter light tinted the graveyard a melancholy blue that seemed all too apt, Father Jim thought, as he walked on the narrow pathway between stones.

"Sylvie called, she's very worried."

"I called her last night. She knows I'm neither dead nor wounded."

"She said you told her to stay in London."

"It seems the safest place for her right now. Belfast is likely to see some bad trouble over the next while."

"I suppose it's inevitable," Father Jim said, thinking of his congregation back in Belfast, those who had teetered on the edge of taking to the gun, the young men he'd slowly tried to coax away from the brink. In one day, the British had managed to wipe out the work of months on his own part, years on the part of others. There would be severe repercussions, of that there was little doubt. And the innocent would suffer, as they always did, caught in the crossfire of history. "It's so senseless, I've had people asking me why all day, and I've no answer to give. I was there and I've no clue what happened."

"Don't you? Ask yourself this—why do you think the Paras opened fire?"

"They lost control, panicked—I don't know," he finished lamely, knowing all the explanations he'd tried to formulate strained even his own credulity.

"Does that make any sense to ye, Father? The Paras don't lose control, don't go berserk, they're trained for much more stressful situations than what occurred yesterday."

"I can't make sense of it any other way, Patrick," he said wearily.

"It makes a great deal of sense if ye look at it from the Brits' perspective. An' by Brits I don't mean even the soldiers themselves, for the truth is they were following commands from higher up."

Father Jim shook his head. "I'm not following you."

"Pretend for a minute ye're the man behind the desk, the one who's supposed to invent the formulas to control the rabble on the other side of the sea. The biggest threat to that is the IRA. The cells are impenetrable, ye can't get yer men inside, ye can't seem to turn enough of the lads on the inside to get at what ye need to start tearin' the organization apart. So what do ye do?" Pat's voice was cool and quiet. The tone of it sent a chill of unease up the priest's spine.

"I don't know."

"In order to place key people within such a tight structure, ye need to have a huge influx of new blood. To create that situation ye stage an event that's goin' to cause a big emotional backlash across the community the organization is tied to. Then ye ride out the resultin' fury, an' when things quiet down ye've achieved exactly what ye wanted. Boys that join in emotional haste will be easier to turn when they've the leisure to repent."

"That's quite a stretch," Father Jim said.

"Maybe so, maybe no," Pat rejoined in the same emotionless tone. "But I traveled about a bit last night. The doors of the IRA in this wee city were bein' knocked down by sheer numbers. Anyone could have predicted it would happen, are ye sayin' the powers that be in Britain couldn't see it clear?"

"Were you one of those boys lined up at the door, Pat?" Father Jim asked.

Pat moved out from under the wet black branches of the oak. "I don't need to knock on the door; it's always been open to me."

"Because of who your father was?"

"Because of who my father was, and my grandfather before him," Pat echoed back the priest's words in the affirmative. A thin layer of snow was lying on his dark hair, the ends etched in pale blue frost. His skin was a ghostly white, as though he was more akin to the people that were beneath the iron hard ground than those who walked above it.

"Is it a door you would choose to walk through?"

The silence that stretched between them was long. Pat's answer when it came was quiet, and released on a breath of crystallized air.

"Not today."

Pat hunched down by a simple headstone that leaned precariously over the gnarled root. It was the resting place of one Martin Herlihy, aged twenty-nine. His was the last grave dug in the small courtyard. Fifty years separated him from the previous internee to these grounds. Father Jim wondered who the lad had been—a relative of one of the monks that had labored here? The byblow of some important family?

His stone told no tales, for it merely held his name, the dates of his birth and death and two lines of Yeats.

Here is...
No place for love or dream at all
For God goes by with white footfall.

He had always loved that poem, yet here the lines seemed rather a bleak way to speak of heaven. Here they seemed to speak simply of the grave, or even the country, for today there seemed little place for love or dreams in this land.

"You need to sleep Pat. If you can't manage it I'll give you a shot of something. It might be best to forget for a few hours."

"No," Pat shook his head. "I don't want it. I don't want to forget just yet."

Father Jim gave him a long look, then walked back into the office. He returned a moment later. "Go inside, there's a fire lit in the study as well as pen and paper waiting for you. Write it down, every bit you can remember, leave nothing out, no matter how trivial it might seem. And then, like it or not, you're getting the shot and going to bed."

Pat followed the priest inside. He settled at the long oak table, where Father Jim had left a glass of whiskey for warmth and comfort. Father Jim sighed, and put his hands to eyes that felt like sandpaper. Outside the sleet fell in icy sheets, the wind wrapping round the thick monastery walls with an eerie moan.

He was so exhausted he'd the odd sense of being separate from his body, of rising above the dark, quiet study, with the peat fire a small glow in the hearth. He could see his own head bent over the desk, the posture one of extreme exhaustion and grief.

After a long time, Pat rose and left the study. The paper and pen sat on the table, blank and abandoned. The whiskey as well was untouched.

Father Jim rubbed his hands hard over his face, trying to return some feeling to his skin. He felt numb all over. Except his heart, which seemed both the size and consistency of a large stone. The truth was he loved this country, but it was breaking his heart. History collapsed in on itself here at least once every other generation, renewing the cycle of blood sacrifice to a greater cause, a cause that could not be defined except through myth. Yesterday Britain's soldiers had relit the torch for this generation. And this too would become myth, its victims added to the pantheon of patriot martyrs that littered the halls of Irish history. He had seen the fire in the faces of the young all over the city today, had heard it in the voice of Patrick Riordan, who had struggled much of his life to avoid what must have seemed inevitable. It depressed him, these children committing themselves to a life of futile violence that always ended the same way. It differed little from what he'd seen in Vietnam—different scale, different voices, same results. Perhaps it was time to leave, settle into a parish somewhere near his old home of Springfield, Massachusetts, to try and forget.

He didn't sense the man in the doorway until he spoke.

"Excuse me, Father."

He looked up startled, blinking to clear his fogged vision.

The man was big. He took up a great deal of the doorframe, both in size and presence. He'd only met him once, and briefly then, but he wasn't a man to be forgot.

"Casey. I suppose you've come for your brother."

"Aye, is he here then?"

"He is."

"How is he?"

"He's been very quiet. He's yet to sleep since all this," he made a helpless gesture with his hands, "happened."

"My da said it wasn't when the Riordans were in a temper that a man need fear them, it was when they got quiet."

The priest heard the truth implicit in the simple statement. Everything had changed for the soft-spoken lad who'd worked so hard to effect fundamental and meaningful change in his neighborhood over these past two years. The abyss of violence that always beckoned in Ulster would be yawning up to the most peaceful of souls at present. He wondered if the lad was right about the reasons behind this attack, and the murder of thirteen souls.

"Father, could ye take me to him?"

"Of course. I'm sorry, we're all a little dazed here."

Father Jim led Casey down the long corridor towards the small sleeping quarters.

"He was exhausted. I think he may have gone to sleep."

Pat was not asleep. His small bag was packed, his coat and boots on. He'd obviously been readying himself to leave, though he stood looking at the small crucifix above the bed, face drained of all expression. A strange peace seemed to have fallen across him. Perhaps fatigue and shock had taken their toll at last.

"Patrick, Casey's here."

He didn't turn, nor acknowledge his brother's presence.

"Patrick," Casey said quietly, though the tone was firm. "I've come to take ye home, lad."

After a long minute, Casey reached out and took his brother's hand.

"Take me home then, brother," Pat said, dark eyes as distant as they'd been the previous night.

Casey nodded as they passed Father Jim, their movement stirring the edges of his soutane. He'd forgotten he still wore it. The garment felt oddly natural today, despite the fact that he'd not worn one in years, a cloak of black mourning for the peace that had seemed only a day ago, possible.

Suddenly he was very afraid of tomorrow.

Chapter Sixty-three

Brick Walls and Broken Doors

ASEY'S RE-ENTRY INTO THE WORLD was destined to be rough, personally as well as politically. The aftershocks of Bloody Sunday had been expected, but were no less tragic for all the knowing. There were protests worldwide, and two days after the massacre in Derry a crowd burned down the British embassy in Dublin. Belfast was ready to blow apart at the seams, with anger surging like a blood tide through the streets. On a more personal level, Pamela was aware her husband seemed as likely to implode as the streets of his city.

His actual physical coming home had been a gradual process. At first he had stayed at a variety of safe houses, with occasional stealthy conjugal visits home during the night. Then he'd begun to spend all his nights at home, disappearing like smoke with the dawn. The next step had been the occasional meal at home, then doing the chores that needed a man's hand, and finally after a month of this routine, he had boldly gone out and about in the day time, had even ventured down to Gallagher's for a pint. The result of this had been an absolute lack of repercussions. This in itself had worried Casey at first, but then as day followed upon day he gradually resumed all the facets of his old life. However, there was a funny smell about the whole situation that started a suspicion growing in his chest with which he was not at all happy.

His emotional journey home had been altogether more difficult. He was prickly as a porcupine, gruff with both Pamela and Lawrence and then instantly repentant and apologetic. This alternated with long spells of silence. After two weeks of this behavior, Pamela wished he would blow up and get it over with.

It was apparent he was having trouble fitting back in with the household in as seamless a manner as he'd expected. She'd come upon him a few times, stopped in the middle of a task, staring into some remote vision that took him several minutes to come back from. The intensity of these spells worried her.

He'd spoken very little about his experiences on the ship, and hadn't responded gracefully to queries about it either. She knew he was going to have to talk about it eventually. For now, though, it was a big enough task for him to find a way back into his old life. As to his current state of mind, she'd an uneasy feeling that she knew what was irking him. It would be up to her to open the issue.

Her moment came when the two of them were knocking about the kitchen together preparing Sunday dinner. Lawrence was in his room, the Beatles *Strawberry Fields Forever* vibrating through his door.

"Do you want to talk about it?" she asked casually, as she peeled potatoes over the sink.

Casey looked up sharply from where he was taking a roast out of its butcher paper. He shook his head and then shrugged his shoulders as though his shirt were suddenly too tight. "About what?"

"What's got you acting like a caged bear."

"Is there any percentage in denyin' it?"

She merely raised an eyebrow at him. He took a heavy breath.

"All right, I suppose I just had this idea in my head, a sort of dream that I clung to on that damn ship, of what it'd be like to be home with the two of ye again. But it's all different, an' it's as though I've stepped into a play where the scenery is familiar but I'm naked an' don't know any of my lines."

"I—" she began, but Casey cut her off. "But I have to say what's really botherin' me here is not knowin' if the friggin' man has paid for my freedom."

There seemed little point in asking just whom the frigging man in question was, so Pamela refrained from doing so.

"What?"

"Don't bother givin' me that puzzled look, woman. Has it not struck ye as odd that I've been home these three weeks an' no one has come lookin' for me?"

It certainly *had* struck her as odd, but she had instinctively shied away from the thought, terrified as she was of losing him once again.

"All the men I escaped with are still holed up in the Republic an' I advise them to stay put there for as long as they are able. I'm here takin' only the barest of precautions—livin' in my own home an' not a soul has come to inquire after me."

"I don't care how your freedom was achieved," she said, "only that it was."

He shook his head angrily. "Well ye'll forgive me if I do give a damn."

"I understand," she said quietly, realizing the words were a mistake the minute they crossed her lips.

"No, I don't think ye do understand," Casey said, dropping the roast into the pan. Small droplets of blood sprayed across the clean countertop.

"Then perhaps you'd trouble to explain it to me," Pamela replied tersely.

At this rather delicate juncture Lawrence came into the kitchen, arms full of the model aircraft he and Jamie had been painstakingly piecing together over the last several Sundays. He cast an eye at the abused roast and opened his mouth before Pamela could stop him.

"We're not goin' to Jamie's for dinner?" he asked in dismay. Pamela shook her head, eyebrows drawn down in warning. It was too late, however, for Casey threw the butcher paper in the sink and left the kitchen. A moment later they heard the back door slam.

"I didn't mean..." Lawrence trailed off uncomfortably, chin stuck in the notch of a miniature propeller.

"It's all right," she said. "He's just a little prickly right now. He knew our lives went along without him, but now he's feeling out of place and uncomfortable in his own home."

"Are ye goin' after him?" Lawrence asked, looking uncertainly at the space where Casey had been.

"No, he needs some time to himself. I'll go out and talk to him when he's calmed down."

"How do ye know..." Lawrence's question died on his lips as a huge thump was heard from outside. "Shouldn't we go see if he's all right?"

Pamela shook her head. "No, he'll not do himself any damage, but I wouldn't lay odds on the survival of the shed."

She gave him a half-hour before donning her shoes and coat and walking out into the wet, brown yard. The air was chill with mist, clinging in droplets to the sodden foliage. She walked slowly, half-dreading what she would find. The shed was quiet; the walls however, were still intact.

She found him inside, standing by the bench, back to her. The door he'd been mending when he was lifted was still lying where he'd left it, six months previous. It was battered beyond recognition at present, though. Casey still held the hammer in his hand, his breath coming in ragged gasps. The knuckles of both hands were bloody and swollen.

"'Twas either this or that damned dresser. I thought ye'd mind the loss of the door less."

She crossed the small space of the shed, not daring to touch him just yet. "Do you want to talk about it?" she asked.

Casey snorted derisively. "Talk about it—what is there to say? I'm gone a few months an' the man has taken over every corner of my life. He's finished the roof on the house, the lad's crazy for him, Finbar's pinin' over him, and he's raised the damn sheep. Would it have been too much for him to leave me a wee sheep for myself?"

Pamela gave an involuntary laugh and Casey whirled, flashing a look of frustrated anger at her. Then he bit his lip and a small laugh escaped. Then another and soon they were both helpless with it. They laughed until tears ran down their faces, the laughter itself taking on a slightly hysterical quality.

Pamela finally sat, weak, sides aching. Casey was still bent over the worktable, back shaking, though silent now. It took a moment before she realized it wasn't laughter that caused him to tremor in such a manner.

She stood and put her hand to his back, smoothing the heavy wool of his sweater under her palm. "Casey?" she said tentatively.

He nodded tersely, and she waited, hand still running the length of his spine in a rhythmic manner, trying to impart through her touch, balm for the pain he was feeling. She left his name hanging in the air, knowing better than to try to push him into talking before he was ready. It took several long moments before she felt the tension in his body begin to ease. Then he spoke, voice hoarse and low.

"I'm grateful that he looked after all of yez, an' then I'm angry to have to be grateful to the man. He took care of all the things I'm supposed to look after, an' he did it smooth as silk."

"Smooth as silk?" It was Pamela's turn to snort. "We were a mess after you were lifted. Lawrence was out at night trying to knock off soldiers."

That stopped Casey cold. "Tryin' to knock off soldiers?"

She nodded and told him briefly of Lawrence's contretemps with the security forces, which had included stone throwing, and a Molotov cocktail or two. She carefully omitted Jamie's role in extricating the boy from a premature death at the hands of an irate security unit and an even more intolerant police force.

"Christ," he breathed out as she finished her tale, "I'd no notion. Ye never said a word in any of yer letters either, woman," he finished accusingly.

She shrugged. "There seemed little point in worrying you about things you couldn't do anything about. We managed."

"Aye," he said dryly, "with Jamie's help."

"And Robin, occasionally," she said, knowing it had to come out at some point.

He tilted his head, eyes narrowed. "Robin?"

"Yes, he kept an eye out for us. He dropped by from time to time, to make sure we were all right."

"Can't say that comforts me."

"The man's your best friend. I think he felt duty bound to keep an eye out for us."

"The man *was* my best friend, there's a lot of years between the boy I knew an' the man he is now. Most parts of him will be a stranger to me. Besides it wasn't him that I asked to look after yez, it was Jamie."

"But it's Jamie you're angry about."

"Aye, well much as it pains me to admit it, I trust the man with my life. Though it'd be comforting if he couldn't handle every damn thing that comes his way with such skill. Here he was juggling about twenty different balls at once, an' I was like a monkey in a cage, impotent to do a damn thing, not a man at all."

"What do you mean 'not a man'? You're as much a man as any male walking the planet."

He shook his head, some of the frustration leaking back into his face. "It makes ye feel helpless to live in such a way. That they could take me from my bed, an' not have to charge me, not have to have anything other than a vague suspicion to lock me behind bars and keep me there like some damn dumb animal without rights."

"I was angry too. There wasn't a thing I could do to stop them. And no legal way of getting you out either. I just kept slamming into brick walls and then when I came to see you and you sent me away..." she trailed off, throat thick with tears.

He pulled her to him, wrapping his arms around her gently. His body still shook with the residue of fury and hurt. "I'm sorry for that," he murmured into her hair. "It was my pride that was at fault, I couldn't stand for ye to see me that way, behind bars, powerless. I felt that I wasna' a proper husband to ye, an' then when ye lost the baby an' I wasn't there to comfort ye..." he took a deep breath, voice husky with emotion.

"It wasn't your fault."

"Aye, the logical part of me knows that, but the male side of me doesn't. I'd never been so helpless before ye, an' I couldn't stand it. I didn't want to think what the screws might have been doin' to ye, an' you not sayin' a word, for a minute or two of time with me. It's—" He faltered, a tremor rippling down the line of his throat. "It's like they've castrated ye in a sense. They've all the power an' ye've none, no matter how much rage ye might feel at it all."

She merely nodded, knowing that protesting wasn't going to change what had been done to his sense of himself, his life and his pride, when he'd been torn from Liam's house that August morning.

They stood that way for a time, the fragile shelter of the shed seeming the extent of the world for those few moments.

"I'm glad you're home," she said finally, "and so is Lawrence."

"I know," he replied, "'tis just my pride's taken a few blows this week, an' I'm feelin' like the proverbial square peg, tryin' to wriggle itself into endless round holes."

"It's going to take time for all of us," she said, feeling some of her own tension ease now that Casey had blown off the worst of his.

"Aye, I know, Jewel. 'Tis just hard on a man to realize that life goes on rather tidily without him, an' the hell of it is that I worried about ye all, an' hoped ye were managin' without me, then when ye go an' do just that, it hurts me to see it."

She nodded, moving away and straightening his sweater, removing a wood splinter that had fixed in its weave. "We manage without you, man, but we don't really live."

He brushed the back of one bruised hand across her cheek, dark eyes as present as she'd seen them since the morning he'd been lifted. "Thank ye for that, Jewel."

"It's only the truth."

He gave her a shaky smile, then looked ruefully at the battered door.

"I suppose I'll have to build ye a new one now."

"I suppose you will," she said, a small smile tugging at the corner of her lips.

"Aye well, first things first," he replied and walked to the doorway of the small shed.

"And what's first?"

He turned and smiled. "What do ye think? I'm goin' to go help the lad build an airplane."

Chapter Sixty-four

Beyond Borders

IT WAS WITH NO LITTLE TREPIDATION that David approached the headquarters of the West Belfast Housing Association. He felt more than a bit ridiculous in the dark wool cap and sunglasses, which were rendered even more absurd by the rain sheeting down like the clouds were attempting to piss themselves out for good and all. However, if it came to a choice between looking like an ass, or being called out on the mat once again by his superiors in London over his 'reckless' association with a known Fenian, David, all things being equal, would take looking like an ass.

There was a soldier strolling the street, eyes narrowed against the streaming rain. One would think Pat really was a notorious rabble-rouser, given the amount of attention the British Army seemed intent upon giving him and his organization.

David waited until the man turned his back to the rain, hunching his shoulders to provide shelter to the cigarette he was lighting. Then David sidled up to the door and tapped on it lightly.

It opened a minute later and a very annoyed looking man glared out at him.

"Hi," David said, feeling suddenly in possession of ten thumbs, two left feet and a Union Jack stamped upon his forehead.

Pat merely continued to glare. He looked thin and tired, but in entirely much better condition than he had been when he'd left the prison.

"Can I come in?"

Pat made a rather sarcastic hand gesture. David decided he would ignore it in the interests of avoiding the soldier, who was likely to turn about any minute now.

He stepped in over the threshold and drew in a shocked breath. "Christ, what happened here?"

"Yer workmates decided to give the place a renovation free of charge. Thoughtful of them, no?"

The small two-roomed office looked as though it had been hit by a hurricane. Books, ledgers, and papers were strewn about. The shelving Pat and his brother had built was smashed and torn away from the walls.

Pat turned his back on him and continued with his work, which was patching a hole in the wall that someone had punched through. David joined him, picking up books that had been torn from their bindings and stacking them on the edge of the big oak desk that he knew had been a present from Jamie Kirkpatrick when Pat had opened the Housing Association. A long ugly scar marred the surface of it. He sighed. There were times this ugly little war was more than he could bear.

"So," Pat's tone was deceptively amiable, "what brings ye down here to slum with the Irish?"

"I just came by to see if you were alive and well," David said, blowing tiny fragments of broken glass off of a copy of Michael Collins' *The Path to Freedom*.

"Alive, yes," Pat stood and faced him, face cold with fury. "*Well?* What the fuck do ye think, David?"

"Fair enough," David replied. "I just wanted to be certain you weren't one of the bodies lying in the morgue."

Pat laughed, a harsh sound that sent skitters of glass down David's spine. "Well it wasn't that yer fine laddies didn't give it their all, I only missed bein' one of them by sheer grace of God. Disappointed?"

"I think you know better than that," David said somewhat stiffly.

"I think I know pretty much fuck all about ye, David. That's what I think."

"I thought we were friends." The hurt in his voice was unmistakable.

"I was wrong. I made a mistake, but I'm clear now. No Englishman, particularly one whose entire existence is riddled with secrets, can be a friend of mine."

"Well," David said, voice near to inaudible, "I'm more sorry than I can say to hear that."

"Not nearly as sorry as I am," Pat said acidly. "I trusted ye, that makes me a right fool, doesn't it?"

David shook his head, feeling suddenly very weary. "No, Pat trusting someone doesn't make you a fool. Thinking that somehow in this mess I could be a friend to you," he shrugged, "well I'm afraid that I'm the real fool here."

"Did you know?"

"Know what?" David asked, though it was more of a reflex, for he knew what Pat meant by his question.

"Know that they brought the Paras in to kill us?"

The dark eyes bored into his own, and David was glad that he did not have to lie to the man; he didn't think he was up for subterfuge today, not here leastwise.

"No, I didn't. How can you think I would sit on that kind of knowledge?"

"Well someone did, didn't they? I mean—" Pat suddenly raised his fist and brought it down hard on the counter next to him. *"What the fuck is it,*

David?! Do we remind you of a part of yourselves that you despise? The part that isn't orderly or predestined for greatness. Do we remind you of the one place where you've failed again and again?"

"Perhaps it's only that you've something in you that we don't. Maybe we resent you for that."

"Aye," Pat snorted, "such as what? Humanity?"

"I hardly think people who bomb their own to pieces have a corner on the humanity market."

"Get out." Pat's voice was flat, but David had seen him so before and knew the man was furious, and likely to strike at the least provocation. David stood, hat in hand both literally and figuratively, wondering if Pat would just finish him off this time altogether. He certainly looked entirely capable of doing so, eyes black with fury and his breath coming in uneven puffs, like a dragon about to shoot fire from his nostrils.

"Is there a reason ye're still standin' there? I told ye to leave. Are ye deaf?"

"It's not that," David said, the corner of his mouth twitching slightly. "It's only that I can't afford to be seen leaving just yet."

Pat raised an eyebrow, the corner of his own mouth quivering suspiciously. "I'd ask why, but I've a feelin' I'm safer in my ignorance." He shook his head and heaved a sigh of capitulation. "Well I'll not have ye thinkin' the Irish have no manners. Would ye like some tea?"

David smiled, ever the polite and charming Englishman. "I'd love some, just don't slip any arsenic in it."

"Don't tempt me," Pat said, filling the kettle from the groaning pipes. "Who is it out there today? The wee redhead or that dark one with the nasty skin?"

"The dark one with the nasty skin. He was off having a fag, so I slipped in when he wasn't looking, but now," David flicked the curtain back into place, "he's on guard and doesn't look to be leaving any time soon."

Pat merely gave him a narrow glance, but didn't comment further.

David continued to clean up as Pat prepared the tea and dug in a cupboard for a packet of biscuits that had escaped the general destruction of the rest of the rooms. A picture of Sylvie, looking positively sprite-like in a yellow cardigan, sat on the desk. The broken glass had been painstakingly removed, though the picture was cut up rather badly anyway. He had to admit they complimented one another, she so small and fair, Pat big and dark, though not as formidable as his brother—a man whom David held in certain regard, mostly composed of fear. Casey's file had crossed his desk in regards to Patrick, during his time in the jail.

"I suppose I owe ye thanks yet again," Pat said gruffly, when they sat to tea. He stirred his tea with more force than was strictly necessary.

David looked up in surprise. "For what?"

"I know ye had a hand in gettin' me released."

David looked down at his teacup, running a finger along the chipped rim. "Not officially I didn't. You're rather lucky to have a friend such as James Kirkpatrick. He's a little daunting when it comes to getting what he wants."

"Aye, he's that." Pat's glance flicked away for a moment and he seemed quite absorbed by the green swirls that decorated the cheap table where they sat. "It seems a great risk for ye to take. I don't imagine yer bosses would be too pleased to know ye helped to free such a dangerous criminal as myself." This last was said with a certain amount of acid.

"It was worth the risk."

"Why?" Pat was looking at him directly now, and David felt the strange slippage in his stomach that he always did when the man looked him in the eye. He swallowed hard; it felt as though something large and sharp was lodged in his throat.

Pat was right about the risk, though even he did not fully appreciate the hazards David had chanced in pulling strings to get him released. Secrecy was a normal, if not natural, part of his life. But there were times, like now, that David wished he could confide it all in someone else. Perhaps though, he thought, squaring his shoulders, there *were* things one could be honest about.

"Because what I feel for you doesn't have a border, nor a flag. It doesn't seem to much care what the conditions or politics of this country or any other are. No," he put a hand up to halt the protest he saw forming on Pat's lips. "I'm not asking you for anything, I don't have expectations. I just needed to tell you—when I thought it might be you dead I regretted that I'd never had a chance to tell you how I feel. Even if all you felt was disgust in return, still I needed to have it said."

"David, ye know that I can never return yer feelins'."

"I know. It doesn't matter though. Or rather it does, but somehow whatever the form of it, love seems a rare commodity in this country of late. So I thought perhaps," his fair skin was flushed, though his eyes still met the stark honesty of Pat's, "it only mattered that it existed at all, and not that it wasn't proper."

"Ye're very brave to just say it out like that, my mood bein' what it is today," Pat said, expression unreadable.

David shrugged. "I did it more for myself than you, truth be told."

"Well ye'll forgive me if I don't quite know how to respond to such an admission."

"You don't have to say anything."

Pat obviously took his words at face value, because he drank his tea without further comment. David supposed it was preferable to the punch on the nose he'd half expected.

"I would hope that," David laughed, though it came out with a fractured note, "despite the travesty in Derry and uncomfortable admissions on my own part, we could still be friends. Unless of course I remind you of a part of yourself *you* despise."

Pat looked at him for a long time, dark eyes giving away nothing of what went on behind them. Finally, he smiled wearily. "Can ye just give me a little time to figure out what that means? Right now, I'm not sure of much in my life an' I'm so angry that I'm afraid of myself. Suddenly it seems I may be capable of things I wouldn't have countenanced a month ago."

It was a huge admission, David knew, for a man who was so intensely private. And who, admittedly, had no reason under the sun at present to trust him.

Except that he loved him, and thought perhaps Pat understood there was no force on earth that would cause David to betray that emotion.

Chapter Sixty-five

Neither Friend nor Enemy

STANDING IN THE RAIN on the Mullabrack Road, some miles beyond Portadown, Pamela was severely questioning the state of her sanity. She was on her way to a meeting with the most infamous Loyalist that had ever come out of the heartland of Protestant extremity. A man who was famous for his 'shoot now, ask questions later' policy.

The phone call that had drawn her here had come in three days earlier at the Tennant Street Station, where she'd been filing her pictures and conferring with one of the constables over a few details in the photos.

She'd answered with her mind still on the dumped body in the photo. The voice on the other end jolted her.

"I hear ye're lookin' into an old murder." The tone was direct, and the phrase was not in the form of a question.

"Who is this?"

"William Bright. Is the name familiar to ye?

"Yes," she'd replied, while a small snake of fear uncoiled in her belly. William Bright was a man one heard of, occasionally saw pictures of, and devoutly hoped to never meet in person.

"Scared yet, lass?"

"A little," she admitted.

The chuckle on the other end of the line was dry.

"If ye want to know what really happened to Brian Riordan, ye'll be on the Mullabrack Road just beyond the walls of Gosford House, Tuesday mornin' round eight o'clock. A couple of my lads will pick ye up."

"How did you know—" she began, then fell silent at the unmistakable click of the receiver going down.

"Problem?" the constable asked, not looking up from the negatives he was going over with a magnifying glass.

"No."

Now standing here on this empty stretch of road, it took all her willpower to not jump back in the car and flee for the relative safety of home. She turned her keys over in her pocket, noting with part of her mind that the leaves on the beeches were beginning to unfurl, lending a soft green mist to the heavily wooded road. Then she wondered if this was the last time she'd see leaves open, or anything else for that matter.

"Get a grip, girl," she told herself sternly under her breath. Just then, she heard the chuggy thrum of a car cresting the small rise. She braced herself, the teeth of her keys cutting deep enough to draw blood from her palm.

There were two men in the car, both hooded and both well armed. The one on the passenger side got out, pistol cocked casually in her direction.

"Get in the back, we're blindfoldin' ye first though."

She'd anticipated this. They wouldn't want her to know where they were taking her. She nodded and walked over to where the man waited for her. The blindfold was a grubby football scarf in the red, royal blue, and white of the Glasgow Rangers. It reeked of stale cigarette smoke and spilled ale.

After the man had fastened the scarf tightly across her eyes, he put a hand to the back of her head and shoved her roughly into the back seat of the small car, getting in behind her and pulling her head down to his knee.

"Don't fuckin' move," he said, "an' don't try anything stupid or I'll shoot ye as ye lie. Understood?"

She nodded, wishing fervently she'd given in to her desire to flee minutes earlier. The car made a lurching u-turn and then took off in the direction it had come from. They were heading back to the carriageway. The man kept a firm hand on the back of her neck, his denim leg hard and smelling strongly of car oil.

The car settled to a steady pace. They were traveling toward Markethill as far as she could determine. An odd choice considering the IRA was extremely strong in that area. Though there were several desperately lonely country roads between here and there, the knowledge of which did little to calm her.

"Nice tits for a Fenian bitch," the man above her said in a conversational tone to the driver. She swallowed hard over the lump of fear in her throat. She didn't dare even wriggle under the hand, though the fear of rape was almost stronger in her than that of death.

"None of that, man. Billy said she's not to be touched for now."

The *for now* chilled her, but she was relieved to know that at least for the present she was kept safe by a hard man's word. Inside her head she began her fifth round of prayer to Our Lady as a way to calm herself and hopefully draw some divine intervention in her direction.

The hand on her neck pulled her back, until her face was only inches from the man's groin. She stiffened her neck and gritted her teeth, knowing it was a game of intimidation, to show fear would be suicidal.

"Squeamish are ye?" he said, with a low throaty chuckle that would have stood the hairs up on her entire body were they not already stiff with fear.

The rest of the ride was accomplished in this fashion, until they turned down a considerably bumpy lane where she could hear the scrape of tree branches along the sides of the car.

"End of the line," the man said as the car lurched to a rough halt.

Her first impression was a heavy smell of sap, which told her they were in a wooded area, with not another human soul around for miles. Not comforting, but what she'd expected.

The man pulled her out of the car by her collar, shoving her blind ahead of him. She stumbled and he caught her roughly by the elbow, shoving her forward again. She could feel the menace in his touch, and knew that only a word or two stood between her and the unpleasant thoughts in his mind becoming real acts.

He pushed her through a doorway. The driver seemed to be staying outside, for the door shut behind them. The scarf was then untied, but left looped around her throat. He put his hands in the waistband of her jeans, then slid them around.

"Have to check ye, boss's orders."

It was too dark to see his face but she could feel his smile as he opened the front of her blouse and put blunt fingers under the bottom edge of her brassiere cups in order to determine if she was wired.

"That'll do Rob," said a man who'd emerged from a shadowed doorway. "She's clean, bring her in."

She was pulled through the open doorway into a room with windows three quarters of the way up the dank walls. She blinked in an effort to adjust her vision to the light, pallid as it was. It took a few seconds for the spots to clear and then she surveyed the man in front of her.

He was bald and barrel-chested with thickset arms sheathed to the wrists in Loyalist tattoos. Union Jacks, a single woman with a rifle facing defiantly forward, a masked gunman, and no less than four red hands between the two arms.

"Sit down," he gestured to a chair that sat in the middle of the room. It was a rickety aluminum framed kitchen chair, covered with cracked and dirty yellow upholstery. She sat gingerly on it. Despite appearances, it was sturdy and her jellied legs were grateful for the support.

"Rob, make tea." He gestured curtly at the man who'd held her down in the backseat of the car.

"So ye want to know what happened to Brian Riordan?"

She nodded. The man had the flat, careful stare of a lizard. His eyes were the clear pale blue that was only found in Ireland. He clearly enjoyed his ability to unnerve, for he was relaxed, hands loosely linked together and one leg cocked up on the other.

"Why do ye want to know? Man's been dead long time. It seems a bit risky pryin' at his coffin lid now."

"It's a trail I'm following up. I stumbled across some information that indicated he'd been murdered rather than the accident it was made to seem at the time."

The man eyed her quietly, not even the slightest flicker of concern or interest creasing his face.

"I'd advise ye not to lie to me girl, or I'll let the boys out there do as they like with ye. Out this way there'll be none to hear ye scream." This was said without emotion or heat, but merely as a statement of fact.

The tea arrived then and William put a finger up to warn her to silence. The man had removed his hood, which worried her somewhat. He handed her a mug of tea. She took it, grateful for the small object that gave her hands something to hold.

"Drink it," William said and it was not a suggestion but an order. She sipped carefully at the hot tea, hoping they'd not drugged it. It had come from the same pot that he now poured his own tea from, so it didn't seem likely.

Rob absented himself from the room, but not before flashing a nasty grin in her direction. She shivered, hoping William Bright's word would hold her all the way back to Belfast.

She took as deep a breath as she could manage and told him the truth.

"Had he lived, he would have been my father-in-law. His sons were led to believe he took his own life, when I found out that wasn't the case I knew I needed to go after the truth."

"And ye think they'll thank ye for it?"

"No maybe not, but I still need find the truth if I can."

"Truth seekers in this country tend to end up dead."

"*You* called *me* here," she said.

His eyes narrowed the slightest bit and then he grinned, showing a tooth crowned in gold. "Fuck me if I didn't, girl."

Pamela chose to ignore the possible connotations contained in that simple Ulsterism.

"I'll tell ye straight, because I'm a straight man, an' if William Bright tells ye a thing on his word, ye know it's true."

She nodded, noting the man's referral to himself in the third person, an oddity that seemed to crop up a lot with the men who ran in paramilitary circles.

"That he was killed comes as no surprise to ye at this point, but why and who killed him may contain a jolt or two."

"So he was murdered?" she asked, needing to confirm it for once and all.

"Aye, shot through the heart—his request ye mind—at point blank range. The bomb malfunctionin' was cover of a sort. Hard to tell that a man's been executed when ye can't even gather all the bits of him together."

She clenched her hands around the teacup until it seemed in imminent danger of shattering under the pressure. Brian Riordan wasn't just a statistic to her, he was the father of Casey and Pat. Through their memories and stories, and judging by the men they had become, she had grown to love and respect the man that she had never had the privilege of meeting. The thought of him on his knees having to choose the method of his own execution made her chest hurt.

"Why would it need to be covered up? Both sides are pretty blunt with their killing. Rather like sticking it in the public arena, I would think."

"Times were different then, an' ye need to ask yerself why it would need covering up. Who is it keeps their face in the shadows at all times?"

"Are you saying the government is behind this?"

He shrugged. "I'm makin' suggestions, you take it where ye want. Maybe it was simply an own-goal an' the IRA didn't want the egg of it on their face."

She gritted her teeth in frustration, had she really risked all this—the ride here, the leering man in the kitchen who'd rape her with little more concern than he'd take brushing his teeth—for suppositions and half-hinted at innuendoes that didn't make the picture any clearer.

"I don't think you'd have called me here if his own side had him murdered."

"I heard ye were a smart girl."

"So not IRA, not your side. That only leaves the British. Which is supposed to be your side, but in this case isn't."

He didn't respond, which she took for leave to continue in the direction she was heading.

"So the who is simple enough, someone in the government. I still don't see the why."

"They say a man is only as wise as the company he keeps, so maybe ye need to look at who he was spendin' time with right before he died."

"How am I to find that out?"

"It's not that long ago, ten years is like a day here."

"I feel like you've handed me a bunch of frayed strings and are asking me to knit them into a first class jumper," she said.

"May be that I have, but ye're a smart lass—put it together. It's a small country. Everything is connected from the top of the hill to the whelp in the gutter."

"But why...how..." she sputtered, trying to gather her thoughts together to see the path he was trying to point her down.

"*Everything's* connected," he repeated emphatically. She knew that to push any further would guarantee his warning coming to fruition about letting the men loose on her. Still, in the jumble of all the pieces, something was missing. Something that was hovering out at the edge of her consciousness and shrinking from coming into the light.

"You knew Brian, didn't you?"

A look of annoyance flicked across the impassive features.

"I was familiar with him for a time."

"Were you friends?"

"I wasn't his friend, but nor was I his enemy. Look," the man leaned forward, eyes snaking to the door and then back to her. "There were a series of meetins' in sixty—sixty-one—people from both governments an' armies, that's where ye need to look. That's how I knew him. There were men involved in those meetins' that were involved in other things, still are. I think yer father-in-law came across some information it'd be better if he'd not. He never seemed a man to let evil lie. Now I think," he continued in a louder tone, which she understood was not for her benefit, "it's time ye left before I get bored with this conversation. Ye didn't meet here with me either. Understand? If I hear that yer tongue's been waggin' I'll hand ye over to Rob. I have mercy, a bullet to the head an' I'm done, but Rob likes to play with his dinner before he eats it."

As threats went, it was fairly effective. She stood, a cold trickle of sweat running down the groove of her backbone.

He escorted her to the door, nodding to Rob who stood outside it. "Ye take her back to her car, an' no funny business mind. I'll break yer head like a melon should I find out otherwise."

She followed Rob down the hall to the heavily fortified door.

"Lass."

She turned back to the man who was quite possibly the most feared Protestant in all of the British Isles.

"Yes?"

"Mind what I said about truth seekers."

THE RIDE BACK WAS ACCOMPLISHED in much the same fashion as the ride there had been. She was blindfolded, head down on the man's knee. Above her, he conversed with the driver about football scores and a tart he'd met up with in the Capstan Lounge. He seemed to take particular relish in telling the story of his conquest in minute detail. One hand was kept firmly on the back of her neck; the other occasionally stroked itself down her arm and the side of her neck.

Then suddenly the driver who'd been entirely silent exclaimed, "Dere's someone in the ditch—" He jerked the car hard right, and they flew off the road into the field.

"Did ye fuckin' tell anyone ye were comin' here?" Rob asked through gritted teeth, the pistol barrel biting sharply into her temple.

"No, I swear it," she said, praying that he'd believe her. She didn't think he'd hesitate to shoot her here and now.

The next few minutes were a blur of the car flying out of control through a hail of bullets. The scarf had come off and she had an impression of the color green, the man above her screaming obscenities and then just as suddenly he was completely silent and she could smell blood and feel the slippery warmth of it on her hands. The car was slowing in a huge spraying arc that made her stomach lurch up to her throat. It crashed into an immovable force and her head slammed into the door with a force that made a million stars explode in front of her eyes.

And then suddenly everything was very, very still and she was miraculously still alive and seemingly in one piece, though her head hurt dreadfully and her ankle felt as though it had been sheared through by a sharp object.

She stayed low, knowing if the man outside saw her he'd shoot and worry about her identity later. She stayed perfectly still, the smell of gas dizzying her. As bad as the pain in her head was, she was thinking clearly enough to realize if she crawled out of the car they'd kill her. She could hear their approach even now. If she played dead would he leave her be, or torch the car? Which might be moot in another minute or two as the smell of gas was increasingly strong, and the car could well explode of its own accord. Should she hope to heaven it didn't and pray he walked away, or take her chances with the man who now sounded like he was only feet from the car? She caught a whiff of smoke and made her decision.

She pulled the scarf up from around her neck and retied it around her eyes. The movement caused her to black out for a second. She struggled to regain her senses and gather her courage to speak.

"Please don't shoot." Her voice was a bare croak and the smell of smoke was getting stronger by the second, it wouldn't be long before some spark found the gas tank and she'd be appealing to St. Peter on a much more permanent basis.

"What the fuck?" she heard the man say and then the door was opened and a rush of air flowed in, the smell of clover now mingling with the blood and fuel. A hand grabbed her and yanked. The pain in her head and ankle exploded like steel-edged stars through her bones. There was a flash of intense heat and her skin shrank back from the assault. Then she was being dragged hard and fast over the bumpy terrain, only to be dumped unceremoniously in what felt like a patch of nettles, where she promptly threw up, the acid flooding out of her in a wave.

"Jaysus!" She could hear the man dart back and felt some small frisson of satisfaction that she'd vomited on his shoes before he killed her. However, her murder didn't seem in his immediate plans, for she could hear him sigh and swear under his breath. She put a hand to her face only to hear a sharp "Leave the blindfold on!" And then, "What the fuck were ye doin' in that car?"

Truth seemed the best option with this man. She wasn't in a fit state to make anything up anyway. "I got a call to meet with them, they said they'd information I'd find interesting about...about..." mentioning her father-in-law's name suddenly seemed a bad idea, "something I'm looking into."

"An' what would that somethin' be?" he nudged her ankle with his boot and she thought she'd pass out from the pain. It must be broken; otherwise she didn't see how it could hurt so horribly.

"An old murder."

"What murder?" The voice was ominously heavy now. Journalists had met their end in such fields as these, of that she was all too aware. She couldn't afford to hedge, his patience seemed tissue thin and they were going to have to get out of here soon. It was likely that he'd just as soon do it without the impediment of an injured woman.

"Brian Riordan."

The silence was palpable, and she could feel him considering what she'd said. A small hope began to rise that he might spare her.

"What was he to you?"

"My father-in-law," she said, knowing the answer would either save her or bring a swift end to things.

"Are ye Casey's wife, then?" the man asked, an odd curiosity in his voice.

"Yes," she said, quite certain that she was going to pass out whether he planned to kill her or not.

"Oh Christ." Which wasn't, under the circumstances, the most comforting sentence, but it eased a little of her fear. "How'd ye get here?"

"My car's nearby, just up the road. Parked by the wall of Gosford House."

"That's a ways yet. Can ye walk?"

She attempted to stand but immediately collapsed back to the nettle patch. "My ankle's broken," she said, something about the manner in which the man spoke bothering her. He sounded vaguely familiar.

He bent down and took the ankle in hands that were gloved. She hissed through her teeth as he prodded it. "That bloody hurts!"

"Aye well it would, though it's not broke," he said, "but there's a good sized bullet hole in it. I expect it's still lodged in there. Don't worry lass, we'll have ye to hospital in no time at all."

The trip to the car was long and painful, impaired a great deal by the fact that he refused to let her take the scarf from her eyes. Beyond the occasional burst of swearing, he didn't speak to her. She didn't mind, and kept her silence as well. The less she asked the better the chances were that he'd not think her a threat. And the bullet in her ankle would be the only one she'd have to worry about.

She only threw up twice more before they arrived at the car. It had begun to rain by then and a cold wind had sprung up, clearing her spinning head slightly.

The man settled her into the passenger seat, belting her in and then taking the driver's side for himself.

"It'll take a bit, I can't afford to take ye anywhere near here, we're goin' to have to drive to Belfast."

"Is that wise?"

"Better that than someone rememberin' our faces around here."

Pamela nodded, feeling another bout of incipient nausea coming on.

"Ready?" he asked, turning the ignition and then downshifting the car.

"Give me a minute," she heard herself say in slow tones, before sticking her head out the door and throwing up yet again. It seemed to require superhuman abilities to shut the door. The man reached across her with yet another muffled oath and slammed it shut.

"Are ye ready now?"

"Think so," she said, voice slurred. "I'm going to sleep a bit, wake me when you're there."

"No lass, I think ye're concussed. I suspect that's why ye keep pukin'. Ye need to stay awake. Drive faster for fock's sake," this last directed sharply at himself, apparently. She stayed somewhere just below the level of consciousness for the rest of the trip, the man talking to her, though she couldn't make out much of what he was saying, the words running into one long stream of nonsense. She'd vague impressions of rain whispering against the windows, a smell of dusty burning and an urgency that she couldn't quite understand.

Then there was the whoosh of opening doors, someone placing her in a chair that moved and she knew she had been left at a hospital. Questions came at her, the doctor's face fading in and out of her vision.

There were lights in her eyes, a prodding at her ankle that made the stars swim merrily in front of her again and then a prick in her arm before she let the blackness take her down into blessedly quiet depths.

Chapter Sixty-six

Happy to Be Alive

WHEN SHE WOKE, CASEY WAS STANDING at the foot of her bed. She was tempted to close her eyes again but knew he'd seen her. Her head, hard as it was to fathom, hurt even worse than it had before, though her ankle was numb and felt very far away down the bed.

"Hello," she whispered groggily, throat feeling as though it had something furry lodged in it. "Where am I?"

"Ye're in hospital," he said shortly.

"I know that, but where?"

"The Royal Victoria. Do ye not remember what happened to ye?"

"Not entirely," she said, wondering if it was possible that an hour long trip had compressed itself down to a few confused minutes for her.

"Ye were dumped off on the doorstep with a bullethole in yer ankle an' a concussion that they couldn't wake ye from. What the hell happened to ye, woman?"

"I...I can't remember all of it right now," she said feebly.

He gave her a look that told her clearly that he didn't believe her for a minute and that they would be discussing this at length in the very near future.

"Are ye happy now?" Casey asked. She winced under his tone, noting that his eyes were the deep heavy gray they turned when he was truly furious. This wasn't going to be pleasant.

"Happy to be alive," she said, regretting the words the minute she spoke them.

"Oh aye, joke about it then. Find it funny, do ye? I got called at the center an' thought ye were lyin' here dyin' the entire trip." He was standing at the end of the bed, but she could see how hard he was shaking even at that distance. "Jaysus woman, can ye never use yer damn brain! If ye weren't lyin' in a hospital bed I'd kill ye myself."

"If you want to lecture me," she said faintly, "that's fine, but do it in a lower tone, will you? My head's a bit sore."

"Yer head's a bit sore?" He snorted derisively. "Yer lucky that's all that's wrong with ye. Ye might have been killed."

"I know," she responded meekly. "But I wasn't, and I think that's the main point, don't you?"

He shook his head, mouth still drawn tight with anger. Then suddenly he dropped his head into his hands, shoulders shaking visibly. "Aye," he said, voice hoarse. "I suppose it is."

"I'm sorry," she said, "but really it's only a scratch, the bullet went straight through, I heard the doctor say so before they gave me the shot."

Casey raised his head, a look of disbelief on his face. "Do ye hear yerself? The bullet went straight through—Jaysus, Mary an' Joseph!"

She sat up, ignoring the nasty throb in her head. "Come here to me, man."

He gave her a narrow look. "What for?"

"Just come here," she said.

He came up the side of the bed, still looking suspicious as though she might be about to box his ears.

"Now sit."

He sat.

"Closer."

He hitched closer.

"Now listen." She put her arms around him and drew him close, "Can you feel me?"

"Of course I can," he said, a slight edge of exasperation in his words. "Do ye have a fever, woman?"

She put her face against his own, his whiskers raspy against her jaw. "I'm here, I'm whole, and I'm relatively unharmed. Okay?"

He nodded and then pulled her tightly against his chest. She could feel how hard he was shaking now and understood his anger was mostly born of fear. "Don't ye ever scare me like that again, woman. I don't think I could manage it. Thought my heart was goin' to come out of my chest, an' then the walk up the stairs here had to be the longest I've ever taken in my life. I wasn't sure if I could face what—" Here his voice broke and she rocked him gently, hand rubbing the taut line of his back.

"Sshh, it's alright now."

He shook his head, but fortunately for her he was still incapable of words. She'd a feeling the ones he'd find would be fairly unpleasant. She breathed deeply, laying her cheek against his hair. He smelled comfortingly of cut wood and apples, with a sharp under note of fear—she *had* scared him badly.

"Lie down with me?" she asked.

"Ye'll get me in hot water with the head nurse," he said. "But I suppose I've encountered scarier people in my life, though none quite so intimidatin'."

"I'll protect you," she said, shifting over as he climbed in behind her. She settled into his embrace with a sigh, feeling safe for the first time in several days. Around her bustled the noises of the hospital, voices over the intercom and the running of feet bent on errands of mercy and deliverance. Here, though, in the narrow bed, with her husband's arms strong around her and his warmth wrapping her in a blanket of comfort, she felt as though she was within a private sanctuary that even the smells of blood and antiseptic could not violate.

"I'm sorry," she whispered. The hand that was smoothing the hair back from her face halted.

"Go to sleep," he said roughly, though his hand was gentle on her face. "I'll be here when ye wake."

AN ASHEN DAWN WAS FILTERING through the heavy curtains when she woke. The pain in her ankle had subsided to a dull throb and her head felt as though it were wrapped in layers of muffling cotton.

She turned her head slowly. Casey was asleep sitting in the chair, head cushioned on his arms on the edge of the bed. His face looked bruised in the faint light, lashes a soft fan against his cheeks.

She brushed a hand over his hair. He was dead to the world, though, and didn't so much as stir at her touch. He slept a full twenty minutes more before blinking and yawning, eyes turning automatically to her.

"Good morning."

"Mornin', Jewel." He reached up and kissed her forehead. "No fever, that's good."

She rolled her eyes at him.

"You didn't sleep in the chair all night, did you?"

He smiled wearily. "I told ye the head nurse was a fearsome beastie. She ordered me out of the bed round midnight, said I ought to know better at my age. Felt like I was back in grammar school with the nuns."

He stood and stretched, touching his hands to the ceiling. Several joints popped and he yawned widely. "An' yerself, Jewel? How's the head this morning?"

"Better," she said. It was true; the fire inside her skull had settled down to a bed of coals that, while uncomfortable, was a decided improvement over yesterday.

"I'm sorry I yelled at ye before," Casey said quietly. "I was so afraid, though, an' the fear made me angry with ye."

"It's all right," she replied. "Where's Lawrence?"

"He went home with Pat, after assuring himself that ye weren't goin' to die. Jamie was by while ye were sleepin'." He added this last with a grin. "The nurse took a wee strip off him as well."

"It was nice of him to stop by." She felt rather glad she had been asleep when Jamie visited, she had a feeling his words for her would be only slightly more pleasant than Casey's.

"I'm goin' down to the cafeteria for some food, I'm starvin'." This assertion was borne out by the sound of a lusty growl from his stomach. "D'ye want somethin' yerself? The nurse said breakfast would be along shortly."

"Just some tea."

"All right then, I'll be back in a few minutes."

The door had barely closed behind Casey when a bald head with kindly blue eyes popped in. It was Constable Fred McGilligan, whom she knew through work and who had always treated her well without ever once enquiring as to her religious affiliations. He was the man she suspected of being the conduit between the note writer and herself. It stood to reason that the man had an inside contact within the station. Over the months since the fire and the hanging, she had been inclined to believe this inside source was Constable Fred, merely because he seemed the least likely suspect in many ways.

He was a kind man with never an ill word for anyone and he had eased her path considerably with the other officers at the station, who had become accustomed to viewing all outsiders with what she supposed was a fairly just suspicion, if not a moderate hostility.

"Ah, there ye are, lassie. Might I step in for a minute?"

"Of course," she said, making a vain attempt to smooth her snarled head. She had a feeling she looked considerably worse for the wear.

"I've just nipped in to see that ye're all right. Johnny said as ye were fine, but I didn't feel right unless I came to see for myself."

"I'm fine, ankle's sore and so is my head, but I'll be fine in no time at all."

"Well that's good then, isn't it? I've brought somethin' along for ye, 'tis just a wee posy from the flower shop, an' the wife sent along some of her lemon scones." He set an aromatic bag on the bed, along with a bouquet of snapdragons and silvery lamb's ears.

"Thank you so much." She held the posy to her face, feeling the soft tickle of the velvet lamb's ears against her cheek. "And please tell your wife I'm very grateful for the scones."

He smiled shyly, the top of his bald head going pink with pleasure. "Will do lass, she'll be pleased to hear it."

A nurse came in then with a glass of water and a shot for the pain, which Pamela with sensation returning to her ankle, was very grateful to see. The nurse pulled the curtains and gave her the shot in the hip, promising that breakfast would be along shortly. Then, all brisk efficiency she continued on her route of mercy.

Constable Fred was pretending a great interest in the hideous watercolor that seemed to be present in every hospital room the world over.

"It's all right, I'm decent now."

"Oh, er that's good then. Now lass, I must talk to ye about the bullet ye took in the ankle."

"Is it common knowledge already?" she asked, trying to quell the panic in her chest. If Casey should walk in while the Constable was questioning her about this, it could go very badly.

There were too many questions she simply could not answer. If anyone in the RUC found out she'd gone to meet William Bright she'd be in the center of an inquiry, and losing her job would be the least of her worries.

"Not just yet lass, but it's inevitable it will get out."

She knew if she was going to trust anyone, now was the time. "It was an accident. I don't even know who shot me."

"Now lass, I may look gullible but I've spent many a year takin' statements an' I know when one doesn't sound quite right."

"It really would be best," her voice was low but forceful, "if it could just be filed as an accident. Case closed so to speak." She wondered momentarily if she'd made an enormous mistake and that this man was not the one who had been leading her down the path to the truth of her father-in-law's death.

"Now I don't think—" he began in protest, but just then Casey returned, hands full with tea and buns. He froze at the sight of the constable. It was the first time he'd encountered anyone from her work and Pamela felt a nervous ticking set up under her eye.

Constable Fred turned and his face drained of all color. Casey met his look with one of his dark inscrutable expressions that always made people nervous.

Pamela didn't think even one of Casey's looks could explain the paleness of the Constable's visage. The man looked as if he'd seen a ghost.

Perhaps he *had* seen a ghost. Though Casey didn't look as much like Brian as Patrick did, still there was a very strong resemblance to his father. So Constable Fred was the link; something very much like relief flooded through her.

"An' you must be the husband?" Constable Fred said quietly, voice trembling ever so slightly.

"Aye," Casey said warily. "I would be that."

He crossed the room depositing the tea and buns onto the small bedside table. The constable turned his hat in his hands, obviously taken aback by Casey's presence.

"I only wanted to be certain ye were doin' alright then, lass."

"I'm fine," she reassured him, trying not to give in to the urge to look at Casey and see how he was assessing the situation. Though never overtly friendly, he was generally courteous to all who crossed his path. The neighborhood he'd grown up in, however, considered friendliness to the local constable an act of treason.

Constable Fred seemed to think now was time to make good his escape.

"We'll see ye when ye're able to work again then, lass. An' I don't see that anyone will bother ye with questions until ye're stronger." He gave her a look of complicity and she nodded, knowing he would now accept whatever explanation she gave him. With luck, it could be swept under the rug as an accidental shooting by some overzealous farmer.

"Thank you for coming by, it was kind of you."

"Good day to ye," he said to Casey, who nodded tersely in his direction. Constable Fred bobbed his bald head in reply and then beat a hasty retreat out the door.

Casey handed her the tea. It was hot and sugary, and she sipped it gratefully. The warmth spread out from her stomach to join the tendrils of pain medication purling through her blood, creating a sense of fuzzy-edged well being.

She turned her head to find Casey looking at her with an odd smile on his lips.

"Ankle better too, darlin'?"

"Yes."

"Good," he said with grim satisfaction.

"Why?" The tea in her stomach shifted uneasily. She didn't like the look on Casey's face at all.

"Because now we're goin' to talk about this." He held up a fist that had a red, blue and white scarf wound around it. "An' about whose blood was all over yer hands."

Chapter Sixty-seven
The Brotherhood of the Ring

PAMELA HAD BEEN UP AND ABOUT for two days, since coming home with her ankle casted. Casey had sternly insisted that she be on bed rest for the first few days out of hospital, despite her assurances that she felt completely fine. She half wondered if he had banished her upstairs in an effort to avoid her. He was still angry, she knew, and it was well evidenced in the fact that he attacked every chore he could find with more than usual vigor. While Casey enjoyed physical labor, she knew he also used it as an avoidance tactic when something was bothering him.

Once she had come downstairs he had spent the majority of his time, when he wasn't at work, outdoors. Mending physical fences while ignoring emotional ones.

This morning she was determined to beard the lion in his den, which today appeared to be the chopping block, where he was splitting wood with a force that made her wince. She paused for a moment on the threshold of the door, admiring the easy arc of his swing that cleaved the wood with one blow.

The day was warm and he was clad only in a thin t-shirt and worn jeans. The long moving lines of his muscles could be clearly seen and the t-shirt clung to his torso with a fine dew of sweat. He paused momentarily to brush a forearm across his brow and then resumed his work. He still made her weak in the knees, both literally and figuratively, just as he had from the moment they'd met.

It took her this way at times, the enormity of what was between them, both physically and emotionally. Time and observation had taught her that what they shared was, as Pat had said, no common thing. Like any couple caught up in the demands of home, jobs and active revolution, she sometimes forgot how fortunate they were to have found such a thing.

She took a deep breath, cutting her pleasant ruminations short. He might well choose to sleep on the sofa tonight, but she was going to clear the air with him one way or the other.

He caught her eye and winked. She kept clear of flying chips, but picked up the pieces that had fallen farther off and carried them to the neatly blocked woodpile Casey had built at the side of the back porch.

He split a fresh log and the smell of pinesap filled the air with a sudden golden tang. "Well, what is it? Ye'd best out with it or it'll go straight to yer spleen."

She stifled a sound of annoyance at this preemptive strike from his corner. She carried more wood over to the growing pile, placing each piece carefully one on top of the other. Behind her she could feel Casey watching her, and knew the time to come clean had arrived. She turned back, dusting slivers of wood from her arms.

"I think you'd better sit down," she said, taking a long breath.

"That bad, is it?" There was a sudden fear in his eyes, and she felt the familiar lurch that came when she suspected he half-knew about Love Hagerty.

"I have to go get something, just give me a minute." She went in the house and retrieved the letter from under a half-knit sweater in the bottom drawer of the sideboard.

Outside Casey sat on the chopping block, looking confused and a little annoyed.

"What's this?" he asked as she handed him the letter.

"Just read it, you'll understand."

It seemed to take a small eternity for him to read it. When he was finished, he looked up, face pale above the dark green of his t-shirt. His eyes were blank with shock.

"How...how long have ye had this, woman?"

"Since October," she said, dreading the next question even as she saw it forming in his face.

"And how did ye come to have it?"

"Someone told me where to look."

The dark eyes narrowed. "An' where exactly was it that ye looked?"

"The file room at the Tennant Street station."

Casey took a deep breath and rubbed his temple with his left hand, while the right still held the letter. "Christ, Pamela."

"I believe that's what Pat said when I showed him," she said in a small voice.

"Why didn't ye tell me sooner?"

"Because you've had enough to deal with since being held on that damn ship and because I thought you'd be angry with me. I was afraid what you might do once you found out. Not to me," she added hastily, "but to whomever did this."

"Angry—maybe a little, but I know ye a bit after these years together, woman, an' I know if ye get a notion in ye there's no force on earth that's goin' to stop ye from followin' it to the bitter end. Angry that ye put yerself in harm's way so many times—definitely. But I've forgiven ye that a few times, and" he gave her a rueful smile, "likely will a few times more."

He reread the letter again, pausing on certain parts longer, his brow furrowed in concentration. She thought she could recite the sentences verbatim that he kept going back to, for they were the same that had made her read again and again, in growing anger, when she'd found the letter. Then suddenly he looked up, eyes dark with pain.

"Were ye—were ye out lookin' for answers when ye lost the baby? Was that what ye were doin' with Jamie at the monastery?"

She took a deep breath and met his eyes, "I was, but I...I was going to lose the baby anyway, Casey. The monk at the abbey confirmed it, but I think I already knew it was just a matter of time."

Casey nodded, a sigh escaping him as though he were trying to breathe out a bit of his pain each time they spoke of the lost child. She knew he had taken the loss very much to heart, feeling that if he'd been free the miscarriage might somehow have been prevented.

"I'm sorry about the letter," she said quietly.

Casey looked up, startled. "Sorry for the letter?"

"For what it says. For the knowing. Which, as it turns out, isn't always better than the wondering."

He shook his head. "I suppose it's no more than I suspected, but didn't want to face. He was never one for walkin' away from someone in need. No matter what the consequences of helpin' that person might be."

"What do you mean?"

"Sometimes he'd help people with legal issues, did he think there was injustice bein' done. It became a sideline really; he never got paid for it, though near the end it was takin' up most of his evenings and weekends. There was one man he was helping maybe four, five months before he died. He started showin' up at our house at all hours, an' Da was real uncomfortable with him. He was always a good judge of character, but I think he felt he'd made a mistake by formin' an acquaintance with this man. Told Pat an' I we were to stay well clear of him should he come around when Da was workin' or if we chanced upon him in the streets."

"Any idea why he was so leery of him?"

"Well, Jewel, the man did come round one day while Da was gone, an' I thought it maybe had somethin' to do with his likin' for young boys."

"Why, did he do something inappropriate?"

"Mmn, it was more a feelin' an' the way he looked at Pat put the hair up on the back of my neck. Ye know when ye can't explain it logically, but somethin' stirs at the top of yer spine an' ye know that the person is not quite right?"

She nodded. She had known more than one person that stirred the cluster of nerves that sat in the core of the primal brain. Instinct, survival, a sixth sense—ignoring those signals had led to tragedy more than once in her own life.

"We told Da the man had been about, an' later I told him I didn't like the way the man had eyed Pat. He seemed like a hungry wolf scenting prey. Well Da got all white-faced an' left a few minutes later. Came back an hour later, calm but with an edge to him that I'd never seen before. He told me that were the man to come again, we weren't to open the door, an' were to call him right away. Though it seemed he really didn't think the man *would* be comin' back. An' then a month later my father was dead."

"Do you think the man had something to do with it?"

Casey shrugged. "He came round after the funeral, an' Pat was home alone. I came in an' he was sittin' in the kitchen drinkin' tea an' Pat was lookin' mighty uncomfortable. I went to my room an' took down the pistol Da had always kept up top his closet, an' I put it to the man's head an' told him my father had never liked him, nor was I disposed to, an' if he valued his life he'd not show his face near our door again. He turned back as he was walking down the front path, an' laughed at me. Didn't say a word, just laughed. Sound chilled me to the core, an' I did wonder at the time, did it mean he'd somethin' to do with my da's death? Though we were *assured* it was an accident." This last was said with no small bitterness, as the police hadn't been particularly sympathetic towards two young men whose father had been a known Republican.

Though the day was relatively fair, Pamela shivered at the faint breeze that moved her hair against her neck. She couldn't escape the feeling that she was missing some small corner of the picture that would make a sense of the whole.

Had Brian stumbled across some dark secret that was so volatile he'd been killed to ensure his silence? He wasn't a man to have stood idly by and allow evil to flourish.

"Listen, Nancy Drew, enough, ye're not in a novel here. Sometimes there are questions that don't have an answer."

"There's one other thing. The man who was killed—he gave me this before he died. I don't know if it means anything." She reached into her coat pocket and handed the ring to Casey. "But I've seen the insignia elsewhere."

Casey had an odd look on his face, and was suddenly very pale. "Where did ye see it?"

"William Bright. He had the ring on a chain around his neck."

Casey stood and walked into the house. She could hear him run up the stairs and come down again a few moments later. He walked toward her wordless, dropping something in the palm of her hand.

She looked down, an icy feeling crawling up her spine. In her palm was a silver ring, plain but for the etched harp and the engraved BOR.

"Casey," she said sharply, "where'd you get this ring?"

His face was grim when he answered. "It was my father's."

NEITHER THE BLAZING FIRE CASEY LIT nor the hot tea Pamela made had done a great deal to warm either of them.

"Who were they?" she asked, worried by the distant look he'd worn since dropping the ring in her hand.

Casey shook his head. "Myth, legend, a band of men that no one was ever certain existed. They seemed like a fairytale—Catholics and Protestants, from all levels of the community, workin' together to come to a peaceful solution. No one really believed they were any more real than Robin Hood and his merry band of outlaws. Some thought it a joke, you know the odd things people will scrawl on buildings that have no basis in reality, but it starts a buzz going."

"Well now we know they did exist and it seems there aren't many of them left."

"Anyone who was part of it, Jewel, wouldn't admit to it these days. Ye said it yerself, most of the people on that list are dead, an' none of them from natural causes. My da included. I'm awfully surprised William Bright would wear it on his person."

"I think he intended I should see it. I don't think that man does anything without forethought."

Casey breathed heavily through his nose, brows drawing down in anger. "What the hell were ye thinkin', woman, to go an' see such a man? He's feared throughout Ulster, an' for good reason. In a land of hard men, he's king."

"I know, I just thought he might have an answer for me."

"So he knew my daddy, did he?" Casey asked softly. Under his words she could hear the half-eager, half-sorrowed note of a child who had lost their parent too soon, and would always be searching for the bits of that person that remained behind in other's memories.

"He did, and rather liked him too. Which I think, considering the source, is no small compliment."

Casey nodded, squeezing her cold hand in reassurance, his own only slightly warmer. In the uncertain light of the fire she saw that he was staring into the distance, seeing not the stones of the fireplace, nor the walls or windows, but a memory that would not let him go.

"Tell me what you're thinking," she said, hand resting over the beat of his heart.

"I am thinking," he replied quietly, "that one man can never really understand the heart of another. Even if that other is his own father. I loved him, lived with him, near to worshipped the ground the man walked on, but there were many things, it would seem, that I didn't know about him."

"Are you angry with him?"

"No, Jewel." He laid his hand over her own. "Even a father has a right to his secrets. I suppose I'm feelin' a little lost is all. I know for certain now that he was murdered. What do I do with that knowledge?"

She felt the familiar clutch of fear in her intestines. And yet how could she deny him his right to know, when she'd risked her own life to try and get at the truth of what had happened to Brian?

"I don't think there are any clear answers. Maybe if I'd had a chance to talk to that man before they killed him I would have gotten the answers."

Casey raised a black brow at her, underneath which was a very black look. "I swear to God, woman, if I have to have ye kneecapped to keep ye in place, I'll do it. An' I know the men to do the job."

She swallowed and managed a tremulous smile. There was only one bit of unfinished business that needed attending to and if that didn't yield any more leads as to what exactly had happened to Brian she would call it a day.

In her pocket, where it had burned from the second William Bright had palmed it, was a piece of paper with an address on it. Under the address was the information that this address was the last place Brian Riordan was known to have visited before his untimely death. Why he hadn't told her this during their terse interview she did not know, but suspected that even William Bright was not entirely free from fear of the past.

"Is that all, woman? Are all the skeletons free from the closet now?" Casey's tone was light, but the look in his eyes was not. And for a moment, she considered telling him about Love just to have it out in the open, so that it would no longer have to fester in her soul. But knowing just as surely that it would fester in his, she did not say the words he asked for, but rather the ones that would keep him safe.

"It's done."

Chapter Sixty-eight

Childhood Ghosts

"I AM NOT," CASEY SAID, FOR THE FOURTH TIME in as many minutes, "goin' to a doctor."

"Why in heaven's name not?" Pamela asked in frustration, feeling a strong need to kick something.

"It's only a wee cold," he insisted stubbornly. "I'll not die from it."

"Here," she said, and stuck a thermometer in his mouth, feeling his forehead with her palm. He was burning up, eyes glassy with fever. He sat now, mutinously, on the bed with a blanket wrapped tight around him, shaking despite his avowal that he was perfectly fine.

"Casey Riordan," she said in exasperation, "you make a terrible sick person."

"I've never been sick before, I don't know how to act," he said grumpily, thermometer bobbing up and down with the force of his words.

"I know you've said it before, but really?" she asked in disbelief. "Not a cold or an earache even?"

He shook his head, the movement precipitating several violent sneezes.

"Not even chicken pox?"

"Is that the one with the itchy red rash all over ye?"

"Yes."

"Oh aye," he nodded. "Pat had that one. I slept beside him every night an' never got so much as a spot. Poor little bugger scratched himself silly, though."

"You must have the constitution of an ox," she said, rubbing eucalyptus oil vigorously between her palms until it was slick with heat.

"Well," he said, eyeing her hands dubiously, "Daddy always did say as I'd the skull of one." The red-tipped nose sniffed the air as she approached. "That's evil smellin' stuff, are ye certain it's not gone off?"

"It's supposed to smell like this. Now take off that blanket, I'm going to rub your chest down with it."

Casey gave her a lopsided grin due to the thermometer and said, "Now I like the sound of that."

An hour later, reeking of eucalyptus oil, Pamela covered up a blissfully slumbering Casey and quietly took her leave of the house.

Pat, as promised, was waiting at the top of the road, car engine idling.

"Christ, it's about time," he said as she slid into the car. "I half froze out here—good Lord, what's that smell?"

"Eucalyptus, and don't ask," she said. "Come on, let's get out of here before either Casey or Lawrence wakes up."

The house was lying in utter darkness as they approached. The car they'd abandoned far back, tucking it in to a road overgrown with rhododendrons. The rest of the way they covered on foot. Both were shivering by the time they came up on the back yard, a large luxuriant stretch of grass, surrounded by well-groomed cedars. They paused for a minute, the gravity of what they were about to do weighing in rather heavily.

The weather, however, was on their side, the fog so thick that the house, even at such a close proximity, was a vague shape with only glimpses of chimney and long casement windows. This was where William Bright's scrap of paper had led them. Suddenly Pamela wasn't sure she wanted to know what secrets were hidden behind the thick stone walls. She had a strange shivery feeling that had nothing to do with the cold, that tonight they might well find answers that were going to prove very hard to live with.

"Christ," Pat breathed out, breath condensing onto his skin instantly. "Is it possible that we've completely lost our minds? I mean, what if we get caught?"

"We can't," she said. "Casey will kill me."

"Me as well." Pat laughed, a sharp sound of nervousness. Somewhere in the distance a dog howled, and the two of them clutched at each other.

Pat snorted. "Fine pair the two of us are. We're like to scare each other to death, never mind if we actually run into someone else. Tell me again what the note says."

"Just the address and the information that the house would be empty for the next week. Nothing else."

"Right." Pat blew on his hands, face grim. "We're completely insane to be here on so little. Let's go inside."

The grass, stiff with icy dew, crunched under their feet as they stole across the lawn.

Pamela slid a narrow leather box out of her pocket and flipped it open. The picks, gold-colored, glowed in the fog like the proverbial needles in a haystack. She pulled out the most likely looking one and fit it to the lock. It slid in easily enough, and only took a minute to catch the tumblers and turn them. Lawrence had made her practice blindfold until she could do each lock in the house in under a minute. The practice served her well now, even though her hands were shaking and her heart was pounding fit to burst from her chest.

"Ye're very good at that," Pat said, looking slightly disconcerted.

"I taught Lawrence how to play backgammon and he taught me how to pick locks."

"Oh, good to see ye do things as a family," Pat said, sarcasm in good form despite the chattering of his teeth.

"Come on." She slipped through the door onto a heavy carpet. She moved into the room so that Pat could get inside. He shut the door behind him with a soft click that—to their overly tuned ears—sounded like a gunshot.

They stood completely still for a long moment, letting their vision adjust to the dark and listening carefully to the silence that surrounded them. There were only the normal sounds of an empty house whose owners are on holiday—the hum of electrical appliances, the creaking boards responding to their intrusion, and the low level prickling that all houses seemed to contain, as if they were living, sentient beings.

"Where should we start?" Pamela asked.

They stood in the dining room, a long wooden table glowing like ebony in the darkness, the dim glow of crystal lighting the far wall.

"This way," Pat said, moving off on cat feet. She followed in his footsteps, knowing he shared his brother's instincts in darkness. Both men had the night sense of a cat, whereas she was likely to trip over the edge of a carpet she wasn't anticipating.

Pat rejected the kitchen, two downstairs powder rooms, and a guestroom as being a waste of their limited time.

"Study, I'm betting," he whispered back over his shoulder as he jiggled the heavy latch of a door at the far east end of the house. "Door's locked. Where's yer wee picks?"

"Less than a minute," she said some fifty-odd seconds later. "Lawrence would be proud."

"Aye, well," Pat said dryly, "that's up for debate, all things considered."

The study smelled of leather, old paper, and disuse. It was much colder than the rest of the house, which was saying something.

"It's like the devil's meat locker in here." Pat breathed out, teeth audibly chattering. Heavy curtains hung on the long casement windows, and they felt safe to turn their torches on. The first impression was that the room was rather cluttered. A desk sat in the center, an enormous antique with dozens of small bird nest holes, filled to overflowing with bits of paper. Scattered around the desk were a bizarre variety of ottomans, chaise lounges and dozens and dozens of large cushions, islands of color on the dark rugs that scrolled out to the edges of the room.

"It looks like some sort of pasha's den in here," Pat said, flicking the torch from one velvet-covered atrocity to the next. "Come on, let's get started with the desk."

She knelt down, Lawrence's set of picks glinting like wicked sharp needles.

The desk was a bit of a challenge, being that a larger barreled key was needed for the ornate locks. She chose the largest of the picks, which had a barrel roughly half the diameter of a screwdriver, and slid it into the top lock, which should, she hoped, unlock the entire set of drawers. The drawer popped open a few seconds later and she sighed with relief.

"Here, you check the desk while I get the filing cabinet." Pamela said.

Pat nodded, already riffling through the top drawer, where a series of manila envelopes with dates on them were stacked a foot deep.

The file cabinet wasn't much of a challenge. The second smallest pick and twenty seconds were all that were needed before the lock popped and the heavy drawers rolled outward.

The top drawer held business documents, as well as the normal run of bills, household expenses, insurance documents etc. Pamela flicked through it quickly, her hands stiffening even with the protection of the gloves. The room was so cold it was akin to standing inside a refrigerator with the door shut.

The second drawer held a disgusting array of racist tracts and religious dogma, pamphlets and books that made her feel soiled just for touching them. Hatred was something she had firsthand experience with; hated for merely being of a certain religion, or more particularly in her case, for being female. But hate on an organized scale—the Third Reich or the KKK, or any of the narrow fundamentalist sects whose foundations rested heavily upon hatred of the Other—was something, even after time in Belfast with its firmly entrenched and ancient tribal schisms, she found much harder to comprehend.

There was nothing of particular interest, though, and nothing to tell her why William Bright had put this address in her hands. Given his reputation, he was no stranger to organized hatred himself. She flicked over the last file, and then understood just where he'd been leading her that day.

The photos were poorly lit amateur shots and yet their impact was not lessened by these qualities. Pictures of boys; boys who had a few things in common, they were all young, all naked, and all posed in a variety of perverse sexual tableaux that made her close her eyes in horror.

"What is it?"

"I...I...just come look."

Pat took the file out and the pictures spilled across the floor. He made an inarticulate, half-choked noise and then quickly shoved them back in the dark brown folder they had been hidden inside.

"Desk is full of film strips, negative an' reels. I imagine they'd be the same as these." He put a gloved fist to his forehead and breathed hard through his nose. And then put his hand out to open the bottom drawer of the file cabinet.

Ropes, handcuffs, leather hoods, whips, and other devices that didn't bear a closer scrutiny, filled the bottom drawer. Pat cursed under his breath and turned abruptly away. Pamela stepped back, wanting distance between herself and what they were seeing. In doing so, she stumbled over one of the low tables and caught up hard on her elbow against the solid shelves built into the wall.

"Ye all right?" Pat whispered, breath a chill fog in front of him.

"I'm okay. But I could swear that bookshelf just gave when I hit it."

Pat frowned, and stepped over the velvet-tasseled ottoman. His skin was stark white against the dark wool of his hat and sweater; his eyes indiscernible from the shadows that clustered about them. He looked the shelf over, pushing on the edge, where it seemingly dovetailed with the one next to it.

The shelf was full of books on the occult, both titles she recognized and some far more obscure that appeared ancient, with cracked leather bindings. Between the books were a variety of macabre stone figures—gargoyles, goblins, harpies, bird heads with long knife-blade beaks, gorgons and some particularly hideous sheela-na-gigs—scarred faces leering out from amidst the dark bindings and mildewed pages.

"It's here." Pat cocked his head toward the wall, listening for the telltale click. He pressed here and there against the wood, pulling out various books, and the macabre ornaments.

It was the tiny gargoyle that glared out from the middle shelf, its eyes two rubies that glowed like spots of blood in the dim. Pat pressed against the monstrous wee face and there was an audible click and the shelf came away from the wall.

He took a deep breath. "Right then, let's see what we have here."

He stepped through the bookshelf opening and disappeared. A cold hand gripped Pamela's nerve endings, and she knew whatever was behind that wall was neither benign nor without ghosts.

She gritted her teeth and followed Pat through the wall.

It was a small, stone-lined chamber, damp and smelling of things that only grew in the dark. It was roughly twelve feet long and five feet wide.

She squinted against the dust, suppressing the urge to sneeze. The torch lit up the entire small, dungeon-like room, the dust so thick in the air that it seemed as if the entire space was filled with a brilliant golden snowfall. A series of cubbyholes were built into the wall, the heavy oak shelving rising all the way to the ceiling. Most of the cubbyholes held long, flat iron lockboxes, though some higher up had wooden boxes, roughly the shape and size of the boxes florists used to send long-stemmed roses. On the end of each box was a small plate engraved with fine print. She peered close, shining her torch on one box in particular.

'*Michael*' it read. She flicked the torch over to the next box, '*Sean*'. The cold hand moved higher up her spine, and the chill spread into her very blood.

Pat slid one of the boxes off the shelf and noted that despite the general dustiness of the room the boxes were clean, as though they were polished on a regular basis.

He laid the box on the floor, clicking his own torch off.

"Shine yer light here," he said, and opened the box. The lid slid back with a well-oiled silence.

"Oh dear Jaysus," Pat breathed out. Pamela put a gloved hand to her mouth. The light picked out the delicate fibula, and she had one single second to think he must have been a long-legged boy this Sean, before the full and horrifying truth hit her.

Pat reached up and took box after box off the shelves, his silence grim. Lid after lid, opening in noiseless terror, held the same story. Small skeletons, all terribly clean and free of the soft flesh that had once clung to them. The name on every box that of a boy—boys who had been abandoned by society, and seemingly by God as well. Boys who no one would notice if they simply disappeared off the face of the planet one day. Boys like Lawrence.

Pamela pushed herself back out of the closet, the urge to scream beating like a frantic bird in her chest. She thought she was going to throw up if she didn't get out of the house immediately.

She crawled to a small hassock, sweat starting to bead under her hair and slick her palms. From inside the stone room she heard the scrape of each box coming down until finally a long and dread silence filled the very motes of the air, and Pamela felt as though her breath was tainted with the blood this house contained.

What seemed a very long time later, Pat emerged with one of the white wooden boxes in his hands. His face was expressionless, his movements slightly jerky, the body's reaction to shock. Pamela looked at him in the dim and dusty torchlight, dreading the words she knew must surely come.

"I think I know what happened to Robin's sister," he said in a voice drained of all emotion.

In reflex she crossed herself.

"Dear God, what do we do now?"

PAMELA WAS RELIEVED TO SEE that the house was still dark, other than the small light over the kitchen sink she had left burning. She crept gratefully through the back door, still shaking with nerves and cold.

She locked the door firmly behind her, standing silent for a moment to listen to the small house noises. The refrigerator hummed happily to itself, and the soft pad of Finbar's feet sounded at the kitchen entryway. The dog blinked sleepily at her, loping across the expanse of shining floor for a pat.

She sighed with relief; her absence seemed to have gone unnoticed.

She put the kettle on before changing out of her damp clothes into her warmest pyjamas: an outfit that consisted of an old thermal undershirt of

Casey's, red flannel bottoms and an ancient rugby jersey that half swallowed her. She checked on Casey and found him still sleeping, breath wheezing in and out of his mouth. His forehead was clammy and considerably cooler than it had been earlier in the evening.

Downstairs she replenished the fire in the sitting room, building it from slumbering coals to a high, hot blaze that began to thaw her face and fingers. With great effort, she pulled the vast Victorian armchair close to the fire and then curled up in it with a cup of hot, sugary tea. The Irish cure for shock and pretty much every other ailment known to mankind.

She took a large mouthful of tea, holding it against her tongue for a second before swallowing, allowing the delicate scent to warm her nose. Finbar came and settled himself by the chair with a sleepy *wumpf*. She took a deep breath and felt some of the horrible tension of the evening begin to give way to shaky gratitude that she was no longer inside the walls of that horrible house.

"Where have ye been?" asked an accusatory voice that seemed to issue forth from the tall cabinet behind her.

She started, slopping tea onto the worn jumper. "Jesus, Lawrence," she said sharply, "you scared me."

Lawrence, wrapped in her Star of David quilt, came around the chair and plunked himself onto the floor beside the fire. His eyes were still glassy with fever, though they looked more accusatory at present than anything else.

"When did you wake up?" she asked, deciding it was of little use to dodge the child's question.

"Just as ye were leavin'." He coughed, and she winced at the heavy sound of his fluid-filled lungs. "Saw ye go up the drive an' get in a car. Looked a bit like a blue Cortina." Here he added a significant sniff.

"Did Casey wake up at all?" she asked, feeling slightly sick. She'd no wish to explain her way out of this particular corner; Casey wouldn't take kindly to the reasons nor the outcome of this night.

"Just the once, but I told him ye'd stepped out for a walk an' he went right back to bed."

"Thank you for that," she said, wondering why he'd kept it secret while being completely grateful that he had.

"Didn't want to upset him when I'd no idea where ye'd gone," he said, in response to her unspoken question. "Where did ye go?" He tried to glare accusingly, an effort somewhat marred by another fit of coughing.

"Before I answer any questions," she said sternly, "I'm going to get you a hot drink and tuck you up in bed."

"I'm fine here by the fire," he said weakly. "Ye'll not make me drink the garlic stuff again, will ye?"

"No, you can have a cup of regular tea."

This statement was greeted with a small upturn of his lips. "With sugar an' cream?"

"Yes. But only if you get in bed first."

She helped him back to his bedroom, his skin hot to the touch, body shaking with fever chill.

"Your shirt is soaked," she said. "Take it off, I'll get you a dry one. You can't go back to bed that way."

He clutched his shirt to his thin chest, a look of panic passing over his face. "I'll change when ye go to get my tea."

She turned from the bureau, handing him fresh pyjamas. "Alright, Mr. Modesty. I'll be back in a minute."

She dashed up the stairs to get a pair of Casey's heavy wool socks. It was part of an old remedy that her father had used on her when she'd had a particularly bad cold. The other part required raw garlic being rubbed on the soles of the afflicted's feet.

She retrieved the socks, Casey's snores echoing around the room like the sound of a congested swarm of bees. She dashed back downstairs to the kitchen for some garlic. Garlic, socks and the jar of eucalyptus oil in hand, she nudged Lawrence's door open with one hip.

She froze, riveted to the spot by shock.

The boy's back was to her. The bedside lamp was on and Lawrence stood in the pool of light, struggling his way into the fresh pyjamas. Despite regular and copious feeding, he was still so thin that the knobs of his spine stood out sharply against his fair skin. Pyjama bottoms clung precariously to his thin hips, riding low enough to expose the top of one milky buttock. It was the sight of this that had arrested her, for there were deep weals in the fair skin, the scarring thick and shiny as twisted wire.

She stepped back, taking care to be silent. How on earth had the boy come by such injuries? She was no fool, and realized that the life he'd led exposed him to a variety of perversions, things that she'd no wish to even know about. What had struck the chill back into her marrow though was that a few of the scars looked to be quite recent. They still had the pink, puckered look of recently healed flesh.

She coughed quietly and called out, "Are you decent?"

"Aye," came the muffled reply.

She stepped into the room to find him snuggled under the quilts, face red with exertion. His eyebrows went up at the sight of the garlic.

"Ye promised me real tea," he said in an accusing tone.

"And you'll get it, once I've got you settled here. Now give me a foot."

One pale foot poked out reluctantly from under the pile of blankets. She rubbed the split clove in measured strokes against the oval heel and elegant arch. Though narrow, his feet were very long, giving him the gait of an awkward puppy at times.

"Ye'll not tell him, will ye?"

She looked up, startled. "Tell who, what?"

"Tell Casey about the scars ye saw on me."

She met his eyes, and knew the glassy sheen wasn't all fever.

"I know ye saw, I heard ye come in an' go back out."

"Are you going to tell me how you got them?"

He looked down at the quilt where one long-fingered hand was splayed against a crimson star, the points neatly dividing between his bones. "Promise me ye won't tell him," he repeated stubbornly.

She sighed. "You know I can't make a promise like that."

"Then I can't promise not to tell him ye snuck off with Pat tonight. I know the two of ye are up to somethin' ye're keepin' from him. An' if ye're keepin' it from him, it must be somethin' that would make him fearful mad if he were to find out."

"You rotten little blackmailer," she said indignantly. She pulled the sock on over his pungent foot and tucked it back under the blanket.

"Do we have a deal then? I keep yer secret, if you keep mine."

She started to shake her head, but a look of pure desperation in the blue eyes stopped her.

"I'll tell ye how I got the marks if ye don't tell him. Otherwise I'll not say a word." The sharp chin, still with the baby-fine skin of a preadolescent, jutted out at her defiantly.

"All right," she said, feeling that she was making a devil's bargain out of which no good could come.

"Well, ye've heard me speak of Morris Jones before?"

She nodded, for although Lawrence hadn't spoken directly to her about the man, Casey had filled her in well enough that the mere name stirred a black rage in her.

Lawrence took a shaky breath. "He's usually not picky about who he's beddin' long as they're male an' young, but for some reason he seems to like me especially, if ye can call it that."

She felt sick at the thought of exactly what 'like me especially' meant in this context.

"Go on," she said, feeling incapable of stringing more than the two words together.

"An' he can only really get excited when he's hurting me. I'm very fair skinned, ye see, an' so the marks are that much worse. An' I seem to bleed a good bit when cut. The less I like it, the more excited he gets. If...if I scream or beg for mercy, he really loves it."

The boy's long throat swallowed over some invisible obstruction, and she knew for the second time in her life that she was capable of murder.

"Why, Lawrence? What's he got over you, that he can force you to do this?"

He hung his head, the crystalline eyes gone a deep blue, like a lake with a storm building below its surface. "He said he'd hurt the both of yez, if I don't do as he wants. He knew things, too," he went on, words coming faster and faster, spilling one on top of the other as though he were afraid that if he stopped he'd never be able to finish what he had to say. "Knows where ye work an' the hours ye keep, knows all about Casey an' the center. An' he even talked about Jamie an' how money didn't make a man impervious to bullets."

"You're not supposed to protect us, Lawrence; we're supposed to protect you. You have to trust that we can do that for you. Casey and I have lived with threat before, and we're still around to tell the tale. So has Jamie, come to that."

"An' what do ye think Casey would do, did he know?"

"Kill the man," she said bluntly. Which she tended to think would be no bad thing.

"An' that's why he can't know. I don't want him endin' up in prison over somethin' I've done. He's only just got his freedom back."

"*You* haven't done anything. It's that bastard who has. You are not to go anywhere near him ever again, do you hear me? If you do, I'll tell Casey directly and let the chips fall where they may."

"Are ye threatenin' me?" he asked, the unreliable voice pitching upwards to an indignant squeak.

"No, I'm making you a promise," she said, making certain her voice carried a gravity the boy could not mistake. And though she had promised not to tell Casey, she had not made that same assertion regarding Jamie. Should Morris Jones disappear, she wouldn't even ask so much as an uncomfortable question.

Lawrence frowned at her, as though he read her thoughts. His eyes were red-rimmed from exhaustion and fever, for he had not cried once while telling her of what amounted to a regular raping of his body over the course of months. He was also, despite his lack of tears, at his emotional limits.

"I think we both could use some sleep," she said, feeling very tired herself, though it was a weariness that had little to do with physical fatigue.

"I...would ye mind lyin' down with me just...just until I get to sleep?" he asked, voice uncertain. "If ye don't think it's inappropriate or anything."

"Why would you think it's inappropriate?" she asked.

"I've never had anyone lie with me to sleep, or for comfort, it's always been for sex."

"Not even your mother?" She felt a bone-deep horror for what his life had been. It made her want to weep for all they could not give back to him, and the things that no amount of love and security were ever going to erase.

"I don't know," he said. "I can't remember back that far."

She cuddled next to the boy, putting an arm around his thin form and gathering him as close as he would allow. She was always very careful not to push past the boundaries Lawrence clearly had.

"Tell me about your dreams," she said. It was a tactic her father had used to calm her before bed and put her mind on pleasant childhood fantasies.

"The sleepin' ones or the wakin'?"

"Both."

His voice started out strong, but soon faded and the distance between half-sentences stretched further and further apart. Considering what his life had shown him, his dreams were, for the most part, reassuringly normal: football, music, girls and tests for which he was not prepared. The darker ones gave her pause: forests he could not find his way out of, and a faceless man.

"Aye, I've had that one as long as I can remember," he said in response to her question about the faceless man. "I don't think I'll ever see his face; any time I get close to him in the dream he turns his back. I've gotten a wee bit superstitious about it. I've a feelin' that if he ever turns around an' I do see his face, somethin' truly awful will happen in the daylight."

"We won't let it," she said fiercely. "You're not going to have anymore faceless men in your life Lawrence."

"Promise?" he said, the word stretching to several syllables. He was halfway asleep already.

"I promise," she said, knowing that he'd heard her at least subconsciously, for his body palpably relaxed.

He muttered one more thing, barely audible, and she knew he was no longer aware of the words he spoke, but they sent a chill down her spine all the same.

His breathing became heavy; his temperature rising enough that she could feel the change in heat that presaged deep sleep. He drifted off to what she hoped were dreams untroubled by evil and vice and the fear that he carried with him during his waking hours.

For long hours after he fell asleep, she lay awake staring into the darkness, where shapes were blurred as though covered in a layer of ash. And she saw in her mind the shape of the white box Pat had discovered in that charnel house that masqueraded as a respectable dwelling.

And inside it a small pair of pink ballerina slippers and the delicate bones of a child who had been born to dance. The remains of Robin's sister and the beautiful satin slippers that Brian Riordan had anonymously given to her so that she might have a moment of grace in a life that had been exceedingly short on that attribute.

The box sat in her darkroom, firmly under lock and key. Even now, the other boxes were being photographed, tagged and loaded into police vans. She and Pat had called the police once they were a safe distance from the house. But this one box containing the bones of Jo Temple they had brought away. She would leave it to Robin whether to bury the bones of the past or to expose them to the harsh light of the justice system.

She curled tighter to Lawrence's thin frame, a flood of protective rage and fear tingling all along her skin. And heard again the last words he'd said to her before drifting off into his uneasy slumber.

I dream that I am not alone.

Chapter Sixty-nine

What Remains...

AFIRE BURNED MERRILY in the hearth, pine knots snapping with the heady scent of resin. The flames reflected cheerily in the teacups on the sideboard, and in the highly polished glow of table and floor. It was a setting entirely incongruous with the sad event that was about to take place within it.

"Tea or whiskey?" Pamela asked, holding a bottle of Connemara Mist in one hand and the kettle in the other.

"Whiskey," Casey said grimly. "I don't think there's a drink appropriate to this sort of news, Jewel. But whiskey might blunt the edge a little."

"Should I stay or go?"

Casey eyed her silently for a moment, as though assessing the choice.

"Stay, Jewel. I've no notion of how he'll receive what's to be told, but it's yerself that found the bones. I think it's right you should be here when he sees them."

She had awakened Casey in the wee hours, the morning after the discovery of all the boxes of bones. She had laid the box containing Jo Temple on a chair in the bedroom and then woke her husband.

It had taken several minutes, deeply asleep as he was and groggy with the cold, for him to understand what she was telling him. He had opened the box then, face blank with shock, and had stood for a very long time, staring down at the fragile skull and tiny bones that testified to the delicacy of the little girl they had once borne through the vagaries of an incredibly harsh world.

And then her husband, strong, stubborn, and able to bear a great deal, had leaned his head down beside the box and cried; a long silent shaking of his body that unleashed her own tears as she sat frozen on the edge of the bed, unable to move, feeling as though she would never again be clean after the things she had seen the previous night.

At long last they had lain down on the bed together, exhausted and beyond the physical forms of grief. And she told him the story in its entirety. At the end of the telling, Casey had taken her face in his hands and turned it toward him none too gently.

"No more, woman—d'ye understand? This has caused enough heartache already. I cannot lose ye—d'ye understand!" He'd given her a shake, causing her teeth to clack together.

"Ouch—yes, I understand."

"Pamela, don't lie to me, woman, nor placate me with words ye don't mean. If I catch ye fiddlin' about in these matters again, I'll not be responsible for what I may do to ye."

"I'm done," she'd said, and meant it.

Casey had pulled her to him fiercely then, and held her for a very long time and so, at last, she had fallen asleep, to escape for a short while from the horror of the preceding hours.

Now, though, it had returned full force, as the two of them awaited the arrival of Robin.

They both heard the sound of a car turning in at the head of the lane, and started simultaneously. Casey took a deep breath and squared his shoulders.

It was a rainy twilight, and Robin's chestnut hair gleamed bright as fire beneath the bare winter branches of the oak. The rain was coming down in a heavy drizzle and he ran toward the door, fist up to knock. But Casey had it open before he could.

Robin's bright white grin slid off his face, as soon as he caught sight of Casey's expression. "What is it?"

"What do ye mean?" Casey asked, ushering Robin in and taking his rain-beaded coat from him to hang by the fire.

Robin snorted. "What do I mean? The last time I saw that expression on yer face, ye were about to tell me I'd gotten Mary Tilney up the spout."

"Will ye sit, man?"

Robin narrowed his eyes suspiciously in response to Casey's grave tone. "No, I can stand an' listen at the same time."

Casey laid a hand on each of Robin's shoulders. For a moment they were still, two big men who looked as though they might bear the brunt of the world on their shoulders together, if they must. They stood near the fire, and it limned them in deep red, touching a match to the flames in Robin's hair and etching Casey's bold features, as though he were inked against the air. And then Casey spoke and the still shattered.

"We've found wee Jo," he said simply, knowing there was no easy way to break such news.

The oddest look flickered across Robin's face, and Pamela saw clearly what he would look like many years hence, when age had laid its ungentle touch upon him.

"How...what...I don't understand what ye mean." Robin's voice was constricted, as though a vice were around his throat, tightening with every breath he took.

"The box on the table—Pamela found it in a house where there were many such boxes. They all had skeletons in them—mostly boys—but this one had yer sister's name on it. So she brought it away for ye to decide what ye will do with it."

The room was so still that the ticking of the clock seemed grotesquely loud, the hiss of rain against the windows as audible as water running from a tap. Then suddenly Robin staggered forward, and Casey reached out to catch him, helping him to a chair. He made certain Robin was able to sit upright before pouring a hefty measure of whiskey into a glass and handing it to him.

"For the shock. Drink it back, man."

Robin threw back the glass, downing the whiskey in one swallow. He gasped and put the glass down with a thunk. He scrubbed his hands vigorously over his face, ruffling the chestnut hair over his brow. He gritted his teeth and reached toward the box, sliding back the lid as though a cobra were within, waiting to strike.

His hand hovered above the bones, trembling visibly. "I can't...oh Jesus," he breathed out, eyes riveted to the lambent glow of a small skull, where the grubby pink velvet which lined the box had fallen away.

Pamela took a deep breath, willing her own hands to cease their shaking. "May I?" she asked.

Robin gave her a quizzical look and then nodded.

She picked the skull up, cradling it gently in her hands. Dark shadows stared back at her from the deep orbital sockets. The skull was a mottled brown, with patches of amber, ivory, and pale fleeting green near the base of the skull. The green was indicative of the remains coming into contact with a mineral contaminant.

She brushed the pad of her right thumb gently over the brow ridge. It was a smooth, high arch that molded down to fleet cheekbones, and flowed on to a delicately pointed chin, the face of a child who'd never had a chance to reach maturity. A child who'd not had a girlhood and had not yet been within sight of the bloom of mature womanhood.

"She'd have been lovely," Pamela said softly, laying the skull back in its velvet bed.

Robin nodded, his hands spread upon the table; broad, capable hands that had been too small to come to the aid of his sister.

"Would that we knew how she ended up there," Casey said softly.

Robin exhaled a heavy breath that he seemed to have been holding since his first sight of the white box. "I do know."

Casey's head snapped up in shock. "What do ye mean ye know?"

"Well I don't know how her bones ended up in that house, but I know how she died."

"You do?" Casey's voice sounded slightly strangled. "Ye never said."

Robin smiled wearily. "Aye, well we've not been in touch a great deal these last years, have we?"

He picked up the bottle of whiskey and refilled his glass. The liquid glowed with small golden lights, capturing the flicker of the fire in the arc of the bowl. Pamela was quite certain that Robin was blind to his environment right now, though, and that his eyes were cast much further back, into a past that held no golden hues whatsoever.

"'Twas my father who told me. He left me a letter. Told me what her last days had been like, couldn't spare me even that, the old bastard. But maybe it's better to know, better to know than to spend the rest of my life imaginin' what had happened, what might have happened."

"Do you want to tell us?" Casey asked.

He stared at Casey, eyes lit like candle wicks, surprise evident in his face. "Why would ye want to hear it?"

"Because ye need to tell someone, man."

He gave Casey a searching look, eyes a deep, unblinkered blue. He had learned distrust at such an early age that it was simply in his nature to second-guess everyone's motives now. Casey met his gaze calmly and clearly.

"We were away playin' rugby; perhaps ye'll remember."

"I'll never forget," Casey replied, the gravity of his tone unmistakable.

Robin turned his blue gaze on Pamela. "The team was in an amateur knock-out tournament, meanin' of course that if we won we kept on playin'. We were gone a full two weeks, an' we were havin' a grand time of it. We were a bit young, even for the amateurs, but we were big, fast an' aggressive so they overlooked our years. Two weeks doesn't seem like it ought to be enough to change yer entire world, does it?"

"Two minutes can change everything," Pamela said with the unfortunate wisdom of experience. Casey's hand found hers under the table and squeezed it in reassurance.

Robin nodded. "I'd a feeling ye knew well of these things yourself. It's odd, ye know, I've always felt guilty that I'd had such a good time those two weeks, an' yet it was really the last time I felt a joy that was unclouded."

"I suspect," Pamela said slowly, "that she would have wanted you to snatch at whatever bit of joy came your way and not waste the opportunity of it."

"Ye've told her a bit then, man?"

Casey nodded. "Aye. I hope ye know I didn't intend to violate any confidences. It's only that—" he stopped, as if uncertain how to explain himself.

"It's only that ye tell her everything that troubles yer soul," Robin finished for him, eyes less flame than smoke now.

"Aye, I suppose I do at that." Casey smiled, and it was her turn to squeeze his hand.

"Tell me what she looked like," Pamela said, thinking it might be the simplest place for him to begin to tell the story of his sister. Robin gave her a grateful glance, cleared his throat, and began to speak of the girl who had been his sister.

"Jo was small for her age; ye know the sort that looks a bit birdlike?"

She nodded. The bones under the dusty velvet showed the outline of someone who'd moved lightly, who'd been meant to dance through life.

"I think she would have always seemed a girl, even when she was full grown, an' yet when ye looked in her eyes there was an old woman there, even when she was no more than ankle kin to a grasshopper. She loved dancin', used to spend hours with a bit of an old scarf of our mam's pinned to her hair, pretendin' she danced with the Russian ballet," he smiled, as though he saw, there on the stage of his mind, his sister again dancing. "She said the Russians were the greatest dancers in the world. Had a wee box that she kept pictures of her favorites in, Nijinsky an' Nureyev, Pavlova an' Balanchine, she'd say the names like they were prayer, somethin' sacred ye know?"

She nodded, not wanting to disrupt the flow of his memories.

"But only girls from the good neighborhoods went to dance class an' even if we could have found a place for her, our parents couldn't have paid for lessons. So she took books out from the library an' Casey's da found her an old recording of *Swan Lake,* an' she taught herself to dance. I don't know anythin' about ballet, but I think maybe she was good at it."

Pamela, seeing the pure, fragile grain and arch of the bones on the table, thought he was likely right. Knowing the difference between a good dancer and a bad one was more a matter of the heart and not the head.

"'Twasn't enough for her, though, after a bit, an' she took to standin' outside this one dance place, was an' old converted house, an' it was girls from Malone Road an' Knockdean Park an' the like that danced there, not girls from shabby, little knock-ups off the Shankill. She'd go an' stand there in rain or sun, peerin' through the windows, watchin' these girls in their pretty little leotards, gazin' at themselves in the mirrors like 'twas a form of worship. Jo could make herself shrink into a corner, so's no one would notice her, it was how she'd survived as long as she had. She did this for weeks an' no one had noticed, she'd stand there for the entire class an' then come home an' repeat the moves she'd learned. She never even told me. The only reason I came to know was I followed her one day, wonderin' what she'd been up to. She was small an' quick as a butterfly, didn't so much walk as dart, an' I'd a hard time keepin' up an' stayin' hid from her at the same time.

"I lost her at one point an' had to poke my head down several laneways before I found her. An' then I saw her," his voice, quiet now, had the consistency of dispersing smoke, "an' almost wished I hadn't. She was there, outside that window where she'd peered in day after day, dancin' in the rocks below the window, followin' instructions she couldn't hear, through stone walls she'd never be allowed inside.

"I just stood there an' watched her, feelin' as if my heart were crackin' right down the middle an' yet..." He smiled softly to himself. "There was a magic about her when she danced that wasn't there normally, as if somethin' else came over her, almost as if someone else inhabited her soul as soon as the music began. Do I sound mad?"

"No, not at all," Pamela reassured him. The feeling often came to her when she held a camera in her hands, as if she were merely the instrument through which some other force operated, a force that pulled things out in her subject that she didn't remember seeing during the actual shoot.

"I thought to just leave, I knew she'd be angry to find me there, but then I realized there were girls up by the window an' they were mimickin' her, makin' fun of this little ragamuffin from the streets who was darin' to put so much as a foot near the threshold of their world. An' I just got angry an' outraged that they should think themselves better than her just because they'd been born into more fortunate circumstances. I couldn't bear to see her humiliated in such a way, so I went an' grabbed her, said we were goin' home an' she wasn't to come to this place anymore.

"But she just planted her feet—she was stubborn, my Jo—an' said she wasn't done her lesson an' wouldn't be goin' anywhere until she did.

"I asked her why she did it, how she could stand them makin' fun of her, an' she looks at me real solemn, just a wee white face with too much hair an' says, 'because when I'm dancin', Robin, I know God loves me, the rest of the time I'm not so sure.' Well, what could I say to that? So I let her go an' do her dancin' in the shadow of that window, knowin' she'd never be allowed inside to dance with the other girls. After all," his voice was as hollow as the bones beneath the cloth, "'twas all she had left that brought her joy. An' I could hardly deny her that."

Robin smoothed a bit of the grimy velvet over the skull, as if he could now protect and cherish his sister as he'd not been allowed to while she lived. "After I got the letter, I was glad I'd left her be. It was the last happiness for her."

"What happened?"

"The letter said they'd not fed her while I was away, she'd gotten smart with him about somethin', though with him that could mean somethin' as simple as her stickin' up for mam. He'd told her she wasn't to have a bite until she came to him on her knees askin' for forgiveness. Well he must have known Jo'd starve to death before she'd do any such thing. They locked her up, he knew she'd run away otherwise. There was a bit of a crawl space beneath the house, it was wide but not high, she'd not have been able to stand up. Chained her to the foundation like an animal." Robin's fist clenched involuntarily, the lines around his mouth going a stark white. "I get sick with rage when I think of how it must have been for her alone in the dark, hungry, thirsty an' afraid, wonderin' why I didn't come back an' save her."

"Oh Robin," Pamela said, throat thick with tears, "you'd no way of knowing."

"But I did," he said dully, "I knew better than any what the bastard was capable of. I knew, an' I left her to him. No food, no water, an' nothin' but darkness for days, they didn't even let her up to relieve herself, just left her to lie in it. Jo was afraid of the dark from the time she was a baby, she'd a powerful imagination an' sometimes it would run off on her an' she'd actually think she saw monsters in the dark. An' I was runnin' about Wicklow, playin' rugby an' havin' a grand time of it altogether." His hand was moving again and again over the velvet. "I dream of her an' I hear her callin' me, an' her voice is so desperate but I never can find her. It's as though she's always a step ahead, somewhere in the darkness that she was so afraid of."

"How," Pamela asked, feeling as though the word was scraping her throat, "how..."

"How did it end?" Robin said, as though he wished to spare her the speaking of the words.

She nodded, knowing he'd waited all these years to tell someone, and that they must allow him to tell it, and also dreading the utterance of the words, for she knew they would not leave her, nor would the spirits of the tortured children he and his sister had been.

"Ten days they left her down there, ten days with neither food nor drink nor light, an' the world movin' past the door laughin', runnin' to work an' the pub, passin' the time of day, an' none the wiser. Then on that last night he dragged her up out of the hole, drunk an' determined to make her do his will. But my Jo, she wouldn't, an' it cost her her life."

Robin's hand hovered over the box, and then he laid it trembling upon the bones of the foot. Pamela could see them form under his hand, as though the unfleshed foot had risen upon the air in the arches and planes that signified movement and breath. The phalanxes—distal, middle, and proximal, the longer slender bones of the metatarsils, the hollow core encircled by the navicular, talus and cubiform, all roughly the size and shape of small rocks. Here the branching bones of the foot gathered in a bundle and fed upward to the larger joints and bones of ankle and leg. Life was such a fragile and chancy thing, a bit of bone cloaked in racing blood and fleeting emotion. Weeping and dancing one day, silent and still the next.

"He hit her in the chest. She was so thin even before they'd chained her up, she must have been terrible frail by then, an' in the letter he said she made a funny noise, like a whoop, an' then they put her back down in that damp, miserable hole. It took them all of the next day to realize it was too quiet in the hole, an' when they checked they found her covered in her own

blood, clots as big as a man's fist he said, as *his* fist he said," Robin's fingers
had curled tightly into the velvet, turning the pink white with tension. "She'd
vomited blood, hemorrhagin' to death. I've done some readin' since, medical
textbooks an' such, even asked a doctor what sort of injury would result in
those symptoms an' he said severe blunt trauma to the chest. Then I asked
him if it was a painful way to die," Robin's voice faltered for a moment. "I
wanted him to say such a death was peaceful, but I knew that wasn't what he
was goin' to tell me. Sometimes ye look into a person's eyes an' ye know what
they're about to say is goin' to be terrible, but that ye have to hear it anyway.

"He said it would be a frightenin' way to die, even in a hospital surrounded
by medical help. That ye'd have stabbin' pains in the chest an' a feelin' as if ye
were suffocatin' particularly if the ribs had been broken and tore a hole into
the lungs. That it'd be like drownin', only it's blood, not water, that's killin'
ye. Yer own blood. It likely took hours for her to die, though eventually she'd
have gone unconscious from losin' all that blood.

"They left her down there for a couple of days, panickin' about what to
do. Mind ye, no one other than myself was likely to miss her for awhile. She'd
missed so much school due to injuries an' nursin' mam through hangovers that
the nuns had pretty much given her up as a lost cause." He choked slightly as
though there were a gag on his next words.

"I have this picture in my head of her lyin' there like a broken doll that
no child wants, like a bit of refuse ye'd step over in the street but pay little
mind to. It keeps me awake at night, that picture. Sometimes I try to drink
it away, or walk it off in the streets, but in the back of my mind I know it's
never goin' away."

"How did he get her out of the house with no one noticing?" Casey asked,
hand stroking the top of Finbar's silky rough head, his face the color of ashes.

"He took her out like refuse too, wrapped her in a dirty old blanket an'
carted her out in the middle of the night when there'd not likely be anyone
about."

"And then," Pamela carefully touched the delicate arch of a metatarsal,
half the thickness of a pencil, that would have run along the outer edge of
the right foot. A soft dust rose from the bone, shimmered in the air for a half-
second and then disappeared, "he burned her remains."

Robin started in surprise, eyes flaring hot as a welding arc, "How in hell
d'ye know that?"

"I've seen burned bones before; they looked similar to these, white and
calcined. The thinner bones take on this checkerboard pattern, and the thicker
bones like the thigh crack in a crescent moon shape from the heat. Do you
know why he didn't put the skull in the furnace with the rest?" she asked,
seeing clearly in memory the dim white glow of those other bones, with the
miasma of incinerated violets thick about them.

"No, he was a sick bastard my father, I never could understand his motives an' I don't suppose I ever will now. He knew a man that worked at the foundry in the shipyard, that's where he took her body. Man never even asked what he was burnin', if ye can imagine it. Or at least that's what he says in the letter."

"How did you survive?"

Robin shrugged. "Ye just keep movin'. Even when ye think ye can't take a step ye force yerself to do it. Even when it feels as if there's a thousand pounds of brick on yer back, ye just keep movin'. Sometimes ye drink, an' for a minute or two ye forget, an' then mornin' comes an' the thousand pounds is there again strapped firmly in place. Then one day ye realize it's never goin' away an' ye accept it, ye'd miss it if it were gone because then ye'd feel as if ye weren't rememberin' properly."

"Ye don't have to pay penance forever, Robin," Casey said softly.

"Don't I?" Robin glanced at him sharply, eyes once again incandescent with heat. "I wasn't there an' my sister died because of it. It's that simple."

"You were a child," Casey said.

"No." He shook his head. "I was a child in body, but never in spirit. The mind is a funny thing, aye? It just keeps on when the rest of ye is broke, like some old boxer that doesn't know the bell's rung an' the fight is over." His voice was adrift, as transient as snow or mist. "I'm awful tired, but my mind can't seem to hear the bell, even though it keeps ringin'."

"Ye owe it to her to go on with your life Robin, ye're what remains of her. For her sake ye need to find some peace."

He nodded, head down, eyes closed, hand convulsed in the folds of velvet. "I know the sense of what ye say," he said hoarsely. "But damned if I know where to look for peace."

Pamela reached across the table and put her own hand over his, feeling the terrible tension that lived beneath his skin.

"You made a good start by telling us about her. One step at a time, it's all you can do."

Under her hand, the tension gave slightly, like a singing wire pausing for breath.

"An' if what remains is not enough?" he whispered.

"It has to be," she said simply, watching as a lone tear slid down his cheek, lending a pure light to the skin beneath.

"A time to weep, and a time to laugh; a time to mourn, and a time to dance," she said, hardly realizing she spoke as the words returned to her from childhood. "Jo knew well enough to dance while she could, now's your time for weeping Robin."

He looked up, the twisted smile in place. "Even if I can only manage the one tear at a time?"

One tear at a time, it was all, she knew, that was given to any of them.

For the man in front of her, she only hoped it was enough. If not, then God help them all.

Chapter Seventy

Cara

PATRICK RIORDAN HAD BEEN in the habit of exercising caution most of his life. It came with the territory of being born into a notoriously republican family in Belfast. Their father hadn't wanted them to grow up paranoid, but had stressed the need for a certain amount of wariness in their daily lives. There were streets you simply didn't travel down, tribal zones you'd have to be a madman to venture into. Not to mention that innocents were caught in the crossfire all the time.

He tried to vary his route every once in awhile, to throw both the Brits and any other disgruntled elements off his trail. This morning though he'd taken the most direct route, stopped for tea and the papers and then continued briskly on his way. He'd gone down Dunmurry way the day before to see a young couple living in a caravan. The thing was ancient and rundown and he'd winced as the young man had opened the door, disbelieving of the conditions some people lived in in the so-called civilized world.

He'd a lead on a two-up two-down in Andersonstown that he was going to have a look at this morning. He'd a busy day facing him, more than a hundred families on wait lists for housing, at least eight phone calls he needed to return, as well as the mountain of paperwork and bureaucratic red tape he had to burrow through on a regular basis.

When he saw the man slouched against the wall by the door of his ramshackle office, he sighed inwardly. Another person whose problems he wouldn't be able to solve, but he'd at least have to offer tea and comfort, which meant a late start to the one hundred and one other things on his plate today.

The man smiled and nodded at his approach. Pat shifted his bag from his right hand to his left, and returned the nod.

"Can I help ye with something?" he asked, fixing a look of polite interest on his face. The man was neatly dressed with good shoes, and didn't wear a look of hopeless desperation like most of Pat's usual clientele.

"I've a message for ye."

The man was extremely soft-spoken and Pat had to lean in to hear him properly.

"Yes, what is it?" Pat fumbled in his pocket for the keys, the man's words sending a chill down his spine. In Belfast those words could be harmless, or they could be the prologue to a neatly placed bullet. He wasn't aware of anyone in particular wanting him dead, but having grown up on these streets he didn't take it for granted that someone *didn't* want him dead either.

"George Barclay said to tell ye—"

Whatever the man had been about to say was cut off by the screech of car tires at the head of the street and the sound of an engine gunning directly their way. Pat didn't dare look round, though the man's eyes flicked up at its approach, a look of surprise flitting across his face.

"Pat, get in the car, he's going to kill you!"

Pat started back, the car was coming up rapidly. He half turned toward the voice, knowing it was David, scared to take his eyes off the man in front of him. The car was in his peripheral vision now and driving erratically. He chanced a look to the side, saw that David's right arm was coming up and that he'd a gun in his hand.

"Get in!" David yelled, car still moving. Pat hesitated, momentarily paralyzed, until he saw the man reach into his pocket.

David was half out of the car now, a pistol leveled across the roof at the man. When he spoke his voice was even and calm. "Patrick, get in the car. Now."

Pat didn't waste another second on thought, he ran and yanked the car door open then leaped into the passenger seat, barking his shin hard on the frame as well as giving his head a good knock. A metallic whine shot past his ear and exploded out the opposite side of the car as David swung back into the car, pistol leveled at the man who was now running toward the car. Pat was vaguely aware of the man dropping to the street, a splotch of red on his forehead before his vision was blurred by the speed of the car.

The car careened around the corner, tilting for a split second onto two wheels. Pat hung onto the dash for dear life as David floored the gas pedal, sending the little car hurtling down the rutted street. He slowed slightly as they approached an intersection.

"It's too quiet," he said, just as a car emerged on their right side, pulling into the street and effectively blocking them off. David stomped on the brake, the car squealing in protest and throwing them both forward.

"Back up, and do it fast," Pat said, adrenaline shooting directly to his chest and making his heart pound madly. "They know ye're Army! For fuck's sake," he yelled, "back up!"

David shifted the car down hard, glancing behind as he rammed his foot on the gas. "Christ there's someone blocking up there too!"

Pat twisted around and saw that two men had stepped out of a car that was t-boning off the top of the street. Each held an Armalite in the crook of his elbow. "It's a setup—Jesus—" He pounded the dash trying to think through the panic flooding his brain.

"Here." David tossed a pistol on Pat's lap, then cranked the wheel of the car hard to the left, causing the car to spin madly. It banged hard off the corner of a warehouse, but its end swung into the narrow alley backing an ancient building.

"What the hell do ye want me to do with this?!"

"Use it," David said tersely. "We're in a blind, there's a wall at the end of the lane."

"We're stuck in here," Pat said in disbelief, as the car ricocheted back and forth down the dark, overhung laneway which ended in a high, very solid brick wall.

"It forces them to come in after us," David replied, seeming remarkably cool, considering four killers were even now converging on them.

The car screeched to a halt, lurching them both toward the dash. David swung his door open and rolled out onto the stinking pavement. "Get out and keep your fucking head down!"

Pat did as he was told, coming up with the pistol just as he heard the first shots crack out at the head of the alley.

He shot blindly, with no idea of whether he was aiming at the men or merely giving the walls a good thumping. He heard a howl of pain from the head of the alley, another sharp report from David's pistol and an answering volley, which sounded as if the gunman were advancing toward them. He could no longer tell which bullets were incoming and which were leaving David's gun. The tang of cordite was thick on the air, air which pulsated with the high-velocity thump of ammunition. A brick exploded by his head and a sharp pain lanced through his neck. For a moment he thought he was hit, but then realized a small sharp chip of brick had cut across his collarbone.

Suddenly it was over, the silence more unsettling than the gunshots had been. The nerves in his shoulders were jumping, his heart still pounding fit to come out of his chest. He turned his head to the right, afraid of what he might find.

David was still cautiously crouched behind the car door. He seemed miraculously free of blood or inconvenient holes in his anatomy.

"Are you all right?"

Pat nodded, brick dust coating his throat and rendering it immobile.

"Good. I'm going to go move the bodies and then we'd best get the hell out of here. When I wave, pull the car up and be ready to drive out of here."

David walked to the head of the alley with his pistol still drawn and cocked, keeping his body tight to the filthy brick walls. Pat held his breath, waiting for another burst of gunfire to erupt into the disturbing stillness. A minute later David waved him up and bent over to pull the first body out of the street opening.

Pat swung down into the driver's seat, closing the door and popping the clutch simultaneously. The car rolled forward, the sudden movement startling to his shattered nerves.

David yanked the driver door open when he hit the head of the alley. "Get over, I'll drive, you don't look in a fit state for it."

Pat got over quickly, despite the car's cramped interior.

David swung the car out into the street. Pat looked about, there didn't seem to be a soul around and there was no sound of sirens in the distance either. It was, in fact, eerily quiet other than the hum of the car's motor as they headed north along the street.

They didn't speak for several minutes. Pat finally managed a terse, "What now?"

"I've got to get us good and clear of Belfast and then I'll figure out what to do."

They continued north, leaving the city behind them. Pat felt strangely blank; the beginnings of shock he supposed. Yet there was a slight horror at the back of it all that he didn't feel more appalled by what had happened. Then again, if David hadn't happened along when he did, it would be him lying in a heap in the street right now.

"How did you happen to come along just then?" he asked, seeing that it was too coincidental to be happenstance.

David did a swift survey of rear and side mirrors before answering. "I had information that you were pissing off some members of the Black Roses. We'd been watching one of them and when he went missing this morning I figured they might have come looking for you."

"The Black Roses?" Pat swallowed, throat suddenly as tight as if it had been neatly noosed. "I thought they were just an unpleasant rumor."

"Unfortunately not," David said grimly. "There's not many of them, but like sharks they don't really need large numbers to do a great deal of damage."

The Black Roses were a radical splinter group that had broken off in the wake of the Provisional split away from the Official IRA. Their name derived from the flowers they often sent to those they had marked for death. The Provos had disowned them and their methods, which bordered on the psychopathic. They were not a group a man wanted to have notice him.

"Why in the hell would they want to kill me?"

"They had a nice little graft situation going on with the construction company that was building your little utopia. When you got the construction company fired they lost their side income. Didn't know what you were starting when you got them fired, did you?"

"No," Pat said rather weakly. It was hard to imagine the domino effect such a minor action could have, but very small things could ripple out in this country, until a man was caught in a riptide of events that drowned him. Or was in a getaway car wondering how many deaths out of four he was responsible for.

David flicked him a sideways glance.

"If it's any consolation, you didn't hit anyone, though there's a few bricks that will never be the same."

"It's been a lot of years since my da taught me to shoot. I didn't like it then, an' I can't say my feelings have changed much over the years. My brother was a crack shot though, never missed a target. My da used to say Casey could take the eye out of a mosquito at sixty paces."

"Can't say that surprises me," David muttered. "On the few occasions I've seen him, he always looks as though he'd *like* to shoot *me*."

"Ye're British an' ye're army. It's not a combination an Irish Catholic can trust."

"Then why do you?"

"Ye've given me no reason not to."

David laughed. "I'd think I've given you *every* reason not to."

"Exactly. Which told me one of two things, either ye were dead awful at yer job or ye weren't actually tryin' to cultivate my trust. I've reason to think, particularly after today, that ye're not inept at whatever it is ye actually do."

They drove up the Antrim Coast, past the small fishing village of Carnlough and continued north along the coast. Fifteen minutes beyond the village David slowed the car.

He turned down a narrow rutted lane that dead-ended in a crumbling pasture fence. He stopped just shy of the fence, shifted the car down and turned the ignition off. The sudden quiet filled the small space between them. Pat could feel the density of it in his lungs. David left the car without a word, the driver door open behind him.

Pat opened his own door and stood, knees feeling distinctly rubbery. The field was dry and thick with over-grown spurge. He stayed by the car for a minute, watching David walk toward a bank crowned with a small stand of stunted birch trees, that lifted suddenly out of the flat pasture.

His entire body felt slippery, the residue of adrenaline pooling in his joints and muscles. He took a few deep breaths before following the trail David had left through the tall plants and new grass.

"Going to have to talk to them about equipping the cars with stun grenades," David said, before flopping onto the ground and lying back in the long grass. "Do you have any cigarettes on you, man?"

"Jaysus Christ," Pat sputtered. "We've left a heap of dead bodies behind us, an' believe me there'll be some ugly retribution for this, an' ye want to know if I've cigarettes? Christ!"

"Well do you?" David persisted.

"No, I don't smoke, an' nor do you. I'm not in the habit of carryin' them about should I need a post massacre hit of nicotine."

David merely raised his eyebrows, before closing his eyes and taking a deep breath.

"Are ye havin' a nap now?" Pat asked in disbelief at the man's calm exterior.

"No," David said patiently. "I just need a few minutes to get myself back together here before I set fire to the car and we start the walk back."

"Before ye set fire to the car?"

"Yes. Forensic evidence you know. It's not likely their deaths will be questioned that closely as they were all Black Roses—violent death is merely an occupational hazard for them. Still, it's best to err on the side of caution."

Pat sat down beside David, legs shaking fit to drop him where he stood. "Grass is wet," he said inanely, feeling like he'd been hurtled without warning into an alternate universe.

"A damp arse is the least of our worries at present," David said, tone still annoyingly calm.

"Ye don't say," Pat responded with no little sarcasm. "Ye'll forgive me if I note that ye don't seem over concerned about anything at present."

"Patrick," David replied wearily, "I've just shot four men, driven like a maniac for an hour and been certain about three times that I was a dead man. I need a minute or two to sort it all out before I have the appropriate hysterics."

"An' ye call Irishmen crazy," Pat said. They both laughed and the charged atmosphere began to dissipate. "I can't believe the security forces didn't descend on us," Pat said, watching David's face for any change of expression that would give him a clue to the things that were puzzling him about the aftermath of their shootout.

David merely shrugged, eyes still closed, hands now crossed over his stomach.

"I thought the cars were equipped with panic buttons," he persisted.

David opened his eyes and gave Pat an odd look. "Most are. Mine isn't. It'd be frowned upon if I was to call in the cavalry, so they make certain there's no temptation to do so."

"What do you mean *frowned upon*?" Pat asked, with a queasy feeling that he knew exactly what David meant.

"I don't exist for all intents and purposes here in Northern Ireland. If you were to go looking for me, my superiors would deny any knowledge of me. Nine times out of ten if you passed me in the street, you wouldn't recognize me."

"Seriously? Then how...why...in the jail I thought ye were regular army, or SAS."

David shook his head, plucking a piece of grass from the verge and rolling it back and forth between his fingers. "No."

"Is that all the explanation I'm to expect?"

"It's all that's safe for you to know," David replied.

"Who the hell are ye? James Bond?"

David smiled grimly. "That's about as close as you'll come. I'd have a hard time explaining it myself, what I'm doing here. And in the end, it's just best if you don't know."

"That leaves me a wee bit puzzled as to why ye took such an interest in myself, to begin with at least," Pat finished awkwardly.

"I wasn't there in any official capacity. They seemed to find you of particular interest, due more to your family history than anything. I can pull rank when I need to, so I offered to conduct the interrogation."

"Too bad you didn't offer a few days earlier," Pat said.

"Yes, I apologize for that."

Pat laughed. "Ye sound very prim an' British at times, ye know."

David smiled. "I suppose because I am very prim and British when it comes right down to it."

"Ye still haven't answered my question."

"Because my career, for lack of a better term, makes friendship, or any sort of relationship really, pretty much impossible. When I saw you in the jail, when I fed you that day, I recognized something in you. I guess I just liked you. It was that simple. And," he looked down at the green stains on his palms, "I was lonely."

"Oh," Pat said quietly.

"Does that bother you?"

"What?"

"That I looked at you and saw something in your face that told me we were destined to be friends? That I was reckless enough not to consider my position or yours, that I didn't see an Irishman when I looked at you, but just a human being?"

"No."

"Really?" David asked, sounding rather surprised. A soft flush lit his fair skin, and he bent his head, suddenly absorbed in a leaf he'd plucked off his pant leg.

"It's ironic," Pat said, voice strangely soft.

"What is?" David asked, putting the pale green leaf to his eye.

"Ye're supposed to be my sworn enemy, but somehow, without my willin' it, ye've become my friend. An' that's the real answer to the question of why I trust ye."

"War makes strange bedfellows at the best of times, and as this is the strangest little war in a strange little country, I don't think our friendship is surprising at all." David reached across and put something in Pat's hand. "Here take this."

Pat looked down to find a book of matches. "What's this for?"

David grinned. "I just thought, being that it's the property of the British Army and all, that you might like to be the one to set the car on fire."

Part Seven

The End of Ordinary Life

Chapter Seventy-one

Just Another Day in Paradise

THE FIRST OF THE BOMBS WENT OFF at precisely ten after two in the afternoon. The last at three o' five. In between, there were twenty-five others. It was a short timetable for terror, and yet extremely effective.

It wasn't the first time Pamela had been called in to photograph the aftermath of a bomb. But she had never seen the sort of devastation that surrounded her now.

She picked her way carefully along, noting bits of cloth, and a pair of eyeglasses which had somehow miraculously survived the explosion, and lay whole and glimmering on top of a chunk of brick. There were other things amongst the rubble that she was afraid to look at directly, though she knew she would have to in a matter of minutes.

The Oxford Street bus station had only been one of the twenty-seven separate explosions that had rocked Belfast to its core only an hour before. The explosions had taken people unawares, and many had run for safety only to find themselves in worse peril. Both men and women were crying openly in the streets, as plumes of smoke still rose around them on the air of a summer afternoon. Most bombs had been set off in cars left parked at the various locations.

The office block adjacent to the bus station was destroyed, the front wall having been blown clear off. Beams, black and smoking, hung in midair or lay shattered on the ground. The station had been crowded when the bomb exploded. Now, other than police, firemen and corpses, it was quiet and deserted.

The dull thuds had sounded at first like firecrackers, but as the ones closer in to the core of the city had detonated there had been a terrible intensity in the air, followed by a great vacuum that inhabited the very molecules of the atmosphere, as though time had been rent apart at its seams and destroyed.

She walked along further, catching a flash of permed blonde hair poking out between a sheet of plaster and a great long shard of glass. She gritted her teeth and kept moving, keeping out an eye for Sergeant Wilbee or Constable Fred.

A fireman, face grubby with ash, was shovelling the remains of what had, only short hours ago, been a human being. The sight stopped her cold at the top of a mound of debris. Before she could stop herself she was sliding down it, and saw to her horror an arm completely detached from its owner, lying at the bottom of the mound, still clothed in a pale blue sleeve. She scrabbled back wildly, thinking if the arm touched her she might well go mad here in the midst of all this destruction.

A hand, large and strong, caught her from behind and pulled her up sharply. She turned and found a policeman, uniform coated in a fine dust, eyes red rimmed with grief, smoke and fatigue, facing her.

"Are ye all right?" he asked gruffly.

"I...I'll do," she managed weakly, swallowing hard on the acid which had flooded her mouth.

"Here, lass." It was Constable Fred coming up behind the man, his florid face kind, though filthy. He took out a handkerchief and handed it to her. "Ye're taken a bit badly, that's all, it's to be expected."

The other man nodded curtly and continued on his way through the massacre, shoulders squared against the horrors still to come.

"I feel a right fool," she said, taking the handkerchief and mopping her face. It smelled comfortingly of limewater, and she took a grateful breath of its starchy folds before handing it back to Constable Fred.

"It's all right lass; I'd worry if it didn't bother you in this way. Ye need to get something in ye for the shock."

Her stomach rebelled at the mere thought of food or drink and she shook her head vehemently.

"Right then, we'll save tea for later. Is there someone you'd like me to call? I can walk you out beyond the barricades but then I'll have to come back. I don't feel right leaving you to yourself, though."

She fought to get a grip on her emotions. Like the good Constable, she had a job to do and she fully intended to do it. "No, I just need a minute, then I'll be fine."

He gave her a dubious look, then nodded at the resolve he saw in her face. "Aye, well wait 'til ye're steady on yer pins, lass."

"I will."

"When ye're ready to go, follow Gerard around. He'll be the short one in the red jacket."

She followed the direction of his finger and saw a man she recognized from his occasional appearance at the Tennant Street Station. She took a short breath and rose to her feet. Still shaky, but given another minute her feet just might agree to carry her around the edges of the huge crater that had once been Oxford Street.

Gerard nodded curtly at her. He was a short man, with a lean, wiry frame and a reputation for being one of the toughest and most thorough men on the job.

"Here," he tossed her a blue glass jar. "Smear some under your nose, then you'll not smell the blood or tissue. Makes it easier for both of us to do our job."

"We'll start here," he pointed to the shell of a ribcage, now open, the entire thoracic spine visible, vertebrae strung together by the yellowy pads of cartilage. Above was air—the head and shoulders blown elsewhere. The legs were untouched, stuck out stiff as a scarecrow and capped with well-polished brown shoes. Her gaze was riveted to those shoes, for suddenly she saw him, whoever he had been, shining his shoes, freshly shaved, anticipating the evening ahead. The girl he might meet, an entire future there in a moment's glance—now gone. A son, a brother, a lover, a carcass, chunks of evidence. The children who would not exist because their future father had been killed by a bunch of hard men who thought blowing up a bus station made some sort of political statement.

"You coming or not?"

Pamela took a deep breath, the menthol stinging her eyes. She put her camera to her eye and began shooting.

The next five hours were a blur of following the red jacket, of taking photos of a catalogue of atrocities her mind could barely take in. A blur of images underlined with the scent of vaporub. Finally Gerard stopped making notes into the tape recorder and nodded wearily to her.

"Come on, we both need a rest. Let's sit."

She followed him over to the open back end of a police tender, which had been used to cart supplies. Later tonight when the scene was finally cleared, it would be reloaded with many of the same supplies, only now they would reek of blood and carnage and the smell of burned human flesh.

She closed her eyes and rubbed them hard. They were burning from the oily smoke and she felt as though the images she'd seen were seared permanently onto her retinas.

Gerard held out a mug of tea one of the constables had passed him.

She shook her head, and he shrugged. "Suit yourself."

For the first time, she noted his accent didn't carry the broad tones of Ulster, but rather a curious combination of clipped English consonants and New York street talk.

"Where are you from?" she asked.

"Born in Ballymena, moved to London when I was five, then to New York when I was ten. Came back here a few years ago. And you?"

"New York, summers here in Clare, then Belfast and Boston, and now Belfast again."

"Can't see what the attraction to this place might be, less you'd family here."

"I married a native," she said.

"Ah, love then."

"Yes, love."

He took a long slug of tea. "Hard to believe such a thing exists on days like today."

There was little doubt in her mind that this was the work of the IRA—that men like Joe, and, God help them all, Robin, had likely planned this for months, blinded by their hardline view that violence was the only means to move toward their goals in the quagmire that was Ulster.

What sort of mind saw this as a means toward anything other than more hatred, more violence, and more pain for a population who no longer knew what it meant to live without these things?

He sighed. "We'd best get back at it, we don't have a lot of light left." He shook his head, "Fucking IRA."

"You think it was them?" she asked, face hidden as she deftly changed her film for the tenth time that day.

"Doesn't matter which set of psychopaths did it, these people are dead all the same. And undoubtedly you and I will be at a similar scene when the other side takes revenge."

He stood and she followed suit, taking a deep breath to calm her nerves before facing the carnage again. Around them the activity was beginning to die down a bit, and the light was indeed starting its slow fade into a summer night. A lone fireman was wending his way amongst the rubble of bricks, mortar and glass that lay in great swathes along the street.

Gerard shook his head. "God have mercy on Belfast."

The death toll would mount as the day came to its close and in all nine people would lose their lives, while one hundred and thirty were injured. Only two of the dead were soldiers, the rest were civilians. The youngest of these a fourteen year old boy. The vast majority of the injured were women and children.

The IRA took responsibility for the bombing, though not for the fact that adequate warning was not given for the twenty-seven bombs that were planted, and that it was next to impossible for the areas to be cleared with the short lapse time between the warning calls and the detonation.

In bombing their own city, the IRA had sought to bring an end to ordinary life in Belfast, to try and force a people who had already suffered too much to rise against the perceived oppressor.

What they really succeeded in doing was to hand the British the excuse they had been looking for to launch forces into the formerly sacred Republican no-go areas of the Bogside and the Creggan. Operation Motorman was launched, and an extra 26,000 troops were deployed.

In the end the IRA had rather effectively, with the events of one bloody hour, turned the racing tide of freedom and unity fully against themselves.

Chapter Seventy-two

Hard Man

PAMELA WAS IN THE KITCHEN separating out the several lemon frost thymes that grew in profusion in the big clay pots on the porch. The sharp citrusy scent was pleasing and tended to clear the head when working with them. Working with plants always gave her a feeling of calm, the soil under her fingers soothing. Such small chores were a world away from events such as Bloody Friday, now a week ago, though she still saw the gruesome images every time she closed her eyes.

The newspapers had indulged in a melodramatic field day in the wake of that terrible Friday, the headlines blaring out black from gritty pages about the *Massacre—Wanton Murder, Hour of Terror, Day of Infamy* and so forth. However lurid the headlines, no one offered any solutions to an untenable situation. The British continued to pour more young men into the narrow city streets, to stumble through tiny back gardens while women and children clanged bin lids in warning to the snipers that took potshots at them from the steeply inclined roofs and then disappeared back into the small jungle that was West Belfast.

Living away from the city provided some small measure of relief, though the tension lived in both she and Casey on a constant basis. It manifested itself in small countless ways that became a part of one's daily routine without an overt consciousness of it. This frightened her more than anything; that looking over her shoulder, that jumping at every loud noise, that looking at every person with whom you were unfamiliar with a jaundiced eye, was becoming ingrained in her, and as natural as brushing her teeth.

Suspecting her husband's long hours were not strictly confined to his work and time at the youth center didn't sit easily with her either, and yet just such a suspicion had been growing like a tiny weed in her for some time now. She knew he was spending more time with Robin of late than he had before internment, and she had a feeling their activities weren't strictly confined to lifting pints or playing at horseshoes.

The door opened, startling her. She jumped and knocked over the bag of potting soil that sat on the counter beside the clay pots.

"Damn it all to hell!" She exclaimed as a dark pour of soil fell out onto the wooden floor. The floor she'd finished washing no more than an hour ago.

"Lawrence, is that you?" she called out.

"No, 'tisn't," came back the reply.

She glanced over at the big wooden clock which sat atop the mantelpiece. It was early for Casey to be home. She wiped her hands on a linen tea towel and craned her head around the door to the boot room.

He was sitting on the narrow boot room bench, work boots still on his feet, lunch bag lying in a heap by the door.

"You're home early."

"Aye, we're waitin' on a load of schist from Derry, truck had an accident near Maghera an' went into the ditch. They sent us home for the rest of the day."

He pulled his boots off, his movements unnaturally stiff.

"Did you have an accident yourself? You're moving oddly."

"Not an accident as such, more of an intentional head-on, ye might say."

"What do you mean?"

"I got in a bit of a fisticuffs with one of the other men." He cricked his neck as though it pained him and stood, stocking-footed. "Will ye put the kettle on, Jewel? I could use a hot cup, an' maybe a bite of somethin'."

"What do you mean 'will ye put the kettle on'? Why on earth were you fighting?"

"Can I come in the house first, woman? Then I'll explain it to ye."

She gave him a gimlet eye and then stood back. In the bright light of the kitchen, she could see clearly that he'd been in more than a 'slight fisticuffs'. His shirt was torn and he still had traces of dried blood on his knuckles, which were skinned and puffy. She pulled his shirt—what was left of it—up out of his jeans and pushed it up to his chest, amid protest on his part.

"Good Lord! How long were you at it?" His ribs were a mottled black and blue down his entire left-hand side.

"The ribs aren't the man's fault. We fell onto a pile of concrete blocks from above—ye should see his one leg, 'tis a deal worse than the wee bruise I've got."

"Wee bruise my arse," she exclaimed, "your ribs look like you've been mauled by a grizzly bear."

"Well I daresay I feel about as bad as if I had been, Tim Piggott not bein' particularly small."

"You were fighting with *Tim*? What on earth for?"

Tim was a big, bluff good-natured fellow that worked hard, and drank harder. Casey had always gotten along quite well with him. How the two of them could have come to blows was something she found hard to countenance.

"He said somethin' I took offense to, an' I smacked him in the mouth but good. An' then he took offence to *that*."

"Yes," she said dryly, "I imagine he would. What exactly did he say?"

"He said my wife was after getting' herself a reputation as the RUC's whore."

"*What?!*"

"Aye. He said he'd a cousin lives down near Crossmaglen, an' yer name came up in conversation recently amongst a certain group of men. An' that there were rumblins' about ye an' that burned out RUC car. Those South Armagh boys are mad as friggin' hatters woman, can ye not stay clear of trouble for more than a minute altogether?"

"Don't deviate off topic here, how exactly did he get round to calling me a whore?"

"His cousin is South Armagh IRA, Pamela, an' if they get a bee up their nose about ye, ye might as well go pick out yer coffin. They'll kill ye for having the temerity to walk about breathin', never mind that ye're pokin' yer face into things they don't want found out. An' twas them called ye the RUC's whore—a Catholic woman doin' the policeman's dirty work. Tim was repeatin' it. I think he meant it as warnin' but it took me the wrong way an' so I hit him."

"I just asked a few questions, people will talk to a woman sometimes when they won't talk to a policeman."

"It's my understandin' ye asked a rather direct question about Noah Murray."

She swallowed, feeling slightly nervous. The truth was she *had* asked if anyone had seen Noah Murray about. Which, in hindsight, had seemed more than a little foolish. Noah Murray was, for all intents and purposes, the godfather of the South Armagh brigade of the IRA. He was known for his ruthlessness and his ghost-like ability to elude the police and prosecution of any sort. It was rumored that even his neighbors never questioned him about the strange nocturnal activities that took place on his farm, for fear they would end up in a body bag in a lonely country ditch somewhere.

"I did."

"Are ye tryin' to commit suicide, woman?!" Casey drove his hands through his hair in frustration, ruffling the short curls into spikes. "The man runs the 'Ra down that way."

She could feel her shoulders creeping upward in defiance and shrugged to ward it off. "If I worried about displeasing them I'd never get my job done."

Casey snorted in disgust. "Displeasing is it? Those men are the law down there, yer wee policemen friends can't protect ye from the likes of them. An' nor can I."

"So we should just stand by and let people be killed, leave murders unsolved?"

"Ye don't understand because ye didn't grow up here," he said, eyes turning smoky gray.

"And that's my greatest sin, isn't it? That I wasn't born here, so I can never understand all the rules."

"Ye damn well *don't* understand the rules, an' that's the plain truth of it." In moments of great emotion his Belfast street brogue got the better of him, rendering his words harsh and angry.

"Sometimes I feel like I don't know you at all," she said, stung by his tone as well as the words.

"Aye well, there are days the feelin' is mutual in that respect."

"I am not talking about my job anymore," she said, with a certain mulishness that had become ingrained over her months of employment.

"My point exactly. Ye have your bits that belong only to you and I have mine. I come from a world, Pamela, where a man's wife would never dream of hiring out to his enemy."

She started back as if slapped. "Is that how you see me? As working for the enemy? If you're not involved with the IRA again, why should anyone be the enemy? And while we're on the topic, exactly what the hell were you doing coming in the house in the wee hours looking like you'd been dragged in by the cat, with charcoal all over your face and brick dust on your shoes?"

"Ye're checkin' my shoes after I've been out? Christ, it's good to know ye trust me."

"I do trust you, I'm just saying not all your activities seem designed to keep you alive and breathing, either."

"That's different."

"How is it different?" She stuck her hands on her hips, a full rolling boil of anger starting to bubble in her veins.

"Because I'm a man, I can take care of myself."

It was her turn to snort derisively. "And I can look after my own self as well. I've had plenty of practice, after all."

"What the hell is that supposed to mean?"

"You know what it means," she said coolly, while inwardly quaking at the thunderstorm that was brewing up dark and violent in his face.

"Jaysus woman!" his fist struck the countertop, making crumbly bits of earth roll across its polished surface. "Do ye not realize the 'Ra will have yer address on file now? That they'll have established yer routine about a week after ye started yer work an' may decide that ye constitute a good hit one of these days?" He was breathing in short angry bursts. "Ye can't be the naïve American over here, it's goin' to get ye killed."

"As," she said acidly, "I'm not allowed to be the naïve American in my own country, I guess you'll have to put up with me here, where I never seem to put a foot right."

Casey's eyes narrowed. "Not *allowed*—what the hell are ye inferrin' by that?"

"I'm not bothering with inference," she said, anger making her feel as if she was floating up off the floor, "I'm saying it straight. You couldn't handle living in Boston, so I brought you back here, where you promptly got in trouble again."

"I knew ye resented leavin' Boston, but I really didn't think ye'd go to these lengths to punish me for it."

"*Punish you*," she sputtered, "is that how you view my job? As a punishment to you?"

"Job," he spit the word out, "yer *job* almost got ye killed. Ye're still limpin' from it. Next time ye're not likely to be so lucky."

She shook her head in mute obstinacy. "I don't come from a world where a woman has to quit her job because it annoys her husband."

"Is that so?" Casey smiled, but there was nothing pleasant in the expression. "Well what do the rules in yer world say about entertainin' another man when yer husband is locked away from the world?"

"What the hell are you talking about?"

"Jamie."

She sighed. "Jamie?"

"Aye Robin tells me he was always about when I was gone."

"Robin?" she said in disbelief. "This is ridiculous. You asked Jamie to keep an eye out for me, which he did. I don't know whether to be flattered at what you seem to think is my ability to attract so many men at one time, or insulted by what you seem to be implying. But if you must know, one man seems more than what's required to plague the life from a woman."

"One man ought to be enough, but is he?" Under the fury that flushed his skin, there was a hesitancy in the words, as if he were afraid of getting an answer to the question.

"What are you saying?" she asked, the blood leaving her face in a rush.

"Only that Robin seems to have been about enough to be annoyed by Jamie, an' Jamie enough to feel Robin was on his territory. In fact the both of them seemed to get a wee bit territorial about ye."

"What's really bothering you here?" she asked, knowing he was skirting the edges of what he actually wanted to say.

He looked at her for a long time, the anger draining from his face to be replaced by something ineffably sad. She was suddenly very afraid of what he was about to say.

"Both you and I know, Pamela, that something is wrong at the core of our marriage. I've racked my brain for two years now trying to decide what it is. After we came back here I wanted to lay the blame at Jamie's door, but I knew something wasn't right between us even in Boston. Can ye tell me what it is? Because I tell ye, woman, I cannot live with not knowin' anymore. If ye let a worm chew at something long enough, eventually there's no substance left."

"I...I don't know what you're talking about," she said, feeling a wave of panic pass over her and lodge itself in the pit of her stomach.

He looked at her for a very long time across the expanse of kitchen which lay between them. "I wish I could believe ye," he said quietly. "But I find that I no longer can."

He moved past her and removed his coat from the hook beside the door.

"Where are you going?"

"I need to think," he said, "an' it wouldn't hurt you to have some space either."

"You're *leaving*?" she said in disbelief. "For how long, exactly?"

"I don't know," he said. "Until I find I can live with secrets or you decide to tell me what it is that's gone wrong between the two of us."

"If you go," she said in a desperation that was half anger and half panic, "don't bother coming back."

"Careful what ye wish for," he said, ramming his feet into his shoes so forcefully that the laces snapped, "ye just may get it."

He opened the door and looked back. "I'm goin' to the center to sleep, if ye—" he stopped taking in the look on her face, then continued in a nasty tone, "if ye need anything, perhaps ye can call on Jamie."

Chapter Seventy-three

Misses Robinson

THE MISSES GEORGINA AND EDWINA ROBINSON lived in a genteely rundown section of Protestant Belfast. Their house was a small, brick Georgian, with the highly desirable quality of being fully detached on a small patch of land that was well away from its neighbors.

The qualities of desirability and convenience were strictly in the eye of the beholder. And the beholder in this case was the Belfast IRA squadron, headed up by Joe Doherty, whose interests in said property were being represented by one Mr. Michael Gillivray, who was more commonly known to his own people as Robin Temple.

Mr. Gillivray was known to the Misses Robinson, as he had approached them some weeks ago with the notion of purchasing their property. While they had insisted in Miss Georgina's budgie chirp, and Miss Edwina's school mistress tones, that they couldn't possibly sell—as their family had owned and lived upon said land for the last one hundred years—still, they being both spinsters and rather lonely, found themselves succumbing to the charms of Mr. Gillivray and looking forward with a most girlish anticipation to his weekly visits.

Casey supposed that it was his own fault that he now found himself sitting in the starchy parlor of said ladies, watching Robin seduce a woman who likely had moths in her drawers.

The brief had been simple enough, and Robin had brought enough of such things to him over the course of the last six months that Casey wasn't surprised and had simply put the shrewd tactical side of his brain into gear and come up with the obvious solution. The problem the Belfast Brigade had presented him with was thus; if the local chapter of the IRA was to effectively protect the Catholic population and prepare itself for what appeared to be an inevitable conflagration with the Loyalist population, they needed the time and space to rebuild their ranks. A way was needed for senior IRA men to travel throughout Belfast and to meet away from the all-seeing eyes of military intelligence.

To Casey the answer was simple; since the IRA had always operated in areas that were staunchly republican, and therefore easily found and targeted for surveillance, the key was to move the safe houses and bases into areas of the city which were predominantly Protestant or middle class, or the rare patches of the city where there were no politically defined boundaries. To that end Robin, in the guise of Michael Gillivray, real estate speculator, had already managed to either buy or rent three separate residences in such areas. The Misses Robinson were his last assignment, and he had persuaded Casey to join him for this final sales pitch, using the argument that it was better than moping about the Youth Center, waiting for his wife to forgive him, or more unlikely yet, ask him to come home.

Casey had known bigger fools than himself in his lifetime. Just at the present moment, though, he couldn't think who any of them might be. His false moustache was itching fiercely and his curls, never well behaved at the best of times, were threatening a full out riot against the pomade with which he'd slicked them down. In addition, the wire-framed spectacles that Robin had provided him with were of a thickness to render sight next to impossible.

"Will ye have a wee spot more of the sherry, Mr. McArthur?" Miss Edwina asked him. Casey thought it was likely that if he had another wee spot of sherry he was going to have to throw up over the back of the antimacassared sofa. Nevertheless, he wasn't about to let queasiness get in the way of the republican cause. He bravely held his small glass out, thinking he would dump it in the potted ficus when Miss Edwina's stiff, damask covered back was turned.

He shifted, grimacing inwardly. There was a spring sticking into his backside, though he hardly saw how such a cement-like sofa could be in possession of a spring. Robin had disappeared into the kitchen about twenty minutes ago, ostensibly to help Miss Georgina wet the tea, but from the giggles and gasps emerging from said room, tea wasn't the only thing getting wet.

Miss Edwina had been left to entertain him, and a more sour-pussed, disapproving woman he could not have countenanced in all his life. She was the sort that could put coal in her arse and come up with a diamond and change a day later.

"Another biscuit, Mr. McArthur—Mr. McArthur, are ye perhaps hard of the hearin'?"

Casey started, realizing he was going to blow his cover. "Oh—erm—no thank ye, ma'am." The proffered biscuits were dreadfully stale and had a whiff of dust in their flavor that Casey was still trying to clear out of his throat.

He glanced toward the kitchen, mentally cursing Robin for leaving him to the mercy of this gray baggage. She'd a face on her like a steel clamp, hard and tight. She reminded him rather forcefully of Sister Ignatia, a grammar school nun who had delighted in the corporal punishment of small, wayward boys.

There seemed to be a distinct absence of noise in the kitchen suddenly. Goddamn Robin, did the man have no limits on where and when he would bed a woman? Though, admittedly, one had to admire the raw nerve of the man.

"D'ye know where yer sister and Mr. Gillivray have gone?" he asked, taking the spectacles off. Miss Edwina's eyes brightened considerably.

"I believe they've gone upstairs."

"Oh—I—urm, it's only that Mr. Gillivray and I have other appointments this afternoon." Casey stuck a finger inside the tight white collar in an effort to loosen it. He was imagining seven different highly imaginative ways in which he planned to kill Robin once they got out of here. "Other prospects, ye know," he finished weakly.

"Other prospects is it, Mr. McArthur? Or other women?"

"I am a married man, Miss Edwina," he said as prohibitively as he could manage.

"Are you, Mr. McArthur?"

"I am." He dug in his suit pocket for a handkerchief, feeling the first frisson of alarm in his innards. There was an avidity in Miss Edwina's face that he knew all too well.

"My sister has no knowledge of men in that respect."

"Erm...pardon me?"

"No bibilical knowledge," she replied, her voice nowhere near as stiff as it had been a moment before.

Casey choked slightly, and unthinkingly took a large swallow of the sherry. He gagged and then blurted out, "Yer sister is a virgin?!"

Good Christ, he peered rather desperately toward the stairs. The woman must be fifty if she was a day. While Casey had some experience of older women, anything beyond forty was outside his ken. Should he create a diversionary emergency on Robin's behalf?

"We both are," Miss Edwina replied stiffly, two small patches of red burning in her powdery cheeks. She eyed Casey in a significant manner.

Despite the relative coolness of the day, Casey felt a fine dew of sweat break out on his forehead. Dear God, the woman couldn't possibly think... could she? Apparently Miss Edwina, tongue lightly flicking the last of the stale biscuit crumbs from her bottom lip, could and did. He wished he'd not taken the spectacles off.

"I *haive* always preferred large men," she said, a faint sheen of perspiration glossing her own brow. Casey began to sweat in earnest. He had a brief vision of Pamela laughing fit to die if she could witness his current predicament. "My state," she continued, the spots in her cheeks flaming now, "is an impediment I should like to be relieved of. My sister will be insufferable if she is no longer a virgin and I remain one."

Despite the utter ridiculousness of the situation, Casey felt sorry for the prim, gray woman across from him. To never have known the love of a man, to never have been touched with tenderness and desire, seemed a terrible tragedy to him. He thought of the heat and joy of his own bed, what it was to know another in that way, and compassion for the woman, who was asking him to relieve her of her virginity, flooded through him.

"I'm flattered by the...ahem," he cleared his throat rather violently, "proposal. But as I said I am a married man, otherwise I should be glad to take you up on yer offer," he finished in a rush, aware that he was blushing to the roots of his hair.

"Would you indeed, Mr. McArthur? I hardly think so; despite the ridiculous disguise I can see that you are a fine looking man. I doubt ye'd spare me a backwards glance should you pass me on the street. Your wife, I assume, is beautiful?"

"Aye, she is," he said, feeling guilty for the answer.

"I thought so," she replied dryly.

"It's not why I love her, though."

She narrowed her eyes at him, tilting her long face to one side in a thoughtful manner. "No, I don't suppose it is, but I've nay doubt it's part of why ye desire her."

Casey opened his mouth to deny this, and then paused. He rarely thought of Pamela as a being with separatable qualities. But he supposed if he were honest with himself, he did take a certain male pride in the way she looked. And that a woman as beautiful as she was found him desirable. But it was so much more than that; without her he was only half of a puzzle, with her the picture completed itself. Yet when he thought of her; the fine white skin, the silky dark hair, the long legs wrapped around him and—he cut his thoughts off abruptly, realizing that the woman was regarding every expression that crossed his face.

"It is part of my desire for her," he said softly, "but I think only a small part."

"I have often wished," she said wistfully, the severe face relaxed into an expression that was oddly attractive, "to have a man look at me with desire. A good man. He wouldn't need to be especially handsome, just kind. It doesn't seem so much to ask, does it?"

"No, it doesn't," Casey agreed.

She gave him a disconcertingly direct look then, pulse visible in the wrinkly hollow of her throat. "But to have a man such as yourself look at me with desire, well that I think might be a very fine thing indeed, Mr. McArthur."

"My name isn't Mr. McArthur."

She shook her head. "No, I think it's best if I don't know your real name. I'm a dreadful liar and when the police ask me, I'd just as soon not know who you actually are."

It was at this rather delicate juncture that Casey noticed a man was standing in the entry to the dark parlor, or rather filling the entry from one side to the other. And he was looking straight at Casey, with an expression as though he'd just caught a whiff of rotten fruit.

"Edwina, where is your sister?!"

Miss Edwina started, sending her sherry flying along with a tumble of stale biscuit onto the cabbage rose rug. "I—she—" she shot a look of pure panic in Casey's direction, as though imploring that he come up with an innocent explanation for the whereabouts of her sister.

"I—I believe that she had taken Mr. Gillivray upstairs to check on a bit of dry rot," he said rather unconvincingly.

"Mr. McArthur, this is my brother Edward," Miss Edwina said rather weakly.

"Mr. McArthur, is it?" The walrus-faced man seemed even less gullible than his sister, and Casey started to assess the distances to the various exits, including the window behind him.

At this unfortunate and apparently cursed moment, a sound that was either a woman being murdered or in the throes of ecstasy issued loudly from the upstairs. The large man turned, looking like nothing so much as an apoplectic walrus, all long quivering moustaches and red, swelling fury. At present, he seemed in great danger of exploding.

Casey stood, estimating his odds of getting to the door and out before the man could lay hands to him. If he left Robin to die, he supposed his odds were fairly good. Unfortunately his Catholic conscience overrode his survival instincts and he found himself saying, "Sorry about this, man," before knocking the walrus man to the side and bounding up the stairs, just ahead of the roars of outrage.

He didn't pause to open the bedroom door, merely gave it a good kick and yelled at a very startled Robin, "Fer fock sake, RUN!"

Robin, who was rather too familiar with this sort of situation, reacted swiftly, leaping off the bed and leaving Miss Georgina clutching the sheet around her virginal bosom. At least Casey—having noted that her knickers were still in place—assumed she hadn't yet given that commodity up to Robin.

Robin paused only long enough to grab his pants and shirt and was down the hall behind Casey like Satan and his pitchfork were directly behind.

There was no way back down the stairs, but Miss Edwina had made it up the stairs ahead of the enraged walrus and waved them toward a gabled window. Casey, having noted the exterior of the house on their arrival, knew the window sat just below the roof ridge.

He pushed Robin, half-naked and cursing, out the window ahead of him, hoping the man had the wits to scramble up to the ridge and not down toward the gutters. Casey paused, one leg over the sash and leaned back to give Miss Edwina a swift kiss on the cheek.

"Sure an' it's been a great pleasure meetin' ye, Edwina."

She flushed and put a hand to her parchment cheek and then he was up and away scrambling for the peak of the roof.

He could see Robin's pale form swing off the peak into the branches of a pine tree that grew mercifully close to the house.

Casey ran along the ridge, thanking God and the fates that the tile was dry and rough, and not slick with wet. He was halfway down the tree when he heard Robin drop from the lower branches onto the ground. Then he heard the distinct *zing* of a bullet whizzing past his ear. He half slid, half fell down the remainder of the tree, hitting the ground at a run behind Robin who was still barefoot, and shaking a fist at the house.

"Run, ye daft bastard!" Casey bellowed, cuffing the back of Robin's head as he flew past him. They vaulted the fence in unison, heading for the thick woods that bordered the property.

Robin kept up a steady stream of curses as rocks cut his feet and branches slapped them both in the face, arms, and legs. Another bullet zinged past and a large branch dropped from a tree and glanced off Casey's shoulder. The pungent tang of resin filled his nostrils, the pain in his shoulder sharp as the scent. His eyes were streaming and his lungs burning, but he didn't dare slow down the slightest bit. He did, however, make a note to quit smoking by tomorrow morning at the latest.

They ran for what seemed a small eternity, crashing through brush and blundering through a stream that made them both gasp with the freezing wet that splashed up on their clothes, and in Robin's case, bare skin. Casey no longer had any notion where they might be, when suddenly Robin stopped abruptly ahead of him. The woods ended on the edge of a moonlit field that opened out under the night.

Behind them, the outraged shouts had died away; the only noise that of the wind ruffling the leafy tree crowns and small twitters of birds disturbed in their precipitous wake.

Casey bent over his knees and drew in one deep shaky breath after another. When he stood upright again, Robin was still half winded but already patting his pockets down for cigarettes.

"Christ, I haven't had that much fun in years," Robin said. Finding no cigarettes, he pulled his pants back on and shrugged his shirt over his head, not bothering with the buttons.

Casey flopped in the grass beside him, laughing. "The expression on the man's face, he looked like a bloody gargoyle that'd swallowed a lime pickle. Here take mine; I think ye dropped yers when we ran." He tossed his cigarettes over and Robin caught them neatly out of the air.

"Well I owe the bastard, I was thinkin' I was really goin' to have to bed the old goose did somethin' not intervene soon."

"I don't suppose they'll consider sellin' to Mr. Gillivray now," Casey said, feeling a fizzing elation in his veins now that the danger to their lives was past.

Robin laughed, rubbing his hands hard through his hair and releasing a shower of fragrant pine needles. "No, I think we'll have to make ourselves exceeding scarce in that neighborhood from now on. How accurate do ye think the sisters will be in their descriptions to the police?"

"Very," Casey said, "yon Miss Edwina was lookin' me over as though I were the prize pig at the autumn fair an' she the head judge on pork flesh."

The two of them were silent for a bit after that, regaining their breath and equilibrium, finishing off their cigarettes. The silence was punctuated by the occasional chuckle as each of them remembered some small detail of the recent fiasco. Casey imagined how he'd tell Pamela, which details to share and which to spare and then, remembering that he wasn't likely to be talking to her about anything in the near future, felt a sudden deflation of the dark fizzing in his blood. He sighed heavily, expelling the last of the smoke from his lungs.

Robin, correctly interpreting the nature of his sigh, said, "Go home an' apologize, ye wee fool." He blew out a perfect smoke ring that wobbled in the air before dissipating into the night.

"Would that it were that simple. I'd crawl over a mile of broken glass if I thought she'd take me back an' that be an end to it."

"An' why shouldn't it be an end to it?"

Casey paused, but the need to tell someone, to relieve for a minute the itch that had ridden under his skin for the last two years, overcame his normal reserve. "I wish I knew. I can only tell ye that somethin' lies between Pamela an' me, that I've felt for some time an' yet I don't know what it is. Ye'd have to understand, when we first met, I'd never known anyone like her. She just came into my life as though she'd been meant for me from the day she was born. It's been that natural all along, an' she'd only ever kept the one secret from me, an' that to protect me. But I always felt as if I had all of her, despite Jamie bein' in her life. Then somethin' shifted, I'm not even sure when I noticed it, an' I've felt like I've not got all of her anymore."

"D'ye not think," Robin flipped over onto his stomach, propped himself on his elbows and looked Casey in the face, "that ye're askin' a wee bit much? She loves ye man, an' ye love her. It can't be a fairytale all the time."

"That's just it, 'twas never a fairytale. It's more real than anything I've known in my life."

Robin cocked a brow at him. "It'll be yer own business I suppose, but I don't see the sense of sleepin' cold every night an' mopin' about like a worm without a puddle when ye could just go home an' say ye're sorry."

"'Tisn't that simple," Casey repeated stubbornly.

"Christ, there are times I think ye're the biggest fockin' eejit this side of the Lagan. Ye're a lucky bastard an' make no mistake of it. I've seen the two of yez, ye're daft for one another. I've never had that, never loved a woman that way and sure as fock have never had one love me that way either."

"Never?" Casey asked, turning his head to the side. Robin was gazing far out over the dark fields, bones arcing shadows against the white skin.

"Never," Robin echoed, a hollow reverberation at the core of the one word that hurt Casey to hear.

"I'm sorry to hear it, man. Still," his voice wobbled the slightest bit, "I think I'm not ready to go home just yet."

Robin eyed him speculatively. "A week or two on the road might go some ways toward curin' ye."

"Playin' ye mean?" Casey asked, feeling a sudden tingle in his fingers for the bodhran, an instrument he'd scarce picked up in the last five years.

"Aye, playin' an' singin'. Unless ye've not the lungs for it anymore." There was a glint in Robin's eyes that made Casey feel sixteen again for one fleeting second.

"Oh I've the lungs for it, question is can *you* still seduce a room?"

Robin grinned, teeth a flash in the night. "Ye just watch me boyo, an' I'll show ye how it's done."

Chapter Seventy-four
God and Green Apples

THE GARDEN HAD BECOME A PLACE of refuge since Casey's abrupt departure. It was one of the few things that gave her peace; to work amongst the bee-laden lavender and the musty thyme, to weed and hoe and carefully dig up the first new potatoes, to water and tend to each plant, to deadhead the flowers and keep the waterweed from damming up the stream. Paudeen often joined her there, broad woolly back and sober black face a comfort, as he munched placidly on the grass at the edge of the plot of furrowed earth.

Finbar was in high dudgeon, as Lawrence had felt he should stay behind for protective reasons on the nights he was in town with Casey. The dog had taken up residence in the shed, refusing all overtures and admonitions to come in at night.

She was employed in pulling up garlic sets when Lawrence's bright ginger head appeared like a small sun under the branches of the ash tree. She stood, back stiff and hands pungent with garlic. Lawrence had become a real diplomat these last few weeks, making every effort to repair relations between her and Casey.

She watched him walk down the winding road. The boy looked as though he'd stretched another two inches in the short time since she'd last seen him. He was hovering about the top of Casey's ear as it was. She sighed. The hems on his pants would have to come down again. And he'd need new shirts; his knobby wrists were sticking out of all his jerseys and sweaters. A new coat too, she thought, as he walked across the yard.

Finbar had emerged from his hidey-hole, bulbous nose high up in the air, sniffing. If joy could be said to infuse the entire being of a dog, then joy did just that to Finbar. He put his head back and emitted an unearthly howl, and then flew across the yard, looking like a bundle of gray rags that had been shot from the mouth of a cannon. He knocked Lawrence flat on his back, and then proceeded to lick his face madly, wriggling with canine ecstasy the entire time.

Lawrence hugged the dog fiercely in an effort to subdue him somewhat.

Finbar, however, had added a high-pitched whine to his mad wriggling, and Lawrence was forced to crawl away and grasp the garden gate to get back on his feet.

"Jaysus Murphy," he gasped, as Finbar jumped up and put his front paws on his shoulders. "Down boy, down I say!"

Finbar finally sat, leaning his bony frame into Lawrence's leg, the great brown eyes fixed in adoration to the boy's face.

"You ought to take him back with you," she said. "He's mourning your absence something fierce. I'll be fine here. Paudeen will let me know if someone's about who oughtn't to be."

"Has someone been about? Have ye felt as though someone's watchin' the house again?" Lawrence gave her a sharp look, trying to assess her for untruths.

"No. For heaven's sake, do you really think I wouldn't tell you if that was the case?"

"Hmmph," was the doubt-filled response. Then he dug in his pocket, the long hand emerging with a fistful of crumpled bills which he held out toward her.

"What," she raised her eyebrows, "is that for?"

He cleared his throat uncomfortably, pale skin flushing scarlet. "He said 'twas for the hay, an' to make certain that Mr. Guderson has put enough aside for ye."

"Got you doing his dirty work, has he then?"

"No, he's not. He told me that he'd not stand in the way of my visitin' ye, as what had taken place wasn't to be my concern. Doesn't mean I can't bring ye a bit of money; he's only tryin' to make certain things stay on keel here."

She sighed, feeling suddenly tired and frustrated all at once. "I'm sorry, Lawrence. Come in the house, I'll make you something to eat."

"Oh no, don't trouble yerself, I just ate."

She merely raised a doubtful eyebrow at him. The child was never full.

"Do ye mind if I take a few of my things while I'm here?"

"Of course not," she said, though the question made her slightly sick, as though the split were of a more permanent nature than she'd thought. Had Casey said something to make the boy think that was the case? She fought back the urge to ask Lawrence about Casey's state of mind. She wasn't quite desperate enough for that, though admittedly, given another day or two she might be willing to sink to that low.

She followed Lawrence into the house, Finbar trailing on his feet and Paudeen bleating loudly as he gambolled after them all. Lawrence paused on the porch to rub Rusty's head. The cat miaowed loudly several times and she wondered irritably why every one of them had to make their disconsolation so desperately clear.

"Ye've changed the lock," Lawrence said with a frown, noting the shiny brass deadlock that glowed brightly against the dark green door. "Why?"

"You know the old one stuck all the time; it needed changing. I just finally got around to having it done."

Lawrence treated her to a narrow look and then stepped through the door.

She stayed in the kitchen while he rustled about in his bedroom, occupying herself with packing up a bag of things she thought he and Casey might need.

Lawrence emerged with a mess of clothes, bedding and records, the strong smell of Polo mints hovering about him.

"Were you smoking in there?"

"No, I swear I wasn't. I think I've just exchanged one addiction for another. Can't do without these bloody mints now."

"Do you want me to run you back into town?" she asked, taking the clothes from him and folding them neatly in a stack.

"No 'tisn't necessary. I got a ride out with Owen, an' Gert says she's got business in town an' will run me back if I meet her up head the lane within the hour."

"Oh, so you're not staying. I thought you could have supper here with me." She knew the disappointment was palpable in her voice, but couldn't quite find it in herself to regret it just now.

He looked miserable. "I can't, I've made plans with a few of the lads from school tonight."

"It's all right," she smiled brightly, though her throat felt unaccountably prickly. "I hope you know none of this is anything to do with you, Lawrence. I'm sorry that you've got caught in the middle of our problems."

He gave her an apologetic look, narrow frame all but invisible behind the roll of clothes and bedding that he held against his chest. "'Tisn't that I think ye're in the wrong, I don't know exactly what the two of ye have fallen out over, but it's only that he needs my help at the center an' all. An' if I'm stayin' here at night an' spendin' all day there..." he shrugged helplessly, face the picture of misery.

"I appreciate that you're in an awkward position, Lawrence. If you want to stay with him, I won't be offended or upset. It won't," she tied a length of twine around the neat roll of blankets she'd sorted for him, "hurt for someone to keep an eye on him."

"If ye'd just let him come home, I'm sure he could explain himself."

"I'm sure," she replied tartly, getting up off her knees, "he could. But until he's got something different to say for himself than he did last time, I don't want to hear it."

There had been a rather spectacularly unsuccessful phone call mid-week between the two of them, when she had ostensibly called him to ask a rather stiff question about the amount of hay needed for the oncoming fall and winter.

"It's hard for him too, ye know," Lawrence said, one foot over the doorstep.

"He misses ye somethin' awful an' he's lost half a stone in weight already. The man cooks like he's expectin' a small army to tea each day, but he never eats any of it."

"Lawrence, I love him too," she said softly, "but it's not that simple. It's a matter of trust, and I—"

Lawrence put a up thin hand. "I don't think I should hear this, it's hard enough dealin' between the two of ye not knowin' what's goin' on. If I do know, though, I'll have to start takin' sides an' I'm not goin' to do that. The two of ye are difficult enough when I don't have a clue, it'll be right impossible if ye start to make some sort of sense."

She handed him a travel bag, grimly refusing to meet his eyes. "His shaving kit's in there and a couple of sweaters, it's chilly in the evenings and he's been prone to colds since he had bronchitis."

Lawrence took the case and said in an uncommonly gentle tone, "The two of you are mad, ye know that don't ye?"

"Aye," she sighed, "I know it."

"He and Robin are goin' on a bit of a run down the west coast, playin' the pubs." Lawrence rummaged in his left hand pocket, "I've written down the towns they'll be in, ye'll note they're playin' Davy O'Brien's."

"I'll note it," she said, raising an eyebrow.

Lawrence shrugged, a faint flush staining the bridge of his nose. "He said he'd taken ye there once. It seemed a good memory, he'd a smile when he spoke of it."

"Did he then?"

"I figure ye're angry now, but that date's a week an' more away, ye might feel differently when the time comes."

She smiled at the boy. "You're too smart for your own good, Lawrence."

He returned the smile with one of his truly heart-stopping grins, that transformed his delicate features into something akin to the first real sunny day of spring.

"Think about it, will ye?"

"I will," she said, and then stood watching as he walked down the laneway, long legs gobbling up the ground, until the bright ginger head disappeared into the gloom of the pines.

She sighed. Suddenly the house felt very empty. And the prickle in her spine that was her constant companion of late returned the minute Lawrence disappeared from view. She hadn't quite told the truth about the replacement of the locks. True, they had been stiff, and required oiling on such a constant basis that changing them had been on the to-do list that Casey had left hanging on the fridge.

She had bought them, and Mr. Guderson had changed them for her. The chill feeling of being observed would have been enough to warrant changing them, merely for the sense of security it gave her, however false that sense might be. It was the impression that someone had been *in* the house, though, that had spurred her to get the locks changed.

It had happened twice now, since Casey had left. The first time she'd been away in the village, shopping, and had stopped to have dinner with Owen and Gert. It was dark when she had pulled the car up to the house.

Inside, at first, she'd thought someone was still in the house and she had almost turned around, got in the car and driven straight in to the youth center. Instead, she chided herself and turned all the lights on, called the dog in, and checked every lock in the house.

Nothing was disturbed, nothing was missing, and yet the unease remained. As if the air had been displaced in her absence with an energy that was, if not malevolent, at least very disturbing.

The next morning she checked the wood where the watcher had been before. There wasn't so much as a bent stalk of grass disturbed. Yet the skin of her backbone said different.

The second time was after a full day's work, during which she'd photographed an ancient set of remains that had turned up at the base of Black Mountain. It was a very old burial site, though the person, if the missing skull was anything to go by, had met a violent end. She had been musing on the possible history of those bones as she came in her front door, and so wasn't paying a great deal of attention to her surroundings.

Stepping in and placing her camera bags on the floor, she had heard an audible click that sounded like the back door closing. She had run to the kitchen without thinking, for the big window provided a panoramic view of the yard and wood beyond. Outside there had been no movement though, other than the gate creaking in the wind.

Finbar, however, had been missing, though he'd turned up at Mr. Guderson's, wet and dirty, some hours later. That, however, wasn't proof of anything sinister. Still, she had the locks changed before she went to bed that night.

She stood now, gazing at the empty road, rubbing the silky fur on Finbar's ears. She was suddenly relieved that Lawrence had not taken him. The dog was agitated, whining softly in the base of this throat, wanting to run down the road after Lawrence.

"I know, boy," she said soothingly. "I miss them too."

It would be twilight soon. She shut the curtains firmly and then scooped up the dog's leash and the keys to the car. She would go spend the evening with Owen and Gert, and maybe this time, when Gert pressed her to stay in their spare room, she would take her up on it.

CASEY WAS SITTING AT THE KITCHEN TABLE, a sheaf of street plans laid out in front of him, and an untouched cup of tea at his right hand. There was something wrong with the layout that was before him, but despite the nagging pain behind his eyes from staring at the papers, the problem still eluded him. It was with relief that he heard the backdoor into the kitchen open and Lawrence's puppy-like gait sound across the floor.

"Where've ye been?" he asked sharply, as Lawrence came in trailing the scents of dirt and fresh air.

"I've gone home for a few minutes," the boy replied, returning Casey's tone with a very blue look over the top of an armload of bags and bedding. "Someone ought to be checkin' to make sure she's all right, an' seein' as ye're too stubborn to bother, I went myself."

"I told ye, ye're welcome to stay there with her."

Lawrence merely raised a ginger brow to this statement, as if to say Casey wasn't to be trusted on his own.

Casually Casey lifted his arms off the street plans, allowing them to roll up of their own accord before he asked in a friendlier tone, "What do ye have there?"

"Pamela sent along a few odds an' ends for the two of us. Why," Lawrence tipped everything willy-nilly onto the table surface, "don't ye look for yerself?"

Casey grunted, noting the boy's inquisitive look at the sheaf of papers he'd been looking over. "Alright then, let's see what we have here."

He itemized the contents of the bag as he piled things on the kitchen table. "Biscuits, scones," he sniffed them, "an' fresh baked too. Green apples an' carrots. Does the woman think we're mules?"

"I believe she mentioned something about the hind end of one," Lawrence said, taking one of the apples and biting through its crisp skin. He propped his size thirteens on the table, slouching comfortably in a chair.

Casey snorted and gave Lawrence's feet a smack. "Put yer feet down, we're not beasts here. Reached the name callin' stage, has she? Means her temper is coolin' a bit. Another month or so an' she'll maybe let me through the door." He continued piling items on the table. A box of Lyons tea was joined by a small bag of sugar, his favorite mug, a bottle of peppermint soap, and half a dozen towels. "She's given me the guest towels, that's not a good sign." Eight packets of raisins followed, as well as two Aran wool sweaters. He shook his head over the sweaters. "It's June, what's the woman thinkin'? Or are they meant as a sort of hair shirt?"

"She said ye're prone to colds since ye had the bronchitis."

Casey surveyed the heaped table with a jaundiced eye. "Well she's seen to it all; body, mind an' spirit. I imagine this is meant to tell me I'm incapable of lookin' after myself."

"I think it was more meant as a way of sayin' she missed ye," Lawrence observed, grabbing another apple and a scone. "Ye've missed somethin'—here," Lawrence tossed a small black bag to him. Casey caught it and knew what it was the second the worn velvet touched his fingers.

He turned from the boy, feeling the unfamiliar pricking of tears at the back of his eyes. Damn the woman, did she have to prove that she knew him as no one else ever could? Did she mean to bring him to his knees and still not allow him into his own home? His hand squeezed convulsively around the little bag, the contents making small dents in his palm.

"What is it?" Lawrence asked quietly.

"My daddy's rosary beads," Casey replied, voice tight, "she knows I don't sleep well without them."

Lawrence wisely held his tongue from response. Though Casey knew the lad's sharp eyes missed little, and he likely had a good idea of just why Casey's back was still turned to him. Casey took a minute to pull himself together and then asked in a gruff tone, "Did she look well?"

"No," Lawrence said bluntly, "she looks as if she hasn't slept a proper minute since ye left, and she's lost weight."

"Aye, the woman never eats well when she's on her own." He took a frustrated breath and scrubbed his hands vigorously through his hair, wishing he could rub the very thoughts from his mind. He turned back to Lawrence, summoning up a grim smile that he was fairly certain convinced neither of them.

Lawrence stood, shrugging his coat back on and tucking another apple into his left hand pocket. Casey treated him to a narrow look.

"Where are ye off to? Ye've not had a decent dinner, nor have ye shown me yer math problems from last night."

The boy's eyes shifted. "Just out with a few of the lads. I'll be back before ye close up an' I'll take another of those scones with me. The math sheet is on my bed, ye can check yerself, I got full marks. I've got an essay due on O'Connell for end of term that I'll need yer help with, s'due next Friday," this last was muffled by dint of Lawrence breaking off half a scone in one bite.

Casey fixed the boy with a gimlet glare. "Don't be tryin' to wheedle round me by flatterin' me with promises of needin' help with yer history. Ye'll be back an hour before I close up here, an' ye'll make a sandwich before ye go. There's ham left from last night an' some fresh milk."

Lawrence suddenly fixed him with a suspicious glance. "An' why are ye bein' so reasonable? Have ye business to attend to tonight?" His eyes flicked to the big sheets of drafting paper that Casey had rolled up when he arrived.

"That's not yer worry," Casey said firmly, "just be back when I told ye, or ye'll be better acquainted with the four walls of yer room then ye ever thought possible."

"Ye can't lock me up," Lawrence said indignantly.

"Ye just try me, boyo," Casey said, sending a stern look in Lawrence's direction, "ye just try me an' see what I can an' cannot do."

Lawrence returned the glare, but to his frustration, found he couldn't stare the man down. "I'll be back before curfew."

After Lawrence left, Casey unrolled the street plans and picked up his pencil. After five minutes of staring blankly at the paper and tapping the pencil on his forehead, however, he gave it up as a lost cause. It was no damn good, he couldn't focus, couldn't sleep, didn't have an appetite. He simply wanted to go home, sleep in his own bed, eat at his own table, put his arms around his wife, and listen to the damned perditious cat howl at the moon.

Several times during the week, he'd fought the urge to crawl home on his knees and beg her forgiveness, but the one time he *had* gone, he'd discovered that his keys no longer fit into the locks. And so he found himself firmly back in the anger zone. That he was locked out of the house he'd built with his own two hands left him speechless with fury.

Then why had he given Lawrence the dates for where and when he and Robin would be playing? He sighed. Likely for the same reason she'd sent over all the bits and bobs for him and the boy, because neither one of them wanted to say the word, but the truth was they were both sorry and missing the other. The woman had a rare temper, it was true, but the things she'd said—then again he'd said a few things himself that made him hot with shame just to remember.

His comments about Jamie, for instance. Why he always threw the man in her face every time he was angered, he didn't know, or rather he did, but didn't want to face that it was jealousy, pure and simple. On a gut level, he knew she'd never cheated on him with the man, and yet, there was a bond there, one that went back years before he'd been in her life, and it bothered him, festering just under the surface like a wound you couldn't see but could damn well feel.

The man loved his wife, Casey could see that clearly. But Jamie had never, to his knowledge, done anything about that love, as much as it must have pained him. He understood it, but it rankled nonetheless. The real rub lay in the fact that Pamela loved the man back, yet even this he understood, for from the little she'd revealed of her past, it seemed Jamie had been the one friend she'd known in her growing years, when impressions went deep and stayed long. That and, he admitted ruefully, the man was not without his charms.

Casey was no fool; he knew men desired his wife. He had known that from the first, for desire had been the thing he'd felt himself from the day he first saw her. He'd wanted her more than he'd ever wanted anything in his life, more than he'd wanted to get out of prison, even more than he wanted happiness for his brother and some kind of peace for his country. It had scared him, still did at times, that one could need another human being to that extent. But he'd taken comfort in the fact that she was his—his to keep, bound to him by vows that went beyond the confines of mortality. And she loved him, of that he had no doubt, loved him in a way that made him wonder why God had decided to so bless him.

Then there was the wee matter of her job. It scared the hell out of him and that was all there was to that. She didn't understand the sort of fire she was playing with, and fire in Belfast didn't just burn, it incinerated. He acknowledged that she was a grown woman capable of making her own decisions, but she was also his wife. It was his job to see her safe. That was what a man did—looked after those who needed his care. Whether they appreciated that care or not was another matter entirely. Why couldn't she understand that?

And admittedly he was angry, and the establishment of the safe houses and areas where the rebels could run to ground had been a small way to vent that anger, to feel that somehow he was doing *something*. That the bastards had not completely unmanned them individually, as a neighborhood, and as a nation.

Part of his rage was a leftover from internment and another part was a gut-level response to the events of Bloody Sunday. Because there was no other way to respond to such an act of inhumanity. The only thing men such as those who'd opened fire on an unarmed crowd understood was a return of their own brutality.

Two wrongs might not make a right, but sometimes it seemed the only language that the other side understood.

He returned his attention to the papers beneath his hands, firmly blocking out thoughts of his wife and his home. His mind turned as a well-oiled machine to the intricacies of revolution and its tiny, yet crucial details. Such as how a man might design a workable drop system that wouldn't require too many extraneous people. The British had discovered their last system far too quickly and damning documents had found their way to the barracks, resulting in the arrest and imprisonment of two key IRA figures in Belfast. Which led Casey to think there was a mole within the ranks.

He had a notion just who the mole might be, and thought he might know how to smoke him out of hiding with the proper bait. It would just take a bit of patience and cunning on his own part.

Chapter Seventy-five

On the Craic

THE PUB WAS FILLED TO CAPACITY by the time Pamela arrived, light and raucous voices spilling out onto the humid summer night. It was after nine and almost the hour that the Irish considered appropriate for getting down to the serious business of music and dedicated drinking. The air inside the pub, impossible as it seemed, was twice as thick and heavy as the air outside. The smell of spilled ale, whiskey sweat, and the general fug of too many happy human bodies in a small space, was overwhelming. She plucked at the bodice of her dress, looking about for a seat in a dark corner, hoping to remain invisible for as long as possible.

It soon became apparent that finding a seat was akin to locating the Holy Grail, and after politely refusing the not-so-polite offers of several male laps, she settled for wedging herself into the dark overhang of a set of stairs. She was barely thus accommodated when there was a stir in the thickest of the throng of people. Robin had taken his seat, and in accordance a hush started to ripple across all assembled. It was their third night here and obviously, the word was spreading. Robin looked cool and nerveless as he set about preparing his fiddle for the first set. Of Casey, there was no sign.

Robin drew the bow in a long shudder across the strings, the extended note shivering across everyone's nerves, setting the anticipation. He settled the instrument more comfortably in the notch of his collarbone, experimenting with another drawn-out note before nodding with satisfaction. He paused for a second, letting the crowd fall into a strung silence, then shot a look of pure blue devilment across his fiddle and launched full throttle into a hard, rollicking tune made to race in the blood. Pamela could feel her heartbeat begin to pulse along with the rhythm, could see others around her start to tap their toes and clap their hands in time with the merciless beat.

She caught sight of Casey seconds later as he took his stool next to Robin, settling his bodhran upon his knee. His fingers, slightly bent, splayed the surface, testing the tension of the skin and he shifted his shoulders under the crisp, white material of his shirt, readying himself for his part in the song.

Robin paused for a half-heartbeat, giving Casey his cue.

While the fiddle rode the stretch of nerves directly along the spine, the drum settled itself in the more primitive parts, low in the belly, deep in the blood. It was primal, calling up the animal that had once danced when fire was the only light for darkness. It was also the most sexual instrument known to man. There was a reason, she knew, that drummers were second only to lead singers in allure. Casey understood the dark nature of the instrument and played it accordingly.

Together the two men performed like nothing she'd ever seen, the energy of one seeming to drive the other. People were clapping, feet flying beneath their chairs, a few up already and dancing, drawing rhythms and patterns with the click of bone against wood that they'd known since childhood. She, however, remained still, despite the hard thrum in her blood and the twitching of her nerves. Casey had yet to look up, but she knew he was as aware of her presence as if she'd sat upon his knee. So she watched him, riveted, and waited.

The tipper, tucked neatly between his index and middle fingers, flew in a blur across the taut skin of the drum, the rhythm flying faster and faster, building to a seemingly impossible crescendo. Both he and Robin's shirts were soaked through by the end of the first melody, faces gleaming with sweat, and the two of them positively crackling with the joy of performance. Robin's bow was such a flurry of movement she half-expected to see sparks and smoke pour off it. '*The man can play like the very devil himself,*' Casey had said, and witnessing it, she was inclined to believe that even Old Scratch would be hard put to match the sheer madness of Robin on the bow and strings. His eyes were shut tight in concentration, brow furrowed, tongue protruding slightly between brilliant white teeth and she knew every woman in the room was wondering if his intensity on the fiddle would be matched between the sheets.

She knew, though, that Robin was completely unaware of the women in the room at present. The music had swallowed him entirely, his every cell and synapse brought to its service.

He met Casey's eyes suddenly, in a look she knew they must have shared a thousand times as boys, and got the answering nod. Robin slowed the tempo, skipping into a new tune without a discernible pause. A flurry of notes flew off the strings like liquid silver and then Casey answered it boldly on the bodhran.

Robin played with the audience, allowing the notes to fall down to the cadence of a lullaby, lulling them all, soothing the blood, tempering them to bend to his will, shaping them to the fit of his palm. It was a fleeting power, but in the moment, awesome in its scope.

They played a set of nine songs through, without pause, seamlessly sewing the end of one song onto the beginning of another. It was a river without respite, running its listeners onto shoals of emotion, extracting them without mercy. They seduced, they coaxed, they enchanted, they enthralled, and not a person in the building wished to be released from the spell. But even Robin's bowing hand had its limits and at the end of the ninth tune, by some unspoken agreement they stopped, laying their instruments down. Robin paused to drain a glass of ale, filled to the point of foam flowing down his hand.

"A song or two more," Robin said, wiping his forehead down with the ale-soaked hand, "an' we'll take a break. Any requests?"

A number of shouts greeted this question, but a comely girl in a low-cut blouse said something in a sassy tone that caught Robin's eye and ear. He sent a wink and a nod in her direction before standing and speaking a word or two over his shoulder to Casey.

Casey in turn picked up his penny whistle, blew a testing breath into it, then nodded at Robin. Robin closed his eyes, head tilted to the side, feeling his way into the opening notes of *Four Green Fields*. Pamela had heard it many times, it was a standard in Irish folk music, but she had never heard it as Robin sang it. He gave himself over to the emotion of it fully, drawing every person in the room with him to those four green fields red with blood and an old woman's grief. His throat throbbed with the pain, crying to heaven then dropping to a whisper of raw feeling. Under his voice the old woman of the song became the Ireland of legend, the one each person still wanted to believe in. Her four sons the four ancient kingdoms of Ireland, the final field that lay in bondage—Ulster always un-free. There was not a dry eye in the house. The man was pure *seanachais*, born to mesmerize with his music. Casey kept the penny whistle deliberately low, following each note hand in hand with Robin. The melody wove like tattered ribbon round the anguish of Robin's words, and the audience succumbed entirely, giving the proprietorship of their hearts over to the two musicians.

Robin bled the song for all it was worth, ending on a hoarse whisper, head down, eyes still closed as if in prayer. The silence was all encompassing. Around Pamela, no one even took a breath. Casey sat still, penny whistle at rest on his knee. Then Robin's head came up, blue eyes open, a weary smile in place. The place exploded in a riot of applause and shouts. Robin nodded his thanks and sat, looking suddenly like a mere mortal, and an exhausted one at that.

"One more then," he said when the crowd quieted, holding up a hand to stave off requests. "Casey, ye've a song to sing for yer wife, have ye not?"

Pamela froze in horror at the words, looking for an escape route. However, a knotted chain of shoulders, arms, heads and legs presented no obvious pathway to deliverance.

Casey whispered to Robin and Robin tucked the fiddle back under his chin. Casey took a swallow of his ale and then, seeking his wife's eyes through the thick haze of smoke and overly warm bodies, began to sing, voice pure and untainted as a first fall of snow.

> *'Come over the hills my bonnie Irish lass,*
> *Come over the hills to your darlin'*
> *You choose the rose love*
> *And I'll make the vow*
> *And I'll be your true love forever.*
> *Red is the rose that in your garden grows*
> *Fair is the lily of the valley*
> *Clear is the water that flows from the Boyne*
> *And my love is fairer than any...'*

Beneath the words the fiddle played lightly with heartstrings, Robin knowing well enough to let Casey's voice do its job.

She knew heads were turning her way, but couldn't see clearly through the tears that clouded her vision. Damn the man, he always knew how to get round her. She knew, though, despite the fact that he was very aware the song would soften her up, he also meant every word he sang, for such was the nature of his emotion. He stood, beginning the second verse, voice stronger, filled with longing, eyes burning a corridor direct between them.

> *'Twas down by Killarney's green woods that we strayed*
> *The moon and the stars they were shining*
> *The moon shone its rays on her locks of raven hair*
> *And she swore she'd be my love forever...'*

He began to move toward her, people melting away before the force of his voice and emotion. She could feel, as a physical entity, the pull of his need through the heat and smoke that wavered between them. She dashed away her tears with an impatient hand. Damn him for doing this in front of an entire roomful of strangers. His body could call her own without words and she knew the chemistry between them was palpable in the air, that people could see it, feel it. It was like being naked and on view for them all, and her body flushed beyond its already elevated temperature. The fine hair on her skin rose as though it too sensed his approach. She met his eyes for one moment and shook her head before fleeing the reach of that gaze and the penetration of his voice.

> *'It's all for the love of my bonnie Irish lass*
> *That my heart is breaking forever...'*

Behind her, she could hear the end of the song, Casey's throat washing the words with heartache and unassailable grief. Fucking bastard, she thought furiously, emotional blackmailer with his silver-tongued Hibernian charm. Well she wasn't so much fool as he was betting on! Yet the thought of him standing there in that crush of people, still singing, heart on display for all who cared to look, wrenched her as little else could have done.

'Clear is the water that flows from the Boyne
And my love is fairer than any
My love is fairer than any...'

The last words slid in her ear like liquid gold, pure and designed to rend down the hardest of hearts. She moved faster, elbowing a few oblivious drunks out of the way. She heard the fiddle start as she trod on someone's stout boot and made it out the door. Casey had left Robin on his own, and was likely hard on her heels. She started to run, determined to get to the car and take swift leave before Casey found her and convinced her to do otherwise.

However, when she reached the grass verge where she'd parked the Citroen, it was to find it firmly clinched between two Cortinas. She glared at the cars, fore and aft, as if the sheer force of her frustration would cause them to move. It didn't, so she kicked the front tire of the aft one, adding a few filthy epithets for good measure.

"Ye can curse at it 'til ye're blue in the face, darlin', an' it'll not be encouraged to move. Ye're stuck here for the present time, so ye'll have to talk to me, like it or no."

"Go away," she muttered tersely, seeing the approach of his reflection in the car window, skin prickling happily at the sound of his voice.

He sighed deeply—a thoroughly taxed and Irish sigh. "How long do ye plan to keep runnin' away from me? I think I can manage a few more minutes of this but not much past that."

"Me?" she swung about filled with indignation, determined not to give him the satisfaction of seeing how badly he'd gotten to her in the pub. "You're the one who's not bloody well seen fit to come home for the last week."

"After ye told me ye'd gut me like a pig on the telephone, did I so much as darken the door again, I thought it wisest to give ye yer space." He snorted. "Or are ye sayin' one thing an' meanin' another, like always?"

"You bastard," she stamped a foot in frustration, "How dare you try to make this my fault!"

He advanced, glowering darkly; she retreated only to find her back up hard against the Cortina. "Oh I see how it is then, ye order me out of our home, tell me ye'd rather consort with a snake than have me ever touch ye again and," he put a hand on either side of her, "then ye have the locks changed just to be certain I've gotten the point, but it's my fault I can't find my way into the house? I've half a mind to turn ye over my knee and give ye a tannin' for what ye've put me through." His mouth was so close to her ear that it stirred the curls she'd tucked behind it. Contrary to his words, he didn't sound the least bit angry.

She was drowning in his proximity, breathing in the heat that came off him in waves. Half fury, half lust, with a pinch of whiskey added in for good measure.

"Why'd you sing to me in there, then?" she asked, clenching her hands tightly in an effort not to touch him.

"Well," he said, lips brushing the sensitive rim of her ear, "I've heard as women are notoriously weak-willed concernin' musicians," he moved, effectively pinning her against the car, where she could have no doubt of his intention.

"Have you?" she said, then uttered a small yelp as he playfully bit her neck. The bastard knew every weak point on her body and was not above using his knowledge to sure advantage.

"Come into the grass with me, Jewel," he murmured in her ear, hands pulling her away from the car and toward the open field that skirted the car park on its south end.

"Are you drunk?" she hissed, casting a glance about her.

"Aye, drunk with need," he replied, pulling her with more determination now.

"Casey Riordan, you madman, we can't just be committing acts of passion in a public field."

He cocked an eyebrow at her. "Why ever not? There's not a soul about, an' no one's likely to emerge from there," he nodded toward the pub, "for a good while."

"Because I—we—it's not respectable," she finished, flustered by the feel of his thumb on the sensitive skin behind her ear. Aware that while walking her backwards into the field he'd managed to undo a fair few of her buttons.

"Respectable? Do ye hear yerself, woman? Take it back," he said, giving her a mock stern look, "or I'll bite ye some place ye *don't* enjoy." And proceeded to bite her somewhere she *did* enjoy. "Ach, woman, where's a haystack when ye need one?" They were some distance into the field now, but the noise and light from the pub were still clearly discernible. He looked about with an aggrieved air, as if indeed a haystack was very little to require of the universe.

"Then where," she said gasping with laughter as he bit her again in a particularly vulnerable spot, "do you propose to commit this act?"

Casey smiled wickedly and hooked a neat leg around the back of her ankles, tipping her over one arm. "Did ye not hear the song in there, Jewel, about love lyin' in the long grass? This grass looks as though it's not been mowed in a good while."

"Casey Riordan, you're not actually proposing to—*mmphm*—right here in this field, are you?"

"If by *mmphm* ye're inferrin'—do I mean to make love to my wife here amongst the buttercups an' the piss-a-beds, then I'd have to say yes. As for proposin'," he angled himself over her as he laid her gently down, the fragrance of dusty grass rising about them, "I don't think I have. Ye must think I've terrible manners," he said and having disposed of the buttons on her dress, proceeded, with a neat flick of thumb and forefinger, to vanquish the clasp on her bra.

His teeth grazed her collarbone and she forgot that only a week before she'd vowed he would never touch her again. Forget all the vulnerabilities he was so well versed in, the man himself was her greatest weakness. From the minute she'd seen him tonight in the pub she'd been lost. And he knew it. Her body rose to the slightest touch, the smell of him raising the hairs on her skin. She'd tried to explain it away as simple chemistry but it was more, so much more than that, and she knew it.

Tongue and teeth were at her breasts now and she was beyond herself, crying softly, scrabbling at his clothing, desperate to tear away any barriers between their respective skins.

"I need you now, Jewel," he said, voice hoarse, "I don't think I can be slow about it."

"Then don't be," she said, reaching up to pull him down to her.

She could smell the music's sweat upon him, ale and tobacco, felt the pound of the drum inside of her and met it quickly, instinctively, with a rhythm that matched and melded to his. She grasped him tight, meeting his need with her own. She could feel the hurt and anger of the last weeks in his touch and in her response.

"Say my name," he whispered in her ear, "I need to hear ye say it."

She could feel the force of desire like a huge wave, the drowning inevitable, and cried his name on the crest of it, and again through the smaller aftershocks as she felt him tremble and shudder between her legs. He slowly lowered himself until their two foreheads rested together and she could feel the pulse of their blood beat in time.

"Lord I've missed ye, woman," he said softly.

"Me too," she whispered back against his mouth, their breath mingling, whiskey and water, strawberries and smoke. Skins slick with the humid night, hearts still thrumming hard in an echo of the drum's feral beat. In moments like this, she could feel her heart break piece by tiny piece and fall away into his keeping yet again.

As their blood calmed the outside world began to make itself felt. Snatches of song drifted from the direction of the pub, the grass sharp and prickling beneath her, the prod of a most unfortunately positioned rock. She released Casey reluctantly, feeling a keen sense of loss as his body left the shelter of her own.

He rolled to the side, collapsing on his back into the grass with a happy sigh.

"I needed ye so bad, Jewel, I thought every person in the pub must see it written on the air between us."

She winced. "I think they did, there was nothing subtle about what happened in there."

"Aye, we charge the atmosphere up now an' again, don't we? Sometimes I think I'm not goin' to make it through without gettin' burned up beyond recognition."

"I know," she agreed ruefully. "I think I can stay mad at you, stay strong and then I see you, touch you, and I'm lost."

He pulled her over so she was half on his chest and brushed her hair gently back behind one ear. "It's not such a bad way to be is it, darlin'? There's a reason we're so powerfully connected, it's not just coincidence."

"I've given up trying to define it."

"You an' I have always understood that there are things beyond words, can ye just accept that what we are to one another is one of those things? There are times I want to tell ye all that's in my heart for you, but I know how naked an' small it'd sound if I said it. An' so I don't, an' maybe that's wrong. But when I touch ye an' it's like bein' inside a livin' flame, I think ye must know all the words caught inside me."

"I do know, Casey," she said softly, "it's the same for me, after all."

"It's hard for me to believe it at times, that ye could feel as I do. An' yet here ye are, in my arms, proof of it."

She laid her head against his chest, tired but happy. The heavy weight in her own chest had ceased for the first time in weeks. Tonight had solved little, she knew, but for now being here, hearing him breathe and the steady thump of his heart beneath her ear, was enough.

"Will ye have me, Pamela?" he asked, voice still husky with sated desire.

She traced the whorls of his chest hair in a series of lazy eights. "I'd say it's a little late for that question."

"That's not what I mean," he said, cupping her face in his palms. "I mean—will ye *have* me?"

"Are you asking me to marry you again?"

"Woman," he brushed the pads of his thumbs across the ridge of bone beneath her eyes, "we've done most things arse-backwards, including you doin' the proposin' an' me the acceptin'. Sometimes I wish we'd had more time, that I'd romanced ye proper an' married ye in a church before God an' several witnesses. That I'd come to ye on bended knee an' asked ye to marry me. But as ye cannot step in the same river twice, I'll do as I can an' ask ye now. Will ye marry me?"

"You bloody man," she whispered through a throat thick with tears.

He quirked an eyebrow at her. "A simple 'yes' would be preferred."

"You know I can't survive without you," she said, half-resentful of the truth contained in the simple statement.

He looked directly in her eyes, his own dark and shadowed. "That's not an answer, woman, an' ye know it."

She closed her eyes and smelled their desire amongst the buttercups and dandelions. Her emotions felt as frail as the dry grass that sighed and bent against the will of the fitful breeze. She would not be able to bend his will, though, she knew it as surely as she knew she couldn't stand another day of this separation.

"Don't ever frighten me like that again," she said, teeth gritted, eyes still closed.

"I wish I could promise ye that I won't, but we'd both know it for a lie. Will ye just believe me when I say I didn't mean to hurt ye, nor frighten ye?"

"I'll believe you," she said, "but I'm a realist, Casey, I knew what coming back to this country would mean."

"I was a coward to let ye take me home," he said, "I knew it, even as I was grateful I knew I shouldn't let ye do it."

"We'd no choice," she said, making an attempt to pull together the sundered halves of her dress. Casey stilled her hands. "Not yet, Jewel, I'd see ye so for another minute." He ran the fingertips of one hand across her collarbone. "You are so beautiful, it's a wonder to me, do ye know that?"

She nodded, not trusting her throat to actual speech.

He sighed, taking a moment to recollect the threads of their conversation. "It may be that Boston was the wrong place for me, or it may be that I made it wrong. Still, there were places to go other than Ireland."

She shook her head, "No, there weren't, Casey, and you know it. You were dying in Boston."

"I don't half understand it, I need you as much as I need this country, an' yet I can't seem to make the two things work together. Ye scare the hell out of me with yer work, an' yet I understand why ye feel the need to do it regardless. I know the force of such a belief myself. Still," he smiled wearily, "it doesn't make the worry any easier to bear, does it?"

"No," she agreed, "it doesn't. Half the time you walk out the door, I'm afraid I'll never see you come back through it."

"Ye still haven't answered my question."

"Casey," she put her hands to his face, feeling the rasp of his whiskers and the tension that lay beneath his skin. "I've been married to you from the minute I first saw you, it just took me a few months to realize it. We don't need another ceremony to confirm it. I'll always be married to you. When I said for better or for worse I meant it."

"Aye, well, I didn't mean for it to be so much of the worse," he replied, sounding quite tired suddenly.

They were quiet for a moment letting the night wash over them to the strains of Robin's fiddle, which was frolicking through the final lines of *I'm a Rover*. Above them, a light summer wind set the leaves to whispering, a soft, soughing noise that seemed made of equal parts yearning and regret.

"It's not been," she said quietly, "the worse I mean. I wouldn't change it—anything—not if it meant something less, between the two of us."

In answer, he brought the palm of her hand to his face, then folded the fingers under his own, holding her knuckles tightly to his lips. She could feel the disquiet of emotion, the words dammed in his throat.

"Lord, woman," he breathed out at last, "ye do break my heart."

The pub was rocking on its foundations now to the tune of *A Nation Once Again*. Even at the distance, they could hear the pounding of fists as they hit the bar or any other handy surface at the end of each line.

"There'll be fightin' soon," Casey sighed, "Bobbie knows that one doesn't mix well with the drink."

"He'll get what he wants from it, though," she said quietly.

"An' what would that be, darlin'? A bunch of wet-behind-the-ears fools who won't remember that they joined up the 'Ra come mornin'. Some black eyes and split lips to puzzle over is all it will amount to."

"Has it been this way every night?"

He nodded. "Aye, he's been stirrin' the pot, don't know what he's after. I've seen money an' information passin' about, but I don't ask an' he don't tell."

From the pub they could hear Robin's hoarse shout of 'sing with me, people, sing.' The people, with eight hundred years of rage and grief stirred in their chests, did so. She wanted to shut the voices out, knew the fire that fuelled their words burned too hotly in her own husband. Knew that the man who plays with fire, or even lingers too long near it, always gets burned. The woman, too. Love, no matter how consuming or fulfilling, could not change that fact. And so she turned her mind to things she did have some control over.

"You're too thin," she said, running her hands down his ribs. "Have you been eating at all?"

"Lawrence is a worse cook than you, if ye can believe it," he said with the air of a man whose digestive tract has become adjusted, if not entirely reconciled, to its martyrdom.

He ducked as she aimed a cuff at his left ear. She settled for giving him a narrowed eye as she did up the last buttons on the hopelessly crushed dress, which now sported several telltale grass stains.

"What about the fight we had—the things we said, the secret you believe I'm keeping." The words almost choked her, saying them went against every instinct she had, but she knew, nevertheless, that they must be said.

He looked at her long, dark eyes inscrutable. "Do ye love me, Pamela?"

"You know I do," she said softly.

"Aye, well, as long as that's true, I think we might manage until ye decide ye've the words to tell me what it is I sense in ye."

"Oh," she said faintly.

He took a deep breath. "I'm glad to have that settled."

He sat up and reached for his crumpled shirt. "Now, woman, I've only the one question left to ask."

She met his eyes there above the dry grass and the scent of desire, and saw that he too was afraid.

"Ask it."

"Do ye think I might come home?"

Chapter Seventy-six

The Stardust Sea

THE REMAINDER OF THE SUMMER was peaceful. Away from Belfast, one could pretend that Ulster wasn't in a state of undeclared war. And here amongst the fields and sheep and the quiet company of the trees, it was easy to turn one's face from the trouble that plagued the city by the Lagan at every turning of the political and historical wheel.

Here one also felt the rhythm of the natural world, both birth and death and the unmistakable change of the seasons. It was a cycle that Pamela had always taken great comfort in, finding the eternal pattern gave her a sense of well-being and order within her own life. She felt a part of things, a small link in an endless chain, at one with the world around her, even if it was only the extent of the world around Coomnablath. For she could feel the land begin its slow drawing inward that signalled the shift from summer to autumn. She could hear it in the papery rustle of leaves and feel it in the brittle stalks of the herbs, could sense that the sap of green things was withdrawing, slowly returning to the roots, conserving lifeblood for the cold sleep of winter. She herself felt the same; that slow inward turning of the spirit toward the dark and contemplative half of the year.

They were slowly gathering in the vegetables and fruit of the garden and fields. Just this afternoon she had put up a dozen jars of strawberry jam and could smell the sticky sweetness still on her hands, along with the starchy green smell of peas. She had shelled ten pounds of the things before dinner.

Soon she would have to take out the extra quilts and heavier coats, and Lawrence would need a new pair of gloves and a scarf to replace the one he'd lost last winter. Casey had culled the dead pine from the woods, and a comfortingly large pile of wood was growing beside the shed. He'd also been crawling about the house, checking for a draft he claimed he'd felt the previous winter.

The day had been one of flawless blue skies and a pleasant heat that was strong enough still to penetrate down to the bones, and place a store of sunshine within the marrow, to be drawn upon during the long winter months.

Dinner had been salmon that Casey had roasted in the firepit. Along with the last of the small new potatoes and fresh carrots basted with butter and dill.

The night was clear, and so Casey and Lawrence had gone outside to attend to a few chores before night fell, leaving her to bake the bread she'd had rising during dinner. She was determined this would be the batch that was a triumph. Gert had patiently taught her over the last few weeks how to make bread that rose in high, snowy mounds and baked to a golden finish.

She eyed the small oblongs of dough dubiously. They looked a little battered, and not at all like the perfect yeasty rounds that Gert made day in, day out with apparently little effort. She sighed, wondering if she would ever develop any talent within the culinary field, beyond the ability to make a good, strong cup of tea.

It was dark by the time she finished the bread, and though it didn't look like Gert's nor smell quite as ambrosial, it didn't look altogether inedible either. It was a triumph of sorts.

Since Casey's return home, she no longer had the sense of being watched. She chalked it up to nervousness on her own part, though she knew it didn't explain the sound of the back door closing that day. Still, the feeling had disappeared and she wasn't going to cause her husband undue worry on account of it.

She looked up at the clock, suddenly realizing how late it was. She wiped her hands on the floury tea towel and stepped out on the back stair. She breathed in the cool night air gratefully, filling her lungs and stretching her back, which was achy and tired from a busy day.

A tracery of movement down towards the stream caught her eye. It was the glimmer of Lawrence's hair against the trunk of an oak tree. Casey sat beside him, his dark coloring rendering him no more than shadow.

Casey was pointing up to the sky, hand moving back and forth in an arcing motion. She could see the pale silhouette of Lawrence's head tilted back on his thin neck. He was motionless, held rapt by whatever it was Casey was saying to him.

She eased herself down on the steps silently. She'd no wish to intrude, only wanted to watch, for a quiet moment, these two men she so dearly loved.

Near the ground the air was still; higher up, though, the leaves rustled softly to and fro in their sleep. Overhead the sky was ablaze, thick with stars in all their shades of blue and gold, red and silver. She could smell freshly turned earth; Casey had hoed the lazy beds after supper.

"Sometimes," Lawrence was saying, "it makes me dizzy, an' I wonder how I can matter at all when the universe is so big? An' then I get scared an' a wee bit sick inside."

"Aye, I've felt that way a time or two myself, I'll admit," Casey replied. "But mostly I find it comfortin', the sky changin' with the seasons, an' knowin' that people have been able to tell for thousands an' thousands of years where they were an' the time of the year by the stars which appeared each season."

"Comfortin'?" Lawrence said. "I feel like I'm fallin', an' if what ye say is true, I really am, what with everything whirlin' an' spinnin', never stoppin' for a minute. Gives me that awful feelin' like my head's swellin' up and my stomach has dropped to me toes. What did ye call it?"

"Vertigo," Casey said. "Perhaps if ye were to think of it as swimmin' through a great endless ocean, rather than fallin' through space, ye might not find it so disconcertin'."

Lawrence snorted. "If that's yer view, I'm surprised ye've the will to get up in the mornin' then, considerin' yer views on water."

Casey chose to ignore this statement. He pointed upward, almost directly overhead and Pamela looked up as well. "Which is that star?" he asked. He'd been teaching Lawrence the constellations, as well as which stars were the guiding posts of each season.

"'Tis Vega," Lawrence said, a small note of pride in his tone, for despite his fear of the vast ocean that was the night sky, he took pride in his ability to discern the different colors of the stars, a talent he hadn't realized not everyone possessed.

"Good lad. Now the Arabs do call Vega by the name *Al Nasr Al Waki*, which means *'the swooping eagle'*. The odd thing there is that Vega really is flyin' or perhaps it's that we're flyin' toward it. It's near the place in the sky that we call the solar apex, an' that is the spot in the galaxy that the sun is movin' toward, an' where our sun goes, so go we."

Vega winked smokily with blue-white fire. It was the epicenter of the northern summer skies and seemed the gateway out into the very universe, as if one might fall through it into eternal night, into the end of all things, or the beginning of something so wondrous it would beggar the imagination. Pamela clutched the doorstep, vertigo spinning her head and dislocating her body from its place in space and time. She felt a sudden sympathy for Lawrence's fears. It took her a minute to regain her equilibrium and attune her ear back to Casey and Lawrence's conversation.

"... a theory I read of once, that there's an infinite number of universes arranged in a hierarchical structure, so that if ye could see inside somethin' so small as an electron, ye'd find within it an entire closed universe, an' within it galaxies and worlds all the way down to wee particles that are universes within themselves, an' so on down infinitely—universes within universes. An' upward as well, so that our own universe is really no more than a wee particle, a bubble on the wind, if ye will, within someone else's universe. And so ye see we are all merely a part of a greater an' lesser whole."

Casey paused to take a drink of his lemonade. "An' if ye think of that starlight as part of yerself, as sweepin' through ye, that entire universes live within the palm of yer hand an' that you yerself live within the larger structure of yet another universe, then it seems to me we will always be alive in some way, that we always *have* been alive. That everything," Casey gestured to the water, the trees, the hills and the great dome of the night above, "is a part of us, and we of it, an' so we matter in the greater scheme of things, an' yet maybe the things that happen to us day by day need not be so big nor matter to us quite so much."

She felt tears of gratitude sting her eyes. She understood what he was saying, what he was attempting to do for the boy. To make him feel as if his past could be wiped clean, and that he might only retain what joy he had known, and thus move forward into his future, whole and unmarked.

The two of them were quiet after that, and she realized that Lawrence had fallen asleep there under the shelter of night and the protection of the one person he had given the gift of his trust to from the first. Casey sat, his hand on the boy's shoulder, for a long time.

She merely stayed sitting, not wanting to disturb the spell of the summer night, with the echo of Casey's words still warm and reassuring in her ear. It was a moment of grace, and she knew well enough to embrace it as it passed.

Some time later Casey folded the blanket over Lawrence's long frame. Then he stood and turned toward where she sat, still caught in the web of stardust woven over the summer hills and swaying trees.

"Come here," he said, voice hushed, as though he did not wish to disturb the great slumbering night about him. She started slightly, realizing he had known she was there the entire time.

She walked to where he stood on the edge of the water, the earthy smell of ferns and moss springing up beneath her footsteps.

"Look just there," he pointed to the east, beyond the ring of trees where their property ended, and the gray stones of Mr. Guderson's fields were a pale ribbon against the long grass and vines that grew against and over them.

A strange light was moving across the fields, coming toward the embankment of trees. It darted back and forth, and then would glide for long stretches high in the air.

"What on earth is that?"

"Ye'll see, should he come closer," Casey said, eyes fixed on the quixotic object. It glowed a soft yellow, like the headlamp of a bicycle bobbing down a country lane. The brightness increased as it approached, lighting the area around for some small circumference.

The light flew lower as it approached the trees, and then it was above their heads, the air moving in great rhythmic susurrations with the beat of large airy wings.

"It's an owl," she exclaimed, for the feathered body was just discernible within the heart of the light. "But why on earth is it glowing like that?"

"No one knows for certain," he said quietly, "some say it's a luminescent fungus that grows on them when they're weak or sickly. Some think they've simply got the gift of light. I've always thought 'twas them that have been called Will o'the Wisp, and that they might be the truth behind the old tales of fetch candles hoverin' about the house of those that are going to die."

He put his arms around her from behind, his face against the side of her head. They stood in comfortable silence, savoring this moment with the quiet of night about them. The bird had lit on a branch above the brook, and glowed there like a fixed lantern.

The wind was still high in the trees, the tops of the pines bending slightly under the pressure. Pamela had a sense of endless movement, of the ground beneath her feet and the fast wind rush of the stars above her head. And in the midst of it all, the time-stopped beauty of a dying bird, shedding light as it flew along invisible pathways through the air.

"Tis a sort of gift, really," Casey said, "to radiate light as they die, to have that beauty even as your life ebbs away. I think it's God's way of makin' poetry."

The light soared away out of the branches, reflecting in the water like a small drowned moon. And then it blinked once, twice against the backdrop of the low hills and winked out in the distance.

Part Eight

How Fragile is the Heart

Chapter Seventy-seven

The Lost Boy

LATER, SHE WOULD THINK how blind humans were about fear. That most often as a species we are terrified of the unknowable: the future, the bend in the road, the next rise of the hill. But it is the past we should fear; the past that trails like the grotesquely angled shadow of a winter tree behind each of us. Gathering within its crevices, its hollows, its crookednesses, a mulitiplication of damage, of pain and disaster. The things that frighten us most have always crept up from behind. The primal brain, sitting low within the fragile skull, knows this, has always known this. It is the past we should fear, it is the past that haunts us.

And it is the past that we cannot escape.

SHE WAS DREAMING OF TREES when Casey shook her awake. Of running in a forest full of falling leaves; the colors a glory of crimson and gold. She could smell the smoke and mellow light and knew, though she could not see him, that a man ran before her, for his footprints were visible in the frost. Ahead was water, she could smell it, could sense the way air was always thicker and purer near water.

Suddenly between two pale-skinned birches she caught a glimpse of the man—lithe and swift upon his feet as thistledown, dodging in and out amongst the trees, his head crowned in scarlet oak leaves, his body smooth as water over dark stone.

She was breathing heavily, slipstreams of fog crystallizing in the air ahead of her. Her heart was beating so hard that it echoed like a drum through the woods and she could smell the hot salt of blood as she ran. She glanced down and saw that the blood lay upon the ground, in hardened drops, like fire opals scattered upon snow with a careless hand. But whether it was the man's or her own, she did not know.

Was she prey or predator? She couldn't tell, only knew that fear filled her, electrifying her nerve endings, making her run on in pursuit of the man, though it felt as if her heart would burst with the effort.

And then, in the odd time-slip way of dreams, she was at the water's edge. The man she pursued stood thigh-deep in the cold stream, blood on his legs and back, pooling in ribbons around his thighs. Closer to, she could see his smooth skin was really a pelt of fine, fawn-colored hair and that he was neither man nor beast, but rather something else that only existed in the netherland of dream. She could see how his body heaved with the effort of breath, and knew he was badly wounded, was dying here where the water froze in delicate geometry against the black earth. She called to him, but could not say what name fell from her tongue, nor how she knew what word would summon him.

And then he turned and she screamed, for he had no face.

She came awake with a start, the dream still pounding in her blood, making her skin feel thin and fragile, and the bones beneath aching as though she really had been running all night.

"Where's Lawrence?" she asked immediately, eyes not focused yet, so that it seemed she still saw the faceless man in front of her, overlaying the dim glow of the peat fire in the hearth.

"I don't know, that's why I woke ye. I felt uneasy about the lad an' so I called Pat—he was supposed to go there, aye? But Pat didn't know anything about it. He said Lawrence hadn't made arrangements with him."

She was all the way awake now. Tree branches were scraping against the window and the wind was moaning about the corners of the house. "We have to find him," she said, fumbling to get out of the bed, limbs still stiff with sleep.

"Aye we do, but I think it'd be best did ye stay here."

"No," she shook her head, "I'm coming with you, and that's an end to it."

Casey gave her a look of taxed patience and she braced herself for an argument. "Jewel, be reasonable, if the boy comes back here an' the place is empty he might pull another runner on us. Ye need to stay here an' keep watch. I won't be long." He leaned forward and kissed her on the forehead.

"No. Casey, I have to come with you."

He gave her a searching look, his own face white with worry. Then he nodded slowly. "All right then, I'll meet ye downstairs once ye're dressed."

Outside, the rain was sweeping in great horizontal draughts, the wind blowing hard enough to steal the breath from her lungs. The car was cold, but Casey did not wait for it to warm, but rather leaned forward wiping the windshield periodically, as they drove down the narrow, dark laneways toward Belfast.

They did not speak, each caught up in the thoughts of what scenario awaited them. It had been months since Lawrence had missed his curfew.

The dream still lingered about Pamela, laying an icy touch upon her skin. And she remembered too clearly the night Lawrence had told her his dream about the faceless man in the woods.

"I've a feelin' that if he ever turns around an' I do see his face, somethin' truly awful will happen in the daylight." The words echoed in her head with the force of prophecy. How had the dream found its way unbidden into the recesses of her own subconscious?

A memory came to her suddenly, of being lost herself. When she was found, her father had first hugged her and then just as swiftly yelled at her, an anger in his face she'd never seen before. It had frightened her, that lightning swift change in him, and she'd burst into tears, and he had hugged her again until the tears stopped. She could still smell him, the warm scent of Bay Rum cologne, and the under note of green things he always seemed to exude from his person. She felt a surge of longing for him, for the reassurance of a father's presence. The arms around you that kept you shielded from the world.

She closed her eyes and prayed silently. *"Please Daddy, please let him be safe. I don't know if Casey can survive it if he isn't. I know I can't."*

She opened her eyes to the sight of a three-storied hotel, sagging about its edges, paint peeling and the odd window stuffed with rags. The sort of place people went when they needed anonymity.

"Why here?" she asked, a choking fear suddenly gripping her throat.

"Because if the boy is in trouble it'll be because of Morris Jones. This is one place he brings boys," Casey said flatly.

"How do you know that?"

"Because I asked around until someone told me."

It was a small hotel, with filthy threadbare carpets in the lobby and a sleeping attendant behind the desk. Casey leaned over the desk and grabbed the man by his dirty collar and yanked him halfway across the desk. "D'ye have a lad upstairs—about fifteen, tall, skinny an' ginger-haired?"

"Ye can't feckin' come in here an'—" whatever protest the goggle-eyed man had been about to make was swiftly cut off by the simple expedient of Casey twisting his collar until the man resembled a blowfish on the verge of explosion.

"Just answer the focking question."

The man twisted his head far enough to look in Casey's face. Something there made him gulp, his Adam's apple bobbing like a cork above the torn blue collar. "Room number four, on the right at the end of the hall."

Casey threw him back and ran up the stairs two at a time. Pamela followed in his wake, nausea clawing its way up her throat. She saw him stop at the door, and then raise a leg to kick it in with a force that made the floor shake all the way down the hall.

"Wait out here," he said to her grimly.

For a long time there was only a dreadful silence from the room, a weight like wet sand clogging up the atmosphere, making it hard to breathe. She put a hand to the door and it must have made some small noise of protest, for

Casey spoke then.

"Don't come in," his voice was hoarse; each syllable limned in fear and something else that made her step back involuntarily. She knew very suddenly that to look beyond the door was to change her perception of the world. And yet there was no way back from this edge place and so she stepped through the doorway.

The scene before her eyes was laid out starkly, grimy sheets that had once been white, arrayed with large crimson blooms. The wallpaper was a nasty shade of brown, peeling at its seams. She noted these things, mind staving off what it was not ready to see. For on the bed, amid crimson-blossoming sheets, lay the nude body of a thin boy, barely into adolescence. The ginger hair was pale against the red that spiralled out from under his head. She opened her mouth but couldn't find sound, couldn't find breath.

His ankles, milk-blue with the absence of life, lay askew, veins already retreating from the surface. There were bruises on the back of the pale thighs. She forced herself to look higher, though she could smell the evidence of what had taken place in this room. The air reeked of it, as well as a colder scent that she knew as the perfume of recent death.

Casey knelt by the bed, hands fisted in front of him. Slowly he uncurled them and she saw how badly they shook. "Pamela, there's a blanket on the chair, pass it to me."

"We can't cover him," she whispered, "we could destroy evidence."

He turned, eyes ablaze with fury. "Fock evidence. I don't need a detective to tell me who did this. Give me the blanket so I can cover the boy."

She retrieved the blanket. The smell of cigarette smoke filled the air as Casey shook it out and laid it gently over Lawrence. He drew it up to the boy's neck, tucking it about him as though he were merely asleep on his own narrow bed at home, and not dead with the smell of sex ripe on the air about him.

Casey brushed a large hand across Lawrence's head, moving the cowlick that had hung over his eyes away. And then the hand, calloused and powerful, lay there trembling.

"I have failed him. I have put him here," Casey said, a terrible hollow at the heart of his words that reverberated in her own chest.

"No you didn't—we couldn't have..." the words died away in her throat though, for she *had* known and had foolishly believed Lawrence's ties to that old world had been severed.

"Aye I did and yes, we should have," Casey said. "Because I promised him he would be safe, but he never really was. And he knew it. And so he kept trying to make things right an' this is where it put him."

The hand on Lawrence's head stilled, and a chill planted itself firmly at the base of her spine, sending quicksilver shots up through her nerves. Though Casey did not speak, she had the strong feeling that he was laying some sort of oath upon the boy, for his eyes were closed and his face wore an inward look that was both a sealed book and a revelation to the core of the man. She knew suddenly that he was swearing vengeance, promising a letting of blood in payment for this murder. His face was touched with a cold fire that simmered like black ice beneath his skin. The chill in her spine was dread; the sense that this night had unlocked a door within Casey which had never been properly shut. He was so still, like a stone figure that had weathered through a thousand years overlooking a barren plain. The constraints of civilization had always ridden uneasily upon his shoulders. She feared the ropes of it had been cut away completely this day.

Casey opened his eyes and stood, and seemed once again only a man. "I must go for the police," he said.

She nodded and then reached out to touch her hand to his face, before turning from her husband and lying down on the bed beside Lawrence. She felt oddly weightless, as though she were a feather, blown about in the winds of chance, resting here in this cold place for a moment before the next gale tore her away.

"Pamela," Casey said hoarsely, "what are ye doin'?"

"I'll not have him alone right now," she said fiercely.

Casey nodded slowly, his face blankly smooth, like the stone man he resembled. But she could see already the rivers of grief that ran beneath, and how they would overswell their channels and crack the foundation of his humanity.

She turned away and clutched Lawrence tighter, the scent of his hair smoky, but with an under note of Polo mints. She closed her eyes, a spasm of pain flashing down her center that made her want to curl up in the dark for all eternity.

"Go get the police," she said, "I'll stay with him."

She heard the scrape of Casey's shoes against the filthy carpet, and a thump as he stumbled into the doorway on his way out. But she did not look round. Some small thing inside warned her to be very still, that somehow if she didn't move she could stop the planet flying off its very axis here in this grubby room. Because she knew once the police came, once they removed Lawrence, it would be real and the core of pain would crack wide in her and then there would be no way to stop the headlong plunge into the frozen abyss of space.

Like all children, he had come into the world trusting in a mother's love, but that mother had gone so long ago that love was not even a memory upon his skin, nor a trace within his blood. And so he had abandoned faith in the world of adults, until he had been pulled toward the warmth and light of she and Casey's home, the intangible one that was not built of stone and wood, but rather of love and trust.

She thought they had brought him within that shelter, but saw now that they had not. That though he had drawn near the windows of family, aglow with the promise of warmth and security; he had somehow found those windows barred and himself unable to enter. Though she thought he had tried over and over, despite the understanding that he could not breach the entry.

Maybe every child abandoned to the cruelties of the world, every child left, abused, neglected was somehow frozen in that place where first they had known the pain the world could inflict on the young, the fragile, the deserted. And if they could not find shelter soon enough, perhaps they were stranded on the shores of Neverland forever, where the Captain Hooks and the crocodiles were all too real.

She laid her cheek against the chill silk of his hair, arm tight around his long, gawky height and began to store him in the mine of her memory. The milk-white skin, the laughter that always cracked into a higher register—Christ his voice hadn't even done breaking yet—the clumsy grace of him, his devotion to Finbar. Oh God, the thought of the dog put a hairline fissure in the core. She took a deep breath; time was short, the police would be here soon and she had something she would say to the boy first.

"It's alright now," she whispered. "Don't stop, don't let anything stop you, you're free to fly now Lawrence. There's nothing to stop you. Just remember," she took his young slender hand in her own, curling its cold resistance to the living warmth of her fingers, "it's the second star from the right and straight on to morning."

And then she simply lay silent, holding a dead child in her arms, knowing that some lost boys could never be found.

Chapter Seventy-eight

Englishman

AT FIRST PAT THOUGHT CHURCH BELLS were ringing, and wondered how he'd slept in so long. Then he realized that it was the phone ringing, and knew it had been ringing on for some time. He stumbled from the bed, cursing as his foot wound up in the sheet and caused him to stumble.

"Are ye all right?" Sylvie murmured.

"Aye," he said, making his way out to the kitchen where the phone sat, still blaring its clarion noise out into the night.

"Hello," he said, peering through the half-light to the clock that hung on the wall above the table. Two am—Christ, it couldn't be good news at this hour.

"Is this Pat Riordan?" asked a whisper on the other end.

"Aye," he said, the voice sending an odd shiver down his spine and waking him up.

"I'm calling from the Barracks. It's about David Kendall."

"I'm listening," Pat said tersely.

There was a deep breath at the other end of the phone and then the voice rushed on. "He was due back here about two hours ago, he's never late. I wouldn't normally worry but this is David and-and..."

"He's never late," Pat finished for him, understanding now what had the caller so frightened.

"No, but it's more where he went tonight."

"Where?" Pat asked, fumbling in the dark for a pen and paper.

"Down South Armagh way, a wee pub called the Two-Step. He was wearing civvies but he had his pistol strapped on. Said he was going off base, but I don't think it was a social occasion if you understand?"

"Aye, I understand," Pat answered heavily. Two hours was a long time to be overdue for a man as punctual as David. Two hours allowed a lot of lag time for any number of things. Torture and death being among the top contenders.

The Two Step was a hornet's nest where only truly hard line Republicans went to wet their whistle, amongst other things. If someone in that pub had made David and his cover was blown, he could be dead already. On the other hand, if he wasn't made and merely had a flat tire somewhere between here and Armagh, Pat could be offering himself up as some sort of sacrifice. He'd a sick feeling it was not a flat tire, though.

"How do I know I'm not walking into some sort of trap here?" Pat asked.

"You don't," said the voice at the other end, "I called you because David trusts you. I've got nothing else to offer you. No one is supposed to know where he's at, so I can't call out the cavalry on this one." There was a slight pause, and then the voice, small with worry asked, "Will you help him, do you think it's too late?"

"I'll try," Pat said and hung up the phone, reaching for pants and shirt even as he did so.

THE DRIVE TO DRUMINTREE SEEMED to last a small eternity. Three times Pat had to pull over and unstick the wiper blades, as they refused to keep up with the deluge that cascaded out of the low black sky. By the time he'd reached his destination the storm had passed over, and the lingering clouds were only spitting the occasional fine spray of rain.

The Two-Step pub was foursquare and snugged into the arms of an elm copse. It was dark as Pat approached, silent except for the remnants of rain pit-pattering from the trees. Low-beamed and solid, it was a pub notorious for its Republican leanings, no small distinction in an area that was legendary for its crack IRA squads. Here a whisper in the wrong place meant death, swift and absolute. The South Armagh Brigade stood apart from the rest of the IRA, bound by generations of communal history and blood ties that made betrayal unthinkable. It was a closed society and strangers were looked upon with a wary, if not hostile eye. Pat knew this, and understood the risk he had undertaken by coming here. However, he also knew that if David had been here in an attempt to cozy up with the locals and extract intelligence, he'd very little time for subtlety and would have to get the information he needed as swiftly as possible. He felt the heavy weight of the Browning against his backbone, like a dark reassurance that he devoutly hoped he would not need.

He gave the door an experimental tug, surprised when it swung out.

"Too late for drinks an' we don't serve breakfast," a voice said from the direction of the back wall. Pat squinted, making out a stocky figure polishing down the bar with hard strokes.

"I know," Pat replied, stepping into the dimly lit room. The place had been closed for some time from the looks of things. Chairs were upended onto clean tables, the floor was swept and all the glasses were cleared away. "I'm not looking to eat, only for a little information."

That got the publican's attention. He was a short, squat man with a bulldog's neck and the beady glare of an unpleasant hawk. "Ye want information laddie—here's some—take the same road out that ye came in on."

Hospitality was obviously not on the menu. However, the man's surliness was no match for Riordan obstinacy. Pat merely smiled and stood his ground, taking in the surroundings quickly in an attempt to ascertain if anyone might be lurking in corners or backrooms.

After a cursory glance, though, it appeared that there was only an old man drooped over a pint of half-done stout, heavy jowled and sad-eyed. The publican nodded in his direction.

"My father-in-law," he said curtly, "he's an old drunk, but he don't harm nobody." The tone of the publican's voice indicated that he might not be as peacefully inclined.

"I'm looking for someone who may have been here last night."

The publican scrubbed harder at the oak beneath his hand. "Lot of faces come an' go man, 'twas a busy night."

"He's on the small side, long fair hair, looks like he'd not offend a flea."

"Unflatterin' portrait ye're paintin', an no I didn't see anyone of that description. Now if ye don't mind, it's been a long one an' I'd like to lock the doors and go to bed."

"Please," Pat said, desperation leaking into his voice, "it's a matter of life an' death."

The man snorted. "In Armagh there's little else."

Pat took a deep breath. "Look, this man likely had no idea what he was wandering into. He's innocent of anything but bein' in the wrong place at the wrong time. If someone's taken him, they're about to make a terrible mistake." Out of superstition, he crossed his fingers, hoping the lie was convincing.

The man gave him a hard look, then capitulated with a grunt. "I don't want it on my conscience, so I'll tell ye what I know, though it's little enough an' if anyone should ask, ye didn't hear it from me an' ye were never within a square mile of this pub, ye understand?"

Pat nodded.

"Round ten or so I went out back to get a keg of ale," the man continued, "an' there were two lads hangin' about in the car park, seemed as if they might be waitin' on somethin' or somebody. Here, ye see people loiterin' it don't pay to get too curious." He shrugged eloquently, "Could be it was yer friend they were watchin out for. Didn't waste time lookin' or askin', though."

"That's what I'm afraid of," Pat muttered.

The man shook his head, "Whoever he is, he's not here now, an' ye'd best leave, man, if ye've a notion of what's good for ye."

Pat nodded, taking the warning as it was intended. In a county full of hard men, this pub was infamous. It wasn't wise to be caught asking questions about things that weren't your business. And unless David was bound and gagged in the washroom, he was no longer here.

He turned and walked out into the night. Behind him, the door slammed and a lock clicked audibly into place. The man was nervy, and there'd been a flicker of fear in his eyes when Pat had described David. Unless his instincts were awry, David *had* been here at some point.

He started to walk back to his car when a dark shape caught the corner of his eye, and he turned toward it, adrenaline starting to pump. He swore under his breath, not happy that he'd been right about the situation.

The wee red Triumph that he recognized as David's sat at the west end of the car park. Pat's hand went automatically to the gun at his waist. He approached the vehicle cautiously, gun now tucked firm to his side, finger crooked on the trigger. It looked empty, but he wasn't taking any chances. The ball of ice in his intestines was now roughly the size of a grapefruit.

Shadows seemed to cluster thickly around the little car, where it sat in the lee of a scraggly looking sapling. Pat cast a quick glance over his shoulder, then closed the gap between himself and the car. The driver's door was slightly ajar, the shadows deeper on the ground near the vehicle.

Pat grabbed the handle, flung the door open, bringing his right hand up sharply with the hammer pulled back on the trigger. The car was empty. He scouted the back seat, the floors, even the dash for any sign of struggle. Nothing presented itself to his eye. He walked the perimeter of the car, checking the tires, lights, mirrors. The left headlight was cracked, glass slightly concave. It meant little, though, the headlight could have been broken long before tonight.

His eyes were drawn down, noting a deeper patch on the ground. He reached into the thick clot of shadow, praying that it was a trick of the dark and his eyes. His fingers touched wet, chill and cold. He brought the fingers to his face, sniffing them. There was a faint iron tang, but still he couldn't be certain. He touched a finger to his tongue and cursed at the unmistakable taste. There was blood on the ground and from the little he could see, a fair amount of it.

"Goddamned Englishman," he muttered to himself. Meddling in things he'd no understanding of. "Damn it, David, where are you?" he asked the world at large, expecting no answer and therefore nearly jumping clear of his skin when he received one.

"Dead by now, I expect."

Pat whirled about, finger hard against the trigger.

The figure backed off, hands held high. "Whoa there boy, I mean no harm."

"Who the hell are you?" Pat asked, voice harsh, arm held out straight so the man could not mistake his intentions.

"I was inside," the man cocked his head back towards the pub.

Pat narrowed his eyes, adjusting his vision. The old man who'd been sitting in the corner, the alcoholic father-in-law.

"What do ye know of the man I'm lookin' for?"

"What John told ye is true enough, there were two lads waitin' on someone out here. I came out for a piss 'bout eleven, an' I could hear a scuffle up round here, like someone was gettin' a hiding—there was four different voices. If those boys were waitin' for yer man, then there was another man joined them, or mebbe he just brought the car that took them all away."

"Did no one see ye?" Pat asked, wondering how they'd missed the presence of someone who'd stood there long enough to take in all that had happened in those few moments.

"Likely they did see me, but it'd not matter. I'm part blind, wouldn't make much of a witness, would I? I'm no more threat than a piece of furniture to them, mebbe they don't know my hearin' is sharper than their eyes any day."

"Were you inside when he came in?"

"Aye, there was a bit of a stillness when he walked in, th'only strangers that come in the Two-Step are fools. Ye could sense the trouble right off. I'm surprised he didn't scarper for it sooner."

"Was he there the whole evening? What I mean is, did he go out and come back in at all?" Pat asked, wondering if David had planned to meet with someone and had been ambushed instead.

"Aye, came in an' stayed. Moved about a bit, talkin' to a few people. Seemed familiar with a few of them. Thought he was with the band at first."

"With the band?" Pat furrowed his brow, wondering if the old man was entirely clear on the events of the evening.

"Aye, but then the boy opened his mouth." The man grimaced slightly. "Laddie didn't have an ear for the singin'," he sighed, "bit of a pity."

"Singing?" Pat echoed, wondering at what point he'd tumbled headfirst down the rabbit hole.

"Aye, yer man was up there yowlin' with the band, sounded like a scalded cat."

Singing with the band?! Had David lost his few wits altogether?

"Sang a couple of republican ones, band called 'im up said he'd come the whole way down from Belfast."

"What made you think he hadn't?"

"Accent was wrong. Mebbe less sensitive ears wouldn't have noticed, but his r's were off. Seemed like they was stuck in his throat. Belfast is a hard accent, an' his voice was a bit too plummy-like. More Lord Muck gone native, if ye take my meanin'. 'Twas more noticeable after he'd had a few drinks."

"How do you know he was drinking?" Pat asked suspiciously.

"He leaned across me lookin' for an ashtray, said 'scuse me' an' I could smell it on him. Besides it'd look odd as hell if ye werena drinkin' in there. That'd raise suspicion quickern' a British uniform. He'd maybe had a wee bit more than was," the old man paused to spit, "strictly necessary to uphold his disguise."

Drunk and singing with the band? Pat didn't know whether to laugh or cry, but it was becoming glaringly apparent that David had exercised no caution whatsoever, in a situation that he knew was of life and death seriousness.

"How'd they get him out of here?"

The old man shook his head, looking like a weary St. Bernard in the dim glow of the car park lights. "I don't think he was conscious anymore when they put him in the car. Sounded like they were throwin' a bag of potatoes in the boot."

Unconscious would be a blessing, the alternative didn't bear thinking about.

"If it's of comfort to ye lad, he didn't beg, he's a real soldier that one."

"Do you know where they took him?" Pat asked sharply.

The man's face was suddenly guarded, eyes blank as milk in the moonlight.

'Don't hold out on me now, you old bugger,' Pat thought, fighting to control his panic. "Where?" he repeated, applying emphasis to the question with a sharp prod of the gun.

"I c—can't b—be certain," the man stuttered.

Pat let the hammer-click make his point for him. "Make yer best guess."

The man swallowed audibly, then seemed to make his mind up to the lesser of two evils. "There's a wee bridge off the Ravensdale road, clump of trees down the left hand bank. That's my best guess."

"Thanks for yer cooperation," Pat said, turning to go.

Behind him, the man cleared his throat. "Ye'd best knock me out before ye go, laddie. Blind I may be, but stupid I'm not."

Pat sighed heavily, knowing the man was right. Blind, deaf *and* mute wouldn't stand in your favor if 'the lads' thought you'd ratted on them.

He turned and said "Thanks again," and brought the butt of the gun down hard on the man's head. The old man crumpled like a rag doll, and Pat stepped over the prone form on his way to the car, hoping to God he wasn't already too late.

THE DRIVE TO THE BRIDGE SEEMED to take hours, though in reality Pat knew it was only about ten minutes. Ten minutes could mean the difference between life and death, though, as he well knew.

The bridge was only a conduit on a narrow country road and therefore not lit. He was on top of it before he even realized it and had to reverse the car off, cursing to himself for every second that passed.

He turned off the ignition, put the car in neutral, and allowed it to slide down the hill and come to rest under a thick copse of trees. He got out of the car, gun in his right hand, finger cold on the trigger.

There was no light beneath the trees. He moved through the heavy murk, nearly jumping out of his skin when a branch brushed across his face. He needed to get a grip on his nerves before he shot the hell out of a sheep or a fence. He stopped and took a deep breath, willing his hands to be steady. The grass was thick with dew, his pant legs soaked and chill against his legs, his breath a damp cloud reaching out before him. Then, beyond a small cluster of elm trees, he saw a faint movement, and heard the rumble of a voice questioning and another replying sharply. He stooped, checking quickly over his shoulder before proceeding any further. He stopped behind a clump of gorse, slowly leaning left until he had the men in view.

There were two of them milling around, one smoking; he could see the tiny coal of his cigarette wink in and out. The third man wasn't visible, though he wasn't likely to be far. The last form was on its knees, forehead propped against a tree trunk. Pat cursed softly under his breath, it was the classic IRA execution position. On your knees, one shot to the back of the head. Still kneeling though, not dead yet. He knew there wasn't time to think, or hope that angels would swoop down from the clouds and intervene. Still he hesitated, knowing that what he was about to do was irrevocable and would change everything in his life. He'd have to be fast and accurate, there was no room for near misses. Both men were armed and ready, all he had was the element of surprise.

He stepped out and aimed, taking out the one that stood directly behind David first. It was a direct shot to the head and the man dropped like a stone. Pat swivelled before the man finished falling, sighting in on the one with the cigarette as a bullet *zinged* past his left ear. His second shot hit dead center in the smoker's chest, sending the man sprawling backwards into the narrow stream behind him. The next bullet aimed toward him grazed his left arm, leaving a burning pain in its wake. He sucked in a sharp hiss of air before shooting off another round and hoping his luck held.

It did. The third man staggered a bit and then went to his knees, finally falling forward into the wet grass on his face.

He ran to David, breath heavy in his chest and panic spreading a fine numbness through all his limbs.

"Are ye all right?"

David had toppled forward into the grass, and appeared to be barely conscious. He was also barely recognizable, he'd been so badly beaten.

"Jaysus," Pat said, but whether in curse or prayer he was not certain. David looked too fragile to be moved, and yet there was no choice in the matter. They had to get out of here, and quickly.

Pat bent, one knee to the ground, and levered David up and over his shoulder as gently as he could manage. The stumble back to the car seemed to take forever.

He put David in the back seat and covered him with a heavy blanket that they kept in the boot for picnics. If he got stopped at any of the checkpoints, God help him, for the soldiers would likely shoot first and ask questions later.

The drive back was an agony, he had to pull over twice to be certain that David was still breathing. Pat wasn't sure what to do, though he knew the man required immediate medical attention. He could drop him off at a hospital and run, though it seemed a dreadful cowardly thing to do. And yet, given the circumstances, what choice did he have? There was a trail leading back to the bloody field that he could not afford to have traced. But how could he, in all good conscience, leave a man so badly injured? What if David succumbed to these injuries and his last contact on earth was with total strangers?

Without having made a conscious decision, he found himself in front of the Royal Hospital. He pulled David out, wincing at each catch of the man's breath, and carried him in his arms through the door.

A nurse looked up, startled, her blue eyes weary at the end of a long shift. She blinked when she saw the man swaddled inside the plaid blanket, blood and swelling obliterating his features. Then she looked sharply at Pat.

He realized how they must appear, David a crumpled bloody heap and himself near as bloody, even though the blood was not his own. "Please help him," he croaked out. The nurse nodded and came around the counter hastily.

She laid her fingers against David's neck. "Pulse is thready," she said matter of factly. "Lay him down over here. I'm going to page the doctor."

The scene quickly became pandemonium, as more nurses came and medical terms were flung about and David was swiftly wheeled off into the bowels of the building. In the melee, it wasn't hard to slip away unnoticed. Pat was neither ill nor badly injured himself, and so did not warrant a great deal of notice.

Later the nurse would remember only a tall, dark-haired man and nothing more.

And certainly David, under a surgeon's knife as they fought to keep him alive, was telling no tales.

"HERE," JAMIE HANDED PAT A LEATHER STRAP, "bite down on this, it's going to hurt like holy hell when I pour the alcohol."

Jamie placed a ceramic basin under Pat's arm, then nodded. Pat obediently bit, stifling a scream. Jamie was right, it did sting like holy hell. He was shaking, beads of sweat gathering on his brow by the time the last of the whiskey evaporated from the furrow in his arm. He had called Jamie in a panic a few blocks from the hospital, not knowing what to do nor where else to go, and unwilling to alarm Sylvie in his current state. Jamie had told him to waste no time and come directly here to Kirkpatrick's Folly.

Jamie had brought him through the back door, then ushered him into the study, gone back out and returned with the whiskey, a basin, a razor blade, and a long length of gauze to bind his arm.

The bullet had taken a neat runnel of flesh from his left shoulder. While it had bled rather copiously, it hadn't damaged the muscle.

"D'ye think," Pat asked weakly, "I could have some of that whiskey in a glass? It seems a terrible waste pourin' it over my arm an' not a drop of it makin' its way to my throat."

Jamie gave him an assessing eye and nodded. "You can have the one, but no more. You've had a bad shock, getting drunk won't improve matters." First he neatly taped and bound the shoulder, which was already stiff and aching like it had been hit full on with a cannonball.

Jamie then poured out two healthy measures of whiskey in heavy crystal tumblers, handing one to Pat. Pat took two large gulps, the fumes making his eyes water. It settled in his belly and steadied him for what he needed to say.

"I've killed three men tonight. I—I suppose I will have to turn myself in to the police." Pat's voice wavered slightly, though he sat firm, injured arm clutched to his chest.

"That sounds rather foolhardy," Jamie said, sitting back on the sofa opposite Pat and taking a swallow from his own glass, "not to mention it would only serve to complicate things."

"*Complicate things!*" Pat sputtered over his drink, "I've killed three men by my count, an' am facin' several years of prison if I make it that far, an' ye say it merely complicates things."

Jamie raised one gull-winged eyebrow. "Yes, it's complicated. Had you actually managed to kill all three men out there tonight, it would have been somewhat less complex. However, you didn't, and that definitely *complicates* things."

"What?" Pat could feel all the blood in his head start a precipitous rush towards his toes.

"I had someone check the field. Two bodies, and a trail of blood that ended in a patch of tall grass. The owner of said blood, however, was rather conspicuous by his absence." Jamie sat his glass down on the splay-legged table at his elbow. "Now what I need to know is if anyone saw your face tonight. And I do mean *anyone.*"

"I—no—well there's the publican an' his father-in-law, though he said he was blind." Below Pat's feet, the lush patterns of the Aubusson rug began to whirl giddily.

"Take a big swallow of your drink," Jamie said brusquely, "and then take a few deep breaths. It's not as though this is something that cannot be fixed."

Pat stared at him incredulously. "Fix it? How the hell do ye suggest I fix this? I've killed tonight, an' short of a miracle there's no fixin' that!"

Jamie took a deep breath, elegant nostrils flaring slightly. Pat got the distinct impression the man was beginning to feel rather annoyed. "Patrick, I'm going to tell you something and you need to listen closely." There was no longer sympathy nor warmth in the man's tone. "Tonight you had a choice, kill or be killed. Allow those men to take a friend's life or take theirs. You chose to save David. Now you're going to have to deal with the consequences."

Pat leaned forward, sloshing his drink in agitation. "An' what the hell do ye mean, ye had men out there? How the hell did ye get someone out there? Do ye have a man in every county?"

"Two," Jamie said, with only a trace of sarcasm, "except for Sligo, there I've got a set of triplets."

Pat blinked, uncertain if the man was in jest or not. "Triplets?" he echoed stupidly.

"Focus man," Jamie retorted curtly. "There's now at least two possible witnesses who can testify that they saw you at the Two-Step last night. They'll need to be dealt with in one manner or another."

"Are ye suggestin' that I should just commit murder," Pat said hoarsely, "an' then act as though it never happened?"

"What exactly did you plan to do? Turn yourself over to the IRA or the police? Either way you'll end up in the same spot as those two men tonight."

"But I—" he stuttered, "David will need me to back him up. He can hardly hide his injuries and the man who called me knew where he'd gone. When his superiors find out there are dead men lying in a field so near there will be questions David cannot answer. I won't let him take the blame for this; he needs me to tell the truth."

"What David doesn't *need*," Jamie said caustically, "is you martyring yourself on the Ulster pyre. David can take care of himself, and if you think the British powers that be give a good goddamn about a few IRA toughs being killed, think again. They'll merely consider it a few points for their side. Not to mention that it would be best if no one knew where David was last night. It could go very badly for him; do you understand?"

Pat nodded, swallowing the whiskey which suddenly tasted very bitter. He had the distinct feeling that Jamie was warning him off, that he had crossed over a line tonight that the man was guarding very carefully. That it was more than just David's wellbeing and future career that was at stake. Much more.

Jamie was sitting back now, green eyes narrowed in speculation, as if he were taking Pat's measure for the first time and wondering if he were made of the proper material to bear through with this. Behind him, dawn had turned to full day, the sun breaking along the horizon like rose and gold watercolors spilled on dull gray paper.

Suddenly, Pat felt one of those odd interior shifts that he recognized as the last piece of a puzzle clicking into place. He buried his face quickly in the fumes of his whiskey glass, knowing Jamie was capable of reading him like an open book.

It was the first time, Pat realized, that he'd actually felt scared of the man.

Chapter Seventy-nine

Blood Brothers

THE HOUSE HAD NOT BEEN THE SAME to Casey since the boy's death. He hated being alone in it now, where before he had liked the occasional silences when it was only himself and perhaps the cat. Today though, Pamela, drawn and white, had taken herself off to the city, though for what reason he couldn't entirely remember. His mind was clouded, and it seemed to him that he couldn't hear people when they spoke, the sounds no longer recognizable as the language he had known all his life.

He felt as though he were under a spell, brewed of equal parts rage and grief. And that the only thing that would break the spell would be to find the man who had killed Lawrence. Find him and kill him. The act would not expiate his grief, but he felt certain it would take away the rage that was consuming all the better parts of him.

He tidied away the morning breakfast dishes and contemplated going outside to work on the barn; there were boards in the hayloft that needed replacing. He sighed and rubbed his temples. He didn't give a good damn about the loft, nor the barn, nor any of the hundred and one tasks that had seemed paramount only weeks ago. Still it was either occupy his hands or go mad. He grabbed his work coat off the peg in the hall, knocking over the canvas bag that had lain untouched on the shoe bench since Lawrence had left it there.

The contents spilled onto the floor and Casey backed away, breath stuck fast in his chest. To see the boy's belongings, the things he'd toted about with him on a daily basis, might well be more than he could bear right now.

A crumply roll of Polo mints lay beside a half-empty pack of Sweet Aftons. A corduroy jacket, the shade of sapphires, was unrolling from the ball it had been thrust into in the bag. An orange, speckled with the white beginnings of mould, rolled drunkenly into a boot. Casey's attention was drawn back to the jacket. He knew how it would smell, tobacco and mints with a strong whiff of Finbar. Sure enough when he bent down to pick the jacket up, it was covered in coarse gray hair. He winced, both for the pain the sight of these things had caused him and for the dog, who'd barely eaten or drank in the two weeks since the boy's death.

He had to grab at the coat twice before he managed to grasp it. Grief had made him clumsy, his hands and feet cold and his limbs uncoordinated with the pain that seemed to weigh heavy in each and every cell of his body.

A flash of white, slipping out of the upended pockets caught his attention. Casey pulled it out and a chill suddenly enveloped him. Lawrence's slapdash handwriting was sprawled across the white. Casey read the words, his brow furrowing. Then he turned the white object over.

It was a photo with four clear images in it. The tale these four images told was one of blood. Blood both spilled and shared; a part of his own past. A story he knew the words of, though the entire plot had not become clear until now.

He froze in place, his hands cold and mind suddenly clear. The taste of vengeance was in his mouth, as bitter and hot as forged iron. What he must do was clear, for the writing of the final chapter in this story was his and his alone.

THE FISH PLANT HAD BEEN CLOSED DOWN for the better part of a year, a sign of the economic ruin that always accompanied violence. Its façade loomed up gray and nasty in the twilight. Fury had carried him this far. This rage had forged something in him that he knew could not be unwrought, for it went to the core of who he was.

There was no one about, the only sound that of water slapping against the rotting wharf. He knew, though, that inside the vast gloom, the man he'd sworn to kill waited for him. He approached the doors with caution, noting they were slightly ajar, as though they had been left so in anticipation of his arrival. He slipped through the gap into utter darkness.

He moved sideways, knowing the day would backlight him and give his opponent more of an advantage than he already possessed. He stood in perfect stillness, giving his breath and heart a moment to calm themselves. He needed a clear and cold head for what lay ahead. And then he sensed a slight movement in front of him, some ways off, but closer than he'd anticipated. He narrowed his eyes, flexing his hands, ready to fend off an attack, keeping the wall tight to his back until he could get a better fix on where the man stood.

For a brief moment it seemed he could hear the other man's heart beating in accord with his own, could feel his pulse from across the space, could claim his blood for his own. Then a light flared briefly in the gloom accompanied by the sulphurous sound of a match striking, and the comforting scent of tobacco burning. There was no comfort to be found, however, in what the match light had so briefly revealed. He only wondered that it had taken him so long to understand what might have, without the cloud of emotion, been terribly obvious.

"Robin," he said, voice flat with unwelcome knowledge.

"Ye expected someone else?" Robin's words were like ether scattering in the vast space. Casey's eyes probed the dark for a glimpse of the red ember of the cigarette. But either Robin had it cupped or behind his back, because he couldn't see a damn thing.

"More fool I am, I prayed it wasn't you."

"Naw," the answer came back, lightly, "'twas always meant to end this way, man."

"Christ, Robin, I really didn't want it to be you."

"Aye well," the tone was wry, "I think we've both learned that things rarely work out the way a man might like. I've been waiting here for ye for a couple of days. Knew ye'd put it together eventually." Robin's voice was conversational, as though Casey had come by for a simple visit and they would sit as they had so many times before, and have a drink and a laugh.

"I'll only ask ye the once, did ye kill the boy?"

"Aye," Robin said, "I did."

Casey had known, he had seen the evidence in the picture that had led to Lawrence's death. So why did it feel like a knife running the length of his chest to hear it confirmed?

From a great distance, he heard a beast roar in rage and pain and then realized as he rushed toward Robin, that it was he who made the terrible noise.

Robin was ready for him. The man had always been his match physically. Casey had only ever had his size to his advantage. And tonight a rage that threatened to incinerate all that lay in its path, including its possessor.

A light blinded him as he crossed the floor toward Robin. It seared his eyes, and he realized Robin had a torch and was using it to disorient him. He shut his eyes, willing the spots away, moving on relentlessly to where he knew Robin stood waiting.

Robin took the first blow without defending himself, allowing Casey to knock him down to the ground, where his own skills of lightning fast reflexes and a catlike ability to whip himself out of tight corners were to his own advantage. Casey, however, did not care if Robin beat him to a pulp as long as the final blow was his.

The floor was rough against his forearm, which he quickly locked around Robin's neck in an effort to immobilize him as much as possible. Robin twisted quickly to the side, though, kicking at Casey's legs and making searing contact with his left ankle. Casey swore and tightened his hold on the man's neck, pushing a knee into his back in an effort to still him.

Robin reared back and caught him on the temple, causing the world to whirl dizzyingly for a second, and giving Robin the split second he needed to scrabble out from under him.

Casey caught him before Robin could get onto his feet, though, twisting his left arm behind his back in a bone-cracking hold that had Robin gasping in pain.

Using the wall in front of them, which Casey could sense looming in the darkness, Robin fought his way upright, dragging Casey by main force with him. Locked in a thrash of fury and limbs and muscle pushed to burning, screaming limits, they were at a stalemate. Casey would not give, however, they could tumble all the way to hell locked together in endless combat and he wasn't going to give the man an inch. Robin's arm, close to cracking, gave suddenly, and Casey fell against him, unprepared for the sudden slack. He ought to have known better.

Robin seized his second and thrust Casey back with all the strength he could muster. Casey caught up hard against a support beam, pain flashing like lightning through his ribs, breath knocked from his body. Robin stood across from him, fighting to keep to his feet. Casey knew he was being assessed for injury. Robin would use any weakness to his gain.

He was panting, breath coming in ragged gasps that seared his throat. The impulse to kill was there in his fingertips, thrumming through muscle and sinew, body taut as a bow ready to release an arrow. Still his mind reeled at the notion that Bobbie had been the one to take Lawrence's life.

For a long moment they were still, each weighing their advantages and disadvantages. The air about them supercharged as though lightning were about to strike and every air molecule tensed at the expected onslaught. His own flesh drawn close to the bone, blood surging with reckless abandon.

In the dark, though, the dance had changed. Casey's body, alert to the last nerve-ending, sensed it. Robin was tiring and would resort to desperate last measures. He could, in his own state, only anticipate so much, but he thought he knew what Robin would do. He'd seen him fight too many times not to know. Yet this was a fight to the finish, and not a bruising that they might hope to recover from. Either way, one of them would not be leaving this building tonight. And the one who did walk out at the end would still leave something behind forever.

Robin came in a rush, a demon in the dark, straight at Casey's front, knocking him hard in the chest, sending them both in an awkward sprawl onto the conveyer belt Casey had been careful to keep at his back. He went down hard taking the brunt of Robin's full weight to his shoulder and felt it pop out with a resounding crunch. He bit down on a scream, praying Robin hadn't heard the shoulder crunch, though even if he hadn't it wouldn't take him long to realize that Casey was fighting one-handed. Two-handed he had the greater strength, though Robin had the advantage of moving swift and light. One-handed, he knew he'd not a prayer. And if his own memory retained the knowledge of Robin's patterns, then certainly the same would be true of Robin.

He quickly brought his left hand into play, wedging it between himself and Robin, knowing it was the only chance he had. At first, all he could find was a handful of wet, torn cloth and sweaty flesh that refused purchase. Then he felt the collarbone and hooked his fingers around it, digging in sharply. Robin cursed and responded by shoving a thumb into Casey's dangling shoulder.

Casey roared in agony and shoved as hard as he could against Robin's collarbone with the heel of his hand. It gave with a sharp crack and Robin was unbalanced for a moment. Only long enough for Casey to grab a breath, though, and then lithe and cunning as a cat, Robin was back on him, hands unerringly on his throat, so that not a thread of air could pass through his windpipe. Snowstars began to whirl in streams before his eyes, the pressure of Robin's hands threatening to blow his ears out. Thought no longer mattered, instinct was all the guide he had left. He scrabbled with his good hand, managing to get it palm flat against Robin's chest. Then inched it up slow until he'd a grip on the other man's neck that bought him a few extra seconds. He hoped to God he had that long.

Sweat or blood was dripping in a steady stream onto his face, he neither knew nor cared which, part of his brain still spinning with the notion that Robin was choking him to death.

The dark tingling increased rapidly, he knew he was only seconds from passing out and beyond that lay a certain death. His right arm was useless and his left quickly tiring. As soon as the pressure eased even a fraction, he knew Robin would seize his advantage and he'd be finished. Even now the cramping in his hand was agonizing, his grip ready to seize. Then above him, Robin's breathing checked and his hands, slick with blood and sweat, slipped. It was what Casey had waited for. He gulped at the air, then brought his good elbow down in a vicious arc onto Robin's collarbone. Robin grunted and reared back slightly, giving Casey the small bit of space he'd sought. He used the gap to lever his legs out and kicked up, knocking Robin off balance, then grasped the opportunity to slam his head into where he thought Robin's face should be. A crunch of bone and a spray of blood confirmed the accuracy of his aim. Robin fell to the side like a stone tipped into a pond, with as little noise when he hit bottom.

Casey lay back, breathing heavily, shoulder a blaze of pain and a warmth spreading across his back that told him he was bleeding a good deal. Robin wasn't moving yet, but was likely only stunned and would soon be up. Casey moved his right arm experimentally, catching his breath at the pain that shot across his back and down his arm to the elbow.

He twisted to the left side, bit down hard on his lip, and shoved himself into a sitting position on the belt. He had to get up before Bobbie did, or he was finished. He managed to find his feet and plant them where he thought the floor should be. Thankfully it was, though he swayed and saw several stars come into view before extinguishing into the turgid air.

In the few seconds that Robin had flashed the torch about earlier, he had taken in what he could of the surrounding area. He staggered to the left, where he thought he'd seen a support beam that would serve his purposes well. If he could just get to it and do what needed doing before Robin came around.

It took a bit of stumbling, good hand out in front of him, seeking for purchase in the dark, but he found the beam a couple of minutes later. He ran his hand over it, looking for any protrusions or sharp edges, but it was broad and smooth and would do nicely.

Getting the arm up and into position was another matter. Sweat ran in beads off his forehead, down to mingle with the drying blood, and his vision blacked on him more than once as he lifted the arm up.

He closed his eyes and threw himself against the beam as hard as his abused body would allow. The shoulder popped in, accompanied by a fresh spurt of blood down his back and he let go a howl that would have shivered the roots of a man's soul, had any been conscious to hear it. The pain reeled him out, threatened to drop him to his knees, then he recovered, head pressed against the beam to stop the world spinning. On the other side of the conveyer belt Robin was moving and making an odd noise, like a beached fish with vocal chords. Casey opened one eye and turned toward the noise, mystified.

It wasn't what he expected. Robin was laughing. Exhausted, bleeding, reeking of fish and sweat, but laughing.

"Mad bastard," Casey muttered through lips still tingling from pent-up oxygen.

"Now that's the pot callin' the kettle names," Robin said, still flat on his back and still laughing. "Jaysus, ye've knocked a tooth out, cracked my collarbone an' broke my nose. Yer da was right, yer head is bone right through."

Casey grunted in reply. "Where's the torch gone?"

"Don't know," Robin replied, "rolled off in the scuffle."

"Scuffle," Casey snorted, flexing his right hand carefully, wincing at the red-hot wires of pain that shot through his arm as a result. "I've not a square inch left to me that isn't broke, bleedin' or painin'."

"Ye gave as good as ye got," Robin said, laughing again with an ominous gurgling under note.

Casey had been moving quietly as he spoke, and now his foot struck something solid which rolled ahead of him across the floor. He bent down, his ribs creaking in virulent protest and crawled under the conveyer belt, feeling on the floor for the torch. He found Robin's hand instead and flinched back as if struck by a cobra.

"It's above my hand, rolled into my ribs."

Was the man trying to trap him? He'd have to take the chance. He couldn't continue on in the suffocating darkness another minute. He grabbed for the torch and switched it on immediately, eyes lighting on Robin's face.

"Christ, ye're a sight," Casey said, appalled by what the dark had hidden from him.

Robin's nose, canted off to the left, was leaking a bright, steady stream of crimson, his right eye almost swollen shut, lips puffy and torn, the rest a slowly weltering mass of broken blood vessels. Robin peered up with his good eye. "Ye're not exactly lookin' like ice cream on Sunday yerself, boyo. Now help me up, I can't breathe proper."

Casey eyed him warily, but Robin merely gave a watery snort in reply. "I'll not do anything, I couldn't even if I wanted to. Give me a minute or two to go back on the defense, I'm not sixteen anymore."

"Aye," Casey responded dryly, "I don't need remindin' of the fact." He hooked his good arm around Robin's chest, bracing against the inevitable pain in his body as soon as he applied any force. "If I help ye up, can ye make it over to where that bundle of sacking is?"

"Aye," Robin replied grimly, though he sounded less than convinced. It took three tries, a great deal of grunting, and an undignified scream on Robin's part before Casey managed to get him on his feet. Then, with Robin's arm looped around his neck, they managed to hobble over to the sacking, where Robin promptly collapsed, gasping for air in the cloud of dust that arose from the burlap bags.

"Well if ye came here to kill me, I'd say the job is about three-quarters done," Robin said, once he'd recovered his powers of speech.

"Luck's with ye," Casey replied wearily, "for I've not the energy to finish off the last quarter. Can ye breathe comfortable now?"

"Comfortable would be stretchin' the point beyond its limits, but aye, I can get enough air for the moment."

Casey stood facing Robin, body too far past its boundaries to understand just how fatigued and damaged it was. He was still tensed, uncertain of what Robin intended, only knowing he didn't have the strength at present to continue what had begun, and must be ended here.

"Would ye take the torch out of my eyes fer Chrissakes," Robin said, "there are things I would tell ye, an' I'd rather not feel that I'm bein' interrogated."

A primal fear shot up Casey's backbone at his words. He'd a feeling that up to now, all the words and actions had merely been a prelude to Robin's real purpose for calling him out with that photo. He was about to find out why he was really here. Despite his dread, he moved the torch, allowing its light to form a shallow pool on the sticky floor.

"Pamela was right about yer da's death."

"What?" Casey felt something cold and heavy settle in the very marrow of his bones.

"I said she was right. In fact, she got so close to the truth she's lucky to still be breathin'. 'Twas fortunate ye made her stop when ye did. She was close to stumblin' across that bastard Morris Jones while tracin' the Brotherhood."

"Ye know about the Brotherhood?"

"Aye, though maybe not so much as yer friend up on the hill."

"What are ye sayin'?"

"That the organization still exists, though it's more secretive than ever. An' that yer man on the hill runs the show nowadays. Now there's a ruthless bastard if ever I've met one. Man thought I was sneakin' about watchin' yer house while ye were locked up on that ship. He kidnapped an' questioned me for hours. Didn't hold so much as a gun or knife on me, but I tell ye, I've rarely sweated out a time as I did that one."

"Do ye know how my da died, then?"

"Aye I do, didn't have anything to do with the Brotherhood in the end, though he did belong, though ye'll know that, for ye've the ring."

Casey tried to breathe and found he could not. "Do ye know who killed him?"

"Aye, I know. Yer da spent a deal of time tryin' to find out what happened to my sister. Durin' the course of his searchin' he found out about the things goin' on at Kincora. He was goin' to go to that wee friend of his that worked for the newspaper. The names he'd come across played like a Who's Who of British aristocracy, government ministers an' celebrities. Men have been killed for far less. They had him shot out in a field. They say he asked no quarter an' gave them no satisfaction." Robin swallowed as though he had a rusty nail lodged in his throat, "'Twas my father who had the shooting of him."

"What?" Casey felt horribly sick, as though the world had tipped out from under his feet without warning.

Robin met his eyes, and Casey saw something old beyond counting in the man's face and knew there were things that time did not have the power to heal.

"And I killed my father, gave him the same treatment as he gave yer daddy. Took him out in a field in the dark an' made him beg for his life, an' he did beg. An' then I shot him. Don't know why he bothered with beggin', he saw his death in my face from the minute I found him."

Casey shook his head slowly, the knowledge of things coming at him too quickly. His daddy on his knees—what had he felt knowing his death was imminent...? Christ, he couldn't think of it now, he had to stay clearheaded, had to stay level, stay standing just a little longer.

"But ye said that yer father died on the street, choked on his own vomit..."

Robin shrugged. "I lied, seemed best then, rather than tellin' ye what had truly happened. Then yer wife kept diggin' about for the truth an' I knew it would have to come out. Yer da was kind to me, an' he was maybe the only adult that gave a damn when Jo disappeared. I owed him vengeance for his death."

"How did ye know all this?"

"Casey, ye know what it is, I'm surprised ye never worked it out before. Maybe it's only that ye didn't want to see it."

"Ye're workin' for the Brits," Casey said, disbelief still strong in his mind. He could hardly connect this with the man he thought he knew, and yet it all fit, every piece that hadn't seemed to form a picture before, now snapped tightly into place. The scenario it presented made him queasy.

"The MRF was runnin' me. I got cozy with Joe an' fed back to them. Now an' again I took somethin' back to Joe, just to keep his trust. It made certain other information easy to come across. They never knew I'd come upon the pedophile ring, that I knew about their filthy parties over the water with all those young boys; I'd have been dead months ago if they knew that. But now I've outworn my usefulness an' they've made it apparent that my services are no longer required."

Casey swallowed back a sick surge. The MRF was the Military Reconnaissance Force, the agency that gathered intelligence and ran agents in Northern Ireland. To work for them, as a Republican, meant you had a pretty big death wish.

"What the hell were ye thinkin', man? Ye can't play those games in this neighborhood, ye know that as well as anyone who grew up on these streets."

"I didn't know the Brits would cut me loose when it was over, I thought I could play both sides for all they were worth an' walk away the winner. Forgot you were the lucky bastard, not me."

"Jesus Christ, Robin, eight hundred years of them throwin' us to the wolves wasn't enough for ye to know how it'd end?"

"Doesn't much matter anymore, man, I know too much to be comfortable for either side. We both know what happens next."

Casey nodded, there was no answer needed, they both did know, and a little too intimately, just what happened next. Robin had always known where this path led, and yet had chosen to keep walking it.

Robin shifted, a grunt of pain escaping his lips along with a slipstream of darker blood that made Casey's stomach lurch. Blood that shade was never the result of a surface injury. "There's another thing I'd tell ye before we're done. Do ye remember how yer da used to say sometimes a man is most blind to what's goin' on right beneath his own nose?"

Something in Robin's tone stopped Casey cold. "Robin, it's too late for games, if ye've somethin' to say, say it."

Robin drew a half-breath and gasped as it caught hard upon the shoals of his smashed ribs. "Yer wife an' Love Hagerty."

Five simple words, but enough in their content to fell a man, to put him on his knees and make him wish he were deaf rather than hear them.

"No," he said, throat stripped raw, heart pounding so hard that it filled his ears with the sound of a roaring vortex. Aware that it did not come as the shock that Robin had intended it to be.

"Every time ye shipped out she was in his bed. He'd an apartment for her, I think the damn fool was actually in love. Then there were the things ye'd seen that he'd rather ye hadn't. An' given that set of circumstances you were lookin' like a mighty large inconvenience."

"How—" he swallowed hard against the bitterness surging at the back of his throat, "how'd ye know?"

Robin shook his head, wiping a crusted hand across his mouth. "Hagerty was no man's fool, though in the end he surely was a woman's." He held up a hand as Casey started forward. "Save it man, I can see by the look on yer face this comes as no great shock. What I mean to say is the man did his homework, he knew all about yer background an' that's where he found me."

"What did he want with ye?"

Robin laughed, a bitter sound that raised the hairs on Casey's neck. "Hired me to follow ye, if ye can believe it. Sad bastard didn't know I was playin' both sides of the coin, followed him too. That's how I found out about him an' Pamela. Watched her come an' go from the flat in Brookline. Sometimes I'd follow him to public events and I'd see how he watched her across the room, or make reasons to be near her. He was obsessed. An' I knew that would be his downfall, she'd only need to feed him a little rope an' he'd hang himself. She can be mighty cold, yer wife, when the need is on her."

"Ye'll keep yer opinions of my wife to yerself," Casey said in a flat tone that brooked no argument. "I've no proof of what ye say, but if she were to do such a thing, she'd have to have a mighty good reason."

"She did—your life."

"What?"

"Did ye not ever wonder why; if Hagerty wanted ye dead, he never managed to accomplish it? The man had connections up an' down the entire eastern seaboard."

"You mean—" Casey paused, unable to finish the sentence, a clear picture of Pamela in Love Hagerty's bed, her body at his bidding, allowing him to touch her in the most intimate of ways. With a great force of will he pushed the picture away, heart turned to lead in his chest.

"She did it to keep ye safe an' whole," Robin continued quietly, eyes taking in the bleak set of Casey's face. "I understood that after I met her, there wouldn't have been anything else that could have induced her to do such a thing. She really loves ye, man."

"How was he killed?" Casey asked, voice dark and hollow.

"Ye know how he was killed, the Bassarelli boys took him out. Wasn't pretty either."

"That's not what I mean an' ye know it. If ye were following her then ye must know if—if she had somethin' to do with it."

Robin nodded slowly. "She visited old man Bassarelli the once. Love Hagerty died later that same evening."

The nausea Casey had suppressed earlier overwhelmed him now, his body understanding truth, though his mind refused it. Beneath his knees, the floor was thick and sticky with years of scales and blood.

"Why tell me now? It can't serve any purpose."

"Long time ago ye told me that if someone were to betray ye, ye'd not want to be the last to know. Both she and I have betrayed ye an' beyond the two of us, there's no one else left alive who knows."

Casey tilted his head, feeling like a cur that's been smacked with an iron pipe. "What do ye mean none left alive? Who else knew?"

"The boy knew I was playin' both sides. He knew I was workin' for the Brits. Saw me one weekend, when he was slurkin' about his old hangouts. 'Twas just happenstance, an unfortunate coincidence."

The world tilted again but he held to his feet, the red haze tinging the corners of his vision once again. "Is that why ye killed him? Because he saw ye playin' out a double-cross?"

"'Twasn't how ye thought, the boy was never in anyone's cards. He just got in the way of things. Knew too much, Morris was afraid of him, only the more so once the boy had joined up with you."

A low moan of pain escaped Casey's lips, Lawrence's ginger hair and pale, clear eyes rearing up stark in his mind. Killed for the inconvenience of his existence. What love or joy had his brief life ever known? "Was it Morris Jones he went to meet?" Casey ground the words out, the sickness surging hard through his system again.

"Aye. The lad was right to be afraid of him. I've known some sick bastards in my life but he was altogether in a league of his own. He's some ugly appetites an' he'd a special spite for the lad. He lured the boy there with some sort of threat, an' then raped him amongst other things. By the time," Robin swallowed, the scene apparently still vivid in his own mind, "I found him he was in a bad way, a very bad way if ye understand my meanin'."

"Ye forget maybe," Casey said harshly, "that 'twas me that found the boy, an' myself an' my wife that buried him."

"An' yerself that loved him," Robin said quietly, "no I've not forgot. Not likely to, am I? For it's what brought you here tonight, the belief that ye'd avenge his death."

"And I will," Casey said, in the tone of an oath.

Robin coughed again, a sound like a sputtering engine, and blood bubbled from the corner of his mouth.

"Robin—"

"Nay," Robin said shortly, "I'll do. Now ye'll have seen enough of fightin' to know there are some men excited by the sight of blood?"

"Aye," Casey replied tersely, the wealed crosshatch of fine silver scars scattered about Lawrence's body all too plain in his memory.

"Well, Morris was that way, but it had to be a boy's blood, I think maybe it started out with a few simple cuts, nothin' that the child couldn't heal physically from, but then like most appetites it built until it was out of control. Lawrence wasn't the first to be hurt at the man's hand."

"He wasn't dead when ye found him?"

"No, but 'twould have been better for him had he been."

"So it was you, then," Casey said, voice flat, a tone that made Robin brace for the expected blow. None came, though. "Why, Robin? He was nothin' to ye, he'd not harmed anyone. He'd kept yer secrets that long, there was no reason he'd have told then."

Robin shook his head. "It wasn't my secrets that I was worried for, don't ye understand?"

"No."

"It was a mercy, do ye see? Ye can't live proper with such scars on yer soul. The boy wasn't going to heal this time, I knew that an' so I did what I had to for him."

"It wasn't for you to decide."

"But it was, who better to know what the boy felt?"

"He wasn't you Robin, ye can't know—"

"Yes, I can know," Robin said wearily, "an' that is why the boy didn't like me. He saw himself, another decade down the road, when he looked in my face."

Casey didn't think he could stand much more revelation tonight. "I didn't know, Robin, why did ye never say? Maybe I couldn't have helped but my da would have gotten ye out."

Robin shook his head, tongue tentatively flicking at the corner of his mouth, causing a fresh stream of blood to trickle down his chin. "Do ye think I could have ever looked ye in the face had ye known? I couldn't bear the thought of ye not treatin' me like an equal anymore, I'd have become somethin' to pity, not to love."

"I knew about Lawrence, all of it, an' it didn't change my love for him."

"Aye, but that's as a man loves a child, we were boys together an' that's a different view. I was hollow before I met ye, but when ye gave me yer friendship, when ye cared for me as though I wasn't," Robin paused to take a ragged breath, "wasn't broken an' filthyw—well there wasn't any secret worth tellin' to sacrifice that."

"Tell me how." Casey said, barely able to force the words past his throat, but needing to know all the same.

"I just held his nose. It was quick an' peaceful, he barely struggled, 'twas more like he slipped off to sleep. He'd not have survived the night anyway. He was damaged real bad. He said yer name just before he went beyond words, just sort of breathed it out. Ye need not worry yerself about Morris neither, I took care of him that night as well. 'Twas him ran the ring that killed all them young boys. He spent a deal of nights at that house where Pamela found my sister's bones."

"Oh Jesus," was all Casey managed to gasp out before the sickness took him firmly in its maw and shook him without mercy. He wished with the force of everything in him that he could erase the sight of Lawrence's ruined body from his mind, that he would never again know that smell, the scent of utter depravity and cruelty. To not know that the boy had died calling his name, wondering why he didn't come to his rescue. But no, he thought as another spasm of nausea clawed his insides, Lawrence had not believed in fairytales. He had known the cavalry didn't rush in at the last minute on white horses, holding salvation in their hands. The child had not had any illusions and somehow that seemed much, much worse than the alternative.

As the retching subsided, he felt Robin's hand on his back and tensed immediately for the blow that would end the night and all things with it. He no longer had the energy to resist it. The dark would be welcome. He realized with a shock that Robin's hand was fast in his hair, the singing tension in his scalp only now registering itself on his ravaged senses. And then there was a knife at his throat, scoring the skin just below his Adam's apple.

Robin's mouth was by his ear, breath as intimate as a lover. Casey could move neither forward nor back and was completely at the man's mercy. The anger that had sustained him for so long was ebbing, swamped in the beginning of a grief that threatened to become a deluge he would surely perish in.

"Do ye have less courage than a wee lassie, then?" Robin hissed in his ear. "She killed without a backward glance to keep ye safe, will ye sell her so short as to let me take ye here an' now?" He yanked back on the handful of hair and Casey grunted, teeth gritted, not daring to swallow with the knife so tight against his throat. "Come on, ye black Irish bastard, ye said ye'd avenge the boy's murder so fight me, fight me!"

Robin let him go so quickly that Casey half fell into the sticky muck on the floor. He was quickly losing feeling in his right arm, which seemed a mercy at this point. He took a shallow breath, aware of the coppery taste of blood on his tongue.

He rose onto his knees to find Robin had circled round to the front of him and was propped against the dusty sacking and empty wire spools. One arm wrapped protectively around his shattered ribs, the other pointed straight at Casey, with a pistol snugged tight in its grip.

His wife's voice was suddenly clear in his head, the words she'd spoken only days ago. Though it seemed a lifetime. She had found him sitting on their bed, pistol in his lap.

"Some night you're going to find it."

"Find what?"

"The bullet with your name on it." And his reply, which in the cold, hard light of what he now faced, seemed naïve and foolhardy.

'Better that than to live afraid for a hundred years." And untrue. He did not want to die, not here and not now, not by the hand of a man who'd been trying to lure him into a fatal death dance from the moment they'd seen one another across that smoky card table. He slowly put down his left hand, not trusting the right to support him, and pushed himself up into a standing position, preternaturally aware the entire time that the gun continued to point at his head. His legs were shaky, but they held him upright and it seemed—if he gave them a minute or two—they might be willing to carry him out of this place.

Robin was speaking again, voice gone soft with fatigue. "Do ye remember the time we were goin' to run off to Liverpool together?"

Casey drew a ragged breath and nodded. "Aye, we'd not the sense of a goose between the two of us, had what—thirty pounds total to call our own in this world? I remember we were goin' to meet down by the Donegal Quay."

"Aye, well I was there, but you never came."

"What?"

The gun dropped between Robin's knees, his eyes shimmering with tears. "Do ye know how long I waited there for ye?"

Casey shook his head, the tension still thrumming hard through his shoulders, down his arms and into his hands.

"Three days I waited, three days," Robin's voice was no more than a hoarse whisper. "I even slept on the goddamn dock, thinkin' if I just gave ye another hour ye'd show up."

"Neither of us was thinkin' clearly, ye knew I'd a powerful fear of the sea, an' when it came down to it I couldn't leave my da an' brother." He sighed, feeling the stab of his lungs against the cracked ribs.

Robin nodded, all the wariness gone from him. Casey dragged over a spool that had once held cable, wincing at the pain the movement caused, until he was only a few feet from where Robin stood slumped against the wall of sacking, the nets under him thick with the smell of diesel and fish guts.

"Ye don't need to waste energy disarmin' me man, I've no fight left in me. Besides, I brought the gun for you."

"What—what do ye mean?" Casey asked, afraid he was finally understanding just where Robin had been leading him tonight.

"How long have we known one another man? Near to twenty years now, an' ye know my secrets. Ye'll know I once had something worth carin' about, even if it's long gone now. I'd rather it was by yer hand, than that of a stranger."

"Jaysus man, how can ye ask me such a thing?"

"That's what ye came here to do, so finish it. Besides I'm already a dead man, Casey," Robin said, face entirely sober now. "Ye know it as well as I do.

It's only a matter of a day or two."

"You could run, man," Casey said desperately, "go back to the States."

"I'm too tired to run anymore, I've been running all my life." He shook his head, the dim light picking out the red in his hair. "D'ye remember what it was we used to say to one another before goin' onto the pitch?"

Casey sucked in a sharp breath. "Aye. Today is a beautiful day to die."

Robin nodded, a strange luminescence in his eyes, the blue of drowned stars. Then he bent down, the pistol still unwavering, and lit the tinder ends of the sacking. The small flames flickered, uncertainly, then realizing the arid landscape they'd lit upon, caught with a fierce will.

"I've thought those words many a time over the years, but I believe," Robin squared his shoulders with conviction and put the gun to his head, "if ye won't do it for me then I must do it for myself. And I believe, after all, that today is a beautiful day to die." He tilted his head toward the fire that was merrily crackling now, feeding itself in ever larger bites. "Ye'll have to go man, or it'll soon be too late."

"Bobbie, those words were never meant, it was said in fun, come on man, give over the gun," Casey edged his way carefully along the crates, heart threatening to come out of his chest, hands out in supplication. But Robin was no longer listening.

He looked up, eyes now aglow like the heart of a candle flame and smiled, the blood still trickling from the corner of his mouth. "You have always been," he said softly, "the brother of my heart. Beyond Jo ye were the only family I ever knew." The breath was stopped in Casey's throat, the blue of Robin's eyes expanding to fill all his senses. "I love ye man, but we will neither of us be free, until I am dead," Robin finished in a whisper.

Time stopped and froze as Robin squeezed the trigger, Casey lunged, legs like lead, pain slicing across his ribcage, the smell of cordite like brimstone on the air. He never knew if he'd screamed 'no' aloud or if it was only the pounding reverberation in his skull. It was a kill-shot though, Robin was well trained in such things. He stopped short of the man who had been his best friend, knowing the boy he'd loved had been dead for a very long time. For Lawrence's sake, he would not touch him, he would not search for a pulse, he would not ask questions that needed no answer, he would let it end here and now.

The fire, rapidly advancing, licked now at the nape of Robin's neck, grasping finally at the ends of his hair. It caught with a lung-collapsing *whoosh*, and Casey, paralyzed to the spot, understood the smell that had lingered like a ghost since he'd opened the doors. Paint spirits.

And so—this now, was how the world ended. But not for him, not tonight. He was still quicker than the fire, though rogue sparks smoldered in his hair and spent themselves on his clothing, his skin taut with the enticement of heat. His body, apart from a mind that was lost in the ash of revelation, moved, turned, lifted limb, sought the sanctuary of the night beyond these walls.

Hand on the door, he turned. The flames had engulfed Robin, lighting the hellish interior of the plant like a throbbing jewel, making of his childhood friend a living, breathing coruscation of flame that spangled the night, as bright as the last explosion of a dying star.

"*Slan leat, mo dearthair*," he whispered, and walked out into the night.

THE SUN WAS SETTING when Pamela arrived home. Though it was only late August she could both feel and see the days drawing down, the night creeping in earlier and earlier. She shivered; she'd been cold since the funeral and couldn't imagine ever feeling warm again.

The house was too quiet, Casey wasn't home yet. She knew that he couldn't bear to be here where there was such a black hole in the universe where Lawrence used to exist. She understood that he needed to be alone with his grief, but missed his physical presence like an ache that nothing would alleviate. It hurt her to think he couldn't turn to her in his pain. Did the man not see that she had lost Lawrence too? That she too had failed to keep the boy safe, when it was as much her responsibility as his?

She went to the kitchen, turning lights on along the way. She filled the kettle directly from the tap, thinking a hot cup of tea might alleviate some of the bone deep cold.

She looked out the window into the yard below. It was full dusk, a light breeze turning leaves silver side up, an unmistakable sign that it would rain before the night was through. Shadows clustered thickly along the roots of trees, clinging to the framework of the half-built shed. The garden gate still hung half repaired, in the same state as Casey had left it the night Lawrence died. It creaked back and forth in the wind, the sound as desolate as the silent house around her.

She still couldn't bear to walk past his empty room, she'd closed the door the night they found him and neither she nor Casey had opened it since.

She froze suddenly, the fine hairs standing up on the back of her neck, realizing what had put her on edge. She turned slowly, seeing what her brain had registered as she'd walked through the hallway into the kitchen.

The door to Lawrence's bedroom stood open. The room beyond it lay in utter darkness.

She stood as if paralyzed, a chill premonition swamping her.

Finally she forced herself to move across the kitchen, loathe to leave its bright interior for what lay beyond that door. She hesitated on the threshold, uncertain if she'd the strength to see Lawrence's room. The untidy boy jumble of clothing and schoolbooks, his rugby uniform and record albums strewn across the carpet just as they'd been the day he'd left them. The smell of grass and jam and dirt and sweetness that he'd exuded even when grimy from an afternoon on the field with the lads.

She turned on the desk lamp, fingers stiff with dread. Light pooled over the room, collecting in the coils of dirty socks, catching upon the rim of a half-empty glass of milk. The milk had soured, mingling its sickly smell with the other scents in the room. But under it, under the stale smell of a room closed off from human energy, from movement and light, she could still smell him. The boy she'd grown to love, every smart-mouthed gangly inch of him. She clasped a hand to her mouth, the grief rising in her gorge like a bitter tide, unstoppable and bent on destruction. The soft fog of disbelief she'd moved in these last two weeks was ripping away. She turned, fighting a wave of dizziness and grasped the headboard of the bed in an effort to steady herself.

On the white pillowcase, a single strand of ginger-gold hair glimmered softly. The sight of it was a blow to the chest. She gasped, dropping to her knees beside the bed. Dry sobs racked her body, forcing her face to the rumpled sheets. The cotton was cold to her skin, the same horrible stillness laying over it as over all the things in this room.

She could feel a terrible howl rising within her, the primeval howl of dreadful pain and anger. That the universe could be so evil as to allow a child's life to be snuffed out in such a horrible way. The injustice of it was beyond comprehension and neither body nor mind could begin to understand how to survive it.

As quickly as it had begun, the rage subsided. She felt an enormous lethargy swamping her every cell, hot tears drying tight and itchy on her face, salt stinging the fine skin across her cheekbones.

She became aware of other sensations, the small heaviness low in her pelvis that she'd ignored with equal parts superstition and fear for the last two weeks, the dull metallic taste on her tongue that said a real storm was about to hit, and a sharp burn that cut across the skin on her right knee.

She bent down, seeing the edge of a photo sticking out from under the bed, its glossy knife edge had sliced her knee, where a thin line of blood now gleamed. She blinked a few times in an effort to see the picture more clearly, finally grasping it and bringing it up where the light could reveal the dim figures in the picture.

There were four men in the picture. The picture had been taken from above them, as though the photographer were suspended somehow. It was obvious the men in the picture had no notion they were under observation. Three stood poised around the fourth, who was kneeling, features obscured by the black cloth hood he wore. The three standing wore balaclavas so they too were unidentifiable. Except that there was something odd about the clothing on two of them. She tilted the picture toward the light. They were wearing uniforms—British Army uniforms. The shooter was in civilians, but the other two men, who must have stood and watched the execution, were unmistakably soldiers.

And then she saw it on the gunman's trigger finger. She backed away on hands and knees, fingertips pulsating where she'd touched the picture. Saw in her mind, hands stroking pink velvet over a delicate skull, hands wrapped around a brandy flask. And on the one hand, a ring. A childhood memento worn on the smallest finger, the only one it would fit. Her stomach was a hollow pit, her entire body weightless and tingling with shock.

Lawrence must have taken the picture, must have followed Robin and somehow Robin had found out. But why on earth would he have been following Robin? She remembered suddenly a conversation she'd had with him some months ago, after Robin had come by the center to drop off some groceries for the terminally emptying pantry.

"I don't like him," Lawrence said bluntly, a wary look pursing the skin around his mouth and nose.

"You don't know him," Pamela said in exasperation.

"Don't need to, to know there's somethin' off with him," Lawrence cast a blue glare in Robin's direction. *"Man's trouble, the bad kind."*

She stumbled backwards, feet turning toward the stairs before she even consciously understood where they were headed. She felt very odd, as though her head were a balloon and her feet filled with lead. It must be shock, she thought muzzily, groping the wall for support on the way up the stairs.

In their bedroom, she scrabbled for the box on top of the closet. But it was gone, the sweaters that had once covered it shoved to the side. She turned; the box lay open on their bed. He'd not bothered to hide what his intentions were.

Her knees started to shake and she uttered a little cry as the world tilted on its axis, Casey's words echoing in her head.

'If ye stop me now I'll only bide my time until ye're back is turned an' do it then.'

Then had terrifyingly become now.

She willed herself to think, to try and force some linear path through the jumble of terror and panic that was scattershot through her brain. The truth was she'd no idea where he'd gone, only what would be in his mind. She could see him clearly in her mind's eye, bent on revenge, needing the taste of blood to purge himself of some of the pain of Lawrence's death, and the racking guilt that he'd not been able to prevent it. He had known violence all his life, had been both its victim and its executioner. Under normal circumstances, he didn't condone it, and channelled his own with discipline and intelligence. But now stripped to his soul, it would be his natural wont. And he would not hesitate to act upon it.

The small heaviness low in her belly, surged suddenly, the taste of hot copper flooding her mouth, forcing her to stagger to the bathroom, where she was violently ill. The nausea passed quickly, though it left her weak and shaky. If she'd needed proof of her suspicions, the sickness had confirmed it. What would have been an occasion for great joy only the week before, now seemed a terrible joke, a wish granted far too late.

She managed to get back to the bed, just as the storm broke with a huge cracking *boom* directly over the house. She huddled against the curving headboard, still dizzy, black spots dancing in front of her eyes. The saying about an Irishman never being drunk as long as he could find a blade of grass to hang onto skittered through her head. She clutched Casey's pillow like it was the proverbial blade, burying her face in its feathery depths. It smelled comfortingly of him, wood shavings and male musk. Over the top of the pillow she spied a dark blot where the pillow had lain. She reached out and clutched the tiny velvet pouch tight in her hand. His father's rosary. The beads felt like small islands of assurance lodged in the lines of her heart and life.

She prayed then, not the well learned prayers of childhood, nor the imprinted cadences of the Church, but a prayer of pure desperation. For her husband, for herself, for the small fragile life that was within her, barely begun. She prayed with eyes open to the night and the rain that flooded the windowpanes and fretted at the walls. Prayed until she drifted almost trancelike, barely aware of the room around her anymore. Seeing her husband in absolute darkness, feeling the fear and rage. Knowing who he had gone to kill, fearing that despite her prayers, there was no redemption for such an act.

Time seemed fragmented, stretching out, then racing past. *Oh God, why didn't Casey come home?* Was he hurt, laying somewhere mortally wounded, was this small quickening in her womb destined to grow up fatherless?

Finally, her body did what her mind could not and dropped a soft blanket of unconsciousness over her. She sank into the depths gratefully.

It was the sound of the door opening below that woke her. The storm had died back, though rain still drummed against the roof. She found she couldn't move from where she'd huddled on the bed for the last three hours. Her legs were cramped, left ankle throbbing but it was fear more than anything that kept her there. Her heart fighting against her ribs like a bird caught in a tight fist. Her hearing was painfully acute. Every step was audible as he moved through the downstairs, tread heavy. Then he mounted the stairs, slowly, as though each step were an effort beyond measure.

He stood in the doorway to their bedroom for what seemed a small eternity. His silence telling her all she needed to know about where he'd been.

"Casey?" she said, voice barely audible.

"Aye," he said, voice insubstantial as smoke, "it's me."

"Are you..." she swallowed, the fear tasting like blood in her mouth, "are you all right?"

He didn't answer, just moved into the room. "I'm goin' to turn a light on," he said quietly.

She wanted to say no, to leave the light off, as though the dark would protect the both of them from the truth. That without light he would be able to turn back the sheets and rest in this bed of lies without discomfort or pain.

She heard the click of the bedside lamp, its rosy glow stamping her eyelids like a brand. She opened her eyes slowly, unable to stifle a gasp at the sight of her husband. His face, in the patches free from drying blood, was black and swollen. One eye was almost closed, his hair matted to his head. He held his arm across his stomach, his hand trembling visibly.

"Oh God, Casey." She lurched across the bed awkwardly, reaching out for him.

"Don't," he said harshly, "don't touch me."

Her hand froze in mid-air at his words, he'd never spoken to her in such a tone, not even in his worst moments of despair or anger. The *why* she'd been about to utter stopped, flayed of its purpose, on her lips. She saw the stiff dark patches on his coat, some still wet, then the smell hit her and with it another wave of nausea. She fought it back, throat thick with the scent. She had known two things—either he would not come home ever again, or he would come home a man changed entirely. Before her stood her answer. A stranger occupied her husband's face.

"It's blood, isn't it?" she managed to whisper hoarsely, feeling as though her heart was going to push its way up into her throat and choke her to death.

"Aye, it's blood," he said, voice still harsh as though its timbre was the only thing holding the fragile thread of its owner's sanity.

"Casey," she bit her bottom lip against the tingling numbness that always preceded a horrible shock, "what have you done?"

"I went to see Robin."

"Is he dead?" she asked, the words sounding like a far off echo to her ears.

"Yes. Ye don't seem shocked. Did ye know he killed the lad?" His voice was flat and accusatory, his undamaged eye remote as the night sky.

"I found the picture. How—did Robin—" she choked on the words, couldn't bring herself to ask what the exact manner of Lawrence's death had been. Couldn't bear to know if he'd cried out, or begged for mercy.

"It doesn't matter," he said, "it's done now, an' nothin' will bring him nor the laddie back.

He..." he faltered for the first time since entering the room, "he told me of another matter that I—I wanted to think him a liar in but couldn't. What he told me made sense of a good many things, an' I think perhaps I knew it, only was too much a coward to look it full in the face."

She never knew if she actually uttered the word 'what?' or if he only sensed the inevitability of it, and the many mutations the word took on upon utterance.

"Yerself an' Love Hagerty."

Four words, she thought, putting her head down to the bed in an effort to control the panicked spinning the words had caused. Four simple words, a minor arrangement of vowels and consonants, and the world beneath your feet tore apart. Ground that had seemed like granite, now quicksand.

"Is it true?" It was just barely a question. She saw that he'd always suspected, but had kept it from himself. In some perverse way, it was almost a relief to have it out. As though someone had finally removed the knife from her belly, and she could now quietly bleed to death. Casey wasn't going to let it be that easy though.

"Look at me woman. Is it true? Ye owe me the truth."

She pulled herself up, scar feeling like a lick of flame along her cheek. He'd had the courage to ask this question, now she must have the courage to answer it. She looked directly into his face.

"Yes, it's true."

He staggered back slightly. "Oh Christ, why—how could you do this to us?"

"I was working for the FBI," she said tonelessly, the words sounding utterly ludicrous. "They said if I could get incriminating information out of him, they'd make sure you never faced any prison time and they'd find a way to keep you out of his reach."

"An' did they ask ye to whore to the man for this information?" he asked, tone horribly calm.

"Yes they did. It seemed a small price to pay to keep you alive," she said, knowing the words were like a slap across his face.

"Why didn't ye tell me?"

She shook her head slowly, wishing she could break the mutual gaze they were locked in. "How could I tell you? You'd have hated me and I couldn't bear the thought of that."

"Lying to me was better?" he said hoarsely.

"Of course it was," she whispered, throat thick and heavy as lead. "Because at least I could still have you, and the burden was only mine to bear. I could manage it. But to have you hate me, to have you look at me," she swallowed against the metallic surging at the back of her throat, "the way you are now. That I couldn't bear."

"You couldn't bear it?" He gave a short strangled laugh. "*You* couldn't. I've just watched a man I loved like a brother take his life in front of me, an' all I can see in my mind's eye is you—you and *him,* a man who tried to have me killed, in bed, him touching you, *inside you,*" he spit the words out, face the color of ashes. "He must have had a good laugh at my expense, here I was tearin' myself up about what I'd seen in his business, what I'd done at his service, an' he was screwing my wife the whole time. I have been such a goddamn fool—*such a fool where ye're concerned!*" His clenched fist shot out, driving into the wardrobe hard enough to rock it on its foundations. "Goddamn it, Pamela, how could ye?!"

"You—you didn't kill Robin?" she stuttered, her mind having grasped at the information as a straw of salvation.

"No, I'd not the courage it seems, so he had it for me. He shot himself in the head. He gave me the choice, his life or my own, an' I discovered that I valued breathin' over a clean conscience." The tone was dry but she heard the tidal wave of emotion that could not stay dammed much longer. His mouth was a grim line. "I'd best pack."

He grabbed a bag from the top of the wardrobe and began to pull clothing off hangers—shirts, pants, sweaters. He yanked open the drawers of the bureau, grabbing handfuls of socks and the white cotton briefs he favored.

"Casey," she said, the panicked bird beating frantically now, "you can't leave."

"No? Why's that?" he asked, grabbing his kit bag without regard for its contents and shoving it into the bag.

For a single moment, she considered telling him about the baby, and then just as quickly rejected the notion. She would not have him stay out of guilt. He would stay for love or he would not stay at all.

"Can't you understand why I did it? I did it to keep you alive. That's all that mattered to me, keeping you alive and whole."

He snorted derisively. "Thanks, but all things considered I think I'd just as soon be dead."

"You forgave Robin when he betrayed you, are you telling me you can't ever forgive me?"

"Robin was my friend an' there was a time I trusted him with my life, it's true. But I trusted you with my heart. It's a fact that I'm still walking about breathin' but whether I've still a heart," he shook his head, rubbing a bruised hand over his eyes, "I cannot say just now."

"Please," she whispered, knowing it was futile, but unable to stop herself all the same, "please don't do this. Casey, I love you, you know that."

"I'll thank ye not to say those words again," he said very coolly, then returned to packing his clothes.

He turned from the bag a moment later, a perfectly pressed white shirt still in his hands. "Do ye know all I could think of when Robin was putting the gun to his head? Do ye know?"

"No," she said quietly.

"You," he said, eyes a hard black that held her at bay, "all I could think was I'd rather crawl back to ye covered in another man's blood than risk never bein' able to see ye again. Do ye know what I did when he told me?"

She shook her head, turning away from him, unable to bear the look in his eyes any longer.

"I threw up, right there at his feet, that's how much the thought of you lyin' in Love Hagerty's bed sickened me, an' do ye know what the man did, he held me like I was a child in need of comfort. Do ye know what it does to ye to have someone tell ye such things an' then watch them put a bullet in their head? Do ye know?"

"No, I don't know what it does to you, but I do know something, Casey. I know what it feels like to have a man inside my body that I loathe, and to have given him permission to be there. I know what it is to hate the man I love above all others in this world for putting me in that position. I know what it is to feel filthy all the time but to know that I'd do it again and again into eternity to keep you safe and alive. I'd do it now if I had to, even now when you look at me as though you hate me."

He was across the room before she was aware he was moving, pushing her back hard against the pillows, his hands pinning her to the bed. "*Don't tell me,*" he said through gritted teeth, face a mask of pain, as though he'd aged a decade in the space of a few short hours. "As much as it must have hurt ye to do what ye did, I cannot hear about it right now. Allow me that much cowardice, will ye?"

She nodded, the movement causing the smell of lilac water to rise up from the linens around the two of them. The scent of it would sicken her for the rest of her life. The pressure of his hands had become painful and she couldn't stop from squirming slightly.

He blinked, then slowly released her, backing away as if he couldn't understand how he'd come to be here. He turned back to the closet, taking the last shirt off its hanger. He stripped himself awkwardly of the coat and torn shirt he wore. His back was to her and in the pale light she could see just how badly he'd been hurt. He managed the left sleeve, though it was awkward, but couldn't get the right. His shoulder was swollen and bruised, blood dark against his skin.

She took the empty sleeve and brought it around to a height his arm could manage, careful not to touch him, knowing he was like tamped gunpowder right now. "Won't you let me at least bind your ribs for you, maybe wash off a little of the blood?"

He stepped away sharply as though she'd hit him, and shook his head. "No, I'll not have ye touch me, for I'm afraid of what might happen were ye to do so. I've not much dignity left to me, but I'll not hurt a woman."

He zipped the bag, dropped it by the doorway, and reached for clean shoes. He took the bloody ones off his feet, wrapped them in the ruined shirt, and placed them in a separate compartment. He stood up then, wincing as his shoulder moved.

"One question," he said, and his voice was very, very soft. "An' ye'll answer me honestly."

"Yes."

"Did ye feel anything when ye lay with him?"

For several seconds she was silent, the time expanding to fill all the world between them. She could hear his breath, weary, as if even filling his lungs was very difficult right now.

"I—I," she stuttered, and found she could not lie anymore, not even for his sake.

"'Tis all right," he said finally, exhaustion like smoke round his words, "the silence spoke for ye."

He moved slowly, pain evident in every line and movement of his body. She moved to the edge of the bed, worried that any sudden move might alarm him in his present state. She felt slightly dazed and not entirely real. As though she hung suspended above the dismantling of her life.

"Where will you go?" she asked quietly, the scene before her eyes oddly surreal, the buckles on his bag seeming as large as fists, the teeth of the zipper brutally sharp and jagged.

"Away," he replied shortly, reaching for his coat, recoiling in revulsion when he touched the wet on it and then picking it up with grim determination.

"Casey," she said, not missing the way he flinched at the intimacy of his name on her tongue, "am I going to see you again?"

The silence was like a hard, flat blow to her stomach. It took all the courage she had left to look up and see the answer in his face. It was the tenderness she found there that frightened her more than any sort of rage would have. There seemed no hope in such a fragile emotion.

"I—I don't know," he said, voice betraying him only the slightest bit.

She thought she might pass out from the sheer weight of the pain she could feel approaching with the force of a hurricane.

"Can you do one thing for me?" she asked, her voice sounding very far away and muffled to her own ears.

He nodded.

"Go quickly," she said, the three syllables breaking off from her tongue like seared iron.

He put his shoes on, tying them with an abrupt economy of movement, then shouldered his bag. She closed her eyes, unable to watch him turn for the door. She felt his approach, and thought the smell of mint soap was the thing that finally broke her heart.

He leaned down, kissed her softly on the top of her head and then, without a word, he left.

Chapter Eighty

The Butcher's Bill

SUNDAY LUNCH AT JAMIE'S HOUSE had become a longstanding tradition for Pat and Sylvie. Sundays they attended mass at Father Jim's parish, where more often of late, Jamie could be found as well. Then they would regroup at his house for dinner. Others came and went. For months Pamela and Lawrence had joined them, Father Jim came at least once a month, and Belinda had been a fixture both before and after Pamela's sojourn there. For the last two weeks, though, she'd been conspicuous by both her absence and Jamie's silence upon that absence.

Pat looked forward to these Sunday afternoons, for somehow all the troubles of the week fell away once seated at the long oak plank table. With good food and wine, and talk of books and music, and shoes and ships and sealing wax, and whether pigs had wings. The one rule that Jamie insisted on at Sunday lunch was that there would be no talk of politics. A rule that they all obeyed with some relief. For Pat those afternoons had become a way of decompressing from all the stresses of the week before.

Today, though, he'd other things on his mind. His brother's continued absence, Pamela's stubborn insistence on staying at the empty house alone, and frankly, the thought that he'd like to lose himself in a long afternoon in bed with Sylvie.

The woman in question, though, had baked a pie, and picked a sheaf of late summer roses for Maggie's table, and wasn't to be gainsaid from delivering either of these things.

"Besides," she said practically, "I need to ask Jamie for the time away."

"Will we tell him today, then?"

"Aye, though I feel right bad not tellin' Pamela at the same time."

"I'm not certain it's right to do so at present, not with the state of things."

"She still hasn't said why Casey left?"

He shook his head frowning. "No, the woman knows how to keep her tongue still when she wants."

"What's wrong?" she asked, watching him pat down his pockets down for the second time.

"I can't find my wallet," he said irritably, "I could have sworn I'd left it in the kitchen."

"Try the bedroom," she said dryly, "ye threw yer jacket an' trousers willy-nilly when we came in last night. I'll wait for ye in the car."

"Hey you," he said as she stepped over the doorsill, just for the pleasure of seeing her turn to him with that particular light in her eyes. She was a picture, his woman, in a pretty summer dress, the pie on one arm, a light cardigan and the spray of roses on the other.

"Hey yerself, boyo," she retorted with some sass.

"I love you, Mrs. Riordan."

She smiled, face flushing as pink as the tea roses that she carried. "I'm pretty fond of you too, Mr. Riordan."

"I'll only be a minute," he said.

In reality he was about three, having finally located the wallet where it had fallen down behind his bedside table, jammed between the baseboard and table leg. Just as he was crossing the kitchen floor, the telephone rang. He debated leaving it but thought it might be Casey, and didn't want to miss his chance of finding out where the man had disappeared to. He picked it up, only to hear a garbled voice on the other end, obviously in a great panic.

"Slow down, I can't understand ye," he said.

"It's Tom—the center's on fire, ye need to get down here now!"

The phone was slammed down, leaving a dead silence and then the fretful hum of the dial tone. Pat put the receiver back in the cradle and turned toward the open door, seeing beyond it the bright summer day, the sleepy heads of daisies nodding in the breeze over the garden path. He heard the car door open and shut and halted, glancing back at the telephone, a vague pricking in his spine.

He shook his head. The center was on fire, becoming ashes even as he stood here. And yet, had the voice sounded like Tom—even a panicked Tom? The vague pricking became more pronounced, a thought that would not surface, but was very close to the light. Then suddenly he understood and ran for the door yelling Sylvie's name.

The knowledge had come, as such things often do, too late. But still he ran, the entire universe stilling, the distance to the car seeming as long as the length of his own life.

Sylvie was in the driver's seat putting the key to the ignition. It happened in the blink of an eye and yet, in memory, it would always seem as though he'd had a small eternity to stop her and still had been unable to.

He was screaming, but the sound seemed distant and feeble. She turned her head to look at him at the last second, just as she turned the key. An instant of eternity etched onto his brain and heart forever. She smiled, brown eyes filled with a question and then the world exploded out from its core and he was falling rapidly into the sky, and all he knew was a hollow echo at the heart of existence and a great and terrible burning.

He came to what seemed a long time later, a neighbor shouting in his ear. The car was still on fire, flames reflecting off the few windows that hadn't shattered in the explosion.

Pain was there hovering way off, threatening to blanket him. He was on his back and amongst the stars that danced in his view, was a thick pall of black smoke coiling across the flawless blue sky.

With what seemed a ridiculous amount of effort, he managed to roll over onto his stomach and lever himself up onto his knees. The neighbor was pulling at his coat now, trying to stop him but he ignored the hands and pushed himself toward the car. Burning fragments lay all over, flower petals coating the ground, blown from the daisies that only moments ago had nodded so prettily over the path. Daisies that Sylvie had planted in the spring.

The smell of burning petrol coated every breath, his lungs feeling as though they would shrivel and crack from the heat. There was a film across his eyes, like a heavy veil dividing the heaven that had been, from the hell that now was.

The doors had blown right off the car, the shell-shocked body of it twisted and rumpled like a rusted tin can, a hundred different colors in the fire that consumed it. Within that fire nothing moved. Still he crawled toward it, looking for a grain of hope on this infinite shore of tragedy.

More hands came then and pulled him away, pulled him back to where the grass was cool and wet, and then they held him down to keep him back from the fire.

He lay there, head pressed to the side, the air shimmering with heat and debris, alight with flaming ash. Through it floated a scrap of blue cloth, fancy-free, spinning, dancing small minuets with black ashes until it came to rest on the ground before his eyes. A few threads from the pretty Sunday dress she'd worn. It was all that remained to prove that she'd been there only minutes before. Nothing more. Not a bright blonde hair, nor a pair of brown eyes, nor the smell of lilac and lemon verbena.

And there he lay, amidst the burning wreckage of a life, and cursed himself for a fool.

For he had forgotten, in the cruel spring of his happiness, that even lovers die.

THE WALLS OF THE ROOM WERE FRESHLY PAINTED a soft robin's egg blue, the chair rail that ran around the room at waist height a pale cream.

Pamela surveyed her handiwork with some satisfaction and no little weariness. She put the lid back on the pail of cream paint, and wiped her hands on a turped rag. She straightened up with a groan, the small of her back stiff and twinging slightly.

She had thrown herself, with grim determination, into fixing up the nursery. First the paint and then when she had a crib, she would put it under the whimsical little half-moon window, and make a rag rug for the floor. She would repaint the pine chest she'd salvaged from Lewis' barn in the blue and cream of the room and get Casey to build a changing table. She sighed and pinched the thought off. It might be that Casey wouldn't be building anything for this room, and she needed to plan as though she were alone. Which, truth be told, she was.

She sat in the ancient walnut rocker that Casey and Pat had been rocked in as babies. Casey had placed it in the room when they'd moved into the house, and had been anticipating the arrival of their own baby. For many long months after she had lost the baby, it had sat still and empty, neither of them with the heart to move it. Now she'd taken to sitting in it to have a cup of tea, or to simply rest from the weariness of painting.

She stretched her legs out, feeling the pleasant burn of tired muscles relaxing. She nibbled half-heartedly at a cracker taken from a pile she kept handy in case she found an appetite between bouts of nausea. She quickly put it down in disgust. Everything made her queasy. Except, oddly enough, the smell of the paint.

She closed her eyes; the fatigue of early pregnancy was never far from her and she found herself dozing at odd moments, though sleep eluded her at night. Eluded her to the point that she had given up on it, and had taken to filling her nights with cleaning the house, which then graduated to readying this room for the baby. She'd also picked up her knitting and the wee hours of the morning were filled with the soft rhythmic clicking of her needles, the huffling snores of Finbar and the rumble of the Aga.

The sound of an expensive motor turning off the lane into their drive broke in on her doze what seemed only a minute later. She glanced at the small clock; she'd been asleep for twenty minutes. She yawned and stood, craning her head to look out the small window.

Late afternoon sun gleamed off the dark green flanks of Jamie's Bentley. He was just now rounding the curve beneath the ash tree. She left the room, shutting the door behind her. She didn't want Jamie seeing the paint and leaping to the obvious conclusion. She was to the landing, midway down the stairs when he called out. "Pamela, are you here?"

She froze in place; it wasn't like Jamie to just walk in. The tone of his voice was of a shade she'd never heard before. She understood without another word or sound from him, that he had come bearing bad news.

She moved to descend the remaining stairs and was swept by a wave of dizziness. She sat down on the top riser and called out weakly, "I'm here on the stairs, Jamie."

She wanted to say Casey's name, to ask the question, but could not utter the two syllables that would destroy what was left of her world.

Jamie found her there and read her face. "It's not Casey. It's Sylvie; she's been killed in an explosion."

"Explosion?" she echoed, not quite understanding.

"There was a bomb planted under their car. I think it was meant for Pat."

"Oh God—is he—"

"He's alive," Jamie said, "but that was all they knew for certain. He was taken to The Royal. I've come to take you there. Do you have any notion where Casey is?"

"But I just saw her three days ago," she said dazedly, "we had tea. How—how can she be gone?"

"Pamela, where is Casey?" he asked again.

"I—I'm afraid I have no idea. He left me over a week ago now."

"What? Why on earth would he do that?"

She met the green eyes that looked at her with both confusion and compassion. "He had his reasons, Jamie. But I really don't know how to find him. Is—is Pat going to die?"

"I don't think so."

Twice on the trip into the hospital, Jamie had to stop the car so she could get out and throw up in the ditch. She was reeling with shock, and simply wanted to lie down amongst the buttercups that grew wild in the tall grass, and close her eyes for a long time. She had not believed that after Lawrence's death and Casey's desertion there was any room left in her for more grief. But there was. An infinite capacity for it, apparently.

Somewhere under the immediate shock and anguish was relief. Relief that it was not Casey. And guilt that she could feel such a thing at all.

A doctor met them at the front desk on the ward.

"He's concussed, and has a few second degree burns on his hands. Mostly he's in shock, I think, and can't hear that well just now. I don't think there's permanent damage to his hearing, but we won't be certain for a few days on that score."

A stern-faced RUC officer stood outside Pat's room. He recognized Pamela, though, and let them in without any fuss.

Inside the room, it was very quiet. Pat lying as still as if he were dead, swathed in bandages and with an IV line feeding into his left arm. His hair was a dark splotch against the starched white linens. Both arms were wrapped in gauze from fingertips to elbow. His face was partially bandaged, the right side exposed. Every bit of visible skin was scraped, bruised and singed looking.

"Pat?"

The sound of her own voice seemed unnaturally loud in the terrible hush of the room. From the bed, there was no response, other than the smallest twitch of the index finger on his left hand.

She was at his bedside in an instant. The one eye that was uncovered stared up at her with a hazy intensity that was equal parts shock and drugs.

He rasped out a solitary word, "Jamie."

"He wants you," she said.

Jamie leaned over Pat, close enough that Pat wouldn't have to exert himself beyond a whisper. He stood there for a long time; the fair head so close to the dark one, like spills of ink against the stark white sheets, one writ in black, the other in dark gold. The story they told one of unutterable grief.

Finally Jamie nodded, and said something in the affirmative that she couldn't quite make out.

He came around the bed and took her arm. "I think we should leave him be for now."

Once they were safely outside the door, she spoke the words they were both thinking. "I'm afraid for him."

"He's going to live," Jamie said bluntly, "only he can decide if that's a blessing or a curse."

IT WAS VERY LATE and Pamela was light-headed with exhaustion. The fluorescent lights were harsh and hurt her eyes, which felt as though they were lined with fine grain sandpaper. She'd come to the waiting room to sit and fight away the worst of the dizziness. The smells of disinfectant and illness, however, were stirring her incipient nausea up again.

Jamie came and sat beside her. Just his presence allowed her to let go a little of the breath she was holding in. He handed her a paper cup full of tea as well as a plain bun wrapped in a napkin.

"You'd better eat," he said, "you're looking rather faint."

"Thank you," she said, cupping her hands around the heat that radiated through the thin-walled cup.

"Were you this sick last time?"

She gasped in shock, and then realized she shouldn't be surprised by his knowledge. "Damn you, Jamie Kirkpatrick," she said wearily. "Taken up midwifery in your spare time, have you?"

"No," he returned calmly. "I'm just not blind, nor trying to be; besides, you've nursery blue paint specks all through your hair. Does Casey know?"

She shook her head miserably. "No, I barely knew myself before—" she made a futile gesture with her free hand, "all this happened. It hardly seemed the time to tell him," she said ruefully. "I—I—."

"Didn't want him to stay for the wrong reasons."

She nodded. "He would have stayed, and then I would always wonder if it was only because of the baby. I don't want him on those terms. Do you think that's silly or vain at this point?"

"No, it's just who you are, you won't compromise, even if not compromising breaks your heart. I can sympathize with that."

"I may end up raising this child alone as a result, though. I'm a little frightened by that prospect."

Jamie looked at her in a straightforward manner. "Even if he doesn't come back, Pamela, you won't be alone."

Green eyes looked long into their kind and saw something there that had neither beginning nor end, something that would not fail and could be counted upon no matter how hard the outside world was brought to bear.

She took his hand and squeezed it gently. "I know, and I thank you for it. Still, I think Belinda might have a thing or two to say about it."

"I rather think Belinda won't care, all things considered."

"What?"

He shook his head. "She's gone, jilted me and run off to Italy. She said there was nothing left here to keep her."

"What? Why? She was mad for you, Jamie, anyone could see that."

He gave a grim smile. "Well, I believe her exact words were that if I'd even once looked at her the way I look at you, it would have been reason to stay. But that as I never had, she wasn't going to settle for being a poor second fiddle."

"Oh Jamie, I'm so sorry," she said, and found that despite the jealousy she'd often felt for the woman, she really was sorry. Jamie deserved to love and be loved freely. "Are you certain?"

Jamie shook his head. "No, she was right. I was cheating her by thinking a half cup would be enough to build a life around. I couldn't give her what she needed, she was wise to go. And I think perhaps it's time for the cripple to try walking without his sticks. And while I have lost a dear friend and lover, Pat has lost his wife."

"What do you mean, *wife?*"

"Yes, his wife. They were married on Friday. I think they were going to announce it at lunch today. That's where they were headed when the car blew up—to my house, for lunch. He told me before they sedated him."

"Oh God," she breathed, the band of grief in her throat winding itself a little tighter, snarling its barbed points through her vocal chords. "Jamie, eventually one of them would have gotten in that car, or if she'd waited a few more minutes to start the ignition, the both of them would have died. It didn't matter where they were going, because they were never going to get there."

Jamie didn't answer, but the hand that held her own gripped a little harder.

A throat cleared itself and they looked up, startled. David Kendall stood before them, worry writ large across his face. His fair hair was rumpled, eyes bleak with fear. Traceries of bruises still stained his skin, and there was a scar near his hairline that hadn't been there a few short weeks ago.

"Is he hurt?"

Pamela extended a hand to him and squeezed his fingers. "Not seriously no, but Sylvie—"

"I know, I heard at the barracks."

"It's perhaps a little risky for you to be here," Jamie said, and Pamela turned at the tone. He was exchanging an odd look with David which seemed full of unspoken disapproval. David's face flushed red.

"I had to know if he was all right."

Jamie nodded, but she could still sense that something wasn't right. He seemed angry.

"I suppose," he said, relenting a little, "Pat could use all the friends he has right now."

"I'll take you in if you'd like to see him," Pamela offered. "He's with the doctors right now, but we can go back in a few more minutes."

David shook his head, hazel eyes sliding away from her own. "No, I won't bother him just now, I'll wait until...until. I'll just wait," he finished helplessly. He looked at Pamela again. "Would it be all right if I called you, to check on his progress?"

"Of course," she said.

"Thank you," he said, "I'll be in touch, and if there's any change?"

"I'll make sure you know right away, if you leave me a number where you can be reached." He scribbled a number on the back of a scrap of paper that she found in her pocket for him. Jamie remained silent throughout this exchange, though his disapproval was palpable in the air.

"You weren't exactly friendly," she said, as David disappeared down the long corridor. "He's a right to worry."

"I just think you need to keep your distance, he's British Army, and not regular channel Army either, if you take my meaning. I don't want to be here visiting you, or worse still burying you."

"You're not saying that Pat's friendship with David had anything to do with the bomb, are you?"

Jamie sighed. "No, but look at it realistically, Pamela, befriending a British soldier isn't looked upon kindly in this city, in fact it's tantamount to suicide. I don't know what possessed him."

"They were meant to be friends, for whatever reason. Sometimes people are just fated that way. Even in Belfast."

"In Belfast," Jamie said, "your friends can get you killed."

She looked at him sharply. "You just said you didn't think he'd anything to do with Sylvie being killed."

Jamie rubbed his eyes, the vertical crease like a cut on his forehead. "I don't know, Pamela, you throw a pebble in a pond five months past, and the damn wave can sweep you from the shore today. That's how this country works."

"No one can look down the road every time they as much as say hello to someone. Casey couldn't have known, when he was a teenager, how his friendship with Robin would end." She realized the mistake of the words the instant they left her tongue.

"Indeed," Jamie said quietly, "and just how *did* that friendship end?"

"In death."

"By Casey's hand?"

"No," she said, "Robin wanted that, but Casey found he couldn't and so Robin did it himself."

"More's the pity," Jamie said. His face was still, but a flicker of something very much like hatred stirred in his eyes.

"Why would you say that?"

"Because in the future, I think Casey may regret not killing the man by his own hand. Some wounds don't heal well unless cauterized first."

"Jamie, you're scaring me."

"Don't listen to me, I'm rambling."

With the tremor of panic had come another swift and engulfing wave of nausea. She bent down, attempting to put her head between her knees. The direct result of this was to make the room swing wildly as a pendulum in front of her.

"You need to lie down," Jamie said briskly. She could see he was glad to have even the smallest of tasks to occupy him, however briefly, and so did not have the heart to tell him that she didn't think she could possibly rest.

To her surprise, however, once an empty room was located and she lay down on the clean, starchy sheets, exhaustion overtook her. It was only a few minutes before she felt herself drifting, like an autumn leaf borne down through dark and chill winter air.

"Jamie."

"Yes?"

"I don't want to be alone."

"You won't be," he replied softly.

SHE AWOKE SOMETIME IN THE WEE HOURS. The lights were off and the door partially shut.

"Jamie?"

"Right here," he said.

"How's Pat?"

"He's resting now; they gave him a mild sedative and are monitoring him closely. How are you feeling?"

"All right," she said, "the nausea is gone for now."

She sat up. Jamie stood by the window, his reflection pale against the glass. His hair was rumpled, shirt half untucked, eyes red-rimmed. It was the first time she'd seen him thus. Defeat and grief had altered the line of him, so that he seemed both terribly young and old at the same time.

The noises of the hospital were distant, as though a layer of cotton lay between them and the world out there where the swiftly padding feet of nurses were ever bent on errands of mercy. Where alarms cried and ambulances—wailing—came and went.

She heard Jamie mumur to himself an old poem about the fevered gods of war, taking both maiden and king, without regard to their station. She knew he spoke not for the sake of her ears, but more to his own grief and to the events his mind was trying to make some sort of sense of.

"Do you think that's what took Sylvie's' life, war?"

"Yes. To paraphrase a countrywoman of yours, the wrong war, at the wrong place, at the wrong time with the wrong enemy, and yet, nevertheless, a war."

"I wish it would end," she said, "I can't make sense of any of it anymore. But I'm not sure anyone here would be comfortable with peace, or know how to make a life without constant pain."

"Who would we Irish be, without our unending little war, what would we have left to make us feel special?" His tone was bitter and weary, that of a man who has tried and failed times beyond counting.

"I wish we'd never come back. I feel somehow if we hadn't Sylvie would still be alive."

"I wish you hadn't either," Jamie said, "but not for the same reasons. Things would have spiralled out of control for Pat and Sylvie regardless, but for your own sake, I wish you'd stayed away. Though I suppose such a wish makes me a dreadful hypocrite."

"Why?"

"Because I rather made certain that you married the one man who would always come back to this country, didn't I? This damnable, demon-haunted land. This is the country of my heart, and yet I don't see how I can continue to live here."

She understood his meaning, for it *was* a demon-haunted country, laden with spirits—those of failure, those of war and bloodshed and all that they left behind. And then there were the ghosts that were more personal—people you'd known in passing, and those you believed you would know forever. Last, there were the ghosts of one's own heart—the lost children, the never forgotten lover, the Husband who could not forgive you.

"There are ghosts everywhere, Jamie."
"Yes, but only some do we call our own."
"And what are we to do with all those ghosts?"
He turned from the window, eyes a heavy glass green.
"We take them with us."

Chapter Eighty-one

In Sunlight or in Shadow

ON EITHER SIDE OF PAT, Pamela and Jamie stood, two sentries guarding against an invisible enemy, backbones stiff against the rain. She could feel it running down her spine where it had leaked inside her collar. Pat seemed oblivious to it, face immobile, dark eyes blank as if he'd drawn into a far place inside from which he'd no wish to emerge. Shock? She didn't know. Pat wasn't an easy read at the best of times and since Sylvie's death he'd said very little, only gone about doing what needed doing with a fierce determination that told her he was holding onto his sanity through sheer dogged will power.

Jamie, as always, exuded a calm dignity, though she knew his show of strength was purely for Pat's sake. This had devastated him in a way few could suspect.

She wondered with a part of her mind that seemed to exist separately if Casey had received word, if he knew by newspaper or television what had happened to Sylvie. He musn't know or he'd be here, and that meant either he wasn't reading papers or watching the television, or that he'd left the country entirely.

David Kendall stood to her left, blonde hair combed smoothly in place, glancing at Pat now and again, though never enough to appear unseemly. He was hopelessly British, but exemplified all that was right with England and had displayed courage of tempered steel in daring to come today. It was possible, the political climate being what it was, that he was risking his very life by attending. She tucked her hand in the crook of his elbow and he gave her a quick smile of gratitude.

Father Jim, now saying the *Rite of Committal*, was bareheaded, brown hair flying wild in the wind, voice ringing through the rain like a deep, clear bell.

Wherefore my heart is glad, and my spirit rejoiceth;
my flesh also shall rest in hope.
Thou shalt show me the path of life;
in thy presence is the fullness of joy,

and at thy right hand there is pleasure for evermore.

She could not quite believe that Sylvie wouldn't slip up any minute, squeezing in beside Pat, flyaway blonde hair tamed by the rain, apologizing breathlessly for her tardiness. She bit hard on the inside of her cheek; she'd not cry, Pat needed her strength, not her tears. She closed her eyes for a minute, taking a breath to calm the grief that was clawing its way relentlessly up the back of her throat. And felt Casey's presence there as surely as if he'd touched her. Her eyes snapped open and certain enough, there he was, a dark, windswept figure in a navy overcoat, face thinner than it had been three weeks ago, eyes as dark as she'd ever known them.

She had to bite back a cry of welcome, even through grief and the dull miasma of shock, everything in her pulled toward him. He was looking at her steadily, face unreadable, though there was no hint of the softness his expression habitually wore around her.

She flinched as the first clod of earth hit Sylvie's coffin, breaking the gaze Casey had locked her in, feeling as though someone had stabbed her repeatedly in the area of her heart. Father Jim was speaking.

"In sure and certain hope of the resurrection to eternal life through our Lord Jesus Christ, we commend to Almighty God our sister Sylvie; and we commit her body to the ground; earth to earth, ashes to ashes, dust to dust. The Lord bless her and keep her, the Lord make his face to shine upon her and be gracious unto her, the Lord lift up his countenance upon her and give her peace. Amen."

Pat stood, mud still clinging to his hand, and Father Jim began the closing words.

"The Lord be with you."

Like the good Catholic children they all were, they responded with the all too familiar words, "And with thy spirit."

Father Jim bowed his head, a tremor in the strong bulge of his Adam's apple.

"Let us pray." Together they all prayed the final communal words that would be spoken over Sylvie.

Our Father, who art in heaven,
hallowed be thy Name,
thy kingdom come,
thy will be done,
on earth as it is in heaven.
Give us this day our daily bread.
And forgive us our trespasses,
as we forgive those who trespass against us.
And lead us not into temptation,

but deliver us from evil.
For thine is the kingdom, and the power, and the glory,
for ever and ever. Amen.

Suddenly she became aware David had laid his hand over hers, and that Father Jim was speaking the words that would dismiss the mourners.

"The God of peace, who brought again from the dead our Lord Jesus Christ, the great Shepherd of the sheep, through the blood of the everlasting covenant: Make you perfect in every good work to do his will, working in you that which is well pleasing in his sight; through Jesus Christ, to whom be glory for ever and ever."

People were moving away from the grave. Pat was nodding mechanically as mourners filed past and offered their last words of comfort.

She turned to Pat, painfully aware of Casey at her back. She squeezed his hand, and was rewarded by a small flicker of his mouth, his hand, however, was slack and unresponsive. She left the graveside and David, offering her his arm, walked her to the edge of the path that ran up toward to cemetery gate.

Father Jim's words of comfort for Pat floated toward her, mixed with rain and the scent of hothouse flowers.

When she turned toward the car, Casey stood directly in her path. Close enough to touch and yet the distance between them now was greater than it had ever been. Despite the lack of emotion in his expression, she knew it was not coincidence that had placed him here. She crossed her arms firmly over her soaked coat, more in an effort not to give in to her longing to throw her arms about him than anything else. David silently slipped away, leaving them alone.

His face had healed, the bruises faded now to pale ocher and watered green.

"How are ye?" he asked, and the mere sound of his voice was enough to break the fragile reserve she barely had a hold on.

She shook her head, biting down on her bottom lip as tears filled her eyes. "Don't ask me that unless you're ready to come home. Are you ready to come home?"

His face was as miserable as her own. "No," he answered and then again, "no, I'm not."

"Then don't ask me how I am," she said, voice cracking despite her best efforts, "when you bloody well know the answer."

He nodded, rain dripping in a steady stream from the ends of his hair into his eyes.

"I never thought it would come to this with us," he said so softly she barely made out the words.

"Nor did I," she replied. She reached into her pocket for the one item she'd tucked there this morning, on the chance he would appear. She took his hand, flinching inwardly at his hesitation to her touch.

Casey gazed blankly at the key she'd placed in his palm. "What's this for?"

"It's the key to the house," she said tightly.

"I know what it is," he said, taking a frustrated breath.

"I thought you might need a place to stay. I'll leave if it makes it easier for you." She took a deep breath, throat thick with unshed tears. "You should feel free to go home."

He shook his head, holding the key back towards her. "If ye're not there, it's hardly home, Jewel."

"Don't call me that," she said, unable to hold back the tears any longer. They fell unchecked, mingling with the icy downpour that had soaked them both.

"Sorry," he muttered, "it's habit."

She touched his cheek, smoothing the rain away from his lashes. He closed his eyes, allowing the contact for a moment. Then he lifted his own hand and gently pushed hers away.

"Pamela I just—I can't—"

She shook her head. "It's all right, I understand. You should be with Pat now."

They both looked toward the grave, the mounded dirt a slick hill of mud, and to the man who stood beside it, head bowed, rose petals wilting at his feet.

She stepped off the path, away from Casey. She stood as he walked past, without another word or glance in her direction. He went to his brother, stood beside him, silent, knowing there were no words in the lexicon of human language that could comfort Pat now. Then Pat turned slightly in Casey's direction.

She saw Casey's hand go gently to the nape of his brother's neck, saw him pull Pat towards him. When Pat bowed his head to his brother's shoulder and Casey's arms came around him protectively, she turned away, unable to bear the sight of them any longer.

Jamie waited by the car, face impassive as she approached.

"Home?" he asked, opening the door.

She shook her head. "I don't think I have one anymore, Jamie."

Chapter Eighty-two

Requiem

"YE NEED TO GO HOME."

Casey sighed, and turned the page of the book he was pretending to read. "I heard ye the first seven times man, I'm startin' to feel a mite unwelcome."

Pat glared at him across the table where they both sat, the dinner Casey had prepared lying untouched between them. Since the funeral, Casey had stayed here with his brother, who had made it clear in all ways that he wanted him gone.

"Ignore me if I'm irritatin' ye so badly."

"Maybe it's that I think ye're a fool eejit," Pat said flatly, "when my own wife is layin' cold in the ground an' yers is alive an' well, an' in need of yer comfort. Ye weren't the only one who lost Lawrence, ye know. We all loved him. Pamela as much as yerself, I warrant. Or would ye rather leave the job of consolin' her to Jamie?"

Casey eyed his brother darkly. "Dinna throw that threat at me, I'll not rise to it. I'm here to look after yerself, an' to make sure ye neither drink nor starve yerself to death, an' there's an end to it. 'Tis nothin' to do with my wife or Jamie."

"Don't be a fool Casey," Pat said quietly. "He has always loved her."

"And she him," Casey said with no little bitterness. "D'ye really think I need remindin' of it?"

Dark eye met dark and neither looked away.

"Then go see her."

Casey shook his head. "No, I can't just yet, seein' her the other day was hard enough, an' if I'm not ready to go home I don't think it serves either of us to see the other."

"Are ye leaving her?"

Casey wouldn't meet his brother's eyes. "I don't know Pat, I've not decided yet."

"It's only yer decision to make?"

Casey nodded, face grim. Pat knew instinctively that to say another word on this subject would be the same as sticking a knife into his brother.

Pat sighed and took another tack. "Tis my life to do with as I please. I don't much care if I die, as long as I don't do it before I find the bastards who killed Sylvie."

"Well perhaps ye'll forgive me if I do give a damn," Casey said, rising to clear away the cold food.

"It's too late now anyway," Pat said quietly, "it was me they meant to kill an' as soon as they figure out how to do it they'll come, might take a week or a month, but they'll come."

"No they won't," Casey said, "ye can do yer healin' in peace. An' maybe if ye can stay clear of the Englishman ye'll not have cause to worry in the future."

Something in Casey's tone roused Pat from the fugue he'd been suspended in since Sylvie's murder. He turned, watching his brother calmly fill the sink with soap and water, a tea towel slung over his shoulder, cuffs rolled up above his elbows.

"What have ye done?"

Casey didn't answer at once, instead he started washing glasses as though they were talking of what groceries needed to be bought. When he did answer, the words struck ice to the core of Pat's soul.

"What needed to be done."

For the first time since Sylvie's death, Pat felt something—utter panic and terror. "When did—was it by yer own hand?" He gasped for air, feeling as though someone had punched him hard in the chest. "How the hell did ye know who to look for?"

Casey gave him a hard look. "Do ye want to know this? Because I don't feel the need to talk about it."

Pat took in the look on his brother's face, and read what lay below it. "No, I don't want to know. But there'll be others, they'd likely have talked."

Casey shook his head. "No, there's nothing to trace back those men to you or David. No one in the pub in Drumintree has a memory of that night."

"Ye've been busy," Pat stood, chair falling over with the sudden violence of his movement. Anger was flooding him, a sharp center in the midst of the leaden shroud he'd been in since Sylvie's death.

"Aye I have been, but now it's done. I've tied up the loose ends an' I leave it to you what to make of yer life."

"Just like that? Did yer wife have to take the pictures, man? Did she have to witness an' record yer handiwork?"

"It was yer handiwork I was takin' care of, laddie, that's what caused this whole mess in the first place. Oh Christ, I'm sorry Pat, ye know I don't mean it."

Pat staggered back, anger swiftly drowned in guilt. "No, don't apologize for tellin' the truth. It's my fault Sylvie's dead, I know it better than anyone."

"Ye did what ye thought right, ye saved a man's life. No one could have seen where it would lead."

"No?" Pat shook his head. "We've lived in this country all our lives, Casey. I more than anyone should have seen exactly what would happen. I was stupid an' naïve an' the price was Sylvie's life. There's no forgiveness or redemption for a mistake like that."

"So ye just throw yerself away? I think ye'd best face facts, laddie, ye've still a life ahead of ye an' ye're goin' to have to make some tough decisions. Decide what it is ye can live with and what ye cannot."

"What of yerself, brother, what is it you can live with?" Pat spat the words out, the taste of them like blood on his tongue.

"It's who I am, Pat, I'm not wove of the same stuff you are. I tried for a long time to be somethin' else an' it never worked. Ye're the poetry in this family, an' I'm the prose. When I see a need I fill it, finish the job so to speak."

"Ye're talkin' mad 'cause of what's happened to Lawrence. And I don't know what's taken place between yerself an' Pamela, but ye need her now as ye never have before."

"Ye've no notion what's gone on," Casey said, tone indicating the topic was not up for conversation.

"No I don't, an' I can see by the way the two of ye are that it's no small thing, but I can tell ye that it's not worth it, whatever it is."

Casey shook his head. "Ye could be forgiven for thinkin' my judgement is clouded an' that I'm not actin' rationally, but despite all that's happened I'm thinkin' clear as I have in a very long time. I didn't agonize over the decision to kill those men, Pat. I just did it. I promised Da I'd look out for ye an' I'll do what it takes to keep that promise."

"Listen to yerself," Pat said, anger pushing out against the leaden shroud harder now, ripping at the casing he'd tried to shelter within. "Ye're talkin' like ye've taken some blood vow to protect me."

"I have," Casey replied quietly, "what is a promise made to yer father if not that?"

"Christ," Pat breathed out, "ye frighten me."

Casey shrugged, face intractable. "If that's the price I pay to keep ye breathin' so be it."

Pat wondered when the transition had happened, when his brother had become this man; tall, broad-shouldered, with nothing of the boy remaining. Strong and ruthless when the necessity presented itself, capable of acts of violence to protect the ones he loved. The fact that he'd not been able to protect Lawrence would be eating him alive, yet nothing of it showed in his face. The years of pain, the time in prison, all the wars both public and personal, had not served to diminish him. Instead, the fires had refined him into this man who was both beloved and terrifying. His brother, and a stranger that he couldn't fathom the motivations of.

"It's everything Daddy didn't want for ye," Pat said bluntly, "he's likely rollin' in his grave."

"No," Casey said, "he'd not be surprised, he always saw what was within me. He knew me better than I did myself. He may have wanted different, but Da was a realist, Patrick, so he tried to equip me for what he knew I was, an' where that might lead."

"And where is that? A life away from the woman you love, in exile, for what? So you can be some sort of vigilante? It's only romantic in movies."

"An' how is it any different from what ye did for David? It was his life or theirs, did ye hesitate?"

"No."

"Well, ye're my brother, an' there was no less I could do."

Pat nodded. Casey meant what he said, to his way of thinking there was no other option. "What now, man?"

"We're on the outside now, Patrick, killin' those men has changed things for the both of us an' that's why I want ye to take this." He fished an envelope from his pocket and threw it on the table in front of Pat.

"It's enough," Casey said gruffly, "to take ye anywhere ye've a mind to go. I want ye to get clear of this godforsaken wee town."

"Where'd ye get this sort of money?"

"I work an' so does Pamela. We don't do so badly, we'd a bit set aside. She wants ye to take it as well. I'd not have given it to ye without askin' her first."

Pat stood, walked over to the desk in the corner of the front room, and took a long, thick envelope from the top drawer. He tossed the package to Casey.

"What are these?"

"Plane tickets to California, 'twas Jamie's wedding gift to Sylvie an' me. I'd told him beforehand that we planned to wed, an' he gave me these a couple of days later. I'd not told her, wanted to surprise her with it. I should have taken her six months ago." He eyed the money that he'd yet to touch. "Seems everyone wants me to run away."

"Will ye go then?"

Pat shook his head. "I know ye think I need to escape, but I cannot just yet. For now, I need to be here, where she was. Can ye understand that?"

Casey sighed. "I understand, but I wish ye'd go anyway."

Pat pushed the money back toward him. "Take it back. Start that construction business ye've talked about. If I thought ye'd leave Belfast yerself, I'd say take it an' run. As for me, for better or worse, my life is here."

"Ye're mad," Casey said shortly, though a weary smile took the sting from his words.

"Can I ask ye a question?"

Casey eyed him warily. "Aye, ye know ye can, though when ye say it in that tone of voice ye scare me."

"Is Robin dead?"

Casey looked away, the line of his jaw suddenly taut.

"Aye," he replied quietly, "dead with none left to mourn him, nor bury him."

"*You* mourn him, ye were the only person on this planet that the man loved, I think, an' it's only you he'd want to grieve him."

"I think I've a full quota on the grieving just now," Casey said lightly, though the tone did not quite come off.

"Still, I am sorry my brother, I know what he once was to ye."

"Aye so am I—for everything."

Chapter Eighty-three

Brother's Keeper

THE BOTANICAL GARDENS LAY DESERTED in the drizzling twilight. David glanced about nervously; where was the damn man anyway? The entire city seemed hushed tonight, but here by the back gate of the gardens, the quiet was unearthly. He shivered; the drizzle was forming a low fog that wrapped around the wrought iron of the gate he'd just scaled.

"David," said a voice directly behind him.

David spun around, though there was only one man who could know he was here. Despite the fact that he'd agreed to meet with him, David was more nervous than he could remember being in a great while.

Casey nodded toward a bench that sat under a hawthorn tree. "Let's sit."

David swallowed over the tension in his throat, still unclear as to why the man had requested this meeting. Nevertheless, he followed and sat beside him, the branches of the tree providing enough shelter that the bench was relatively dry.

David waited for Casey to begin, knowing that polite conversational preambles were not a route to take with this man. He snuck a sideways glance. Being an expert in matters of grief, David noted all the signs in the man's face.

"Ye know I don't like yer relationship with my brother," Casey said bluntly, eyes hard.

"Yes," David replied dryly, "I'm aware of your feelings on the subject. But I—"

Casey held up a hand. "I don't want to hear yer justifications; you an' I both know how this whole tragedy got started, don't we?"

David nodded tersely. Unfortunately, that was only too true. From the moment he had walked into the Two Step pub that rainy night, events had careened out of control.

"Right now my only concern is my brother. He's grievin' badly an' not thinkin' straight. I'm afraid for him, an' more afraid of what he might do in such a state."

David saw that despite the hard façade, the man *was* afraid, he loved his brother and was terrified of what Pat might do to himself. It was a fear that had kept David awake well into the dawn every night since Sylvie's death.

"And what do you want me to do?" David asked.

"Well, it seems that he respects yer opinion, an' I think," Casey swallowed as if there were something very bitter lodged in his throat, "I think maybe this is where ye can help him where others cannot."

David could only fathom what it had taken for this man to come and ask his help. He could well imagine the pain it caused Casey to know he could not save his brother in this situation. Though David was hard-pressed to see how *he* might be of any greater value.

"I should like for you to go and see him." Casey cleared his throat and David realized he'd managed to discomfit a man that few had likely ever ruffled.

"I can do that," David replied quietly, "though I doubt he'll welcome my presence."

"Maybe not, but I think, right now, what he thinks he wants or doesn't want isn't the point."

"No, perhaps not. I'll go then. I wanted to say goodbye anyway. I'm being sent home—best for all, I'm certain. I've become a bit of a liability for the government just at present."

Casey nodded, expression unreadable.

David sighed, the bitter smell of hawthorn filling his senses. "I'll go tomorrow."

Casey stood, and David thought he would leave without so much as another word or backward glance, but he turned back, the curling leaves of the tree rippling in dark shadows across his face. "It changes nothing that I feel about ye, but I thank ye for this. I'll always be in yer debt an' should ye need help someday," he nodded brusquely, "ye'll have only to ask."

"My seeing him may make no difference," David returned softly.

"It has to, ye're my last hope."

And that, thought David, was an indication of how truly desperate they'd all become.

Chapter Eighty-four
How Lonely People Make a Life

D
AVID HAD TO POUND ON THE DOOR for several long minutes before he heard even the slightest noise from within the small abode. Then he had to wait several more minutes before Pat unlocked and opened the door.

Pat's shirt was rumpled and a rather heavy fug of whiskey hung about him. He stood there silent, as though he couldn't fathom what David might be doing on his doorstep.

David stepped past him into the narrow entry. He removed his gloves and coat, the latter heavy with the rain that had fallen all bloody day, as though even the weather had grieved the loss of the bright-haired girl who'd loved this man in front of him. Much as he himself did. That it was entirely possible that his love had cost this man his own was a fact that weighed heavily on his heart.

Pat shuffled to his right toward the small living room that fronted the narrow two-up, two-down he'd shared with Sylvie.

David took a deep breath, knowing his words would not be welcome, yet seeing no choice but to say them. "Pat you have to stop this—stop punishing yourself. You need sleep, you need food. Everyone is worried sick over you."

Pat was shuffling restively around the small room, shins bumping into furniture every few seconds.

"Patrick, please stop for a minute."

Pat whirled, despair contorting his features. "Jaysus, David, don't ye see? We were actin' like it was all a game, but both of us knew better. It's inexcusable. It's my fault that my wife is layin' under—under," he choked, the words beyond him.

"I know," David responded quietly.

That brought Pat's relentless pacing to a sudden halt. "Ye know, do ye? Did ye not come here to tell me how it's not my fault, how it could have happened anytime, anywhere?"

David shook his head. "No, I think you realize by now, Patrick, that I can't lie to you. You're right, we acted like fools, acted like we could be young and not have to pay the consequences of that. We acted," he took a deep breath, "like this was a normal country in a normal world. But it isn't. We forgot that for a few minutes and now you're having to pay the price, and I'm having to watch you pay it. But none of it changes the fact that Sylvie is laying six feet under a pile of dirt."

Pat glared at him in disbelief for a moment, then his face crumpled. "Nice try, David, but the reverse psychology bit won't work. It was my fault, plain an' simple, that's the fact of it." Pat continued his aimless shuffle around the room, picking up small ornaments and putting them down without looking at them. The photos of Sylvie were clustered, shrine-like, on one small table.

"How old are you, Pat?" he asked softly.

Pat staggered slightly against the sofa, body gone beyond its limits and starting to fail him. "Ye know how old I am."

"Yes, but do you?"

"I'm twenty-three," he said crossly, continuing his pacing again, feet scuffing against the floor.

"That's young, you have no idea how young that is."

"Not young enough for what I've done."

"Why? Are you Cassandra that you should be able to predict every disaster that might happen? Should you be able to see the ripple effect of every bloody thing you do?"

"Yes," Pat yelled hoarsely. "Because I should have fucking known better! I fucking *did* know better and yet that never stopped me."

"Come on, Patrick, nobody is clean in this little game. You always knew I wasn't, but you were willing to risk my friendship for some reason. Was it the excitement, knowing you were part of something bigger than you, something you couldn't control?"

Pat turned his head slowly, eyes suddenly focussed with a terrible intensity. "What exactly are you saying?"

"That Sylvie knew what she was getting into when she chose you. She knew your history, who your family was, and what that meant in this fucked up country. She wasn't completely innocent."

"Don't you dare," Pat said, each word hard as a bullet. "Don't you dare even imply that she was in any way at fault here."

David swallowed over the thickness in his throat, he hated what he was doing and yet felt a small frisson of triumph at the anger that flared in the other man's eyes. Anger meant Pat could still feel enough to care. Slender as that thread might be, it was enough to hang onto.

"Why not? She was a grown woman, and from all accounts an intelligent one. She moves in with a known Republican agitator during the worst spate of violence this country has ever seen and expects to live happily ever after? Come on Pat, no one is that naïve. She knew."

Pat came at him in a rush, but David was ready for it, though the slamming of his back into the wall still winded him. The years of intensive training at the hand of British Special Forces wasn't all for naught, however. David grabbed Pat's arm and put him facedown on the floor within seconds. He held him there for a minute, feeling the strain in the man's body, the heavy pounding of blood in his own ears. He relaxed a little, easing the tension he'd exerted, and Pat took his opening.

Even in the complete exhaustion of grief the man had the reflexes of a cat. David was on his knees before he knew what had happened, Pat's hand like tensile steel on the back of his neck. Try as he might David couldn't move his head, couldn't avoid the black look that seemed to burn right through him and see all the darkest corners of his soul.

"You can have it," Pat said, "what you've dreamed of," a terrible smile formed itself on his lips. "It doesn't matter to me anymore, why shouldn't I at least give ye a moment of happiness?"

David closed his eyes, the one line of defense open to him at present. Still he was only inches from the man, unable to escape the intense heat of his skin and the scent that he'd memorized like some pathetic schoolboy.

He wasn't prepared for what Pat did next. The shock of the man's mouth on his own was so great he didn't realize what was happening at first, couldn't fathom that such a thing could happen.

David held the kiss for a moment, allowing himself a hint of what was being offered, an understanding of what timeless hours could be created within the force of such a passion. And knowing the passion would be built only on grief and bottomless pain, found the decency to push it away.

He sat back on his knees, breath coming in ragged gasps, blood thundering through his veins like an unstoppable tide. He ran a hand over his face, then looked down at the man prostrate on the floor.

Pat's eyes were closed, mouth set in a grim line.

"Christ, David," he whispered, "I'm sorry."

David shook his head. "I'm not. You're exhausted and grief-stricken, in the morning it'll be as though it never happened."

Pat shook his head, eyes open now. "No, it won't be. We both know ye can't erase such moments."

David shrugged and then softly said, "If it's all the same to you, I don't want to erase it."

Pat didn't respond. He turned his head away and the long frame, so pale in the gathering dusk, began to shake. David merely laid a hand on his shoulder, knowing that anything more would be a grave mistake.

"I've sinned," Pat said dully, "an' this is how I'm to pay for it. Yet it's Sylvie who's paid the greatest cost."

"How very Catholic of you," David responded dryly. "The only sin here was the one of trying to be human in a system that doesn't allow for such weakness."

"Now who's bein' naïve?" Pat asked, eyes still closed, though the trembling in his body had ceased and he lay very still as the ebb tide of fatigue finally caught him in its net.

"Even being born here doesn't prepare one for this country," David replied, feeling profoundly weary himself. He still had to return to base and pack up; he was to leave for London tonight. However he couldn't, at present, find the words to tell this man he was leaving and would not be returning in a fashion that would allow them to maintain their friendship.

"Will ye—will ye just sit here with me for a bit?" Pat asked, startling David out of his thoughts. "I could try to stand but I don't think my legs would hold me up right now."

"I'll sit here all night, if you need me to," David replied.

They were silent for a long time. When the darkness came, David could feel it settle like a living thing, its touch soft upon his face. The rooms around them seemed to retreat, the furniture blurred into indefinable shapes. Beyond the walls, he could hear the sound of a mother calling her child home out of the night. If the child came at once all would be fine, but if he didn't her voice would soon grow panicked, for like all mothers she knew that some children went out to play and never did return home.

In the dark, Pat spoke, voice hollowed out with grief and exhaustion.

"How," he asked, "am I to live now?"

David paused, considered a lie, and then knew despite the necessity of it, he'd told the truth earlier. He could not lie to this man.

"However it is that lonely people make a life."

Chapter Eighty-five
Here in the Dark

THE HOUSE LAY STILL ABOUT HER, the only noise that of the water gently lapping at the edges of the big tub. The water was up to her throat, awash with lavender heads, spicily fragrant in the steam. But even the warm bath couldn't erase the chill that went bone deep in her now. Despite the exhaustion of early pregnancy, she still lay awake much of every night, listening for a step on the stair which never came.

A week ago, she had cleaned Lawrence's room, tidying away the jumble, washing the dirty clothes and placing them back in the drawers. She'd even made the bed, though she'd not had the heart to take the indent out of the pillow where his head had lain so recently. Then she had closed the door and not opened it since.

She stepped out of the bath, the gurgle of the escaping water the only noise in the great hush that surrounded her. The house felt like a fragile shell around her which would shatter at the slightest touch.

She looked in the steam-smudged mirror and sighed. She felt like the survivor of a shipwreck, cast ashore on an abandoned island. She looked the part too, she thought, hair a wet tangle of black, face thin and white, eyes hollowed out with grief and exhaustion.

Yesterday she'd finally gone to the doctor and had confirmed that which she had already known. She was most definitely pregnant. The baby was due in early April, conceived, she was certain, on the night she and Casey had made love in the field, with the sound of Robin's lament washing over them.

She towelled off, eyeing her body in the mirror. Her breasts were unmistakably those of a woman with child, warm and painfully tender; the traceries of blue vein like bruised rivers weaving through a snowy landscape. Her stomach was only beginning to round itself out, in promise of the fertile mound it would become.

She slid a flannel nightgown over her head, an ancient garment which was flecked with tiny blue forget-me-nots and was as soft and comforting as a child's blanket. It clung to her bath warm skin as she padded downstairs to let Finbar in. The dog ambled in, his gait much less spritely than it had been only weeks before. He looked at her with mutely pleading eyes and she shook her head. He sighed as if in understanding, and walked dispiritedly over to the locked door of Lawrence's room, whined and then curled up in front of it, the spot he'd slept in every night since the boy's death. It seemed even her thoughts had become filled with those words—before, since, after, all the words which divided time and became a part of the vocabulary of loss.

She filled an old stone gin jar with water that was bubbling away on the Aga. The nights were turning cold, and she couldn't seem to warm of her own volition these days.

She turned off the lights as she walked through the house on her nightly journey. The route a map of comfort, lodestones on the roads and streams and mountains of a life—here in the half-whittled lark Casey had been working on before Lawrence's death, there in the ashes of the fire they'd talked beside when the summer nights had begun to cool. In his mug still in the sink, because she could not bear to wash it and put it away. In the telescope lenses, coddled on a velvet cloth, that he and Lawrence had been painstakingly grinding together. In the stairs they climbed together at night, talking the small pre-sleep talk of a married couple, or the times they barely made the door before tumbling to the bed, mute with need.

She stood now in the dark of their bedroom, wondering if it was possible that she had been so happy only six weeks ago. How had their world burned down so quickly? Leaving them to stand in the charred ruins without a clue of how to act, or speak or breathe.

She slid the gin jar down between the sheets. The heat released the smell of soap and lemons from the smooth cotton. She got in, pulling the blankets up around her ears, sticking her feet on the small warmth of the jar.

The house was so quiet she could hear her pulse thudding against the walls of her skin, deep and heavy, feeding the small life within. This tiny being who tethered her to her own mortality, that made her feel both comforted and more alone than ever, all at the same time.

In his pen beside the shed, Paudeen gave a long *mehhhh*. The poor thing was lonely and made his disconsolation clear several times a day. She turned in the bed with a sigh, toes curling tighter to the gin jar. There was no way she was going out into that dark misty night to comfort him. He was tucked up snug with a new bale of hay, he'd just have to cry himself into exhaustion like the rest of them had been doing of late.

She sat up in bed a minute later, all senses on alert. Paudeen's bleat had been cut short and she could hear the squeak of his pen gate. Someone was in the yard. She got out of bed, legs shaking and went to the window.

A man was walking across the yard below. His head was bowed, hair too dark to be distinguishable in the moonless night, but she knew the line of that body and the long strides that ate up the yard in a few steps.

She got back into bed, feeling suddenly breathless, hands and feet cold with panic. Torn between the desire to rush down the stairs and the desire to stay firmly put and avoid what he may have come to say.

She heard him murmur to the dog and then the sound of his tread on the stairs. It was the step she'd waited for all these weeks and now lay frozen in a welter of blankets, hearing it. Had he come to get his things, to say goodbye? To tell her they could no longer be a family, or grow old together. He was here though; perhaps that in itself was a good sign. He was, however, not a man to avoid unpleasantness, and would tell her to her face if he'd decided to make their separation permanent. But surely not in the middle of the night, creeping up the stairs like a thief?

The door creaked open, and a tall form stepped in. She could hear him take a deep breath and the tiny hairs on her body rose in expectation.

"Pamela, it's me," he said quietly, "are ye awake?"

She turned toward him, sheets rustling with her movement. "Yes, I'm awake." Her voice was high and tight with a mix of fear and anticipation.

She could make out his outline. Tall and broad-shouldered, but even in the dark the lines of fatigue were evident. He still wore his coat, though he'd climbed the stairs in his stocking feet. For a moment they simply stared at one another, wordless with grief. Finally Casey cleared his throat and spoke.

"May I stay the night?" he asked, his voice smoke-soft with weariness.

She nodded, pinpricks of tears gathering in a flood behind her eyes.

"Of course you can." She put a hand to her eyes, pressing against them to still the tears.

She could hear his clothes drop to the floor, heard him bend to pull off his socks. Then there was just the smooth slip of skin against sheet, the feel of his body settling to rest beside her. The skin, the weight that shifted behind her, the movements more familiar to her than her own. He'd come in through the pine copse, she could smell the sharp clean tang of it on him. And wasn't entirely sober if the underlying note of whiskey was anything by which to judge.

All that she could manage was, "Why?"

"Pat told me ye'd not slept well since I left," he said simply, "I thought if I came to lie with ye, ye might be able to rest."

"Pat knows where you are?" she asked.

"No," he said, "no one does."

She wanted to ask if he would be there come morning, if his presence here in the bed signalled the beginning of a thaw, but was afraid of what the answers might be and so the questions remained stuck in her chest, like a big cold ball of ice that threatened to choke her with uncertainty.

"Casey, I—" she began, but a finger touched her lips softly in the dark.

"Hush *macushla*, there's no need for words tonight. Just sleep, I'll bide."

He settled an arm around her, pulling her tight to the comfort of his body. Despite the painful gulf which stretched between them, their skin understood another language altogether and her body relaxed instinctively into his own. Much as she longed to speak, to beg him to put an end to this self-imposed exile, she knew he wasn't ready to listen. She derived some small comfort in his calling her *macushla*, the literal translation was 'my pulse', or 'my heartbeat', but the common usage meant 'my beloved'. He couldn't have decided to leave her permanently if he still loved her enough to speak an endearment he'd only used previously in the most tender of moments.

With the warmth of his skin against her, the steady beat of his heart echoing in her own blood, sleep came readily, her exhausted mind and body slipping into a deep and dreamless slumber.

Somewhere in the wee hours when the light was ashy, she heard him murmur, but was so lost to sleep she couldn't make out the words. But the hand that traced along her neck and cheek was gentle and the voice was that of a man whose heart was broken in two.

She awoke late in the morning, the sun shining warm and thick on the blankets and her shoulder. She turned over in the bed, hoping against hope.

But Casey was gone.

Chapter Eighty-six
The Tenth Commandment

THE FEELING OF SOMETHING CRAWLING across his face was the first thing that demanded Casey's attention. He swatted irritably at whatever it was and rolled over. He was tired and was certain it could be no more than half-five in the morning. He wasn't due at O'Connell's farm until half-seven. Though to be sure, the idea of digging potatoes for twelve hours straight didn't sound too appealing right now, not when his head felt as though someone had replaced it with molten lead during the night. Once his conscious mind truly awoke, though, he found that unremitting, mind-numbing physical labor was the only thing that could wipe thoughts of Pamela from his head. He'd been working for the O'Connell's as an odd jobs man for a month now. He'd promised them another two weeks at the least.

Something tweaked his ear none too gently. He cursed and flipped over on his back. What the hell sort of bug had that kind of a grip to it?

He squinted through the haze of what promised to be a particularly brutal hangover. Someone was sitting by his bedside, someone who even at this ungodly hour looked entirely composed. Casey swore again. This time, though, the epithets had a direction.

"My, your language is almost as foul as your smell," Jamie Kirkpatrick said, one long leg canted over the other, while he tapped a pair of gloves against his flannel clad shin. "Now get up."

"What? Ye have a nerve comin' in here—"

"Get up," Jamie repeated, voice cold as ice. His tone sent a shiver of warning down Casey's spine. The man had not come to play.

Casey sat up, hands clutching his head to stop the room spinning. A crash brought his head up, nausea surging at the back of his throat and pain breaking like an anvil across his skull.

Jamie had quite deliberately tipped over the table, which had been loaded with a stunning variety of empty bottles.

"Hey, what the hell was that for?"

Cool green eyes, without a hint of a thaw, met his own.

"For behaving like a perfect jackass for the last month. I gave you that long, thinking even a thick-headed bastard like yourself would have to come to his senses, but apparently I," he gave a glittering smile that was not friendly, "underestimated the depth of your stupidity. Now get up."

The man had stood at some point himself, and though his pose was relaxed, Casey knew Jamie was coiled and ready to strike.

Casey stood, a small cauldron of anger beginning to brew in his stomach along with the nausea. Jamie's left hand came up so quickly that Casey felt a jarring pain through his face before he realized what had happened. He blinked, feeling like a dazed owl, hand coming away from his lip smeared with blood.

"Ye hit me," he said in shocked indignation.

"Well at least you've the faculties left to state the obvious," Jamie replied dryly, flexing his fingers as though they were merely cramped from the blow. He looked about the room in distaste. "Is it too much to hope that you've coffee hidden somewhere in this sludge pile?"

"Aye," Casey said, still gingerly dabbing at his rapidly swelling lip, "it's in the cupboard above the stove."

Jamie moved about the small area swiftly, scooping coffee into the filter, tipping a pile of rubbish into the garbage, stacking bottles under the sink and rinsing the coffee pot several times before he was happy with the condition of its interior.

"Now," he said, voice like shattered crystal, gleaming and razor-sharp, "I'm going to pour coffee into you until I'm satisfied you're sober and then I'm going to lay a proposal before you."

"What sort of proposal?" Casey asked warily, not liking the look on the man's face at all, at all.

"The sort that requires an action either in the negative or positive, and those aspects I'll leave entirely to your own judgement, but without gray areas."

"Listen, if ye've come on behalf—" Casey began, words fading away under Jamie's glacial look.

"I'll talk and you'll listen. When I'm finished you can make any comment you like, realizing in advance that nothing you say will change the course of action I've chosen."

A moment later Casey found himself with a mug of coffee in hand which bore an unpleasant resemblance to tar, and a strong feeling he wasn't going to like the words he was about to hear.

"I've not come on behalf of your wife. I daresay she wouldn't like to think of me here, she's not even spoken your name."

Casey flinched visibly. "Point taken man, there's no need for cruelty."

"Isn't there?" Jamie asked coolly. "You didn't seem to mind being cruel a month ago. Perhaps you can imagine what these days have been like for Pamela. Then again, perhaps that's why you did it." He paused to take a drink of his own coffee, green eyes never leaving Casey's face. Eyes that had all the warmth of a dissecting scalpel, and all the mercy.

"What lies between my wife an' myself is none of yer concern," Casey said, some fine thread of anger beginning to run through his veins.

"Isn't it? You once told me that though she was your wife and lay in your bed, you still weren't so big of a fool as to not know you were sharing her with me. I've always been careful not to take advantage of that particular fact. I find I'm not inclined to be quite so generous anymore."

Casey uttered a short bark of laughter. "Christ, Robin once said ye were the most ruthless bastard any of us was likely to be acquainted with, but I told him no, ye were too civilized for it. I see he was a better judge of character than me."

"You'd do well to remember his words, perhaps then you'll take what I have to say seriously."

"So what is it ye feel ye have to say to me?" Casey asked with no little belligerence.

"You're not the first man to deal with a wife's infidelity."

Casey felt as though he'd been hit hard in the chest. "Christ, ye waste no time in comin' to the point, do ye? Did she tell ye?"

Jamie shook his head. "No, but I'm not a fool. It's been obvious to me she's been carrying a secret that was eating her up since the two of you came back to Belfast. It wasn't terribly hard to piece it together. I daresay you knew on some level yourself. Every time the woman looked at you, it was as though she was afraid you were going to break."

Casey nodded, granting the man that much. "Aye, I knew something was wrong but I didn't want it to be this. Do ye know that she also arranged to have the man killed when she was done with him?"

Jamie eyed him calmly. "I rather think she didn't have much choice in the matter. I think she saw it as either him or you. Not much in the way of choosing there."

"Ye say it so calm-like, as if it's of no great surprise to ye."

"What is it you know about her now that you didn't before? That she's capable of killing to protect the people she loves? Can you honestly tell me you didn't know that before? She's your equal in all things, man, and you're more fool than I suspect if you didn't know it on some level. I knew."

Casey took a breath and gritted his teeth. The last two words were intended as pure provocation, and as determined as he was not to rise to the man's bait, he could feel the pure need to choke the bastard quickly getting the better of him.

"I know what she's capable of. I have always seen the echo of yerself in her. An' the echo of my own self and what I am capable of doing. I'd have done no less, and yet—" he stumbled on the words, because the truth was he still could not bear the thought of another man touching her, using her in such a fashion, because of the mistakes he himself had made.

"So what is it, then, that you cannot face?" Jamie asked, tone slightly softer but still edged with razor sharpness.

"I can't face her because I cannot face myself. She bought my life for me an' I've used it cheaply, I'd no notion of what she'd done. Oh, I wasn't so blind that I couldn't see he'd an eye for her, but after these years I'm used to men starin' plenty."

"You never suspected that he wanted more, that he'd do whatever he could to have her?" Jamie all but snorted. "You had good reason to know how unscrupled the man was in every area of his life; did you somehow think he'd respect the boundaries of marriage? You left your wife at the mercy of a wolf, and you know it."

"Aye," Casey said in a flat voice, "I do know it. I suppose you'd have found a way to keep her out of harm's way?"

"I'd have killed him before I let him touch her," Jamie said softly, but Casey was left in no doubt that the man meant exactly what he said.

"Would you? Or am I naïve to ask such a question? After all, you've killed to avenge her before, haven't ye?"

Jamie's expression did not change, but Casey felt the tension in the room creep upward a notch or two. "There were four men on that train that night," Jamie said, voice low and tight. "I know the fate of two, and the fair Reverend took care of the one both you and I really wanted dead. However, I never did manage to find the whereabouts of the fourth man. I've always wondered if you had taken care of that detail yourself."

The words were not framed in the form of a question, and so Casey did not answer them. It was his opinion that the man in front of him did not rest until everything had been finished to his satisfaction, and that Jamie knew as well as anyone might what the fate of that fourth man had been.

"I guess that makes you the white knight," Casey said bitterly. "Always there at the ready to catch her when she falls."

"And what does that make you?" Jamie asked, voice polite but eyes alight with a fury so cold Casey could feel the prick of it along his spine.

"The fool that causes her to fall in the first place. But then ye've always known that. I've played my part admirably well, made it very easy for ye didn't I?"

"At times you have."

Casey sighed. "I've had about enough of yer honesty for today."

"Too damn bad. I'm going to say one more thing whether you want to hear it or not. All those times I've rushed to the rescue, every time I've fixed a situation it's been because of her, not you. She wanted you, and so I gave her into your arms, knowing even as I did it that I'd regret it over and over."

"And now," Casey's voice was tight as corded wire, "ye've decided to take her back, is that it?"

"If you don't return, I see no reason not to. I'll give her time to mend, but she's still feelings for me so I don't think I'll have to wait that long. You walked away from her, which ought to cut the time for guilt down considerably. Two, maybe three months, a touch here, a glance that lingers too long there, and," Jamie shrugged, a suggestive smile on his lips, "nature will take her usual course."

"Ye bloody bastard!" Casey rose to his feet, anger thundering along muscle and vein, in blood and marrow, the urge to kill opening and closing his fists. "Who the hell do ye think ye are to come here an' say such things?"

Jamie looked at him sharply, no movement rustling the lines of his body, and yet Casey instinctively knew that he was as ready to spring as a cat with the scent of blood up its nose. "I think," Jamie said slowly, each word a cut to a psyche already bruised, "the more pertinent question is who the hell do you think you are?"

"I—" Casey began hotly and then stopped seeing the point clearly that Jamie was making. "I don't know," he said quietly, fists uncurling to hang limply by his sides. "I don't seem to know who I am anymore. Between findin' out what she'd done, an' knowin' 'twas me put her in that position, an' not bein' there when Lawrence needed me the most..." his voice cracked on this last sentence.

"No, you weren't there when the lad needed you most, but neither were any of the rest of us who loved him. We're all going to live with the guilt of that for the rest of our lives. Perhaps rightly so. You were his hero, though, and so you're going to pay dearest for it."

Casey cast his eyes about, feeling the familiar shaking start in his hands. He desperately needed a drink.

"Is that how you intend to honor Lawrence's memory?"

Casey flinched as if Jamie had struck him.

"Don't think it's helping you, because it isn't. It seems a safe place to hide from the world—I know, I've tried it—but one day you wake and find out your safe place has become prison walls. You need to grieve the boy, drinking won't change that one bit. The minute you sober up long enough, it'll be waiting for you."

Casey staggered forward, wanting to hit the man until the cutting pain in his chest subsided. But the grief had flooded in from the edges of his consciousness and it caught him full force, taking him to his knees. Jamie caught him as he fell, going to his own knees as Casey's weight bore him down.

"Oh—Christ—oh God," Casey gasped, the very breath sucked from his lungs. His entire frame shook with a cold that emanated out from his core, laying waste to all it touched in its passing. Jamie took him in his arms and held him tightly as the worst of the spasms shook him like a leaf in a gale. He was oddly grateful for the man's touch, as though it was all that tethered him within this storm of grief and rage.

The tears, when they came, were foreign, a thing he had forgotten. They burst the dam he'd so carefully constructed, overflowing and rushing forth from the great sea of things withheld, suppressed, and not allowed within his personal universe. It was this loss of control that he had always been afraid of, that once started the tears would be impossible to stop, that he would no longer know where he ended and the grief began. He was, simply, afraid of drowning in the pain.

"Let them go," Jamie said above him, still holding him, bracing him against the flood. And so he did, knowing that, though he would carry them with him for all his days, he had held them too tightly and not given them the grief nor the joy owed to those whom we love and lose.

His father, his brother who had grown to manhood without him, his own missed youth. The boy who had been the best friend he'd ever known. Deirdre and the baby they'd lost while he was interned. Lawrence, who had been an odd mix of wise friend and son. The trust he and Pamela had known, and a marriage that now stood on shifting sands so that he felt he could not recognize the form of it, nor to whom such a marriage might belong. And, God help him, he even cried for the mother who had left him so long ago.

He lay for a time after the tears subsided, too weak and exhausted to move. The world came back to him in pieces. His jaw was throbbing where Jamie had hit it and his head still hurt like holy hell. The pain in his chest had receded a bit though, and he drew his first full breath in months. He levered himself up, aching in every joint and muscle. Felling as though he'd been mercilessly beaten.

He slumped against the bed frame. He felt terribly fragile and yet knew that somehow he had been restored to himself in the last few minutes. That Jamie had unlocked his grief and in doing so had placed the shore of redemption within sight. There was one last thing, however, that he needed to know.

"How much?" Casey said softly, voice drained of all emotion. "How much money did ye pay to buy my freedom?"

"Two hundred thousand pounds," Jamie said. "You were far more expensive than your compatriots."

"What?"

Jamie eyed him dispassionately. "They were only ten thousand a head, you were far more. You wanted to know and now you know. Has it set you properly free?"

"Why—why would ye do such a thing?"

"For her. I didn't think she could bear losing you again, after she got you back. It seemed a small price to give her peace of mind."

"To whom did ye give this money?"

Jamie raised an eyebrow. "It's not the sort of thing for which they issue receipts."

He sighed. It seemed he owed the bastard yet again.

"You're going to survive this," Jamie said gently, "something has already decided that for you. Now you have to decide how to live with it."

And there, Casey thought, was the rub.

Jamie stood and straightened his shirt, then slung his overcoat casually over his forearm. "If you're inclined," he said, "to prolong your suffering and stay out here in the wilds, perhaps it will motivate you to think of her living under my roof, eating at my table, spending her mornings, noons and nights in my company."

"Sleeping in yer bed?" Casey retorted between gritted teeth.

"If it comes to that, then yes," Jamie replied, "sleeping and waking in my bed."

"One question before ye go," Casey said wearily, head throbbing like an anvil.

"Yes," Jamie said, green eyes meeting his coolly.

"Do ye love her enough to give me a day or two to get myself together? Do ye love her enough to wait a bit?"

"I love her enough," Jamie said quietly, "to wait forever. But you my good man have until Hallowe'en to make a decision and act upon it."

TWO DAYS AFTER JAMIE'S VISIT, Casey looked down the laneway to see Matty's little car humping its way through the ruts.

"Jaysus, Mary an' Joseph," Casey said aloud to the air. "Will they never leave a body alone?" He heaved a sigh of frustration, and then pinned a smile of welcome on his face as Matty got out of his car. "I don't suppose ye just happened to be passin' through the neighborhood?"

Matty smiled, looking like nothing more than a cherubic garden gnome, laced in butterflies. "Desmond an' I talk now an' again."

"Do ye indeed?" Casey said dryly, thinking Dez's promise not to interfere had lasted about as long as it took for Casey to shut the door behind him. The man had been down to visit and proffer his own advice the week past. When Casey had enquired as to how he knew where to find him, Dez had smiled in an annoyed Cheshire manner, which told Casey exactly who had given out the directions to his hideaway.

"Aye we do, an' the both of us came to the one conclusion—that the way ye're behavin' isn't somethin' yer daddy would like to see, nor would he want for ye the sort of life ye're headin' for, if ye don't take stock here."

Casey sighed, a breath of frustration that seemed to work its way up from his very toes. "An' what do ye suppose the man wanted for me?"

"I imagine that he wanted for ye what most parents want for their children. That ye find happiness and someone to love. Might not seem much in the grand scheme of things, but it's all that really matters when the day is done."

"Mmphhm," Casey said, in what might be grudging agreement, or outright irritation.

"Ye may think I'm meddlin' where I'm not concerned," Matty avoided Casey's gaze as he said this. "But I was there after that bastard opened yer back up for ye, an' we didn't know for a good bit whether ye'd live or die."

"Yer point, Matty," Casey said impatiently.

"My point is when a man's brought so low as that, well that's when he knows what matters in his life, gives ye a clarity that canna be achieved in other ways. An' my point is that ye yelled her name, even while ye were unconscious. Ye kept callin' her over an' over until ye were hoarse—fair drove Declan mad, ye did. I'd always heard as ye'd made a love match, but I knew what it meant after those three days. Maybe lad," Matty fumbled with his knit cap, "ye'll not know that doesn't happen for everyone, in fact I'd wager it only happens to a very lucky few."

"I do know that," Casey said quietly, "but somehow, Matty, it only makes what she's done that much worse. I feel like she's gutted me."

"I don't know what she's done, but I'll ask ye—does she still love ye?"

"Aye, she does."

"An' do you still love her?"

"Aye, I do."

"Then I think ye can forgive it, whatever it might be."

"Matty, I appreciate ye takin' the time to—"

Matty cut him off with a raised hand. "I've said my bit, an' ye can take it or leave it. Now, would ye have a drink about the place, man?"

Casey laughed. "No, the bloody bastard that sent ye here, an' I think we both know I'm not speakin' of Desmond, poured every drop of it down the sink. I can make ye a cup of tea if ye'd like, though."

Matty smiled. "That'd be grand, lad."

When Casey returned with the tea, Matty was still sitting on the stone wall, face turned toward the sun, which was bright but held little warmth this late in the autumn. His wispy hair lifted in the breeze, heightening his gnome-like countenance. It struck Casey that the man was starting to look old. He wondered with a sudden tightness in his throat what his own daddy would have looked like had he lived to this age.

"Here's yer tea then," Casey said gruffly, handing Matty a mug that steamed in the cool air.

"Yer daddy gave me a bit of advice once that I'm goin' to pass on to yerself today."

"Aye?"

"He told me to go home an' save my marriage before I found I didn't have one. I didn't listen, an' I've had a lifetime to regret it. I'd not see ye make the same mistake. I felt I owed ye that much."

"Ye don't owe me anything, man."

"Aye, that's as may be or no, but I owed yer da. Were he here, he'd tell ye much as I have today."

"An' likely cuff me upside the head just to be sure the point had gotten across."

"Aye, well a man might see the temptation. Ye're a stubborn laddie."

"I suppose I am at that," he admitted ruefully.

"There's stubborn an' then there's just plain stupid, make certain ye know the difference, son."

"I'm trying, Matty."

Matty reached across and patted his hand. "I know ye are laddie, just don't be too long about it, though."

Chapter Eighty-seven

Good Night Moon

SEPTEMBER BECAME OCTOBER and the days slipped from soft fog and slow sun to chill frost and early nights. And still there was no word from Casey, and still Jamie would say to her sleepless eyes and overstrained nerves, 'He'll come.' But as the days of October melted off the calendar and drew themselves down toward November, her doubts took over and she began to believe Casey had made his decision and by not coming was telling her just what that decision was. So when the bell rang in the early evening of a late October night she thought very little of it.

"Will you get that or shall I?" she asked, stretching lazily, the print of the book in her lap beginning to swim in front of her eyes.

"I believe it's for you," Jamie said, calmly turning the page in his own book.

"How do you know—" she began and then stopped just as suddenly, a constriction in her throat. There was only one way he could be certain. She stood, the book falling to the floor unheeded, her pulse suddenly throbbing in her ears. Her legs felt as insubstantial as blown glass, as if they could not possibly make the short trip to the hall, and yet they did so, moving of their own accord across the polished floor and along the Turkish runner. The door seemed a mile away and far too close at the same time. She put her hand upon the great carved knob and taking a deep breath, opened it.

He stood on the doorstep, hands rammed in his pockets, nerves apparent in every line of him. She stood wordless, confronted with his physical presence. Common sense took its leave gracefully and small talk seemed utterly beyond her abilities.

"The night is fine," he said softly, "will ye walk with me?"

Silence gripped her throat in a painful vise. This was the moment she had wanted and yet now that it was here, it terrified her.

"Please," he added, and it was the uncertainty in his voice that broke the spell for her.

"Yes," she nodded, hand gripping the doorknob tightly still, afraid her legs would not support her if she let go.

"Ye'll want a coat, it's cold," he said, the proof of his words displaying itself in small puffing clouds of breath.

"I'll just be a minute," she said, awkward in the face of the man who knew her better than any other, who'd seen her at her finest and at her very worst.

"I'll wait," he replied, and she understood that the words extended far past their immediate implication.

She headed towards the stairs, meaning to fly up them, only to halt, uncertain, in the doorway of the study, knowing there weren't any words to properly express the jumble of violent emotion that had her shivering and burning all at once.

Jamie looked up, green eyes bemused, the recently lit fire sparking gold off his hair and the ring on his finger. "Take a sweater," he said gently, "it's chilly in the evenings now."

"Jamie I—thank you."

He gave a wry smile. "That, as they say, is what friends are for. Now go, don't keep the poor man waiting any longer."

Casey, as he'd promised, waited just beyond the stairs where the garden lights made shallow ivoried pools in the hollows between fallen leaves and dew-iced grass.

"It's good to see ye," he said as she drew near, his tone that of a hesitant half-stranger.

"It's good to see you too." His awkwardness had translated itself to her and she found her hands flapping uselessly at her sides, then realized it was because she was used to slipping one automatically into his. And now did not know if she could, or should.

"I've a place in mind that I'd like to take ye, if ye'll allow it." She understood the words which lay unspoken between them, 'trust me this little,' he was saying.

"That would be grand," she said softly.

He'd left the car at the bottom of the drive, near the cypress gate. The gate he'd waited for her at in the early days of their courtship. He gave her a hand into the car and she could feel the burn of his touch even through the layers of material which separated their respective skins. She was awash with the need to touch him suddenly, to be able to bridge the abyss that had widened to an impasse on the night Robin had told him about Love Hagerty. She knew, though, the move would have to be his.

The ride was quiet, both painfully aware they were far beyond the point in their relationship where small talk was an option for smoothing ruffled nerves. Casey drove quickly, eyes on the road, face set in the lines that meant he was deep inside his own mind. Soon they'd left the lights of Belfast far behind, to turn down a country lane that was heavily overhung with ragged hedgerows and brown, wilted fuchsia. The lane was so constricted that the trees bent back against the sides of the car and after a few minutes of this, Casey stopped the car and turned off the engine.

"We'll have to walk, car can't go any further," he said and squeezed out his side into the pitch-black tunnel of leaves.

She joined him in front of the car, still rubbing at a stinging spot on her scalp where a particularly vindictive branch had tried to extract a generous patch of hair.

The silence was absolute, the night creatures burrowed down against the chill of winter. Under her feet, the ground was hard as tempered steel.

"Are ye all right, then?" Casey asked, his voice almost a shock in the dark.

"I'm fine," she murmured, tucking her hands into her pockets and following as he set off purposefully up the narrow rutted pathway.

He walked a little ahead of her, visible only in flashes where the moon's light, chill and thick as hoarfrost, penetrated the murk of the surrounding flora. His time away had changed him. So attuned was she to his variety of nuances that she could sense it even in the way he held his shoulders, the way the deep groove of his backbone was apparent through his shirt. She remembered the last time she'd run her fingertips in that hollow, each vertebrae round and smooth beneath her hands. The odd silkiness of old scars, pale against the brown of his skin. She remembered the heat and damp of their two bodies and felt the familiar rush of weakness that always came with the thought of what that body could do to her, had done to her.

She stumbled slightly, a loose stone in the pathway catching her unawares. He reached back a hand and caught her, giving her his own hand to guide her through the tangle of frostbitten broom and gorse which cluttered the path in front of them. The feel of his palm, smooth and hard with calluses, was like coming home after a particularly long absence, slightly unfamiliar and yet entirely comforting.

They came upon the cottage suddenly, around a bend in the narrow track. Here the moonlight was dense, delineating the smallest blade of grass and the finest whisper of breath, the white so stark that all it touched seemed without weight or depth. The cottage appeared to be floating on top of a slight knoll, half-hidden by the bare bones of the trees that emerged from the whitened landscape like rheumatic bones. The little house seemed to hunch in on itself, as if trying to elude the grasp of the curving tree branches.

That it was abandoned was at once apparent, it had the odd eyeless look of a house with its windows broken out. The ancient reeds of the roof were rotted, and gaping holes, like untended wounds, perforated the little building.

She looked at him, the question clearly written upon her face.

He responded as though she'd spoken aloud. "It's neither your territory nor mine, it belongs only to ghosts. I thought neutral ground was only fair. Come," he gestured toward the door, his voice no more than a whisper, as if he felt the need not to disturb any spirits that might be lingering.

Inside the cottage, moonlight poured through the rotten reeds of the roof, molten and lambent, it lay thickly over every surface. The white light bent around dust-shrouded shelves and a table which still held a bowl and cup and a stub of a candle. The strange stillness was here as well, only heavier, as if this sad, abandoned home were the source of its emanation. She moved carefully, hardly daring to breathe, to take that strange, still light into her lungs.

"You'd think no one had been here in a hundred years," she whispered, and even that low tone sounded like a shout to her ears. Dust stirred in a delicate eddy under her fingertips as she passed them above the table. The light was such that each mote was limned as though it danced its spiral dance in broad rays of sunlight.

"It's like that no one has been," Casey said, voice somber. "There's houses like this all about the country, Jewel, families that just up an' left an' wee houses that wait forever for their people to come back."

"Just left, with food still on the table?" She gestured toward the bowl and cup, thickly shrouded in cobweb.

"Aye, at times. Not that there was likely much food to be had."

"But what could drive a family so quickly from their home?"

"Despair," he said simply, "do ye not feel it? Ye're usually extra sensitive to it. The wee house feels it, aye?"

She was silent for a moment, allowing thought and feeling to flow in rather than out. Her eyes absorbed each object, its angles and shades, the way the cobweb lay in fragile sheets, overlaid by years of grime, glimmering like fairy dust in the moonlight. She took a deep breath, smelling the disuse, the mildew, the rot—the scent, as Casey had said, of despair. It was almost palpable, the little house had felt disappointment which over the days, months and years had become despair. The pain was very nearly physical, a deep empty void just below her ribcage.

"Why did they go, do you think?"

Casey shook his head, moonlight painting him in silver and black. "The Famine maybe, so many left then an' so many after because they could not feed their children, nor themselves. Can ye imagine what it was to look into yer child's face an' know ye'd not a bite to feed them, while grain lay rotting in the harbors? There's a poem by Jack Stuart aye, perhaps ye'll know it? It's called *An Gorta Mor* an' it lists the things that were sent to England in one year—

> *Four thousand ships they say,*
> *Left for a land that year*
> *Salmon and honey flowed from*
> *A Land that could not feed its own...'*

Casey quoted quietly, his dark eyes far away, as though he saw the wretched people even now as they died on the roadsides and in the shelter of their own homes, which had become prisons of pestilence and agony.

> *'Wheat and barley by the sheaves,*
> *Sailing down in Shannon's lee...'*

she continued for him, her voice low as though she spoke in the presence of death.

"Ah, so ye do know it?" Casey's face was unfathomable in the odd light, his eyes the only point of color, and they an impenetrable black. "My da always thought that 'twas the Famine more than anything which made peace between England an' Ireland impossible, he said 'twas like a sword that lay between the two, an' it would cut from either side."

"What do you think it is that makes peace so impossible?"

He shook his head, one lock of hair catching the light and laying it like a kiss against his forehead. "It's that the English memory is very short an' the Irish very long. They don't want us an' yet they won't acknowledge that we are separate, a people apart from them, but then England will hold tight even when the holdin' is blisterin' her palms. They have never understood us, they've never assimilated nor subdued us—conquered us, aye, an' almost succeeded in wipin' us off the face of the earth, but never made us British. An' I think maybe that's what they hate about us, that we have no desire to be them. An' yet," he sighed, "I've known many a good Englishman in my life an' many an Irishman that I'd not dare turn my back on. But I suppose the conquered are never in a position to feel charitable toward the conqueror."

"No," she agreed quietly, "I don't suppose they are."

Casey took a step toward her, the still light suddenly broken by his movement. She could feel the displacement of air, aware to the last fiber of her being of his presence. As things were, she thought wryly, so they shall be again.

"Do ye suppose there is any charity left between the two of us?" he asked quietly, voice constrained, though not without emotion.

"It depends," she responded, her own voice tart with nerves, "upon how you define charity, I imagine."

"Well, as I remember, the dictionary had a few things to say about it, but the one that comes to mind at present is makin' allowances for other's shortcomins' an' a disposition to think favorably of men in general."

"Mankind," she corrected primly, "I believe you are taking liberties with the text."

"I'd rather," he said, with a ghost of his old grin, "be takin' liberties with you." The look she gave him was enough to freeze the grin in place. "I didn't mean to make a joke of things, darlin', only I don't know," he rubbed his temples in frustration, "how to be around ye anymore. I feel like a schoolboy standin' out in the rain on some disapprovin' father's doorstep."

"Why did you bring me here?" she asked, voice slightly less hostile.

He took a deep breath and stepped forward, reaching out, his hands palm up, white as bone in the stark light. She understood the choice he was giving her by not taking her hands himself.

'Not impassable,' Jamie had said, *'you only have to find the way across, one step, one oar stroke at a time. He'll meet you halfway.'*

And her question in response, syllables built entirely of fear. *'And if he doesn't?'* And Jamie had given the answer that had likely cost him more than she could count.

'He will.'

She laid her hands, open, in his own, felt the strength of his fingers, and how the strength was held in check.

A tremor shook him, the broad shoulders trembling visibly. "I was so afraid ye'd given up on me."

She shook her head. "No, never that."

He took a long, shaky breath, fought for mastery of his emotions, eyes on the hands that rested quietly in his own. "When my mam an' da fought he used to say to her, 'Will ye still grow old with me, Deirdre?' It was his way of makin' it up, of askin' would she still have him, through the bad as well as the good. An' I suppose," he glanced up from her hands, his dark eyes tired and afraid, "that's what I'm askin' ye now, Jewel, is will ye still grow old with me? Will ye take me durin' the bad as well as the good?" His hands gripped her own tightly, his body still, so still, as if all the moments that had gone and all the ones to come were weighed in her answer.

"Yes," she said quietly, "I'll grow old with you Casey Riordan, I'll take you in bad times as well as good. I don't think that's the question though, I think the real question here is will *you* grow old with me?"

"I know I've given ye ample reason to doubt any words I say, but I can only give ye the answer of any man with the frailties of bein' human. All the days of my allotment on this earth are yours." His eyes held her own, the light making it impossible to hide the tears that stood in them. "On our weddin' night I told ye that as long as there was breath in my body an' blood in my veins it was yers for the askin'."

"I remember," she said softly, giving his hands a gentle squeeze, which he returned with a strength that seemed to promise something or all things.

"I meant it, ye know, it wasn't just idle words said in the heat of passion. I meant it then an' I failed to keep that promise. But I make it again tonight, an' I intend to live up to it this time." He said the words, the grit of emotion darkening them and making her shiver slightly. It sounded in the night like something that couldn't be reversed, a blood oath, the sort his ancestors would have made thousands of years ago, before they went out to do battle. And she heard what was left unspoken, *'Show me that you believe me, for words have never been our kingdom...'*

She sought his mouth there in the abandoned cottage, with the ghosts of a nation thick about them. Gave to him once again her trust and all the intangibles that went with it: her heart, her soul, her very life, relinquished anew into his safekeeping.

"I once told you that you were my shelter, you were my home," she said, feeling the shiver of his hands as they bared her skin to the night and his touch.

"Aye, I too remember," he said as the rhythm of his breathing changed, accelerated, drew out.

She arched against him, length to length, their hands, interlaced in prayer or promise, caught between them. She breathed softly against his mouth and gave him back his vow.

"It's still true."

OUTSIDE, THE LITTLE HOUSE seemed no less haunted. Once its roof had sheltered laughter and tears, joy and pain, love and hate. Once it had known life. Now it merely seemed a crumbling monument to desolation. The white-washed stones had long ago given over to the forces of nature. Lichen, deep and squelchy green, filled the cracks and smoothed the gnarled stones to a velvet finish. The dirt track they had walked in on seemed, in the still light, only to lead away, to another world and another time. The hills surrounding them glowed a soft dull pink, their tops rimed with a fine dusting of snow. Winter had come early this year and she felt the chill of it down to her marrow. Casey often joked that she froze in October and didn't feel the hint of a thaw until late May. Somehow it was different this year though, a subterranean cold that seemed to emanate from the inside out. Beneath her feet, she could feel the earth itself shiver.

She remembered suddenly the words of an astronomer she had read recently.

'Some night you'll look out there and you will feel the planet beneath your feet as you have never felt it before, you will know the flow and stretch of it, and feel the roundness of its bones, you will know we hang by a single thread, this pale blue accident on the shores of infinity, held up by God's grace alone.'

One atom, he had said, one atom in the infinite. That is what we are.

"A ripple," Casey said behind her, his voice seeming part of the night, echoing her thoughts, "an' yet it matters greatly." His arms came around her, strong and secure, her port in every storm. He smelled of smoke and damp and the fresh cut of the season's first snow. The urgency of the flesh was there, magnified by denial, but for the moment, it would wait.

"When it's like this it seems as if the whole world is alive an' breathin', the trees an' the stars, the grass an' even the dirt beneath my feet. An' I wish I knew the right prayer, a blessin' that fit with the night an' its rhythms."

She tipped her face up to the strange still light, felt a chill breeze ripple across her skin like slow-moving champagne, and smiled.

"I know one," she said.

"Do ye?"

"I do."

His hands moved along her forearms, down until they covered her own, pressing her fingers into the crumbling stone. "Will ye speak it to me then?"

"I will," she said and took a deep breath, closing her eyes, seeking the one ripple in the river of memory that held a childhood prayer. She found it, shimmering softly like a flash of silver, heard in memory her father's voice warming and wrapping the words, even as she spoke them.

"Goodnight moon..." She began and her voice continued on, weaving quietly through the story, each phrase accompanied by small puffs of purling fog.

Silence held them softly in the wake of the words, the scent of the pines sharp on the air. Against the sky, the trees were a soft delineation, smudges of dry ink, weary sentinels of a hundred years duty.

His hand drifted from hers and touched, gently, the side of her face, his head bent into the cloud of her hair. "'Tis a lovely prayer, thank you."

She turned and slid her arms around his waist, breathing deep of the night and his sudden warmth, grateful to her very core for this moment, where it seemed the world spun separately from them around a fixed axis. For them, in this one minute, time was stopped, moved neither forward nor back, was a thing neither looking over its shoulder nor trying to grasp the future. It was merely, in and of itself, whole and perfect.

He rested his chin on her head, the stubble of his beard rasping on the sensitive skin of her scalp. "Say goodnight to the moon, darlin'," he whispered, "an' then take my hand, for I'm takin' ye home."

Above them, like a candle melting down one side, hung the moon one week after its fertile fullness, now waning and gibbous. She could make out the bare edge of the great illuminated darkness of Mare Tranquillatis and to the left the blast site of Kepler's crater, so lucent that it seemed it might have been struck only moments ago rather than eight hundred years before. And all the unending oceans and seas, valleys and mountains. Purveyor of time and blood, it hung weary, shedding light as its orbit diminished the viewable surface. And suddenly the silver light, at first eerie, seemed a blessing bestowed by a hand of ancient and indefinable wisdom, by one who had seen too much of the affairs of man to truly believe in happiness, and yet would wish him luck despite the fact.

"Goodnight moon," she said and took the hand of her husband, turning towards home.

A ripple, and yet it matters greatly.

Epilogue

DAVID HAD NEVER APPROACHED THE HOUSE in daylight. Their meetings, through the necessity for secrecy, had always taken place at night, and only rarely in the man's house. Those two occasions had been unqualified emergencies or neither of them would have risked it.

The fog was beginning to dissipate, though shreds of it still wound through the lower branches of the trees, higher up it was shot through with the rare sun of a November morning. The house wore the aspect of a cathedral in the diaphanous gold light. It was as though he'd stepped out of time as soon as he'd come up through the garden gate. The somnolent hush of the morning was broken only by the occasional soft croak of a crow and the muffled crunch of pine needles beneath his thick-soled shoes. Summer's birds had long flown.

The grounds were immaculate, flower beds banked, the more delicate shrubs covered, the amber stones of the house muted to beige under lowering winter skies.

He went to the servant's entrance and rang the bell, he was expected.

"Ye're to go in the study," Maggie said, and pointed toward the set of double doors that led off the end of the long hall. David nodded and thanked her.

The room was empty and far tidier than David was used to seeing it. The books had been replaced on the shelves, the papers tidied away into cabinets and drawers. The desk itself was empty, except for a solitary sheet of stationary, propped against a full bottle of whiskey. On the neck of the bottle was a silver ring, David didn't need to look to know the initials that would be carved into its face.

He drew near the table with reluctance. He had a feeling he wasn't going to be happy with whatever that piece of paper had to say. There was an absence of energy in the air, as though the light had shrunk and become less substantial than before.

The stationary was Jamie's own, thick and watermarked with the graceful scrawling *K* of the House of Kirkpatrick. It contained only two words. David read them and smiled in spite of himself. Bloody Irish bastard, the man was as unpredictable as any of them.

He recognized the absence of light and energy now for what it truly was. This room and all the rest of the house seemed to understand in some way that its master was gone, and was not likely to return any time soon.

A light breeze, stirred by the closing of the door, lifted the paper and swept it from the table. It drifted across the floor, coming to rest by the ashes in the fireplace. It landed facedown, but the words remained unchanged, just two of them.

Gone fishing.

About the Author

Cindy Brandner lives in the interior of British Columbia with her husband and three children, as well as a plethora of pets. She is currently working on the continuation of the Exit Unicorns series.

Praise for Exit Unicorns

Here is a riveting read filled with the politics of conflict, the drama of the human condition, the depth of character, and the story of mid-twentieth century Northern Ireland struggling from freedom and peace amidst the rubble of armed conflict and the politics of terrorism and suppression.

- Midwest Book Review

'Exit Unicorns', unlike many contemporary books on the subject, brings colour and energy to the Irish struggle... The reader is caught up in the intertwined lives of these characters, each of which pursues their own agenda in the struggle for personal, religious and cultural freedom.

- The Cariboo Observer

The contrast of these wonderful characters propels the one story forward from many interesting directions - book-smart and street-smart, rich and poor, old and young, Irish and American. Regardless, the dreams of freedom and equality remain the same. This is a story of passion and loyalty to one another, to ones heritage and to a country. Mix in a bit of warmth and humor, Celtic legends, exquisite poetry and you've got one hell of a book.

- Amazon reader reviews

Praise for Mermaid in a Bowl of Tears

'Mermaid in a Bowl of Tears' quickly immerses you into the vicious inner circle of 1969 Irish-American politics of South Boston, leaving you desperate for the shores of a gem across the Atlantic; those of the Emerald Isle. However, Ireland remains much the same as generations past, presenting beloved characters with trials and tribulations of love, life and fierce reality. Cindy Brandner skillfully plays an emotional tug-of-war with your heart strings on Irish and American shores, creating a roller coaster ride that you will not soon forget.

- Shannon Curtis, Shamrocks and Stones

Praise for Flights of Angels

Cindy Brandner has written Exit Unicorns, Mermaid in a Bowl of Tears and now Flights of Angels in this Irish series and I am already anxiously awaiting the fourth book. You MUST read the first two books if you have not already! Flights of Angels is a novel to be cherished not only for the authentic portrayal of the struggles of Ireland and Russia as nations, but also the personal, emotional, and mental struggles and triumphs of each of the beloved characters - in particular Jamie Kirkpatrick, Casey Riordan, Pamela Riordan and Patrick Riordan. Cindy writes with such a wonderful, descriptive fluency that minutes of reading turns into hours of reading and without knowing, you are whisked away to a gulag in Russia or a cottage in Ireland. You will enjoy how the history and politics of Ireland and Russia are weaved throughout the story and lives of the characters along with the intrigue of how enemies and friends play amongst each other in high stakes games. Cindy Brandner's writing is masterful and I highly recommend Flights of Angels for the captivating page-turner it is. The only downfall in the reading experience is that you will not want the story to end!

- Amazon reader review

Winner of the Dan Poynter's 2012 Global Ebook Awards

CPSIA information can be obtained
at www.ICGtesting.com
Printed in the USA
LVHW01*2259060618
579889LV00001B/1/P